HERETICAL FISHING

A COZY GUIDE TO ANNOYING THE CULTS, OUTSMARTING THE FISH, AND ALIENATING ONESELF

BOOK 2

HAYLOCK JOBSON

Podium

Published in 2024 by Podium Publishing
Los Angeles, CA

Cover design by Mary Cruz

ISBN: 978-1-0394-5313-5

www.podiumentertainment.com

Podium

This book is dedicated to dogs;

all of 'em, even the naughty ones.

PROLOGUE

The sun beat down from above and blanketed me in its warmth. A soft, calming breeze blew over the sandy flat by my home, bringing with it the scents of salt, ocean air, and deep-fried fish.

A crunch rang out, and my heart pounded. Maria's eyes went wide at the taste of the fish, then she closed them and let out a soft *mmm*, raising her face toward the sun's rays.

"This is the best tasting meal yet, Fischer. I—"

Her gaze went distant, causing my heart to climb into my throat. Something tugged at my core, the faintest whisper of pressure that originated from Maria. Fast as it had come, the hint of power disappeared, and I held my breath, every sense focused on her.

She shook her head and blinked, her eyes still somewhat distant. "That was . . . *wow* . . ."

My pulse beat in my ears, and I wiped sweaty palms on my thighs. "You . . ." I swallowed. "You got the message?"

Her gaze snapped to mine, and she gave me a small nod. "I did."

". . . and?"

"And I'm a cultivator now, I suppose."

"How do you, uh . . . feel?"

"I feel the same, honestly . . . though I suppose I have to get used to the new name I picked."

"Wait, you picked a new name?"

She nodded, her face serious. "Yeah, it might be a bit jarring for people to start calling me 'Fish Queen,' but I'm sure they'll get used to it."

I blinked; she blinked back.

"Please tell me you're joking."

Her mask of indifference shattered, and she covered her mouth as she snorted a laugh. "Your face, Fischer." She cackled, roaring her delight toward the sky as she leaned back in the sand. Corporal Claws chittered from her lap, one paw pointing at me as her hissed laughs joined Maria.

I glared at them. "You two are as bad as each other."

* * *

A week later, in a room high atop the capital of Gormona's castle, a construct worked tirelessly.

Since its reawakening, the relic had been processing the world's essence, not pausing for a single second. As the power continued building, it approached a milestone.

If a construct could experience emotion, it would be elated. But . . . such things were not possible for this artifact, so it continued on incessantly, taking neither joy nor pride in its task.

It gathered the final trickle necessary and added it to the pool of collected essence. The construct pushed it out, forcing the power into another relic across the room. That relic, which had sat dormant for millennia, sputtered to life.

A screen that had sat unused for time immemorial turned on and began printing text.

Boosting power relay . . .

. . .

. . .

. . .

Success! Relay area increased!

That evening, a frosty breeze flitted through the streets of Gormona. Candlelit lamps lined the roads, half of which had burned out, either extinguished by the wind or lacking the requisite fuel to make it past the early hours of morning. A half-moon shone down from above, adding an ethereal air to everything it touched.

It was on these streets, hugging himself and regretting his choice of clothing, that a hooded man strode. "By Zeus's forked beard—it's *freezing.*"

Talking to himself didn't help his predicament. If anything, it put him at risk of being discovered, so he clamped his jaw shut and trudged on.

By the time he reached his destination, his fingers were numb. When he pounded on the door, numbness transformed into a bone-deep aching. There was no answer, so he pulled his fist back once more, but then a muffled voice spoke from inside.

"What's the password?" Number Two asked.

"Mellow yellow banana," he hissed through chattering teeth.

"That's the old password, Number Four. What's the new one?"

"Don't be daft," another voice said from inside. "We can hear his voice and we know who it is. Besides, I'm Four—he's Three. If you insist on using these silly code names for the mission, at least get them right."

Number Three fought down the urge to kick in the door, but before he could complain, Two spoke again.

"Right, sorry about that mix-up. What's the new password, Number Three?"

Another breeze kicked up, chilling Three to his core—what paltry amount of patience he had dwindled further. "You didn't tell me the new password, Keith, now let me in before I freeze to death!"

"I must insist you use our correct names, Number Three, and if you don't know the password, I cannot admit you."

"Gods above, Keith," came the exasperated voice of Four. "Just open the door and let him in!"

Two, also known as Keith, harrumphed. "There's a reason we're taking such care to protect our identities, and your blatant disregard for the rules is making me begin to doubt this entire endeavor."

The last vestige of Three's patience withered like a noble under questioning, and he started pounding on the door.

"Let me in, Keith, you administrative wind knot! So help me Poseidon, I will cut every last one of your—"

The door swung open, and Four's arm reached out and pulled Three inside.

Three rushed to the small fireplace, extending his hands toward the licking flames. The warmth was pure bliss, and he let out a relieved sigh.

Two was pouting, leaning against the wall where Four had doubtless pushed him. "I really don't see why it's so hard to follow the rules. We don't have that many to follow, and they're put in place for all of our safety . . ."

Another knock came on the door, and Two darted to it, reinvigorated by the mere thought of bureaucratic pedantry. "Password?" he demanded.

Three grit his teeth. "For the love of—"

"Fresh tasty bread," the voice answered from outside.

"See?" Two demanded, scowling at both Three and Four as he opened the door. "This is how things are supposed to work."

Number One came inside, a broad grin plastered over his face.

"Good morning. Are we all ready to go . . . ?" He looked around the room, his face going from elated to confused. "What has got everyone in such a dour mood? We are about to embark on the most important mission of our lives—show some enthusiasm!"

"They're ignoring protocols, One!" Two said. "It's chaos, I tell you! Absolute *chaos!*"

"Ah, I see." He walked over and clapped Two on the shoulder. "I know it is hard on you to bend the rules—forgive them, all right? We are all doing our best."

He took off a backpack and removed three robes, then threw one to everyone.

Three put his on; it was oversized, lined with fur, and decidedly warmer than the thin one he'd previously worn.

"Thank you, One."

"You're most welcome."

Two still bristled, his impressive mustache making the pout look more than a little ridiculous.

"Has Five arrived yet?" One asked.

"No. Not yet. He is the one in charge of the cart—"

Another knock on the door.

"Fresh roasted bread," Five said from outside before anyone could demand a password.

"That's the wrong phrase," Two said, getting to his feet and crossing his arms.

"It was close enough," One replied, swinging the door open to admit the last squad member.

A horse-drawn cart sat on the street beyond. It was laden with supplies, and Three smiled at Five's organizational skills.

"How did everyone go?" Five asked. "Did we get everything we needed?"

They all nodded.

"Right. The cart is ready, so I think we're good to go. What about you, One?" Five's deep voice transformed into a whisper. "*Did you get the artifact from the king?*"

One beamed, reached into his backpack, and removed a small rectangular object. "I did."

Three gazed down at it. It was something he'd only heard of before, but it was just as the tales told. There were two bulbs, one below the image of a human, the other beneath a series of animals. The first was blinking, likely responding to the cultivators within the capital.

"With this," One said, "we'll be able to locate the cultivator with ease."

Three grinned.

This trip to the village known as Tropica was going to be *fun.*

CHAPTER ONE

ASCENSION

The shade of the forest's canopy was a welcome relief from the sun's heat as I strode forward. I had a bucket in hand, my trusty straw hat atop my head, and excitement bubbling up from within.

It had been a week since Maria's ascension, and for the first time since my arrival in Tropica, I'd taken some time to relax. Well, I told myself it was relaxing, but after two days of lounging around and working on nothing, I'd gone a bit stir crazy.

The accidental pillar of light that exploded from me during our time away had been a wake-up call. Even *if* it was just a side effect of ascending and had nothing to do with the uncomfortable truths I'd been avoiding, I had to ensure it would *never* happen again.

With my self-imposed vacation finally at an end, it was time to get back into it. With that thought in mind, a grin spread over my face. I hastened my steps, and within minutes I found my quarry.

"G'day, Barry! How are ya?"

My farming neighbor spun, cutting his conversation off mid-sentence.

"Fischer! Thanks for coming, mate! I'm good—how ya doin'?"

I smiled at his adopted vernacular; Aussie slang was pleasing to the soul.

"I'm wonderful, thanks." I turned to the other man. "You must be Leroy. I've heard a bunch about you, mate." I strode forward, holding out a hand.

He grasped it and shook, giving me a friendly smile. "Likewise, Fischer. It's a pleasure to finally meet you."

"Pleasure is all mine, my man. Were you gonna join us today, Barry?"

He shook his head. "I've gotta get tilling on the new fields, but I might see you later?"

"Sounds good! Pop by if you need a break."

Barry gave us a wave and jogged off, his pace clearly identifying him as a cultivator.

I turned to Leroy. "So, Barry tells me you have some sort of nature power?"

"That's right. It's not as advanced as Corporal Claws's lightning or Sergeant Snips's water, though."

"Mate, I'd be surprised if it was. Those two are kinda terrifying."

"They're certainly impressive . . ."

A gust blew and rustled the trees above. Leroy's eyes watched them as he took a deep breath, and a small smile crossed his lips. I let the silence stretch, similarly enjoying the sights, sounds, and scents of the forest.

"It's so nice to be back," he said, his voice wistful.

"I can only imagine, mate. I only know a hint of what you've been through, but I'm glad you've earned your freedom."

"Earned?" He let out a chuckle. "If not for those 'terrifying' creatures of yours, I'd be on my way back to the capital by now."

"I'm sure you'd have found a way eventually—or Barry and Helen would have busted you out. Those two are scary in their own right when they get an idea in their heads."

He barked a laugh. "You're not wrong there, Fischer."

Another silence stretched, and before it could get awkward, I broke it. "Well, should we get going?"

He nodded. "Aye. Lead the way."

I led us a little out of the way so I could show Leroy something, and when we reached it, he let out a whistle.

"This is the pond you made?"

"Yeah, mate."

The morning sun peeked through the leaves, lighting the water, rocks, plants, and the log with a soundly sleeping Corporal Claws atop it. She glanced at us through lidded eyes, chirped a greeting with a raised paw, then rolled over and showed us her back.

"Is this the one that heals?" Leroy asked.

"Nah, that's the saltwater one. I don't actually know what this one does, but it does . . . something. I'm pretty sure it helped Claws ascend."

"Interesting . . ."

Claws half sat up to scratch her ear, then flopped back to the log.

"Let's leave Claws to her nap—the patch I wanted to show you isn't far off."

We kept moving, heading further south toward where I wanted to try my little experiment.

When we caught sight of it, I pointed. "That's the spot, mate."

A large tree sat amid the others, its hue identifying it as a different species. Its trunk was thicker than most and covered in a thin veneer of blue bark. Other than the color, another thing made it stand out against the rest of the forest: its canopy sprawled out, spreading out on thick branches laden with fat, glossy leaves. A large circle of grass was left clear around its base, the other trees giving it space.

"Know anything about this tree, mate?" I asked.

Leroy nodded, his eyes fixed on it. "They're called sapphire mesh trees. It's considered terrible luck to fell one."

"Sapphire mesh . . . ? I get the sapphire bit, but why mesh?"

"I couldn't say—maybe something to do with their wood? If it's mesh-like, it'd make sense why people think it's bad luck to cut one—they'd be almost impossible to work with."

"Yeah . . . maybe . . ."

I gazed over the trunk, remembering the sensations I'd felt when seeking trees to harvest. "When I was looking for wood to use for my fence, I came here. Before I could even think of cutting it, this tree pushed me away, like it was warning me from taking it down."

"Really . . . ?" Leroy stepped forward and placed a hand against the tree. He closed his eyes, a line forming between his eyebrows as he concentrated.

"Feel anything, mate?" I asked when the moment stretched on.

"Nothing," he answered, smiling at himself. "My abilities lend me some nature knowledge, but it's more like instinct, if that makes sense. I know what plants need to keep them happy. More sun, less water, fertilizer—that sort of thing."

"Did they let you do that in the capital?"

He snorted. "No, though I did come across plenty of trees and plants when we'd go out on expeditions."

I winced at the bitterness in his tone. "Sorry, mate. I shouldn't have asked."

He took a deep breath, and as he exhaled, the bitterness left him entirely. "It's fine, Fischer. It's just a little aggravating to think about."

"Well, do your 'nature instincts' or whatever tell you where it would be a good place to plant a lemon tree?" I asked, not-so-smoothly changing the subject.

"Lemon . . . ?"

"Yeah, mate. I got some seeds from a few lemons I bought."

"Fischer . . ." He gave me a friendly smile, but it was the kind you'd give a child when they said something adorably stupid. "You can't grow lemons from seeds. The lemons they sell are modified to not produce more trees."

"Oh, yeah, I know that, mate."

"You do? Why are you planting them, then?"

"Leroy . . . I have a crab pal that shoots aura blades, a lobster companion that shoots blasts from his claws like an anime protagonist, and an otter friend that rides the lightning like some sort of Metallica fangirl."

He blinked at me, his face blank.

"I don't know what most of that meant, but I think I get the idea. Stranger things have happened, right?"

"Exactly. It can't hurt to try, and with your nature power, I was hoping you might have some insight. So . . . any ideas?"

"Can I see them?"

I reached into a pocket, then dropped the four seeds I'd brought with me into his open palm. He moved them around with one finger, then closed his eyes, his brow once more creasing.

He blinked, looking around the clearing.

"Huh . . ."

"What is it?"

"I'm pretty sure the whole area surrounding the tree is a good place, but I'm not certain . . ." He shrugged. "It's vague."

I grinned. "Good enough for me!"

I stepped back and grabbed a spade from my back pocket, then started digging a small hole in the ground.

"I've been meaning to ask," Leroy said. "What's in that bucket you're carrying? It smells terrible."

"That would be our fertilizer, mate." I moved the wet tea towel aside and removed part of a cichlid's frame. "Leftover fish is a great source of nutrients."

I dropped it in the hole, layered dirt atop it, then poked my finger into the aerated earth.

"If you'd do the honors," I said, gesturing at the ground.

Leroy dropped a seed in and tenderly covered it.

"Would you meditate on it with me, mate?" I asked.

His head cocked to the side, and he gave me a strange look. "Meditate . . . ?"

"Yeah. I'm pretty sure that's how my pond ended up transforming. Just close your eyes and imagine life pouring into the seed. I'll do the same."

"Oh . . . sure."

I held both hands out, willing life and sustenance toward the seed. I pictured it turning into a mighty tree, bearing countless citrus, and sending thick roots deep into the earth. The thoughts took me over, and I leaned into the pleasant musings. Time stretched, and though I didn't feel any shifts in the world, it was an enjoyable moment of peace.

"Er, how do we know if it works, Fischer?"

"Oh, sorry. It happened pretty quick last time—it might not be working." I rubbed the back of my head. "I've kinda been making it up as I go."

We repeated the process three more times, creating an invisible square around the light-blue tree.

After we planted the last seed, Leroy cleared his throat. "Do you want to try meditating toward the tree?"

"The tree? I mean, I'm down, but why?"

"Just a hunch."

"My man, considering you have the ability to ride vines like some sort of superhero, I'll trust your hunches on anything plant related."

He gave me an abashed smile. "Someone told you about that?"

"Corporal Claws hasn't shut up about it. Considering how much she chitters and chirps about you, I'm surprised she didn't launch herself at you when we went to the pond."

He let out a soft chuckle. "It's not as impressive as it sounds, especially compared to the abilities of your animals . . ."

"You're being too humble, my man. But I get it—anyone would down-sell their cultivator abilities if it was something so scorned by society." I shook my head. "I'm taking us off course—let's meditate."

We sat down at the tree's base, and I leaned my back against it. Its bark was smooth and firm against my spine, and I closed my eyes, easily slipping into a meditative state.

* * *

In a place of darkness, surrounded by the comforting scents of wood and dirt, something ancient stirred. Though it remembered neither who nor what it was, one thing was certain: it had been asleep for a very, *very* long time.

Something was nudging it, calling it from its slumber, and it reluctantly listened. Its senses expanded as it reached out, seeking what had disturbed its rest. Something was just beside it. Touching it. Reaching out and offering power.

No, not something, the ancient thing realized. *Two beings.*

A part of its soul—an instinctual nexus hidden deep within—rejoiced at the offering. But then, it tasted what they had to offer.

The tribute was pitiful.

Even without any memories, it knew the power offered was a mere trickle of the torrents it had once consumed. It scoffed at the insult and went back to sleep, content to wait until the world's essence was properly restored.

My eye twitched, and I darted a glance at Leroy.

Did I just feel something?

It had been a tiny blip, and quick as it had come, it vanished.

Maybe it was just my imagination . . .

I gazed up at the sky; the sun had climbed halfway into the sky, so I stretched and let out a soft groan to get Leroy's attention. When he peered at me through sleepy eyes, I gave him a grin.

"The meditation was fruitless, but what do you say we try a bit of fishing?"

CHAPTER TWO

HERETICAL FRIENDS

Leroy's face was more than a little confused as he looked down at the tangle of tackle connected to my fishing rod. I had the smaller rod with the sabiki rig attached. I'd bound a rock on the end of the main line, which was currently the object of Leroy's scrutiny.

"I understand what the hook is for, but what is this bit?" he asked, pointing down at the rock.

"That's the sinker, mate. It helps you cast it out further and keeps the bait in place once it's in the water. This thing's called a sabiki rig, and in this case, if there wasn't a sinker attached, the lines would get all tangled up the moment they hit the water. We probably wouldn't catch a single baitfish without it."

" . . . baitfish? Is that a type of fish?"

"Nah, mate. Baitfish refers to any of the smaller fish we use as bait to catch the bigger ones. I figured if I was going to teach you fishing, we'd start from the beginning. Actually, now that I think of it . . ." With a deft movement, I cut one hook off with a knife. "I think I should show you the knot. That way, if you're ever stranded in the wilderness with gear, you can create your own."

I took a length of line and showed him an "improved cinch knot."

"Reckon you can do that?"

"This is kinda cheating," I admitted as I slipped cuts of common eel onto the hook Leroy had reattached. "But we have the bait, so we may as well use it. See the short bits of metal attached near to the hooks' eyes?"

He nodded.

I moved one back and forth under the sun's rays; it shone. "You can use these without bait. The fish will still bite, thinking the sun is reflecting from a smaller fish's scales."

"I see . . ."

I looked down at my "Bamboo Rod of the Fisher." Leroy could have just used a stick of bamboo as a rod, but I wanted him to get practice with a proper reel before we tried fishing for something big. "All right, mate—it's ready to go."

He picked up the rod and flicked the reel into the open position, as I'd shown. "Like this?"

"Yep!"

He walked to the edge of the headland's rocky shore, pursed his lips in concentration, then flicked the line out into the water. It flew straight and hit the water with a soft *plop.*

Line continued to spool out, and he tried to flick the reel back into place, but it held firm.

"Other way," I said, reaching over and shifting it back into position.

"Oh—right. Sorry."

"No need to apologize—today's a day for learning. Reel in the loose line and wait for a bite."

He did so, the serious expression never leaving his face.

Despite Leroy being the one fishing, the calm that always came with the act washed over me. The soft murmuring of waves lapping the shore, combined with the gusts of wind fitfully washing over my skin, made the corner of my lips curl into a smile. I took a deep breath, and the salty air made joy spread over my entire face.

"Gods above, I love it here, Leroy."

He glanced at me for only a moment before returning his attention to the rod, but I didn't miss the hint of anticipation coloring his features.

"The ocean is calming, isn't it? Even before they took me to the capital, I always found its movement and sounds soothing."

I raised an eyebrow at him. "That's rather heretical of you to say, mate."

He snorted and smirked at me. "You're one to talk."

"Yeah, but you can't blame a heretic for also being a little hypocritical. I'm bound to have more than one personality red flag."

" . . . red flag?"

"Yeah, like a warning sign. For example, you're fishing and enjoying yourself right now—major red flag to anyone of sound mind, mate."

"Well, lucky no one of sound mind is here, then."

I nodded, trying to keep my face serious. "Exactly. We heretical friends have to stick together; otherwise we'd have no one to talk to."

His smile turned wistful, and I immediately realized my mistake. "Sorry, mate. I know it must be hard having to hide away from everyone."

Though Claws had removed Leroy's slave collar, the villagers were all too aware he'd awakened as a cultivator. He was technically free, yet he couldn't return to the way his life had been pre-awakening.

"It's fine, Fischer," Leroy said. "I should be grateful to be here, but if I'm being honest, it's a little hard not being able to walk around openly."

"Well, you're always welcome here. Consider my fence your fence—you can come hang with the awakened gang or do some fishing whenever you like."

A moment of silence stretched out before Leroy responded. "Thank you, Fischer. That means more than you know."

"Don't mention it. You've been through a lot, and if there's anything else I can do, just let me know, yeah?"

He nodded and took a deep breath, letting it out with a slow, calming sigh.

A tear formed in his eye and he swept it away with one hand. "Sorry. It's been overwhelming."

I put a hand on his shoulder and squeezed lightly. "You're all good, mate. I'm gonna have to start up an apology jar. Every time you apologize unnecessarily, you'll have to chuck a copper in."

He laughed and shot me a coy look. "Can I apologize for saying sorry too much, or is that also a—*whoa!*"

The rod's tip shot down as something bit. The fish was small, likely a juvenile cichlid from its size, but that didn't stop Leroy's eyes from going wide.

"What do I do?" he yelled, his voice anything but calm.

"Reel it in slowly. The fish thrashing might attract other fish to the other hooks on the—"

"*Whoa!*" Leroy yelled again, cutting me off as something much larger hit the line.

The rod bent down, tugged incessantly by the creatures beneath the water.

"Reel it in fast and keep the line tight! That's what we were looking for!"

Leroy wound the reel's handle, his body tense and shoulders hunched.

I caught a flash of silver, and as more of the line came from the water, I smiled at what had bitten down on the lowest hook. "Flick it up on the shore!"

He did so, and as I dashed for the creature, my eyes were drawn into it.

Common Eel
Common
Found in the brackish waters of the Kallis Realm, this eel's flesh has high oil content and a strong scent, making it unpalatable food but excellent bait.

As my vision cleared, I picked the twice-common eel up and removed my trusty nail. "If you spike its brain right here, it'll . . . *uh, Leroy?* You all right?"

His gaze was distant, but then his eyes snapped to me.

"What is it . . . ?" I asked as I dispatched the eel, not wanting it to suffer more than was necessary.

"The System just spoke to me . . ."

"Wait. *What?*"

I unhooked the juvenile cichlid and threw it back into the water, then looked up at Leroy. "What did it say?"

"Yeah . . . my eyes were just kind of, I don't know, pulled into it? It gave me a description of the common eel."

"Oh, yeah—it does that. You've never seen that before?"

"No . . ."

"What about the rod? Have you tried looking at it?"

He scrunched his forehead and raised it to his face.

"Nothing?" I asked.

"Not yet . . ."

He pulled it closer, going cross-eyed and trembling with the effort.

I couldn't help but laugh at him. I focused on the rod, checking I still had the ability to inspect it.

Bamboo Rod of the Fisher
Rare
A bamboo rod paired with an iron wood reel. This fishing rod provides boosts to both fishing and luck.
+10 fishing
+2 luck

"You don't need to force it," I said. "That thing transformed when I made it, and I can inspect it the same way you inspected the eel."

He lowered the rod. "Yeah, Barry mentioned that . . ."

"Oh? What did he say?" I paused, then held up my hands. "Wait, never mind—I don't want to know."

Leroy gave me a funny look. "You're kind of weird, Fischer. You know that?"

"Oh, yeah. I couldn't agree more. Which weirdness are you referring to, though?"

"That my brother-in-law is trying to turn you into some sort of god, and you want to know nothing about it. Don't give me that look. I know you don't enjoy talking about it, and I won't bring it up again, but still . . . I feel like most people would want to be involved."

I smoothed the scowl that had crossed my face unbidden. "Oh, that's easy to explain. I just want to fish and make friends. I'm not gonna actively stop Barry from doing what he pleases, but that's because he's doing it for everyone's safety. It's selfish of me to stay here, knowing I am what I am, so the least I can do is let him ensure everyone is as protected as possible."

"And if he—no, if *we* succeed in causing you to ascend . . . what then?"

"Then you'll still find me here, catching fishies, hanging with my pals, and having a good time."

He shook his head, smiling at me. "You really mean that, don't you?"

"Sure do."

"Yep. You're definitely weird."

I barked a laugh. "I'm downright strange, mate, but I wouldn't have it any other way."

When Leroy finished tying the knot, I nodded; he'd reattached the large hook and sinker flawlessly.

"Am I missing anything?" he asked as he slid a chunk of eel onto the hook.

"Nope. It's good to go."

He got to his feet, reeled in the line, then flicked the reel sideways. "How far do I cast it?"

"Aim for the river mouth—where the freshwater hits the ocean is a magnet for big fish."

He held the rod back, paused a moment, then launched it. The line and sinker flew high, soaring almost all the way to the other side of the river.

He winced as he turned to me. "Too far?"

"A little, but it's all good—reel it back until it's about halfway."

When the bait was in the middle of the channel, I set up two of the folding chairs Greg and Brad, the village woodworkers, had kindly let me keep.

We sat down and I leaned back, stretching as I enjoyed the serious expression on Leroy's face. I understood his feeling entirely; there was nothing else in the world quite like waiting for a fish to strike.

"You know, Fischer . . . I wasn't sure what to expect when Barry said you'd invited me to go fishing."

"It's better than you thought, isn't it?"

He smirked at me. "That's an understatement. How can something be so relaxing yet so exciting at the same time?"

"I'd say it was to do with it being heretical, and therefore more exciting, but honestly, it was the same in my previous life, and it was totally chill to fish there."

He narrowed his eyes in confusion. "What made it cold?"

" . . . what? *Ohhhh.* Chill in that context means allowed—society as a whole wouldn't look down on you for doing it."

"I still can't believe you're . . ." He trailed off. "Sorry, I didn't mean to bring it up."

"It's fine, mate. It's pretty wild that I'm from a different world, huh?"

"That's putting it mildly."

I shrugged. "I'm used to it, and I've only been here for like a month or something. Two months? I've honestly lost track—the days have been so busy and enjoyable."

We fell into a comfortable silence, our thoughts taking us to distant places. Eventually, movement caught my attention, and my eyes moved to the rod tip.

"Leroy . . ."

He stared at nothing, his eyes dull. "Yeah, Fischer?"

"You should hold your finger to the line."

"Oh . . . ? Why's that?"

"Because there's a fish having a cheeky little nibble of your bait."

He shot upright, his eyes widening as they focused on the rod. His index finger drifted to the line, and when he felt the tiny tugs, a toothy grin appeared. "When do I set the hook?"

"You'll know. Wait for it . . ."

The fish was getting more confident, taking bigger and bigger bites of the bait.

Bump.

"Wait for it . . ."

Bump.

"Not yet . . ."

There was a pause, and I thought the fish had stolen the bait, but then the rod dipped, almost bending in half as the fish took off.

"*Now!*" I yelled.

CHAPTER THREE

QUANTIFICATION

Time seemed to freeze as I watched Leroy lift the rod and set the hook. The muscles in his arms bulged, and he leaned back, bracing against the fish's mighty run. A gust of wind blew his short hair back, revealing a smile of sheer, child-like joy on his face.

The fish redoubled its efforts, swimming out to sea and dragging Leroy stumbling across the slick rocks.

"Let some of the line out," I instructed.

He did so, easing the tension. "What in Poseidon's salt-washed back hair is this thing?"

"A big bloody fish. Move with it if you need."

He stepped to the side, but with his eyes moving between the reel and ocean, he slipped.

I caught him before he could fall over. "The rocks are slippery, mate—cultivator's body or not."

He showed no embarrassment, only anticipation and palpable excitement.

Despite the open waters surrounding the river mouth, the fish never changed direction; it swam in a straight line out to sea, attempting to take Leroy with it.

Leroy started the fight off clumsily, but as the battle dragged on, his footing grew more sure. He adjusted his stance, and while Leroy's technique improved, the fish grew sluggish.

Without me instructing him, Leroy started taking some line back, pumping the rod up, then winding the reel in as he lowered it. Each time the fish caught sight of the shore, it would tear off again, dipping deep into its energy reserves to escape.

The grin never left Leroy's face, and despite his enhanced body, sweat peppered his brow, glistening under the sun's light.

I'd still not caught sight of the fish yet, so as Leroy wound it close to land once more, I jogged along the shore, trying to spy it. Its muscular body kicked again, taking off toward the depths—but not before the sun reflected from its silver body.

It. Was. *Huge.*

Actually, huge was probably doing the fish a disservice—it was gigantic, long as a man and half as tall.

My eyes went wide as I turned to Leroy; his were even wider, his mouth hanging ajar.

"What in Hades's hounds is that?" he demanded. "Fish get that big?"

"It's the biggest I've ever seen, Leroy! Keep winding!"

He clenched his jaw and focused on the fight, his grin disappearing for the first time since he'd hooked the monstrous thing.

One turn of the reel at a time, he pulled it back toward us. The fish swam languidly across the shoreline, clearly exhausted, and we got our first good look at it.

It had a rounded head, angular fins, and triangular spines running down to its tail. The fish looked too big for us to pull it up without hurting it, so without a second thought, I got down to my jocks and jumped into the river mouth.

The freezing water made a wave of adrenaline wash over me as I swam forward and put my hands under the fish, taking care to avoid the spines and fins. I kicked my legs toward the rocks and lifted it up above the waterline.

Leroy grabbed it and hauled it onto the shore, and I pulled myself up onto the headland. Water cascaded down my body and I shook my head, clearing it of salty water as I wiped my eyes.

Leroy hugged the fish tight to his body, his mouth still wide, his eyes staring down at the fish vacantly.

It drew my attention, and my gaze went distant as a screen popped up before me.

Mature Giant Trevally
Rare
Found in the oceans of the Kallis Realm, this fish is a prized sport fish for anglers everywhere. Its flesh is undesirable, and it is considered bad luck to harm them.

When my eyes cleared, Leroy was waddling down to the water with the fish still in his arms. I dashed past him and jumped into the water, then we eased it down together.

"Help me move it back and forth in the water," I said, showing him how. "Forcing water through its gills helps it release better."

I treaded water as we moved the fish. Neither of us spoke, and all I could assume was that Leroy was as awed as I was. The trevally's body was as thick as my head, and feeling the lean muscles hidden beneath its scales, I completely understood how it had put up such a fight. It would be like a dart beneath the waves, and I didn't envy the fish this thing must hunt to sustain itself.

Abruptly, the trevally tried to swim, so I let go and swam back. It kicked its tail only three times, but that was enough to lose sight of the fish as it melded into the deep blue water of the river mouth.

My mind went blank as I continued treading water, uncomprehending of what we'd just witnessed. I looked up at Leroy, who was beaming down at me, one hand extended. I grasped it, and he hauled me up to the rocks.

We blinked at each other, then both yelled at the same time.

"What the hell, Leroy!"

"What was that, Fischer!"

We laughed and jumped up and down on the spot, slowly spinning in a circle as we giggled wordlessly.

"Uhhh . . ." came a feminine voice, and we both stopped, peering at the intruder.

Maria's eyebrows shot up to her hairline as she stared at us. ". . . am I interrupting something?" Her eyes narrowed on me. "And where are your clothes . . . ?"

Despite wearing only a set of thin jocks, being drenched in salt water, and having been caught dancing like a child with my new pal, I grinned at her. "Feeling jealous?"

I ran over and wrapped her in a hug.

"Fischer! You're soaking!" She batted at me ineffectually and laughed as I pressed my soaking body into her. "Put me down!"

I set her back on the sand. "You missed it! Leroy just caught the biggest fish I've ever seen! It was as long as the Lady of the Lake, but even taller!"

Her annoyance was immediately washed away.

"What was it? How big was it? Where did it go?"

Maria pouted as I finished drying myself, and I shot her a wink. She rolled her eyes, but the hint of a smile tugged at her lips.

"I help my dad in the fields for one morning, and you go and catch a new fish without me!"

I held my hands up. "Hey, it was Leroy's fault, not mine. The man is a natural."

Leroy rubbed the back of his head. "Hi—it's Maria, right?"

"Oh! You two haven't met? Where are my manners?" I pointed to Leroy. "This is Leroy. He's Helen's brother, Barry's brother-in-law, a fellow cultivator, and fisherman extraordinaire."

I gestured at Maria haphazardly. "This is the neighbor girl. I forget her name, and she's kind of annoying, but she's okay at fishing too, I guess. I usually just tune her voice—*oof*."

She cut me off with an elbow to the ribs, and it actually kind of hurt given her enhanced body.

"Ow, you little terror! Watch your strength."

"That's what you get for disrespecting a young lady." She lifted her nose in a facade of disdain, but rubbed where she'd elbowed in apology.

"Well, it's nice to meet you finally, Maria," Leroy said. "I've heard a lot from Sharon."

"All good things, no doubt."

"Of course." He gave us both a smile. "I'll leave you guys to it, then. Thanks for this morning, Fischer."

I held up a hand. "Whoa, where do you think you're going, my man?"

"I don't want to impose—I was just going to see if Barry needed any help in the . . ." He trailed off as I shook my head emphatically.

"You've not yet caught a fish for dinner! As your fishing trainer, I couldn't stand for such an incomplete lesson."

He raised an eyebrow, and Maria piled on. "I couldn't agree more. Fischer is a bit useless as a trainer, so the more experience you get, the better."

I nodded along. "It's true. This is your first time fishing, and you've already caught a fish bigger than my personal best."

"You're sure?" he asked. "I don't want to eat into your alone time . . ."

"Oh, if anything, you'll be doing me a favor!" I grinned. "Being alone with this one is like being stuck in an elevator with a honey badger, but she's even more—*joking! I'm joking!*" I dashed away from her raised backhand, hiding behind Leroy to avoid her wrath.

I smiled as the afternoon sun beamed down on us. I'd set up another chair for Maria, and all three of us sat in a comfortable silence; the waves, wind, and birds high above created a pleasant symphony.

Maria's hand rested atop my arm, and she moved one finger back and forth. Her touch was both welcome and comforting, and my breaths came slowly as my body's sensations lulled me further into a state of mindfulness.

Leroy shot to his feet, and I directed a half-lidded glance toward him.

"Fish!" he said, his voice filled with elation.

I stayed sitting, content to watch the fight from afar. The rod dipped as the fish fought to escape; it was big, but nowhere near as large as the giant trevally.

Leroy easily wrestled it to the shore, and as I caught sight of it, I smiled. "It has no teeth—you can pick it up by the mouth."

He bent and grabbed it with one hand, resting his other under the belly as he hauled it up.

Mature Shore Fish
Uncommon
Found along the ocean shores of the Kallis Realm, this fish is a staple source of both food and bait.

"What . . . ?" Maria asked, turning toward me.

"What's wrong?"

She swallowed, her eyes darting between me and the fish. "I inspected it . . ."

It was the first time she'd been able to accomplish such a feat.

I shrugged. "Huh . . . Leroy could too. Neat."

She gave me a flat stare. "Neat? What do you mean, *neat?*"

"It's kind of cool, right? More people can inspect fish now. Maybe you two earned enough fishing skills or some other nonsense. Who really knows with the System being more broken than Xin Zhao on release?"

She scowled at me for a long moment before turning to Leroy, not taking the bait. "Please tell me I'm not crazy and you're just as shocked."

He shrugged. "I've only been back just over a week, and I'm already desensitized to the happenings around Fischer."

She let out a long-suffering sigh. "I guess you have a point."

"Wait . . ." Leroy said. "It said staple source of food—does that mean we can eat it?"

"It certainly does, mate."

He grinned, Maria put her head in her hands, and I strode over to Leroy. "Do you want to try dispatching it?"

He nodded, so I passed him the spike.

"Poke it right here, swift and decisive."

He did so, and the fish immediately went limp.

"All right," I said. "I'll show you how to prepare it."

As Leroy watched Maria and Fischer bicker good-naturedly across the campfire, he couldn't help but smirk. Fischer was singing some song about complimenting a chef and acting like Maria was the weird one for not having heard it, despite it having the weirdest cadence and lyrics Leroy had ever heard.

Definitely a song from his previous world, Leroy decided, shaking his head.

He looked down at the shallow-frying fish, and his mouth watered at the aroma rising from the pan.

After showing Leroy how to gut and scale the catch, Fischer had crumbed and thrown the fish into a tallow-filled pan and was keeping an eye on it as he continued stirring up Maria.

The System nudged Leroy for the fourth time today, and he rolled his eyes. Despite willing his notifications to be silent, the System's attempts at communication were still an annoying occurrence. He checked them with a mild flex of will, expecting to see the usual "insufficient power" message.

"All right," Fischer said, jostling the pan's handle as he turned to Maria. "I reckon it's finished—what do you think?"

Leroy barely heard the words.

Maria leaned over, peering down at the fish's golden crumbs. "Looks good to me!"

Fischer nodded and removed the fish with a pair of tongs. He set the fish down on a board, and after a minute of letting the fat drain from the steaming fish, he smiled up at Leroy. "After you, mate. It was your catch."

Leroy's eyes were still distant, looking at a screen occupying his field of view.

"Er . . . Leroy? You right, mate?"

Again, Leroy barely heard the words; he stared at his System notifications, unbelieving.

A series of lines had printed out, and he read them again.

You have learned fishing!
You have advanced to fishing 2!
You have advanced to fishing 3!
You have advanced to fishing 4!

CHAPTER FOUR

BURDENS

I leaned down, eyebrows knitted as I stared at Leroy.

I clicked my fingers softly before his face. "You with us, mate?"

Leroy startled and his eyes cleared. "O-oh. Sorry. My mind went elsewhere for a moment."

It's not surprising that there's some lingering damage from his time in the capital, I thought.

"No need to apologize. The fish is ready, and seeing as though you caught it, I thought you should have the first bite."

He returned to his senses swiftly, giving me a broad grin as he accepted the fish. "Thank you."

Leroy cut through the crumbed fish with the side of a fork. It crunched, and as he separated a chunk of the flaky flesh, steam billowed from it. He tentatively lifted it to his mouth, blew once, then bit down.

As his expression melted from anticipation to pure bliss, I darted a look at Maria. She was already looking my way, and we shared a knowing grin.

"*Mmmmm,*" Leroy said, moving his head side to side in a little dance.

"Yep," Maria said. "Looks like he's definitely a heretic."

I nodded seriously. "Now that we have proof, we'll have to let the kingdom know."

"It's not my fault, officers," Leroy said, covering his mouth. "It's too delicious—I was left absent choice."

Maria raised an eyebrow at me. "I guess we'll have to try it then. Just to make sure he's telling the truth, you know?"

I nodded again, a smile coloring my features. "That would only be prudent—well said, Officer Maria."

I used my fork to break apart the fish, and as steam rushed up to assault me, I breathed deep. I still had a tray of herbs and spices I hadn't used yet, so I'd added three previously untested flavors to the crumbs before frying the fish. Their faint aromas wafted up, and I closed my eyes, focusing more on the scents. There was a hint of smokiness, something like rosemary but slightly more floral, and another that smelled of caramelized onion. I raised an eyebrow at the latter, but it wasn't unpleasant, just surprising.

I placed the fish in my mouth, and before I could even start chewing, the flavors exploded. As I bit down, the fish's juices and the golden crumbing fused with and calmed the herbs and spices fighting for dominance.

Maria let out a noise of delight, but I barely heard it; I was busy analyzing the tastes.

"Needs more of the caramelized onion and less of the floral rosemary . . ." I mused aloud after swallowing.

"Sorry, what?" Maria asked, her eyes half-lidded.

"Just taking notes." I pulled out my collar and peered down. "Did you get that, Cinnamon? Don't let me forget."

Her head popped out as she blinked sleep from her eyes, then she gave me a serious nod.

"*Cinnamon!*"

At Maria's voice, the little bunny flew from my chest with a deft kick. She sailed at Maria, who caught her and let out a lilting giggle.

She scratched behind Cinnamon's ear, and the bunny's back leg kicked incessantly as she leaned into the touch.

"So this is Cinnamon?" Leroy asked. "You're the only one I haven't met yet—it's a pleasure."

Cinnamon raised her ears and turned to take in the cultivator. She spun her body, braced herself against Maria's thigh, and started wiggling her fluffy little tooshie.

Knowing what would come next, I turned to look at Leroy, and was delighted when his eyes went wide at the bunny-turned-torpedo that sailed his way. He leaned back in shock and she crashed into his chest, causing him to topple onto his back on the sand.

He let out an *oof,* then chuckled as he reached up to pet her.

"I bet you get along with Corporal Claws, don't you?" he asked, and I couldn't help but laugh.

Over the last week, Cinnamon's personality had flourished, and I could scarcely remember the terrified, injured rabbit we'd found out in the forest.

"Cinnamon and Claws have become fast friends—I'm not sure if it's Claws's influence rubbing off on her, or if their similarities are why they bonded, but the result remains the same: she's a little trickster."

Cinnamon turned to look at me with one eye, and the corner of her mouth curled into a cheeky little smirk.

Joel, the head priest of the Church of Carcinization's Tropica branch, sat in solemn silence. He had shuttered each window and door of the cult's headquarters. The air was still, and as he took a breath, the scent of something unpleasant washed over him.

Rather than recoil from the disgusting smell, he leaned into it, focusing all his attention on the odors flooding the room.

Jess, his lead disciple, made a retching sound.

Joel peered out through a slitted eye. "I know it's unpleasant, but this is all part of our worship."

"I know," she replied, her voice muffled as she covered her mouth with an arm. "How did you even catch these?"

Joel glanced at the three fish sitting on a tray in the center of the room. "I caught them last night on a fishing rod."

Jess's eyes and above were the only part of her face visible, and her forehead scrunched in thought. "That's . . . I suppose it's fine given that we're a church, but still . . ."

Joel nodded. "I know—it still feels antithetical to our beliefs, but the doctrine is clear—once a crab deity is identified, all other rules go out the window. The most important thing is nourishing the emerging ascendant."

"How did you even know how to make a fishing rod? Were there instructions in the doctrine?"

"Uh . . . *yes.*"

In truth, he'd asked Fischer, but he didn't feel the need to divulge that information.

"Where they came from doesn't matter," he continued. "We need to meditate on and suffuse this fish with our will before offering it to our deity."

"Right. Sorry . . ." Jess removed her arm, scrunching her nose as the fish's smell hit her once more. "Let's resume."

Joel flared his nostrils and closed his eyes as he breathed in the unpleasant aroma, willing himself to become one with the fish.

With the sun having set, two cowled individuals walked through the empty streets of Tropica with a smelly payload. Joel held one side of the tray, Jess the other, and each time the wind changed direction, one of them dry heaved.

"How is the smell getting worse?" Jess demanded, trying to bury her face against her shoulder.

"That is the scent of our devotion—remember it well."

"Our devotion smells like Poseidon's swarthy sack."

Joel made to chastise her heresy, but a breeze kicked up and wafted the fish's scent toward him. He held his breath, lest he desecrate the offering with his lunch.

"Yeah, it smells pretty bad," he forced out, facing his head away.

One horrible-smelling breath at a time, they made their way between the buildings of Tropica and down toward the coast.

As they passed a house on the southern side of town, a northerly wind hit them. It swept the smell of decaying fish away, and they both breathed a sigh of relief.

Joel led Jess down to the water's edge, and they set the tray down.

"What do we do now?" Jess asked.

"Now, we offer one to the ocean, and we hope the deity hears our call."

Joel grabbed a fish and lobbed it into the shallows. Small waves crashed and lapped at the shore, dragging the fish—and hopefully its scent—out to sea. He placed another fish on the beach, creating a trail back to the offering-laden tray.

He lowered himself to the sand and shuffled his feet as he took the stance of a crab. "Let us meditate, Jess."

She nodded and squatted down.

As hours passed, the moon rose higher in the sky. A sudden breeze kicked up and sent a shiver down Joel's spine. He opened his eyes, intent on gauging the passage of time by the moon's movement, but something in the waves caught his attention.

Two mighty claws reached out from the salty waters, opening and closing with incessant regularity as if demanding more of their worship. Joel nudged Jess's thigh, and when she raised a questioning eyebrow at him, he nodded toward the claws.

Her annoyed glare turned awe-filled when she saw it, and as one, they threw themselves to the sand in prostration.

Rocky had been out patrolling the bay for his beloved mistress when a delicious scent wafted his way. She had instructed him not to bother with the nighttime guard duty following his ascension, as his time was—in her opinion—better spent gaining power. He disagreed with this. If anything were to happen to his spiky matriarch, the world would grow dull and empty. Better to ensure no harm befell her, even if it meant he missed out on some sleep.

When the scent hit him, he immediately followed it. Not because he was hungry, of course—it was because he had to make sure some devious actor wasn't setting a trap for his beloved. On the off chance he found a tasty treat, he'd have to indulge and ensure it wasn't poisoned. Such were the burdens of Rocky, yet he welcomed them.

He followed the delicious aroma all the way back to Tropica, and when he spied the two cultists sitting on the beach, he paused. He had been explicitly forbidden from contacting the two following their introduction to Sergeant Snips, but given the possibility they could be trying to offer her poisoned fish, he was left absent choice.

Rocky couldn't smell any poison coming from the offering, but it was better to be safe than sorry. It definitely had *nothing* to do with the fish's pungent allure and his desire to taste it.

With both his claws held high in a violent warning above the waves, he began eating the possibly poisoned fish that had been thrown into the ocean.

Joel chanced a glance from his prone position, and when he saw the claws still held high in welcoming approval, he slammed his forehead back down.

"Remain prostrate, Jess. This may be another test of our devotion."

"You remain prostrate! I saw you peeking just now."

"How did you know I was stealing a glance unless you were also peeking?"

Having eaten the fish beneath the waves—and detecting no poison—Rocky moved to test the rest of the delicious-smelling food.

He scuttled up the beach with silent steps, watching the humans for any unexpected movement. With his claws still held high in a promise of impending violence, he noticed they were talking to each other in hushed tones, so he hissed a warning for them to cease their planning, then indulged in the aromatic meal—to test for poison, of course.

* * *

The deity hissed a greeting, and Joel slowly lifted his head. The crab still had its claws held high; she opened and closed them, praising their continued worship as she began eating their offering.

A cloud that had been obscuring the moon moved aside, and a soft-white light illuminated the scene. As it did so, Joel's eyes went wide. The crab's spikes were gone, its eyepatch was nowhere to be seen, and if Joel's memory didn't deceive him, it had shrunk in size.

Realization drove an icicle into his spine, and he froze as his vision tunneled in on the deity before him.

Rocky delighted in the terror and awe in the humans' eyes. They were the correct emotions to show, and he puffed himself up as he continued eating, devouring every bite of the offering to ensure there was nary a drop of poison present.

He turned to leave, but a devious thought crossed his mind, and he slowly turned back toward them. Their gazes were still locked on his magnificent form as he grabbed the tray and slowly approached them.

Swifter than either of the humans could see, he lifted the metal tray high, then slammed it down on the male's head.

CHAPTER FIVE

PATIENCE AND FORTITUDE

A cool breeze caressed Rocky's body; it was a welcome sensation following his feast. Moonlight shone down from above, reflecting off of the thin metal tray he held high.

Swifter than either of the humans could see, Rocky smacked them both on the head—not hard enough to hurt, but firm enough to make a satisfying noise. He dropped the tray, jumped back, then lowered his claws to the ground and slammed them shut.

Two explosions ripped into existence, sand sprayed everywhere, and Rocky flew backward, propelled out over the ocean.

He hissed and bubbled with laughter as he spun over the water's surface, trailing salty tears of joy as he imagined the looks on their faces.

Bonk.

Donk.

Joel flinched as the deity smacked him on the head with the serving tray. A sharp detonation sounded, and sand sprayed everywhere. Grains fell, and he tentatively lifted his head, squinting out at the world through narrowed eyes. The deity was nowhere to be seen, but then the moon reflected from something high above the bay. It was the crab, having somehow ejected itself from the beach and granted itself flight. It arced down, and after another breath, splashed down noiselessly.

"I can't believe it . . ." Jess said, sitting up and rubbing her head. "There's two of them, and that one is a maniac . . ."

Joel slowly turned to her, giving a knowing smile.

"I think you've misread the situation, Jess."

"I have? How?"

"That was the same crab, merely in a different form."

" . . . a different form? What do you mean?"

He nodded. "It's not your fault—some of the doctrine is off-limits to anyone but head priests. When creatures ascend to a certain level, they can alter their appearance."

Jess's mouth moved noiselessly, the words refusing to come forth.

"That's right, Jess. It was another test to see how we'd react."

Joel grinned, his features going manic.

"Our deity, this 'Sergeant Snips,' is even more advanced in her ascension than we thought."

* * *

For the second time in recent memory, an ancient being of the forest stirred. It knew not what had roused it, and as its awareness slowly grew, it looked for the source of its awakening. It extended tendrils in search of the two beings from earlier, but neither were present.

Confusion bloomed, and it was just about to go back to sleep when it felt something . . . *underground?*

There was a source of energy near one of its roots. It took a chance and exerted what little power remained to it, sending a root up to quest toward the anomaly. When it reached the source of its confusion, joy bloomed like a springtime flower. It was a source of energy, and though it was small in size, it was *potent.*

The ancient being drank deep, using some of the power to extend more tendrils in pursuit of further discoveries. It found three more in the surrounding earth, spaced evenly apart. Each was small, powerful, and left it wanting more.

The being shivered in delight, and if anyone were present, they'd have noticed a peculiar sight: a light-blue tree's leaves swaying in a breeze that didn't exist.

The meal was over entirely too soon, and with its hunger somewhat satiated, the being withdrew its awareness and slipped back into a restful slumber.

Corporal Claws was resting atop her favored perch when something curious occurred. A strange power tickled at her awareness, and she darted her head toward it, trying to gauge its source. The resonance was coming from somewhere to the south, and she leaped from her log before slinking off toward the anomaly.

She slipped from shadow to shadow, utilizing her unparalleled skills in reconnaissance. She was the night. She was silence incarnate. She was—Corporal Claws froze, her body going stiff as an oyster's shell. The source of the strange energy was before her, and she peered from under a fallen log, ensuring her entire body lay in shadow.

Pinpricks of moonlight shone down through the canopy, revealing a light-blue tree. Whatever was causing the disturbance had to be hiding behind it, so she snuck—rather sneakily, by her estimation—around the perimeter, keeping her peepers pinned on the offending trunk. No matter which angle she viewed it from, however, there was nothing to be seen.

There were four patches of disturbed earth surrounding the tree, which were undoubtedly where her master had tried planting the lemon seeds he'd spent the last week talking about. Was it possible that their growth had been what she felt . . . ?

No, she decided immediately. It had been an intelligent creature acting upon the world. There was no answer for what the creature was or where it went. Her ears twitched in frustration.

She was just contemplating her next move when the tree *shook.* The entire thing shivered like an otter with no fur emerging from a frosty stream, so she hunched low to the ground. There wasn't something behind the tree—it was *in* the tree!

She wiggled her body and lay flat as her pupils dilated. She would wait the creature out—such was the patience and fortitude of Corporal Claws, fuzziest and cutest disciple of Fischer.

Half an hour later, Claws crept forward toward the trunk, having had her fill of waiting. It was just so *boring.* She held her power at bay, not wanting to spark with energy and warn her unseen foe. On silent paws, she approached. A small grin tugged at her lip as the thrill of the hunt flooded through her. She bent her legs, wiggled her tooshie, then leaped into the tree's branches. She had a haughty expression across her face, intending to appear smug to whatever was hiding there, but upon landing, her visage transformed to annoyance.

Corporal Claws darted from branch to branch, but no matter how hard she looked, there was no creature to find. Her nose twitched as she worked to catch a scent, but other than earth, foliage, and her own wonderful aroma, she detected nothing.

She looked around, blinked, then let out an indignant chirp.

There were shenanigans afoot.

I woke to something warm and fuzzy curled up between my arm and body, snoring. I stroked Cinnamon's velvety fur with one hand as I let out a yawn, and she nuzzled into me, letting out a quiet peep to protest the arrival of morning.

Carefully, I extricated myself from the bed and placed pillows around Cinnamon before tucking her back in. She wiggled, and within seconds, resumed her quiet snores, easily falling back asleep.

The moment I opened my front door, I was buffeted by a cool breeze. I stepped into the sun, and its warmth stole some of the wind's frigid touch as I stretched. With my eyes closed and arms extended to the sky, I luxuriated in the sensations of my body.

The serendipity was shattered when something collided with my chest, and I let out a laugh as I fell to the sand. "Good morning, Snips. Sleep well?"

She bubbled her greeting from atop my chest and lowered her carapace, snuggling into me.

I petted the top of her head, taking comfort in her sturdy shell. "I have some stuff to build, so I'll be gone most of the day."

She nodded her understanding and hugged me tight, so I held her back with both arms.

I heard a hiss from my left. Rocky was approaching, his snippers raised and bubbles of fury spewing from his mouth. "You want a pet too, mate?"

I reached out to pat his head, but he clacked his claws in warning. "Whoa. Grumpy little fella, aren't—"

Snips, as a blur of blue and orange, halted before him, scooped him up with one claw, then flung him out to sea with a vicious overhand throw. I watched his body rocket out toward the horizon, his angular carapace rather stunning under the morning sun's light.

"You don't have to send him for six every time he tries to nip me, Snips."

She brushed her claws as if wiping off dirt, the very picture of indignation.

"I think he's a little jealous of our friendship," I said, laughing.

She shook her head and hissed in exasperation, and I laughed again.

After one more reassuring rub of her carapace, I set off for Tropica.

"Morning, Fischer!"

"G'day, Sue!" I replied from the back of the line.

She was a coffee-pouring, order-taking, pastry-slinging whirlwind behind the bakery counter, and I couldn't help but smile. "You're getting faster!"

"I have no choice—business is booming!"

Before I could respond, someone with a gruff voice cleared their throat behind me.

How does he make an ahem *sound annoyed?* I thought, turning.

"How ya doing, Roger?"

"I'm well, Fischer." He paused, his mouth moving as if he had gristle stuck in his teeth. "How are you?"

"I'm fantastic, mate! Are the ladies up yet?"

"They're not, no."

I didn't let his unimpressed attitude bring me down. "Well, hopefully they'll be up when we bring them a coffee and croissant."

His face remained still, but something was burning in his eyes. "I believe it's my turn to pay."

I'd been taking them a coffee and pastry every day for the past week. Each morning, Roger and I played out this little dance. I'd be chipper, he'd be grumpy. I'd offer to buy brekkie, he'd insist it was his turn. The last three days, I'd paid—Sue was on my side, after all, and she had final say in the domain of caffeine and baked goods.

I figured it was time I gave Roger a win. "Are you sure, mate? I'm flush with dosh, and I'm more than happy to shout. It brings me joy—"

"I'm sure," he interrupted, staring at me.

"Well, thank you, mate. I appreciate it."

That I didn't have to pay for my coffee or croissant because of my arrangement with Sue, and that I'd basically just agreed to let Roger buy his family their own brekkie, went unsaid.

"Just the usual, thanks Sue!" I said when we reached the counter.

"Coming right up!"

As she slid four coffees and croissants toward us, she peered at Roger's proffered coin, then raised an eyebrow at me. I gave a small nod, and she beamed in response.

"Thank you, Roger. I'll just get your change."

The sun peeked over the rows of sugarcane as Roger and I walked between them, and I took a deep breath of the morning air.

I had a coffee in hand. It was a beautiful day. And I was on the way to see my favorite human; given all this, I was unaffected by the disgruntled father of said human stomping beside me.

"What are your plans for the day, mate?"

"Farming," he replied matter-of-factly.

"Nice. How are the crops doing?"

"Good."

"Happy to hear it. I'm gonna make some stuff today, I reckon."

He made a non-committal grunt.

"You know, Roger, you'd be more than welcome to come give fishing a try if you wanted to."

"And why would I do that?"

"If nothing else, fish is a fantastic fertilizer—you could think of it as an extension of farming if it makes the whole 'heretical' aspect of things any better."

"No." His scowl somehow deepened even further. "I don't think I will."

"Suit yourself! The offer is always open if you change your mind. Think of my sand as your sand."

He snorted, and I smiled in response. We went the rest of the way in silence.

"Maria! Fischer's here!" Sharon yelled from the kitchen as Roger and I went inside.

Her head shot from her door. She wore pajamas, a beautiful grin, and an absolute mess of hair. "Be out in a moment!"

She emerged a minute later, hair smoothed, pajamas swapped out for daywear, and the stunning smile still present.

I held out the coffee; she ignored it entirely, stepping past my outstretched hand and pressing her lips to my cheek. "Thank you," she said, taking the coffee as she withdrew.

Heat rose to my face, and I pointedly looked at her and not her parents, who had gone quiet in the kitchen. It was the first time she'd displayed affection in front of them, and despite it being merely a peck, it left me poleaxed.

Sharon laughed and I chanced a look. She leaned on Roger's shoulder for support, her other hand covering her mouth. "Your face, Fischer—you're redder than passiona jam."

I opened my mouth to respond, but nothing came out.

Maria stepped back in and wrapped her arms around my waist. "Don't be so mean, Mom."

"Sorry," she said, her cheeks glowing with mirth from behind her raised hand. "It's just funny seeing a fearless heretic brought low by a mere kiss. Come on, Roger. Let's go finish our breakfast outside."

As they passed, Roger shot me an unreadable look that I took as a warning, and I gave him an awkward smile in response.

"So," Maria said, releasing me from her cuddle. "What are the plans today, oh *'fearless heretic'*?" She smiled up at me as she took a sip of coffee, and the embarrassment slowly left me.

"Well, I did have some light teasing in the itinerary, but seeing as that's been taken care of, we can skip to phase two."

She nodded, giving me a knowing look. "My efficiency knows no bounds. I thought it best to get the teasing out of the way, lest I become the target." She took another sip, closed her eyes, and let out a light sigh. "What does phase two entail?"

"Oh, nothing major—I thought you might like to make your own fishing rod. If that's not to your liking, though . . ." I trailed off, delighting as her eyes went wide and a grin grew across her freckled face.

CHAPTER SIX

RARE COMMODITIES

Both of my arms and Maria's were full as we strode toward Tropica. The rising sun had crested the horizon, allowing me to steal glances at Maria and the obvious joy and anticipation spread over her face.

"You know, if someone saw you smiling so hard about creating heretical objects, they might make some terrible assumptions."

"It's horrible, isn't it?" she asked, still beaming. "Your bad influence is spreading."

"Truly a travesty," I agreed, laughing.

As our footing swapped from sand and soil to cobblestones, we started passing people in the street. We were greeted with smiling faces, waves, and more than a few good-mornings as we made our way toward the woodworkers' shop.

I knocked on the door, and it swung open to reveal Brad, coffee in hand and apron already dirty with wood chips and shavings. "I was wondering when you were going to visit! Come on in."

We followed him inside. A workstation was already cleared and set up with myriad tools.

"I wasn't aware you were coming too, Maria. Did you want me to make some space for you?"

"Nah, you're all good," I answered. "We can make room if she wants to try it herself—I don't want to impose on you more than necessary."

"You're never imposing, Fischer. I wasn't joking when I said you don't have to ask to use it." He fumbled in a back pocket. "That's why I wanted to give you this."

My eyebrows shot up at what was in his hand. "What's this, mate?"

"A key to the workshop."

"Woah," I said, stopping. "I appreciate it, but you've already done so much."

"Nonsense." He dropped it into my top pocket, which I was unable to block given the crate of fittings, bearings, and other knickknacks occupying my arms. "Think of it this way—it's a weight off my shoulders because I won't need to let you in if you have work to do at odd hours."

"Sounds like he's trapped you, Fischer," Maria said, setting her bamboo poles down and patting me on the shoulder. "Turning it down now would be downright rude, which a proper, god-fearing citizen like yourself would *never* be . . . right?"

She grinned at us, and Brad barked a laugh. "Couldn't have said it better myself."

"Mate . . . I don't know what to say . . ."

"You could say thank you," Maria suggested, elbowing me lightly in the side.

I put my crate down and turned to him. "You a hugger, Brad?"

"Er, I mean—" He cut off as I wrapped him up, gave him a few pats on the back, then let go.

"Thank you, mate. I appreciate the trust."

"You're welcome." He rubbed the back of his head. "It's the least I can do given how much you've helped Tropica."

"All right, that's enough flirting, you two," Maria said, shooting us a wink. "I'm sure you've got orders to fill, Brad. And we've got *rods* to make!"

"Sorry, mate," I said to Brad. "She's terribly jealous."

"It's true," Maria agreed, unpacking the contents of my crate.

He opened his mouth to speak, closed it again, and shook his head. "I'm just gonna keep sanding these chairs down—I don't even know what to say to you two."

Maria and I shared a grin as he turned away.

I started helping her unpack and organize the components.

"Are these the offcuts we can use?" I asked from my kneeling position by a bench after my workspace was set up.

"Aye," Brad said, still focused on his work.

"You didn't even look . . ."

"That's because you can use whatever you want—there are more chunks of ironbark riddled in there at the back."

"Thanks, mate, but I think we'll try using something a little easier to work with—they don't need to be works of art. I'll definitely take one for Maria's reel, though."

I shot her a wink.

She held a hand to her chest and mouthed, *"Who, me?"*

I collected an armful of offcuts that were roughly the correct shape: six softwoods, and an ironbark one for Maria. A softwood one went in the vice first, and after winding it firmly closed, I picked up a handsaw and started shaping.

"So," I instructed, "it's best to get a rough shape before we start filing and shaving." My enhanced body easily pushed the saw's teeth through the soft wood, and within minutes, the block was roughly circular. "Do you want to try doing one?"

Maria nodded, picked up the saw, and started cutting into the next block.

As Maria's arm moved forward and back, she marveled at the strength of her body. It had been over a week since she'd become a cultivator, and the awe she felt hadn't yet diminished. Her small muscles didn't grow tired as she cut away at the chunk of wood, and though she took longer to complete it than Fischer did, it was still at a speed that would have been impossible before indulging in Fischer's food.

"Perfect," Fischer said.

She set down the saw, unwound the vice, then picked up and cast her gaze over the soon-to-be reel. There were jutting sections, hanging splinters where the offcuts weren't severed cleanly, and parts that were lower on one side than the other.

"It's not as smooth as yours . . ."

"It doesn't matter," Fischer said, placing a reassuring hand on her shoulder. "All you had to do was remove any excess wood, and we'll take care of the rest when we sand and shave it down. Here, I'll show you on the one I did."

A deep sense of calm overcame me as I used a plane to shave down the block of wood. I continually spun it in the vice as I worked different sections, and with each sliver of wood removed, the reel came closer to its final form. Before I knew it, the block of wood was blurring and morphing, becoming something else entirely.

Pine Reel of the Fisher
Uncommon
Crafted of pine, this reel contributes bonuses to both fishing and luck.
+2 fishing
+1 luck

"Whoa . . ." Maria said as my vision cleared.

Her gaze was distant, and as her awareness returned, she focused on me.

"What does it mean by 'requisite knowledge'?"

"Did it say something like, 'this has many purposes to those with the requisite knowledge'?"

"It didn't say that for you?"

"No, but it used to."

When I inspected any of my non-fishing-related constructions, I still received the same message, but ever since I'd created my fishing rod, I could see the 'stats' granted by all of my fishing-related creations. Only a week and a half ago, I had been pushing the change—and its implications—from my mind. Since confronting Barry and Sharon about their involvement in the cult, or whatever it was they were doing, I had spent my week off considering what it meant. I'd reached a conclusion pretty easily, and after only a moment's thought, I decided I should share with Maria.

"My running theory is that you can see the stats if you're high enough in the related skill. I can't see the stats of Snips's eyepatch, or a ring I made, for example, because I think my skills are probably too low."

As I spoke, her eyebrows continually lowered, until she looked at me with sheer incredulity. I cocked my head in response.

"What's up?"

" . . . you made Snips's eyepatch?"

"Yeah, why?"

"It's actually pretty good . . ."

"Hey!" I said, laughing. "What's that supposed to mean?"

"I'd assumed it was just something she was born into this world with, or was created upon her ascension." She shot me a teasing grin. "I saw the fence you made before my dad had to come fix it for you. I figured any clothes made by you would be similarly, uh, structurally challenged."

I held a hand up and gasped in mock affront. "My lady, you *wound* me."

Maria giggled as she stepped in close, placing her palm to my chest. "I'm only kidding."

"I know. You're right, though. Steven helped me with the eyepatch, and the System took over and made it transform into an actual usable item. Still, the point remains—I'm relatively sure it's your hidden skill level that determines whether you have the 'requisite knowledge.'"

"What does it say for you?"

"It gives two points to fishing and one to luck."

She scrunched her nose in thought. "It gives luck? That . . . that's a lot to take in."

"It has some implications, huh?"

Maria nodded, her face serious. "It certainly does. I wonder if the luck bonus is only active when you're fishing . . ."

I blinked at her, and she cocked her head. "What's the look for?"

"Oh, nothing," I replied. "You just reminded me how smooth-brained I can be at times."

"What does asking about the luck bonus have to do with how smooth you are?"

"Wait . . . what? Oh! I don't mean I'm smooth with my words; I mean my *brain* is smooth. A wrinkly brain is very much preferred, and having a smooth brain implies I'm an idiot."

She gave me a flat stare. "Fischer."

"Yeah?"

"What on Kallis are you talking about?"

"It's basic biology. Having a wrinkly brain means there's more of a surface-to-volume ratio, which allows room for more neurons while decreasing the relative distance between them. Though, there is an argument that having a smooth brain is a defense mechanism that makes you more aerodynamic, allowing insults to slip right off—"

"Nope," she said, holding up a hand.

" . . . nope?"

"Nope," she repeated. "I've heard enough, and I won't be letting you take us any further off track from my glorious fishing rod we're *definitely* making today. Understood?" A smile curled the corner of her lip as she raised an eyebrow at me.

"Understood, boss."

"Good. Before we continue, why did asking about the luck bonus make you feel like an idiot?"

I opened my mouth, and she held up a finger, signaling me to wait. "I will allow you to explain it in seven words—no more, no less."

"My lady would allow me to speak *seven* words? This lowly one thanks elder sister."

I bowed at the waist, and she giggled. She cut it off and cleared her throat as she tried to hide her amusement behind a mask of indifference.

I rubbed my chin in exaggerated thought, planning my seven words carefully.

"Fischer can wear fishing rod," I said with the intonation of a caveman. "Increase luck."

She nodded, then responded with the same cadence.

"Luck good. Fischer smart."

"No—Fischer dumb. It Maria idea."

I paused for effect, rubbing my chin as if I was channeling every ounce of intellect into my next words.

"Maria *smart.*"

Brad shook his head as he listened to the two go back and forth. He had been adjusting to the abilities and strength of his newfound body over the past week. One such ability was his enhanced hearing, which he was currently using to eavesdrop. He was all the way at the other side of the workshop, and by all rights, shouldn't be able to hear their conversation.

He'd intended to search for nuggets of wisdom, and to that end, he'd succeeded. Knowing that gaining levels in a skill would allow one to read created items' bonuses was intel he couldn't wait to share with Barry.

Despite the insight, and despite the possibility of further knowledge to come, he found himself more interested in their playful bickering. Genuine connection and conversation were rare commodities. He felt guilt for listening in on such intimate moments, but as he began traversing that internal rabbit hole, he shook himself.

Focus, Brad, he thought. *Keep your mind on the mission at hand.*

"All right," Fischer said, laughing. "Let's put this reel on the rod and see what happens."

Brad refocused, his hands moving of their own accord across the leg of a chair atop his workbench as he listened in.

I started by binding the rod's eyelets. "These are what you run the line through. When either you or the fish pull, the rod will flex and take most of the pressure from the line."

Maria nodded intently, her eyes focused on what I was doing.

Next, I attached the bracket that I'd asked Fergus, the blacksmith, to create for me. It, along with the others I'd had him make, was slightly smaller than the one on my fishing rod.

"This is what allows the reel to flick sideways and let the line spool out freely."

She said nothing, merely watching.

My heart hammered in my chest as I picked up the reel and slid a bearing into it. The fitting was seamless, and I took a deep breath as I slotted it onto the metal bracket. Exhaling, I focused on what I wanted the rod to become. The world listened, and it blurred before my eyes. The shape expanded, then contracted and sharpened.

My vision was drawn into my newest creation.

CHAPTER SEVEN

SCALING

Corporal Claws, chosen of Fischer and warden of the forest surrounding her beloved pond, grinned mischievously. Last night, something had eluded her. She knew not what it was, but the creature would be punished for its hubris.

She released her arms, and a pile of fish fell to the forest floor at the base of the light-blue tree's trunk. From behind her ear, she removed the stalk of sugarcane she had requisitioned from Barry's private stock.

Following her master's reprimanding of the farmer for allowing a wild bunny to ascend, Barry had built a giant wall around his crop. He'd dug a trench around the field's perimeter and filled it with rocks to stop any creatures from burrowing below. Above the stones, wooden palings extended a good two meters from the soil. Such roadblocks were nothing to Claws, and she'd leaped over it with a single bound, not even needing her lightning powers.

With the fish and the sugarcane, she had bait to lure the creature back in. Whether it was a glorious fish eater like herself, or a lowly muncher of vegetation, it mattered not; she had prepared for both possibilities.

She made to dash back to her hidey-hole beneath the fallen log but paused. Her paw darted out to requisition one of the fish, then she slunk back to her scouting position. With a sparkle in her eye and anticipation in her heart, she crunched into the fish, chewing it quietly as she awaited her quarry's arrival.

Maria took a sharp inhale of breath, and a grin spread over my face as I inspected the rod.

Bamboo Training Rod of the Fisher
Uncommon
A bamboo rod paired with a pine reel. This fishing rod provides boosts to both fishing and luck.
+5 fishing
+1 luck

The System tried to get my attention—as it so often did—but I ignored it, instead turning to Maria.

Her vision was clear; she was no longer looking at the item's description. Her eyes were wide and her mouth was slightly open. "Wow . . . it really worked."

"It did," I agreed, smiling at my work. "I wanted it to be an easy rod for anyone to use, and it looks like that intent was reflected in its name."

"Can . . . can I hold it?"

"Of course!"

I held it out, and she took it timidly, running her hands along its different components. "It's so . . . is smooth the right word? I can't find any flaws." She held it up to her face and peered at it through squinted eyes. "Even the eyelets transformed . . ."

"Yeah, I know what you mean, and smooth is the word I'd use."

Her fingers ran deftly along its length as she continued marveling at its quality. A strand of hair slipped from behind her ear, but focused as she was, she didn't sweep it back into place.

Just as the rod had consumed her attention, I was consumed by her beauty. My heart sang at the way her nose crinkled in concentration, shifting her freckled and suntanned skin.

"So," I said, "how do you feel about trying to make one without my help?"

Not even a minute later, Maria's sun-bleached hair swayed back and forth as she used a plane to shave down the chunk of wood.

She had already sawn off the corners, and one sliver at a time, she reduced the block down. I said nothing—I didn't need to. She was intently focused, and I was content letting her work it out for herself.

An hour went by, and with each passing second, the wooden block looked more like a reel. She lifted the plane but stopped, cocking her head to the side as she looked down at it.

Just in time for it to transform.

As with every time the System intervened, the reel's lines blurred and grew vague. In the space of a single breath, it shrank back down and tightened. A wave of resonance shot from Maria, and my core hummed in response.

She gasped and held a hand to her abdomen. "Wh-what was that?"

"Totally normal," I said, laying a reassuring hand on her back. "It does that sometimes—I'm pretty sure it coincides with System advancements."

"What does it mean . . . ?"

"Honestly? No clue. That you learned woodworking? That you became a fishing artisan? With the System dysfunctional as it is, it's hard to tell. More importantly . . ." I pointed at the reel. "I think you should have a look at what you made."

Her eyes went wide, and her head darted down to the reel.

I gazed at it too, letting it pull me in.

Pine Reel of the Apprentice
Uncommon
Crafted of pine, this reel provides a boost to fishing.
+2 fishing

My vision cleared to see Maria blinking up at me, her face anxious.

"What did it say? I can't read it!"

"It gives two fishing—nothing else, luck or otherwise."

Her face remained shocked.

"Don't let it dishearten you," I said. "I've been making them longer, which is probably why mine have more—"

" . . . *dishearten?*" her voice was soft, a little flat, and entirely incredulous. "Dishearten?" she repeated, laughing. "Fischer, I just made a—"

She cut herself off and darted a look toward Brad; the woodworker was bent over, sanding a chair and paying us no mind.

She leaned toward me, whispering urgently. "I just created a magic item! An actual real-life item created with the System! I . . . I can't believe it!"

"I'm not surprised—I never doubted you for a moment."

She chewed her lip in thought, her eyes staring at my chest vacantly as her thoughts roiled.

"If you're excited now," I said, "wait until you make a fishing rod out of it."

Her gaze rose to meet mine, and a beatific grin spread across her face.

"Are you sure? What do I do? Am I ready? It's all so much—"

I cut her off with a side hug, laughing as I pulled her close. "You're ready. Just do what I did and the System will handle the rest."

She leaned her head against my shoulder, then broke off with a skip and began gathering the components.

Excitement bubbled up within Leroy as he strode beneath the midmorning sun. He'd slept fitfully last night, but despite his distinct lack of sleep, he was full of energy as he made his way to Barry and Helen's home.

He reached a hand out to brush sugarcane leaves in his passing, taking comfort in their touch and how content the crops seemed to be. When he focused on any plant life, he could tell what they needed to flourish and grow.

When it came to Barry's crops, he didn't need to extend his awareness; they sang their health and contentedness toward him. With his senses engulfed by the sugarcane's joy, he lost all sense of time.

"Good morning, Leroy," Barry said, yanking him back to reality some time later.

His brother-in-law leaned on a hoe and smiled over at him from a field of sandy soil he was tilling.

"O-oh. Morning, Barry."

"Are you all right?"

"Yes. What makes you ask?"

"You have bags under your eyes bigger than a field mouse."

"That obvious, is it?" Leroy asked, rubbing the back of his head. "I didn't sleep too well after spending the day fishing."

"Really? I would have thought you'd have slept better than ever. Did something happen with Fischer?"

"Aye . . ." Leroy took a moment, inhaling and exhaling a deep breath before he dove headfirst into the conversation. "Has the System spoken up to you at all?"

Barry raised an eyebrow. "I mean, yeah, but nothing other than the usual 'insufficient power' message. Why?"

"Have you received any over the last twenty-four hours?"

"No . . ."

"Well, I have . . ."

Leroy willed the log to show, and a box appeared before his eyes.

You have learned fishing!
You have advanced to fishing 2!
You have advanced to fishing 3!
You have advanced to fishing 4!

"Oh?" Barry said, peering at Leroy intently. "What did it say?"

"After spending the day with Fischer, it said I learned 'fishing,' and that I advanced to level four in it."

Barry froze on the spot, his hoe falling from his hand and thumping to the ground. "You're serious?"

"Serious as the wet season, Barry. I'm sorry I didn't come to you sooner. It brought up a lot of inner turmoil about my time in the capital, and I just needed some time to—"

"Mate, you don't need to apologize. Does Fischer know?"

Relief flooded Leroy at Barry's easy acceptance, and a tension he wasn't aware of melted away as his shoulders dipped. "No. I'm aware he wants nothing to do with your plans, though I'm sure he'll catch on soon enough."

"Maybe not," Barry said, rubbing his chin in thought. "It might just be happening to you, and even if it's everyone, Fischer told me he has his notifications turned off."

"Wait, why would it just be me?"

Barry shrugged. "Who knows when it comes to the System, but if there's enough power for it to work . . ." he trailed off as the implications hit him.

Leroy nodded. "The possibilities are why I didn't sleep much last night."

"Our plans may be working much sooner than we'd expected . . ."

Leaves rustled as something came barreling through a field of cane to the west, and both men darted their heads toward it. Helen appeared, shoving stalks aside. Her eyes were wide, and despite her cultivator's body, she was breathing heavily. As she saw them, she skidded to a stop.

"Helen?" Barry asked, stepping forward. "What's wrong?"

"M-my bread . . ."

"Your bread? What about your bread?"

"I made some bread, and when I finished . . ." She swallowed, her face pale. "The System told me I reached 'baking seven' . . ."

* * *

I fought to keep down my excitement as Maria started putting the rod together. The only sound in the woodworking shop was that of Brad's sanding from across the room, but I barely heard it.

Maria easily twisted the hooks into place along the rod's shaft. She attached the bracket next, the screwdriver in her hand winding the threads into place. She took her time, ensuring she didn't split the thin stick of bamboo. When the screw was held tight against the bracket, she set the rod down and grabbed the reel. With a deft push of her thumb, the bearing slipped into the reel's center, making a soft *thunk* as it hit the wooden lip that stopped it going all the way through.

She set the reel down, then closed her eyes and took a deep breath. As she exhaled, she looked out at the world and collected the reel once more. She held it to the bracket and connected the two with a bolt, then started twisting the nut over its threading.

When she finished, I held my breath. Nothing happened for a long moment, and just as she turned to raise an eyebrow at me, the rod transformed.

It was over in a matter of seconds.

Bamboo Training Rod of the Apprentice
Uncommon
A bamboo rod paired with a pine reel. This fishing rod provides boosts to both fishing and luck.
+3 fishing
+1 luck

I noted the wording and stats, and before my vision could clear, Maria made an excited noise. I dismissed the inspection to see her bouncing side to side on her toes, the rod in hand and held up before her.

"I did it!"

"You did! Congratulations!"

"It's amazing!" She squealed quietly and hugged it to her chest, still dancing on the spot. "My very first rod! What are the stats?"

"Three fishing, one luck."

Part of me expected her to be disappointed, but her foot-to-foot dance only increased. I held a hand up and she high fived it with entirely too much vigor.

"Hey!" I said, laughing. "If I wasn't so strong, you might have dislocated my shoulder with that."

"Oh! Sorry!" She grinned up at me. "I'm just. *So. Excited!*"

She held the rod up and looked it over, peering at the seamless qualities of its new form.

She spun on me with a fervent gaze. "Can I make another?"

The day passed by like a calm breeze as Maria and I made more rods. Brad helped me clear a space for her to work from before he left to get some lunch, and I matched her pace, content to take my time and let her get more experience. Each subsequent rod she made took less time, and as she finished her third rod of the day, she let out a soft gasp.

"Fischer! Look!"

She held it up before me, and it immediately drew my eyes in. It was the same as before, but gave four instead of three to fishing.

"Hey! You're getting better."

She nodded chaotically, hair bouncing around her face in her excitement. "I am!"

"Well, with those six rods finished, it just leaves one more to make."

Her body language sobered in an instant. "You should make it—it will come out better."

"You know, I thought about that, but I have another idea."

Her eyebrows furrowed and her head tilted to the side. "What?"

"I was thinking we could do it together."

Excitement bloomed across her face and she nodded sharply.

We took turns shaving down the reel. The ironbark was much more difficult to work with, but given our enhanced bodies, it never stood a chance.

When it was almost finished, she turned a curious gazc on me. "Who should do the last bit?"

"I've been thinking about that too . . ."

I unwound the vice and removed the reel, holding it out to her. "You hold it for me and focus your will on what you want it to become, and I'll do the last bit of sanding."

She held it firm and rotated it as I took fine sandpaper to the reel's surface. Bit by bit, the hardwood smoothed, and with a final scrape along its surface, it transformed.

Ironbark Reel of the Fisher's Apprentice
Rare
Crafted of ironbark, this reel provides an unknown benefit. Combine it with a rod to learn more.

As both our visions cleared, we blinked at each other, then grinned at the same time. Without a word, we started constructing the rod.

Maria attached the hooks as I screwed in the bracket, and as with the reel, she held the rod firm as I attached the last piece of the puzzle. Her eyes were closed and her brow was wrinkled in concentration as I wound the nut into place. It pressed against the bearing, and I was just about to rotate my hand again when the transformation began.

The rod seemed to vibrate and my fingers tingled where they touched it. The lines blurred more than normal, and it seemed to drink light from the room as it shifted and expanded. My eyes went wide as confusion hit me, but quick as the change had started, the lines snapped back into place sharply.

A wave of elation rolled out from my abdomen, but it was completely drowned out by Maria. A tidal wave of force billowed from her and collided with my core, causing my whole body to buzz with its resonance.

"W-what . . . ?" we both asked.

Before I could speak another word, the rod's description consumed my vision.

Bamboo Rod of the Fisher's Apprentice
Rare
A bamboo rod paired with an ironbark reel. This fishing rod provides boosts to both fishing and luck. The stats provided will grow with the skill of the user.
+? fishing
+? luck

"*What?*" we both asked again, darting looks from the rod to each other.

"Holy shit, Maria . . . you got a scaling item."

She rested back against the bench, leaning on it for support. "Fischer . . . that's insane, right?"

I took a seat beside her, lifting myself up onto the bench. "Yeah, it really is. Pretty sure it will out-scale my rod, given time."

"What was the wave that rushed out of me? I felt a smaller one from you, but mine . . ." She shook her head, trying to clear it. "I've never felt anything like it."

"Also normal. It usually coincides with a message from the System reminding you how out-of-power and useless it is."

Her gaze went distant, and I guessed she was checking said message.

She took a sharp intake of breath as she whirled on me. "Fischer . . . it said something."

"Yeah, you'll get used to those messages. They're always the same, unfortunately."

"No, Fischer—you don't get it. It *said* something—a lot of things, actually. I learned woodworking and advanced to level ten in fishing."

"Wait, *what?*" I almost yelled the last word, and I quickly willed my System notifications to show.

Lines printed out before me, and my mouth went dry.

CHAPTER EIGHT

PUNGENT

Sawdust and the scent of wood filled the air, and as I read the System messages again, my mouth grew dry.

You have become a woodworking trainer!
You have advanced to woodworking 8!
You have advanced to fishing 57!

If I wasn't sitting atop the workbench, I would have fallen to my knees. I leaned back, bracing myself against the tabletop.

"Fischer, are you okay?" Maria's face was concerned as she held a hand atop mine. "What did it say?"

I told her. As I said them out loud, the truth hammered into me. I had already leveled my fishing so much, and I had become a woodworking trainer? What did that mean?

Maria spoke, drawing me from my introspection.

"If it listed them for you too . . . does that mean what I think it does?"

I nodded, clenching my jaw. "The System is regaining power—for everyone."

I checked the messages again, still not believing what I saw. On a hunch, I willed a "stat screen" to show. If this world were anything like the books and stories I'd read on Earth, there would be a way to quantifiably track progress. As I focused my mind on the task, I felt something respond. It was there, just out of reach, so I redoubled my efforts, forcing the waking world out of my awareness as I closed my eyes.

That's when it happened—the System spoke up, responding to my request.

[Error: Insufficient power. Superfluous systems offline.]

I barked a laugh, and Maria raised an eyebrow at me. "What's so funny?"

"It's nothing—I tried to see all my skill levels, but the System responded with its usual 'insufficient power' nonsense. I guess we don't have to worry about the world returning to the days before the gods' departure anytime soon . . ." I grinned. "Still—pretty neat to see notifications, huh?"

"That's all you have to say?" Maria asked, a smile quirking her lips.

"Yeah. Why?"

"You just learned that the System, something that has been dysfunctional for thousands of years, has started working again . . . and all you can say is *neat*?"

"What? You don't think it's neat?" I blew air from my lips. "You're hard to impress."

I laughed as she slapped me on the arm.

"No, you goof, I think it's beyond neat—it's downright *astounding.*"

If it weren't for Brad's cultivator body, he'd have fallen over and accidentally announced his presence. He had made an excuse to leave over an hour ago, saying he had to grab some lunch. It was a lie, of course, and while he didn't feel good about deceiving two people he considered friends—and one he considered a god just waiting to happen—it was a necessary evil. He needed to gather intel, and that was that.

Brad's hands were braced against his knees, and he was taking deep, silent breaths to steady himself. That Maria had become a cultivator wasn't surprising—the Church of Fischer had suspected as much, but it was good to hear it confirmed. What had him buckled over and fighting to not pass out was the knowledge that the System was regaining power.

He gathered his strength and left on shaky legs, heading for Barry's.

As excited as I was, Maria had to be even more excited; she practically danced as we made our way from the woodworking shop. We received a few odd looks when traveling through Tropica with our rod-laden arms, but neither of us was bothered—we had some new tools to test.

After dropping off the extra rods at my home and collecting my tackle box, we set off toward the coast. I walked with a quick gait, while Maria skipped beside me, unable to contain her energy.

"Where should we fish?" she asked. "Would the saltwater or freshwater suit my rod better?"

"Where would you like to fish? They'll work in either area."

"Hmmm . . ." Her skipping stopped abruptly, and she cocked her head to the side in thought. "The river! I haven't had a chance to go fishing there yet."

"As my lady wishes," I said with a small bow, and she whacked me on the back with the butt of her rod.

"Your *lady* demands you stop teasing her."

I grinned. "As my lady commands."

When we arrived at the rocky shore, I removed a sabiki rig. "We're all out of bait—you wanna fish for some? We'll need some more bait-catching rigs for our fellow heretics-to-be, so I might make another while you catch us some eel."

She nodded fervently. "Want me to tie it myself?"

"Do you remember the knots?"

She rocked back in mock hurt. "Do *I* remember the *knots?* You wound me, manservant. You're talking to a bona fide fisherwoman."

"My apologies—I forgot how talented, learned, and downright attractive your teacher is. Of course you remember the knots."

She gave me a sidelong glance. "Don't forget how humble he is."

"And humble," I agreed, passing her the sabiki rig with a grin.

Ten minutes later, a steady breeze blew from the ocean, so I faced my back to it as I tied small lengths of line to each other. My tackle box was freshly stocked with hooks and small offcuts, all courtesy of Fergus and Duncan at the smithy. I would have to thank them again the next time I saw them.

I shook my head and focused on the task at hand; my fingers moved deftly through each knot, connecting small bits of metal to smithy-forged hooks. I used three hooks in total, all connected to an individual line running from the main one. As I tied the last line and cinched the knot tight, what I'd been hoping for occurred.

Sabiki Rig of the Fisher
Common
A rig used to catch baitfish off the shores of the Kallis Realm. This rig boosts the attraction rate of baitfish and provides a boost to fishing.
+3 attraction
+1 fishing

My vision cleared, and I gazed down at the System-created item. The only change was the small metal offcuts I'd attached, but boy was it a change.

The metal had completely transformed, shrinking in size and folding around the eye of the hook. I held one up to my face; it had a reflective pattern that shifted in the sun, some patches shining the light back toward me while others stayed dull. I moved it around, and the other sections lit up while previously shining ones turned dull.

"You have *got* to be kidding me!" Maria said, striding over. "I only just got my line in the water! How did you—"

She cut off as something bit one of her hooks, and her head shot to look at the water. A moment later, the rod's tip dipped heavily as something else bit another hook and thrashed to escape. Her hand wound the reel in, and with a flick of her arms, a cichlid and an eel flopped up onto the rocks.

Swifter than I'd ever seen her move, she unhooked the cichlid, threw it back into the river, then dispatched the eel with a nail I'd given her.

She dashed back over with her rod in hand, her eyes going distant as she peered at the rig.

"How do I look?" I asked.

She shook her head, returning to the present. "What?"

"How do I look?" I repeated, deadpan.

"Uhm . . . good? Why do you ask?"

"I mean, it gives me an extra three 'attraction,' right? I thought it might have an effect."

She groaned. "Save the dad jokes for actual dads, Fischer. That was horrible."

I beamed up at her, entirely too pleased with myself.

"By way of apology, would you like to have the inaugural test run of this rig? We could use an extra eel as bait for the crab pot."

Her annoyance disappeared, replaced with a smile as she gave a sharp nod.

I stood beside Maria as she cast her line out. The sun had begun to descend from its peak, its warmth hitting the right side of our bodies as we faced south. The reflective strips of the newly created sabiki rig twinkled in the light as they flew over the water and landed with an inaudible splash.

"So, how does the new rod feel?"

Maria's eyes were closed, a soft smile on her face as she angled her cheek toward the sun. "I didn't realize it before, but the rod you made is a bit big for me, I think. This one feels just right."

I shared her sense of calm, and I watched the tip of her rod with relaxed eyes, waiting for a fish to bite. The movement of the water beyond drew me in, its chaotic shifting and swirling making a sense of ease course through me.

The bonus to attraction must have kicked in, because we didn't have to wait long; the rod bounced and twitched as a small fish bit one of the hooks. She waited for more to bite before reeling it in, and her patience was rewarded.

Something bigger joined the fray, bending the rod almost in half as it tried to escape. Maria's eyes went wide, while mine narrowed in thought. I couldn't say why, but the way the rod moved made me think a new species was hooked. She wound the line up, but as the hooks neared the water's surface, the hooked creature swam for its life, darting down and away in a sporadic dash.

At the fish's movement, my eyebrows narrowed further; it was *definitely* something new.

Maria stepped toward the water, giving the creature room to move. As swimming down didn't let it get away, the fish tried going out to sea, but upon finding that course just as fruitless, it darted back up the river. The line cut through the water with its movement, holding firm as Maria expertly stepped to and fro on the shore.

The fish soon grew tired, and while it still took runs, they were shorter and more sporadic. Maria meticulously wore it down, and with a final lift of her rod, something long, brown, slimy, and repulsively hideous slid up onto the rocks.

"What the . . ."

Pungent Monkeyface Eel
Rare
Found in the brackish waters of the Kallis Realm, this mature variation of the Common Eel has high oil content and a pungent scent, making it unpalatable food but excellent bait.

"Whoa," Maria said, drawing me from my inspection as she dispatched it. "It's a mature version, and it says it's rare! I wonder how good—" Her words cut off as she gagged and covered her mouth. "*By the gods,*" came her muffled voice. "*It stinks!*"

I leaned down, the impulse to sniff it working against my self-preservation instincts.

"It can't be that bad. It's only a—*hyuk!*" I shot back as if physically struck. A scent of ammonia reminiscent of smelling salts with a hint of ripe garbage crashed into me, and I similarly covered my mouth. "All right—it's *really* that bad."

I stared at the creature, its visage somehow making its scent even more repulsive. For lack of a better descriptor, the eel looked like some errant god had made its face by combining a primate's head with the bottom of a foot. It was covered in wrinkles and slime, looking like a hand gone pruney after staying underwater for too long.

"Fish can't really like eating this, can they?" Maria asked, incredulous. "It smells like death."

"I know how to find out . . ." I cupped my hands to my mouth. "Sniiiiiips! Assistance needed at the river mouth!"

Maria and I moved upwind from the nasally offensive sea creature, and before I could take a seat in the sand, something flew from the water and crashed into my chest. I'd seen her coming, so I braced my legs and easily caught her.

Sergeant Snips, my ever-reliable guard crab, hissed her greeting up at me. She withdrew her power, blue billows of water sucking back into her carapace.

"You got here fast—were you close by?"

She shook her sturdy head and blew negative bubbles, pointing out to sea.

"You were off exploring, huh? Well, thanks for coming. We have a question for you."

She cocked her entire body and peered at me with her visible eye, her curiosity evident.

I nodded at the foot-looking eel. "We want to know if that tastes good or not—fair warning, though: smell it first. The System says it's good bait, but we're struggling to believe it."

Snips jumped to the rocks and puffed herself up, taking pride in the task. With sure steps, she approached the pungent monkeyface eel.

CHAPTER NINE

FUZZ

The sun beat down on Sergeant Snips as she approached a rather silly looking creature. It had already been taken care of, and its lifeless mouth hung slightly ajar, revealing black flesh and sharp teeth within.

Her master had said the System called it "excellent bait," which meant it would likely be a tasty little afternoon snack for Snips. Just then, the wind changed direction, and she immediately reassessed how tasty a treat it would be. The smell was suffocating, and she froze on the spot, the scent overwhelming.

Part of Snips could tell that in the not-so-distant past, this eel would have been a pleasure upon her senses. As she was now, however, that wasn't the case. Her palate had changed following the introduction of Fischer's varied foods. Whatever this creature was, it was no longer on the menu.

She turned and headed back for Fischer and Maria, shaking her head emphatically.

"It's not nice . . . ?" I asked.

"See?" Maria said. "I told you! It's way too stinky."

Snips held up a claw, halting us. She made a series of gestures between her and the water, blowing hisses and bubbles that I understood.

"It'll taste good to fish, but not you?"

She nodded in confirmation, blowing another series of bubbles.

When I caught their meaning, I laughed and bent down to pat her head. "Thanks, Snips."

"What did she say?" Maria asked. "All I got was that she was happy about something."

"She says my cooking has made food she once loved taste terrible. Probably the best compliment you could give a chef."

I stretched and took a deep breath; the salty air leveled me out, and a smile came to my face as I exhaled slowly. "All right. Now that we know the eel is good for fishing, shall we?"

Maria grinned. "Let's do it."

Cutting the eel into hook-sized pieces without getting a whiff was a convoluted process involving a leaf glove, facing my back to the wind, and no small amount of concentration.

With a leaf cupped in my hand, I slid a chunk of flesh onto Maria's hook. She had swapped the sabiki rig for a drop rig, and with the bait's addition, her rod was ready to go. She walked to the rocky edge, flicked the reel forward, drew her arms back, then sent the hook and sinker sailing out over the water.

The sun was descending behind us, making its inexorable way toward the western mountains. The sky was tinged with hints of purple and pink, and I knew we would witness a stunning sunset over the next couple of hours. Beneath the beautiful colors of the afternoon sky, Maria's bait hit the water and sank toward the river mouth's floor.

After placing some pungent eel on my hook, I stood to the left of Maria and cast my line further out to sea, ensuring our lines wouldn't get tangled. I flicked the reel back into place and spun to my fishing partner.

She was beaming a serene smile at me, and I raised an eyebrow, smiling back. "What's up?"

"This is really nice, Fischer."

I took a deep breath, the joy spreading wider on my face.

"It is, isn't it? It's nice fishing by yourself, but there's just something about doing it with a friend. Oh, don't give me that look—you know what I mean."

She sniffed, attempting to appear unimpressed, but the corner of her lip twitched in amusement. It was almost unnoticeable on her sun-kissed skin.

"Just a friend, huh? Wait until my lord father hears about this."

I shot my eyes wide open and gaped at her. "Please, *my lady,* anything but that—King Roger would have my head!"

Her amusement broke through, and she covered her mouth with the back of her hand as she giggled. "I will take pity, but just this once. Next time you won't be so—"

The words died in her throat as the tip of her rod twitched. It tugged down, slight but repetitive.

"It looks like baitfish have found it . . ." I said, watching her rod. "Wait it out. They may bite the pointy end by accident."

As we both watched the chaotic twitching of her rod, the fish found my bait too, and both tips bounced in a staccato rhythm.

"Does this usually happen?" Maria asked.

"Not really, no. Maybe the bait is too effective and it's luring the baitfish all the way from the shore to the middle of the channel?"

Maria's rod stilled, and after a few more tugs, mine did too.

"What happened?" she asked.

"I'm pretty sure the little buggers stole our bait . . ."

She made an annoyed noise and began to wind her line back in, but it went slack. Maria cocked her head in response, her hair falling freely.

"Huh?"

She wound the line until it went taut, then tugged the rod up a few times, but it didn't budge.

"I think I'm stuck on something—*whoa!*"

She was almost pulled into the river and had to let go of the reel's handle as something colossal moved away, taking the line with it.

"You're stuck on something, all right," I said. "A massive fish!"

"Th-this is a fish?" she asked, her eyes going wide. She made a few testing tugs on the rod. "Feels like I'm hooked on a log . . ."

The "log" changed directions, and her eyes went even wider. She moved along the shore toward me as it swam out to sea.

Focused as I was on the thing Maria had hooked, I'd completely forgotten about my rod—until something tried to yank it from my hands.

"W-whoa! Fish on!"

I set the hook, and something large took an immediate run further into the river mouth.

"Go under," I said to Maria as I walked toward her and held my rod high. She slipped underneath, crouching low.

I felt a moment of conflict as I stared after her, feeling a need to assist with her fight, but also wanting to focus on my own. With a shake of my head, I cleared it. I had to give my full attention to my battle, lest I lose or hurt the fish. Breathing deep of the salty air, I focused on the slick rocks beneath my bare feet and the fitful breeze whipping around me.

The fish felt like nothing I'd ever hooked before. With each kick of its powerful tail, my rod bounced. Anticipation and glee rose up from within; I used them to further ground myself in the moment, each sensation of my mind and body tunneling me in on the present.

As the fish moved further upriver, my footing changed from rock to sand, and I followed along, letting the fish tire itself as I kept the line taut. Its strength slowly began to waver, so I started pumping the rod up and down as I wound the reel. It came closer and closer to shore, and I squinted out in the fading light of day as it drew near.

I caught a glimpse for just a moment, but it made the blood pound in my ears. A powerful tail, spotted and muscular, kicked away as it left the shallows for the depths. I wound the reel backward, both letting the fish tire itself further and decreasing the chances of my line snapping.

Exhausted as it must be, its power remained unbelievable. Each kick of its tail was slower now but still made the rod shift and sway. Eventually, even its kicks grew sluggish, and I reeled it into the shallows.

The fish swam with the shoreline only two meters from me, and I let out a soft whistle. The sky had turned a brilliant pink, causing its light-colored body to absorb and reflect the hues above. The fish was covered in spots and had an enormous mouth and tail. I wound the line in further, stepped into the shallows, and lifted it up onto the shore.

It kicked feebly as my eyes drew into it.

Juvenile Goliath Grouper
Rare
Usually found in the deepest reefs of the ocean, these fish grow to become true monsters of the deep. It is said they can live to be centuries old.

"You're a *juvenile?*" I asked, incredulity clear in my voice. "Just how big do you get?"

The fish kicked its body in response, and I walked it back down to the water. I'd eaten juvenile fish before, but knowing this thing had such a long life ahead of it, releasing it felt like the right thing to do. If my friends or I were starving, that would be a different story, but as the saying went, there were always more fish in the sea.

I dipped its head beneath the water and moved it back and forth to get water running through its gills. At the same time, I looked toward the river mouth in search of Maria.

"Where has she gotten to . . . ?" I mused aloud.

Just then, the fish kicked off. Its tail moved sluggishly, but as long as it could swim forward, I knew it would survive the release.

"Thanks, fishy," I called after it, watching as its light-gray speckled body disappeared beneath the waves.

An immense wave of gratitude flooded me, and I smiled out at the dark water for a long moment before I took off, running for the river mouth.

When I rounded the headland, the sky had turned from a light pink to a vibrant shade of violet as the sun got lower in the western sky. Maria was just up the coast, leaning back as she tried to heave the fish she'd hooked toward land. I ran to meet her.

"Have you seen it yet?"

"*No!*" she grunted through clenched teeth, then dipped her rod down to wind in more line. "It's like the thing is glued to the ocean floor . . ."

I had an idea of what it probably was, but I didn't want to spoil the surprise.

Their dance continued, and bit by bit, Maria got the heavy creature closer to shore. Sensing it would soon be caught, the fish abandoned its tactic of sucking its body to the floor, instead trying to glide away. Maria pounced on the moment of weakness, pumping and winding the rod. A massive shadow lifted toward the water's surface, and she let out a gasp as she caught sight of it.

"What in Nereus's rich bounty is that?"

"That," I answered, "is a stingray."

She blinked down at the thing as she continued winding, bringing it to the shallows. It was a meter wide, so dark a brown as to be almost black, with thick wings surrounding a raised body.

Maria practically vibrated with excitement, and a full-body shiver overtook her.

"You right?" I asked, smirking at her.

"*I'm overwhelmed!*" she yelled back, so loud I may have assumed she was angry if not for the open-mouthed smile betraying her true feelings.

She continued heaving, and when the stingray was half out of the water, I leaned down, grabbed the line, and hauled it up onto the sand.

Common Stingray
Common
Found in the coastal waters of the Kallis Realm, these stingrays are a staple source of food.

"Watch out for its tail," I said as my eyes cleared. "That's where the name comes from."

"How do you know so much about it?" Maria asked, bouncing from foot to foot. "Have you caught one before?"

"No—I've caught a shovelnose ray before, but it was much thinner with a long, meaty tail. I know about these from Earth."

"Is it edible? The description said they're a staple source of food . . ." Her eyes grew intense. "Are they *tasty?*"

I grinned at her. "It looks like you've caught us dinner."

Corporal Claws, most lusciously furred of all of Fischer's disciples—*Yes, including Cinnamon,* she thought, who was clearly covered in fuzz, *not* fur—returned to her watch post as the sun set.

She'd had to leave for a moment to obtain sustenance; it would be downright negligent to attempt an overnight watch on an empty stomach. She smiled to herself as she munched on the fish she'd caught in the river and cast her gaze out over the clearing, the light-blue tree in the center, and her pile of bait.

Some hours later, with half-lidded eyes and a deep sense of weariness, she slapped herself across the face, shaking her head as she willed herself to wake up. Despite her intention of waiting all night—and her best efforts at staying true to that ideal—doing nothing was just so *boring.*

She took a deep breath and let it out in a hissing sigh, not at all looking forward to the rest of the night.

It was just then, her attention waning and wakefulness fading, that the creature's presence returned. Corporal Claws's eyes dilated, and she was immediately flooded with focus and determination.

The strange power started as a trickle, like the first drop of rain that fell from the sky and hit your arm, leaving you unsure if you imagined it. The trickle became a stream, and the stream became an immutable torrent.

Corporal Claws's confusion only grew. The exertion of will came not from around the tree, but within its magnificent trunk. The power seemed to spread through the ground, climbing up toward the forest floor. Finally, it burst through the carpet of grass.

A single root, thin as a piece of straw, exited right beside her pile of bait. It moved with prehensile grace, seeming to taste the air before plunging into the fish. Claws let out an indignant chirp, ignited her body with crackling energy, then launched herself at the creature.

CHAPTER TEN

DISTASTEFUL

The being within the light-blue tree stretched her awareness out as she woke from her slumber, thoughts addled and mind foggy. It hadn't been long since her last moment of awareness.

Despite the insignificant stretch of time, she immediately noticed something: the latent energy suffusing the world had increased. It was still far below the levels of old, but compared to that of the last few thousand years, it was as a bonfire beside a smoldering log.

As she extended her senses further, feeling the ebbs and flows in the surrounding world, she made a delightful discovery: someone had brought her an offering. As with the morsels she'd found beneath the earth, the offering was of fish, along with a single stalk of chi-infused plant matter. If she had a mouth, it would have watered as she extended a thin root out, questing for the power offered.

Her root rose above the earth, tasted the air, then plunged deep into the fish's flesh. She was immediately disappointed. The power within was paltry, nothing compared to the preceding chunks of fish. She redirected the root, twisting out of the fish and into the green stalk of cane. Her spirit shivered as she tasted the sweet juices within, drank of the will intertwined with its very fibers, relished in—

Power exploded from somewhere in the surrounding forest, and an unidentified creature flew directly at her.

Corporal Claws, wreathed in lightning and promising justice for the egregious slight of tricking her, trilled a battle cry as she flew headfirst for the light-blue trunk.

Sergeant Snips was fond of telling her violence wasn't always the answer. Sure—not *always.* Sometimes, however . . . sometimes swift violence was the solution.

Claws grinned, exposing needle-sharp teeth as she rocketed at the invader, her chittering war cry not pausing for a moment.

What is this feeling? the ancient being thought as she watched the otter approach. She tasted the emotion, rolling it around her consciousness. It had been so very long since she'd felt anything.

Ahhhh, she realized. *It is amusement. I am amused.*

The otter continued to fly, claws extending and teeth bared in a promise of impending violence.

Even after having been asleep for millennia, her awareness was more than capable of keeping up with the pup before her—enhanced by lightning or not. The lightning element was what made the situation so amusing and the only thing she felt as the otter flew closer was anticipation.

The being bared her soul as the otter's collision neared, opening up her very core.

Come, then.

Corporal Claws's battle cry turned into a laugh of glee as she soared at the blue-tinted trunk. She imagined herself obliterating the tree, tearing the wood to splinters, ejecting the creature, demolishing—

The lightning surrounding her arced out and touched the trunk, and the moment it did, the power flooding her drained away. Within the blink of an eye, her ability was sucked from her body and into the tree.

No, not the tree, she thought. *The creature within.*

While it had stolen her lightning, it had—unfortunately—done nothing to reduce her velocity.

Crack!

Claws's vision blurred as she bounced back from the tree and tumbled ass over whiskers.

Delight flooded the being as she cycled the lightning down into her core. The nature power tingled, nourishing everywhere it touched.

The moment she'd seen the lightning surrounding the creature, she knew she was in for a treat; lightning was of nature chi, and very much within her Domain. What she didn't know, however, was just how much power the otter would possess. The mammal felt like a newly awakened being, and she had expected a matching level of essence.

Just what had occurred in the time she was asleep?

She had been drifting in and out of wakefulness over what must have been a few days, and the revelations in that insignificant amount of time made little sense. Her memory was littered with gaps. She could not pinpoint exactly what was off about the situation she found herself in, but it felt wrong nonetheless.

The otter, having rolled almost out of the clearing following the collision, shook her head as she got back to all fours. The being hoped she would attack again, summon forth more lightning that she could absorb, but she was left disappointed. The otter turned and ran, fleeing.

Using part of the energy harvested, the being within the tree extended a root through the humid earth. It lifted up right under the otter, just in time to catch her front paw. The otter tripped, tumbled, then stared daggers at the trunk as she got back to her feet. She chirped an insult before wreathing herself in lightning and launching herself away.

Exuberance flooded the ancient being, and her leaves shivered in amusement.

* * *

"Um," Maria said, staring down at the ray. "What part of this thing do we even eat?"

"The wings," I replied, poking the body and feeling the flesh. "They have a layer of cartilage running between the upper and lower sections of meat, so we cut off the wings, then remove the cartilage and skin."

"That sounds . . . complicated. How'd they do it in the video you watched?"

"Well, the bloke in the video went full Florida-man with an electric saw. I'm just gonna use a knife, though."

Maria narrowed her eyes at me. "Do I even want to know what any of that means?"

"Not really, but the sentence was fun to say."

She lightly backhanded me, trying not to let her smile show.

Despite how sharp my knife was, it took well over an hour to separate all the flesh from the inedible bits. I had Maria to keep me company, so the time flew by as we joked and talked about small things.

With an absolute mound of fish on one tray and all the trimmings held in a bucket, we headed back to the campfire Sergeant Snips was tending. My trusty guard crab had come and found us when the ray was half processed, and I'd told her to gather the rest of our animal pals. We were going to have a feast.

Sergeant Snips, Private Pistachio, Rocky, and Cinnamon were arrayed around the fire, and I beamed a smile at all of them.

"No Corporal Claws?"

Snips shrugged and blew bubbles I understood—she hadn't been able to find her.

"No matter," I said. "I bet she'll come running once she smells the food."

I seasoned the meat with a mixture of herbs and spices that I thought would go well with the unique flavor of ray, then placed it on a hotplate atop the flames.

Maria stroked Cinnamon's fur as I sat down next to the campfire, and I reached a hand over, scratching right between her floppy ears. Cinnamon leaned into it, arching her neck in delight. Snips hissed, demanding a scratch from my other side. I happily obliged, letting out a soft chuckle as I rubbed the top of her sturdy carapace.

The scent of ray and spice wafted up from the hotplate, and my mouth began to water. I'd placed sections of cartilage atop the fire, and Rocky leaned down before one of them, leaking anticipatory bubbles.

"You know, Rocky, you can eat those whenever you like. You don't have to wait for them to cook."

He turned to face Snips, his bubbles increasing. She hissed a sigh and nodded, giving him permission. Rocky became a blur of movement as he snatched a section from the fire and began crunching.

"Same goes for you, Pistachio. Help yourself if you like."

The giant lobster shook his head; he was content waiting.

I stood and started turning the chunks of ray with my trusty tongs. The cooked sides were a deep, golden brown, and the uncooked sides would only take a few minutes to complete. The herbs and spices had a savory punch, packed with an umami hit that made my mouth water even more.

Everyone was silent as I lifted a chunk from the hotplate and split it open, checking to see if the inside was cooked. The flaky meat parted easily, and steam rose from the white flesh. I removed the ray from the hotplate, but just as I was about to dish them out, something made itself known from the west.

My head darted to the side, peering out into the dark to see what approached. I only felt a moment of worry before I recognized who it was. Corporal Claws, wrapped in lightning and babbling an incomprehensible series of chirps, slammed into my chest. She dismissed the lightning just before hitting me, and I caught her easily, wrapping her in my arms.

"What's wrong, Claws?"

Tears sprung from her eyes as she pointed toward the forest, hissing and chirping at me so swiftly I only caught a few words.

I clenched my jaw in response. "Show me who hurt you."

From her perch in my arms, the aggrieved otter directed us through the forest. As we traveled—and I recognized the path—my confusion grew. Surely we weren't headed where I thought . . .

Eventually, we emerged into the clearing where I'd planted my lemon seeds—just where I'd suspected. I raised an eyebrow at a pile of fish on the forest floor. Claws leaped from my arms and chirped her indignation, completely ignoring the fish as she pointed at the light-blue tree, accusation clear on her fuzzy little face.

I looked at her, the tree, then back at her. "Uhhh, Claws? Are you sure the—"

A presence exerted itself on the world, and the words died in my throat. Something within the tree stirred and wielded its will. A hole opened up under the pile of fish, making it disappear into the earth. Roots churned underneath, and the patch of grass was pressed back up to obscure the hole.

I gaped, and Claws strode forward, puffing out her chest. She babbled a series of trill sounds, pointed at me, then mimed punching the tree. She slid to the spot she'd punched, then extended her arms and splayed her fingers in the approximation of an explosion.

"Stay here, Claws," I said, bending to pat her head. I glanced back at everyone else. "You guys, too—keep clear just in case."

"Fischer . . ." Maria took a step forward, but I shook my head.

"I'll be okay—I promise. Just keep your distance, yeah?"

She chewed her cheek, but nodded, her eyes serious.

As I strode past Claws, she shadowboxed the air and cheered me on with high-pitched chirps. I stopped walking as I got to one of my lemon seeds and I dug my fingers into the earth. The seed was still there, ungerminated, but just as I'd suspected, the fish fertilizer was completely gone.

As I brushed dirt from my hands, the beginning of an idea sprouted in my mind, and my enhanced awareness quickly expanded the idea until it formed a plan. Well, the possibility of one, but it was worth a try.

I stood and faced the tree. "You found my fish to your liking?"

No response came, so I crept forward on light feet.

"You know, I put that fish there to help my trees grow. I'm not upset that you took it, and I'd be happy to bring you more."

Still, the tree made no reply—not that I knew how a damned tree was supposed to communicate.

"If you want more food from me, there's a cost. I want you to help cultivate the seeds I planted into fruit trees. Can you do that for me?"

The ancient being looked on at the procession of strange creatures littering its clearing. A myriad of newly awakened creatures, one of which was one of the humans that had been present earlier.

Weak, she thought, remembering the human's power.

The man strode forward, speaking to her. She understood the language, but found his words . . . distasteful. He compared himself—but a sapling on the path of ascendance—to a mighty spirit of her station.

Using some of the power she'd harvested from the otter, she raised a mighty root, thick around as the man's arms. The ground shook and the earth split to allow its exit. She held it up before him, letting him inspect its magnificence. His face registered surprise, but his spirit was unshaken.

This annoyed the spirit, so she flicked the root at his chest. It should knock him away, but given he was a cultivator, it wouldn't hurt him . . . probably.

CHAPTER ELEVEN

DISTRACTION

Pinpricks of moonlight broke through the canopy above, illuminating the root thundering toward my chest. Thick as an otter, the root would tear through most men.

I appraised the root further as it tore through the air. If not for my enhanced body, I wouldn't have been able to spot it. Lucky for me, that wasn't the case. I grinned at the challenge and lifted one hand calmly, raising my palm where the root would strike my sternum.

The being's amusement turned to worry as the cultivator lifted an arm to block her attack. She'd aimed the blow at his center of mass, not intending to hurt him and only meaning to put him in his place. When the root struck his chest, it would knock the wind from his lungs, but his vital points would be spared. The arm, however, wouldn't fare so well; bones would break, if not shatter.

She had neither the time nor the power to withdraw her blow—all she could do was hope the devastation was minimal. A grin spread over the man's face, and she felt pity for the fool until the root struck his open palm.

Crack!

Air exploded from the collision, blowing the cultivator's hair back. His eyes didn't flinch, his footing remained sturdy, and the grin never left his face.

Realization and terror washed over the ancient being, and her leaves shook, entirely out of her control. The cultivator, this man so new on the path of ascension, had halted her blow with a single hand. Worse, she had felt his ability—the power he possessed. It was blank; pure; lacking any sort of elemental touch. The power of one's will came from the element tied to their chi, so how was it possible for this man, having not even a whisper of elemental power, to possess such strength? In her uncountable years of life, she'd never heard of such a thing.

She shuddered, her entire trunk vibrating. What kind of demon had she found herself in the presence of? One thing was certain: she wasn't safe in this human's presence.

"Well, that was pretty rude," I said, raising an eyebrow. "You could at least take me out to dinner before trying to root me."

I turned to Maria and waggled my eyebrows expectantly, but she just scowled in response. "I don't know what that means, Fischer, but I'm gonna assume it was uncouth, vulgar, and perhaps a little gross."

"Oh, you're getting *good* at this."

"No, I'm not—your immaturity is getting predictable."

The tree shuddered, and I spun to face it. The thick root that struck at my chest withdrew into the ground, slithering out of sight. Its presence minimized, and I got the impression it was departing.

"Hey! Hold up, lil' tree dude. My offer is still on the table. I really want to grow some lemons, and I'm willing to bring you snacks as payment."

I strode forward and pressed my palm to the bark, pouring my will into the tree.

"Is . . . is that something you can do?"

The being heard his words, yet still withdrew, feeling an instinctive need to get away. Her kind lived longer than most, and there was a reason for that: they didn't get involved in the games and machinations of those like the one before her.

She willed herself back to sleep, knowing her best chance of survival was avoidance. His star would either burn out too soon, or he would ascend. Either way, he would be gone and she would remain.

But then he placed his palm against the bark of her firm trunk. His intent flowed out, and it stopped her in place. Was . . . was this some kind of trick? His desires, what he wanted from life . . . was that even possible from a man possessing so much potential?

Tentatively, with great care, she extended part of herself, wanting to know more of the man. Given how fresh he was to ascendency, he likely didn't know the gravity of what he was doing—what he was exposing himself to by opening up so candidly.

She pounced at the opportunity.

As I poured myself into the tree, I felt the thing inside reach out. It was hesitant, as if testing the heat of a stovetop with a fingertip. Our souls mingled, and it—*No, she,* I thought—poked around my will, examining it. She offered some of herself up in exchange, and a hint of understanding rose from the depths of my consciousness.

As quick as it had begun, her attention withdrew, but her presence returned as she made a metaphorical step forward, returning her awareness to the center of the tree's trunk.

Her will stirred, and something sprouted from the tree. A stem extended, unfurling with small leaves. A bulb grew from the tip, and within the space of a breath, it unfurled, revealing a beautiful, light-blue flower.

I bent and sniffed it; it smelled of the forest. The condensed scent of earth, grass, trees, and life were held within the flower, and as I continued breathing in, the stem severed and fell. I caught it in one hand, holding the stunning flower out before me.

"Er, is that a yes?"

The tree seemed thoughtful. Its leaves shook a single time, and I took that as confirmation.

"All right—I'll bring some food by soon. My name is Fischer, by the—"

Corporal Claws unleashed an indignant chirp. She pointed at the tree, then punched a closed paw into her open palm, demanding retribution.

"I don't think she meant any harm, Claws."

She dashed toward me, jumped into my arms, and chirped what I thought was an expletive at the trunk. The being's awareness stirred, and a second stem extended from the tree, unfurling into another blue flower.

"See?" I said, catching the flower as it fell. I held it out to Claws. "She made a peace offering."

Corporal Claws raised a furry eyebrow, assessing the gift. She sniffed the flower, nodded, and turned her back to the trunk, dismissing it.

I pet her head. "We're gonna go have some dinner, tree, then we'll bring you some fish, all right?"

There was no response, so I shrugged and left.

"So," Maria said as we strode beneath the forest's canopy. "Are you going to explain what the frack just happened?"

"It looks like we might have made a new friend."

She raised an eyebrow at me as she stepped over a fallen log.

"Are you sure that thing is friendly? I'm pretty sure it tried to kill you . . ."

"Nah, it wasn't trying to actually hurt me. It felt a fair bit of regret when I raised my arm—it thought my bones would crack if I tried to block the blow."

"And you know that *how?*"

"It was the vibe I got when I held my hand to the tree. We kind of . . . spoke to each other? Without words. I don't really know, to be honest—it was pretty neat, though."

She took a deep breath and sighed it out. "If you call one more shocking event *neat* I might explode. You're annoyingly calm about this kind of stuff."

"I just have even more important things to focus on, like the pretty lady walking beside me, my trusty animal pals, and the delicious ray waiting for us back at home."

Claws and Snips chirped and bubbled their agreement. Cinnamon nodded from her spot in Maria's arms. Pistachio lumbered on behind us, stoic as ever. Rocky initially made no reply, but Snips darted a look at him, clicking one claw in a threat. He grumbled and nodded a single time, agreeing under the threat of violence.

Maria scoffed. "You think flattery will get you out of this?"

"Did it?"

"Hmmm." She rubbed her chin in exaggerated thought. "Not yet, but feel free to keep trying."

Despite how cold the ray had gotten while we were gone, it was still one of the best meals I'd ever had. As I took another bite of the firm flesh, I let out a soft *mmm,* focusing on the flavors. It was reminiscent of the shovelnose ray I'd previously eaten, and the herbs and spices paired perfectly with its unique yet mild taste.

"It's almost perfect," Maria said, leaning back on the sand as she assessed the lingering flavor in her mouth. "It's just missing one thing."

"Oh? What's that?"

She smirked at me. "Lemon."

"Yeah, I think you're right . . . good thing we planted some seeds, huh?"

The creatures arrayed around the fire crunched and chewed on parts of the ray. The cacophony they made was comforting, and as I gazed around at their content expressions, a grin formed on my face.

"Do you really think the seeds will grow?" Maria asked.

"I'm not positive, but I have a good feeling about it."

"Let me guess—it was the 'vibe' you got?"

I beamed. "That's right—you *are* getting good at this."

I took another bite of ray as Maria shook her head at me, and the savory flavors whisked me away, bringing me to a place of serendipity. We lapsed into silence, the only noises that of the crackling fire and my loudly eating animal pals.

As I lay in my bed that night, sleep was being elusive. My mind was awhirl with the things I'd learned today, and I couldn't shut my brain off long enough for slumber to take me.

We'd taken the ray's body to the tree when our meal was finished, and the ground had opened up beneath the offering, swallowing it whole. Based on the way the tree shuddered and shook, it was safe to assume it enjoyed the meal.

Realizing my thoughts were going in loops, I sighed and sat up, tucking in Cinnamon so she didn't get cold. The bunny was softly snoring as I stepped from my bedroom and quietly shut the door behind me.

When I crept outside, a cool breeze hit me, sending a shiver down my spine. I leaned into the chilly night as I walked down to the waterfront, hoping it would stop my mind from spinning. It didn't.

I had long suspected that the System's "insufficient power" messages were the result of skill advancements, but to have that fact confirmed . . . well, it had implications I didn't necessarily like. That I had become a "trainer" of woodworking had even more meaning, and my overactive mind immediately dove down the rabbit hole.

I'm probably a fishing trainer too, right? I wondered. *If I'm a trainer and someone I trained gains levels, does that mean I get part of their experience? Would it be more efficient to train everyone, or to train one other person that can then train others, like a pyramid scheme, or a multi-level marketing operation?*

I sighed, shaking my head and trying to dismiss the thoughts. I had no desire to become some powerful being in this new world I found myself in. I didn't want to worry about min-maxing, optimizing advancement, or organizational structures. I just wanted to fish, make friends, and be a positive influence on the lives of those around me.

Another thought popped into my consciousness, and I cocked my head, letting it unfold and expand. A grin spread over my face, and a full-body shiver took me as a massive gust of wind kicked up, swirling around me and covering my body in goose bumps.

"That just might work . . ." I said aloud through chattering teeth, turning and jogging back to the warmth of my bed.

The following morning, I woke to a slight headache, more than a little brain fog, and a plan firmly rooted in mind. I snuck from the bed, not wanting to wake the still-snoring bunny. Her butt poked vertically from between two pillows, two back legs and her fluffy tail extending into the air.

I had to suppress a laugh at the way she was sleeping as I slipped from the bedroom into the predawn light. When I stepped outside, I covered my mouth and let out a yawn.

"I guess I should ask for permission before I begin construction . . ."

"Thanks, Sue!" I said as I grabbed the offered coffee. "If you see Roger, tell him I've already been and gone—I have a meeting this morning."

She laughed. "I'm sure he'll be happy at the chance to buy his own food and coffee for once. I'll let him know. You have a great day, Fischer! Good luck with your meeting."

"Cheers—you too!"

I took a bite of the croissant; its flaky, buttery pastry was as welcome as ever, and as I washed it down with a swig of coffee, I let out a content sigh. The sun was just peeking over the rooftops, warming me and granting the world a golden hue.

"What a beautiful morning."

I walked slowly, taking the time to finish my breakfast before I arrived. I chewed on the last bite as I strode up the steps to the front door. I swallowed, then took another mouthful of coffee. After a moment's pause to appreciate its nutty, mellow flavor, I knocked on the door.

Heavy steps ran down the stairs, and fumbling could be heard from inside. The door swung open slowly, revealing the pallid, wide-eyed face of George, the lord of Tropica.

"G'day, George. How ya been?"

CHAPTER TWELVE

HOUSE KRAKEN

As the sun peeked in through his tent's opening, Number Three rubbed tired eyes. Each day since they had left Gormona, he'd woken with a smile on his face and a racing heart. Today was no different.

He still couldn't believe they were really doing it—truly leaving the capital on a mission so exhilarating, terrifying, and fraught with danger. Those anxiety-inducing thoughts were running through his mind when a friendly face poked into his tent.

"Good morning, Ellis," Number Three said.

"Good morning, Three. I'm 'One,' by the way." Ellis gently chided. "Don't let Keith hear you using any other name."

Three barked a laugh. "Right—we wouldn't want to upset the cantankerous Number Two. Is it time to pack up?"

"Not yet. Four is making breakfast, and I was just coming to see if you were awake."

"Be out in a moment."

After Ellis—er, One—departed, Three took a moment to stretch, then tidied his camping roll before stepping out. He stood upright under the sun's rays; their warmth smothered any lingering anxiety he felt about their mission.

"Good morning, everyone," he said, striding toward the campfire and the men surrounding it.

They all called back greetings—except Four, who didn't look up from making breakfast, clearly having not heard him. Two, who was wringing his hands and staring at the ground, merely grunted.

Three raised an eyebrow at the obviously conflicted man. "How are you feeling, Two?"

"Good, thanks."

Three snorted. His training as a crown auditor had begun before he was a grown man, and as a result, he could read the truth in Two's body language.

"You remember I'm an auditor, right? It's no use lying to me."

Two's eyes shot up, then narrowed. "I do *not* consent to you reading my thoughts."

"That's not how it works, Keith," Five said as he removed the pegs holding down one of the tents. "Besides, I'm not a trained auditor, and even I can tell you've got a burr in your smallclothes this morning."

"Don't call me that!" Keith—er, Two—hissed. "It's Two! I'm *Two!*"

Five held both his hands up. "Whoa. My bad. No need to go all royal on me."

"Do *not* call me royal! That's an identifying trait!"

"I don't think it was until you said so . . ." Three said. When Two turned his furious gaze on him, Three gave the royal a kind smile. "We're out in the wilderness, Two. I'm sure there's no one around to hear us."

Two adjusted his shirt, smoothing creases that didn't exist. "Procedures exist for a reason, Three. If we don't follow the rules, things will descend into chaos. *Chaos,* I tell you!"

"Worry not, gentlemen," One said, his voice deep and calming. "We will leave this location as soon as we've replenished our reserves with some delicious food. Is it almost ready, Four?"

Four's eyes jolted up from his pan, oozing incomprehension. "What now?"

"I asked if breakfast is almost ready," One repeated, tone patient and slow.

"Oh—right! It is! I'm just wilting some spinach."

Five let out a soft groan and stood to his full height, towering over the collapsed tent. "We lucked out having a gourmet chef join us on the mission."

"I wouldn't say I'm a gourmet . . ."

Five snorted. "We both know you'd have been running the royal kitchen long ago if not for that bastard head chef taking the credit for all your ideas."

"You flatter me."

Five turned to Three. "Was I lying?"

Three shook his head. "He told the truth, or at the very least believed he did."

"Well, that's kind of you to say," Four said, removing a heavy pan from the heat. "I'd say we're just as lucky to have the capital's quartermaster on board. I'd never have been able to organize every—"

"*Stop!*" Two hissed, shooting to his feet. "No more identifying traits!"

Five snapped to attention and gave a crisp salute. "Sorry, my prince! It won't happen again, my prince!"

A vein pulsed in Two's forehead and his eye started to twitch. His mouth flew open, closed, then dropped open again, trying to find words sufficient enough for the requisite chastising.

Five held his salute, and Three couldn't hold it in any longer. He laughed loud, long, and without reserve. By the end, everyone but Two had joined in, but Three noted the smile threatening to curl the prince's lip.

It is going to be another wonderful day, he thought, beaming at all of his friends.

George, the lord of Tropica and noble of House Kraken, had spent the last two weeks fortifying his resolve. Even now, in the early hours of morning, he was awake and practicing the techniques passed down from father to son since time immemorial. He had never used them prior to his confirmation of Fischer's position as a crown agent, but with the anxiety that revelation brought, he had been willing to try anything.

"I'm so glad we tried this . . ." Geraldine said, echoing his sentiments.

George cracked one eye, peering out at his beautiful wife. Even without communicating, their thoughts were joined, and a well of gratitude opened up within him; he may never have made it through the last two weeks if not for her steadying presence.

"I am too—I wish we'd read House Kraken's manuals sooner." He lay a hand on her plump knee, and she opened startlingly green eyes that crinkled as she smiled at him.

She giggled, covering her mouth with a voluptuous hand. "I never thought I'd hear those words from you. You've always been so adamant that your family's teachings were the reason for their diminishing position."

He gave her a rueful grin. "Relying on the meditations has been an . . . enlightening experience."

She laid her hand atop his, pressing it down against her knee. "I feel the same, my love. No matter what happens with Fischer and the other crown agents, I know we'll be just fine—"

Three sharp knocks came on the front door, and George's calm was shattered like the hardened glazing of a donut dropped to the floor. Geraldine hissed and patted his hand, and he realized he'd dug his fingers into her leg.

"S-sorry . . ." He took a deep breath, trying to recenter himself.

It didn't work.

Geraldine sighed. "Speak of the devil. Do you want me to get it?"

"No, my love. I can face him."

George got to his feet with no small amount of effort, grunting as he leaned on both plump arms. He got to his feet, inhaled, and released another measured breath. Again, it didn't help. He smoothed his clothes and stood tall, resigned to at least appear composed. "I'll be back in a moment."

Geraldine squeezed his calf with one hand, then closed her eyes, returning to her meditation.

George strode for the stairs, relying on the railing to hold his weight, shaky as his traitorous legs were being. When he reached the door, his fingers fumbled over the locks, and he took a moment to steady them. They still shook, but with exacting movements, he carefully removed the final latch and swung the door open.

"G'day, mate," Fischer said, giving George a predatory smile. "How ya been?"

"I have been well, Fischer, and you?"

"Great, mate. I've been great. Sorry to skip right to the heart of the issue, but I've got a bit of a big day planned today. I was hoping to talk to you about a project."

George's stomach dropped. He swallowed, buying time to compose himself.

"You have? What, uh, project are you talking about?" Even George could hear the slight quiver in his voice, and he leaned on the doorframe for support.

"Oh, nothing major, just a wall to fish from."

Despite his uneasy state, confusion still washed over George. "A . . . wall? To fish from?"

"Yeah, mate. A wall."

Fischer smiled, and George realized the crown agent wasn't going to elaborate.

"What kind of wall? Where?"

"A rock wall in the ocean, extending from the headland and running in line with the river's bank. I'm pretty sure no one would care given how disregarded the ocean is, but I figured it couldn't hurt to ask—make sure it was legal, you know?"

"H-How does that help with fishing?"

If George's wits had been about, he'd have simply given permission and moved on. Unfortunately, his thoughts were addled, and Fischer was all too happy to continue the ruse and elaborate.

"It helps immensely—it's actually really beneficial for the sea life of the area in general. You build it using large boulders, and the gaps between them provide room for all sorts of species to live in." Fischer's eyes were practically shining, and his hands moved animatedly with every other word. "It's also great for erosion! Sediment builds up at the base of the wall, and it stops sand from washing away from the river mouth!"

If George didn't know better, and he wasn't aware that Fischer was some sort of senior crown auditor, he might have believed what appeared to be a passionate speech. But George was far too clever for that. He didn't know what trap was being prepared, what rope Fischer was dangling with which George could hang himself, but he wasn't going to fall for it.

He schooled his face and nodded. "You can do what you want with the ocean, Fischer. There are no explicit laws regarding the ocean and its ownership." Along with his meditations, George had spent the last two weeks reading and rereading the crown laws, and he wouldn't be fooled into giving incorrect information. "Was that all?"

"Oh, for real?" Fischer beamed the smile of a wolf. "Yeah, mate! That's all I had to ask!" He turned and jogged from the step, looking over a shoulder to give George one last grin. "See ya, mate!"

As he disappeared around a corner, George closed the door, the soft *click* of the lock sounding far away.

His back itched and tingled as sweat sprouted. With each step upstairs, his legs felt more and more like they belonged to someone else. The sense of his body was numbed as he shuffled along. He knew not where he was going, and his legs moved of their own accord, taking him . . . somewhere. He started tipping over, and his arm shot out, trying to grab anything for support.

Something . . . no, *someone* caught him. Voluptuous arms held him tight, and as he realized it was Geraldine, his awareness returned to his body in a rush.

"You're okay, George," she said, rubbing his back.

He stood tall and squeezed her, taking solace in her touch. "Thank you, my love. I was a little . . . lightheaded. I'm all right now."

She helped him sit down, and he crossed his legs, easily falling into the House Kraken meditation position. Despite his worries, he felt a twinge of amusement that he'd been practicing for less than two weeks and his flexibility had already improved enough for him to sit cross-legged. It was still far from the optimal stance, but he was much closer to achieving it after such an insignificant amount of time.

"What happened?" Geraldine asked, drawing him from his musings.

He relayed everything without embellishment, leaving out his assumptions and thoughts; he wanted to hear her untainted opinion on everything Fischer had said.

Geraldine leaned back and stared at the roof for a long moment, considering what he told her.

"What do you think, George?" she asked, still looking up.

"I want to hear your opinion first."

She nodded, and after a moment, sighed. "I have not the faintest idea."

He chuckled, shaking his head. "Neither do I. At first, I'd assumed it another trap for me to fall into, but when I think about it . . . what end would that serve? I've already been caught lying about and *doing* much worse."

"My thoughts exactly . . ."

The more he sat and tried to work it out, the worse George felt. His stomach was doing flips, and his breaths felt shallow, like he couldn't get enough oxygen. He rubbed his hands through thinning hair, making a frustrated noise and trying to banish the troublesome thoughts.

"What are we to do, Geraldine? I was just starting to feel more equalized, but a single visit from our tormentor and I'm back at square one. It feels hopeless . . ."

She crossed the floor faster than someone of her impressive form had any right traveling, and she leaned into him, hugging him tight.

"I'm sorry it feels that way, but don't let your thoughts deceive you." She pulled back and stared into his eyes. "Why don't you read your house's manual again? It's what got us through the last two weeks, is it not?"

He didn't feel the motivation to do so, but nodded, knowing it would probably help. He stood and strolled to a table across the room, taking a seat and flicking open the large tome atop it. Flicking through pages, he stopped when he saw the heading he was looking for—Chapter 4: Navigating and Harnessing Times of Great Stress. He took a deep breath and held it for four seconds—just as the book instructed toward the end of the chapter—then released it slowly and began reading.

CHAPTER THIRTEEN

THRILL

Cool air tickled my skin as I soared through the air. I smiled at the water rushing up to meet me before I splashed into the ocean. Its icy temperature sent a thrill coursing through my body, and I arched my back, curving up through the water column to breach the surface. I gasped instinctively, taking shallow breaths as I shivered, acclimatizing to the ocean's frosty touch. Corporal Claws's head popped up next to me. Her cheeks were puffed out.

"Claws? Why do you look like— "

She pressed a forepaw to either cheek and squeezed—a torrent of seawater slammed into my face.

"You little rascal!" I slapped my hand against the water, intending to splash her back—instead, my hand made an ear-splitting *slap* as it struck, and water flew in every direction, including into my open mouth.

I coughed and wiped my eyes, bobbing up and down on a now-roiling patch of ocean. Corporal Claws floated on her back, chittering with laughter and pointing at me with one paw.

Two extended claws poked above the ocean, and I turned to greet Sergeant Snips. The words died in my throat as I saw it was Rocky, blowing *very* pissed-off bubbles. One claw pointed at me, the other at the still-giggling otter. He slammed them closed. Twin explosions rang out, and another wash of water assaulted me, but I'd had time to turn my face away.

Despite the lack of playfulness in his clacking, I turned back to smile at Rocky—just in time to see him lifted from the water. Sergeant Snips, spewing bubbles and seething with fury, flung him upward. He soared five meters into the air, and as he fell back down, blue water billowed from Snips's body. She darted up to meet him, swung a claw up, then slammed it into Rocky's undercarriage.

Like a slingshot, she launched Rocky parallel to the ocean's surface. He didn't lose height for a long moment, but then he dipped rapidly. He skipped across the water like a flat stone, getting smaller and smaller as he bounced out toward the horizon.

"Nice shot, Snips."

She blew a single bubble filled with anger, then held a claw to my shoulder, apologizing for her subordinate's actions.

"No need to say sorry, Snips—it was actually kinda funny."

Claws nodded her agreement, letting out a shrill chirp and revealing her pointed teeth. Something large and surprisingly buoyant bobbed the surface, and I reached a fist out toward it.

"How ya going, Pistachio? Good to see ya, mate!"

He reached a claw out ponderously and fist-bumped me, blowing a small stream of greeting bubbles.

"All right, here's the plan, gang . . ." I paused, realizing one of the construction crew had just been yeeted out toward international waters. "Would you relay the plan to Rocky when he gets back, Snips?"

She nodded curtly, clearly unhappy to be reminded of the crab's existence.

I lifted my face toward the sun as I treaded water, delighting in its warmth. "It's such a beautiful day. Anyway, the plan is to check out the ocean floor from here to about fifty meters that way." I pointed out to sea. "We're just making sure it's all clear to put some rocks down. If it is, we're going to find some boulders and move them here. We're going to need *a lot* of rock, so we may have to create a quarry somewhere."

All three of the creatures bubbled or chirped as one, voicing the same question.

I grinned. "You'll just have to wait and see what it's for, but I promise you'll all love it."

Sergeant Snips's and Corporal Claws's eyes shone, and even Private Pistachio's face became filled with intrigue.

I took a deep breath and started swimming down. The frosty water hitting my face spiked my adrenaline, but it wasn't unenjoyable; I smiled as I approached the ocean floor, my powerful body easily gliding through the water.

I realized my eyes had improved since I'd first become a cultivator—I could now see underwater as if wearing goggles. Each time I'd gone underwater in recent memory, I'd closed my eyes, not wanting them to sting under the saltwater's assault.

How long have I been able to do this, but didn't know? I wondered.

It was a startling but welcome discovery, and a sense of awe flooded through me as I gazed around. Small fish darted away at my approach, and I stretched my fingers out toward them, delighting at the water flowing past me.

Corporal Claws, completely misunderstanding my intent, sped past me at unbelievable speed. She caught a fish in her paws, swam over to me, and held it out, grinning wide. I scratched the top of her head and extended cupped hands. She released the fish, and relief flooded me as I saw it was uninjured. It swam around my palms, flitting to and fro with small kicks of its tail.

When I opened my hands, it dashed away, swimming off to find its friends. Claws glided over to me, upside down and still grinning; the angle, combined with her toothy smile, made her look ridiculous. I laughed noiselessly underwater.

She collided with me, and I scooped her up in one hand, using the other to scritch her belly as I kicked my legs and propelled us along the ocean floor. My body seemed to slip through the streams of water; I didn't feel the drag I expected to hit my body. Rather than disorienting, it was thrilling, calming, and everything in between. I stopped kicking my legs and swam like a dolphin through the sea, enjoying the experience more than I could put into words. I scooped up Snips as I soared over her, and she wiggled happily, wrapping her legs around my abdomen.

By the time I'd swum the length of the would-be wall, I had forgotten all about it. We swam together beneath the waves, traveling farther and farther out to sea. I followed the path of the ocean floor, and the surroundings got darker as the bay got deeper. Bommies of rock and coral began sprouting up, resembling the tops of bouquets, and I slowed, gazing at them intently.

Coral and anemone of an unbelievable variety swayed in the underwater currents. There were patches of orange, purple, green, blue, and even pink of different shades, sizes, and shapes. Uncountable species of fish used the bommies as shelter.

Small fish you'd see in aquariums back on earth swam around the coral. Clown fish hid in the anemone, not at all bothered by our appearance. Fish bigger than my hand poked their heads from holes in the rock, and upon noticing us, disappeared back into their holes. Larger fish, of which I only caught glimpses, swam away at blistering speeds, finding another place to use as shelter now that we, who they undoubtedly viewed as predators, had come to visit their waters.

I reached out and touched some coral; it was soft and squishy, and I smiled at the pleasant texture. My lungs started to complain for oxygen, so I swam up, careful not to disturb the water too much with my excessively powerful body. When I breached the surface, I took a deep breath, squinting my eyes against the oppressive daylight.

"Huh . . ." I said when I looked back toward the shore.

I had lost track of time while swimming, and I hadn't realized just how long I'd been holding my breath. The rock of my headland was the size of a marble in the distance. I could just make out a welcome sight on the shore; Maria stood with who I had to assume was Cinnamon in one arm, the other held high in the air, waving at me.

I held my animal pals tight and dipped back below the water. When I got back to the headland, I kicked off the ocean floor, still holding Snips and Claws to my chest as I shot from the bay. A gout of water followed me as I landed on the rocks, and I bent my knees to soften the impact.

"Good morning! I see Cinnamon found you."

"She certainly did . . ." Maria replied, raising an eyebrow and looking down at my stomach.

"Uh . . . something wrong?"

"Just admiring the muscles. Have you gotten stronger?"

I glanced down and shrugged. "I think I've been pretty muscular since awakening—it's nothing new."

"Yeah, that's a straight up lie. I saw your stomach when we were on that camping trip, and it was lean, sure . . . but this?" She stepped forward and slapped my stomach lightly. "That's just ridiculous."

"Must be the lighting. Anyway, my washboard abs and impressive physique aren't important right now—I need your help with something."

"Oh? What's that?"

I grinned. "I just found something beautiful, and you *have* to come see it."

I held a hand up to Maria, intending to help her into the water. She bent down, then gave me an odd smirk. I didn't like the look in her eyes. She launched from the shore, tucking her legs up and holding them to her chest. She cannonballed into the waves beside me, holding strong eye contact and that same expression the entire time. I accepted my fate and let the wave of water slam into me.

I wiped my eyes and gave her a flat stare, which only increased the vigor of her giggling.

"Do you feel good about yourself?" I asked.

"I feel amazing." She gave me a full-faced smile. "Thanks for asking. How are you?"

"Feeling rather refreshed, thank you."

She swam over and ran her hand over my head, smoothing my hair. "Glad to hear it. So, what did you have to show me?"

"Follow me."

I took a deep breath and sank down. Maria followed, and a smile quirked my lips as I saw her eyes firmly squeezed shut. My right hand darted toward her, and I spread one of her delicate eyelids open.

Her immediate reaction was to try to bat my hand away, but she froze, opening both eyes and blinking. Her head spun and mouth dropped open as she looked around, awe clear on her features. I pointed at her and gave her a thumbs up, cocking my head in question. She nodded vigorously, and her head began darting around, taking in our surroundings.

I held a hand out, and her fingers intertwined with mine. Starting out slowly, I swam like a dolphin through the water, and she mimicked my movement. We picked up the pace as I led her out to sea.

The path was just as pleasant as before, and I could tell Maria felt the same; a peaceful smile covered her face, mingled with a calm serenity. I picked up Snips again from the ocean floor in passing, and Claws swam circles around us, similarly delighting in the sensation of swimming.

Halfway to our destination, Maria went to the surface to get a breath. She quickly rejoined me, and we continued our passage. When we arrived at the colorful bommie, she let out a muffled noise of surprise.

Rather than look at the swaying coral and anemone, I watched her. The look of wonder on her face was everything I had hoped for, and my heart fluttered in response. When I glanced at the bommie, my eyebrows furrowed in confusion, and I swam to the surface.

"What is it?" Maria asked when she joined me. "You look concerned . . ."

"All the fish are gone . . ."

"What do you mean?"

"There were hundreds of fish before, and now there are what? Like ten?"

Maria opened her mouth to respond, but the head of a belligerent otter popped up and let out a trill noise I'd not heard from her before.

"Claws?" I reached out to touch her, but she moved her head away, her eyes going wide. "What's wrong?"

She pointed down with one paw, chirping incoherently. Maria and I shot a worried look at each other, then both put our faces beneath the water's surface and peered down.

Despite my enhanced body, a spike of fear stabbed into my core at what was lurking below us.

CHAPTER FOURTEEN

APEX PREDATOR

A lump formed in my throat, and my body involuntarily froze as a wave of adrenaline washed over me. The water seemed to change temperature; where its cool touch was previously welcome, it now felt intolerably freezing as the shadow shifted beneath us.

Even with my eyes still adjusting, I'd seen enough footage of the terrifying creatures to identify one by shape alone. A shark of monstrous proportions swam through the bay. Twice as long as I was tall, the thing barely needed to kick its tail to send its gigantic form gliding through the water.

Maria moved beside me and latched onto my hand. I squeezed, trying to reassure her. Corporal Claws clung to my back, also wanting nothing to do with said shark. Sergeant Snips lacked the same sense of self-preservation, and she sank to the ocean floor, both clackers extended and poised to deliver violence. Pistachio was also beneath us, and his head slowly turned, following the shark's movement.

Meanwhile, the shark continued its passage, unaware or uncaring of our existence as it moved with the ease of an apex predator. It slowly faded from view, swimming far enough away for us to lose vision of it. Snips swam back up to meet us, and we kicked to the surface, emerging as one while Pistachio remained below.

"Snips—can you keep an eye out and warn us if it comes back?"

Water sprayed my face as she gave me a crisp salute, then disappeared beneath the water.

"What in Hades's influence was *that?*" Maria hissed, keeping her voice soft.

Claws chirped her agreement, poking her head around from where she clung to my back.

"You haven't seen one before?" I asked.

Both of them shook their heads, their eyes wide.

"It's a shark. They're pretty common in the ocean where I'm from. I'm pretty surprised you hadn't seen one, Claws."

"They're common?" Maria asked. "I never want to get in the ocean again—I'm honestly rethinking my whole love of fishing right now."

"I think we'd be all right considering we're cultivators, but still . . ." My entire body shook with an involuntary shiver. "Something about seeing such a large creature in the water beneath us makes my brain go into nope mode."

Maria shuddered too.

"If Snips and Pistachio weren't beneath us keeping watch right now, I'd be swimming back to shore as fast as I could."

"That'd probably be a bad move. From what I know, they don't usually attack humans—they only do so when desperate, or they mistake you for prey they'd usually hunt. Splashing around to get away might make you seem like a seal or an injured fish."

She glared at me. "Not helping, Fischer."

Claws batted the side of my face, chirping her agreement and scowling.

"Sorry," I said, laughing. "I couldn't help myself. Let's get back to shore—I haven't even told you what I want to build yet."

Maria leaped at the extended branch, happy for any distraction. "You have something you want to build?"

I grinned. "I do—something to help us fish."

A measure of fear left her face in an instant, and her eyes began glimmering beneath the morning sun. "Go on . . ."

We swam past the river mouth and made our way south, following the shore as sand transformed into scattered rock, and scattered rock transformed into sheer cliff. Snips had mentioned we could find boulders this way, and while I'd believed her, I hadn't expected there to be so many. All along the cliff's base there were what had to be hundreds of tons worth of giant stones that had fallen from the jagged cliffs.

Rocky had returned from his Snips-empowered trip out to sea, and he now acted as guard crab against any wayward sharks. He was flanked by Snips and Pistachio, and I smiled down at the reliable crustaceans.

I swam down and tried lifting a boulder that was as wide as I was tall, and I easily brought it up. Maria was watching me, so I hefted it above my head with one hand, flexing my other arm in a Herculean pose. A white wash of bubbles exploded from her mouth as she laughed at me, bending at the waist and holding a hand to her stomach.

Dropping the rock, I kicked off the sandy floor. A moment after I breached the surface, Maria joined me, and she gave me a grin reflecting the excitement I felt. "Are these boulders the right size?" she asked.

"They're *perfect,* and there's enough that I don't think we'll need to quarry any more."

She shimmied her shoulders, unable to contain the anticipation. "How do we start this construction, and when are you going to tell me what it actually is?"

I'd been extremely vague with my explanation, wanting to keep the details a surprise.

"To answer your first question, we just have to put the boulders there. To answer the second . . ." I shot her a wink. "You'll just have to wait and see, but I promise that you'll love it."

She shimmied again, and I couldn't help but smile.

"Let's get started."

* * *

Sergeant Snips and Private Pistachio joined the boulder-hauling efforts, leaving the rather irritable-looking Rocky as the main defender against shark-related threats. It wasn't that his role as defender annoyed the neurodivergent crab. I suspected it was anything but—he just always looked like someone had insulted his ancestry and spit in his soup.

Even with the cultivator's strength of our respective fleshy—and carapacey—bodies, it was a long process; we could each carry one boulder at a time, and it was quite a distance back to the river mouth.

Despite also being on the path of ascension, Maria couldn't carry some of the boulders I could; her arms were shorter and her cultivation less advanced. The largest one I found was half again as wide as I was tall, and I easily held it in my arms. When Maria tried to carry one slightly smaller, the best she could manage was repeatedly throwing it short distances. Snips had the same issue but worked together with Claws, who stabilized the boulders by swimming around them, correcting the positioning if they leaned too far in any direction. Pistachio had no such issue, and he easily threw massive rocks atop his back and scuttled along the ocean floor.

A few hours later, I threw a boulder down, adding it to the line extending from the headland. We were creating the base layer first; it was roughly five meters wide and ten meters long so far. Maria, Snips, Claws, and Pistachio arrived shortly after, and they carefully placed their loads down.

I pointed to the shore and they followed me up. Cinnamon greeted us with a squeak, her long ears upright as we emerged from the water. She was lounging in the sun but got to her feet and jumped to a stack of towels, nuzzling them with her cute little nose.

"Thanks, Cinnamon," I said, reaching down to rub her head after I dried my hand. She leaned into me, closing her eyes in delight as my pat turned into a good scritching.

She then walked over and dipped her chin, inviting Corporal Claws to pet her. The otter cocked her head but reached out to oblige the soft little bunny. Said bunny's expression turned downright malicious, and faster than a normal eye could see, she spun and kicked out her back legs, spraying Claws with more sand than such a small creature had any right displacing.

Cinnamon tore off across the shore, angling around the headland as Claws went stock-still. The otter ran paws over her face, wiping away sand. Her eyebrow twitched, and her lip curled to reveal needle-sharp teeth. She hunched and gathered power in her legs, her entire body shaking, causing more sand to fall away.

Lightning sparked out, and she rocketed from the headland. Her form curved and twisted; she flew like a heat-seeking missile for the trail of kicked-up sand that was Cinnamon trying to escape. Corporal Claws arced high, then slammed down on top of the bunny. A mushroom cloud of sand and dust sprayed up, obscuring whatever was happening within.

"Uhhhh," Maria said. "Is Cinnamon going to be okay?"

"She'll be fine—Claws wouldn't hurt her."

Maria shook her head, letting out a light sigh. "I can't believe our daughter has become such a prankster. I thought we raised her right . . ."

"Claws has no one to blame but herself." I chuckled softly. "She set Cinnamon on the path of treachery, so now she has to deal with the consequences."

The sand started to clear, revealing a slap battle happening in the distance. Both creatures were up on their rear legs, batting at each other in a blur of forelimbs.

"Should we get lunch started?" I asked. "I'm sure they'll be hungry when they're finished."

"I don't know about them, but I'm *starving* after you forced me into physical labor all morning. The least you could do is prepare me a snack."

"Forced, huh? I recall you shimmying so hard you created waves."

"Shimmying? Oh, no—I was shaking in fear of what you'd do if I refused your orders."

I bent down toward Snips, giving her a conspiratorial glance. "Take note, Snips. If you want your subordinates to behave, the threat of unmitigated violence is unparalleled as a motivator."

Rocky rubbed his chin with one claw, then nodded his agreement to the statement.

Snips walked over to Maria and patted her leg, blowing bubbles of solidarity.

"I know," Maria said, bending to rub Snips's carapace. "We're surrounded by clowns, but I'm glad to have you here for support."

"Clowns? I have *never*." I raised a hand to my chest in mock affront. "Would a clown make you a feast of sand crabs for lunch?"

Both ladies froze, their farce failing before the promise of a delicious meal.

Maria raised an eyebrow at Snips. "Perhaps clowns was a bit . . . aggressive."

Snips's head bobbed up and down energetically, her mouth blowing hungry bubbles.

After we got dressed, we made our way over to the crab pot, and butterflies took flight in my stomach as I pulled in the line. Ever since Maria had started joining me daily, we had been catching a *lot* of fish. As a result, I hadn't been using the crab pot, not wanting to waste any meat. After finding the new type of bait in the pungent eel, however, I just *had* to try it out.

The cage at the end of the line felt heavy; the butterflies within me multiplied, and a broad grin spread over my face.

"How does it feel?" Maria asked, whispering from beside me.

I turned to look at her, and when she spied the look on my face, her eyes crinkled in delight. We cast our gaze back toward the shallows just as the first corner of the crab pot became visible. It was impossible to make anything else out, so I kept pulling, bringing the cage closer to us.

My excitement dwindled as it came into view. The back half of the trap was filled with sand, somehow getting caught on the ocean floor and dredging it up in passing. Then a claw extended from the mass of sand, and the entire pile seemed to move and undulate.

I realized the truth of it: it wasn't a pile of sand—it was a pile of sand *crabs!* There were so many as to fill half the trap, and before I could make a sound, Maria let out a loud *whoop!*

"There's so many, Fischer! Demeter's harvest—I've never seen so many!"

I grasped the handle and dragged the crab pot up onto the shore. There had to be dozens of them, all of which were unhappy about being removed from the water. Those on top of the stack held their claws high, warding off any would-be attackers.

"Holy frack," I eventually said. "That bait wasn't kidding about being effective."

Corporal Claws dashed to the cage, running around it and twisting her head at strange angles to inspect the pile of creatures. Cinnamon was atop her back, also cocking her head to peer down at the crabs. The two had worked out their differences and were once more the best of pals. Their eyes were alight, and following their example, the rest of the creatures stepped forward.

Pistachio watched the sand crabs with an intent gaze; there was always a startling intelligence hidden within the stoic lobster's eyes, and I once more wondered at the depth of his thoughts.

Snips and Rocky were much easier to read; they both blew hungry bubbles as they scuttled up to the cage.

Not wanting to drag it out any further, I opened the cage up and started sorting them.

"Come closer, everyone." I gestured for Maria to stand beside me. "Snips already knows, but I'll show you how to differentiate between male and female. Females are breeders, so we let them go."

Corporal Claws—trickster of the sands and espionage extraordinaire—dashed over the dunes.

She had a freshly cooked sand crab held under one claw, and thinking of the meal to come, she redoubled her speed. Her master had promised they'd wait for her return before feasting, but it would be downright rude to make everyone else delay longer than necessary. Her haste had absolutely *nothing* to do with her desire, nay, her *need* to partake of the crab.

With a spark of lightning, she activated her ability and flew between the trees, bouncing from trunk to trunk. As she catapulted into the clearing, her eyes locked onto something before the tree. She lost control of her power, and the lightning surrounding her guttered out and died.

Corporal Claws slammed into the tree and slid down its trunk. She blinked dumbly as she took in the scene, not once taking her eyes off what had arrested her attention.

CHAPTER FIFTEEN

QUARTERED

The world was upside down, and Corporal Claws gazed out at it. She rested on her head at the base of the light-blue tree, a cooked crab clutched tight, and her back feet dangling above her, twitching of their own accord. No matter how many times she blinked, the scene didn't change.

She rolled over slowly, her eyes not once leaving the twin leaves that grew from a mound of churned soil. She left the offering of crab at the base of the tree and padded over to the disturbed patch of earth. She circled the seedling, not seeing any defects or damage. She was a blur as she sprinted around the tree, checking on the other three seeds.

Each of them had germinated; their leaves and stalks were a vibrant green—a testament to their health.

She looked back at the tree and the crab she'd left beneath it. Roots extended from the ground and plunged between gaps in the crab's carapace, and the tree's leaves twitched and vibrated in what appeared to be delight.

Claws held a paw to the firm trunk, chirped her thanks for the tree's hard work, then dashed away toward the sand, her mouth spread in a wide smile.

"How did you go, Claws?" I asked as she returned.

She chirped joyously and sat in the shade beside me, not elaborating on her mission.

It must have been straightforward, then . . . I thought.

Returning to the present, I started cutting the crabs into sections. After releasing the females, we had fifteen crabs—a veritable feast. I pressed down lightly on the sections of crab, cracking shell and exposing the meat within.

"What are you doing?" Maria asked, her face alight with curiosity.

I grinned back at her. "I'll show you in a moment."

I strode to the campfire and removed the large pot I'd put atop it. With my nose above its opening, the scents of butter, garlic, a mild hint of chili, and onion rose up to greet me. My mouth immediately began watering, and I set the pot down on the sand.

"I cut the crab and broke the shell so the butter can get in and suffuse the meat with its flavors."

Maria leaned in to smell the steam rising from the pot. Her face softened, and she let out a sigh. "Okay—that smells *divine.* How long does it need to cook in the butter for?"

"That's the best part—it doesn't."

I reached in with tongs and removed the first chunk of crab. It was a large forequarter, and golden liquid streamed from the front claw as I lifted it from the mixture. I put it on a plate, which I passed to Maria. "I already added salt to the butter pot, but feel free to add more to your taste."

I took out more sections, passing one to Snips, Claws, Pistachio, and Rocky. The latter raised a buttery leg to his mouth, but Snips slapped him on the back of his head before he could bite into it.

I removed another and placed it on a plate before me, then flicked a stalk of cane to Cinnamon, who caught it mid-air and started chewing without delay.

"Dig in, guys—you didn't have to wait."

"Food tastes better when eaten together," Maria replied, pulling a claw apart with her hands. She lifted the white meat to her mouth and bit down. Her entire body relaxed like a weight had been lifted from her shoulders, and she let out a soft *mmmm.*

My animal pals crunched down, their eyes fervent and movement harried.

I couldn't wait any longer.

With my mouth watering and body demanding, I removed the tip of a claw and bit into the crab's white, buttery flesh. The butter exploded throughout my mouth, and the garlic joined it to lead the charge. The hint of smoky paprika and onion followed the advance, dancing and weaving behind the more-pronounced tastes. As my tastebuds became accustomed to the rest of the flavors, the crab's meat made itself known. The flesh was subtle yet undeniable, bringing with it a unique umami that raised the entire experience from enjoyable to otherworldly.

No one said a word as we continued eating. Sounds of carapace cracking, the slurping of meat, and my animal pals' loud chewing were the only sounds that one could hear, but even they were hard to notice with how all-encompassing the meal's flavors were. Each time someone finished their bit of crab, I'd pass them another, and before I knew it, I was passing the last chunk of crab to Pistachio.

The giant lobster brought the quartered crab to his mouth and chomped a claw whole. His mouth undulated as he chewed and ground down the food.

"All right, Fischer." Maria sucked the tips of her fingers, then leaned back, her mouth spreading into a content smile. "I changed my mind—*that* was the best meal I've ever had."

"You seem to keep saying that . . ." I narrowed my eyes at her playfully. "I'm starting to think you're lying to save my feelings."

She snorted. "It's not my fault you keep outdoing yourself. I swear your food gets better and more delicious every time you make me something."

I willed the System notifications to show—they had nudged me halfway through the meal, but I'd ignored it.

You have advanced to cooking 32!
You have advanced to fishing 58!

"Well, thank you," I replied, pushing the notifications away. "I would cook for you regardless. There's something so rejuvenating about making food for others, but it's even more rewarding when it's appreciated."

"*Appreciated* may be an understatement. I can't imagine going back to not eating seafood."

I arched an eyebrow and let out my best evil-antagonist chuckle. "The plan to turn you into a heretic is coming together."

She shook her head and smiled at me before closing her eyes and laying down.

Snips scuttled over lazily and leaned against my leg, blowing happy little bubbles as she closed her eye. Claws leaned against Maria, and Cinnamon sat atop the otter, extending a paw to touch Maria's knee. Never one to turn down a good midday nap, I lay back. The sand was cool against my exposed neck, and before I knew it, sleep took me.

I woke with the sun high in the sky, a content sleepiness blanketed over me, and a crab blowing joyous bubbles from atop my chest.

"Mornin', Snips," I said through a yawn, covering my mouth.

"Afternoon, technically," Maria said, bending at the waist to look me in the eye.

Her hair hung down around her face, and her freckles shifted as she gave me a stunning grin. A soft breeze kicked up, swaying the strands of her sun-kissed hair in a hypnotic pattern. Despite my half-awake state, heat rose to my face at the sight of her.

"What?" she asked, cocking her head to the side and somehow appearing even more adorable.

I would like to think that if my mind weren't so addled, I'd have said something equal parts charming and endearing. "How long did we sleep for?" I asked instead.

"An hour or so. I thought I should wake you up so you wouldn't be up all night."

"Thank you." Snips jumped from me as I stood and stretched, willing the lingering vestiges of sleep to leave my body. "I'm gonna keep moving boulders, but you can leave if you'd like."

"And miss out on the finished product? Nice try!"

I rubbed the back of my head. "I don't think we'll be able to finish it today."

"Wait, what? How big is it going to be? I thought we just needed to add more layers of stone."

"We've only done the first section—I intend for it to be a lot longer."

"It's going to be that big?" Rather than become disheartened, her face brightened at the news. "All the more reason to stay and help." She flexed an arm, exaggerating the effort it took with a soft *hnggg*. "Your noodle arms will take too long to finish without the great Maria's assistance."

I barked a laugh, making her smile grow even wider.

"How could I turn down the *great Maria?*" I clapped her on the shoulder as I walked past. "I'll have to rely on you."

She nodded seriously and turned to my animal pals. "Are you coming too? Fischer could use all the help he can get."

Sergeant Snips hissed her agreement, Corporal Claws chirped and puffed out her chest, and Private Pistachio nodded his lumbering head. Rocky scratched his behind.

The sun warmed my back as we made our way back to the shore.

The forest air was damp and still, and as the sun climbed down from its peak in the sky, its warmth only increased the humidity.

The sun above, the rising temperature, and the birdsong coming from every direction were a welcome cascade of sensation for the ancient being within the light-blue tree—well, they should have been.

Despite being asleep for so long, and despite how enthralling the return of her awareness had every right to be, all of her attention was elsewhere. The otter, that freshly ascendant creature, had delivered something previously unknown. In all her many, *many* years, she had never experienced this particular meal. Most of her memories were unreachable, likely locked away due to the lack of power in the surrounding world, yet she knew this as a fact. She would have recalled partaking of such an odd creature.

Even more startling was the strength it held. As with fish caught by the cultivating human and delivered by the otter, the hard-shelled meal contained a staggering amount of power. Though it was small in volume, the chi was potent, immutable, and, most importantly, *delicious.*

Her thin roots penetrated the creature's armor all over, piercing holes in the connective tissue between plates of carapace. She funneled the essence back to her core, where it circled and gathered. She transformed it to nature chi, which then flooded out and suffused the rest of her body.

As per the agreement, she had extended her network of roots to include the four seeds that surrounded her. Already, they had germinated into seedlings. Even now, she felt their growth; they absorbed her nature chi like cracked and dried earth would soak up the first rains after a drought. Time blurred and lost all meaning as she continued feasting and channeling chi toward the four plants.

Something tugged at her awareness, and as she returned to the present, she realized the day was almost done. The sun's warmth had depleted, and darkness was creeping into the clearing around her tree. She cast about the earth, trying to find what had tugged and pulled enough to rouse her.

Four points around her were calling out—the four seedlings, she realized. Something was happening, and she leaned toward all of them, trying to understand. She sent out a testing wave of chi, and the moment it left her core, they absorbed it entirely.

Confusion ran through her every fiber, so she sent out more, seeing what would happen. Again, the moment the chi left her, the sprouts absorbed it like sponges. Despite her lack of memory, she knew this to be . . . peculiar. Such young plants shouldn't be able to hold so much, and they visibly grew each time she sent a pulse of power out toward them.

She shook her leaves to expend some nervous energy as she watched them and let out another trickle of nature chi. It was gone as soon as she let it out, and they grew once more. All four seedlings were now as tall as the otter, and more leaves had sprouted from their small yet sturdy stems.

She felt an impulse, and following her curiosity, she indulged it. Rather than open the gates to her core, then close them after releasing a small burst of chi, she left the metaphorical gate open a crack, letting the trees absorb it directly.

The response was immediate.

They sucked at the essence, and she felt a growing understanding of them. It was terrifying.

They were as bottomless pits, great yawning maws that could never be filled, no matter how much they devoured. With her curiosity assuaged, she tried to close the floodgates, but her core didn't respond.

Panic surged through her as she tried again to close the door, but the seedlings held it open—the force with which they drew on her chi was too great. Sensing her attempt to push them out, their hunger increased, and they drew ever more on her reserves.

The gates to her core were thrown wide open, and they began consuming her very essence. She was getting torn apart in four distinct directions, and with one last desperate force of will, she tried to slam the doors to her very soul closed.

She failed, and they tore her apart.

CHAPTER SIXTEEN

GROWTH

An ancient being stirred. She returned to herself slowly, and as her awareness bloomed, memories returned. The last she recalled, she was being torn apart, and terror reigned as she sent her awareness down, inspecting the damage.

Her core was . . . changed.

She feared she would find utter destruction. Instead, she found it open and whole. Four channels had been carved into her, creating permanent pathways out. She followed these channels, finding what she expected yet feared at the end of each: the four seedlings.

What she didn't anticipate was for her understanding to extend beyond the pathways and into the plants. As she reached the foreign bodies, her vision and awareness split, becoming a kaleidoscopic mesh of sights and sensations. Time seemed to alter and warp as four distinct experiences joined her own, all playing out simultaneously. It was a disorienting experience, and the moment her sense of self returned, she threw herself back from them. With a minor flex of will, she easily departed and returned to her original perspective.

As she returned to the previous bounds of her body, she pondered the sensations of the four plants.

Lemon trees, the ancient being said internally, tasting the syllables.

Each of them were individuals with their own personalities, wants, and needs—perhaps those weren't the correct words, as the trees weren't as advanced as she or other sapient beings were. Still, there *was* an aspect of individuality granted them.

This merger, whatever this joining of souls was, it felt neither wrong nor right. The ancient being tried to push into her memories, to crack whatever boundary locked them away, but if such a thing existed, she couldn't find it.

Intent on exploring this new bond, she tried to send a tendril of awareness out to one of the saplings, using her significant willpower to keep the other three pathways closed.

I woke to a chill in the air, and I pulled my blanket up, soaking in the warmth it provided. I lay in a half-asleep state for an indeterminate amount of time, lapping up the rest after a long day of hauling boulders under the ocean. When I remembered the half-built wall, a spike of wakefulness pierced my slumber, and I threw the blankets off.

I immediately regretted my decision; the part of my brain that demanded comfort told me to crawl back under the covers and curl into a ball. Ignoring the impulse, I stood and stretched, unleashing a mighty yawn as I tensed every muscle in my body. I glanced back at the bed, seeking the lump that would tell of a cute little bunny hiding within, but Cinnamon was nowhere to be found.

"I guess she's already gone to Maria's . . ." I mused.

Roger's fields required work over the next week or so, and as a result, Maria wouldn't have much free time. Cinnamon was free to do as she pleased, and I knew she'd much rather spend time in the fields with Maria than sit around on the shore waiting for me to return.

I opened my bedroom door and stepped out into an even colder room. The large window of my living room provided little insulation, and the night's chill had well and truly crept within my walls. It was my first taste of winter, and it hinted at a cold few months to follow.

I went back to my room and rummaged through sets of sheets, towels, and the thin, everyday clothes I usually wore, having to reach for the back of my wardrobe to find a jacket I'd bought from the tailors what felt like months ago.

I put it on, quickly made my bed, then left for Tropica.

As I walked back home, a croissant and coffee in hand, the sun peeked its head over the eastern horizon. Purple and pink hues spread throughout the sky, so I turned and strode toward the coast, intent on watching the sunrise. As I walked over the last dune, I saw some friends.

"G'day, everyone!" I said, walking down to meet them.

Barry, his wife Helen, his brother-in-law Leroy, and Leroy's wife, Barbara, all sat on the dry sand, heads turned to look at me. Barry's son peered over his father's shoulder, and he grinned wide, revealing the beginnings of a tooth growing where a gap had been.

"Hello, Fischer!" Paul yelled.

"Hey, mate! I see you're getting a new tooth there."

He nodded fervently, exploring the tooth with his tongue. "I am! Dad says it means I'm growing up!"

Barry smiled at his overenthusiastic son, and I nodded. "It certainly does—it's your last adult tooth. You'll be a grown fella before you know it."

"Would you like to join us?" Helen asked.

"I'd love to. I came here for the sunrise, but having some friends to experience it with is a happy accident."

I took a seat on the sand; it still held the night's chill, and a shiver took me. "It's bloody cold."

"Winter is coming," Barry agreed, staring stoically at the horizon.

I let out a soft laugh. "Hopefully the long night doesn't come with it."

"The what?" Barry asked, narrowing his eyes in confusion.

"Never mind. Do the winters get very cold here? I assumed they wouldn't be too bad given the tropical climate."

"Aye, they get a bit colder than this, but never enough for frost. The wind can make it feel cooler than it is, though."

As if summoned, a breeze kicked up, rushing past us and making Paul lean back into his father's lap.

We lapsed into silence, all watching the sun as it climbed ever higher in the sky. The pink and purple hues consuming the horizon turned to orange and yellow as the great orb rose above the ocean, shining its warmth down upon us.

I noticed Barbara shooting furtive glances in my direction.

So, I thought. *She knows about me.*

It was hard to pinpoint the emotions brought on by the realization, but they weren't good ones. I thought about it more as the silence stretched, reminding myself that it was entirely reasonable to be hesitant of a bloke that could shoot anime finishing moves from his body.

"I forgot to tell you guys," I said, swirling the last dregs of coffee around in my cup. "I made more fishing rods."

I shot a look toward Leroy just in time for his head to whirl on me, and I nodded, giving him a knowing smile. "You're all welcome to use them whenever you like—they're on my back deck."

"Maybe I'll take you up on that offer." He nudged his wife. "I'd be happy to show you."

Barbara made a non-committal noise and leaned into his shoulder.

"Paul," I said. "Seeing as though you're almost a man, could I give you a task, mate?"

His eyes lit up, and he nodded so hard I thought his head might fall off. "Could you go buy four coffees and five croissants? I wanna buy everyone some brekkie."

I flicked him a coin, which he deftly caught.

"You don't have to do that, Fischer," Helen tried.

"I don't have to, but I'd like to. It makes me feel good treating my friends." I shrugged. "Call it a selfish request you begrudgingly accept."

"All right," she conceded, knowing me well enough to understand I wouldn't back down. "You be quick, Paul."

He was already sprinting away, coin in hand and responsibility powering his stride.

When the young lad was out of earshot, I spun to Leroy. "One more thing—pretty sure there's some sort of ancient tree spirit living in that light-blue tree we planted the lemon seeds around. I've been feeding it fish in the hopes it helps the lemons grow. Maybe you should check it out?"

My statement had the desired effect, and all four heads turned to me, giving me various looks between confusion, bewilderment, and doubt.

I laughed. "Really? After everything you've all learned over the last few weeks, *that's* what surprises you?"

Barbara was white as a sheet, her lips pursed.

"It's nice to meet you, by the way," I said, smiling at her. "I'm not sure we've been introduced . . ."

"O-oh," Barry said, coming back to himself. "Sorry. I'd totally forgotten—as you said, it's been a crazy few weeks." He pointed at his sister-in-law, then me. "Fischer, Barbara. Barbara, this is Fischer."

"Nice to meet you too," she replied softly, some of her color returning.

"The pleasure is all mine!"

Before I could say more, Leroy leaned all the way forward, planting his hands in the sand. "What in Hades's realm do you mean there's an ancient spirit living in the tree?"

"It's pretty straightforward, mate."

I kept my face straight, causing Leroy to grow even more incredulous. "Why are you acting as though that's the most normal thing in the world? A plant spirit? What does that even mean? Is it already ascended? It must be, right? How else could a plant gain sapience? When did it . . ." His voice lowered, and he continued rambling too softly for me to hear.

While watching her husband's impassioned mutterings, Barbara's mask shattered for the first time; she practically glowed, her eyes bright and blood returning to her cheeks.

"Well, I'd better get going." I stood and brushed off my pants. "Lots of work to do and all that."

"I-it really was nice meeting you, Fischer," Barbara said, so I turned to her.

"Likewise! Come around for a fish or a chin wag any time."

" . . . a what?"

"A yarn," Barry answered.

" . . . that doesn't help, Barry."

He and I both laughed.

"It's fun, right?" I asked.

Helen batted me on the leg. "Stop leading my husband astray, you."

Barry patted her on the shoulder reassuringly before turning back to me. "What are you working on?"

"Me?" I smiled, delighting in the confusion that would follow. "A big underwater wall made of boulders."

I turned and strode away before anyone could ask what I was talking about. "Catch ya later!"

Barry, Helen, and Barbara blinked after me, while Leroy raised a single hand to wave goodbye, still muttering to himself beneath a furrowed brow.

With my body low, I snuck up on my quarry. I walked into the breeze, ensuring I was downwind from my prey. The sun continued its rise before me, meaning my shadow wouldn't give me away. I grinned, hunched, prepared to leap . . . and the hunter became the hunted.

Sergeant Snips, billowing blue clouds of power, flew from the water, hissing with victory. She slammed into my chest, and given my utter defeat, I let her throw me from my feet.

I let out an *oof* as I hit the sand, then groaned with Bollywood-level dramatic flair. Snips let out a hissed giggle, puffing her body up and flexing her claws.

"Oh, the pain! Woe is me who attempted hunting Sergeant Snips, protector of the pond!"

Rocky leaped from the saltwater pond, streaming water as he went. The moment he landed, he began nodding gravely, having heard our conversation and agreeing wholeheartedly. She smacked him lightly on the head, and he blew bubbles of thanks.

"All right, you two—are you up for another day of moving rocks?"

Snips hissed and danced from side to side, ever happy to help. Rocky peered down at a claw and projected indifference despite the fact everyone knew he'd do whatever Snips did. The pond's water roiled and the head of a Leviathan emerged. I held out a fist and Pistachio bumped it.

"You free too, mate?"

He nodded immediately, dipping his impressive body to do so.

I glanced toward the distant tree line, wondering for a moment if I should go get a particular otter, but I decided against it—she might need more rest if she tended to the weird tree-spirit-thing last night. She'd come and find us when she was ready.

"Cheers, everyone. I don't know what I'd do without ya. How about I make us all some delicious lunch and dinner as payment?"

Three heads bobbed up and down—even Rocky was unable to resist the temptation of a good meal.

I set off for the shore with three crustaceans scuttling after me.

CHAPTER SEVENTEEN

EMBROIDERY

Corporal Claws, master of the log and guardian of the pond, luxuriated on her favored perch. A cool breeze wound its way through the forest, but given her superior body, she barely noticed it. She rolled onto her back, letting a ray of sun land on her belly fluff. With a chirp of sheer contentment, she wiggled her body, settling further into the groove of her perch.

With her ascension, knowledge had poured into her body in a steady stream, making her, by her own approximation, the smartest of Fischer's students. Because of her vast intellect, she knew that as a mammal, she had subterranean fat.

Claws raised an eyebrow—that wasn't right.

Sub-cute-angus fat? Sub . . . sub-cretaceous? Her face crinkled in annoyance—they weren't right either.

Whatever—she was aware of her fat. She rubbed her belly for emphasis, grinning as she ran both paws through her illustrious fur and massaged the layers of fatty insulation beneath. She thought of the cultists in town claiming that crabs were the superior form, then let out a chittering chuckle—the poor fools.

She slipped back into a state of half slumber, smiling at the world's sensations as they blanketed her. Some time later, she heard a twig break. She raised her head to see a man departing, so chirped to get his attention.

Leroy froze on the spot and spun, giving her a guilty look. "Sorry—I saw you sleeping and didn't want to wake you."

She waved a dismissive paw and rolled over before stretching, arching her back and shaking with effort. When the stretch was well and truly complete, she settled back on her hindquarters and cocked her head at Leroy. Thankfully, he understood her unspoken question—such things were to be expected of her minions.

"Fischer told me that there was a spirit in the light-blue tree." Leroy shook his head. "Man, saying that out loud makes me sound insane. I figured it might be able to help the lemon trees grow, so I came to help."

Claws's body became wreathed in lightning and she crossed her arms, staring down at the deliverer of terrible news.

Leroy took a step back. "Uh . . . Claws? Everything okay?"

Corporal Claws, queen of the forest and matriarch of the pond, shook with indignation. She had wanted to raise the lemon trees without anyone knowing, then surprise her master.

As quick as her frustration had come, it drained away, as did the lightning surrounding her. It wasn't Leroy's fault; her master was simply too intelligent, too prepared and calculating to be surprised in such a way. She leaped from her perch atop the log, landing silently before Leroy. She chirped once, nodded for Leroy to follow, then set off for the clearing.

They traveled in silence. Each time Claws glanced back at Leroy, he was looking up, a smile on his face as he appreciated the beauty of the forest. She approved of his wonder; her forest was magnificent indeed. Pride suffused her, and she held her head a little higher as she led him on. When they arrived at the clearing, her pride scattered like a school of fish upon seeing her deadly form beneath the waves.

"What the frack . . ." Leroy said from behind her, echoing her thoughts.

The clearing was no longer a clearing.

Where the forest floor surrounding the light-blue tree had previously been clear, four saplings now stood. She slunk toward one, overly cautious of the unexpected growth. When she reached it, she stood on her hind legs, and even stretching to her full height, the sapling was taller. All of its leaves were glossy, a light green that indicated fresh growth. She wrapped a padded paw around the trunk and pushed softly; it held firm, not moving even a little.

There was a blur of green and something swung down toward her. She chirped in alarm and tried to scurry away, but off balance as she was, she never stood a chance—the twig smacked her right between the eyes. Corporal Claws rolled backward with the hit. As she got to her feet, she rubbed her stinging forehead, frowning at the impudent tree. The sapling's leaves shook with mirth, as did those of the light-blue tree.

Leroy stumbled further into the clearing, his gaze distant and eyes wide.

"There . . . there really is a tree spirit?" His head darted between the two shaking canopies. "No—there are *two?*"

Claws shook her head with a chirp. She recognized that sadistic humor—it was just like the time the spirit tripped her with a root. The same cheeky being had somehow taken over control of the lemon sapling that whacked her, if not all of them.

"No?" Leroy asked. "What do you mean?"

She pointed at all the trees, then brought her paws together, clasping them.

"You're saying it's the one spirit?"

Claws nodded. So did the sapling—an entirely unnerving action for a tree to make.

Leroy stared at the small lemon tree, his face etched with incredulity. "Y-you can hear us . . . ?"

Again, the sapling nodded.

Seeing Leroy's awe, the whispers of a plan started forming in Claws's magnificent mind. Perhaps her plan to surprise her master wasn't ruined after all . . . She rubbed her chin with one paw, just as she'd seen Fischer do when lost in thought. Corporal Claws grinned, exposing her needle-sharp teeth as the plan further unfurled.

* * *

I bent my knees, braced my core, and lifted. Sand cascaded from the boulder as it left the ocean floor. Wasting no time, I strode off toward the headland.

Despite the frigid night just gone, the ocean was a pleasant temperature, especially compared to the freezing wind blowing above. Sergeant Snips and Rocky scuttled past me as they headed for another boulder. Snips blew happy little bubbles and waved a claw at me. Rocky gave me a rude gesture, which caused me to snort. Snips spun to bonk him on the head, and I thoroughly enjoyed the reproachful hisses and clicks coming from her as I strode on.

One step at a time, my powered legs launched me high above the sand, and the boulder's weight brought me back down. The temporary weightlessness made me think of an astronaut traversing the moon, and a smile came to my face unbidden.

Before I knew it, I'd arrived at the pile of boulders. Rather than place a second layer on the already constructed portion, we had started extending the base layer out to sea. It was now fifteen meters or so from the shore, and as I approached, movement caught my eye. I placed the boulder and swam over to where I thought I'd seen something. My head was tilted to the side, and as I locked eyes with a creature, a smile slowly spread over my face.

A common eel peeked out between a gap, going still in its hidey-hole as it watched me. I looked further toward shore and spotted baitfish flitting around the base layer of rocks, using them for protection. Fish were already using the new habitat despite it being nowhere near finished.

I stood there for a long moment, soaking in my surroundings. Juvenile shore fish darted from gaps in the wall before dashing back inside. The common eel slowly slunk away, not wanting anything to do with me. Different schools of unknown baitfish continued flitting around continually.

A sense of deep calm washed over me and I lost track of time.

The form of Pistachio glided through my peripheral vision and dropped his boulder. He came up beside me and joined my moment of contemplation. I glanced to the side, seeing an endless stream of curious bubbles coming from his mouth. The lobster was quiet compared to my other animal pals, but I knew that behind his mask of stoicism, a vast intellect dwelled. Of all the ascendant creatures, he likely best understood the breadth of what this structure represented for the local marine life.

The need to take a breath climbed into my awareness, so I kicked off the ocean floor gently, not wanting to spook any surrounding fish.

The midmorning sun greeted me atop the churning ocean, and I closed my eyes as I turned my face toward it. A cool breeze was still present, but the sun's heat canceled it out. I floated on my back, exposing my body to more of the rays. My ears went below the water, muffling the cries of seagulls circling high above.

It was truly a beautiful day.

Gary, the leader of the Cult of the Leviathan's Tropica branch, gazed out at the ocean—it was beautiful. He stood atop the stone walkway on the eastern side of

Tropica, both forearms leaning against the low wall. Birds circled above, and a strong breeze made white foam form atop waves all the way out to the horizon. He breathed deep of the sea spray, then turned and strode for the cult's headquarters.

As he swung the new door open, he marveled at the metal bracing on its internal face. Despite it being installed over a fortnight ago, he still found the addition a stark contrast to the thin, weatherbeaten door that Pistachio had annihilated when shooting Sebastian through it.

Firmly closing the door behind him, he gazed out at the room. If not for his being there, he'd never have believed the entire bottom floor had been almost demolished less than a month ago. He looked at the wall that a creature of legend had flown through—as with the room itself, no signs of destruction remained.

Memories of that evening flashed through his mind. His former master, Sebastian, hadn't made it through. Despite Gary's continued efforts to turn Sebastian from his murderous path, the man's hubris had been his downfall. Gary still partially blamed himself for that, but as he recognized that thought bubbling up, he focused instead on the present.

He traipsed toward a newly constructed bench and looked down at the contents of the tank. His fresh batch of baby lobsters scuttled about within, exploring their home. Now that he was in charge of the cult, Gary had first and final say for the environment the lobsters grew in. Previous batches had been kept in small, overcrowded tanks with no structure to hide or forage in.

Gary took a deep breath, pride swelling as he smiled down at the tank he'd created. It was twice as long as he was tall. A layer of sand covered the bottom, with rocks, shells, and patches of seaweed added that the baby lobsters could use to hide in. The lobsters in the old tanks made by Sebastian were sedentary creatures; they sat still most of the day, only moving when pellets of food were added. He had assumed that to just be what baby lobsters did. He couldn't have been more wrong.

The twenty-four lobsters within the new tank constantly moved around, searching their environment. Though he couldn't tell for sure, he thought they seemed happy. He sprinkled half a handful of pellets into the tank and watched with delight as his cute little pets scuttled from their hiding spots.

A loud knock came from the door, jolting him from his reverie. He shook his head as he strode toward it, still feeling somewhat disconnected from the present. When he opened the door, that changed.

"How are ya going, Gary?" Barry asked.

"Hi, er . . . sir?"

Barry laughed.

"Just Barry is fine, mate."

"Right. Sorry. What can I do for you?"

"Would you mind following me for a bit? I need help tending the weeds."

Recognizing the code phrase, Gary nodded and stepped through the doorway to join Barry outside. He closed the door and locked it.

"After you, sir—er, *Barry.*"

Gary followed his church leader through the streets of Tropica, his heart thumping and palms clammy. It was well past the morning bustle of the village, and most of the south-side residents were off tending to their fields. Barry waved at the bakery owner, Sue, as he passed, and Gary gave her a nod of greeting. The friendly lady waved back, beaming a smile at them.

They eventually came to the woodworking shop, and Barry held the door open for him. As he stepped inside, he was met with a sea of faces: both woodworkers, Brad and Greg; the tailors, Ruby and Steven; Barry's wife, Helen; her sister-in-law, Barbara; and Sharon. All smiled or nodded at him, and he dipped his head in response.

"Now that we're all here," Barry said, "would you like to start, Ruby?"

The middle-aged woman's smile went wide as she bent and picked up a box.

"I've finally finished the robes! The stitchwork took longer than expected, but I suppose that's not really a surprise—we had to source some fine materials."

"Fine indeed," Steven, her husband, agreed.

"And that's not even the best part!" Ruby continued. "The *effects!* Each transformed, and they give a bonus to luck and cultivation speed, whatever that means. The embroidery is royal blue, with just a hint of gold added in to reflect the—"

Steven cleared his throat.

"You're rambling, dear."

She shot him a venomous look, but then sighed to herself. "I suppose I was." She started walking around the room and passing out small bundles. "Let me know if they don't fit. They should, though, if the measurements you gave me were correct."

As Gary accepted his robe, a great weight was shed from his shoulders. Despite his ready acceptance of joining the church, each time he was called to a meeting, a sense of anxiety rose from within. He supposed it was a remnant of the scary stories his drunk auntie would tell about churches when he was a child.

He unfolded the bundle, running his hands along the expensive-feeling fabric as he did so. The main robe was as dark as the ocean's depths—more colorless than the night sky. On the front, right above where his heart would be, a stylized pattern had been embroidered. It was the light-blue of the ocean and depicted a fishing rod with a fish hooked on the end. To the top left of the embroidery, a golden sun shone down, beaming its rays toward the fishing rod. Gary felt his anxiety recede further; the pattern filled him with a sense of deep calm.

His moment of peace lasted less than half a breath.

"So," Barry said. "Shall we vote on how we're going to deal with the blacksmiths?"

CHAPTER EIGHTEEN

CONGREGATION

The night's cold air lingered within the woodworking shop. It was punctuated by the scents of unknown woods and lacquers, a soothing yet unfamiliar mix. A layer of shavings lay scattered over the floor beneath Gary, and he stared down at them, not trusting himself to mask the emotions roiling within him.

The moment Barry had mentioned *dealing* with the blacksmiths, fear had bloomed, trailed swiftly by a cloying sense of unease. The silence within the room thickened the air, and his stomach churned, twisted.

Barry sighed. "Knowing what they do, we can't let them be."

Gary's eyes flicked up, scanning the surrounding congregation. What he found made his last flicker of hope die.

He had expected someone to voice their concern, to rail against the condemnation of two innocent men. Instead, acceptance was plastered across the faces of everyone present. Some even nodded, physically declaring their complaisance.

"The only question is," Sharon said, "who is going to do it?"

Despite himself, Gary's head shot toward her. A woman who had always seemed so kind in their meetings, yet she was so easily agreeing to something so heinous. He stared at her, his incredulity overriding the fear of what he'd gotten himself into.

Noticing him, she stared back, tilting her head to the side. "What's wrong?"

Everyone turned to look at him. There were only eight others present, but they may as well have been an entire village for how their gazes made him feel. Beneath the weight of their eyes, something within him snapped: his self-preservation faltered, and he stood taller, bracing himself for what was to come.

"I can't go along with this. It's despicable. If you're going to be *dealing* with innocent villagers, I regret ever agreeing to join you." He closed his eyes and extended his head. "Please do it quickly."

Seconds that felt like minutes passed by, and he squeezed his eyes tight, knowing the death blow would come at any moment.

"Gary . . ." Sharon said. "What do you think Barry meant when he said they had to be dealt with?"

Gary cracked an eye, seeing her head cocked to the side and eyebrows furrowed.

He set his jaw and doubled down. "You intend to kill them, and for what? Knowing information? I can't stand by and be . . ."

He trailed off as Sharon covered her mouth and her eyes crinkled in . . . was that amusement? He glanced around the room, seeing faces transform. "What's so funny?"

Sharon's entire body shook, and in the time it took for his resolute defiance to change into sheer incomprehension, the entire room was lost in laughter. The worst were the two woodworkers who leaned on each other for support, and Sharon, who was still cackling like a madwoman.

"Gary . . ." Barry stepped forward and took a deep breath, banishing his mirth. "We aren't going to hurt them."

Gary opened his mouth to respond but closed and opened it a few more times before the words came. "You're . . . you're not?"

"No," Brad replied, wiping a tear from his eye. "We're not."

"What are you going to do, then? What does *dealing* with someone mean?"

Barry gave him a kind smile. "We're going to ask them to join us, Gary. They've seen Fischer make things, and we know they harbor suspicions about his nature—they said as much to Brad and Greg."

The woodworking brothers nodded, and seeing as though Greg was still lost in a fit of silent laughter, Brad spoke.

"We're pretty close. They asked us the other night if Fischer's creations in our shop had transformed. Naturally, we played dumb—"

"I played dumb," Greg corrected. "You were just being yourself."

Brad slapped his brother on the back of the head, which only made Greg's smile spread wider.

"The point being," Brad continued, "that they suspect Fischer, and rather than try to convince them otherwise, we'd like to invite them to join the church. They're good blokes, as Fischer would say."

Barry nodded. "What we meant by *dealing* with them is how we'll tell them."

"And who will tell them," Sharon added.

Gary blinked at them for a long moment—then he started laughing too. Elation and relief washed away his concerns.

"There's one more thing," Barry said. "I was going to surprise you at the end of the meeting, but I suppose now is as good a time as any."

"Oh?" he said, still chuckling at himself. "What's that?"

"Oh—nothing major." Barry grinned. "I just wanted to know if you were ready to become a cultivator."

With the afternoon sun beating down and a strong current sweeping to the north, I placed my last boulder for the day.

As I sat on the ocean floor and waited for the crustaceans to join me, I watched the movement of baitfish. A curious eel even peeked its head out from between rocks as I waited, bringing a smile to my face.

Pistachio lumbered forward first, his streamlined body easily hunkering down against the current. He placed his boulder at the end of the line and blew a single, questioning bubble. I pointed to the shore, indicating that we were done for the day. Pistachio nodded and joined me, also watching the fish with curious eyes.

When Rocky and Snips approached, I couldn't help but laugh. A cloud of bubbles escaped my throat, and Rocky spun to glare at me. Snips was on the other side of the boulder they held, pushing it forward. With the force of her and the sweeping ocean behind it, Rocky was stumbling and struggling to keep it upright.

His glare never left me, and I just smiled back at him. Something about the animosity coming from such a cute little crab just tickled me pink.

He and Snips put the boulder down, and seeing me and Pistachio waiting for them, Snips swam over and latched onto my arm. She blew contented bubbles, and I rubbed the top of her head as I strode toward the shore. I held my other hand out, offering for Rocky to join. He crossed his foreclaws and turned away from me, showing me his back as he scuttled from the water.

I hauled myself up to the rocky headland to be greeted by a flock of seagulls. They squawked and crooned at our arrival as those closest to us took flight, landing further away from our position. I couldn't blame them—if I was a bird and a giant lobster crawled from the ocean, I'd probably freak out too.

Not for the first time, I considered feeding one some fish and having it awaken. As with the previous times, I dismissed it almost immediately. I pictured a sapient seagull with the ability to demand chippies, and a shiver ran down my spine.

Talk about annoying . . .

The seagulls had begun posturing and positioning against one another, some bending down and making a grunting noise as they challenged others for their spot on the rocks. I watched them for a long moment, enjoying their belligerence.

Perhaps because he wanted to assert his dominance, or perhaps because he was just as belligerent, Rocky joined the fray. He scuttled at them with his claws held high and clacking chaotically. He didn't use his explosive ability, so I let him go.

Maybe he won't be so angsty all the time if he burns off some energy . . .

Snips shook her head at her subordinate, and I laid a reassuring hand atop her head. "He's a handful, huh?"

She nodded gravely and blew bubbles of resignation.

A wind kicked up, and my body shook as it wicked the water from my skin. I walked to my towel and started drying off, never taking my eyes from the battle between the persistent birds and a single angry crab.

By the time I finished drying myself, the seagulls had won the war of attrition. No matter how many times Rocky chased them down, clacking away with his pincers, the seagulls would just fly five meters away and begin the battle anew. After only a minute or two, power swelled within his claws, but before he could slam his clackers closed and turn the birds into nuggets, Snips attacked. She flew at him, put a claw under his carapace, and launched him out toward the horizon with practiced ease.

"Eeee—" was all Rocky could get out before he was forcefully ejected from hearing range.

"Damn, Snips—that throwing arm of yours is getting better."

She preened, puffing her body up and shimmying in delight at my praise.

The show of strength was enough for the gulls, and they all took flight, letting the southerly wind blow them north. They sailed high over Tropica, heading further beyond the village.

"How long do you think it'll take him to get back?"

She shrugged, clearly not caring.

"Well, it's no matter—I was going to make us some dinner regardless. I suppose we can just save some for him . . ."

At my mention of dinner, both Snips and Pistachio perked up, so I grinned down at them.

"Would you like fish or sand crab for dinner?"

Ten minutes later, I stood on the river's shore as my animal pals tended the fire.

"That was a silly question," I mused. "Of course they'd choose both."

Both of my feet were planted in the cold sand, and I dug them further in. The sun was setting over the western mountains, lending orange and pink pastel hues to the sky. Scattered clouds above were tinged with the colors, and as I gazed up at them, a sense of ease settled over me. I held one finger to the line and waited patiently for a fish to bite.

With my eyes closed, I leaned further into the present moment. The strong wind was whipping up waves, and as they crashed into the headland just to the left of me, water sprayed up and onto my legs. I focused on their kiss as they flicked into me, their cool touch the antithesis of the warmth my upper body felt beneath layers of clothing. My sense of ease turned to contentment, and I smiled out at the world.

Something bumped my line.

My eyes flew open. They took a moment to focus on the rod before me, and just as they did, the fish took another nibble. I leaned forward and tensed my arms, ready should the fish eat the hook.

Bump.

Bump. Bump.

There was a big tug, but it ended before I could set the hook. I waited, my excitement making patience almost impossible to grasp.

Just as I was starting to think the fish had retreated for good, it returned. My rod bent down as the fish ate the hook. I lifted the pole just enough to keep tension, and anticipation bubbled up from within. The fish felt big, but nothing so large as to give my improved body and System-enhanced rod any issue. It took small runs to either side, but I reeled it in with ease, never once losing line or my position on the sand.

As the fish came closer to shore, I leaned forward, peering down into the water and trying to catch a glimpse. A flash of silver, then the fish swam down, making one last desperate attempt to get away. I reeled and lifted the rod, and its body became visible once more. Even before I hauled it from the river, I knew what it was, and I smiled down at it.

With a flick of the bamboo pole, the fish was up on the shore.

Mature Cichlid
Uncommon
Found in the fresh and brackish waters of the Kallis Realm, this fish is a staple source of both food and bait.

I bent and grasped the fish in one hand, dispatched it swiftly with the other, then held up the sizable cichlid. It was short and fat, just larger than Rocky's body. It was equal in size to the biggest I'd caught so far.

I bounced on my heels, unable to stay still. Despite it being tied with my personal best, the fight told me just how much my fishing ability had improved; where before I'd had to let out line and move along the shore to stop the fish from escaping, catching this one had been a walk in the park. I knew I had a quantifiable skill level now, but seeing the improvement from one catch to another was undeniable proof of my progression.

I turned to grab my knife but jolted back when I saw what stood behind me.

"*W-whoa!*"

The creature startled at my exclamation and leaned back, but with its eyes locked on my catch, it soon stretched its neck forward again.

"You want my fish, huh?"

The wild animal, completely unaware of what I was saying, merely watched the fish and waited for the chance to steal it.

CHAPTER NINETEEN

THE ALCHEMIST

The magnificent creature stared at me with inhuman eyes in the last hints of daylight peeking over the western mountains. Its white plumage was accentuated by black feathers on either side of its body. It stretched its wings wide and opened its long beak, revealing the inside of a tan-colored pouch.

The pelican and I blinked at each other as I contemplated the repercussions of giving it some food. Its gaze strayed back down to the fish I held, and I gave it a rueful smile.

"I'm not sure how my friends would feel about me letting you have their dinner . . ."

The pelican stretched its head and puffed its pouch out, getting closer to the cichlid I held.

"Tell you what—if you can wait a little while, I'll let you have some leftovers. How does that sound?"

A croaking noise came from its throat as it took another step forward, lowering its head. It snapped its beak at me, and I dodged back, avoiding the sharp point on the end. "Hey! That's not very nice, mate."

A blur of orange came from my left, and the raging form of Rocky scuttled at the pelican, his claws held high and a stream of angry bubbles spewing from his mouth. It took flight, its wings beating heavily as it rose into the air. With a single glance back at the fish, it continued on, flapping toward the river mouth then angling south as it soared along the coastline.

I put my hands on my hips and stared down at the degenerate crab. "That was a dick move, Rocky."

He made a snorting noise—which I wasn't even aware a crab could do—then crossed his claws in defiance. I recalled Snips having a visceral reaction to the seagulls when she was freshly awakened—perhaps rock crabs and birds were mortal enemies.

"Don't chase the pelican away unless it's in self-defense, all right?"

He turned away, ignoring me, so I crouched down and plucked him from the sand. I turned him to face me. "I mean it, mate. I know you're technically Snips's subordinate, and I find your independent nature rather endearing, but if you chase that pelican away again we're gonna have problems."

He squinted his eyes at me.

"And no killing the seagulls," I added. "You can chase them, but no killing anything you don't intend to eat. I won't stand for sociopathic crabs. If you can't agree to that, you can't live here. That means no delicious food and no sharing a pond with your beloved Snips."

He didn't respond for a long moment, but under my steady glare, he eventually agreed with a single affirmative bubble, averting his eyes as he did so.

"Good lad." I let him go and he scuttled sullenly back to the fire. Snips and I locked eyes from where she tended the flames. She gave me a subtle nod, and I returned it.

Rocky caught the interaction, so he spun toward me, giving me a decidedly rude gesture as he scuttled backward.

Snips's arm shot out in a blur.

Crack.

A pair of tongs collided with Rocky and sent him sprawling in the sand. As he lay on his back, unmoving and accepting his fate, his eyes locked onto mine. He gave me the same gesture, but from where Snips couldn't see this time.

I barked a laugh. "Fair play."

As I was removing the crab and fish from the grill, a lithe form came tearing across the sand. Corporal Claws, cycs crinkled in delight and lips spread in a grin, launched herself at me. I dropped the tongs and caught her, spinning to absorb the force. "Claws! We missed you today! Where have you been?"

She chirped her love at me and pointed back at the forest, answering my question.

"With the tree all day? Any news?"

She shook her head, but as she did so, her whiskers twitched forward and stayed there, betraying the truth.

"Nothing, huh?" I asked, hiding my smile. "Well, maybe the food you bring it tonight will garner some results."

She climbed to my shoulder as I bent to grasp the tongs.

"I'll tell you all about our progress on the wall today while we eat dinner."

She nodded vigorously, then nuzzled into my neck, cooing with affection.

In a room filled with acrid smoke and the smell of sulfur, a lone man toiled. He had long ago become accustomed to the scents, and though his throat still stung when breathing in the byproducts of his research, it was a small price to pay for immortality.

The alchemist focused on his cauldron as he smothered the flames beneath it. Today, he was seeing if the removal of heat impacted his concoction, and he watched the thick sludge as he swirled it around his pot.

This is the potion, he thought to himself. *This is the one that will break me past the barrier and allow me to take steps toward the path of ascension.*

For years he had hidden away in this coastal town, assigned the outpost by the leaders of the Cult of the Alchemist. Where some would take it as a slight to be sent to such a distant area, Solomon saw it in a different light: being sent to a coastal town afforded him all manner of exotic ingredients to experiment with.

For hundreds if not thousands of years, his forebears had tried and failed to reach immortality with the usual fare: common herbs; animal products, some from farmed animals, some harvested from the wild; and the local ingredients that could be found in the market of any large village. Having alchemists work to attain their goals in coastal villages was a relatively new assignment—a sign of what some members had called desperation.

"Call it what you like, fools. When I become the Alchemist, they'll know the truth." His voice was raspy even to his own ears, but that was just a sign of his devotion to his craft.

He chuckled as he continued stirring, watching the mixture intently for any changes. His dry chuckle turned into a racking cough as he leaned in too close and inhaled some of the acidic vapors wafting from his concoction. He choked and sputtered and his eyes welled with tears, but the smile never left his face.

With my mouth watering, I cracked the claw of a sand crab. The smell of its sweet juices joined that of the herb-laced butter I'd coated it in, and a deep contentment washed over me.

All around me, my animal pals were crunching down on their food, and I couldn't help but smile at the symphony of what most would probably consider to be repulsive sounds.

To me, they were pure bliss.

I bit down into the crab's soft flesh, delighting in the flavors that danced over my tongue. I'd tried not cracking the crab shells before tossing them in the buttery mixture this time, intent on seeing if trapping the juices in changed the flavor profile at all—it did. The sweet liquids trapped within the shell mingled in my mouth rather than in the pot, providing an entirely new experience. A soft *mmm* escaped my throat, but my enjoyment was interrupted when someone cleared their throat behind me.

"I'm not too late, am I?" Maria approached with the fuzzy form of Cinnamon cradled in her arms.

Quickly swallowing my food, I patted the sand beside me. "I wasn't sure you'd come tonight, but I saved dinner for you just in case."

As she settled on the ground, I went to the fire and made up a plate of food. When I placed it on the sand before her, Maria's eyes lit up.

"This is just what I needed after working the fields all day."

I watched her as she lifted the plate. Steam rose from the food, visible by the light of the fire. She inhaled through her nose, breathing deep of the scents, and a smile slowly spread over her face. "This smells wonderful, Fischer."

I returned the smile. "Wait until you taste it."

She cracked a claw and raised it to her mouth. As she bit down, her shoulders dropped and she let out a sigh.

"Good?" I asked.

She chewed slowly, not rushing the mouthful. "Amazing," she eventually replied. She gave me a warm smile, then took another bite.

That night, despite a day spent doing physical labor, I found myself unable to sleep. Cinnamon was snoring softly beside me, and I petted her head with one hand as the other drifted toward my lips. My heart thumped in my chest as I replayed the kiss Maria had given me before departing. Though thinking of her made my blood pound, she wasn't the source of my sleeplessness.

Well, not the only source, anyway.

I'd started the rock wall with the intention of banishing my churning thoughts, and, thankfully, it had worked, but it wasn't that I was overthinking—I felt as though I'd just had five double shots of espresso from Sue's bakery.

Maybe I need to cut back on the caffeine? I thought. *I haven't been drinking that much, though . . .*

Abruptly, I sat up, feeling as though I needed to burn some energy. Not knowing why, I flung the door to my wardrobe open, and something caught my attention. There was a glow coming from the back of the closet, and I bent down, my eyebrows furrowing as I cast aside shirts and other bits of clothing.

I found a familiar chest back there, but as the layers of material had been removed, the glow dissipated entirely.

"Was I imagining it . . . ?"

I'd long ago hidden the chest in my room, but hadn't given it much thought since then. Not wanting to make any noise and wake Cinnamon, I picked it up and took it to the living room.

The night air was cool beyond my bedroom, and the ethereal moonlight shining in through my glass windows seemed to add a layer of frost to everything it touched. I set the chest down and sat before it.

An overwhelming amount of wealth lay within when I opened it. The moonlight reflected off pearls and silver, giving the assorted jewelry an enchanting appearance. One ring in particular stood out, and I picked it up, lifting it so it shone beneath the moon. It was the one I'd made with the help of Fergus, and it drew my eyes in.

Iridescent Ring of Silver

Rare

A ring of precious metal, adorned by one of the most sought-after stones found in the Kallis Realm. More than just a symbol of wealth, this ring has a multitude of purposes for those with the requisite knowledge.

I slid the ring on one finger, taking comfort in its cool touch.

Returning my attention to the chest, I lifted a small pouch from within and opened it. I removed a gold coin from inside and held it up to the light. On one side, an unfamiliar face stared back at me, and on the other, the image of a scythe was raised in gold. There were twenty-six coins in total, only one of which was a remnant of the coins I'd received when arriving in this strange world. The rest had appeared from nowhere when I created the freshwater pond Claws now called home; the System had seen fit to generate them for a reason entirely unknown to me.

I recalled how wishing for and imagining a home had resulted in my house being built, and an idea struck me. Focusing on the pile of coins before me, I closed my eyes and took a deep breath. With my legs crossed, spine upright, and palms facing up, I settled into the stereotypical meditative pose from Earth.

Trying to replicate what I'd done when accidentally building a home, I imagined what I wanted to create. I immediately hit a wall; I had no idea what I wanted. I had more friends than I could count, my own oceanfront land, and all the time in the world to spend fishing. I cocked my head to the side, unable to sit still as I searched for what more I could possibly need.

All I want is to protect what I already have, I decided.

With this realization, my core seemed to vibrate. A tendril of power shot out from my abdomen, seeking . . . something. I let it go, focusing on the sensations of my body and the desire to protect the life I'd found here in Tropica.

The tendril extended further out, and I jolted as it made contact with something. It paused for but a moment, then started pouring power into the connection.

CHAPTER TWENTY

REFUGE

Barry woke to a strange sensation. Something was tugging at his core, and he sat up slowly, rubbing bleary eyes.

The moon shone down through the thin curtains of his bedroom. Helen murmured softly, so he reached over and smoothed her hair, willing her to not wake.

The tugging in his core became more insistent, so he climbed from his bed and shuffled through the open door from his bedroom. He closed it behind himself and went to the kitchen, hoping to find a drink of water. The urn was empty, so he made his way out into the cold and still night air.

The moon lit the landscape, shining down its white light on everything he could see. The sugarcane crop directly to the west was only half grown, allowing him to see far into the distance until an older crop grew high. He smiled at the vista's layered beauty.

His steps felt more sure as he went to the well and lowered a bucket. He pulled it up and splashed his face before taking a drink, willing whatever was happening within him to dissipate.

I cracked an eye as something interrupted my meditation. There was a tug at my awareness, as if my core was being pulled to the northwest. It was almost . . . pleasant, and I cocked my head at the indescribable sensation.

I glanced around with a furrowed brow but saw nothing that would explain it. As I looked about, I started losing my connection to that which coaxed me on, so I closed my eyes and settled back within myself.

Taking a steady breath, I poured every ounce of my attention into whatever the connection was, trusting my instincts to not lead me astray.

Barry held his breath, hoping whatever this episode was would pass. Instead, the pressure increased and twisted. He doubled over, his knees driving into the earth. He struggled to keep himself upright, struggled to breathe, and the force only grew stronger.

Though his body was suppressed, his thoughts raced. Whatever this was, he had to overcome it. There was so much he had yet to do, so many things he had to accomplish—both for himself, his family, and the world at large.

He reached within and held onto those ideals for dear life. Part of the pressure receded, so he delved further into his desires.

A religion that the world had not seen for millennia. The ascension of a god, one that truly held love for the humans of Kallis. His next project had been a church. A physical building that declared their intent—that screamed it at the very heavens.

The only reason he hadn't started the construction was because he hadn't found a suitable location, somewhere he could build a structure that was still hidden from sight. He now regretted not doing so sooner; he may not live to see the sunrise.

At this thought, the thing tugging on his core seemed to find purchase and snap into place.

And the next thing Barry knew was pain.

All at once, the power coursed through me. As something in the connection shifted, the world became blinding. A light brighter than the sun bloomed from the treasure-filled chest; the golden rays flowed into me, then were thrust along the pathway stemming from my core.

I gritted my teeth, struggling to stay upright as my vision waned. Though I wasn't aware how, I knew I had to stay conscious for whatever was happening to work. The blinding light slowly faded, as did the power pumping through me. With shaky breaths and trembling arms, I leaned against the wooden floor, just barely stopping myself from slumping over.

"Just . . . a little . . . more . . ."

Barry's abdomen felt like it was smoldering from within as power beyond his control rushed through him. He focused on what he wanted, somehow knowing that to be his only chance.

A building . . . for worship . . .

He clenched his jaw against the white-hot agony.

Hidden. Unseen. Grand.

He braced his core against the onslaught threatening to fold him in two.

A refuge for the congregation . . .

The searing pain began to dull, as did the torrent flowing through him. It became more manageable by the second, but before it could fade away entirely, a bone-deep weariness washed over him.

No . . . he thought. *I need to stay awake.*

His vision started to fade.

. . . just . . . a little . . . more . . .

Beneath the ethereal light of the moon, trembling on all fours and desperate to stay conscious, Barry failed.

The dark of night took him.

The golden hues bled from the room, slowly fading as the ocean of power flowing through me turned into a river. The river became a stream, and the stream became a trickle. Before I knew it, there was nothing left.

As the power fled me, so too did my strength. I tried to lower myself to the floor, but my arms failed me. I fell before the now-dull chest.

I . . . I did it . . .

With a sigh of relief and a half-formed smile, I let sleep take me.

"*Barry!*"

Someone was shaking Barry's shoulder, and he groaned, willing them to leave him alone.

"Barry, please—please wake up!"

He recognized the voice. It was Helen.

"Stop . . ." he slurred with a mouth that felt full of cotton. "I'm fine, just . . . tired . . ."

"Thank the gods." She lay atop him, her body trembling. "I thought I'd lost you. What happened, Barry?"

Barry slowly came back to himself, and he registered that Helen's voice was frantic.

Why? he wondered. *I just need some sleep . . .*

But then, all at once, he recalled what had happened. A spike of adrenaline shot through him. He rolled over to his back with a groan, opening bleary eyes to stare up. The moon was high in the sky; hours had passed since he'd passed out . . . *since he'd failed.*

He shifted again and made to stand, and Helen helped him, lifting him easily now that she, too, was a cultivator. She slung his arm around her shoulder, turned to help him inside, then paused.

"What . . . ?" she asked.

"What's wrong?"

She didn't respond for a long moment, merely stared to their right. With great effort, Barry turned his head to see what she was looking at . . . and then he understood.

"When did you build a new shed?" she asked, gaping at the ornate bricks where their wooden shed had previously been.

"I didn't."

They stared at each other wide-eyed, and without another word, turned and made their way toward the building. Barry's steps were shuffling, but Helen held him upright. When they got to it, he let go to lean on the wall. The stones were cool to the touch, their surface smooth and uniform.

"What kind of stones are these?" Helen asked, her voice filled with awe.

"I have no idea. I've never seen anything like it."

The stones were carved into perfect bricks, and unlike those comprising most of the buildings in Tropica, they weren't porous river stone. Barry raised an eyebrow as he leaned closer to inspect the gaps between them—if they were held together by mortar, he couldn't see any. He reached his left hand out to touch the door. It was made of dark wood and had intricate swirls of banded metal around every edge.

Helen stepped around him and grabbed its handle, then pulled. The door swung open on silent hinges, and as the metal coverings glinted in the moonlight, she inhaled sharply. "Is that . . . ?"

"Gold," Barry answered. "It's covered in gold."

He leaned against the entrance and peered inside. All of his equipment and tools were still there, set atop a raised bench that ran around the room. Right in the center, descending into the earth below, was a stairwell.

Barry ambled forward and Helen grabbed his arm, helping him approach. The stairs stretched down, obscured by shadow. They stood there for a long moment, both lost in thought.

"Do you want to rest before we explore?" Helen asked, rubbing his shoulder. "It'll still be here in the morning . . ."

He glanced at her and, seeing the unmistakable glint of curiosity in her eye, forced a grin.

"Let's get a torch."

As I cracked an eye, a thumping headache made itself known. My mouth was dry and tasted like I'd been drinking Barry's rum all night, so I rolled over and slowly climbed to my feet. With ambling steps, I made my way to the kitchen and bent down, drinking straight from the tap. I drank until I needed to take a breath, then drank just as much again.

Wiping my mouth and rubbing my eyes, I stumbled back toward the chest. I picked up the empty bag beside it.

The coins were gone.

"Yeah, that checks out . . ." I groaned.

I trailed off, my eyes going as wide as my throbbing headache would allow. I knelt down, looking directly at the contents of the chest. The jewelry was still there and the precious metals that served as their foundation were untouched. Each piece had been worth a fortune to a commoner, given they were inset with illustrious pearls.

. . . were.

I shuffled the jewelry around, confirming my suspicions. Every single pearl had disappeared, leaving behind empty sockets and indents in the pieces of silver and gold they'd once adorned.

"Well, ain't that something . . ."

I held up my right hand, peering at the Iridescent Ring of Silver on my index finger. The pearl was still there, and when I inspected it, it remained intact.

I sat down heavily and covered my eyes, willing my headache to recede so I could properly think. The door to my bedroom clicked open, and a moment later, the fuzzy form of Cinnamon crawled over my knee and curled up in my lap. I stroked her head with one hand as the other covered my eyes, blocking out the building light of day.

She made a questioning peep, and I peered down at her. Her neck was extended, and she gazed down at the empty-socketed jewelry I'd dropped on the ground before me. She turned to stare at me with an intelligent gleam.

I bobbed my head in a nod as slow as I could, trying not to aggravate my already pounding head. "Something downright fracky happened last night, Cinnamon, and I'm pretty sure I know where I need to go to find out what it was."

She cocked her head, and I let out a sigh as I slowly stood, holding her in my arms. She leaned into me, so I held her tight.

"All right—let's go."

I knocked on the door softly; my headache was thankfully receding, but was very much still present. The door opened, and Helen looked up at me with tired eyes.

"Oh—morning, Fischer."

"Hey, Helen. Is Barry about?"

"Oh, uhhh, he's a bit busy this morning, but he should be back later . . ."

I rubbed the bridge of my nose. "It's fine, Helen. I know something happened last night—I felt the power coming this—" My brain seemed to thump against my skull, and I winced. "It doesn't matter. I just really need to talk to Barry."

"Are you sure, Fischer?" She gave me a look my pounding head couldn't properly parse. "I know you didn't want to be involved . . ."

"It's fine. My head hurts too much for me to care right now."

She chewed her lip for a long moment, then gave a single nod. "He's around back."

She led me through their home and I stepped out the back door. Barry was hammering away at his shed, which confused me for a moment, but then my eyes adjusted to the growing daylight.

Where his shed had been, a stone building was now erected. Barry was adding a wooden facade to obscure the shed's transformation. In the side facing toward his well, a wooden door was set in the stone. Its edges were accented with intricate golden swirls, and confusion warred with my overwhelming headache.

A shed?

All those coins . . . All those pearls . . .

For a shed?

It made little sense, but before I could think about it any longer, the door swung open. Ruby strode out wearing a black robe and drying her hair with a towel. The robe had a pattern embroidered atop her heart: in blue, a rod with a fish on the end of the line; in gold, the sun shining down its brilliant rays.

"Hygieia's smooth skin, those showers are *amazing!*" she said.

"The pressure is amazing, isn't it?" Barry asked, reaching up to hammer in another plank.

She let out a contented sigh, started winding the towel around her head, then glanced up.

We locked eyes, and she froze. With the stunned look of a kid caught with their hand in the cookie jar, she made not a move.

I blinked; she blinked.

I narrowed my eyes; her eyebrows rose.

She took a step backward, then another. She slowly disappeared from sight, and the door made a soft *click* as she closed it, sealing herself inside the building.

Barry bent down to grab another plank of wood.

"We just need to hide this shed before Fischer just happens to stroll along—that'd be just my luck."

Helen cleared her throat from behind me. "Uhhh, dear?"

"Yes, honey?" he asked, glancing up. "What's—"

Barry and I locked eyes, and he, too, froze. His shoulders almost immediately slumped in defeat. "*Frack me . . .*"

CHAPTER TWENTY-ONE

EXPLORATION

The midmorning sun beamed down from above. I held a hand to my forehead, shielding my eyes. A sparse cloud drifted before the light, providing a modicum of relief. A soft breeze blew across the fields and the sugarcane leaves rustled and shifted around us, highlighting the silence that stretched between Barry, Helen, and me.

"So . . ." I said, drawing the word out. "New building, huh?"

Barry sighed. "How did you know?"

As I went to answer, the cloud partially shielding the sun was swept away, and I squeezed my eyes shut.

"Is there somewhere we can talk inside?" I gestured at the ornate door. "I have a splitting headache and it's bright as hell out here."

"Are you sure you want to see?"

"If it means we can get out of the sun? Yeah."

"All right." Barry turned to Helen. "Would you mind taking Fischer down? I'll just finish concealing the outside, then come join you."

"You two go ahead," she replied. "I'll finish up out here."

"You're sure?"

She arched an eyebrow, giving him a dangerous look. "Are you implying I can't do it as well as you, dear?"

Wisely, Barry hopped off the ladder and put down his hammer. "Thank you, my love."

She nodded and rolled up her sleeves, and Barry led me to the door. It swung outward, and as we stepped inside, I gave Ruby a polite nod. "Mornin'."

She stood wide-eyed against a wall, her still-wet hair bound in a towel. "Er—good, uh . . . morning?"

As Barry closed the door behind me, the light of day was blessedly banished. A soft orange glow suffused the chamber, climbing up from a stairwell that led down into the depths of the earth.

"There's a place for us to sit downstairs," Barry said, giving Ruby a wincing smile in passing.

I gave her a little wave. "See ya later."

She raised her hand haltingly. "Yeah . . . later . . ."

As we walked down the stairs made of the same smooth brick, a soft orange glow came from sconces set in the wall. I stopped at one, cocking my head at the small flame inside. It burned behind a shield of glass, and there was no wick or coil from which the fire could be fueled. I leaned in closer and spotted a tiny hole in the stone brick beneath the flame.

Gas? I wondered. *Or some sort of magical Xianxia land tomfoolery?*

"Barry . . . ?"

"No idea," he answered. "They lit by themselves when I first came down and seem to turn off when someone hasn't passed in a while."

"And they turn back on when someone approaches again?"

"Just so."

"Huh. Neat."

Step after step, we made our way farther down. I expected it to get colder as we went, but the air remained pleasantly warm. We reached a flat section of floor, and a long, spacious hallway met us. It stretched out an impressive distance and had open doorways intermittently placed on either wall.

"So," Barry said, looking down the hallway and avoiding my eyes. "How did you know?"

"I felt the power coming in this direction, so I had a hunch it was you."

"Oh . . ." He slowly turned to me. "It came from you?"

"By 'it,' do you mean that ungodly amount of essence or whatever that came your way? Yeah, mate. My bad on that one. I hope it wasn't too much."

He barked a laugh, and some of his weariness disappeared. "It was entirely too much. But hey, look at the result." He breathed deep, then let out a slow breath. "How did you do it?"

"Did I ever tell you how I made my house?"

"No."

I opened my mouth to tell him, but then I looked into the first room. A colossal round table made of what appeared to be a single piece of timber took up most of the space. Dozens of chairs surrounded it, and at the far end of the room, seven eyes went wide as they saw me: with her gaze locked on me, Sharon started rolling up a giant parchment she had been animatedly gesturing at. Private Pistachio nodded in greeting, his stoic features revealing nothing. Sergeant Snips slowly lowered from sight, her eye wide as it retreated from view. Rocky stared at me with a hint of accusation, daring me to say something, but then Snips's claw shot up and dragged him from sight.

The sound of something hard smacking carapace rang out through the room, and Rocky let out a very feminine squeak.

We walked past the doorway, and I shook my head in amusement. I turned to Barry and started telling him all about my accidental house creation, sparing no detail. Barry's forehead grew more and more lined as I spoke.

"Gold coins with a scythe and a face? Never heard of anything like it. Do you have any more?"

"Er . . . I did?" I gave him a rueful smile. "They were all consumed in building this place."

"If you pictured a house and it built itself, what did you imagine last night?"

"Uh, that's a little less straightforward. I couldn't sleep, so I tried meditating on the coins. I realized I already had everything I needed, so I focused on protecting what I had."

"Protecting what you had . . ." Barry repeated, tasting the words. "And it sent the power my way . . ."

We strode onward, and I glanced into a room with a . . .

You have got *to be kidding me.*

Steam rose from a pool that took up most of the room. There was an underground hot spring, complete with a trickling waterfall and shower cubicles on the far wall. Boulders protruded from the water's surface sporadically. I glimpsed a familiar shower head through one of the open doors, which was presumably where Ruby had come from.

Just when did they recruit her? I thought. *I wonder if they also got Steven . . .*

My thoughts trailed off as I noticed someone in the pool.

In the center of the hot spring, with his arms held out to his sides, the man in question let out a happy sigh. Steven opened his eyes and peered out at the world with a half-lidded gaze and a ridiculously relaxed smile on his face. It disappeared the moment he caught sight of me.

His entire body went rigid and everything but his head dipped below the water's surface. He slowly shifted, making his way around a boulder and disappearing behind it, never once taking his eyes off me.

Having missed the show, Barry was still gazing into the distance and walking along, so I jogged to catch up, laughing under my breath. "What happened on your end last night?"

He shook his head as his eyes cleared. "I was woken up by something tugging on my core—the power you were channeling my way, from what it sounds like. I went to the well to get a drink and the weight of your will folded me like a croissant."

"Oh . . ."

"It's fine. I started thinking about all the things I had yet to do, and when I pictured creating a church for the . . . uh . . ."

He shot a look at me, and I sighed. "It's fine, mate. I already know about the culty churchy shenanigans you've got going on. So you thought about building . . . what? A place for your heresy?"

I shot him a wink, and he gave me a small smile. "That pretty much sums it up, yeah. I wanted to create something hidden for everyone."

"So I wanted to protect the life I've carved out for myself here, and the System recognized that what you're doing would do so. That's . . . kind of a big deal."

He grinned, and for the first time that morning, he looked as carefree as usual. "Agreed."

I ran my hand along the stones as we walked on. They were cool and smooth, and as we approached a door, they grew even colder. I poked my head around the doorway, curious as to what I'd find.

A humid breeze blew out from an underground forest. The room was the biggest yet in both width and height, and saplings of different varieties sprouted up sporadically from the lush green grass covering the floor. In the center of the room sat the only mature tree, its trunk wider than any I'd seen in this world. Great roots extended down into the ground in every direction, and the tree's bark was the deepest brown imaginable. It reminded me of the giant fig trees you'd so often see growing in the subtropical climate of Australia.

I gazed up at the roof as I stepped into the room; golden light beamed down from tiles set in the ceiling high above, so bright that they were hard to look at.

"That's . . . wow."

"That's not even half of it, Fischer. This place . . ." Barry knelt down next to one of the saplings and touched its bark. "It's already astounding, and I don't think any of us are even close to understanding the whole of it yet."

"Does that mean you don't know the purpose of this tree room yet?"

He raised an eyebrow. "Do you?"

I grinned. "No bloody clue, mate."

"That makes two of us," he replied, laughing.

I gazed down at the different saplings as we strode toward the tree in the middle of the room, and the air grew cooler with each step forward. I hadn't properly appreciated the tree's majesty from afar, but a sense of awe was inescapable when standing at its base. I reached out with one hand, pressed my palm against its smooth bark, and took a deep breath. The air smelled sweet, and I got the impression it was filled with life.

"How many more secrets are hidden down here, Barry?"

He didn't respond, so I turned to look at him. His lips were pressed into a firm line, and they shifted as he considered something, his eyebrows furrowed.

I cocked my head. ". . . mate?"

His eyes snapped up, his gaze firm. "Do you trust me, Fischer?"

I didn't have to think about it long. "I do."

He slowly nodded, his eyes unfocusing as he thought on what to say next. "I don't think you should go further in."

My head rocked back. "Can't lie, mate—I didn't expect that. There's stuff I wouldn't want to see?"

"Just that. I know how much you value your peaceful life here, and I respect that. I don't want to introduce any unnecessary worries."

I tongued my cheek as I considered for a long moment. "Is it something that puts anyone in danger?"

His lips pursed, then he smiled. "No one is in danger, no."

One side of my mouth curled up as I looked at him and fought down an undeniable sense of curiosity. I swept it aside.

"Okay, mate. I trust you. If you think it's for the best, we can end our little tour here."

"Thank you, Fischer."

"Nah. Thank *you*, mate. I appreciate everything you're doing here to keep everyone safe." The last hints of my headache were finally receding, and I stretched high as I stood from where I knelt by the tree. "Seeing as though my tour is over, I think I'll go mess with Snips a little bit before I leave—she's entirely too cute when she's guilty."

Barry let out a soft chuckle. "I'm guessing they'll have retreated by now, but you're more than welcome to try."

"Oh, one more thing, Barry."

"Yeah?"

"You should start collecting pearls."

" . . . Pearls?"

"Yeah, mate. Pearls."

Barry stopped walking and he shot me a confused look. "What the frack are pearls?"

"Oh! My bad. You guys call them iridescent stones."

Barry's confusion turned to incredulity. "Where on Kallis would I get iridescent stones?"

"You should ask Snips and Claws about that."

"Okay . . . but why are we collecting them?"

"Because they function the same as those strange golden coins. Whatever we did last night consumed dozens of pearls I had stashed away."

" . . . You had dozens of iridescent stones?"

"Yeah, something like that. But that's not important." I waved my hands dismissively, delighting in the look on Barry's face. "What's important, mate, is that you get more."

In a room made of smooth bricks, Trent, the first in line to the throne of Gormona—and not at all resembling a toe by his estimate—sniffed. "I suppose it's a *little* better."

Leroy gave him a flat stare. "A little better?"

"That's right."

Leroy glanced around at the room's features. A shower and a toilet, both of which had running water. A gigantic bed that was comfier than any Leroy had ever felt before. Space and equipment for exercise. And even a small garden with one of those golden tiles that the room two doors down was decorated with.

"You know, Trent, I think I hate you."

Trent crossed his arms like a petulant child. "You dare say such things to the crown prince of your kingdom?"

Leroy sighed. "Yeah, I definitely hate you."

"Pah!" Trent threw up his hands. "How am I supposed to be happy about being thrown into another prison?"

Leroy looked at the door and the black metal bars blocking the escape, then turned back to the idiot. "You were locked in the last room too, but there you had to pee in a bucket."

"The bucket doubled as a drum, and without it, you've removed my only source of fun."

"You're saying you'd be happier here if I got your pee bucket back?"

"It's a percussive instrument, cultivator scum—*not* a pee bucket."

Before Leroy could hit him back with some snark, a beautiful form entered the door beyond the bars of Trent's prison cell. Barbara.

"I've brought lunch."

Leroy smiled at his wife.

"Finally!" Trent said, perking up. "There better be something sweet this time." He snapped his fingers at Leroy. "Fetch it for me, cultivator."

Leroy gave him a sickly sweet grin. "Gladly, prince."

Trent's toe-like face became even more detestable as he frowned at Leroy, clearly not expecting the polite response.

Leroy reached the bars, and Barbara passed him a plate with a croissant and dollop of jam, and a cup filled almost to the brim. He strode to Trent, set them on the ground, then made his way back to the bars.

"Before you get any ideas . . ." Leroy's arm muscles bulged, and he swung with all his power at the black metal. The room reverberated with the strike, yet the bars held firm.

Trent's eyes went wide and he gulped

Leroy smirked. "There's no chance of escape. You may as well get comfy down here."

Trent's fear was swiftly hidden behind a strained smile, and he sat down before his food. "Wait . . ." he looked down at the cup. "Why in Demeter's busty chest is this water green, cultivator?"

He sniffed the contents, then took a tentative sip with raised eyebrows. As the flavor hit his tongue, he let out an appreciative *mmm.*

"That isn't water," Leroy answered. "It's sugarcane juice."

"It's . . . it's delicious!" Trent said, then started sculling the sweet liquid.

Leroy shot a look at Barbara, and both their faces crinkled in shared amusement.

CHAPTER TWENTY-TWO

NEW BEGINNINGS

It was a pleasantly cool day in Tropica—until a heat like that of the sun bloomed. Fergus squinted and leaned back from the forge's glow as he threw another shovel of coal into the hearth. He stepped to the side, wiping sweat from his brow with a burly forearm. "Ready, Duncan?"

"Aye!" his apprentice responded and started placing lengths of iron into a crucible.

Fergus watched carefully as Duncan added pinches of phosphorus and sulfur; there was a hint of hesitation in his movements.

"You've got this." Fergus gave him a reassuring smile. "It's the same as any other alloy."

Duncan's hand froze, and he looked up, his gaze wavering. "You're sure? I don't want to ruin—"

"When was the last time you ruined anything in this smithy?" Fergus interrupted.

"I, uh . . . I can't remember."

"Neither can I. Besides, you thinking you're not ready is calling into question my superior and flawless judgment." Fergus shot him a wink. "That's a paddlin'."

Duncan's uncertainty melted away, replaced by a flat stare. "Just you try to paddle me."

Roaring with laughter, Fergus clapped his apprentice on the shoulder. "Just kidding, lad. You're ready, all right? Let's do it."

Duncan set his jaw and nodded, so Fergus took up position by the bellows. As the apprentice put his goggles and thick gloves on, Fergus moved the bellows slowly, causing the added coal to glow red at the edges. When Duncan strode to the forge with the crucible held in a set of large tongs, his steps were sure and filled with purpose. He extended the crucible into the furnace, and Fergus began working the bellows in earnest.

Less than an hour later, a thin sheen of sweat covered Fergus's body as he watched Duncan pour the molten metal into the molds they had prepared. The liquid was bright yellow and of uniform viscosity. The alloy's creation had been a success.

Fergus said not a word, intent on watching the process. During the years he had been teaching Duncan the art of blacksmithing, he had slowly but surely grown to see the boy like a son.

No, not a boy, he reminded himself, looking over Duncan's muscled arms.

He had been a boy when he first came to his smithy, but now he was a man—and a blacksmith—in his own right. The waif of a boy that had shown up in his workshop was now a distant memory, and a smile came to Fergus's face as he compared the bull of a man before him to the bag of bones that first walked in the door all those years ago.

The last dregs on the molten metal dribbled down in the final mold, and Duncan breathed a sigh of relief as he set the tongs and crucible down.

"Perfect, lad," Fergus said.

"You're not just saying that?"

Fergus snorted, and so did the bunny.

Wait, what?

The smith's head darted to the side; a bunny had joined them on the bench and was peering down at the molds. She looked up at them and nodded a greeting.

"Uhhh," both men said, the sound dragging out as their brains tried to comprehend what was going on.

The bunny cocked her head, causing her ears to flop to the side. She hopped to the first mold, tapped it lightly with one paw, then bobbed her head up and down in approval.

"Hello?" came a voice from behind them, and Fergus whirled.

Sharon, with a large bag slung over one shoulder, smiled and waved.

"Hi, guys. I was hoping I could talk to you for a . . ." She trailed off as she saw the bunny sitting on the bench. "Cinnamon! What in Hades's cursed realm are you doing?"

Fergus glanced back at the bunny. The creature, Cinnamon, seemed to shimmy in delight, her little tail wiggling away. There was a blur of brown and blue, and another creature appeared behind the bunny. An otter, shaking her head and chirping indignantly, put one forepaw around Cinnamon's waist and covered the bunny's mouth with another.

The fuzzy little bunny let the otter drag her down from the bench, shaking in what appeared to be laughter as muffled peeps escaped her throat.

Sharon let out a heavy sigh. "Well, so much for the plan."

Sharon closed and barred the door, and from the bag slung over her shoulder, something horrific emerged. A crab the size of a small dog poked its entire body out and began shaking a claw menacingly at them, blowing a steady stream of bubbles. Something smacked the crab from below, making it fly up into the rafters at terrifying speed. Another crab emerged from the bag, wearing an eye patch and covered in spikes.

There was a loud *crack,* and the first crab fell down to the smithy floor, as did something else. An object of monstrous proportions slammed into the ground with a loud *thud.* A wave of dust sprang up from the collision, and as it slowly cleared, Fergus realized his mistake. It wasn't an object that had fallen—it was a creature.

A lobster as long as he was tall stared up at him from its back, unblinking. Other than the eye patch–wearing crab that was hissing and berating the crab it had flung—and was once more shaking a claw at the smiths—the entire room froze. The silence was broken when Sharon let out another sigh. She rubbed her temples and shook her head. "Well, that couldn't have gone any worse—"

From the corner of Fergus's eye, he saw the bunny break free from the otter's grasp and launch across the room. It slammed into the upside-down lobster and kicked off his side, flipping the crustacean right side up and throwing itself skyward. As its body rotated in the air, there was an unmistakable grin on the bunny's face.

The otter, chirping at the top of her lungs and trailing lightning, slammed into Cinnamon. They sailed across the room into a stack of metal-filled crates, obliterating them in a cloud of splintered wood, metal bars, and furred limbs.

Fergus raised an eyebrow as he slowly turned back to Sharon. She blinked at the carnage, spun to meet his gaze, and shrugged.

"Fergus and Duncan, meet Fischer's ascendant animal friends. As you can see from their behavior, they're *clearly* his. Everyone, this is Fergus and Duncan."

"Ascendent creatures . . . ?" Duncan asked, sounding as numb as Fergus felt. "Does that mean . . . ?"

The pieces of the puzzle slammed into place, and Fergus's eyes went wide. "I knew it!" He slapped Duncan lightly on the chest. "I told you Fischer was a cultivator!"

His apprentice looked around the room with his jaw hanging open. He swallowed. "I don't think that's the issue at hand, Fergus . . ."

"It's not so dire as it appears," Sharon said, sweeping hair behind her ear and giving them what was likely intended to be a reassuring smile.

"Let me explain . . ."

With the midday sun beating down on my skin, my steps were surprisingly light given the events of the last twenty-four hours. I took a bite of my freshly warmed croissant and washed it down with a mouthful of coffee. I closed my eyes and focused on the soft breeze tickling the hair of my arms. As I walked over the sand, my thoughts roiled with implications and worries about the future. Rather than push them away and pretend they didn't exist, I acknowledged them, allowed my anxiety to swell, then let the thoughts go as I refocused on the sensations of my body.

I narrowed my attention on each step, feeling the shifting sand beneath my feet. The wind picked up, wicking away sweat and causing grains of sand to strike my lower legs. A sense of calm replaced my anxieties, and I shielded my eyes with one hand as I peered down at the saltwater pond. No one was home, but that was to be expected—I imagined my pals might be a little busy for the next few days after an underground base appeared out of nowhere. I chuckled and shook my head, continuing toward the coast.

When I arrived, I took a moment to sit in the dry sand and gaze out at the water. Small waves lapped the shore, and the bay was calm all the way out to the horizon. I took a deep breath; the sea spray on the air seemed to suffuse my entire being.

Unbidden, a smile came to my face, and my eyes unfocused, my entire visual field becoming a single sheet of light, shadow, and color. The joy spread to encompass my entire face, and I stretched as I got to my feet. "All right. Time for a little harvesting."

I took off my outer clothes and, after one more good stretch, walked into the small waves peppering the shoreline. The water was pleasantly cool, and the moment I got up to my knees, I collapsed beneath it. As I sprang back up, a whole-body shiver took me, and I walked farther out into the ocean. When I could no longer walk, I swam, and I reached my destination in no time at all. Large wooden poles marked the spot, and as I caught sight of the cages strung between them, I couldn't believe my eyes.

The oyster cages were one of the first things I constructed after coming to Tropica. I'd created them for two reasons: replenishing the oyster population a certain otter was decimating, and, more importantly, *pearls*. At the time, I'd thought pearls were a source of gold, but as it turned out, they were much, *much* more valuable than that. I hadn't checked the cages because, well, what was the point? We had plenty of food, I didn't want or need more gold, and I thought they'd take a fair while to grow. My understanding was that oysters took years to reach maturity.

My understanding was wrong.

All six cages strung up before me were filled to the brim with massive oysters. I yelled excitedly underwater, and it came out in a garbled stream of bubbles.

I started untying the first cage, picturing the look on my animal pals' faces when I presented them with an entire *cage* of freshly shucked oysters.

Number Three breathed deep of the afternoon air, delighting in the humidity and scents of the forest. The sun was setting behind them, and as he looked at the surrounding faces, he saw similar looks of contentment. As much as their personalities could clash at times, they were unified in their mission, and being so close to their destination had picked up their moods greatly.

Even Two, whose patience had become shorter with each passing day—and each time someone slipped up and didn't use a code name—sat with a small smile on his face, bathing in the afternoon sun.

Three couldn't help himself. "You look almost serene, Keith."

Two, the human formerly known as Keith, sputtered with indignation. "Number Two!" he boomed, glancing at the surrounding trees. "My name is Two!"

By his estimate, Three did a fantastic job of hiding his amusement behind the appropriate amount of chagrin, but then Four burst into laughter and he couldn't help but join in. Five joined in soon after, and even One, who was engrossed in one of his large tomes, arched an amused eyebrow over his book.

Two's face went beet red, and he rounded on their expedition leader. "You too, One? I thought you were above their childish games!"

"Normally I would err on the side of caution, but I believe I recognize the mountain we are about to crest."

"So?" Two demanded, his fury still hot. "What does that have to do with anything?"

Three gave One an appreciative look. "I have to admit, I'm a little surprised. How did you know?"

One spun the tome he was reading, revealing a topographical map of Kallis's eastern coast. They smiled at each other, and Two made a series of exasperated noises.

"Will you both stop speaking in riddles and explain why the mountain we're on has a godsdamned thing to do with revealing my true name?" He hissed the last two words, as if merely speaking them would bring about ruin.

Just then, the cart shifted angles. They started moving downhill, and the other side of the mountain came into view. Rolling fields of green and yellow crops swayed in an unseen breeze. A smattering of buildings were bunched together, some of which had gray streaks of smoke rising from their chimneys. Most notable of all was the far distance, where the sky was pink and orange above an endless sea of blue and green.

"Because, Keith . . ." Theo, the man also known as Three, answered with a broad grin. "We've arrived at Tropica."

CHAPTER TWENTY-THREE

THE FISHING CLUB

With the wind at his back and butterflies in his stomach, Theo strode across the sand. His closest friends in the world were at his side, and despite how different the men could be, they were unified under a single ideal. Five men of different stations, with different backgrounds and ambitions, had become the closest of allies since finding each other that one fateful day so long ago.

No words were needed as they strode toward the southern headland. They spied a fence, and Theo whistled at the size of it; Fischer had been keeping himself busy. As they let themselves in, Theo cast his gaze around for Fischer's home, but saw nothing that denoted a house.

"You are sure this is where he lived?" Ellis inquired, his large tome still open in his hands.

"I'm sure. He said by the river mouth . . ."

"There," Peter said, pointing at the rocky headland as he shifted his bag onto one shoulder.

"I don't see anything, Four," Keith said, squinting.

"We're here now—call me Peter again. There's a hint of light coming from behind the headland, likely a fire."

Theo looked closer, and sure enough, now that the sun had set further behind the western mountains, a soft orange light flickered to the right of the large rock.

With a grin spreading over his face, he took a step forward, then abruptly stopped. Something had appeared in front of them. A small bunny blocked their path forward, and it stared at them intently, its ears alert.

"What are you doing out here, little one?" Peter asked, shifting his bag to the other shoulder.

Danny, the man formerly known as Five, squinted at the unmoving creature. " . . . Why isn't it running away?"

The bunny responded by going back on its haunches and stretching its forelimbs in an entirely too-human-like manner. It started boxing the air, unleashing little jabs as it ducked and weaved its head.

Keith took a step back. "Oh, no—"

The bunny shot forward faster than Theo could register, and the next thing he knew, Keith's unconscious body hit the floor. Ellis was next, and all Theo saw of the attack was a blur. He stared uncomprehendingly as, one by one, the rest of the men dropped to the sand. The bunny stared at Theo, cracked its neck threateningly, and grinned.

I smiled as I walked from the ocean with an entire cage of oysters on my back. The sun was setting over the mountains to the west, and I took a moment to appreciate the sky's beauty. I grabbed my outer clothes from the sand and set off for home with thoughts of the feast to come fueling my stride.

The warm glow of a lit fire greeted me as I rounded the headland from the northwest, and I squinted down at the illuminated ground. There were large grooves dragged through the sand.

Did someone bring whole trees for the fire? I wondered.

I heard a chirped and hissed conversation as I got closer, and a wide smile came to my face.

Claws and Snips were here already. Then I heard Barry speak, and a sense of excitement bloomed. The last time I'd given the man an oyster, it had been raw and he'd found it disgusting. I had already mentally picked out some herbs to cook this new batch of oysters in—I couldn't wait to redeem myself.

"G'day, everyone," I said, stepping into view of the fire. "Have I got a surprise for you guys . . . *what the fuck?*"

Barry, Sergeant Snips, Corporal Claws, Private Pistachio, and Rocky were arrayed around a pile of lifeless forms. Cinnamon sat atop the one in the middle, and when she caught sight of me, she puffed up her chest, downright preening with pride.

I recognized the person she sat on. "Theo?" I dashed forward and laid my finger against his neck. When I felt a pulse, I let out my breath. "Thank god . . ."

At my words, he stirred.

Theo was having the strangest dream, filled with even weirder noises. A myriad of what sounded like animal calls that were periodically interrupted by human speech. He couldn't make out any of the words, but then someone called his name.

"Theo?"

A hand touched his neck and the contact called to him. When Theo opened his eyes, his vision was blurry. There was a face right before him, and as he rapidly blinked, it came into focus. "Fischer . . . ?"

Lines of worry disappeared from Fischer's face, and he let out a relieved laugh. "Theo—long time no see, mate. How are ya?"

Before he could respond, a bunny's fuzzy little face leaned forward and took up his entire field of view. All at once, his memory returned. He yelled wordlessly and scrambled backward on the sand.

Fischer laid a hand on his shoulder; his firm grip held Theo still. "You're all good, mate. You're not in danger."

Despite Theo's addled state, he recognized Fischer's words.

He is telling the truth . . .

Fischer looked up and to the right. "What the hell happened, Barry?"

Theo spun to see who Fischer was looking at.

A man in farmer's garb gave a rueful smile. "Cinnamon found them inside your fence line. She knocked them out and came to find me."

The bunny—whose name was apparently Cinnamon—let out a triumphant peep from atop Theo's chest.

He gulped. "An ascendant creature . . . so it's true?"

"What's true, mate?"

"You're a cultivator."

Fischer opened his mouth and raised a finger. Theo saw the lie forming in the lines of his face, but then Fischer let out a sigh and nodded. "Yeah, mate. I'm a cultivator." His face moved almost imperceptibly, and anyone but a crown auditor wouldn't have noticed the conflict etched in his features. "What are you doing here, Theo?"

Ellis bolted upright. "No candles in the library!" he boomed, his voice deep and commanding. He blinked and looked around, his brow narrowing lower and lower. "Oh, uh… my apologies."

"Ellis," Theo said, forcing urgency into his tone. "This is Fischer. Fischer, this is the leader of Gormona's fishing club and the former head archivist of the royal library. The bunny's name is Cinnamon, and she's an ascendant creature." He pointed at Barry. "That's Barry. I don't know him, but it seems he's aware of Fischer's status as a cultivator."

Ellis looked at each of them as they were introduced, giving them a curt nod. "A pleasure to meet you."

Fischer frowned at him. "That's all? You're not surprised?"

"Well, I do have one question." Ellis pointed over Theo's shoulder. "Who are they?"

With his eyebrows lowering in confusion, Theo turned to the left. When he saw the faces staring at him, any chance of a coherent response fled.

Theo's jaw went slack when his eyes landed on my arrayed animal pals, and I couldn't help but chuckle. I still wasn't sure what was going on, and I had more than a few questions, but I didn't get the impression Theo was here for nefarious reasons.

"Everyone, this is my friend, Theo."

Snips hissed and dipped her head.

"That's Sergeant Snips, my ever-reliable guard crab."

Rocky gave him a rude gesture, and Sergeant Snips threw him out into the river.

"That was Rocky. He's kind of a dick."

Claws dashed forward and chirped a greeting. She dipped her head and pointed for Theo to rub behind her ear. He complied, his mouth still hanging open.

"That's Corporal Claws, lightning wielder and resident prankster."

Finally, Pistachio dipped his head. I noted the positioning of his claw—he was prepared to fire a blast on short notice if required.

"Private Pistachio is the stoic and trustworthy lobster."

It was the other man, Ellis, that responded with the enthusiasm I had hoped Theo would.

"Amazing. Absolutely marvelous!" He removed a notepad from his pocket and started writing. "Unheard of. To have so many awakened creatures, all of which appear to be subservient. This is much better than we could have anticipated . . ." he trailed off, mumbling under his breath as he took notes.

"Er, I don't really like the term subservient," I said, rubbing the back of my head. "We're more like pals working together."

Theo turned back to me, his eyes still wide. His mouth worked, but no words came out.

"I'm glad to see you again, mate," I said. "But I have to ask again: why are you here?"

Ellis cleared his throat. "I may be able to answer that."

I nodded, looking at him properly for the first time. The easiest way for me to describe his look would be cracked-out Gandalf. He had the exact hair, beard, and a similar face, but he was mostly skin and bone. Even the robes all the men wore were giving off wizardy vibes.

"So," Ellis said, "it all started when—"

"The bunny is awakened!" another man cried, shooting upright from his state of unconsciousness.

Cinnamon hopped into his lap and nodded her agreement; she was, in fact, awakened. He stared down at her, his jaw dropping.

"We know, Keith," Theo said. "She's a friend, apparently."

Keith was the youngest of the newcomers. Likely in his early twenties, the man had hair so blond it was almost white, and a strong jawline that, even as I was watching, fell further open in indignation.

"Not a danger? She *attacked* me!"

Theo tossed his head side to side. "Yeah, you've got a point there. She's not a danger *anymore*. She's Fischer's pet."

"Not my pet," I tried to correct, but Cinnamon shot me a venomous glare and punched one paw into another menacingly, so I held up my hands. "Okay, got it—you're mine. My bad."

"Also . . ." Theo pointed over his shoulder. "You should probably look behind you."

Keith's head snapped around fast enough that I thought he might get whiplash. "Phobos's lathered horses. Are they all—"

"Weevils in the wheat!" a fourth man yelled, jumping all the way to his feet.

"Isolate the grain immediately!" the fifth demanded, waking from his stupor and also launching upright. His face was bright red and his eyes darted around, presumably looking for said weevils.

"Whoa!" Theo stood and gestured for them to calm. "You're fine. We found Fischer. See?"

He pointed to me, and I waved. "G'day, fellas."

"Where are the weevils?" The fifth man demanded, his breaths coming heavy.

Theo rubbed his eyes. "There aren't any weevils, Danny. Peter yelled that in his sleep."

Keith cocked his head. "What's the big deal with weevils? Aren't they just bugs?"

"Just bugs?" Danny repeated, a firm line forming below his bald head. "They can decimate an entire city's grain stores! They're a damned plague!"

Theo turned to me and started explaining.

"Danny is—*was* the head quartermaster of Gormona's guards."

Danny gave a curt nod.

"The one that yelled about weevils is Peter," Theo continued. "He was the sous chef in the royal castle."

Keith sniffed. "What about me and Ellis?"

"I already introduced Ellis," Theo replied, smirking.

Before Keith could protest, Peter bellowed a laugh. "I can introduce you, your greatness. Keith is cousin to the main royal line, and seventeenth in line to the thro—"

"Sixteenth," Keith corrected.

"Oh, my apologies, my lord!" Peter gave an exaggerated bow. "How could I have—Medusa's pickled tit! Look at the size of that lobster!"

"Awakened creature!" Danny bellowed, pointing at Pistachio, whom they'd only just noticed. "Defensive positions!"

After things somewhat calmed down, what followed was a short round of introductions, reintroductions, and assurances that the animals arrayed before them were friendly.

"How can we know they're safe?" Keith asked, watching them intently. "I came under the assumption that we were coming to meet a cultivator, not a cadre of spirit beasts."

"You don't," Barry answered. "If it makes you feel any better, if they had violence in mind, they already would have disposed of and eaten you."

Claws grinned and made a loud *clack* with her needle-sharp chompers. Keith audibly swallowed.

"All right, all right." I shook my head at her, trying not to smile. "That's enough messing with them for one day, Claws." I spun back to the archivist, Ellis. "You said you could explain why you came here. You're all awake now, so it seems like the perfect time, yeah?"

He nodded. "I will keep this brief—I do not wish to impose any further on such a magnificent one's time."

I held up both hands. "You can drop the 'magnificent one' stuff. I'm just a regular bloke doing regular bloke things."

He cocked an eyebrow, but Theo nodded. "See? I told you. Tell him why we're here, Ellis."

"Hmmm." Ellis stroked his beard. "All right then. It all started when Theo returned from his trip to Tropica Village. He told us of a strange man that seemed to bend the world around him."

I grimaced at Theo. "What did I say that gave me away?"

"Nothing."

"It was this . . ." Ellis rummaged around in his pocket and withdrew a leather pouch. He unfolded it, then held his hand up, displaying a single hook.

It was one of the hooks I'd created and given Theo. The campfire's orange light gleamed off its curved edges, appearing as new as the day I'd made it.

"As an official of the royal library, I have access to restricted information. This hook, along with Theo's description of its creation, made me and the rest of the fishing club test whether we could break it. Can you guess what happened?"

"I'm guessing it didn't."

Danny grunted. "The only thing it broke was one of my favorite hammers."

"Precisely," Ellis said. "Even for a regular cultivator from before the gods' departure, such a creation would be quite a feat. Certain volumes listed in great detail what the cultivators of old could do, especially those called 'travelers.' Do you know what that is?"

I sighed. "I do."

"Wait, you do?" Barry asked, his head rocking back.

"Yeah, mate—people that were isekai'd by truck-kun and transmigrated to another world, right?"

" . . . What?"

"I'm from another world. Keep up, Barry—you already knew that."

Barry frowned at me, and I beamed a smile.

Ellis resumed stroking his beard. "So, it is true then?"

"It is, but you still haven't answered why you came here."

"Nor," Barry added, "why it was with such a collection of important people. The royal library's head archivist, a crown auditor, a royal chef, the capital's quartermaster, and an actual royal. Forgive me for saying so, but what you've stated so far doesn't add up."

I gave Barry an appreciating glance. My man was spitting straight facts. "Yeah. That."

"I suppose I should get to the point, then." Ellis's eyes bore into me. "We have abandoned our kingdom. We have left our posts, and if we are ever caught, our lives are forfeit. We have done all this for a singular purpose . . ."

Ellis stood taller, as did the other men. He took a deep breath, cast his gaze over everyone, then narrowed his vision on me. Despite his frail stature, he demanded my attention.

"We have come for you, Fischer. Though you know what a traveler is, I do not believe you understand the vast implications." He steepled his fingers before his face and narrowed his eyes at me. "We have come to start a church and raise you, Fischer, to the pantheon. We wish to make you a *god*."

A silence stretched over the sand. The wind vanished, the campfire's flames dulled, and no birds could be heard overhead. Even the waves gently lapping at the shore seemed to still.

Barry and I looked at each other, and as one, we erupted into laughter.

CHAPTER TWENTY-FOUR

BREAKING BREAD

I shook so hard with laughter that my legs collapsed beneath me. Snips and Claws made their way to me, chirping and hissing their delight as they leaned against my torso. Barry laughed harder than I'd ever seen—he took shallow, halting breaths, trying to get oxygen to his lungs as tears streamed from his eyes.

I lay on my back in the sand, delighting in the shaking forms of Snips and Claws as they similarly lost themselves to mirth. Minutes must have passed, and when I sat back up, the grandiose posture of the fishing club had entirely deflated.

"I'm—I'm sorry." I wiped tears from my eyes. "We're not laughing at you."

"Then what are you laughing at?" Keith's face was red, his lips pressed into a firm line. He turned his anger on Barry. "You. Who even are you? Why is Fischer's neighbor laughing at a *royal?*"

Theo snorted. "What happened to the Keith that said 'the monarchy is nothing but a farce set up to suppress the common folk'?"

"I'm annoyed, all right?" he snapped. "I don't understand what's going on!"

I walked toward the fire, sat down before it, and gestured for them to follow. As everyone took a seat, I smiled at the ridiculousness of the situation I found myself in. "I introduced Barry as my neighbor. That's true, but he's also more than that."

Danny smacked a fist down onto his open palm. "Oh! He's a cultivator too?"

"No—wait, yes. He is." I made a dismissive gesture. "But that's not what is important. Barry, behind my back and with the help of Sergeant Snips, started a cult. Or a church. I'm still not too sure, but that's by design."

"Church," Barry declared.

I watched the fishing club closely, scanning for a hint of annoyance or malice, but all I saw on their faces was disbelief.

"Remarkable," Ellis said. He picked up his pencil and watched the farmer intently. "What gave you the idea, Barry? How did you conclude that to be the correct course of action?"

"Timeout!" I held up a hand. "It's a long story, but—wait, it's not a long story at all. I wanna know as little as possible about the whole cult thing Barry has going on."

"Church," Barry parroted.

I waved a dismissive hand. "Sure. Church. I told you he set it up in secret, right? That's because he knows me, and he understands that all I want to do is fish and make friends. You guys are more than welcome to discuss cult stuff, but I'd prefer it be done while I'm not around."

Ellis's eyes locked onto me, and he lowered his book, stroking his beard with one hand.

"You do not have any desire to shape and mold the direction of your own church?"

"Not even a little bit."

Barry smiled at me. "We thought we were being sneaky, but Fischer knew we were doing it for quite a while and turned a blind eye."

I snorted. "That's a nice way of putting it. In truth, I was putting my head in the sand and pretending my problems didn't exist. That ended up being a mistake—I accidentally obliterated a tree in front of a friend of mine and—"

"A friend?" Barry interrupted, his eyes glittering.

"Oh, shush. The point is, pretending it wasn't happening only caused me grief. So I let Barry know that I knew, and I've asked him to inform me if anything happens that would put anyone's life at risk. Short of that, I'm blissfully unaware." I took a deep breath and exhaled with a sigh. "It's quite nice, really."

Theo slapped Keith's arm. "I told you Fischer was a good man, didn't I?"

Keith scowled at him. "Are you saying that was all the truth?"

"It was, though Barry was right to call out Fischer's use of the word *friend*."

I gave him a flat stare. "Whose side are you on?"

"A real crown auditor . . ." Barry said before Theo could respond. "It's true you can tell if someone is lying?"

"I can."

"That would prove more than a little useful." Barry rubbed his chin, and I could almost see the schemes coming together in his head. "Would you be willing to—"

"Barry," interrupted. "I'm still here, mate."

"Oh. Right. My bad."

Danny chuckled. It was deep and rough, like he'd spent a lifetime yelling at the top of his lungs, which I suppose may have been the case for a man organizing the guards of a capital city. "It looks to me like we've made the right call in coming here."

A smile crossed all of their faces; their joy was infectious, and I joined in.

"Now that all the boring details are taken care of," I said, "should we talk about the actually important stuff?"

Theo frowned, cocking his head to the side. "What do you mean?"

"What else could I mean?" My smile transformed into a conspiratorial grin. "I'm talking about fishing."

"You're always talking about fishing!" a feminine voice called from the darkness.

Everyone's heads turned, and when Maria strode around the headland, her skipping steps came to an abrupt end. "Oh. Er . . . hi?"

"Everyone, this is Maria."

"Fischer's 'friend,'" Barry added.

"'Friend'?" she asked, raising an eyebrow at me.

"Maria, remember how I told you about Theo?"

She slowly nodded. "I do."

"And remember how I told you he was part of a fishing club in the capital city?"

Her eyes went wide and her face lit up.

"No. Way! Which one is Theo?"

He raised his hand. "It's a pleasure to meet you, Maria. I—"

"What kind of fish did you catch in the capital?" she interrupted, unable to contain her curiosity as she dashed to join the circle. "What kind of equipment do you use? What bait? Are there eels so far up? Wait, what kind of water do you fish in?" She vibrated with excitement. "I have too many questions! Where do I even begin?"

"Ah," Ellis said with well-worn smile lines crinkling his eyes. "A woman of culture. It is always a joy to meet another fishing enthusiast."

"Why don't we catch up and compare notes over some dinner?" I suggested.

Before anyone could answer, I turned and strode into the darkness. When I returned to the light of the fire, I was met with a wall of confused faces. The first to recognize what I held was Corporal Claws, and she let out a shrill chirp as she launched herself at me. She landed on the cage and put her eye right up to one of the gaps, peering wide-eyed at the oysters within.

"I have a job for you, Claws. Are you up to it?"

She chirped again and snapped a crisp salute.

"I knew I could rely on you. You know where the oyster cages are, right? I think we'll need at least one more for the—"

She leaped from the cage. The moment she hit the sand, lightning engulfed her body and she zapped out of sight, flying directly toward the ocean.

"By Zeus's regal beard . . ." Danny said, his face blanching.

"You . . ." Theo swallowed. "I knew you weren't lying when you said Corporal Claws wielded lightning, but this . . ."

Maria, Barry, and I exchanged amused glances as the men went silent, the only sound that of Ellis's pencil scratching away on his notepad.

"I guess this might kind of encroach on culty churchy duties," I said to Barry. "I assume it's all good if I give them oysters?"

Barry nodded immediately. "Of course, though we should probably warn them . . ."

"Warn us?" Theo asked. "About what?"

"Oh, nothing major." I shrugged, fighting to keep my face straight. "It's just that the food I make kinda causes people to become cultivators?" I pointed at Cinnamon, who was curled up in Maria's lap and enjoying a good scritching. "Creatures too, obviously."

Another silence stretched, and one by one, the fishermen turned to stare at Theo, whose eyes never left me.

"He's . . . telling the truth."

Ellis's arms trembled, and the tip of his pencil snapped against the pages of his pocketbook.

"The texts said nothing of this . . ." he mumbled, his eyes going distant. "The implications of such an ability . . ."

I shrugged. "Yeah, I try not to think too much about it, but if you guys were planning to start a cult or a church for me, I'm guessing you'll want to join Barry's.

He has a bad habit of helping people become cultivators. I assume you were going to turn them with your magical juice, mate?"

"Wait, what?" Maria looked around the circle, then burst into laughter. "You came here to start a church? Oh, man—I wish I was here to see your faces when you realized Barry beat you to the punch."

With a rueful smile, Barry nodded. "Assuming they wanted to join, I would have offered for them to ascend, yes."

Ellis, still looking into the far distance, closed his pocketbook with a sigh. "We may need to think about this more . . ."

"Not me!" Peter almost yelled. "I get to try new food *and* wield lightning? Sign me up!"

"Aye," Danny agreed. "We've come this far, so we may as well go all the way."

Theo gave me a strained smile. "I might consider it a while."

"Me too," Keith agreed, his complexion pallid and troubled.

I nodded. "There's no pressure—it's totally up to you guys. You can have as little or as much as you like."

"Are . . . are you going to season them?" Maria asked.

"I am. I've already planned a few different flavor combinations to—"

"I'll get the spices!" she interrupted, sprinting for the house.

Theo's head darted to the side at her explosive exit, and he slowly turned to face me, the question clear on his face.

"Yep," I answered. "She's a cultivator. Maria isn't a member of the church, but as you can tell, she's pretty keen on my cooking."

Ellis stared after her departure. "Astounding . . ."

"If you think that's good, mate," Barry said. "Wait until you try Fischer's food."

I left the fire to shuck the cage of oysters, and with each one I opened, my hopes were dampened a little further. Considering the Xianxia shenanigans I had grown used to, I half expected each mollusk to contain a pearl.

That wasn't the case.

Am I really annoyed that each oyster—of which I have hundreds—doesn't contain a stone worth more than a farmer might make in a decade?

I shook my head at myself and strode over to the fire with twenty freshly shucked mollusks.

"Where I'm from, it's pretty normal to eat them raw, but it's definitely not for everyone—just ask Barry."

"Not for everyone," he agreed, grimacing.

I laughed. "It might be a bit of an acquired taste, and they'll definitely taste better to the vast majority of people when cooked and seasoned."

"Do you have any formal training?" Peter asked, peering down at the raw oysters.

"Not at all, but I've unlocked the cooking skill and leveled it a fair bit."

"All right, that's enough." Theo crossed his arms and frowned at me, but I saw the hint of a smile on his face. "You're hitting us with too many knowledge bombs for one evening."

"Not at all," Elis countered, sharpening his pencil. "Please continue. You say you have skills?"

"Yeah, the System or whatever seems to have started working again over the last few days. I'm pretty sure I was constantly gaining skills, but it only started listing them recently. Before that, it just said some bullshit about 'insufficient power.'"

Ellis finished sharpening and blew on the tip of his pencil. "That is . . . troubling," he said, scratching away at his pad. "If it is happening everywhere, that could mean we have to—"

"Hey!" I interrupted. "No scheming, planning, or plotting in my presence!"

"Oh. My apologies."

"It's all good. So, who wants to try the oysters?"

Snips and Pistachio scuttled forward first, each of them noisily eating one. Rocky had returned, and he remained on the sand, claws crossed and attempting to look unimpressed, but his eyes were glued to the mollusk Snips ate beside him.

"Help yourself, Rocky."

He turned his head away, but Snips nudged him forward, and with her suggestion, he scuttled forward and snatched one. As he ate it, his facade of indifference shifted to genuine bliss, and Maria and I shared a smirk at the cantankerous crab.

I grabbed an oyster, as did Maria and Peter.

"I think I'll wait for the cooked ones," Danny said, scrunching his face at what was clearly an unappetizing sight.

I ate mine first. As fresh as they were, there was no hint of the ammonia flavor that could sometimes accompany raw oysters. I watched Maria closely—her face bunched up, then she chewed and quickly swallowed.

"Yeah, I don't know how I feel about that . . ."

"Interesting . . ." Peter said, biting down on the oyster in his mouth. He tossed his head from side to side. "Not a great texture, but the flavor has a lot of potential."

My eyes lit up. "You like it?"

He nodded. "I can see why it's off-putting to some, but I didn't hate it."

"Mate, anything short of downright despising it on your first try is a good sign. You and I are going to get along."

"Is it all right if I have another?"

"Help yourself!"

Everyone but Maria grabbed more, and as I was just lifting one to my mouth, a chirping from behind me drew my attention.

My favorite otter had returned, beaming a needle-sharp grin and dragging a cage across the sand.

CHAPTER TWENTY-FIVE

FORMER STRANGERS

With a delicious taste lingering in my mouth and the campfire warming my skin, I beamed a smile at Corporal Claws.

"What took so long, you little scamp? We've already started . . ." I trailed off and pursed my lips, glaring at the cage she dragged behind her. "Claws . . ."

She cocked her head, giving me a full-toothed grin.

"Did you stop for a little snack of oysters on your way here?"

She glanced back at the notably bare patch of cage.

Yes, she chirped, her grin never disappearing.

"You scoundrel! We have guests!"

She bowed her head in shame but slipped one paw into the cage and removed another oyster. With her head still bowed, she snicked it open with a claw, slurped it into her mouth, then threw it over one shoulder, discarding the evidence.

I shook my head. "You can apologize to our new friends here by helping me shuck the rest. Come on."

When the cage I'd retrieved earlier was almost empty, we found our first treasure. Claws chirped to get my attention, and as I glanced over, I caught the shine of a pearl slipping into her pocket.

"Good girl," I whispered, reaching over.

She preened at my praise, leaning into the scratch I gave her.

"Let's open the rest. We might find more."

Her eyes gleamed, and we raced to shuck the remaining mollusks. It didn't take me long to conclude that she was much faster than I was. Despite how deft I had become with my small knife, I was no match for the sharp claws of an oyster-munching machine.

"A shame we didn't find any more pearls . . ." I said to her as I plated up the last of the oysters.

As if waiting for the complaint, mischief sparkled in her eyes. She put a paw in her pocket, and when she withdrew it, three little orbs reflected in the moonlight.

"Three? From those two cages?"

She radiated delight as she nodded.

"Oh, you are the *best* girl."

I rubbed her all over and she leaned every which way, following my scratches as they moved. We turned to make our way back to the fire just in time for Maria to yell.

"You're a *what?*"

"A royal," Keith answered, straightening his back.

"A royal!" she repeated. "Ares's shield, did you know Keith is a royal, Fischer?"

I smiled at her wide-eyed amazement. "They all have rather impressive backgrounds."

"You flatter us," Ellis said, not looking up from his pocketbook.

"We *had* rather impressive backgrounds," Theo corrected, smirking at Keith's posture. "We left that behind to become common fishermen."

I snorted. "And to raise some poor bloke to godhood."

"That too."

I set the oysters down next to my arrayed spices, shaking my head at how easily he agreed to such a ridiculous statement. "All right. I have a few different ideas for ways to prepare them, but I'm lacking some necessary ingredients—I'll just make one kind tonight and hope it works out. If the first batch sucks, I'll have to try another combination." I turned to Peter. "To address the elephant in the room, you're probably a much better chef than I am, mate, but I'd still love to make a meal for you."

"I can help, even if you just want me to chop ingredients."

"Nonsense, mate—this is a welcoming feast for my soon-to-be-pals of the fishing club. Let me handle the food. I'm open to any critique you have afterward, though!"

Before he could offer resistance, I started preparing the meal.

"That smells divine, Fischer," Theo said, sniffing the aroma in the air as I added a clumpy powder and dried herbs to the pot some time later.

"Will you tell us what it is already?" Maria demanded, her patience well and truly at its limits.

I chuckled softly. "I suppose I can, now that it's ready." I nodded at the pot as I spooned some of the sauce atop the arrayed oysters. "I'm attempting a bastardization of what my world calls a roux. Do you know what that is, Peter?"

He raised an eyebrow, confusion clear on his face. "It's one of the first things you learn to make when training in the royal kitchens, but it's, uh, supposed to be a secret—a closely guarded one at that. You combine fat and flour in equal parts as a thickening base, right?"

"Right. What I've made here is like that, but I've used much less flour than beef tallow." I put the tray of oysters on the fire, then covered them with another tray, sealing the heat in. "The sauce should be thick and packed with flavor, especially after what I just added. Do you know what béchamel sauce is? Mornay?"

"No."

I grinned. "Well, I'll have to get some milk and cheese before I make oysters again, because I'm about to blow this world's cuisine wide open."

Ellis's eyes got a dangerous gleam and his fingers literally twitched around his pencil, but he managed to rein in his questions for another time.

I lifted the cover and peered down at the oysters; small bubbles were forming at the sides. Peter leaned forward, smelling the rising vapors. He closed his eyes and let out a content sigh. "What spices did you add? The aroma is delightful."

"Chives and nutritional yeast."

He cocked his head. "I know what chives are, but what is nutritional yeast?"

"That's what I was cooking in that pan earlier. Heating yeast over a fire deactivates it and gives it a richer flavor. That's all this was. Beef tallow, flour, nutritional yeast, chives, and a sprinkle of salt."

With that, I lifted the cover from the oysters again. Bubbles roiled in each shell, and when I poked an oyster's flesh with my tongs, it was firm. I fanned them with the tray, and before long, they were cool.

"All right! They're ready, gang!"

Maria, Peter, Danny, Barry, and I each grabbed one, as did my animal pals—including Rocky, whose feigned indifference hadn't returned since tasting his first oyster.

I lifted one and poured the contents into my mouth. The flavors exploded across my taste buds, and I made an involuntary noise. The tallow's beefy taste was cut by the cheesy, nutty flavor of the nutritional yeast. The chives danced along across every other ingredient, uplifting and enhancing them. I bit down into the oyster, and the flavor profile immediately shifted.

As if the ocean's essence was trapped within its flesh, juices rushed from the mollusk and joined the sauce it was cooked in. I could hear the ocean in my ears, gulls flying high above, and in my mind's eye, I saw crashing waves beneath a midday sun. I chewed it slowly and lost all sense of self as the tastes consumed me.

"Hestia's welcoming hearth," someone said dreamily. "What on Kallis was *that?*"

I opened my eyes, and the vision of a sunny day melted away. The night was dark, lit only by the campfire's flickering flames.

It was Peter who had spoken, and he looked up at the moon, tears welling in his eyes. "I . . . I don't . . ." He blinked rapidly, causing a tear to roll down his cheek.

Danny reached over and put a hand on his shoulder, a look of awe plastered on his face. He turned to Theo and Keith, who were looking confused, then Ellis, who was scribbling away in his notepad while watching everyone.

"You need to try one." Danny swallowed. "That . . . that was . . . wow."

"I'm repeating myself here," Maria said, "but that was the tastiest thing I've ever eaten."

Barry and my animal pals nodded vigorously—including Rocky, I happily noted.

I may have dismissed it for polite praise, but I'd eaten one too. I wholeheartedly agreed with the sentiment.

"I'm glad it worked out," I replied, rubbing the back of my head as the memory of a sunlit ocean faded. "I wasn't sure if the tallow would be too fatty or the flour would make it too—"

"Perfection." Peter took a deep breath before looking down from the moon and staring at me. "That was perfection."

I grinned. "That's high praise coming from you, mate. Help yourself to another—there is plenty to go around."

Theo swallowed with flared nostrils, and I raised an eyebrow at him. "Wanna try one, mate?"

"I probably shouldn't. I don't mean to insult your cooking, Fischer, but Ellis told us that the royal library had reports of people getting sick from eating fish. One of us should abstain, just in case."

Sensing his weakness as he stared at the oysters, I went for the jugular. "I mean, even if you were to *somehow* get sick, ascending seems to cure you of all illnesses and ailments."

Ellis leaned forward, and despite me dropping a knowledge bomb on him, the pencil in his hand was still. His eyes lasered in on me. "You are sure? It cures all sickness?"

"Positive, mate. Maria's mum here was dying, but Barry saved her life by giving her juice from sugarcane I fertilized with fish."

Ellis turned to Theo, raising an eyebrow.

"He's telling the truth," Theo said, answering the unspoken question.

Ellis swallowed. "W-well, I suppose it would not hurt to *try* one . . ."

I grinned like a fox in a chicken coop. "Exactly! Give one a try. It'd be a shame for them to go to waste."

I caught Maria smirking at my salesmanship, and I shot her a wink. Everyone reached for an oyster this time, and before I ate my own, I watched Theo, Keith, and Ellis for their reactions. All three men melted before the onslaught of flavors, their bodies relaxing and breath slowing. The hint of a tear formed in Ellis's eye.

I averted my gaze and slipped an oyster into my mouth. I was greeted by the same sensations as last time. They weren't at all diminished by having experienced it once before, and I marveled at how vivid the ocean vista was in my mind's eye. The makeshift roux had cooled and thickened slightly, but it wasn't an unwelcome change—just different.

"Why doesn't your food taste this good, Peter?" Keith asked.

"I'd like to say it's because you've only eaten my campfire cooking," he replied, then gestured at the fire before him. "But these were also cooked on a campfire, and they are the tastiest thing I've ever had."

"Is all his food this good?" Theo asked, glancing between Barry and Maria.

The former nodded, the latter grimaced.

"Unfortunately," she said, winking at me. "It's enough to give someone an inferiority complex."

"Tell me about it . . ." Peter mumbled, staring down at the sand.

Danny boomed a laugh and slapped him on the back. "We'll get you on the path of ascension and acquire you some cooking skills before you know it."

"He's right, mate," I said. "You'll likely put my food to shame in no time at all, especially considering your background. I only learned to cook from watching videos."

" . . . videos?" Theo asked. "What are videos—"

"Don't!" Barry and Maria both yelled, getting in the way of the obfuscating response already forming in my mind.

A laugh bubbled up from within me, and as it subsided, I let out a content sigh. "Don't worry about it—I'm sure Barry can explain when he gives you the tour later."

“The tour?” Ellis asked, but I just shook my head.

“You’ll have to wait and see—until then, we have a bunch more oysters . . .”

“Thanks again, Fischer,” Barry said, nursing his overfull stomach. “Sorry we ate so much.”

“Nonsense, mate.” Fischer gave him a wide grin. “Food is there to be eaten, and Claws was all too happy to fetch another batch.”

They’d swiftly eaten through the first two cages, and at seeing their readiness to continue eating, Fischer had sent the otter off to fetch more without hesitation.

“Well, we’d better get going,” Barry said. “I’ve yet to show them around.”

“Of course!” Fischer cast his gaze over the newly arrived fishermen. “It was really nice meeting you guys.”

“It was,” Maria agreed, putting her arm around Fischer’s waist and hugging him right. “We’ll have to go fishing soon! I’m curious what techniques you guys use!”

The five former strangers all said their goodbyes, and Barry led them away from the fire. Theo lingered a moment longer than the rest, watching Fischer and Maria walk toward the coast with their hands entwined.

“Something wrong?” Barry asked.

Theo gave him a smile. “Nothing, Barry—I’m just glad to see Fischer happy. So much of what we came here to do had moral questionability surrounding it, but seeing the man we plan to raise to godhood living a normal life . . . it washed most of my hesitation away.”

“You still feel hesitation, though?”

Theo nodded. “Who wouldn’t? We don’t truly know what ascension entails and how it could impact him.”

Barry shrugged. “I haven’t known Fischer for long, but I’ve stopped doubting him.”

“I hope you’re right.”

“To steal his words, Theo—you’re a good bloke. Just the fact that you consider such things lifts you in my eyes.”

A silence stretched across the sand as Barry led them toward his house beneath the moonlit sky. When they reached his home, he led them around back and strode toward the shed.

“You wish for us to sleep in a shed?” Keith asked.

Without another word, Barry flung the door open. When the five men saw the contents of the shed and the inside of the now-disguised door, their dispositions shifted. Every eye went wide, and Ellis took an involuntary step forward, craning his neck.

“You recognize what this is?” Barry asked.

All nodded, and Ellis slipped forward. He put his hand against the inside of the door and put his eye so close to the gilding that it was almost touching. “An ancient building. Unbelievable . . . outstanding . . .”

“I take it there are buildings like this in the capital?”

“There are.” Ellis ran his hands along the golden edging, his aged fingers moving with grace. "They are strictly off-limits to the general public, but part of the inner library is made of such material. To think there was one like it out here . . . how long has it been here?"

"Since last night."

Ellis's hands froze. He whirled faster than a man of his age had any right moving, and his eyes drilled into Barry.

"Theo. He tells the truth?"

"He . . . he does."

"If you think that's impressive . . ." Barry waggled his eyebrows and pointed down at the descending stairwell they hadn't yet noticed. "Wait until you see the rest of it."

CHAPTER TWENTY-SIX

TEST OF ALLEGIANCE

As Barry led the men further down the underground tunnel, Ellis sharpened his pencil violently. Keith, who had the unfortunate position of being behind the overeager archivist, batted ineffectually at the barrage of shavings flying his way.

"Good gods, Ellis—can you aim that elsewhere?"

"No time," he replied, eyes focused on his pencil. He removed it, pocketed the sharpener, and immediately started writing again.

Barry smiled at his eagerness. They'd just come from the underground forest, and Ellis had spent a full fifteen minutes documenting every feature of the giant trcc within it before his friends finally convinced him to keep moving.

Barry took a deep breath, knowing this next room was going to be a final test of sorts.

If they don't agree with my methods . . . he thought, but then he shook his head, dismissing it. *I can deal with that possibility when and if it comes to pass.*

Barry's steps slowed, and he came to a stop, spinning toward them. "I have something to admit."

"What's that?" Ellis asked, not looking up from his frenzied writing.

"You aren't the first group to come from the capital. Another royal came, Keith." Barry turned and continued walking, making his way toward the door. "He was accompanied by two cultivators."

"Don't tell me . . ." Keith uttered.

Barry reached out, swung the door open, and stepped back. Keith rushed forward, peering out into the room.

"Finally!" came a nasally voice from within. "Where's my desert? I was promised more *sweet water juice!*"

Keith immediately recognized the voice.

"It's called sugarcane juice, Trent," Barry replied with a slight shake of his head.

Though Keith knew who he'd find, when he spied the speaker, his mouth still went dry.

Trent—his eldest cousin and childhood tormentor—sat in a rich wooden chair. He fanned his face with a book, putting on an air of poise and dignity that looked ridiculous on him.

Keith fought to keep his face still. "I didn't think to find you here, cousin."

At the words, Trent shot to his feet faster than Keith had ever seen him move. Even as a child, Trent had always been prodigiously pudgy, but he'd lost weight since last he'd seen him.

"Keith! Thank Poseidon's slick shaft you're here! Did Father and Uncle come?" Trent rose from the chair and lurched forward, grabbing the metal bars. He leaned closer, whispering. "They're creating cultivators here, cousin. I hope you've brought a large retinue of the collared with you."

"He knows what we're doing, Trent," Barry said, stepping into view.

The prince let out an *eep* and jumped back from the bars. "Run, cousin! Make haste!" Trent took a deep breath, puffed out his chest, then bellowed. "Faaaather! I'm underground! I require assistaaaance!"

Theo peeked his head around the corner. "He's not too bright, is he, Keith?"

"Not particularly, no."

"I have always found it fascinating," Ellis mused, craning his neck to see past Theo. "That those of the same lineage can grow to have such contrasting dispositions."

Trent stared at Keith, his face contorting in thought like a dog trying to work out whose tail it was chasing. "Ah, I see." He snapped his fingers and let out a facetious chuckle. "You're a cultivator with the ability to shapeshift. Very clever, but not clever enough to fool the crown prince." He narrowed his eyes on Barry. "Shame on you, coming down here and trying to use a man's relatives against him." He pointed at Ellis. "And who are you pretending to be? Some evil wizard of old? Jokes on you, pretender—I didn't study the histories!"

Ellis watched him patiently. "I am well aware you did not study the histories, Prince. I do not think you studied anything. If you had spent a second in your family's archives, maybe you would know who I am."

Keith rubbed his temples. "Trent—when you were ten years old, you got your head stuck in a vase when trying to lick the last vestiges of syrup from its wall. You wouldn't let us get help and we had to break it for you to escape. You cried. A lot."

The prince's head darted up to stare at his cousin with wide eyes. "Poseidon's sweaty sack—it's really you!" He narrowed his eyes. "Hang on a damned second—you swore an oath to never tell that to anyone!"

"Under duress of my head being squashed by your well-fed rump, if I recall."

Trent's gaze shot toward Barry, to the rest of the men peering into the room, then back to Keith. "Betrayer . . ." he whispered.

"That's right," Keith agreed. "I've betrayed the capital and the royal family."

"How far does this plot go? Is this your father's doing, finally coming for the crown? Oh, when my father the king catches wind of this, you'll be sorely—"

Keith closed the door, cutting off Trent's impassioned speech.

Tension he wasn't aware of left Barry's body.

"I'm assuming this was one last test of our allegiance?" Keith asked.

Barry made a so-so gesture. "I wouldn't call it a test, but I did need to see how you would react to his imprisonment. It doesn't bother you?"

"By itself, no, but I do have a question for you." Keith's face turned serious. "Do you plan to torture him?"

"Reasonable question. I'll answer bluntly—no. We've been extracting information from him in exchange for sweet treats, and we plan on eventually bringing him over to our side." Barry's eyebrows twitched of their own accord as the problem with Trent sprang to mind. "He has been a real pain, if I'm being honest, but that's not really important right now."

A silence stretched through the corridor, only marginally interrupted by the muffled, indignant yelling of Trent from the other side of the door.

"For what it's worth," Theo said, "both of you are telling the truth."

Barry smiled, but Theo continued.

"However . . . there's a little more to what you were saying, Barry. You said he's been a pain and that it wasn't important right now. It is though, isn't it?"

Barry sighed. "It is, but I didn't leave it out for nefarious reasons."

He raised an eyebrow at Theo.

"True," the former auditor confirmed.

Barry nodded. "We've been giving him endless cups of sugarcane juice, multiple a day, yet he hasn't awakened. And we have absolutely no idea *why.* It has worked for everyone else, just not him."

"Fascinating . . ." Ellis said.

"I'd say infuriating," Barry replied with a wry smile. "But we will have plenty of time to explore that in the coming days. Let's continue the tour."

When Ellis read the plaque set beside the next door, he let out a hiss of air. He lunged forward, grabbed the handle, and threw the door wide. His body stood rigid as his eyes scanned the room beyond.

Barry gave him an understanding smile. "I had the same reaction when I saw that the library came without books."

Ellis's shoulders slumped, and his head hung.

"A true shame. I had hoped . . ."

"Me too, mate."

Barry stepped inside and gestured for the others to follow him. The room's walls were covered by lacquered shelves of dark wood; they stretched from the floor all the way to the high ceiling. On each wall, there were large ladders to allow the placement and retrieval of books.

"As with the other rooms, the air in this one appears to be magically altered," Barry said. "It's dry. *Really* dry. I spent an hour here today reading and my throat started feeling scratchy."

"Remarkable. It is perfectly acclimatized for the preservation of vellum, yet it did not come with any books." He let out a bone-deep sigh, his body looking its age as he stood with great effort. "At least I will have a place to store the books I brought with me." He turned to Barry, his eyes half-lidded. "Is there much more to see, Barry? I find myself ready for rest."

"There are more rooms, yes, but they're mostly...well, you'll see. We can make it quick."

Giving Ellis an arm to lean on, he led the men from the room.

The next stretch of hallway consisted of five doors, and as Barry reached the first, he opened it. Beyond the door was . . . nothing.

Theo strode forward and touched the smooth stone. "They lead to a solid wall? Why?"

"Couldn't tell you," Barry answered. "My best guess is that we can add more rooms, given time."

He expected Ellis to comment that it was remarkable, astounding, or some other synonym for his amazement, but the aged man merely watched, leaning on Barry for support.

"All right," Barry said. "Other than the mysterious doors to nothing, the rest are sleeping quarters and bathrooms. Let's go straight there."

After Barry's departure, Theo looked around the room with unbelieving eyes. Ten luxurious beds lined the room, all of which were as opulent as the next. He ran his hands over the silk-smooth cover he sat on, unsure if he was dreaming.

"This is real, right?" Danny asked, doing the same thing with his hands on the next bed over.

Peter launched himself and crashed down on a pile of plush pillows across the room. "Feels real to me! Gods, I've never had such an amazing shower. If it wasn't so late, I may have slept under the running water."

Theo couldn't disagree; after weeks of travel, the shower had been an unexpected yet welcomed relief. He glanced over at Ellis. The former archivist was already asleep, snoring peacefully in the farthest bed.

Pete followed his gaze and grimaced. "I'm sure he's all right . . ."

"He got worse while we were traveling. He did well to hide his sickness from us for so long, but it's hard to ignore when someone coughs up blood . . ."

"Well," Danny said, leaning back on his bed. "With any luck, he'll ascend."

Theo nodded. "I'll ask Barry about some of that sugarcane juice tomorrow. There's no rush for us, but after seeing how weak Ellis got today, I'm more than a little worried."

Peter and Danny grunted their agreement, and realizing he hadn't heard from Keith in a while, Theo glanced his way. The royal was fast asleep.

Peter covered his mouth as a yawn escaped him. "I suppose we should get some sleep too."

"Aye," Danny agreed, throwing back his covers and climbing in.

As if listening in on their conversation, the flames set in the walls dimmed. Theo slid between the sheets of his bed. His body rejoiced the moment he lay down, and before he knew it, his consciousness faded.

When Theo opened his eyes again, his mouth was dry, and he sat up, searching for something to drink. As his vision cleared, he took in the surrounding room. Everyone was asleep, their bedding crinkled and in various states of disarray.

He stood and walked for the door, intent on heading to a tap for a drink, when something in his peripheral vision caught his attention. In the far corner of the room, a dark form moved. Theo froze, staring at the blob of darkness hiding between Ellis's bed and the wall. He tiptoed to Danny's bed and shook the burly man. His larger friend opened his eyes immediately, and they locked onto Theo, who held a finger to his own lips.

Danny understood; he slipped his blanket aside silently and climbed to his feet. Theo gestured at the murky blob, and as Danny noticed it, his body tensed. The former guard crept forward, ready to deliver violence. As they got closer, a soft whispering sound came from the shape.

Danny stilled, holding a hand up to stop Theo.

Theo looked between the dark mass and his muscular friend, not comprehending what was going through the latter's mind. After a tense moment, Danny shook his head, let out a sigh and walked forward, all of his stealth abandoned.

"What the hells are you doing, Ellis?" He reached down. "You scared the piss out of us."

As Danny lifted the blanket covering their friend, the flickering orange light of a candle danced against the walls.

"Careful!" the archivist hissed. "I have an open flame and paper out!"

As soon as paper was mentioned, Theo realized what the whispering had been—the scratching of graphite on a pocketbook.

He let out a relieved sigh. "What *are* you doing, Ellis? You need your rest."

Ellis spun on the spot with the agility of a gymnast. "I don't, actually."

"Huh?" Danny asked. "What are you talking about?"

Theo knew.

His lifetime of training let him see the twinkle in Ellis's eye, the speed with which he spun, the firm set of his shoulders, and the subtle changes to the muscles of his friend's arms.

"You didn't . . ."

Ellis beamed. "I did."

"You awakened?" Danny hissed. "You're a *cultivator?*"

"An astute observation. I have been testing and documenting for the last few hours." Ellis clenched his fists and released them, staring down at the muscles of his forearms. "It feels rather good."

Just then, something tugged at Theo, and words consumed his vision.

"No way."

He blinked and rubbed his eyes, yet the words remained.

Please select a name.

CHAPTER TWENTY-SEVEN

NAMES

Barry paused before the wooden facade covering the church's entrance. He turned and gazed toward the western mountains, absorbing their beauty. The sun rose at his back, peeking its head over his house and warming his body. A gust of wind kicked up, ruffling his hair and lending him a sense of tranquility. The breeze sputtered out, and as he inhaled through his nose, the scents of coffee and fresh-baked pastries made his mouth water.

The door to the church opened, so he looked over his shoulder. "Morning, Ruby."

"Good morning, Barry. How did you sleep—*ooh!* Are one of those for me?"

Barry held out the coffee and croissant laden tray. "Help yourself."

She slid forward and grabbed one of each. "Thank you."

After sipping the coffee, she let out a full-bodied sigh. "What did we ever do without this stuff?"

"Honestly, I have no idea. Is Steven still inside?"

She rolled her eyes with a playful smile. "He is. I swear, that man could sleep the day away."

"I'll drop him off some breakfast. Did you meet the new arrivals yet?"

She lowered the cup from her lips. "I didn't meet them yet, but they're up and sounding quite lively this morning."

"Really? I thought they'd sleep in given they spent weeks traveling . . ."

Ruby shrugged. "The door to their room was closed, so I didn't burst in to introduce myself, but they certainly *sounded* awake."

She took a bite of a croissant, and her shoulders slumped as she let out a quiet *mmm.* Barry watched her with a growing smile, excited for his own pastry after delivering breakfast to the rest of the congregation.

Ruby washed the croissant down with a sip of coffee. "Well, I'd better open the shop while that husband of mine sleeps the day away." She grinned. "See you, Barry!"

He bid Ruby farewell, and as she closed the door behind him, Barry gazed at the surrounding room. As with the gust outside, the flickering light of the walls' naked flames brought him a sense of calm. He oozed gratitude as he made his way down the stairs.

Distracted by the scents wafting up from his tray, Barry reached their room before he knew it. Muffled conversation and grunts came through the thick door, and Barry opened it with a raised eyebrow.

All the beds had been moved to the back of the room, leaving an empty space of smooth stone. Theo and Peter lay on their stomachs close to the door, their right hands clasped and ready to arm wrestle. Danny and Keith stood just past them, the former's feet firmly planted and the latter bouncing on his heels. Ellis was furthest from Barry; he sat on a bed with his legs crossed, his right hand gripping a pencil and ready to take notes.

Barry grinned at the unfolding scene. "Good morn—"

"Go!" Ellis yelled.

Keith launched across the room and drove a fist into Danny's stomach.

The former quartermaster hunched, braced for the impact, then let out a grunt as he flew across the room and slammed into a wall. Theo and Peter's arms bulged, and they clenched their teeth as they fought to force the other's hand down to the stones. All the while, Ellis's eyes darted around the room, his hand a blur as it wrote in his notepad.

Barry almost dropped the tray, but he quickly readjusted, catching the assortment of breakfasts before a drop of coffee could spill.

"Oh! Hello, Barry," Ellis said, still writing.

"Er—I brought food and coffee . . . ?"

Ellis closed his notepad and set it down. "Let's pause for breakfast, gentlemen."

Danny got to his feet at the base of the wall and brushed himself off with a smile. "Nice hit!"

Keith gave him a grin, rubbing his knuckles. "Not as good as your defense—it feels like punching a boulder."

"Another tie," Peter said. He stood, easily helping Theo up.

Barry entered the room, looking over the men before him. Now that he knew what to look for, the signs were obvious. Their bodies were already changing after becoming cultivators. Most distinctive was Ellis, whose previously thin frame was nowhere to be seen.

His shoulders had lost their hunch, and he came to meet Barry with sure steps. "Are these the famous Sue's baked goods and coffee? Theo has talked them up quite fervently."

Barry just nodded.

"Are you all right, mate?" Theo asked with a grin, taking a coffee. "You look like you've just seen a whole gang of cultivators."

The rest of the fishing club burst into laughter as they grabbed a coffee and pastry.

Barry couldn't help but smile at them. "When did it happen? I didn't think it'd occur so soon."

"In the middle of the night," Ellis answered with crema-colored foam covering the lower half of his mustache. Theo pointed at his lip, and the archivist wiped it away. "We've been testing and documenting ever since."

"Unreal . . ." Barry set down the tray and grabbed his own croissant and coffee. He strode to the piled-up beds and sat down. "I planned to help you ascend today . . . I can't believe a single meal of Fischer's oysters worked."

With the rest of the men biting down into their pastries, Theo answered. "Well, we did eat a *lot* of oysters."

"Still . . ." Barry took a sip, his eyes growing unfocused. "I think it means his cooking is getting stronger. We'll have to be careful with that."

Ellis resumed scribbling in his book, never one to miss an opportunity to take notes.

"These are damned delicious together," Keith said around a mouthful. "Forget our ascensions—I can't believe the peasants here can afford to eat and drink these every day."

Peter cringed. "For the love of everything we're doing here, please don't refer to the common folk as peasants."

Keith swallowed and washed his pastry down with a swig of coffee. "Wait, that's a bad term?"

"Quite derogatory," Ellis confirmed.

"Oh . . . sorry, Barry."

"It's fine with me, but some of the townsfolk won't take kindly to it."

"I won't use it anymore." He sighed. "It's hard to shake my upbringing at times."

"Tell me about it," Theo said. "You can be a real prick."

Keith slapped Theo's shoulder with one hand playfully—it sent him flying into the wall. The room shook and the last dregs of Theo's coffee spattered across the floor, the cup having been knocked loose during his unplanned flight.

Keith rushed over. "Are you all right, Theo? I'm so sorry—"

Theo's booming laughter cut the sentence off as he stared out at the room, upside down and slumped against the floor. Keith helped him up and offered up the rest of his coffee.

"It's fine—I only had a mouthful left," Theo said. "We'll have to watch our strength, huh?"

Barry nodded. "There's an adjustment period."

As a realization bubbled up within him, the smile died on his lips. The men must have sensed his mental shift; their faces sobered.

"What is it?" Theo asked.

"I didn't think to warn you because I thought there was no chance you would awaken so swiftly . . ." He winced. "Trent slipped up and gave us some important intel: there's a construct back in the capital that prints out the name you give to the System. I don't suppose you chose names other than your own . . . ?"

The silence that followed could have been cut with a knife.

Charles, head servant to the king of Gormona, rubbed his temples as he traversed the upper levels of the castle. The echo of metal footsteps came from down the hall, and he gazed up, eyeing the rushing guard as he rounded a corner.

"Guard!" Charles calmed his features, hiding his worry. "Report. Have you found any sign of the missing?"

"N-no, sir!" the guard stuttered.

Charles made to dismiss him, but the guard's wild eyes made him pause. "What is it? Do you have something else to report?"

"Y-yes, sir."

Charles's nostrils flared at the insufficient answer, but he quickly schooled his features once more. "Well? Out with it."

The guard, sensing his frustration, snapped a hurried salute.

"Yes, sir! I—I think it's best you see it yourself, sir."

What has him so shaken? Charles wondered.

"Very well—lead on."

Two long hallways later, the guard opened a door and gestured within. Light filtered into the room through a lone window, the sun shining down on a smattering of old furniture.

Charles's eyes narrowed. He strode in, and as he looked closer at the objects, he immediately recognized what this was. It wasn't furniture at all—it was a storage room for inert constructs. As old as the kingdom was, of course such relics existed, but he'd never seen so many in one place.

"What did you bring me here for?" he demanded, turning on the guard. "Why have useless relics of the past shaken you so?"

"Uhhh," another voice came from behind him.

Charles turned on the source; another guard stood up from behind a relic, his face lit by an odd-colored light.

The second guard smiled like a fool. "They aren't all useless."

"Explain."

The guard pointed down. "I think you might need to see it for yourself."

Though Charles suspected he'd find nothing of use, something about the guard's demeanor—and the green-tinted light illuminating him—made curiosity swell within him.

"Why did you two even look in here?" he asked, bending to crawl between gaps in the constructs.

"Well, sir," the second guard answered, "It's been weeks since the men deserted—"

"Disappeared!" Charles corrected, his tone brooking no discourse. "We know not what happened to them."

"Er—right. Sorry, sir. It's been weeks since they, uh, disappeared, and we've found no sign of them, so when we found this room of relics, we decided to check if they were hiding inside."

Charles caught sight of the guard's armored legs as he crawled toward them. He shuffled up beside the man, fighting for space.

"Sorry, sir. Bit of a tight fit."

Charles clenched his jaw. "Whatever you wanted to show me had better be . . ." he trailed off as he stood to his full height, and as he stared at the source of the soft light, his jaw dropped. "Is this . . . ?"

"Looks like it, sir," the guard answered.

* * *

As the silence stretched in the fishing club's quarters, Barry's pulse quickened. He glanced between the freshly awakened men, but at what he saw on their faces, his brow furrowed. Were they . . . smiling?

Theo started laughing first, and the rest of them quickly followed. Ellis's chuckle was deep and rich, a stark contrast to his raspy laughter the day before.

"Worry not, Barry," the archivist said. "We considered that possibility and named ourselves accordingly."

"*You* considered that possibility, you mean," Theo corrected, wiping a tear from his eye.

"We all contributed to the names." Ellis shrugged, giving a wicked grin. "It was quite fun, really."

"What did you name yourselves . . . ?"

They all glanced at each other, amusement clear in their eyes. Ellis bowed at the waist, giving a flourish with his hand. "Lizard Wizard greets you."

"Glare Bear," the burly Danny said, his eyes anything but glaring.

Theo held his hand out. "Pleasure to meet you, Barry. I'm Bog Dog."

Barry's face grew more and more confused as he shook the offered hand, but the onslaught continued.

"Hurtle the Turtle," Keith said. He made his upper lip protrude in the approximation of a turtle's v-shaped mouth.

Peter barked a laugh. Inspired by his friend's antics, he dropped to all fours, looking up at Barry with vacant eyes as he chewed pretend cud. "Boat Goat." He tried to bleat, but it turned into a choked laugh.

Barry dropped his head into his hands as the rest of the fishermen joined in, giggling like children.

"Gods above. You're all definitely Fischer's friends."

CHAPTER TWENTY-EIGHT

FRIENDSHIP CHAIN

"You called yourselves *what?*" I demanded. Laughter bubbled up from within me as I saw the arrayed smiles, and I let it come, delighting in the feeling.

"*Why?*" I asked when I could speak again. "Why animals, and what's up with the rhyming?"

"Loathe as I am to admit it—it's genius," Barry said, shaking his head. "If someone happens across the ancient construct, there's no chance that they'll link it back to them."

"And if we're lucky," Ellis added, "they'll assume it's a handful of awakened creatures. That would put a real burr in the king's breeches."

I laughed again, picturing a procession of guards sent from the capital in search of phantom beasts. "There's no way they're that daft, but it's certainly a fun idea."

Keith opened his mouth to speak, but Ellis's hand darted to cover it.

I raised an eyebrow. "Culty stuff I probably don't want to know?"

Keith winced. "Yeah, sorry."

"Don't mention it, my man! Well, I was going to suggest we all have a fish today, but now that you're all cultivators . . ." I gave them a grin. "How do you feel about helping me construct something that'll let us fish deeper waters?"

The gleam in their eyes was all the answer I needed.

Sweat poured from Charles as he ran through corridors, down spiraling stairs, and past confused servants that dashed out of the way.

He reached the antechamber to the throne room and threw open the door. The servant posted there quirked an eyebrow at the uncouth arrival, but upon seeing Charles, his back straightened. "The king is in a meeting, sir."

Charles strode forward, unerring. "I must see him. Now."

"Sir, I'm sure he won't be—"

At the glare Charles leveled his way, the servant's words died in his throat. "Of course. Right this way, please."

The door groaned as the servant pushed them open with a bowed head. The king had been speaking, but his hushed words cut off the moment he noticed the interruption.

"What is the meaning of this?" he demanded, his voice commanding attention.

The servant opened his mouth to respond, but no sound came out, his lip quivering.

"My king," Charles said, striding forward. "I have vital information that cannot—" As he noticed the man standing before his ruler, Charles's chest constricted. He cleared his throat, gathering his courage. "I have vital information that cannot wait."

Augustus Reginald Gormona, the reigning king of Gormona and lord of these lands, glared at him. If Charles wasn't so exhausted, he would have withered beneath the king's attention. His breaths were labored as he bowed at the waist, fighting the urge to wipe sweat from his brow.

The king sighed. "Very well. My apologies, Tom. We will have to resume this conversation at a later date."

"Of course, my king," Lord Osnan responded, not missing a beat as he gave a sweeping bow. Turning on his heel, he strode toward the exit.

Charles felt Tom Osnan's eyes boring into him in passing; he kept his face downward—to antagonize the lord of the Osnan household was to court ruin.

The influential lord's footsteps receded, and the door groaned again as the servant closed it behind them, leaving Charles and his king alone in the throne room.

"Approach, Charles."

He raised his head and obeyed. Light shone down from stained glass windows, illuminating his king's white mane of hair from behind. The ruler's face was unreadable; he stroked his colorless beard as he watched Charles's approach. The closer he got, the more the air seemed to grow thick—his legs shook, so he slowed his stride.

When Charles arrived before the throne, Augustus Reginald Gormona peered down at him like a wolf would consider a sheep. "Are you well, Charles?"

"Apologies, my king." He bowed at the waist again. "I ran here from the upper floors."

"Dispense with the formalities. What has burdened you so?"

He snapped upright. "As you will. In searching for the vanished men, two guards discovered a room filled with artifacts."

The king made a gesture to get on with it. "Yes, I know the room. What of it?"

"One of the relics was active, and the screen show—"

The king shot to his feet. "*Active?*"

An almost physical pressure pushed down on Charles, and he cleared his throat. "The guards are bringing it here—"

The king's eyes went wide, and the pressure seemed to double. "Stop them!" The air almost vibrated with the ruler's voice. "Tell them to return it *exactly* where it was!"

"Y-yes, my king!"

Charles sprinted for the door that was already opening, the servant having heard the booming order. A shiver coursed through his limbs as fear replaced his weariness.

As Augustus Reginald Gormona gazed down at the screen, his eyebrow twitched. A path had been cleared to the relic, and inert artifacts lay scattered against the far wall.

"This was its exact position when you found it?"

He looked up; Charles and one of the guards winced.

The other shrugged. "Pretty sure, yeah."

Red-hot needles pin-pricked Augustus Reginald Gormona's skin as rage coursed through his veins. "I don't need *pretty sure,* fool! Was this where the artifact was?"

Charles and the other guard withered.

The flippant guard snapped a salute. "Yes, king."

He stared at them for a long moment before returning his attention to the construct. Above the screen, in an ancient script only one other in his kingdom could read, were two simple words: *newly awoken.*

More importantly, five names were listed on the screen.

Lizard Wizard
Bog Dog
Glare Bear
Hurtle the Turtle
Boat Goat

"Tell me, Charles," he said, his voice soft. "What do you make of this?"

"I dare not presume—"

"Presume!" he ordered, not looking away from the printed text.

Charles audibly swallowed. "Judging by the names, I believe that multiple spirit beasts may have awakened."

Though he suspected the same, hearing the words spoken aloud hammered the reality into Augustus's brain. He tottered over, catching himself on one of the lifeless constructs behind him.

"My king!" Charles dashed forward, but Augustus held up his other hand, halting him.

"Fetch runners and send for every handler in the city." His vision blurred and eyes went distant as he thought out loud. "If they are able to gather power, to gain strength . . . we may all be doomed . . ."

"Yes, my king!" Charles replied.

Three sets of hurried footsteps dragged him back to the present.

"Wait!" the king called, commanding obeisance.

They all stopped and turned.

"On pain of death," Augustus continued, "none of you are to speak a word of this."

"Yes, my king!" all three replied.

"Very good. You two." He pointed at the guards. "This room is now your post. No one is to enter without my permission and nothing is to be touched. *Nothing,* you understand?"

One nodded silently, while the other snapped a salute and grinned.

The king walked from the room as Charles took off, sprinting away to enact his orders. He clenched his jaw and flared his nostrils, not caring to keep his fury under control.

There were spirit beasts in his lands.

It was time to go on the offensive.

Just by the numbers alone, I had assumed the construction would be much more productive with the help of my new friends. As I watched Keith and Theo launch Peter like a torpedo, I was forced to admit just how wrong I was.

The chef, his eyes wide and mouth spread in a manic grin, rocketed right into Danny. The former quartermaster tried to catch the chef-turned-projectile, but was blown off his feet, and both men slammed into the shore's rocky cliff. Ellis was unable to take notes, underwater as he was, but he watched on with keen eyes, no doubt storing the information away for later.

Corporal Claws, never one to let a chance for mischief pass her by, swam up to Theo and Peter. She pointed at herself, then at Rocky, who was hauling a small boulder by himself. Theo and Peter connected their hands, and Claws sat her furry little tooshie in the makeshift sling. A moment later, she was gliding through the water at previously unseen speeds. She spun like a torpedo, her body becoming a blur. She angled herself upward, and instead of striking the unsuspecting crab, she shot right into the boulder he carried.

A loud *crack* split the water, and the humongous rock disintegrated in a shower of pebbles. Claws shot through it, dragging a plume of spiraling dust in her wake. She came back in a large circle and slammed down next to Rocky, then gazed up to inspect her work.

Rocky froze, his clackers twitching in the open water. Claws ignored him, staring up at the dispersing cloud of sediment and rubbing her chin. With glacial speed, her gaze shifted to give Rocky a side-eyed glance.

When the corner of her lip twitched up, Rocky could contain his anger no longer. Twin explosions rang out, aimed behind him. The propulsion shot him at her like a bullet with too many limbs, all of which were poised to latch onto her. She chittered a laugh and kicked off the sands, easily gliding away from the apoplectic crab.

I shook my head, as I watched Claws's tactical retreat and Rocky's unceasing pursuit. All five of the fishing club members tracked the fight—or was it a flight?—with growing amusement. I watched their faces for a long moment, only stopping when they went up for air.

As Claws and Rocky's chase extended out of sight, I was left alone on the ocean floor. I crossed my legs and sat down, letting the muscles of my body relax. The water undulated softly, pushing my body this way and that. A deep well of thankfulness opened up within me, and I sat with it for a moment, appreciating it in its entirety. I let out a breath; the bubbles tickled my face in their passing. With a content grin, I got back to my feet and searched for another boulder.

The midday sun warmed my shoulders as I took my pot off the boil. Steam rose from its roiling surface, bringing with it the sweet yet savory scent of the cooked sand crabs within.

When the sun had just started to approach its zenith in the sky, I'd snuck off to prepare a surprise lunch. Busy as everyone was with taking turns launching each other at walls, piles of sand, rocks—or anything else unlucky enough to be within view of the chaotically aligned fishermen—they hadn't noticed my departure. Sergeant Snips and Pistachio did, but they'd simply nodded at me when I held a finger to my lips, telling them to keep it quiet.

I heard—and felt—another *thump,* no doubt caused by someone getting flung into the cliff like a boulder from a trebuchet. I laughed, picturing the scene in my mind. One by one, I removed the cooked crabs and placed them into another pot of fresh salt water to cool, then set off to fetch my pals.

I searched close to the shore, but the only life I came across were the schools of fish flitting around the base of the wall. I set off further south, and the moment I found them, my eyes went wide.

You've gotta be kidding me . . .

Everyone—five cultivators and two awakened creatures—had formed a line. They were throwing boulders from one end to another, making a living chain. They'd long since found their rhythm, and the giant rocks bounced along the line hypnotically. At the beginning, Snips launched them a ridiculous distance to Pistachio. The Leviathan-sized lobster easily caught and lobbed it along. Each boulder went to Theo, Peter, Danny, Keith, and finally Ellis, who placed it down atop a growing pile.

There had to be almost a hundred giant stones there already.

Where did they get so many in such a small amount of time? I wondered.

I glanced at the start of the line with a furrowed brow, and then I saw it. I'd been too transfixed by the fluid teamwork to notice the cliff had changed. Though it still denoted the barrier between land and sea, meters of rock had been demolished and lay in a pile right next to Snips, who was easily picking up boulders and throwing them to Pistachio.

She noticed me, froze, then blew a stream of hesitant bubbles. Realizing she wasn't sure if I was going to be mad, I darted toward her and scooped her up in a hug. A stream of relieved bubbles tickled my face as she leaned into my embrace. I kicked off the sand, and as we breached the surface, I smiled down at her.

"We probably would have had to demolish some stone eventually, Snips. I'm not upset. You guys have done an *amazing* amount of work."

Someone cleared their throat behind me, and I turned to see all five men looking rather sheepish.

Theo rubbed the back of his head. "That, uh, may have been my fault. Well, my head's fault."

"Your head?" I asked with a wry smile. "I think you're taking too much blame, mate. Is it safe to assume you were launched by two overenthusiastic cultivators?"

"Oh, it was all four of us, actually," Ellis said matter-of-factly. "His velocity was astounding."

Theo grimaced. "I tried spinning in the water like Claws did earlier. It, uh, worked."

"No harm, no foul, right?" I asked Snips.

She nodded in response, blowing happy bubbles as she rubbed her carapace against my shoulder.

I glanced up at the surrounding faces. "I don't know if you guys are interested, but I've cooked up a feast of crab for lunch—"

"Last one there has to be the subject of Ellis's aerial test!" Theo yelled, cutting me off.

" . . . aerial test?" I asked, but they were already gone, swimming to shore in a chaotic wash of flailing arms and kicking legs.

After a feast of crab, I joined in on the boulder-throwing work chain. Claws and Rocky had returned too, no doubt lured in by the smell. Rocky was still trying to catch and/or maim her when he scuttled up from the ocean, but she squashed the beef by throwing a cooked crab directly at his face, which subsequently exploded in a storm of meat and carapace. I had thought it would further antagonize him, but he'd simply started plucking up chunks and throwing them into his mouth.

With their addition to the line, we were able to reach all the way from the first pile to the base of the wall. I was at the end of the line, catching rocks thrown by Claws and Rocky together, who had put their differences aside for the promise of a good scritching and a tasty meal. The wall took shape before my eyes, and as the hours passed, it neared completion—the boulders protruded above the ocean's surface, stretching a full fifty meters from the shore.

All of a sudden, no rock came, and when I looked back down the line, Sergeant Snips approached. She and Pistachio held a colossal boulder, and something shone from it, reflecting the sun's light. Each person they passed joined and helped carry it to the wall. When the procession reached Claws and Rocky, I realized what the light was reflecting from.

A streak of silvery metal ran through the rock. The moment Ellis noticed the streak he jumped atop the load. His head hung down, peering intently at the anomaly. I joined in to haul the boulder up from the water and onto the wall.

As soon as we got there, I turned to Ellis. "You know what it is, mate?"

"I believe so," he answered, his eyes still glued to the vein. "It's iron."

"Really? I thought it was silver—isn't iron more . . . dull?"

"Ah, that is what I had first assumed as well. See the red tint to some of the boulders? That is the result of iron oxidizing. It is a rather dense vein, which is why it appears so metallic. It will lose its shine swiftly now that we have exposed it to air and salt water. Based on how rich its iron content is, I would guess that it's hematite."

I turned, grinning as I surveyed the area. The ocean surrounded us. Small waves crashed into the rocks and the wind sprayed us with their droplets. I breathed deep of the salty air, closing my eyes and extending my arms to either side. I stood like that for a handful of slow breaths, but then something nudged my core.

I arched an eyebrow and looked out at the world. Everyone had their eyes closed and a look of serene calm on their face, losing themselves to the moment. The nudge came again, but this time it pulled me toward the boulder.

I walked between my pals, taking careful steps across the uneven rocks. When I reached the giant boulder, I closed my eyes and leaned my forehead against it, picturing what I wanted to create: a sturdy surface from which to fish, with gaps in the rocks below for sea life to shelter in. A place of friendship, fun, and species diversity.

Knowing what would come next, I thought myself ready for the rush of power that would leave my core.

I was wrong.

The world quivered, and my vision went black.

CHAPTER TWENTY-NINE

REVELATION

"F*ischer!*"

The voice came from far away.

Not right now, I thought back. *I need to rest.*

"*Fischer!*"

I tried to roll over, but my body wouldn't respond. Something hard smacked me in the face, followed by an angry hiss, a loud *crack,* and a soft *eeeeeee* that faded from hearing.

My eyes fluttered open—Snips was atop my chest, shaking her claw out at the ocean.

"Did . . ." I rubbed my face, willing my vision to focus. "Did Rocky just slap me?"

"Aye," Peter confirmed. "Slapped the piss out of you, if you forgive my saying. I half thought your head would fly off toward the horizon like he just did."

"Little scoundrel . . ." My voice came out raspy and ended in a cough. "What happened?"

"Why don't you take a look?" Theo asked, raising his eyebrows.

I squinted and glanced down.

"Wait . . . what?"

I lay on a surface of dark-gray rock. It was smooth and uniform, and as I shakily got to my feet, I gazed out at the transformed scene.

A colossal slab of stone—around fifty meters long and three meters wide—led back to the shore. On either side, boulders tapered down at a forty-five-degree angle toward the ocean. It was high tide, yet we stood a full two meters above the small waves crashing against the rocks.

I turned to take in the fishermen; sensing my attention, they looked back. When I'd met most of them for the first time last night, there had been bouts of awe and joy, but even Theo's face had held some hesitation hidden deep within the lines of his eyes.

When I studied them now, I saw neither doubt, reluctance, nor mistrust. Hands twitched, weight shifted from foot to foot, nostrils flared, and jaws clenched and unclenched, but they weren't agitated—they *radiated* anticipation.

My mouth split in a grin as I realized what they were waiting for. "So, fellas, what do you say we take this rock wall for a test spin?"

Theo swallowed and licked his lips. "Do you mean . . . ?"

I nodded, beaming as they seemed to lean in, waiting for me to voice the words.

"Let's go fishing."

When I saw the answering looks on their faces, I ran to fetch the training rods Maria and I had made. Not even five minutes later, all five of them had a line in the water.

"What the . . . ?" Danny punctuated his question by pulling on his fishing rod; it bent, but the line didn't budge. "I think the hook is stuck on something . . ."

I nodded. "Yeah, looks like you've got a snag, mate. The bad news is I won't let anyone cut their line and potentially hurt some sea creatures, but the good news is we have a gang of hook retrievers."

I turned to Snips. She was wedged between two rocks in the tidal zone, her eye closed in bliss as the small waves crashed over her.

"Snips, would you mind—"

"Hold that thought . . ." Theo said, raising a finger. "I seem to recall someone losing our race to the shore earlier." His eyes crinkled as he turned to the side. "What was the wager again, Peter?"

The chef grinned maliciously. "The loser was to be the volunteer for Ellis's aerial test."

Keith blanched, taking an involuntary step back. "Now, just hang on one second."

The four men had mischief in their eyes as they approached him from all sides.

"W-we can talk about this, gents. I—no! Wait!"

With Theo and Peter holding his arms, Danny and Ellis picked up a leg each.

"What are the parameters, Ellis?" Theo asked.

"I-I do not consent to this barbarity!" Keith's eyes were panicked. "Unhand me this instant—"

"Subject is to remain rigid," Ellis replied, ignoring Keith's pleas. "This will allow optimal transference of energy."

Peter raised an eyebrow. "On three?"

"On three," Ellis confirmed, adjusting his grip on Keith's ankle.

If I didn't know Danny to be Keith's friend, I'd have assumed the smirk on his face was murderous.

Keith saw the look and his eyes went wide.

"One . . ." they said, lifting him.

Keith tugged his arms, trying to escape—it was ineffective.

"Two . . ." Again, they lifted.

Accepting his fate, Keith's face scrunched up and a soft whimper came from his throat.

"Three!"

They wrenched upward, letting go of his limbs just as Corporal Claws appeared on Keith's chest, a toothy grin plastered on her face and a single paw raised to wave me goodbye.

"Huh . . ." I said, watching Keith and Claws rocket toward the stratosphere.

Keith's rather high-pitched scream was punctuated by chittering laughter, and within a second, their voices left hearing range. The royal's limbs pinwheeled, spinning rapidly with his ascent.

"Is he gonna be all right . . . ?"

Ellis nodded, his eyes staring skyward. "We have been thorough in our testing.

Even if he were to hit terminal velocity . . ." Ellis held up a hand, interrupting himself. "*When* he hits terminal velocity, he will not be wounded by striking the water."

"Huh. Neat."

"Can you still see him?" Theo asked.

"Yeah, mate. His spinning has slowed, but he's still going up."

"Marvelous . . ." Ellis replied, scratching away at his notepad.

Just as his flight was about to turn into a freefall, Corporal Claws hunched her limbs and electricity sparked from her joints.

"Oh . . . that's not great."

"What isn't?" Ellis asked, still scrawling.

As if in answer, Claws's muscled legs kicked off of Keith's chest. She went soaring higher yet, lightning wreathing her limbs as she rocketed upward. Unfortunately for Keith, the law of equivalent exchange appeared to be active in this world, and he was sent spiraling down toward the ocean's surface at startling speed.

"Claws just used him as a springboard," I answered, not taking my eyes off the human missile hurtling toward us.

Keith spread his limbs out wide, trying to slow himself. I let out a relieved breath; she hadn't shocked him unconscious.

"Is that him?" Peter asked, squinting up at the rapidly descending cultivator.

Danny grunted. "Definitely him."

Despite his best efforts at wind resistance, Keith approached with terrible speed.

I raised an eyebrow at Ellis. "Is he still going to be okay?"

"Hmmm?" Ellis asked, looking up.

I pointed at Keith. "Do you want me to catch him, or is he all right?"

"Oh. No, he should be fine."

Keith started flapping his arms, trying to right his posture, but fast as he was going, he'd mistimed the landing.

"aaaaaaaaaaaAAAAAAAAAH—"

Slap.

He belly flopped with a thunder-like clap. A crater formed on the surface at the impact site, and I held up a hand to block the torrent of salt water that sprayed up. A collective groan escaped us as we cringed at the hit, and with a synchronized step forward, we all leaned out and stared down at the ocean.

Keith's head breached the surface and he took deep breaths, treading water.

I squinted at his body, seeing no injuries. "You, uh . . . you all right, man?"

He let out a laugh, more surprised than joyous.

"I think so. I just need to rest a moment—my nerves are frayed."

His torso lifted upward, and he floated on his back with his eyes closed.

I looked up into the sky, glanced down at Keith, then shot a look at Ellis. "Should we tell him?"

Ellis returned the look, his eyes sparkling and a smile barely hidden beneath an indifferent facade. "Tell him what, Fischer?"

I grinned, returning my attention skyward.

Other than Ellis, no one had noticed. That changed when they heard the high-pitched squeal of one Corporal Claws, mischief incarnate. Wreathed in lightning and giving a malevolently toothy grin, she spiraled directly down, her predatory gaze locked onto her target.

At the sound, Keith's eyes snapped open and his body jolted, his limbs not working cohesively to get him out of the way.

"No—" was all he had time to get out.

Claws slammed down into him, flattening her body to reduce the impact.

"*Oof!*" Keith grunted, his body folding in half like the layers of a croissant.

He reappeared at the surface a moment later with an entirely too-happy otter lifting him by the armpit.

Theo hissed in a breath. "You, uhhh, all right, Keith?"

He shook his head as Claws lifted him up onto the rocks. Theo and I went down and grabbed a hand each to haul him up. He collapsed on the walkway, wheezing breaths and clearly winded.

Claws reached into a pocket and rummaged around, then held out an opalescent rock.

Peter cocked his head at it. "Is she saying sorry?"

"Sorry?" I asked, laughing. "No—she doesn't say sorry. She's saying thank you for the fun, I'm guessing?"

Claws chirped and grinned at me, content I knew her so well.

Keith opened a shaky palm, and she placed the stone atop it, pushing it further toward him with little nudges of her padded paws.

"Thanks," Keith croaked, his face colorless.

Ellis, who hadn't stopped furiously scribbling since Keith's orbital strike, flipped his notepad closed.

"All right. The aerial test was a success. Shall we get on with fish—oh, are you well, Keith?"

The royal gave a thumbs up, still looking anything but okay.

A half hour later, the shifting current tugged at my line, pulling and pushing it back and forth every few breaths. I swayed with the motion, my body reflecting the tide's relentless movement. The day's light was just fading as the sun descended in the western sky, heading for the mountains it would soon set behind.

A deep calm washed over me and I let out a sigh. "I can't believe fishing is so frowned upon here. How do people enjoy life without it?"

"It is truly a shame," Ellis said, his face calm as he held a finger to his line. "But such was the weight of the water gods' betrayal and the war that followed."

I turned toward him, raising an eyebrow—as did Theo, Peter, and Danny.

" . . . what?" I asked.

"The gods' betrayal," Ellis replied, still relaxed.

"Not that," Theo answered, lowering his fishing rod. "The *war.* Last we spoke, you knew nothing more than the common knowledge that the water gods had betrayed us all somehow."

Ellis's eyes popped open, and he blinked at all of us. "Oh, I didn't tell you? I must have forgotten with all the excitement of arriving."

"Tell us *what?*" Theo demanded, exasperated.

"About the division in the pantheon and the scope of the war that followed. I have known for quite some time, but when I was still a royal archivist . . ." He shrugged. "It went against my oaths. Now that we have abandoned such things, I no longer feel the need to keep it a secret."

We waited for him to continue, but as the silence stretched on, Peter's patience ended.

"For the love of—" He cut himself off, taking a calming breath. "What happened, Ellis? What are the details?"

"Ah, of course. My apologies." He opened his eyes, smiling out at the ocean. "Though the details are uncertain, one thing is clear: the gods aligned with water betrayed the other gods, humanity, and the world at large. Before they left, a war broke out that encompassed the entire globe."

As I considered the scope of such a war, we fell into silence. I pictured battlefields of cultivators fighting, the carnage it must have wrought, and the countless lives that must have been lost. A breeze kicked up, and a shiver ran down my spine.

"A holy war with cultivators . . ." I shook my head. "That's horrific."

"Just so," Ellis agreed. "Eventually, the non-water-aligned gods, what are known as the 'allied gods,' formed a pact. As their final gambit, they fled from this world. With their departure, there wasn't enough power to sustain the treacherous gods, so they were dragged away too—banished forever to another realm."

"So the allied gods sacrificed themselves?" Theo asked, rubbing his chin.

"So it would appear. Only a god could truly comprehend how many lives they saved in doing so, but as a result, they left our world unpowered—barren."

"That's all it said?"

"That's all?" Ellis asked, raising both eyebrows at me. "That was information hidden within the depths of the royal archive, most of which were almost desolate, which I suspect is the only reason they survived being purged."

"Purged? You mean the information was destroyed?"

"Just so," Ellis replied, and for the first time, I saw a hint of fury in the calm archivist's features. "At some point in the millennia past, a ruler—or an archivist—saw fit to scrub the records. Luckily for us, they were as useless as they are stupid for attempting such a thing in the first place."

I shook my head. "What's a monarchy without a bit of censorship and oppression?"

Ellis sighed. "I wish it weren't so."

A silence stretched between us as everyone became lost in their own thoughts.

"F-fish on!" Theo yelled. His shrill voice cut through the outward melody of crashing waves and the inward musings of revelation both.

"On ya, Theo!" I called back, leaning into the fortunate distraction.

Theo reeled it in, easily handling what appeared to be a small fish on the other end of the line. Its scales flashed at the water's surface, and with a flick of his rod, he lifted it up to the walkway.

Juvenile Shore Fish
Common
Found along the ocean shores of the Kallis Realm, this fish is a staple source of both food and bait.

I dismissed the message and darted a glance at the men.

Peter's eyes cleared first. "What . . . ?"

"Yeah, I guess I forgot to mention that detail. We can kind of inspect stuff—especially fish."

Theo was the last to return his attention from the screen he was no doubt watching, and a broad grin spread over his face. "I got three levels in fishing!"

I raised an eyebrow. "Not bad, mate! I wonder if it took past experience into account?"

Ellis nodded his agreement as he scribbled away in his notepad.

I peered down at the fish and cocked my head to the side—the hook was nowhere to be seen. I picked it up and looked into its mouth. "Ah, frack."

"What's wrong?" Theo asked.

"It swallowed the hook. I don't feel good about eating fish this size unless it's necessary, but there's little to no chance of it surviving."

Already, its life was leaking away, so I dispatched it with a swift movement. "Sorry, little fella."

"It's probably my fault." Theo winced and shook his head. "I was listening to Ellis speak, then I got distracted by my thoughts—I didn't notice the first bite."

"All we can do is learn from it, I guess. I don't know about you guys, but I don't feel good about bringing unnecessary pain or suffering."

They all nodded, and Theo grimaced.

"It's all right, man. You didn't do it intention . . . ally . . ." I trailed off as a winged form glided down onto the walkway beside us.

Covered in white feathers with accents of black on its sides, the pelican stretched its wings out and took a hesitant step forward, peering at the fish with one eye, its head sideways and neck outstretched.

I looked at the fish, then back up at the pelican as a smile lit my features.

CHAPTER THIRTY

THE BLADE

With the sun setting at my back and a cool breeze tickling my skin, I smiled at the pelican. With a deft cut of my knife, I cut into the fish, removed the hook from its throat, and lobbed the fish into the air.

The bird's neck craned forward and its beak opened, easily catching the fish within its pouch. It tossed its head twice before swallowing the fish whole.

"What in Acanthis's feathered form is *that?*" Theo demanded.

I raised an eyebrow at him. "You've never seen one?"

"I believe it is a pelican," Ellis answered. "I've not seen one either, but I recognize it from a compendium back in the capital."

"Bingo, mate. It's a pelican." I grinned. "And I intend to make it a pal."

The large water bird peered at us, uninterested in our conversation yet hanging around to see if we had more fish. On seeing there were no more snacks, or perhaps because we were staring at it a little too much, it took flight. Two huge wings beat at the air, and within a few breaths, it was high above, gliding across unseen currents.

Corporal Claws dashed up beside me, resting her forepaws on my leg as she stared up at the pelican's flight. She let out a dreamy coo.

"It'd be wondrous to fly, wouldn't it?" I asked, understanding her thoughts.

She gave an affirmative chirp, still watching the bird as it sailed away.

"You flew no longer than an hour ago when you used me as a launch platform, you little shi—" Keith cut off when Claws shot him a warning glance, and he held up both hands defensively. "Er—shining light! I was going to say shining light!"

She walked forward and held out a paw. She pointed at it emphatically, extending it further toward him and raising her chin, somehow looking down at him from her position on the ground. Keith sighed and gave her back the opalescent stone she'd gifted him.

I shook my head. "Claws is a fickle mistress."

She nodded, grinning as she pocketed the rock and leaped into the water, disappearing without a splash.

That afternoon, as the last vestiges of light faded from the sky, Theo hooked another.

"Oh! Fish on!"

I was down at the water, cleaning two mature shore fish that Peter and Keith had already caught. Theo shifted his weight backward as the rod bent almost in half with the fish's weight. His eyes were alight with expectation, and I couldn't help but smile as I continued removing scales.

"Looks like a big one, mate."

"Feels like a big one!" he replied, holding his rod high so the line didn't touch the rocks.

The fish took a massive run, each kick of its tail and shake of its head causing the rod's tip to jerk down. Just before the light left the sky, I saw the flash of silver on the ocean's surface, right by where I was cleaning the fish. While it was the same shape as a shore fish, I raised an eyebrow at the size.

"It-it's a monster!" Danny roared, his voice tinged with awe.

I leaned forward, hoping for another look. It swam right up before me, but beneath the amethyst sky and dwindling light, I still couldn't make out what it was. The fish, noticing the rocks—or me, leaning down and having a good peep—tore off with heavy swishes of its tail. As determined as the fish was, Theo was more resolute, and he had the tools to back up his claims. He let line out before reeling the fish back to shore, letting it expend energy.

Seeing how exhausted the fish was getting, I grabbed the line with one hand, lifted it, then grasped the fish around the gills with the other. If not for my enhanced body, I'd never have been able to raise it one handed—it was *gigantic.*

Ancient Shore Fish
Rare
Found along the ocean shores of the Kallis Realm, this fish is a staple source of both food and bait.

"Holy hell, Theo . . ." I said, my eyes clearing.

I hefted the ancient fish up for everyone to see, and their excited clamoring silenced as their vision went distant.

"Ancient?" Theo asked.

Ellis, ever the reliable sort, started scribbling in his notepad. "And rare! Age may appear to increase the classification of . . ." his voice trailed off as it lowered to a mutter.

"What do you reckon, Theo?"

He turned to me, cocking his head to the side. "About what?"

"Your catch, your call—is this fella dinner?"

His grin returned and he nodded so hard I thought his head might topple off.

Not long after, as I set the three cleaned fish in a pan and put it atop the campfire, a welcome voice came rolling over the sands.

"Yoohoo!" Maria called, her voice singsong and brimming with joy.

She walked around the corner of the headland with Corporal Claws lazing in one arm. In the other, she held a tray that immediately drew my attention in.

"What have you got there?"

She grinned at me as we all sat down by the fire. "See if you can guess."

She passed the tray around, and I peered down at the enticing pastries. A sweet, complex scent radiated up from them, telling me they were not long removed from the oven.

I had no idea what they were, though. "I give up. What are they?"

"Cinnamon rolls."

At the mention of her name, Cinnamon's head popped out of Maria's pocket. She launched herself at me, and I easily caught the tiny bunny. I rubbed the velvet-smooth patch of fur between her ears, delighting in the way she pressed into my touch.

"Well," Maria continued, "it's cinnamon if I stole the correct seasoning from your kitchen. I asked Peter this morning what would pair well with a sweet pastry. They're made using sugar refined from your fertilized cane."

Peter broke one in half and breathed deep of the rising vapors. He let out a long sigh. "Definitely cinnamon, and *definitely* going to be delicious. These are a common pastry in the capital and would be the closest thing to the croissants Sue makes. They're made using a cheap spice, so they're affordable to even the poorest of the capital's citizens." He gazed down at the rising steam. "I can't wait any longer."

He blew on the open pastry, then took a small bite. His posture immediately melted; he leaned back in the sand and let out a content *mmm*.

Seeing his reaction, I broke mine in half. The vapors immediately rose to greet me, and I breathed them in, welcoming the scents.

The first smells that hit me were of flour, butter, and sugar—those alone would have been enough to make my mouth water. With the addition of cinnamon's complex scent, it was enough to turn my salivary glands into faucets, and I couldn't help but immediately bite into the pastry.

The surface was crusted with granular sugar, and they crunched between my teeth, highlighting just how soft and pillowy the dough was. The cinnamon came through next; it wiped out all conscious thought. I breathed slowly as I chewed the mouthful, lost to the sensations and flavors. When I swallowed, I opened my eyes. I had lain back on the sand, my hands still holding half a roll each and resting atop my chest.

"What's the verdict?" Maria asked, leaning over me with a smirk.

The campfire's dancing flames lit her face from below, giving her skin and freckled face a golden glow; the rising moon lit her from behind, casting its ethereal light about the hair hanging down around her.

"Perfect," I replied, my eyes crinkling in delight.

Augustus Reginald Gormona peered down at a tray covered in dozens of fresh pastries, his mouth dry and brain awash with worries. He picked one up, his usual favorite, and took a bite. The pastry was smothered in a passiona jam reduction, and it was the finest treat his kingdom had to offer.

It tasted bland.

He let go, allowing the sugary pastry to fall down to the tray. It landed the wrong side up, and jam splattered over the surrounding pastries. He pushed the tray away, letting out a discontent sigh.

A creak drew his attention, and the great doors to his throne room swung open. His servant on duty led someone in, then snapped to attention.

"Handler Aisa to see the king!"

Augustus nodded and gestured for the servant to leave them. Aisa bowed at the waist and remained so, waiting for permission to approach.

"Come," he said.

"Yes, my king." She marched forward, stopping right before the throne and standing at attention.

"Thank you for coming on such short notice, Aisa."

"Of course, king. I am your blade to wield."

Her words were curt and clipped, as he knew her general demeanor to be. Which was exactly why he called on her to complete this task. Augustus gave her an appreciative smile.

"We find ourselves in dire straits, Aisa. The very kingdom may be at risk. If there was any time for a blade to be brandished, it is now."

His words had the desired effect; her gaze turned flinty and she set her jaw. Despite her passion, she waited patiently for him to continue.

"If I were to tell you that I believe a number of spirit beasts have awakened close enough to our capital to be a threat, what would you say?"

She chewed her lip for a long moment, considering the statement and question in their entirety. "If anyone else were to make such a claim, my king, I would dismiss them as a fool. From you . . ." her eyes grew sharp once more, "I ask their whereabouts and what your orders are."

He let his gratitude show, grinning at the answer. "In that case, I'll get right into it. Five spirit beasts have awakened, all of which I believe to be nearby."

He watched her closely, and though the shock was clear in her eyes, determination swiftly returned, banishing any doubt.

"I have a particular target in mind for you," he continued. "I've chosen this target for you to dispatch because of your proven efficacy in dealing with powerful renegade cultivators. Based on the information we have access to, this spirit beast will be the most magically gifted of the threats."

"Where shall I go in search of this spirit beast?"

"I don't have an exact location, but I believe the most likely location to be the desert beyond the southern range."

She nodded. "Would you like me to take the usual squad of four cultivators, or does this threat require more?"

"As many as you desire. Due to the danger posed, you will have first pick of the collared."

"Forgive my insolence, my king." Aisa bowed her head. "May I ask a question?"

He waved her concern away. "Of course—please do."

"Thank you, king. Will my sisters and the other handlers also be going on similar missions to eliminate threats?"

"They will be, yes."

"Then I will leave their favored cultivators. Though some are more powerful than my regular team, we will be more effective overall if we take collared whose abilities we know well."

Augustus leaned back in his chair and sighed, letting his facade of calm assurance drop. "Thank you, Aisa. As always, I appreciate your insight." He sat up straight, resuming his regal posture. "Do you have any more questions before you depart?"

"Just one, my king: what is the name of my target?"

Augustus straightened further, stretching his spine to its vertical limits. He gazed up at the stained glass windows for a long moment.

"Remember this name well, Aisa. If not for your intervention, it could go down in the records as the beast that ended the kingdom of Gormona. The name of your target is . . ."

He locked eyes with her, clenching and unclenching his jaw. Finally, he ground out the name of his dreaded foe.

"Lizard Wizard."

CHAPTER THIRTY-ONE

A BLIND FOOL

Barry smiled to himself as he fed sugarcane into his juicer. His life had felt chaotic of late, especially following the arrival of Gormona's fishing club. Thinking of the five men made his grin widen. They had slotted seamlessly into the church, and it already felt as though he'd known them for years, not days. Even now, they were off with Fischer, no doubt having a wonderful time partaking in some heretical activities.

"What's got you so cheery?" Helen asked from beside him.

She was sitting on the bench, and Barry turned his amusement her way.

"I was just thinking about the fishing club and how much fun they're probably having right now."

"Are you sure you don't want to join them?" she asked, kicking her legs. "The offer still stands."

"Thank you, love, but it's okay." He wound the juicer's handle, feeding a stalk of cane in with his other hand. "I know this is technically work, but something about it is relaxing."

Mischief sparkled behind Helen's eyes. "If you're not careful, people might assume you're a simple farmer that enjoys working with his hands, not the leader of a cult."

"Not you too!" He feigned dismay. "Church! It's a *church!*"

She giggled, covering her mouth as she shimmied. "I know, but Fischer makes messing with you look so fun."

"Ah, my wife torments me." Barry let out a theatrical sigh. "What did I do to be wedded to such a treacherous woman?"

She snorted, rolling her eyes at him.

They shared a glance as Barry added another stalk of cane to the juicer, and his heart seemed to skip a beat as he took in her beauty.

"Something wrong, husband?" she asked, smirking.

"Just daydreaming about this woman I saw in Tropica the other day. She had these *massive—*"

Helen whacked him on the arm, cutting him off.

"Ow!" He rubbed his shoulder, laughing. "Watch your strength!"

"You're the one courting death by talking about other women around your heretical cultivator of a wife." She tried to pout, but her smile ruined it. "You got off easy this time."

"Speaking of heretical cultivators, we should deliver this sugarcane juice."

"I suppose we should." She hopped off the bench as Barry wound the handle.

Yellow juice flowed from the spout, and when none of the stalk remained, the cup it flowed into was almost full.

Hand in hand, they walked down the hallway. Before they arrived at their destination, the sound of wood rhythmically striking metal bounced off the walls. They shared an amused glance as they entered the doorway.

Trent had a wooden cup in hand and was running it along the metal bars of his prison.

Dink. Dink. Dink. Dink. Dink. Dink. Dink—

"Oh!" He noticed them and halted his percussive performance. "About time!"

"Hello, Trent," Helen said, smiling at the simple prince.

"Is that mine?" he asked, pointing at the cup in Barry's hands.

"You know," Barry said, "it's usually considered polite to greet someone back."

"Yeah? Well it's also considered polite not to put a *collar* around someone's neck and *imprison* them, *Barry!*"

"He's got you there," Helen noted.

Shaking his head, Barry held out the cup.

Trent snatched it from his hand and immediately chugged it, somehow not spilling a drop. "Ahhh," he sighed not even five seconds later. "When is dinner?"

"How do you feel?" Barry asked, ignoring the question.

"Huh? I feel hungry, which is why I asked when dinner was . . . ?" Trent gave him some bombastic side-eye. "You're pretty dumb, aren't you?"

"Sounds like a failure to me," Helen said.

"Yep," Barry agreed.

They turned and left together, ignoring the prince's squawked insults that chased them down the hallway.

Helen squeezed Barry's hand. "So, do you have any theories?"

"None." Barry shook his head, looking at the roof as they walked. "No one has any clue why he won't awaken."

She looped her arm through his and rested her head on his shoulder. "Don't stress over it. It'll work eventually."

He took a deep breath and slowly exhaled. "I hope so . . ."

The room's walls were bathed in flickering candlelight, and George let out a sigh as he rubbed his eyes. Geraldine lay a supportive hand on his shoulder, and he leaned against it with his prodigious jowls.

"Maybe we should go to bed for the night," she suggested.

"You're likely correct, my love—as always."

"What is it you were reading?" She set her own book down, leaning over to peer at his family's manual. "I thought you might scowl your eyebrows right off your face."

He pursed his lips, but when he realized his forehead was knitting once more, he let out another sigh. "It's the same entry that continuously vexes me."

"Hmmm. The same one as yesterday?"

He put a hand into her lap, their fingers intertwining. "And the day before."

She scrunched her nose at the book. "It irks me that I can't read it . . ."

"Sorry, love. The ancient language is notoriously tricky, and I only know it because my father drilled it into me from a young age."

"I just wish I could help—it's infuriating to sit by and lose myself in fiction while you struggle."

He turned to look at Geraldine. The candle lit her ample face, and love for the woman before him flowed out like thick custard from a piping bag. "Just having you by my side is enough."

She leaned in and kissed him, her lips tugging up in a smile. When she pulled away, the love he felt for her was reflected in her eyes.

"Would you read me the part that you've been poring over?"

"Of course." He skimmed the open page until he found the sentence constantly replaying in his head. "I feel the entire chapter is reflected in this line here."

He cleared his throat.

"It translates roughly as: 'To conspire against your fellow man is to court ruin; to benefit from them unfairly is to invite ruin into your home.' 'Ruin' isn't exactly correct, though—there isn't a word in the common tongue to reflect its potency. It doesn't mean just physical ruin, but also desolation of one's very soul."

She swallowed, licking her lips. "I . . . I can see why it troubles you."

He pushed the book forward, wanting physical distance from the words that assailed him.

"Before I saw the wisdom held in the rest of this book, I assumed all of it to be the fancy of a long-diminished household. But now . . ." He ran fingers through his thinning hair. "Now I can't help but wonder if we brought all our problems into existence with our actions since arriving in Tropica."

Geraldine sucked her teeth, and as he watched her, she appeared lost in thought. When her gaze locked with his, her eyes were morose. "I've been meaning to speak to you about that . . ."

"My love? Talk about what?"

"As you've been lost in the book most days, I've been busying myself by wandering the village. I've spent some time lingering among the south siders, and the more time I spend there . . ." She gave him a wincing smile. "Well, I came to a similar conclusion."

" . . . you did?"

She nodded, looking away and staring at the wall as she continued. "I had assumed that all peasants were just the glum sort. What did it matter if we took extra gold if they wouldn't enjoy it? At least we could use the funds to improve our own standing and try to claw our way back to the capital, right?" She shook her head, and the weariness etched in her features made George's heart break.

A tear welled in her eye, and she wiped it away with a plump hand. "They're happy, George—truly happy. They gather around that damned bakery like clumps of sugar on a fresh donut, laughing and joking merrily as they eat unsweetened pastries and drink coffee made by a peasant. Seeing the joy such small improvements brought them . . . it makes me feel terrible about what we did."

George stared at her for a long moment. She peered back, her head cocked to the side, seeing something on his face she didn't understand. Suddenly, laughter bubbled up from within him. Her curiosity morphed into anger as he lost himself to mirth, but every time he tried to explain himself, his voice was cut off by choked laughter.

"I was being serious, George." Her tone was clipped as she leaned away from him. "I don't appreciate being laughed at."

"No. I'm not laughing at you, my love—I'm laughing at myself."

She narrowed her eyes, clearly skeptical, so he continued. "I've been lost in this book, gleaning the writings of generations of my ancestors for the truth, and all you had to do was just go for a walk." He blew air from his nose, shaking his head at himself. "I'm a blind fool."

A moment of silence stretched between them as she considered his words.

"You're no fool, husband," she whispered, pulling him into a hug. "If you were, I'd not have married you."

"Given how long it's been taking me to digest the words in this manual versus how you understood the truth by just opening your eyes, I'd beg to differ."

"We all have different strengths, love."

She squeezed him tight, and he returned the embrace.

"All right—I've decided," he said, pulling away.

She gave him a confused look. "Decided what?"

"I'm going to teach you the ancient language—if you're willing, of course."

Her eyes went wide. "George . . . I thought you said that was only for blood relatives to know? I don't want to get you in trouble . . ."

"In trouble from who? My mother and father have passed, and we have no idea where my brother is, let alone if he still lives. Besides, as far as I'm concerned, you are of my blood, Geraldine. I love you, and without you, I would be lost."

Tears welled in her eyes, but this time, she didn't wipe them away.

"Oh, George . . ." Her lip quivered, and she wrapped her voluptuous arms around him, drawing him into an embrace. "I love you too."

As I lay in bed that night, my body felt leaden. I spread my arms out to either side, delighting in the plush doona and pillows surrounding me. Cinnamon wiggled beneath my armpit, turning into the cutest dang loaf I'd ever seen. As with most nights in recent memory, my mind replayed the soft kiss Maria had planted on me before going home, and a warm, fuzzy feeling unrelated to my bedding washed over me.

With sleep calling to me, my thoughts strayed toward the revelations Ellis had dropped on us. According to the information hidden within the royal library, the water-aligned gods had betrayed not only their kin, but humanity itself. If that were true, it made sense why the world at large had shunned anything to do with them—fishing included.

"But to continue doing so, thousands of years later . . ." I yawned. "It makes no sense unless their betrayal was particularly savage . . ."

Cinnamon wiggled, and I lay a reassuring hand atop her fluffy back, willing her to go back to sleep.

After the day I'd had, my consciousness started to fade, and I released the worries. It didn't matter what happened all those years ago. I was here now, and I was going to continue living my life. When sleep finally took me, I was smiling, beyond content with the little slice of paradise I'd carved for myself in Tropica.

With the arrival of the sun, Corporal Claws, queen of the forest and conqueror of the sky, let out a magnificent yawn. She rolled onto her back, allowing the sun's rays the privilege of warming her tummy fur. Using both paws, she rubbed her face, finding it both amusing and comforting to shift her malleable cheeks around. After her tum was sufficiently heated and her face was stretched enough for the day to come, she sat up, chirping a good morning to the world.

She immediately felt the need to go find her master and demand scritches, but then she spied the fish frame sitting beneath a tree. She had delivered one to the tree spirit last night, and wanting to space out its meals—and keep the cheeky thing's ego in check—she had kept another for this fine morning. She leaped from her log, hit the ground running, and snatched the frame in her jaws as she passed. The sooner she delivered the fish, the sooner she could see Fischer and receive her deserved pats.

As she jumped from tree to tree, amplifying her passage with small bursts of electricity, something curious caught her attention. She slowed her pace, gazing up at a trail of small insects that buzzed their way beneath the forest canopy. She had seen bees before, but never flying in tandem like the ocean birds sometimes did high above the waves.

Matching their pace, she followed them, too curious to let them go unwitnessed. Before long, the canopy opened up, and she raised both eyebrows as she realized the bees were flying for the lemon saplings. When she looked up at the trees, her mouth dropped open and the fish fell to the grass.

CHAPTER THIRTY-TWO

FLIGHT OF THE BUMBLEBEE

Five weeks earlier, in a land far to the northeast of Tropica, a lone bumblebee followed a terrific scent. He flew around trees, through grassy meadows, and over a giant wall, the sweet scent's allure inescapable. Every male bumblebee of his species operated on a series of hierarchical needs that could be boiled down to a single goal: the proliferation of the species. For this bumblebee to do that, he needed to attract a queen. To attract a queen, he needed to create his magnum opus—royal jelly.

Not that he was aware of this; he was a bumblebee.

What he was aware of, however, was that he had an instinctive desire to create the sweetest royal jelly that there ever was. Such an act would broadcast his virility and attract potential queens.

So, when the lone bumblebee caught the scent of fresh honey in the air—a fuel source he could use to make his queen-attracting jelly—it was only natural that he went to steal some.

His instincts told him to prepare for a fight; for honey to be exposed to the air meant that something large had broken into a hive. Despite his size, the bumblebee was agile, and he could utilize that speed to requisition some precious honey for his proliferation endeavors.

As he reached the source of the smell, the bumblebee paused and scanned his surroundings—there was no movement, neither predator nor bee. A series of containers sat within an open crate, and an unmistakably viscous liquid dripped down their sides.

Honey.

The bumblebee darted forward, landed on one of the golden trails, and began its feast.

Suddenly, there was movement from above as something large enough to occupy the entire sky appeared. The bumblebee tried to take flight, tried to flee, but his legs got caught in the honey for just long enough to seal his fate. He bumped into the sky-obscuring object and spiraled down to fall among the jars.

Darkness engulfed the prison he found himself in.

A mercenary captain scanned the surrounding faces as his client checked the last crate loaded onto his wagon by a well-dressed merchant. He had five subordinates with him: four veterans and a fresh recruit.

"What do you think that one holds?" the recruit whispered.

"It's honey," another mercenary answered. "Worth its weight in gold, that stuff."

"Wow . . ." The recruit's voice was filled with wonder. "The king's coffers are something else . . ."

"Eyes forward," the captain growled, gazing at the pedestrians traversing the street.

Each mercenary snapped to attention and made themselves busy, recognizing the threat of discipline in his voice.

The recruit, having been sufficiently chastised, made sure to cast a suitably suspicious gaze over the capital's citizens as they passed by. Many of them looked at the cart and guards with curiosity, but upon seeing the butt-chewing, rock-splitting expression on his captain's face, all averted their eyes.

The form of a plump yet nimble insect caught his attention, and he cocked his head, watching a bumblebee make a beeline for the open crate. He smiled at his wordplay, but then the client, who his captain had repeatedly insisted was someone rather important in the royal retinue, picked up the crate's lid and set it down, sealing the bumblebee inside.

"Wait!" the recruit said, taking a step forward.

In the blink of an eye, four swords were drawn. The captain's body grew tense, and the sea of passing faces froze.

"Report!" the captain roared, glancing at the recruit for a fraction of a second before turning to scan his surroundings.

The recruit winced.

"There was a bumblebee in the crate when it was sealed. It won't survive the trip—our client is going over . . ." he trailed off as he recalled at the last possible moment that the client's overseas destination was a secret. He flicked a glance at the sea of citizens watching before returning his attention to the client and his captain—both of their faces turned murderous, and the latter grabbed him by the collar.

"Stand down," he ordered the others, then pulled the recruit aside.

"Keep moving, everyone," another mercenary yelled to the crowd of onlookers. "There's nothing to see."

The captain shoved the recruit beside the cart, where nobody else could hear. "One more mistake, recruit, and you're out. I won't have you jeopardizing our lucrative contracts with the crown." He pointed at the hammer and pile of nails that had been used to seal each crate after the client approved their contents. "Nail the lid in place and return to your post."

"Yes, sir."

He grabbed the hammer and a nail.

"Sorry, friend," he said under his breath to the bumblebee as he hammered the first nail home.

With each passing day, the bumblebee grew more agitated. Most weren't aware that bees—including this species of bumblebee—had an endogenous clock independent of its environment. Well, the bumblebee wasn't aware of that fact either—it was a bee—but it *was* aware of the passing of time despite the lack of light.

Each day within the place of darkness made a sense of urgency grow within the insect, pushing it to find a way out. No matter how much it chewed at the walls of its prison, however, the hardwood didn't give way before its small but powerful mandibles.

The world itself continually shifted, sometimes causing the jars to clank together softly. One day, after a couple weeks of confinement, the movement became unbearable. The jars bouncing together in the confined space made such a loud noise that the bumblebee became completely overwhelmed by the cacophony.

The only break in the monotony of continuous black was immediately after a two-day span of violent shaking. There was a creaking noise, and the lid to his prison came free. If the bumblebee had been well, it could have easily escaped. Instead, it merely lay at the bottom of the crate, its nervous system too overburdened to move.

Odd-tasting air flowed into the crate, cool and thick with salt. The head of a giant peered down, and after moving some jars around, the lid was returned, and darkness came with it.

The only consolation to his confinement was the delicious drops of honey lining some lids—even that small reprieve also vexed the bumblebee, however. He had the means with which to craft royal jelly, yet no suitable hole to build a hive in. If the denizens of the world were aware of the bumblebee's plight, those with a shred of decency would unequivocally recognize the injustice. It was, as the common folk would say, a bunch of bullshit. Alas, the bumblebee was alone, and there were no gods left to witness his predicament.

When his faculties returned, the bumblebee flew up to a jar and vibrated his wings in annoyance. He drank deep of the last drop of honey within his prison, relishing its sweet flavor.

When its prison opened again weeks later, the bumblebee was ready. There was no more food, and the second the lid made a creaking noise, it prepared for flight. Light streamed in through a tiny crack—the bumblebee darted through it and out into the sun's rays.

He immediately flew headlong into something gigantic.

The man's legs trembled. He had been at sea for much longer than expected.

"Damned Zeus and his storms," he muttered, sitting down on a crate and massaging his knees.

He'd dragged his sloop up onto the beach and started unloading the contents. It was a slow endeavor without his land legs. After a brief rest, he looked down at the crate he sat upon. It was made of a dark, reinforced hardwood, and its contents were the most expensive of all his cargo. He'd checked it after the storm, ensuring none of the honey jars had broken—thankfully, they'd survived the tempest.

"I suppose I should check it again . . ."

He went searching in the sloop for his crowbar, and as soon as he returned, he forced it into the crack between crate and lid. He pushed down on the bar, and nails creaked as the lid came free. The moment it did, something came flying out. He leaned back instinctively as a bumblebee—a damned *bumblebee*—bumped into him, knocking him to the sand. He rolled over, watching his yellow and black assailant as it flew for the trees.

He shook his head, and all he could do was laugh. "Brought low by an insect—what would my master say?"

He got back to his feet and brushed sand from his leathers. He didn't know how long it would take his contact to arrive, so he'd need to set up a camp and get his wares out of the weather.

After removing rings from his waist pouch and sliding them onto his fingers, he resumed unloading crates.

The bumblebee's exuberance at freedom was steadily diminishing as he flew from flower to flower. There was something wrong with the nectar here. No matter how much nectar and pollen he fed on, his hunger was never satiated. He tried flowers of every color and variety, yet each time, the result was the same. After three days of traveling, he began to grow weary. His usually rapid speed slowed as his body went into maintenance mode. All the while, he tried every new flower, hoping one of them would alleviate his starvation.

Over a week after regaining his freedom, he was sluggishly droning beneath the forest's canopy when he caught the scent of his salvation. At first, the smell was but a whisper on the breeze, but after only minutes of searching, the taste in the air was undeniable.

He had once more found honey.

He trailed its scent, getting closer and closer with every wingbeat, eventually coming to an unguarded hole. The bumblebee landed far from the opening and walked forward silently, not wishing to alert any defenders of his presence. The opening was large, and he crawled inside, his wings twitching from anticipation.

He didn't have far to travel before finding the life-saving goo; mere seconds from the surface, he came across the hive. It was tiny, consisting of only five chambers, but that was more than enough to replenish his energy. As the bumblebee raced forward to the undefended gold, he came face to face with death.

A wasp, even larger than the rotund body of the bumblebee, stared at the intruder with compound eyes. Before the bee had a chance to react, the wasp's wings buzzed in alarm. The bumblebee turned and fled. He had to escape the hole, had to get back to the canopy of the forest before he was swarmed.

Just as the entrance came into view, the first defender arrived. A wasp zipped inside, the beat of its wings making a low drone and relaying the alarm to any surrounding wasps. With its mandibles open and legs spread wide, the wasp attacked. The bumblebee tapped into its reserves and took flight; he slammed into the approaching insect. Barbed legs grabbed at him, but he tore free and continued out into the open air.

Just in time for the rest of the defenders to arrive.

Too many wasps to count had come in defense of their hive, and each of them lunged. Barbed feet grasped, mandibles closed, and stingers lashed out. His speed slowed as countless wasps attempted to engulf him. The bumblebee's striped body was a blur as he twisted and spun in response, doing everything he could to get away. Just as he made it through the tangle, his flight hitched to the side.

There was a tear in his right wing, and now that he was past the cloud of wasps, pain coursed through his entire body from the myriad of scratches and punctures. His hunger forgotten, the bumblebee fled.

With each passing day, the bumblebee grew more delirious. Scholars could spend days, weeks, and possibly even years arguing whether it was possible for an insect to be beset by delirium—unfortunately for the bumblebee, the opinions of scholarly naysayers didn't alleviate his condition.

Wasp venom coursed through his circulatory system where a stinger had punctured his side, and given that he'd eaten nothing he could properly digest in weeks, his body hadn't had the chance to cleanse it. With a halting, almost-drunken flight, the bumblebee flew in no particular direction. Lacking a sense of time and space, the bumblebee followed his basic instincts, continuing to move despite the carnage wrought within and without his body.

An unknowable amount of time later, something pierced through the bumblebee's delirium. A scent, as sweet as it was familiar, called out to him. He bobbed along beneath the canopy, slowly but surely heeding the call.

CHAPTER THIRTY-THREE

POLLEN

The morning sun filtered through the gap in the canopy above the clearing, and the fish frame made a wet *slap* as its tail smacked the ground. Corporal Claws let out a loud chirp that, if spoken in common, would have roughly translated to: "*What the frack?*"

Each day since the tree spirit had somehow incorporated the lemon trees into its being, the saplings had grown a little in size. Today was no different in that regard. What *was* different, however, was the carpet of white flowers covering each sapling. The clearing was abuzz with insects, and they darted around chaotically, pausing only to collect the yellow pollen peppering each flower.

She picked up the fish and crept forward, not wanting to spook the bees away from their task. As she walked between two of the saplings, the insects' movement engulfed her vision, and she paused, transfixed by the sight. The buzz of so many individual pollinators combined became a cacophony, and she stood there for a long moment, happily losing her sense of self.

But then a root slapped her across the face.

Claws darted her head toward the blue-barked tree, chirping with indignation. The root that had struck her was wrapped around the fallen fish frame, dragging it back toward its trunk. Claws glared her annoyance at the impatient tree. There was no response, so she walked up to it. Reluctantly, she patted its bark, praising it for a job well done. After all, her master had wanted to grow lemons.

Claws gave a toothy grin as she continued petting the tree, looking back at the flowers and wondering if they would fruit.

With sleep still fogging my mind and a rather cute bunny cradled to my chest, I gazed out at the ocean. The sun hadn't breached the horizon, yet its yellow and orange glow already tinted the world. A fitful breeze kicked up as Cinnamon lifted her head and sniffed the air, her little nose twitching away. I rubbed between her ears with one hand, delighting in the velvety fur I found there.

Together, we watched the sunrise. With our position at the end of the rock wall, it was as if we stood on the ocean; small waves peaked all around us, reflecting the sun's light from countless undulating points. I inhaled through my nose, smiling at the world as the scents of salt and fresh air assaulted me.

"It's a beautiful day," I said, still rubbing Cinnamon's head.

She squeaked her agreement and wiggled backward, settling further into the crook of my arm.

"Did you want to hide in my shirt while I get a coffee and some brekkie? I can take you to Maria's if you wanna spend the day with her in the fields again."

In response, she crawled up my torso, planted a tiny peck on my chin, then crawled into my open collar. I patted her through my shirt as I set off, lured on by the promise of caffeine, a fantasy croissant, and Maria.

"G'day, Fischer!" Sue called as I reached the front of the line.

"*G'day?*" I repeated. "Where did a lovely young lady like yourself hear such a barbaric word?"

"Lovely?" Sturgill, her husband, called from the back of the bakery. "You should hear the words she uses in private. You'd never look at her the same—whoa!"

He cut off as he dodged—or was struck by—the pair of tongs Sue hurled at him from around the corner.

She turned back to me with a venomous grin as Sturgill cackled with laughter from the back. "The poor man has an odd sense of humor. I took pity on him, which is why I agreed to marry him—*isn't that right, husband?*"

"Yes, dear!" he called back, still laughing.

She rolled her eyes, but a smile had firmly taken root on her features. "What did you want today, Fischer?"

"Has Roger been by yet?"

"I'm sorry to say he has—he came before dawn." Her smile turned conspiratorial. "If I were a betting woman, I'd guess he was trying to stop a certain fisherman from buying his comely daughter a coffee."

"Hmmm. This fisherman sounds like an intelligent and proactive fella."

"And humble," she added.

"Naturally." Our eyes locked and the twinkle in hers reflected my own. "I suppose I'll just grab a coffee and croissant for me, then."

"Won't be a moment!"

I stepped back as she became a coffee-slinging blur, and when I spun to take in the sun's beauty, an unexpected visitor approached.

"Good morning, Fischer," George said.

"G'day, mate!" I turned to the woman beside him. "Geraldine, right? How's it going?"

She gave me a tight smile. "I am well this morning, thank you."

No one spoke for an awkward moment, and their body language grew slightly agitated.

Oh, no, I thought. *She gets social anxiety too, the poor thing.*

Hoping to make the interaction as carefree for them as possible, I let my mouth do its thing. "Lovely day today, isn't it?" I asked, smiling up at the still-rising sun.

"Y-yes," George replied. "Quite pleasant."

"So," I continued, not leaving a second of downtime for them to overthink. "What are you two up to? Have you come to try Sue's famous coffee and croissant combo?"

"Yes." Geraldine nodded, her features firming. "We have, actually."

I arched an eyebrow. "You have?"

"*You have?*" Sue repeated from behind the coffee machine, her eyes wide.

"Whoa, Sue!" I shot her a smirk. "I didn't take you for the eavesdropping sort."

"Oh, shush." She threw a coffee bean at me. "I can't help but overhear your annoying voice when it prattles away. I was just surprised—the lord and lady of the village have never paid my little bakery a visit."

Geraldine set her jaw. "We mean to rectify that. Is that the line?"

The two farmers in the queue behind me blanched as Geraldine pointed their way.

"It is," I answered.

The married couple shared a glance, nodded, and made their way to the back of the line.

"Good seeing you, Fischer," George said.

Geraldine nodded. "Farewell, Fischer."

It was my turn to feel awkward—they took two steps past me before reaching the end of the line, still very much within arm's length.

"Er, yeah. See you guys . . . later?"

Blessedly, Sue came to my rescue. "Coffee and croissant up, Fischer!"

As I collected my brekkie treats, Sue arched an eyebrow at me, and I just shrugged.

"No clue . . ." I whispered, then shot her a wink. "Good luck."

As I walked past George and Geraldine, I noted the resolute set to their jaws, and when I stepped between the first set of fields, realization struck me.

"Ohhh! They're trying to push past their social anxiety!" I shook my head, feeling a fool for not realizing sooner. "Good for them. I hope it helps them feel more comfortable around people."

Cinnamon's head popped up from my collar. She nodded sagely, agreeing with my assessment.

In a sea of common honeybees, a lone bumblebee flew from flower to flower. The beats of his wings were slow and sporadic, a far cry from his usually steady wingbeats. The simplest answer to his state of being was that he was a long way from home. There was a complicated tale, too: one of a tasty treat, an accidental bee-napping, and a fight for life and death. The bumblebee, being an insect with little to no cognition, was aware of almost none of this, of course.

With a shaky and halting flight, he had been on the verge of his final rest when he caught the scent of something downright delicious in the air—honey. Though the scent of another hive's honey had initially lured him along, something even more enticing soon caught his attention—something that wouldn't require a fight to the death.

Pollen.

Blessed, harvestable pollen. It smelled of home, and following its scent, the bumblebee found a reserve of strength he wasn't aware he possessed. There was a carpet of white flowers spread out before him, and a sea of other bees harvesting pollen from them. Unlike the ground wasps he had encountered, the common honeybees didn't bother him—they were busy collecting the means to feed their hive.

That first sip of nectar had been the most delicious thing he'd ever tasted—better even than the honey he had eaten while confined in the wooden prison. He buzzed with delight, a large portion of his exhaustion falling away like flower petals after pollination.

When his rear legs were filled to the brim with pollen and both his stomachs were filled with nectar, he looked for a nook to create a hive. Once he could create some royal jelly, the bumblebee could recover from his wounded state. More importantly, the royal jelly could attract a mate. Of course, the bumblebee was too far away for the scent of his creation to reach a female of his kind. As always, he was but a bee, so he was blissfully unaware of this tragic detail.

With the promise of survival and the prospect of creating a hive that would attract a mate, the bumblebee took flight, his movement even slower now that his legs were full of blessed pollen. He followed the path of the honeybees, knowing that if he found a nook near their hive, the other colony could serve as a natural defense.

A more devious creature would also consider that the smell of their honey would be much more enticing should a predator come knocking, but this bumblebee just wasn't that sort of insect. Or perhaps he didn't have the requisite brain for devious planning, but the result was ostensibly the same.

The honeybees he followed streamed into a thick trunk, and as he watched their comings and goings, something caught the bumblebee's attention.

Right next to the beehive, set on the grass beside the trunk, was a white box with a tiny hole. No honeybees entered or left the box as the bumblebee made his ponderous approach. The moment he landed on the hole and crawled inside, he knew he had found his new home.

He ambled forward on faltering legs, climbed onto a sheet he could make wax chambers on, and, tapping into his last reserve of strength, began creating his first ever batch of royal jelly.

Beneath the midday sun, I took a deep breath. The fishing club had returned in the morning, and after a couple days of working with her father, Maria had asked for the day off to come fishing. I'd been impressed with Roger's lack of a blow up—he only called me a fool twice during the entire interaction. Well, he had implied it a couple more times, but that was progress.

By our combined efforts, we'd caught four more fish to have for lunch, along with a bunch of undersized ones we let go. The smell of them roasting over the fire made my mouth water.

I'd kept a single juvenile shore fish; it had been bitten by something while Theo reeled it in, and I doubted it would survive. Because of its small size, it had cooked faster than the rest of the fish, and it now sat cooling on the campfire's edge.

Returning my attention to the task at hand, I pressed the head of my small axe down against the tip of some bamboo I'd harvested, and with one last push, a sliver of fibrous material flew off. I glanced down at the bamboo's sharpened end, nodding.

"Excuse me, Fischer," Ellis said.

"What's up?" I asked, peering back at him.

"What exactly are you doing?"

I poked the sharpened end of a bamboo pole into a raw, unscaled fish on the sand before me and lifted it up. "I'm fishing, mate."

He blinked at me for a long moment, and just when I thought he was going to ask another question, he shrugged.

"That's it?" I asked. "You're not going to inquire further?"

Maria snorted. "He's already worked out that asking questions is just going to lead to a frustrating answer, and that he's better off just waiting to see what happens."

"Quite," Ellis agreed, reading his pocketbook.

I leveled a glare at them. "You guys aren't any fun at all."

"In our defense," Theo said. "Your idea of fun is just confusing the frack out of everyone."

"I thought that was everyone's idea of a good time. It's not my fault you guys have terrible taste."

I planted the unsharpened end of bamboo into the sand and started waving it around slowly with the fish high above.

"Okay, I'll bite." Keith's eyes shot between me and the top of the pole. "What on Kallis are you doing?"

"I told you, Keith—fishing."

"Right. What are you fishing for?"

"Birds—well, *a* bird, I guess."

Danny rubbed his chin. "Wouldn't that be called birding?"

"Don't be ridiculous, mate—that's . . ." I cocked my head. "Huh. Yeah, that might actually be correct, but I think *birding* is used by people that like watching birds."

"There are people that like watching birds?" Ellis asked.

Maria rubbed her temples, and when she looked back up at me, I shot her a wink.

Her eyes moved past me, narrowing on something in the distance. "Is that . . . ?"

I turned, and the moment I spied it, a grin split my face.

"Here it comes . . ."

CHAPTER THIRTY-FOUR

ABDUCTION

The sun high above cast a broad shadow as the pelican circled the sky around my patented fish-on-a-pole technology. It flew around a few more times, then swooped down, landing on the sand gracefully for such an enormous bird.

The pelican looked up at the fish, then back down at me. Its head turned to the side, its inhuman eye weighing me. I slowly lowered the pole, shuffling it backward until I could grab the fish and throw it toward the bird.

I held the fish in one hand as I reached down with the other to grab the cooked fish from the campfire's edge, then threw the raw fish to the bird. With a snap of its beak, the fish disappeared into the pelican's pouch, and its neck bobbed up and down, the fish vanishing down its gullet. I licked my lips and held my breath as I grabbed the cooked fish from the fire, then held it up in offering. The pelican watched it intently, and with an underhand throw, I threw it to the bird.

It didn't catch it.

The fish landed with a soft *thud* on the sand as the pelican flapped its wings and waddled to the side. It stepped in close after the sand had settled, peering down at the cooked fish. It poked the flesh with its spiked beak, but when the meat parted, it lost all interest and returned its attention to me.

"It's fish!" I gestured down at the abandoned meal. "You like fish!"

It glanced around at everyone, and seeing no more snacks forthcoming, the pelican turned and took flight.

I let out a sigh. "Picky thing . . ."

Maria laid a hand on my shoulder. "What is it you said to me once? There's always more fish in the sea?"

"Or birds in the sky," Danny offered, entirely unhelpfully.

"But I don't want just any old bird—I wanna be pals with that one!" I yelled, intentionally petulant.

Maria petted me, nodding her understanding. "You'll just have to keep birding, dear."

High above the waves, a pelican soared on unseen currents of air. After spending the morning hunting for food, he had been on the way back to his roost when a silver gleam caught his attention—the unmistakable flash of fish scales. Naturally, the pelican had gone to investigate.

He now had a belly full of fish and was on an express path to a well-deserved nap.

The weird, two-legged creature was as clumsy as ever, and it had fumbled another delicious meal the pelican's way. It had dropped something else, too, but after investigating, the pelican deemed it inedible. It had smelled good, but lacked even the smallest of reflective scales, which was just unacceptable.

As he caught sight of his nest on the cliffside overhang he'd called home for as long as he could remember, bile rose in his gullet.

Someone had invaded his home.

He beat his wings, climbing higher into the air to get a better view. Two birds sat among his carefully curated twigs, their brown feathers an anathematic stain on the illustrious nest. They were similar to his wondrous form; both birds had long beaks with large pouches that could expand to scoop up fish. As with their feathers, though, the pouches were a dirty shade of brown.

The closer he got to the two pelicans rearranging his nest, the more incensed he became. By the time he landed beside them, rational thought had been replaced by the immutable desire to evict them and reclaim his territory. He let out a mighty grunt and clacked his bill together, asserting his dominance.

If an outside observer had been present, they would have seen an awkward and gangly battle. Overlarge bills lashed out, webbed feet scrambled for purchase, and feathers flew. After only a short exchange of ineffective blows, the white and black pelican withdrew, overwhelmed by its two adversaries.

If a bird could feel shame, the oceanic pelican certainly did. He retreated back toward the north, intent on finding a place to lick his proverbial wounds.

"What are you guys up to for the rest of the day?" I asked, savoring the flavor of the fish we'd just eaten.

"We have some business to attend to, unfortunately," Ellis replied, similarly lounging.

Theo let out a sigh. "I wish we could spend the day fishing, but Ellis is right."

"No worries," I said, then turned to Maria. "You too?"

"Unfortunately. I got the morning off, but if I'm gone this afternoon too, Dad might have an apoplectic fit."

"The last thing I want to do is set your dad off—I feel like he's finally coming around to me."

She laughed. "That's one way of putting it, but I think each time you buy us all breakfast is two steps back."

"Ah," Theo said. "In-law troubles—a universal constant."

I sent a smirk Maria's way, but she gazed down at the sand, a furious blush rising to her cheeks. I wondered at the response. She had taken every previous insinuation of us being in a relationship in stride, often joking along.

Theo noticed her reaction and immediately turned a meaning-laden grin my way. I glared at him, but it only made his grin intensify.

Peter, the ever-empathetic chef, took pity on me—or perhaps her. "What will you get up to for the rest of the day, Fischer?"

I smiled at him, pointedly not looking at Maria. "I have a few projects going on that I've been neglecting, so I might take a trip to the smithy and have a little wander afterward."

"All right," Theo said, getting to his feet and brushing sand from his pants. "Shall we, gentlemen?"

We said our goodbyes, and as the fishing club strode away, I turned to Maria. "Are you okay?"

Her hands were intertwined in front of her, and she nodded.

"I'm fine, just have a lot of work to do, is all. I'll see you later."

"Yeah . . . see ya later."

She chewed her lip for a moment, then darted forward and gave me a light kiss on the cheek. She barely made contact, then turned and walked away, her posture rigid.

I stared after her, wondering at the shift in demeanor.

As I pottered around beneath the early afternoon sun, my overactive mind was left pleasantly occupied by the sun's warmth, the cool breeze, and the feeling of sand beneath my bare feet.

I lost myself further as I walked between rows of sugarcane. My vision was engulfed by their swaying leaves and the soft rustle they made when sliding against one another. By the time I reached the smithy, there was a pleasant smile stretched across my face.

"G'day, fellas," I said, stepping inside.

Fergus had his goggles on and was removing a bar of red-hot metal from the forge. Duncan was bending a thin piece of iron at the back of the workshop by hitting it with a hammer. At my words, both men's heads shot to me, and a silence sprang into being, then stretched out uncomfortably.

"You guys all right?" I asked, letting out a small laugh. "You look like you've seen a ghost."

"Sorry, Fischer," Fergus replied, lifting his metal and taking it over to the anvil. "I was in the zone and you surprised me."

"Aye," Duncan said. "Same."

Fergus lifted a small hammer and started striking the still-red metal, focusing on its square angles to smooth it out.

I waited for him to finish, and after a few moments of the hammer falling, he placed the bar back into the forge. He smiled at me as he removed his goggles and gloves, coming over to meet me at his bench.

"What can I do for you?"

"Remember those cages we made a few weeks back? I created six of them."

He gave me an unreadable look that was quickly swept away. "Aye, I remember. Is there something wrong with them? We can always patch—"

I held up both hands, cutting him off. "Nah, mate. They're perfect. I want more."

"More, huh . . . ?" He rubbed his bearded chin. "We're running a bit low on bars, so you might need to wait for the merchant's visit—it's only a few days out."

"That's all good, my man! I don't want to leave you without the materials for your regular jobs, but I'm happy to pay, as always."

"Well, how many do you want to make?"

I gave him a wide grin. "*All* of them."

His eyes narrowed. "Define what you mean by all of them . . ."

"Just that," I replied, laughing. "I want to make as many as you have the metal to facilitate."

He shook his head at me with a small smile.

"I'm not sure Marcus will stock enough mesh for *all* of them. I'm sure he'd be happy to make a custom order if you pay upfront, but that would mean you'd need to wait another month for their delivery."

"That's all good, my man! I'd love to make them as soon as possible, but there's no rush if the materials can't be sourced."

He nodded as he strode back to the forge, putting his gloves and goggles back on before removing the glowing-red bar.

"Is there anything else I can help you with?"

"Hmmm. There was something else I wanted to make, but if you're low on materials, it might need to wait until after the merchant's visit."

"Oh? What did you want to create?" he asked, striding back toward his anvil.

"A bloody big barbecue plate, mate."

" . . . a what?"

"I'll tell you all about it when you have the materials." I grinned and waved goodbye. "See ya later, fellas!"

"Oh. Right. Bye, then . . ." Fergus said.

"Bye, Fischer!" Duncan yelled from the back of the workshop, giving me an exuberant wave with one hand.

I shook my head as I stepped beneath the shade of the forest canopy.

"Everyone's a little off today . . ." I mused, thinking back on both the smiths and Maria. I breathed a slow sigh, then inhaled the cool, earth-scented air always present between the trees. "Ah well. Nothing to be done about it, I suppose."

The further I strode from the sand flats, the more distant my worries grew, and before I knew it, the sound of constant buzzing came rolling out between the trees' sturdy trunks. I smiled and picked up the pace. When I caught sight of the beehive, both my eyebrows tried to leave my face.

"Wow, you lot are some busy bees today, huh?"

I smirked at myself, watching the stream of bees leaving and returning to the tree they called home. The industrious little insects were always active, but never this much; a veritable cloud of the honeybees milled around the hive's entrance, waiting for their turn to enter the tiny opening.

I couldn't help but feel a little disappointed when I looked down at the hive I'd made. Not a single bee came or went from its entrance; the colony had yet to expand into it.

Carefully stepping around the back of the tree, I made my way to the unoccupied hive and, with the glacial speed of an iceberg, lifted its lid. As I had expected, there was no sign of life within, so I replaced the lid, not wanting to get my scent anywhere on the internal components.

Just as I let go of the wooden lid, I heard a buzzing that stuck out from the symphony of noise the honeybees were making. I cocked my head to the side, just in time for something small, yellow, black, and furious to fly directly at my head.

The bumblebee's stomachs were full and his legs were absolutely covered in pollen as he made his way home. His hive was well and truly under construction—he had even produced the first few drops of his mate-attracting royal jelly. He happily bobbed along within the stream of common honeybees.

But that all changed when he caught sight of his home.

A giant stood behind it and was actively breaking in. His royal jelly had attracted someone, all right, but it wasn't a mate—it was a *predator.* The bumblebee saw red and his wingbeats increased in frequency.

He charged, willing to risk it all for his hive.

I leaned back from the angry bee, one hand darting up of its own accord. I caught it between my thumb and index finger, narrowing my eyes as I peered down to inspect the clearly irate insect. It was too large to be a regular bee. Its mandibles opened and closed as it turned its head every which way, trying to get a hold of my fingers. It vibrated within my grasp, still making the low buzzing sound that had alerted me to its presence.

"Angry little dude, huh?"

I thought for a moment that it might be a soldier of the regular bees, but it was too large and different to be the same species. I realized it hadn't stung me, so I looked at its abdomen. It was trying to grip me with its legs and barbed feet, but was lacking the requisite stinger to inject me with venom.

"What even are you? A bumblebee?"

The only response was more buzzing and attempts to bite me, so I decided it was time to let go. I softly pitched it away, hoping it would continue flying in that direction now that it was released.

The bumblebee had different ideas.

It turned on a dime and flew straight for my head again, and I ducked out of the way, letting it soar above. I spun to watch it. The bumblebee spun too, but it didn't have curiosity in its heart; it had only violence in mind. I ducked again, avoiding the tenacious little thing. Ensuring I didn't hurt it, I ran away, giggling the entire time. The bumblebee trailed, emitting the same low drone as I escaped its pursuit.

The pelican soared down to a familiar headland, gliding on the wind to preserve its strength. It may have possessed the brain of a bird, but it still dreamed of justice. After resting, it could attempt to win possession of its nest once more—no, it *had* to reclaim its nest.

It angled low over the waves, and with a few flaps of its broad wings, the pelican landed atop the headland's raised rocks. It lowered itself and got comfortable—well, as comfortable as it could be without being in a carefully crafted nest of twigs and grasses.

Just as the pelican closed its eyes, something hard grabbed it by the neck. The pelican tried to escape, tried to kick and bite its attacker, but it was pinned tight. It attempted to grunt and screech, to make a fuss loud enough to scare off its ambusher, but all that came out was a strained growl.

Its attacker, strong as a rock and immutable as the passage of time, dragged it away.

CHAPTER THIRTY-FIVE

LIBERATION

Wind rushed past me as I ran from the canopy's protection and out into the afternoon sun. With each step I took, a plan came together. I was home in no time, and as I entered the kitchen, I beheld a scene of pure chaos.

Sergeant Snips was hissing loudly while softly pulling at Rocky. I raised an eyebrow—she was never one to pull her punches when chastising the insubordinate crustacean.

When I saw what Rocky held, I understood.

His claws and most of his legs were wrapped around a pelican, while his free limbs wrestled with the lid of a pot. He was attempting to shove the bird inside, but Snips was stopping him from doing so, using her strength sparingly so she didn't hurt the panicked bird. Metal clanged against metal, Snips hissed urgently, and the pelican made low grunts. The sounds combined and bounced off the walls in a tumultuous cacophony.

"What the fuck, Rocky?"

At my voice, everyone froze—except for the pelican, who took the opportunity to try to escape. It was no use; Rocky was a black belt in whatever godsforsaken jujitsu he was using to restrain the bird.

Snips blew a small stream of pleading bubbles at me. Her eye was frantic, showing genuine worry for the bird's safety.

"Rocky," I said, appearing at his side. "You need to let go."

He blew his own stream of bubbles as he looked between me and the pelican, hissing quietly. The frustration in his message was clear, but a deep confusion was even more prevalent.

At once, I understood.

"Oh. I get it. You caught the pelican so I could feed it food and awaken it, right? That's . . . I mean, the intention was nice, I suppose, but this is the wrong way to go about it, mate. We can't catch wild creatures and force them to . . ."

I trailed off as Rocky started shaking. Laughter hissed out from his treacherous little mouth. When the hisses subsided, he shook his head, then mimed eating something with his claw.

I gave him a flat look. "You just wanted to eat it."

He nodded, shrugging as if to say *duh.*

"Let go of the bird, Rocky. Now."

His mouth parts undulated in annoyance, but after only a moment of further consideration, he released the stunned pelican into my arms. As soon as he was clear of the bird, Snips jumped him. She held him down against the bench, looking up at me for orders.

"Your call, Snips. He technically listened to my orders not to harm any wildlife—if we ignore psychological trauma, anyway."

She nodded and started carrying him outside, no doubt intending to throw him into orbit. She didn't need to restrain his limbs because he wouldn't go against her wishes now that a potential meal wasn't involved, meaning both his claws were free. He used this freedom to make rather rude and threatening gestures as she hauled him out of the kitchen and through the back door.

I looked down at the pelican in my arms, who was silently staring up at me.

"I'm sorry, mate. If Snips or I weren't here, that little idiot might have turned you into a rotisserie chicken." It blinked as I ran one hand over the back of its head, trying to soothe it. "All right—let's set you free."

It didn't struggle as I walked it outside. Snips was down at the riverbank, chastising the quarrelsome Rocky. I couldn't hear the intent in her hisses from so far away, but Rocky was shrinking beneath the onslaught. It was the closest thing to genuine remorse I'd ever seen on the crab. Before I could consider it any further, Snips flew into action.

Blue power flowed from her carapace, then sharpened and flared backward. Her body shot at Rocky, and she grabbed him in both claws, spinning to gain momentum. Their bodies became a blur, and just when I thought they wouldn't go any faster, she released. Rocky resembled nothing so much as a beyblade as he soared out over the ocean.

Or perhaps a frisbee, I thought, watching his limbs splayed outward from centrifugal force.

The pelican tried to move its head, so I let it go. "Please don't bite me . . ."

Instead of violence, its head moved to track Rocky's forced departure. For a second, I thought it was growing friendly, but I grimaced when I realized it was likely shock or exhaustion stopping it from trying to escape.

I strode down to the ocean with smooth movements and dug in the sand, quickly finding the bait I'd buried there. The pelican peered down at the pungent eel as I bent to pick it up. I washed the sand from it in the river, then offered it to the pelican.

It didn't open its beak, merely staring at the lifeless bait.

I let out another sigh. "I'll probably never see you again after the treatment Rocky gave you, but I hope you live a long and happy life." I set the eel down on the sand beside the pelican and backed away. "Sorry again for the trouble, mate."

The pelican fluffed its feathers and shook itself, stretching its wings. It turned away and flapped, then paused. Almost as an afterthought, it tested the eel with its overlarge bill. In a single swift movement, it scooped the eel up. The bait disappeared down its gullet, and it spared me one last glance before taking flight.

With heavy beats of its wings, the pelican rose into the air above the river mouth.

It flew to the south, and I stood watching until it was a speck in the far distance. Snips came to stand beside me, and she patted me on the leg reassuringly.

"Thanks, Snips. It's okay, though." I rubbed the top of her carapace. "A pelican pal would have been neat, but I guess it wasn't meant to be."

I scooped her up, and she settled into the cradle of my arm.

"Are you free for a bit? There's something I wanna try—it might be a pleasant distraction."

She gazed up at me, blowing inquisitive bubbles.

I smiled and rubbed her head. "Remember those bees I showed a while back? I have a plan."

Snips pointed at the jar in my other hand as I carried her over the sands. Her eye was filled with curiosity, and she blew a questioning bubble.

"It's sugar water," I explained. "Bees should love it, and I'm hoping to lure them into the hive I made. I have no clue if honeybees will even expand into another hive, but maybe they do, or perhaps I can lure another queen to make a hive there?" I shrugged. "It's worth a crack."

She dipped her claw into the sludge and tasted it. Her mouth pieces moved as she considered the sweet flavor, then she shook her head, blowing negative bubbles.

I laughed. "Not a fan of sweets, huh? It might've tasted better to you if I used sugar from Barry's sequestered crop, but I intentionally used regular old sugar."

Why, she asked with a hiss.

"Because I don't want to awaken a bunch of bees accidentally. Who knows what would happen if a cultivator bee stung a villager."

She nodded along with my train of thought. I ran a hand along the top of her head, and she leaned into it, letting out a soft noise of delight.

"I'll be silent when we get to the box, all right? I don't want to spook the bees. Also, I got attacked by a bumblebee earlier when I was there."

She perked up, casting her gaze about and opening her claws in anticipation.

"Don't worry," I laughed, tickling her head with a finger. "It can't hurt either of us—I just don't want to accidentally smoosh it."

When we caught sight of the honeybees streaming to and from the tree, Snips's eye gleamed. She watched them intently as I strode wide around their hive, giving them plenty of space.

I set her down on the grass and crept forward, keeping my ears peeled for the telltale drone of the bumblebee's approach. All I could hear was the constant buzz of the honeybees, so I silently lifted the hive's lid. I poured half the sugar water down the back wall, then tipped more in the corners closest to the entrance.

The entire time, I dreamed of honey.

If a bumblebee could feel pride, he would have preened. The insect had protected his home by chasing away the giant invader. A more intelligent being may have worried about the glee with which the invader retreated; the bumblebee held no such concern.

He was hunched toward the back of his hive, completely absorbed in the creation of his royal jelly, when the invader returned. His roof was ripped off, and the bumblebee froze.

All of his energy was going into his royal jelly, so he lacked the means to defend himself or chase away the attacker. All he could do was sit and hope the giant didn't find him or his blessed batch of jelly. Something oozed down beside him, and he stepped forward, putting himself between the invading force and the fruits of his labor. It poured toward him, and he walked toward it on painfully sluggish legs. He bit into the growing puddle with his mandibles as it reached him.

The moment he did, he paused—it was delicious.

He immediately began drinking it, refilling his now-empty stomachs. It was so tasty that he completely forgot about the invader.

As he continued drinking, the roof was placed back atop his hive, and darkness returned.

I scooped up Snips and snuck away with hushed steps.

"Mission accomplished," I whispered, holding up a fist which Snips bumped with a claw.

I took us back around to the front of the hive, and we stood there together in companionable silence, watching the hypnotic flight of the honeybees.

After a few moments, I hummed contentedly. "Should we get going? Maybe we can see how that tree spirit thingy is doing on the way back."

She blew a steady stream of anticipatory bubbles, and I let out a laugh.

"I feel the same—let's go."

As we made our way beneath the forest canopy, there were honeybees absolutely everywhere.

"The little suckers are active, huh?"

Snips nodded, her eye once more transfixed by their movement. We walked past Corporal Claws's favored pond, and I wondered about her whereabouts as I stared at the empty perch she had taken to sleeping on. My unspoken question was almost immediately answered as an otter, wreathed in lightning and grinning malevolently, slammed into my chest.

"*Oof!*"

I stumbled backward, having not been expecting the blow. Claws writhed in my arms, rubbing herself against both me and Snips rather aggressively.

"I was just thinking about you, Claws," I said, beaming at her. "What have you been up to?"

She shrugged coyly, giving me a sidelong glance.

"Ooh, a secret?" I reached a hand up to rub my chin. "It wouldn't have anything to do with the tree, would it?"

She froze, blinked rapidly, then gave an unconvincing chirp.

"Not the tree, huh? I guess it won't matter if we go have a peek at its progress, then—"

Her body went rigid and her eyes flew wide.

I barked a laugh. "You have a terrible poker face, Claws."

She opened and closed her mouth, searching for the chirps that would convince me her secret activities weren't tree-spirit related, but then she slumped and let out a resigned coo.

I laughed again. "It's fine, Claws. We don't have to go see the tree if you're cooking up a surprise."

She sighed in relief.

I scratched both her and Snips's heads. "I love you girls—you know that, right?"

They chirped and hissed their affections back at me, their companionship making my chest warm and my steps light.

As the pelican flew above the ocean, the sun began to set. After the earlier encounter, he hadn't felt safe enough to land. He rested while soaring on unseen currents, letting the food in his stomach digest. An odd sensation bubbled up within his abdomen, but he ignored it.

Though the eel presented by the two-legged creature hadn't been covered in scales, the pelican recognized it as a fish he had hunted on numerous occasions. He had never been able to actually catch one, so he'd snatched it up before taking flight.

The odd sensation in his abdomen swelled, and the pelican considered landing to regurgitate the meal.

He didn't have the chance.

White light engulfed him, and a loud *pop* tore into existence, cutting through the wind's ever-present howling.

CHAPTER THIRTY-SIX

INVADERS

When the pelican's awareness returned, he was gliding on unseen currents high above the ocean. The sun was setting over the western mountains, and as he gazed at the surrounding sky, the colors struck him as . . . beautiful?

That was an odd thought—as was the recognition of thought at all, he realized. Information was blossoming in his mind.

As he continued riding unseen winds, the few drops of information grew into a trickle, then from a trickle to a small stream. Meanwhile, he gazed out at the wondrous landscape below. The sky was a deep orange immediately around the sun's enlarged form, and it faded to mixed tones of pink and purple that slowly bled to blue to the east.

East . . .

He tasted the word as it coursed through his awareness. He had always known directions—it was an inherent function of his body—yet he'd never had words to describe them. The sun lowered further, and the colors shifted again, the blue fading to lilac. As he circled in the wind, his burgeoning intelligence only grew, and his thoughts turned to the strange two-legged creature—human—that he'd been interacting with over the last few days.

It hadn't been a mistake each time a fish had come sailing his way; the human had been intentionally sharing food. More astounding were the human's other actions. When the pelican was grappling with a crab he now *knew* had intended to eat him, the human had saved him, even chastised the crab for the attempt. As had the spiky crab, who appeared to be the murderous crustacean's boss.

Thinking back on it, there had been several creatures that were also awakened. Their actions spoke of higher awareness, as well as physical prowess transcending the limits of regular animals.

The pelican flapped its wings, testing his body. It was hard to tell if it was his imagination, but he certainly felt larger and stronger. The pelican knew of one way to find out for certain; his eyes narrowed, and he angled down, pinning his wings in a dive toward the ground.

A brown pelican looked on lovingly at her partner as she settled down in their new nest. She was the most desirable of her entire flock, which was the reason he had chosen her. Her mate was the strongest bird she had ever seen, making him the ideal partner. The moment he chose to be one of her suitors, the others hadn't stood a chance. The courtship walks, swims, and flights had only solidified her choice, and after they had paired off, they left for distant lands to find a suitable nesting spot.

For weeks they'd flown, a feat only possible because of their physical superiority. They traveled far from any of the territories their species frequented, even crossing a vast stretch of ocean to arrive where they were. The instant she spied the cliff—and the pitifully decorated nest atop it—she knew they'd found the place to hatch a clutch of eggs.

As she sat in the nest they'd just finished renovating, her mate sat on the edge of the cliff, overlooking their lands. His feathers were slightly puffed, giving him an impressive silhouette against the setting sun.

Even rocketing toward the ground like an arrow in flight, information continued to pour into the newly awakened pelican's mind. All manner of anecdotes, memories, and data points streamed in, finding places to nest within his brain. Some seemed useless, and he wondered at their necessity. Other information, however, was almost unbelievable in its timeliness.

Focusing on one such memory, he adjusted his form as he approached his target. He retracted one leg while extending the other forward. His wings stretched behind him, pointing skyward. Finally, he tucked his head against his body with his beak running along his stomach and angled toward his leading foot.

His speed was tremendous, and his eyes sparkled with delight as his target got closer and closer.

Vengeance was nigh.

With her partner watching the land for danger, the female pelican laid her first egg. She would lay more over the coming days, and given the strength of both parents, each of their glorious chicks should survive to maturity. She stood for a moment, gazing down to make sure it was still there. It was, and she honked her joy out at the world. Her partner looked back at her, and they shared a blissful moment, their pride overwhelming them.

With his eyes locked on her, the male pelican had no hope of seeing the blur of white and black retribution that rocketed from above to land a flying kick of immaculate form. A pitiful *honk* escaped her mate's throat as he was thrown from the ledge, leaving behind only a handful of brown feathers and his pride.

The female blinked at the bird now standing in his place among the falling feathers. He flapped his wings, and in his eyes, she saw death.

She took flight with honks of alarm, her maternal instincts entirely swept away before the weight of self-preservation.

The white and black pelican watched the brown interlopers retreat over the ocean. Not wanting to injure a creature so far beneath him, he'd slowed himself at the last possible moment. He was grateful he had. The blow had been more than he was expecting, and if he used even an ounce more strength, the male brown pelican would have been killed on impact.

He collected his foe's feathers from the ground and hopped toward his nest. They had ruined his home, filling it with undesirable grasses that would itch his delicate feet. Worse, they'd left something else behind that made his blood boil—an egg. He looked down at it with conflicting thoughts. It was the product of his two hated enemies, yet given they'd come here to reproduce, it was likely fertile. He felt the urge to expel it, to fling it from his overhang and be done with it.

But his newly found empathy railed against the compulsion.

He removed each offending strand of grass from his nest and replaced them with his brown trophies of war, ensuring he didn't jostle or damage the egg. With grumpy resignation, he lowered himself to sit atop his adversaries' progeny.

He no longer fit in his own nest, so he shot to his feet in a huff. As he bent down to fix whatever vile renovations the egg's mother had enacted, he paused, blinking. The nest was exactly the same; it was his body that had grown. He started moving sticks around, and as he did so, he realized it wasn't just his size that had changed. His bill was longer, the webbing of his feet seemed thicker, and at the end of his gloriously enlarged bill, there was a downward curving spike.

With his chest held high and his feathers puffed out, he lowered himself into the adjusted nest, taking care not to damage the egg.

Within the seclusion of his hive, the bumblebee feasted. He knew not where the delicious treat had come from, but neither did he care—such were not the musings of a bumblebee. Each time he filled his stomachs, he would return to his royal jelly, using the contents of one stomach and some of the pollen on his legs to craft more of his magnum opus. When he would finish, his stomach and crop were both empty, so he refilled them once more.

He continued on like this all night, losing himself to the process as he gradually turned the sugar water into his mate-attracting royal jelly. When most of it was finished, and only a small section of one puddle remained, the bumblebee froze.

An alien sensation swelled within.

The bumblebee's wings buzzed with anxiety, and he braced himelf, waiting for an attacker to make itself known. Instead, a white light engulfed him, and a soft *pop* echoed off the wooden walls of his hive. The bumblebee stilled once more. He gazed around his hive, looking for the attacker he thought may be there, but then the trickle of information began pouring in. The bumblebee hunched down, going completely still as it processed the trickle-turned-stream flooding his awareness.

Hours later, when he realized just how far he was from his lands, and that he'd been taken on an overseas trip, despair took the bumblebee. He hadn't seen any other bumblebees since arriving in this land. When he considered the nectar and pollen offered by the flowers here, it wasn't surprising; even if a bumblebee somehow made it over the ocean, they would soon starve to death unless they found the lone patch of trees he had.

The bumblebee was all alone.

He sat with that fact for a long time. The only movement in the hive was that of his wings when they sporadically moved and stretched of their own accord. Just as the cloud in his mind threatened to engulf him, he forced his awareness toward other things. The easiest target was the strange man that had been peering down into the hive he called home.

Now that the bumblebee had received a torrent of information over the past few hours, he knew that the box he crafted his royal jelly in wasn't a natural object. It had all the trappings of a man-made creation and was likely built by the human he'd attacked when still a simple insect. Considering the human had added a sweet liquid, and the internal trays of the hive appeared to be made specifically for crafting honeycomb atop, the bumblebee was fairly certain the human was trying to lure honeybees inside.

Now that he thought about it, similar man-made objects existed in the land he'd come from. A flash of a memory told him he'd glimpsed the inside of one, perhaps when it was being constructed, perhaps after it was cracked open by a predator. It had been nowhere near as advanced as the one this strange human created.

Strange . . . the bumblebee thought.

If nothing else, the human was definitely an oddity. When the bumblebee had attacked with the blind fury of an insect having its home invaded, the man had simply caught him, let him go, then run away, giggling. He was a cultivator, as was the title for anyone able to move with such speed and grace. From the information pouring into his mind, this was not how cultivators acted—they were supposed to be egotistical, aggressive, and vengeful. It made no sense.

As the bumblebee further considered the man's actions, he began idly making more royal jelly. The process was smoother now that he had more knowledge, and he was able to concentrate it by absorbing the liquid from his crop into his stomach. He used an empty honeycomb for the new batch, and as the process continued, his thoughts disappeared.

The bumblebee lost himself to his work, focused entirely on creating the best royal jelly possible. He dismissed the nagging voice telling him there was no point. Even if there were no females on this land, he'd just have to make jelly potent enough to lure them from over the ocean. Just as he was pushing the last mouthful into the comb before sealing it, a low droning erupted outside.

The bumblebee listened for a long moment—something had the honeybees in an uproar.

With curiosity tugging at the bumblebee, he crawled out of his hive's entrance. The honeybees' furious droning came from within the hive. Only a few bees were outside, and they huddled around the entrance into the tree. He buzzed in close, his body tilting to the side in confusion as he watched them work.

The honeybees on the outside were chewing at a yellow gunk that plugged the hole. As the bees tried to bite at and clear it, the sticky substance got caught in their mandibles, leaving them useless. Suddenly, the noise of the hive bloomed even louder. It was coming from the other side of the tree, so he zipped around it.

The sound was coming from a hole at the hive's rear that he'd never seen before. He wondered if the bees had successfully bored an exit, but then he caught movement inside. Something black, orange, and entirely too large to be a honeybee ambled past. A predator had infiltrated the honeybee's hive. Despite it not being his hive, righteous fury rushed forth, and the bumblebee flew for the hole.

The moment he was inside, he dashed directly for the giant hornet's neck. It saw him coming, yet never stood a chance. The bumblebee bit down at the base of its head, severing its body in two. He didn't pause for even a second, continuing on toward the angry buzz of wings further in. The bodies of worker bees were strewn all over, meeting a similar end to the hornet he had dispatched. With each lifeless insect he passed, he grew more incensed. To create honey was a noble calling, and the fallen honeybees lining the tunnel had only been trying to protect and serve their hive.

These invaders, on the other hand, were predators. Some species of hornet were peaceful, even shy creatures. Given the effectiveness of their attack, these hornets were anything but. They'd plugged the hole after the bees had returned for the night, then chewed their way through the back of the hive like it was made of soft wax.

If he knew hornets—which, due to the steady stream of knowledge pouring into his mind, he did—the invaders would go for the queen. The death of the honeybee's matriarch would mean the slow death of the entire colony if another wasn't raised, so he increased his pace, becoming a blur between ancient layers of comb and wood. When the bumblebee entered a golden chamber, he paused, his eyes wanting to linger on the walls of honey surrounding him.

But then he saw the bodies.

The lifeless forms of what had to be hundreds of workers lined the room, and it made his wings undulate in outrage. A dozen or so remained alive, and they gathered around their matriarch, doing their best to shield her from a single giant hornet. All the bumblebee could do was watch as another hornet appeared from a tunnel above and lunged, plunging its stinger right into the queen's abdomen.

The bumblebee's fury turned to wrath, and his body flew into action. He appeared above the hornet and bit down on the back of its neck, easily severing the head. He spun, looking for the other hornet, but it found him.

The last invader had broken through the line of defenders and had moved to defend its brethren. Its stinger was buried in his abdomen, bulging as it pumped venom into him.

At once, the pain hit him.

CHAPTER THIRTY-SEVEN

AIRSTRIKE

The smell of honey within the hive was almost as intense as the pain lancing the bumblebee's side. With speed the hornet couldn't hope to match, the bumblebee retreated. The envenomed stinger pulled from his abdomen, and sharp lines of agony ran the length of his body. He ignored them. He buzzed behind the hornet's back at diminished speed, just fast enough that the invader couldn't react in time. The bumblebee's mandibles tore through the exoskeleton connecting the hornet's head to its body, and both parts of it fell to the floor, lifeless.

Every worker left in the chamber was either dead or dying, and the queen stood among a bed of fallen drones, the stingless males whose job it was to mate with the queen. Despite their lack of stingers, they had stood to defend their matriarch.

For their selflessness, they had been slaughtered.

The scene stirred something within the bumblebee, and he decided then and there to do everything he could to save the queen. The buzz of workers came from elsewhere within the hive, but with their numbers so diminished, they likely lacked the resources to raise another leader.

The bumblebee flew onto the queen's back, fighting off the pain lancing through him as he grabbed hold of her thorax. She struggled, but even if he wasn't awakened, she would have been too weak to escape. The bumblebee took flight, perhaps for the last time, and he flew out of the chamber. He moved as fast as possible, yet it was still agonizingly slow because of the wound in his side. All the while, spears of pain shot from his body and out into each limb.

The venom was spreading.

When they exited the hive, the first rays of daylight were filtering down through the canopy above. It should have been a time of activity for the honeybees, but as he flew wide around the entrance, not a single insect could be seen. Those that had been trying to clear the sticky substance from the opening lay on the grass below, their bodies twitching.

The bumblebee fought off a surge of despair, knowing it would only hinder his flight and put the queen at risk if his wings vibrated with his true feelings. When they reached his man-made hive, he put the queen down gently, crawled inside, and dragged her within.

He lifted the queen to his comb with halting movements; his limbs twitched as the venom wreaked havoc on his nervous system. When they reached the combs of royal jelly, the bumblebee paused. Even with his own body failing, his instincts screamed to protect his precious liquid, to leave it there for the bumblebee princess that would one day answer its call.

Ignoring his every base instinct, he lowered the queen's head into the last batch of royal jelly he'd made—his most potent brew. His eyes grew unfocused and his compound vision overlapped as the venom bore deeper into him. The moment he saw the queen's proboscis extend in response to the royal jelly's unmatched sweetness, he turned his attention to the other combs.

Whether it was his vision or his body shaking, he didn't know. That question was immediately answered when his legs gave out, and he fell down into one of the earlier batches of royal jelly. He pushed his straw-like appendage out, rejoicing when it reached the sweet liquid just beneath him.

He drank, and even with his body failing him, his wings quivered in delight—his royal jelly was more delicious than he could have ever imagined. More of the viscous goo traveled into his stomach, warming him from within and combating the lines of venom racing up and down his body.

As the first rays of light peeked over the eastern horizon, the pelican stirred. He opened his eyes, and with his groggy mind slowly clearing, he recalled the events of the previous day. He shifted his body and peered down, confirming that there was, in fact, an egg there. His bill stretched wide with a colossal yawn as he shook his feathers out. He had stayed up later last night than he'd have liked to, but that was only natural.

There had been a lot to consider.

Before the blessed darkness of rest took him, he'd reached a decision. He stood to his full height, stretching his wings and bathing in the predawn glow of the day to come. Before the egg could cool, he bent down and carefully clutched it in his beak. Stretching his head high, his adversaries' unhatched child disappeared into his pouch.

He took flight, scanning the surrounding cliffs for an appropriate-sized rock as he headed north.

The soft smile on my face grew as the sun poked the top of its head over the ocean. By some miracle, all of my animal pals had assembled to watch the sunrise with me.

"No, I'm serious," I said, looking at the mixed look of confusion and awe on Claws's face. "Rocky really tried to get me to cook that pelican."

Claws cackled with chittering laughter and leaned up against the crab in question. His clackers opened, showing his annoyance, but the cantankerous crustacean wisely decided not to pinch her—she was likely to do more than just yeet him out toward the depths.

I didn't miss the hint of a smile curling Cinnamon's lip as she shuffled back into the warmth of my lap; she also found the tale enjoyable. Snips shook her head and started hissing away at Claws, no doubt commiserating about the struggles of having such a devious subordinate. Claws nodded and chirped in response, petting the top of Snips's carapace reassuringly.

I watched them both. Only weeks ago, their relationship had been strained, to say the least. Snips was a straightforward sort, while Claws had the heart of a trickster buried deep within her chest. Their friendship had been blossoming lately and it sparked joy deep in my soul. As their chittered and hissed conversation continued—and Rocky's body hunched further down into the sand in frustration—I turned toward Pistachio.

The Leviathan lobster was as stoic as ever, and rather than watch or take part in the morning's hijinks, his unreadable gaze was turned toward the colorful sky above.

"How are you doing, Pistachio? We haven't had a chat in a while."

He blew a single bubble I took to mean *good.*

"Yeah? Glad to hear it, my man. The sunrise is always stunning, isn't it?"

He made a so-so gesture.

"Not that into it, huh?"

In response, he turned to look at me, cocking his head as if considering something. His eyes shifted back toward the sky, and he pointed upward with a single claw. Raising an eyebrow, I glanced up just in time to see the descending boulder.

If I'd been expecting it, maybe I would have been able to stop it, but my brain simply watched the falling rock, unable to process its mysterious existence. I'm sure Pistachio could have stopped it too, given the power and accuracy his rifle of a claw held. Instead, we were both spectators as it slammed down atop Rocky's head.

The thump was so mighty I felt its reverberations in the sand, and we all went silent, looking at the boulder occupying the spot that Rocky had been a moment ago. The rock shook, shuddered, then exploded into a million pieces. I shielded my eyes with one hand and Cinnamon with the other. When the pebbles and dust were no longer forming, I peered out through slitted vision.

Rocky stood upright in a crater, body heaving up and down as a constant stream of pissed-off bubbles frothed from his undulating mouth.

Claws, Snips, Cinnamon, and I all shared a confused look, then turned our heads skyward.

High above, the pelican circled its way down toward us.

The pelican's eye gleamed as the mass of rock descended toward his foe. When he had found a patch of rocks, he was shocked by just how much weight he could handle. He knew he was stronger than before he had awakened, but the sheer size of the boulder . . . it defied logic.

The pelican might have dropped it from less of a height, but the lobster's keen eyes had been tracking his passage since he'd come into view. Even if the boulder were to go off course—which he doubted—the gigantic crustacean shouldn't have any trouble stopping it. So, trusting his calculations and the lobster to intervene should he somehow be wrong, he had released the payload.

There was only a small amount of wind, and even if there had been more of a gust, the rock wouldn't have moved much—such was its sheer mass. As the boulder slammed down atop the adversarial crab, the pelican let out a muffled grunt of amusement; it was a direct hit. A moment later, the *thud* of its impact reached his ears, and he grunted even louder.

The pelican flew down to meet his peers.

My heart thundered in my chest, and all I could do was watch as the pelican approached. Cinnamon climbed atop my shoulder and leaned her front paws atop my head to get a good view. No one made a sound—except for Rocky, who was pinned down by Sergeant Snips and Corporal Claws. The former held the enraged crab's snippers firmly closed, while the latter held his body still.

As the pelican landed on the shore before us, the changes were immediately visible. His body was almost a third larger. His bill was longer, and the tip of it had a wickedly curved hook. The webbing of his feet appeared thicker. And most notable of all, his eyes held the keen spark of intelligence.

"G'day, mate . . ." I said, my voice awestruck.

He nodded and raised a wing in greeting, then opened his bill and dropped something on the sand before us.

I peered down at the egg, my eyes going wide. "That . . . is that yours?"

He shook his head.

"Not yours, then. Is it . . . fertile?"

He nodded, then tensed up as Cinnamon hopped forward to sniff it. She shifted around it, her little nose twitching away.

"She won't hurt it," I said, trying to reassure the freshly awakened bird.

Its eyes rose to meet me and it nodded again, accepting my words.

"Do you, uh, have a name, mate?"

It grunted, and I could hear a hint of its meaning: *no.*

I licked my lips and made to respond, but then Rocky broke free.

Transfixed as they were on the pelican, his jailers had let their attentions lapse. He dashed for the bird, both claws held high and gathering power. Everyone burst into motion, but I was the fastest.

I appeared behind him and grabbed both his rear flippers in one hand, then raised him high. He started releasing rapid-fire explosions in protest. I let him get his anger out, and as the pelican looked at me with wide eyes, I held up one finger and tried to say, "one moment," but my voice was drowned out by the *boom, boom, boom* of Rocky's angst made manifest.

After a few breaths, his blasts slowed, and after half a minute, they had stopped entirely. I lowered the now-exhausted crab, shaking my head at him.

"You tried to *eat* him yesterday, mate. A boulder to the noggin is the least you deserved. I reckon he let you off lightly."

His body had gone limp, clearly having overexerted himself, but he still glared hatred at the pelican.

"I expressly forbid you from hurting our pelican pal, Rocky. Remember my promise—if you hurt or kill any creatures, you're banished, my guy."

I set him down on the sand, and the beginnings of a rude gesture formed, but then he slumped. I shook my head at the soft snores coming from his unconscious form and returned my attention to the pelican.

"Sorry, man. He's kind of a maniac. You're a male, right?"

After giving Rocky one last wary glance, the pelican turned to me and nodded.

"Right. Well, as I was going to say before Rocky went all Rocky on us, everyone here has a name."

I gestured at the other animals. They smiled, made small greeting noises, and waved. The pelican and I locked eyes.

"Would you like one? A name, I mean."

He didn't respond for a long moment, weighing his options. Just when I thought he wouldn't respond, he gave a single, sharp nod of his head.

I grinned.

I'd already picked one out.

CHAPTER THIRTY-EIGHT

HAT TRICK

I beamed at the pelican on the sand before me. The sun was entirely over the horizon now, lighting his feathers from behind and giving him an almost holy appearance. I licked my lips.

"How do you feel about the name—"

"Fischer!" came a booming voice from somewhere behind me.

"Fischer!" a much more beautiful voice called, and I turned, raising an eyebrow.

"Over here!" I yelled back. A moment later, a small army came running from either side of the headland.

Maria, the entire fishing club, and every member of the cult I was aware of came sprinting into view. There were newcomers too, and I narrowed my eyes at them. "You four . . . ?"

Fergus, Duncan, Brad, and Greg all froze, their eyes going wide.

"Er," Fergus began, then Barry stepped forward.

"Are you okay? Is anyone hurt? We heard a series of blasts . . ."

"Oh, that?" I waved his concern away with one hand. "Rocky threw a bit of a hissy fit after my new pelican pal dropped a boulder on his head from like a kilometer up. You should have seen it."

Maria had come to my side, and at my mention of a pelican pal, her eyes went wide.

Barry's eyes drifted to the crab's lifeless form. "Is . . . is he dead?"

I laughed. "Unfortunately, no. He exhausted himself with all those blasts and is having a little crab nap." I stood and brushed my pants off. "Now that you're all here, I suppose we should do some introductions."

I pointed at Ruby and Steven. "I knew you two had joined the cult—"

"Church," Barry corrected.

"Whatever, man. I knew you two had joined, but you four . . ." I trailed off, raising an eyebrow at the smiths and the woodworkers. "When did that happen?"

Brad crossed his arms and gave me a grin. "We don't recall, do we Greg?"

"Not even a little," his brother answered, scratching his inner ear before inspecting a fingernail.

Fergus rubbed the back of his head. "Er, it's been a few days for us. Sorry, Fischer."

"You don't need to apologize, mate. I—hang on a second . . ." I narrowed my eyes at the blacksmiths. "Those other jobs you needed all the metal for . . . were you already making oyster cages?"

Barry raised a finger and opened his mouth to protest, then let out a sigh. "Your desire to be kept out of the loop doesn't work if you keep coming to the correct conclusions, Fischer."

"Yeah . . . if it makes you feel any better, I annoy myself, too." I put my hands on my hips and looked out at the rising sun. "Ah well, nothing to be done about it now, I suppose. Have you guys met all of my animal pals?" I asked, looking between the newcomers.

"Everyone but the pelican . . ."

"Huh. That makes things easy, I guess."

"What's her name?" Barry asked.

"Mate, did you just assume Warrant Officer Williams's gender? He's a bloke."

"But . . ." Maria said. "There's an egg on the sand."

I turned to the pelican. "Sorry about that—Barry's a good fella and Maria is okay too, I guess—*ow!*" I rubbed my arm where Maria had pinched me, then looked back at the pelican. "They're just a little confused, is all."

Barry frowned, then attempted to forge past his faux pas. "Wait, did you just say his name is Warrant Officer Williams? Fischer, if you're going to choose ridiculous names like Snips and Claws, can you at least stay consistent?"

Snips and Claws both hissed a warning, and Barry held his hands up in apology. "I love your names, but they're . . . unique."

My lips formed a line as I did my best to keep my face neutral. "What do you mean, Barry? I did stay consistent. Army rank and alliteration—what else are you looking for?"

"You named him Williams! How is that anything like Snips or Claws?"

"Because, Barry . . ." I beamed a grin at him. "His name is Warrant Officer Williams—or Bill, for short."

Barry put his head in his hands as I cackled with laughter. A few giggles, snorts, and even a few groans came from the crowd—the groans were my favorite.

" . . . Bill?" Barry looked at the massive sea bird and shook his head in misplaced commiseration. "I'm so sorry about the name. Fischer is notoriously terrible at them."

"Hey! I choose the best names, thank you very much!"

Snips and Claws nodded, pouting at Barry.

"I *love* it!" Maria said, smiling at Bill.

I cocked my head at him. "I just realized I didn't introduce everyone—how rude of me."

I quickly ran through the names of everyone present, making sure to enunciate the names of my animal pals—all of which were definitely good names and *not* terrible, thank you very much—with the requisite amount of grandiosity.

"You like the name, don't you?" I asked Bill. "All jokes aside, if you don't like it, we choose another."

Bill had been slowly backing away since the crowd arrived, but the longer our conversation dragged on, the more comfortable he seemed to become. At my question, he paused, once more taking his time to consider.

* * *

Warrant Officer Williams—Bill—pondered the name. It seemed to fit with the other animals, and something about it felt . . . right. He puffed out his feathers, stood to his full height, and stretched his wings as wide as they would go. With his increased size, his wingspan cast a vast shadow that covered much of the shore.

He let out a deep, rumbling grunt, broadcasting his approval out into the world.

Some may have found the noise coming from Bill terrifying. It was guttural, like the sound you'd expect to hear from a creature of Hades, not from a large bird with pretty feathers. I was not most men, however; I found the sound comforting, especially considering the meaning it held.

Bill approved of his name.

"Well, there you have it, Barry." I pouted and raised my nose at him. "Some people—and pelicans—have good taste."

Barry rubbed the bridge of his nose. "I'm glad you're okay, but this is not how I expected this morning to go."

"Nothing wrong with a happy little accident, mate. Bob Ross would be proud."

"Who?" Maria asked, shooting me a glance as she crept toward Bill.

I smiled at her and her obvious intentions—she was angling to give Bill a good scritching.

"Bob Ross was a world-renowned artist where I'm from. He was as good a bloke as he was a painter. Anyhoo, look at me blabbering on . . ." I cast my gaze over everyone present, creatures and humans both. "What do you say we have a little feast to celebrate our new friend's awakening? I know you guys are part of the cult or church or whatever now, so there's no reason we can't have a good potluck."

My words painted confusion over a lot of the faces, but the eyes of those who had eaten my food before lit up.

Time stretched on at an agonizing pace for the bumblebee. Though his own pain was slowly receding before the blessed sweetness of his royal jelly, the queen had yet to show improvement. She still drank of his creation, yet her consumption had slowed. When he finished the cell he was drinking from, he stumbled over to her, his legs sluggish but working properly once more.

Following an impulse that came from somewhere unknown, he rubbed her thorax in what he believed was a reassuring way. The tiny hairs covering her body were soft beneath his barbed feet, and he stroked her slowly, willing her to recover. Against all hope, she seemed to drink deeper. Her legs started to tremble, which he also took as a good sign.

He buzzed to her other side, and what he saw there made his stomachs drop. The hole in her abdomen was a vicious thing. The hornet's stinger hadn't plunged in and out cleanly and had torn free of her exoskeleton at an angle, leaving a ripped and oozing hole. Her legs trembled as she made to stand, and he tried to hold her down, to keep her still, all the while stroking her back.

An odd sensation blossomed from outside of his body, similar to what he'd felt prior to awakening. Before he could question it, his world was engulfed by a bright white light, and a loud *pop* came from the queen, stunning him.

The thought patterns of a honeybee queen are more complicated than most would suspect. It is easy for a human to look at an insect with a brain the size of a poppy seed and presume that there isn't a whole bunch going on within. That presumption, as with many of the deductions produced by the average human's conceit, is wrong. Even worker honeybees, who are hive members denoted by their hard work and low position, have the critical thinking abilities to solve a startling range of problems that might arise.

Given all this, the queen of the honeybees was quite aware of the predicament she was in. Her hive had been invaded, her defenders had been slaughtered, and she had been abducted. When the strange bumblebee had entered her chamber, she hadn't thought for a moment that he was doing it for her. He was an opportunist coming to steal her hive's lifeblood. If anything, that made him worse than the parasitic hornets, who at least had the gall to initiate the attack.

But then the bumblebee had defended her, receiving a potentially fatal wound as a result. The moments following that were a confusing blur to her. Hornet venom ran through her body, causing her synapses to misfire, her body to twitch, and her consciousness to wane.

The next thing she'd known, she was flying, but not of her own accord. The bumblebee, that strange insect whose actions made little sense, had been carrying her. It was a short flight, and after he had dragged her into a dark room, she knew her end was coming. She tried to gather the strength to sting the bumblebee, to finish him off so she could return to her hive and recover, but the hornet venom had well and truly taken control by that point.

Suddenly, her face had dropped into something sweet. Not just sweet—the most delicious substance she had ever tasted. Whatever the bumblebee's plans were, he had made a fatal mistake. She would drink of this boon, recover her strength, and then she would kill him. His honey would be used to rebuild her hive before the workers could raise another queen. One sip at a time, the queen bee drained the comb before her.

Part of her awareness returned as her body digested the viscous liquid entering her stomach. But with that awareness came pain. The only benefit of the venom waging war on her nervous system was that it numbed her, and with her body sufficiently fueled and fighting off the venom, lines of agony ran through her.

The worst of the damage was where the hornet had lanced her with its stinger. Waves of pain radiated from the hole left behind in her exoskeleton, and she harbored doubts she'd live through the damage. An odd tingling came from her thorax, and she directed her attention there. The bumblebee was beside her, running a leg through the small hairs of her back.

Good—if her strength returned, it was within striking distance of her deadly stinger. With a bolstered sense of purpose, she drank deeper through her proboscis, her body never seeming to tire of the delicious jelly.

Then, all at once, her world was engulfed by white.

When the queen's vision returned, the world had transformed. The space she found herself in had shrunk, and her wings buzzed with curiosity. She noticed for the first time that she was within an entirely alien environment. There were wooden racks hanging down from above, running in parallel to one another. Everything around her, including the wall, were all sharp corners and flat surfaces, making it a decidedly unnatural creation.

Information seemed to stream into her mind. The strange hive was made by . . . a creature. The name for it escaped her, so she returned her attention outwards. There was a row of honeycomb lining the floor, but they were not made by honeybees.

In an instant, she remembered where she was.

She whirled, her wings buzzing to spin her as fast as possible. She prepared for an attack by moving venom down toward the tip of her stinger, but no attack came. Then she spotted the bumblebee—well, part of it, anyway.

The bumblebee was content watching from afar. After recovering from the flash of white light, he had retreated immediately, not wanting the queen to attack. The wound at her side had completely healed, and as with his own awakening—which he was certain the queen had just experienced—her body had transformed. Her form was even larger, her wings had grown longer, and the stinger at the end of her abdomen was downright horrifying. It had doubled in length and become even smoother, tapering down to the needlelike tip that could inject venom.

After a long wait, the queen bee finally stirred. Her body twitched at first, but then she got to her feet and gazed around, her antennae tasting the air as she moved her head. He witnessed the moment she remembered his existence; she whirled on the spot with terrifying speed, scanning the hive for him. He leaned backward subconsciously, not wanting to pose a threat.

When she spotted him, he didn't know how to react. Feeling more awkward than he knew he could, the bumblebee lowered a leg into view and wiggled it around.

The queen honeybee watched the bumblebee with growing hesitation. The atypical insect was peeking down from the furthest away rack, only visible up to its compound eyes. One of its foremost legs dropped into view. She prepared herself, thinking it might be making its move finally, but then it just shook the appendage back and forth. Flashes of the gesture ran through her mind, gleaned from the knowledge still pouring into her.

It was a wave—a gesture of greeting.

The queen raised her own foreleg and waved back, not entirely understanding why she felt obligated to do so.

CHAPTER THIRTY-NINE

TRADE DEAL

With careful steps, the bumblebee approached the honeybee queen. She watched him keenly, with a promise of violence held in her posture. When he was within three of her body lengths—her needlelike stinger included—he stopped. They weighed each other from afar, and as the moment stretched on, the bumblebee vibrated his wings in what he knew to mean friendship. He hoped she understood, hoped she didn't misunderstand the message.

A wave of anxiety washed through him, but then her wings moved.

They shook, quivering with the same frequency. *Friendship.* As one, their body language relaxed, and they met each other in the middle of his hive. He stopped, but she stepped in, her antennae feeling his face all over. He was taken aback for a second, but then recalled that there was a delay in the knowledge pouring in. Even now, he was receiving more information from an unknown source. She had been awakened, what, five minutes ago? It was natural for her to still act as a regular bee would.

Her head twisted to the side in an obvious question: *why aren't you greeting me back?* Feeling social pressure—a rather unpleasant side effect of his ascension—the bumblebee caressed her face with his antennae. Surprisingly, he found it natural—calming. He got a greater understanding of the queen before him, and as he did, his wings buzzed in delight. Because of his timely intervention, and more than a little luck, she had survived. Because of his actions—and, by extension, the actions of the human that had gifted him food, an entire hive would live on.

As if she, too, had the same thought, the queen turned. She gazed at the entrance, then shot a questioning look his way.

Yes, he buzzed with his wings. He led the way out into the morning sun, ensuring the path to her hive was free of enemies.

Before they left his hive, the bumblebee's thoughts were consumed with gratitude. Entering the honeybee's hive, however, had been a sobering experience. Before they even took a step inside, they were greeted by the bodies of slain defenders. The surviving workers had wasted no time in expelling the dead from the hole the hornets had made, and a pile of insects lay at the trunk's base, honeybee and hornet both.

Workers greeted them at the entrance, and after examining the queen and deciding that she was theirs, they turned their attention to him. They approached with clear hostility, but the queen vibrated her wings, making the workers immediately recognize him as a friend. A worker escorted them back to the queen's chamber, and each time they met another worker, it greeted them by relaying the same sequence of vibrations the queen had given.

Now that he was no longer in a fight to the death, the bumblebee gazed around the chamber they entered. Walls of golden honeycomb climbed to the roof of the hollow, stunning the bumblebee with the hive's wealth. He had never imagined a single place of so much honey existed. The honeybees had been industrious in their endeavors, and the fruit of their labor was well and truly on display. Even now, having expanded his awareness and base instincts, the bumblebee felt the need to dive headfirst into one of the combs and drink his fill.

As he stared at a half-filled and yet unsealed comb, he felt a nudge on his abdomen. When he turned, the queen pointed at him, the comb, then buzzed her wings in approval. He didn't need to consider the offer; he took a small flight, then plunged his proboscis into the golden liquid. It was entirely different to his royal jelly, yet neither better nor worse.

Okay, that was a lie—it was objectively worse, but it also had some redeeming qualities.

The honey, despite being viscous and rich, had an almost . . . refreshing quality to it. The flavor was less concentrated and much thinner than the jelly he had made. It easily entered his stomach and left him feeling light and energized. He returned his attention to the queen, who he found was wasting no time in tending to the hive. She checked on the pupae, who were likely the successors to the male drones that had been annihilated.

He left her to it, heading toward the usual entrance to the hive. His worker bee guide followed him, dashing forward to let every other honeybee they came across know that he was one of them. With each wall of honeycomb they passed, the bumblebee grew increasingly astounded. The queen's chamber alone was more honey than he could comprehend, yet it was only a fraction of the hive's wealth. After the tenth ceiling-high comb, he gave up counting and focused on where they were going.

As he caught sight of the entrance, his wings let out a low buzz of their own accord. Scores of honeybees were there, piled to either side of the filled-in hole. Their mandibles all had one thing in common: they were covered in the goo the hornets had used to plug up the hive. He felt one of the bees with his antennae and it twitched in response. Another was stirring, slowly getting to its feet.

Good, his wings buzzed—they were only temporarily paralyzed by the toxins.

He ambled up to the horrible-smelling gunk, and after only a moment's hesitation, bit down into it. The flavor was even worse than the smell. The hornet venom suffusing the sticky substance was acidic and immediately made his mouth go numb. As with the honeybees, it clung to him, and he removed as much as he could by scraping himself against the hive's walls. It was painstaking work, but he didn't stop until enough was cleared away for the passage to once more be open.

He dashed off to gather loads of dirt, covering what slivers of hornet gunk remained. As he finished his last trip, the honeybee workers were getting to their feet. Others of the hive carried the recovering deeper inside, no doubt taking them to combs they could drain the honey from. With nothing else to be done, the bumblebee returned to the queen.

She was sequestered in a corner and surrounded by workers. He wondered at her actions, but then he noticed her abdomen undulate and expel a tiny white egg. He let out a shocked buzz and spun, averting his eyes. Unsure if he should be witnessing such a private moment, he had his back to her when the hive shook with a booming voice.

"*What in the frack?*"

I had been unable to contain my excitement when I woke, and in the predawn light, I set off for the hive. I'd only put the sugar water in there yesterday, but the prospect of the bees getting lured into it and making me some delicious honey filled me with anticipation. Before I could make it around the back of the tree, the pile of what had to be hundreds of honeybees brought me up short.

"What in the frack?" I yelled, my stealth forgotten as I bent down.

They were unmoving, clearly dead.

"Where did they come from . . . ?"

I looked up at the tree and spotted it immediately. Something had bored a hole into the back of the hive. The opening was large, and I leaned in closer, my stomach dropping.

The bumblebee flew toward the hornet-made entrance as fast as he could. The breach was too close to the queen's chamber, and a random human poking around inside could spell the end of the hive if they accidentally damaged the queen. He dashed into view of the hole, buzzing his wings in threat and ready to attack if need be. When he saw the giant eye peering into the hive, he recognized it immediately; it belonged to the benevolent human that had shown him kindness before he had awakened.

The eye came even closer, and he froze, feeling naked beneath the weight of a cultivator's gaze.

"Yooo! Is that you, Bumblebro?"

The bumblebee raised an arm, paused, then waved.

The sight of the bumblebee appearing to wave made my head dip backward, and despite the dire situation, I let out a chuckle. "That almost looked like a wave."

Yes, he buzzed.

"Right? It totally—wait, *what?*"

I blinked, and Bumblebro nodded.

"You can't be serious . . ." I leaned back and rubbed my head in frustration, letting out a groan. "Did you drink that sugar water I put in the hive next door?"

Yes, he buzzed. The noise had an affirmative sound to it, and given the fact he'd waved and nodded, I knew it wasn't just my imagination.

"Mate . . ."

I leaned down, going eye to compound eye with the insect. With how close I was,

I noticed the changes to his body that I'd somehow missed—he was definitely bigger than when I'd held him between my fingers yesterday. His mandibles appeared deadly and they could have easily torn through the rear of the hive.

"I realize you've probably got a crazy amount of strength for a bee now, but just because you're strong doesn't mean you can go breaking into innocent honeybee hives and murdering the denizens. That's super messed up, man."

I rubbed my eyes. "This is exactly what I was afraid of . . . I can't believe using regular sugar made you awaken . . ."

The bumblebee made no move, merely sitting in the entrance and watching me intently.

No, he suddenly buzzed, then took flight.

I prepared myself, ready to bat away the little deviant if he tried to attack me, but he flew down to the ground.

No, he buzzed again.

He went to the pile of bodies below and started moving honeybees aside. He did it with a tremendous amount of care, seeming to show respect for the departed.

No, he kept buzzing. *No. No. No.*

One last bee was lifted and set aside with reverence, revealing something violently yellow. He grabbed it in his mandibles and hauled out the headless body of a gigantic hornet. He pointed at it, gestured up at the hive, and let out a low drone with his wings that was laden with anger.

"Oh! The hornets did it?"

Yes.

"And you were just looting the honey after . . ." I winced, imagining the queen likely didn't survive.

No, he buzzed.

"No . . . ?"

He let out a ponderous vibration with his wings that I understood to mean: *wait.*

My eyebrows furrowed as I watched him go, disappearing back inside the hive.

As Bumblebro went to fetch the queen, his mind roiled. The cultivator's kind nature had been one thing, but learning that he had been the cause of the bumblebee's awakening . . . it defied logic. The torrent of information pouring into his brain had slowed to a trickle, and of the myriad things he now knew to be true, a cultivator causing the ascension of other beings was *not* one of them.

When he reached the queen, he let out a thankful buzz that she was no longer laying eggs. She looked up at him, likely sensing the urgency held in the vibrations of his wings.

Her wings made a questioning tone.

Friend, he buzzed, pointing to the path leading outside.

Friend?

Yes, he responded, his wings' frequency holding a hint of urgency. *Come.*

Together, they flew out of the chamber.

* * *

When Bumblebro returned, I cocked my head to the side. "What's up, man? What did you want to show . . ."

I trailed off as the head of another insect peeked out. Bumblebro flew outside, and the queen joined him. They hovered before me, and after a moment's hesitation, she waved.

A smile slowly spread over my face and a laugh tore from my throat. I tried to explain myself to the clearly confused insects, but each time I tried to speak, the laughter interrupted me.

"S-sorry," I eventually got out. "I'm just so happy—this is amazing."

They cocked their heads and both made the same questioning tone with their wings.

"All right." I clapped my hands together. "I have so many questions to ask you two, and I'm sure you have some questions for me . . ."

Yes, they both agreed.

"Well, we can get to that, but more importantly, I have a trade deal to propose."

I steepled my fingers, referencing a meme that went right over the insects' fuzzy little heads, but that didn't matter. I was still enjoying myself.

"Me and a bunch of the gang—well, it's actually the whole gang, I suppose . . ." I shook my head and waved the tangent away. "Sorry, that's not important—I'm just really excited right now."

I smiled at the queen and got right to the point. "How do you feel about trading some of your delicious honey to me?"

She made an unsure buzz.

"You can still say no, but after you get a taste of what I'm offering, I doubt you'll be able to refuse."

Both insects vibrated with curiosity, and my smile turned predatory.

CHAPTER FORTY

UN-BEE-LIEVABLE

I took a deep breath as I gazed at the western mountain range, an undeniable smile crossing my face. There wasn't a cloud to be seen, and the setting sun painted the sky with a swath of soft pastel colors.

"Ho, Fischer!"

I turned toward Barry's voice, raising an indignant hand to my chest. "What did you just call me?"

He cocked his head in response. " . . . what?"

"Don't worry, mate. I'm just feeling a little giddy."

He shook his head at my antics. "If you're giddy now, wait until you see what Helen has cooked up."

I raised an appreciative eyebrow. I knew she was making something sweet, but had no idea what. "I didn't take too much of your sugar, did I?"

"Not at all. We still have plenty left over, even after everyone pillaged it for their cooking." He shot me a conspiratorial glance. "Are you going to tell me what you used the sugar for yet?"

"Nope! Rest assured, though—the result is un-bee-lievable."

My eyes must have sparkled with mirth because he squinted at me. As his stare narrowed further, the fishing club arrived.

"G'day, fellas!" I said, turning from Barry's scrupulous gaze.

They all gave me hearty greetings, except for Peter, whose attention was lasered in on the covered tray in his hands.

"Ooh, what you got there?" I asked, finally drawing his attention.

He reverently placed the tray down on the table I'd set up, then let out a relieved sigh. "That depends—are you going to tell me what you did with the cultivator sugar?"

Ellis's face grew annoyed. "I have told you countless times that *chi sugar* is a much more accurate name."

"I don't know, Ellis," Theo said, rubbing his chin. "I'm with Peter on this one—who in Athena's wealth of wisdom even knows what chi is?"

"It's the historically correct term for the essence that suffuses the world and allows cultivation."

I looked between the group, smiling. "Bit of debate on the terminology, huh?"

Ellis sighed. "Quite."

"Well, let me settle it for you—you're all wrong."

They blinked at me, and Theo's head tilted to the side. "We are . . . ?"

"I'm afraid so."

"Well, what do you call it then?"

"Pew-pew sand."

A sea of blank stares met me.

"*Pew-pew sand?*" Barry asked, his voice full of incredulity.

"Yeah, mate. It has the consistency of sand and gives you pew-pew powers."

Everyone's faces adopted a look somewhere between annoyed, confused, and downright befuddled—except for Ellis.

He removed his notebook. "What is *pew-pew?* Do you have access to information that we do not?"

"You're damn right I do." I made finger guns, then started firing them. "*Pew. Pew-pew.*"

Ellis stopped taking notes. "Er—right. If sugar is pew-pew sand, what is the rum Barry makes?"

"That's easy, mate—it's pew-pew juice."

Silence stretched over the gathering.

Theo raised his arm. "Those in favor of disregarding every single one of Fischer's name suggestions—past, future, and present?"

"Aye," came their responses, punctuated by an ocean of raised arms.

"Heretics!" I gasped, my eyes going wide. "You would defy the heavens?"

Someone cleared their throat behind me, and I whirled, beaming at the only person in Tropica who could make clearing their throat sound cute.

"Do I even want to know?" Maria asked, quirking a brow.

I gave her my most charming smile. "Probably not."

With the warm light of the tiki torches guiding the way, the rest of the cult—er, church—slowly trickled in. Fergus and Duncan were the last to arrive, and I spread my arms wide as they walked around the headland.

"Welcome, fellas!" I pointed at the trays held in their hands. "You can put the food down on the table if you . . ." I trailed off as I realized the entire thing was covered in bowls, plates, cups, and bottles of rum.

"I'll make room!" Helen said, rushing over. "I told you there wasn't enough room for the rum, Barry!"

The cult . . . er, church leader—I was really struggling with the terminology—shrugged.

"You're right, as always, my love."

"Smart man," Fergus added. His eyes widened as he realized he'd said it aloud. "Oh. Uh . . . sorry."

"No need to apologize," Helen said, setting the crate of rum down on the sand. She walked over and slipped an arm around Barry's waist. "He is smart—that's why I married him."

I smiled at the smiths, who were still looking a little like fish out of water.

I guess they haven't adjusted to the group dynamic yet . . .

My hands clapped together sharply, gathering everyone's attention. "All right—shall we get this dinner started?"

As I lifted the tray covering my dishes, steam billowed out, bringing with it a cornucopia of scents. Those who were close enough to smell it leaned in, their eyes fixed on the feast of fish.

I looked over the rest of the table. One entire side was loaded with the savory dishes; piles of baked vegetables, a delicious-smelling stew, dinner rolls, what looked like a beef stir-fry, and a mound of sea salt I'd prepared.

"I thought we could all help ourselves," I said, gesturing at the stack of plates, then at the seafood I'd just unveiled. "There are two kinds of crab—one cooked in sea water, the other tossed in butter. Then there are four kinds of fish. Three were cooked over the fire with different seasoning combinations that pair well together. And the fourth . . ." I let a silence stretch, building the anticipation. "The last kind, these ones here covered in golden breading, were shallow fried in beef tallow. I'd recommend eating them first as they're best fresh."

"Anyone who hasn't tried the fried fish should get some now," Maria suggested. "It's life changing."

The fishing club, trailed by the tailors and the smiths, lined up and filled their plates. Bill was either feeling too shy or saw himself as less than the humans for some reason, as he remained seated, his namesake resting across his feathered body. Before I could intervene, Sergeant Snips, ever the reliable crab, jumped up onto the table and filled a plate for him. I gave her a smile and mouthed *thank you.* She winked and gave a happy hiss.

"Don't hold back," I said when I noticed they were all waiting patiently in their seats for the rest of us to get food. "Eat up! The sooner you dig in, the better it'll taste."

Though that wasn't a lie, my motivations were partially selfish—I couldn't wait a moment longer to see their reactions. I remained seated, watching intently but trying not to be too obvious.

Maria elbowed me in the side. "Could you stare any harder?" she whispered, grinning at me.

"Shh!" I hissed back, giving her a sly look. "I need this."

She covered her mouth to hide her smile and we watched together.

The first to give in was Peter. The royal chef lifted a chunk of fried fish to gaze at it. He flicked the breading, pursing his lips and narrowing his eyes at the firm surface. Then, with no small amount of hesitation, he bit into it.

Crunch.

He closed his eyes as a drawn out *mmmm* escaped him. He chewed sporadically, letting the flavors spread over his palate. His gaze darted from the meal, to his friends, to the meal, to the far distance, then to me. He blinked at me, still chewing, and I gave him a broad grin.

"Pretty good, huh?"

He nodded, and without a word, took another bite. He sank back in his chair, closing his eyes again to focus on the food. The rest of the fishing club had also taken bites, and they were having the same reaction as Peter, if a little muted compared to the culinarily inclined chef. The tailors, Ruby and Steven, were slumped back in their chairs as well. They had the same airy smile on their faces, and they ate slowly, savoring the moment.

The smiths gave the best reaction of all. Fergus and Duncan, who before tasting the fish had seemed rather reserved, stared at each other in clear shock. They let out muffled giggles through food-filled mouths, and rather than pause to let their mirth out, they shoveled more fish in, quickly finishing the fried sections and moving onto the spiced and grilled portions.

Then Bill tried the food, and his response quickly tied itself with the smiths. He ate a chunk of fried fish whole, and as the flavor hit him, he raised his bill to the sky and let out a mighty grunt. Everyone who had tasted it before understood what he was experiencing, and they all let out soft laughs or smiled along with his enjoyment. Bill set about devouring the rest of the plate, his wings held out wide and his feathers puffed out.

I turned to Maria, who looped an arm in mine and pulled herself close.

"Was that everything you were hoping for?" she asked softly so only I could hear.

"Even better than I'd imagined."

She squeezed my bicep. "I'm glad."

"I wanted to ask . . ." I leaned in close, talking under my breath. "Do you guys have plans to tell your dad about, well . . . everything? It's a shame your parents can't be here."

She took a deep breath and sighed. "Yeah, it's a shame Mom had to play decoy tonight, but she doesn't think he's ready yet."

"Still . . ." I cocked my head, trying to find the right words. "I guess it just feels bad—like we're all sneaking around behind his back."

"Well, we kind of are," she replied with a small grimace. "But that's how it goes sometimes. I'm sure he'll eventually understand when Mom decides he's ready."

She was right, of course; tonight was a night for celebration. I acknowledged the worry, then let it go.

When Snips jumped down from the table, a plate in her claw and a length of a sand crab hanging from her mouth, Maria rubbed my back. "C'mon. Let's get some too."

We worked as a team, me putting fish on both plates, her loading us up with vegetables, and so on. We both had a bit of everything when we sat back in our chairs, and I wasted no more time. I bit down into the fried fish, and even with it having cooled slightly, the outside was crisp. And the inside . . . good heavens, the *inside.*

Fat and juices exploded throughout my mouth, absolutely smothering my taste buds in blissful warmth. The flavors were overwhelming, and as I chewed the crunchy breading and the melt-in-your-mouth flesh hidden beneath it, I let out a content sigh. Though the night had well and truly descended, my mind's eye took me to my shoreline beneath the midday sun. Its rays shone down on my entire body, somehow warming me from the core. Small waves lapped at the sands while a soft breeze tickled my hair.

Someone sniffed across from me, shattering the illusion, and I glanced up. Peter's lip was trembling and tears streamed down his face.

"You're okay, buddy," Danny said, patting his back.

"I . . . I know . . ." he got out. "It's just . . . so . . ." He broke off, sobs drowning out his words.

Theo reached over from his other side, laying a reassuring hand on his shoulder. "It's delicious, isn't it?"

Peter nodded, his face contorting in what almost looked like grief.

All present, animals and humans both, cast gazes around the circle. We all understood the significance of the moment; a royal chef, someone in charge of crafting the king's own food, had been brought to tears by the overwhelming taste of seafood.

Maria leaned a head on my shoulder, watching the inconsolable Peter. She squeezed my arm, and I laid a hand atop hers. As his sniffling subsided, the feast resumed, and I tried the rest of the dishes on my plate. The roasted vegetables, to my utter delight, had been caramelized. By the distinct flavor, it was clear they'd used chi sugar.

"All right—who had the idea of cooking the veggies with pew-pew sand? It's fracking delightful."

Helen smirked at me, and Barry sighed. "We did, but it's not *pew-pew sand.*"

I waved his protest away with a smug grin. "Details. The point is it's delicious."

Maria took a bite of a glistening carrot and let out an *mmph,* her body melting back into her chair. "Good," was all she said before putting another piece in her mouth.

Peter, who was only just recovering from his emotional moment, took a bite of said vegetables.

His lip quivered again.

With the savory portion of the feast concluded, we rested on the sand. I couldn't recall who had started it, but before I knew it, everyone was on their backs and caressing distended stomachs.

"I regret nothing," Maria said.

"Couldn't have said it better myself."

A carpet of stars spread out above us, and I stared at their flickering forms, wondering at the distance and composition of the foreign constellations. It was a sobering moment that reminded me just how far I was from Earth. For some, perhaps most, that would have been a horrifying thought. To me, it was anything but.

As if sensing my thoughts, Maria rolled over. She settled into the nook of my arm and laid her head atop my chest. I reached up to pet her hair, marveling at how soft it was. The scent of her shampoo reached my nose—something earthy and floral.

"It's a lovely night," she said.

"Isn't it?" With my other hand, I took turns petting Claws and Snips, who were leaning against my other side. "The only thing that could make it sweeter would be my secret condiment."

She jolted upright and peered down at me. "Are you finally going to tell us? The mystery has been plaguing my thoughts all day."

I raised a hand and wiggled my fingers. "A magician never reveals his tricks, but I suppose I *could* show you if you're ready for dessert."

"I certainly am," Barry said from across the sands.

"Hey!" I lifted my head to glare at him. "No eavesdropping!"

He also raised his, giving me a smirk. "Then you shouldn't have fed me fish and turned me into a heretical cultivator. I couldn't not hear you if I tried."

"Hmmm. That's a good point." I sat up, stretching my arms toward the heavens. "What do you say, everyone? Time for sweets?"

As one, we stood at a decidedly lethargic pace.

"All right, gang. If I could please have your attention."

I gave everyone time to amble over to the table, taking great joy in the anticipation on their faces despite how much we'd already eaten.

"You said condiment, didn't you?" Barry asked, glancing between the two covered trays I stood behind. "I thought you made a dish . . . ?"

"Nope!" I replied, grinning. "That was subterfuge. I've procured something we can add to the no doubt irresistible dishes you've all prepared."

Peter leaned forward, staring at the two metal coverings with greed. So did Ellis, his pencil and notepad ready to go. "Procured?" Barry asked. "I don't like the sound of that."

Maria gasped. "Don't tell me . . ." She leaned in close, shielding her mouth and whispering. "The hive . . . ?"

I shot her a wink. "That's right, my learned student of all things heretical."

Half expecting an elbow to the ribs in response, I braced my core, but Maria was too stunned, staring wide-eyed at the coverings before me.

I looked up at the sea of faces, slowly reaching down to grasp the left tray. "I give you . . . *honey!*"

I lifted the cover high, revealing the golden liquid in all its glory.

"Er—Fischer?"

"What's up, Barry? I'm kinda trying to be dramatic here . . ."

"Isn't that just water . . . and what are those insects?"

I looked down.

Sure enough, a cup of what appeared to be water sat on the plate. Half of it had been drunk, and laying before it, clearly food coma'd out of their minds, were two bees.

"Oh, my bad. Wrong tray." I lifted the other covering. "I give you . . . *honey!*"

"Are those bees?" Maria asked, ignoring the pot of honey and bending down to stare at them. "Are they dead?"

"Oh, them? That's just Bumblebro and Queen Bee." I waved away her concern. "They're having a nap, I believe."

They both stirred, slowly getting to their feet.

"How are you guys?" I asked, bending down so I was eye level with them. "I told you sugar water was good stuff!"

They both let out a sluggish buzz, unequivocally agreeing.

"Wait . . ." Barry said. "Don't tell me . . ."

I looked around the group, but they only had eyes for the two bees. Corporal Claws leaped onto the table and twisted her head, letting out curious coos while trying to see them from every possible perspective.

"Are you guys serious?" I threw my hands up but couldn't keep the smirk from my lips. "I broker a trade deal with sapient insects for something this godsforsaken world hasn't worked out can be farmed, and all you care about is my new pals?"

Some looked at me for a moment, but their attention was quickly rearrested by the two honey makers.

"Ah, well, I guess it can't be helped." I let out a deep, theatrical sigh. "Bumblebro, Queen Bee—this is everyone. Everyone, these are our newest pals: Bumblebro and Queen Bee."

They both raised a limb and waved, making a greeting buzz with their wings.

CHAPTER FORTY-ONE

NO PUN INTENDED

Lit by the warm glow of tiki torches and the half-moon high above, a silence stretched between us that was only interrupted by the soft buzz of Bumblebro and Queen Bee.

Barry shook his head at me. "Are you serious, Fischer?"

"Uhhh . . . I think so?"

"This is why you're banned from naming things!"

I raised my eyebrows, giving him an appalled stare. "How *dare* you?" I caught both insects and shielded them with my hand. "Don't listen to him, guys—he's just upset he has a basic-bitch name like Barry."

Maria leaned over, peeking around the back of my finger shield. "It's nice to meet you—I'm Maria."

They flew out and buzzed a *hello* her way.

She giggled, covering her mouth. "You're both super cute. Did you make that honey?"

Bumblebro shrugged—which I had to admit *was* super cute—and pointed at Queen Bee. The honeybee matriarch tilted from side to side in a so-so gesture.

"Queen Bee's hive did," I answered. "Seeing as though she's the queen, that kinda makes it hers. And Bumblebro is being humble—a humblebee, if you will."

"Get out," Maria said, pointing toward the ocean.

"Hey, this is my land!"

"I don't care—get."

She made a shooing motion, but I caught the smile wrinkling her eyes.

"Anyway," I continued, "as I was saying, Bumblebro is a humble—sorry, sorry!" I held my hands up, warding off the backhand Maria was threatening to send my way. "He was showing humility when he deferred to Queen Bee. He saved her life, and every drop of her honey, when the hive was attacked last night."

"What attack?" Ellis asked, his eyes furrowed as he scribbled in his notepad.

"A gang of hornets. They sealed the bees in with something toxic, then burrowed into the back of the hive."

"Ah," the former archivist said. "Tree-borer hornets. Horrifying insects."

I gave him an appraising glance. "You've heard of them?"

"Oh, yes. There was a plague eighty or so years ago, and they wreaked havoc on the insects the Osnan family uses for pollination. There was a rather thrilling recounting back in the capital of the steps taken to reduce their numbers."

"Thrilling?" Keith shook his head. "Your brain is terrifying, you know that?"

Ellis scoffed. "Hardly. The records of it are stored in the general library—you could have read it yourself if you had felt so inclined."

"No one other than you would feel so inclined," Theo added, laughing. "Still, it's pretty amazing that the bumblebee—er, that Bumblebro—was able to fight them off."

I gave a wincing smile. "Yeaaah, I may have caused him to awaken before that . . ."

I relayed the story from mine and Bumblebro's perspective. I'd spent a large chunk of the morning conversing with the little bumblebee. It had been surprisingly easy to understand each other, given that he spoke in buzzes. Supplemented by my growing understanding of the local language—and Bumblebro's ability to write in said language—we had communicated the entire tale within a couple of hours.

When I got up to Bumblebro's awakening, Barry spoke up. "With just regular sugar?" he asked. "That's . . . new."

"Astounding," Ellis said, scrawling.

"Correct on both counts," I replied, scratching the back of my head. "Not entirely a welcome change, if I'm being completely honest. The last thing I want to do is accidentally awaken an army." I shrugged. "I got lucky with Bumblebro, though. Wait until you hear how Queen Bee took steps on the path of ascension or whatever . . ."

I regaled them with the rest of the story, and as I went over Bumblebro's actions, the audience got more and more engrossed. No one spoke until I was finished.

"Wow!" Maria said, reaching over carefully to rub his head. "You're a little hero!"

He let out an embarrassed buzz, and Queen Bee bobbed up and down on the spot, agreeing fervently.

"So, there you have it—I tried to lure in honeybees, accidentally made Bumblebro ascend, and he crafted some jelly that made her ascend. Pretty unbelievable, really, but if that ain't indicative of my life here, I don't know what is."

A far cry from his humble attitude earlier, Bumblebro's chest—er, thorax?—was held high as he hovered on the spot. He'd moved a little closer to Queen Bee, who was also preening beneath the attention. Small conversations had started up around the circle, people pairing off to discuss the developments with those closest to them. Gazes continually flicked back to the two ascendant insects, who buzzed ever closer to each other. I clapped my hands one more time, regathering everyone's attention.

"I feel there's one more tale to regale you with while you're all here."

Every eye was on me as I slowly turned toward my animal pals.

"Bill—I feel you've flown under the radar a bit, mate. Would you come here for a moment?"

He waddled over to me, his namesake dipped down and his gait awkward. When he reached my side, I patted him on the head. "I also spent some time with Bill today, and he told me a story of trespass, thievery, and renovations most foul."

Maria narrowed her eyes at me, and I raised my hands. "Whoa! Foul with a *u!* No pun intended!"

She squinted and raised a backhand jokingly, causing a smattering of laughs to come from the crowd. I launched into the tale, using colorful and overly verbose language to retell the last twenty-four hours of Bill's life. As I went over the theft of his nest, Theo started booing, and almost everyone joined in—even Ellis, who stopped writing for a moment to cup his mouth and protest. When I went over his earthward flying kick, Barry laughed and turned toward Ellis.

"Maybe you shouldn't write that down—keep in mind that Fischer loves embellishing his stories."

I grinned and glanced down at Bill. As with Bumblebro, his body had straightened as I went over his exploits.

"That's usually true—you shouldn't let the truth get in the way of a good story, after all. In this case, though, I *am* telling the truth. I had Bill here demonstrate what he did, but without pulling his power from the blow." I pointed behind me at a patch of rocks smattering the sands. "That was a boulder until Bill hit it with a flying kick."

Ellis raised his eyes to meet mine. "You're serious?" He turned to Theo. "He's telling the truth?"

Theo's eyebrows were raised so high they threatened to leave his face. "He is . . ."

"Remarkable . . ." Ellis replied, his eyes returning to the notepad. "Such power so soon after awakening—and facilitated by the information streaming into him . . ." He trailed off as his hand became a blur, documenting all that he'd heard.

"What can I say?" I grinned at Bill, then turned toward the rest of the creatures present. "My animal pals are all as impressive as each other."

Claws and Snips chirped and hissed as they nodded, agreeing with my assessment.

I continued, detailing the changes in his body, the found egg, and his dropping of a boulder on Rocky. Said crab made an annoyed hiss but showed a sliver of restraint for once and didn't outright attack.

"And that's when all of you came over, following the sound of Rocky's rapid-fire explosions."

"What did you do with the egg?" Ruby asked, arching a sculpted brow.

"Oh, that?" I unbuttoned the top half of my shirt and pulled it down.

Cinnamon, chewing a stick of sugarcane and laying limp over the egg, squeaked and nodded in greeting.

"There you are!" Maria said, leaning over to scratch Cinnamon between the ears. "I thought Fischer was just getting a bit of a belly."

"Not yet, but maybe after this dessert . . ."

All eyes returned to the table, and I smirked.

"What do you say we get started on the sweets?"

As we stood around the desserts, everyone took turns explaining their contributions. There were cakes, sweet buns, and even one of Helen's berry pies—all of which used either sugar or sugarcane juice from the secret crop. Finally, it was Peter's turn. I couldn't help but stare at him as he stood behind the tray he'd shown so much care for when arriving.

"This dish was the king's favorite dessert," he said, bending down slowly to grab the cover.

I leaned in—as did anyone with common sense. With a single smooth movement, he revealed the contents for all to see. Rows of ramekins lined the trays, and porous, golden-brown cakes rose from within them.

I swallowed. "Is that . . . ?"

"Soufflés," he answered. "The exact recipe favored by generations of Gormona's rulers, with one small adjustment." He set the lid down and gazed at his precious desserts. "I sweetened them with Barry's sugar."

I swallowed, my mouth watering at the sight of them. Soufflé pancakes and ice cream with a drizzle of honey was my favorite dessert on Earth, and I hadn't realized I'd been craving it until I saw the fluffy little dish before me.

"Great," Maria said. "You broke Fischer."

My eyes cleared, and I looked up to see a smattering of amused faces watching me. "What? You've never seen a man have an existential crisis over food before?"

Danny snorted. "We saw Peter have one not a half hour ago."

"I had at *least* two, thank you very much." Peter smiled at himself. "Now, before we go any further off course, these will be best before they cool down."

I let out a heavy sigh. "All right—I *suppose* I can eat one now."

When my plate was absolutely covered in dessert, I lowered my new dipper into the honey.

"Thanks for making this for me, Brad," I said to the woodworker. "It just wouldn't be the same without it."

He smiled at me and removed the previously jam-covered finger from his mouth. "You're most welcome—I was wondering what it was for, but I'd never have guessed it was for honey."

"The grooves let you collect more of it," I replied, removing the dipper from the jar. "And that lets you drizzle the perfect amount."

I circled it over my plate, smothering part of each dessert in copious amounts of the sweet liquid. Following my action, everyone did the same, and I stayed there to help my animal pals—it could be an awkward thing to wield without opposable thumbs.

As I sat down, I couldn't wait any longer, and I dug my spoon into the soufflé. It went in like a hot knife through butter, and I dipped the spoon into a puddle of honey. Without further ado, I put it into my mouth. The moment the honey hit my tongue, my eyes watered. It was sweet—almost too sweet after not having honey for so long, but that quickly faded when I chewed the soufflé. It was as fluffy as it looked—on par with those served by Michelin starred restaurants back on Earth.

I closed my eyes as the flavors swept me away. It was like eating a cloud, and no matter how much I chewed, the soufflé seemed to remain fluffy. Hints of vanilla, cinnamon, and something else joined the overbearing taste of honey. I must have kept shoveling more in because it never seemed to end, and any awareness of time escaped me as my body floated on the inescapable sensations.

Something touched my cheek, and I opened my eyes, returning to my spot by the fire.

“Are you okay?” Maria asked softly. Her face was tender, and I blinked, causing a tear to fall down my other cheek. She leaned over and wiped it away.

“Y-yeah—I’m good . . .” I peered down at my plate, seeing I’d only taken a single bite of the dessert-filled ramekin.

“Good, right?” Peter asked from across the fire, beaming at my reaction.

“Mate . . . good doesn’t even begin to cut it.”

I took a deep breath, then focused on my spoon again, getting another honey-smothered mouthful ready.

CHAPTER FORTY-TWO

SCANDALIZED

In a throne room high in the royal capital, Augustus Reginald Gormona shifted in his chair. His usually comfy chair had felt hard and uninviting lately, as if it protested his very existence. The colorful light that bathed the room during the day had long departed, and with the darkness of night covering the land, the harsh glow of candles flickered. He straightened his posture, trying to reduce the ache in his lower back, then sighed.

"It's useless . . ."

"Er—what is, my king?"

Augustus looked up, turning his displeasure onto the dignitary. "The expeditions are. You said there has been no news of the spirit beasts—has every report been received?"

"Y-yes, my king. The last one came in this afternoon regarding the search for Lizard Wizard."

The throne's armrests seemed to grow sharp and angled beneath him, so the king moved.

It didn't help. "This is more dire a situation than we expected."

The dignitary didn't speak; the man had been in his family's employ for decades, so knew to hold his tongue around his betters.

"What is your name again, servant?"

"Charles, my king."

"Right. You were the one who came to me with news of the artifact room, correct?"

"Yes, my king."

Augustus Reginald Gormona sighed and ran his hands through his white hair.

"Keep up the good work then, Charles. Come to me the moment you receive any more reports."

The dignitary snapped a salute. "Yes, my king."

"You are dismissed."

The man turned on his heel and strode out of the open door. The waiting-room servant closed it behind him, leaving the king alone with the flickering of candles.

Augustus's nose twitched. Of all the spirit beasts, he had expected to find Lizard Wizard and Bog Dog. There was only one desert and swampland within the kingdom's borders. Boat Goat, Hurtle the Turtle, and Glare Bear could be difficult to find, given how much water and forest there was to search . . . but to find *none* of them?

It was unacceptable.

He reached over and picked up a soufflé. A tray of them had been sitting there for hours, and though they had cooled, he still enjoyed them when not fresh. He took a spoonful and placed it in his mouth. He chewed three times, swallowed, then launched the ramekin at the wall. It bounced off ineffectively, and Augustus Reginald Gormona, seething, lifted the entire tray and threw it across the room. The wooden ramekins rolled along the floor, spilling their golden filling everywhere.

"Servant!" he yelled, heaving with anger.

The door swung in, and the man appeared, bowing at the waist. "Yes, my king?"

"What happened to the ceramic ramekins?" he boomed, not bothering to hide his fury.

"Th-they went missing, king. More have been ordered."

He glared at the man. "Went missing? What do you mean, *they went missing?* Can this castle not even keep track of crockery, servant?"

"I apologize for our ineptitude, king."

Augustus Reginald Gormona shuddered, and all at once, he slumped on his throne. "Do not bring me any more soufflés until they can be served in ceramic."

"Yes, my king."

The servant closed the door behind himself, having worked directly with the king long enough to know a dismissal.

"Gods above," the king muttered. "How you vex me . . ."

"Where did you even find these ramekins, Peter?" I asked, looking down at my now-empty plate. "They look posh as hell."

He peered out through a half-closed eye as he caressed his dessert-filled belly. "I may have procured them from the royal kitchen."

I laughed, then winced and held my stomach. "The king's own bowls, huh?" I held it up in the firelight, appreciating its uniformity. "Neat."

"That's not all," Barry said, getting to his feet and stretching.

"It isn't?" I raised an eyebrow at Peter. "What other goodies did you bring with you, scoundrel?"

"Why, all manner of crockery—though I suspect what Barry's talking about is the glasses."

In response, Barry lifted a crate onto the table. He reached down, making the contents clink together before removing a beautiful object from within. He held up what looked like a crystal tumbler. Its angles caught and reflected the different sources of light surrounding us, making it seem to glow.

"How does everyone feel about some of my special reserve rum?" Barry asked, smiling around the circle.

"I'd love some," Maria replied, "though I feel like I shouldn't be able to drink a drop given how much food I've eaten . . ."

I shrugged. "I'm pretty sure it's either our cultivator bodies, the nature of the food, or both—whatever the cause, I'm down for some special reserve, Barry."

Barry, with a smile wrinkling his eyes, started to pour.

Ten minutes later, Fergus slung one meaty arm over my shoulder and raised his glass high. "To Fischer!" he slurred, his first cup of rum and sugarcane juice already well in effect.

"To Fischer!" everyone else replied.

I grinned and raised my glass to join them. "To *fishing!*"

"*To fishing!*" Theo and his pals repeated, their cheeks flushed.

After the last time I'd indulged in Barry's drink—and the absolute brick-to-the-brain hangover that resulted—I was content nursing my drink. Even just sipping at it, a warmth ran through my body, bringing a relaxed contentedness with it.

Maria, already on her second drink, wobbled over and poked a finger into Fergus's chest. "You trying to steal my man, Smith?" She tried to keep a straight face but swiftly descended into giggles.

"Your man?" He bellowed a laugh. "We are brothers bonded by the forge! Your affections are nothing before the alloy of our friendship."

"I *knew* it!" Theo yelled, pointing a finger at me from across the campfire. "You *have* been seeing other friends!"

I shook my head, not even knowing where to begin.

"Jokes on you, blacksmith!" Theo continued, striding over. "The bond you've forged is nothing before the ties that bind fishermen to one another. Like a wind knot, our friendship will never be untangled."

Brad and Greg, returning from a wander down to the shoreline midway through the tirade, jumped right in.

"Knots of fishing line?" Brad demanded, then bellowed a theatrical laugh. "Easily severed, those."

Greg nodded. "Exactly—unlike the knots formed in wood, which only our friendship with Fischer could hope to match."

"Not just any wood, mind you," Brad continued, leaning in conspiratorially. "Hardwood—ironwood, even."

Maria nodded sagely.

"It's true—which is exactly why Fischer is mine." She let out a downright villainous chuckle. "We've bonded over each of those things! You all never stood a chance."

"It's no good, gentlemen." Theo clutched at his heart as if struck by an arrow. "She has too much power."

She hunched down low and faced her head toward the sky as her evil chuckle rang out once more, even deeper than before. I had no idea what she was going for, but I couldn't help but join in.

I had expected Barry to reign everyone in a bit considering they were technically members of his church and were no doubt up to some dastardly schemes. In retrospect, it was probably a terrible idea to expect restraint from the man that was brewing bootleg cultivator moonshine out of his back shed.

Barry hooted and hollered as he danced over the sand, refilling cups in a terrifyingly efficient manner. Rum flowed, laughter reigned, and good times were aplenty as the night stretched on. At one point, I found myself standing by the fireside alone, simply looking out over the different conversations taking place. There were no cliques, and it was a joy to watch those I saw as friends bond with one another.

Maria was across the fire with Danny and Peter, locked in a fierce discussion. Though their cheeks were flushed, their eyes were filled with passion. From the hand gestures she was making, they were discussing the methods of crumbing fish, comparing dough kneading techniques, or practicing some sort of strange dance.

As Maria continued, Peter called over to Ellis. The former archivist strode over with strong—if a little wobbly—strides, and I smiled at him. Most of this world—maybe everyone except for those gathered around the campfire before me—saw taking steps on the path of ascension as some terrible, life-ending malady. Ellis's vigor flew in the face of that belief, and I was beyond grateful that my contributions helped cure the illness that had ailed him.

As Ellis reached them, Peter mimed for him to start recording their discussion. With the dexterity of a wacky-waving-arm-inflatable-tube-man in a stiff breeze, Ellis jotted down the steps they were going over. Maria would make a gesture and Peter would copy it—all the while, Ellis's hand was a drunken blur, and he nodded along sporadically, making his body sway each time.

Someone tapped me on the shoulder; I turned to see Ruby and Steven.

"Hey, guys," I said, cocking a head at their nervous expressions. "Everything all good?"

Ruby gave me a strained look. "We're well. I just wanted to come have a chat—it feels a bit . . ."

"Awkward," Steven blurted.

"Steven!" She nudged him in the ribs. "You're the only awkward one here, you big oaf!"

Steven's grin only grew wider as she turned back to me, shaking her head. "I don't know if awkward is the right word, but it does feel a bit . . ."

I swallowed a sip of my drink and gave them a reassuring smile.

"It's fine; I get it. We were neighbors, perhaps even friends—I saw you that way, anyway—but then you suddenly get brought into a church that sees me as some great being. It's . . . well, it's a lot."

Ruby let out a light laugh. "It is, isn't it? And we also saw you as a friend, for what it's worth. I've not felt comfortable around you lately, but it's not because of anything you did."

"It's more what we did," Steven added. "Sneaking behind your back and all."

I tossed my head from side to side. "Well, yeah, but that's only because I specifically asked to be left in the dark. It's not as though you did it with malicious intent."

"I guess you're right . . ." she said, resting a hand on her abdomen.

"I'm definitely right—you shouldn't feel bad for the choices you've made. I agree with them wholeheartedly."

"If you say so . . ."

Though her words were still pensive, some of the hesitancy had left her expression.

"Are you guys having a good night?" I asked, eyeing Steven's rosy cheeks and Ruby's lack thereof. My eyes drifted down to her hand that still rested just above her stomach. "Hang on a second—you're not drinking . . ." My eyes darted up to meet hers. "You're not . . ." I leaned in. "*Are you?*"

Her eyes went wide and her hand drifted down.

Steven made an '*oh, shit*' face, then he snorted. "He creates cultivators like Sue creates pastries—are you really surprised he saw through you, Ruby?"

"Oh, shush, Steven! Don't be so loud!" She leaned in, her pupils dilated despite her lack of drink. "I am—it's only early days, though, so we're keeping it to ourselves."

"Guys!" I hissed, moving in to whisper. "That's unreal! Congratulations!"

Though she hadn't partaken of any rum, when Ruby smiled up at me, her cheeks were the rosiest of all. "Thank you, Fischer. There are still a lot of questions because, well, we're both cultivators now, and it's still so early in the pregnancy, but I have a feeling it's all going to work out."

She rubbed her stomach lovingly, and I went to shake Steven's hand, but then pulled them both into a hug instead. They were both cultivators, so I gave them a good squeeze.

"I'm over the moon for both of you—I can't imagine how you must be feeling." I let them go, a sigh escaping me as I did so. "You know, Fischer is a great unisex name."

Steven, who had just taken a sip of his drink, choked.

"Kidding! Just kidding!" I laughed.

Ruby patted him on the back as she giggled. "He rarely drinks."

"I'm fine," he said, still coughing. "I was just a little surprised."

"What did I miss?" Maria asked, slipping an arm around mine and raising an eyebrow. "Good news?"

"Errr," I said, rather dumbly.

"Oh, I don't expect you to keep it a secret from Maria, Fischer," Ruby said, taking pity on me. She leaned in close to Maria. "Can you keep a secret?"

At the prospect, she leaned in close, wobbling a little. "Of course!"

"I'm pregnant!" Ruby hissed in a rush, unable to keep it in any longer.

Maria froze. "You're serious?"

Steven nodded. "She is. As we told Fischer, it's only early days, but—"

"Artemis's quivering bow!" Maria yelled, cutting him off. Realizing how loud she was, she leaned in, shushing us as if *we'd* had the outburst. "Oh. My. Goodness!" She grabbed Ruby's hands and danced from foot to foot as she let out an almost-silent squeal. "That's amazing news! I can't believe it!"

Maria dragged Ruby off to the side as she peppered her with questions, leaving Steven and I alone.

"Loved the robes, by the way," I said, referencing the midnight-colored outfit with an embroidered rod and fish I'd caught Ruby in when she walked from the new church.

"Ah. Thank you. The pattern was all Ruby, but I made most of them. They were a delight to create."

"Do you, uh . . . think I could get one?"

He raised an eyebrow and smirked at me, his eyes a little distant from the drink. "Oh-ho! The heretic wants nothing to do with the church but wants a robe?"

I raised my hands.

"That may be true, but they look comfy . . . and pretty damn cool."

"They are comfy," he agreed, nodding. "And they do look pretty damn cool."

"So can I get one?"

"I'll see what I can do. I *suppose* I can rustle one up—for a price."

I rolled my eyes playfully at the amusement writ clear on his face. "What are you trying to get out of me, miser?"

"Oh, you know, I'm sure I'll think of something." He snapped his fingers, as if just remembering something. "What's that thing you like doing? With the rods and the water."

" . . . fishing?"

"Yeah! That's what it's called! I guess if you brought me a cooked fish or two, we could use that food as energy to make you a robe. The wife is pregnant, you see? I don't want to leave her without the nutrients necessary to grow a child . . ."

The grin he gave me was downright wolfish, and laughter tore free of my lips. "You've got yourself a deal, mate."

We shook hands, and before I could joke about his shrewdness, Maria and Ruby returned, the former leaning on the latter for support.

"I don't feel so good . . ." Maria mumbled, looking down at the sand.

"She downed a drink in celebration," Ruby said, rubbing her back. "I don't think it agreed with her."

"Do you want me to take you home?" I asked.

"Sh-shower," she replied, covering her mouth.

"Come on—we can go to mine." I turned to Ruby. "Would you mind coming with? She might need a hand . . ."

"Of course!"

I picked Maria up, not wanting the pregnant Ruby to have to support her. We all made our way inside, and I led them to the guest shower.

"There's a towel in there—I'll just go get some clean clothes," I said as I put Maria down.

When I returned with a fresh set of pajamas, Ruby took them, put an arm under Maria's shoulder, then led her inside. The door closed with a soft *click,* and a moment later, the calming sound of water falling rang out.

"I can't believe you have a shower . . ." Steven said, frowning at the door and rubbing his mustache. "I heard you had a System-built house, but to think you've had a shower this whole time . . ."

"They're unreal, right? If you think that's crazy, wait until you see this . . ."

* * *

"You're all right, dear," Ruby said, helping slide Fischer's shirt over Maria's head.

"I'm sorry . . ." Maria mumbled for what had to be the twentieth time.

"You have nothing to apologize for—I know I fell for the same trap a few times when I was your age."

"I know . . . it's just . . . sorry."

The poor girl's face was slack, and Ruby stroked her wet hair. "You'll feel better after some rest. Were you going home tonight?"

"I was going to ask Fischer to stay . . ."

"That's probably a good idea. I'm not sure how your dad would react if you turned up in a bad way. We can say you slept over at my place. Come on—let's get you to bed."

As Ruby opened the door and helped Maria out, Steven was yelling from another room. Raising an eyebrow, she followed the sound. Steven was at an open door on the other side of a bed, and Fischer was booming with laughter.

"What's got you so animated?" she asked, looking at her clearly drunk husband.

Steven turned to face her and gestured at the open door emphatically. "He has another shower in here, Ruby! Right beside his bed!"

Fischer laughed again, and Ruby rolled her eyes.

"Is it okay if Maria stays here, Fischer? She doesn't want to go home."

"Of course! She can sleep in the spare bed."

I led Ruby and Maria to the bedroom beside mine and threw back the covers. Ruby helped her into the bed. I reached into my shirt and withdrew the egg—and the bunny flopped over the top of it—then put them under the covers.

"Are you okay from here?" Ruby asked.

"Yeah—thanks for all the help. I'm sure she'll be fine after a little rest. Besides . . ." I reached over to pet Cinnamon. "This little mother can keep an eye on her."

Cinnamon looked out through blissfully slitted eyes, nodding.

"All right," Ruby said. "We'll leave you to it. Come calling if you need any help!"

As they walked out of the bedroom and through the front door, Steven's voice came trailing in. "*Two* showers!" he whisper-yelled, clearly shocked. "Two! And only the gods know how many beds!"

"Yes, dear," Ruby replied, patting his arm as she closed the door behind them.

Maria mumbled something, so I turned back and leaned in closer. "What was that?"

"Do you not like me, Fischer?"

The question brought me up short. "What? Of course I like you."

"It's okay if you don't . . ." Her words were soft and filled with resignation. "I just wanted to know—that's all."

I rested a hand on her arm. "What makes you think I don't?"

Cinnamon lifted her head from beneath the blanket and looked between us with narrowed eyes. She scooched the egg against Maria's leg for warmth before hopping out the door and closing it behind her, leaving the room plunged in shadow.

"Because . . ." Maria continued. "You haven't tried to . . . you know . . ."

I swallowed, my words failing me.

"You could—if you wanted to, I mean," she mumbled, her words laden with sleep.

I squeezed her hand reassuringly as my heart pounded in my chest. "It—it wouldn't be right with you so intoxicated, but I do like you Maria—more than I can put into words."

"Hmmm," she replied dreamily.

Silence took over, and all I could hear was my pulse thumping in my ears.

"Maria?" I asked, but she didn't reply, her breaths coming slow and steady.

I sighed and stood, paused, then bent back down to kiss her softly on the forehead. "Goodnight, Maria."

As I left the room, Cinnamon was sitting in a corner, staring at me. She raised her eyebrows, looking downright scandalized.

"Shush, you. Go lay on your egg and come get me if she's sick or needs help."

With a smirk she didn't bother hiding, Cinnamon hopped past me into the room and closed the door behind her.

CHAPTER FORTY-THREE

CITRUS

The ancient spirit, for what she thought was the first time in millennia, was completely content.

Compared to the span of her life, her time since reawakening had been turbulent, to say the least. She had been indifferent, angry, humbled, grateful, and, worst of all, almost torn apart by mere saplings. That moment of fear, of thinking that her life would come to an end at the hand of newborns, only stood to highlight just how happy she now was.

The spirit had become linked with the saplings. With each passing day that she continued providing them sustenance and power, their understanding of one another grew and blossomed, just as the flowers did atop their small canopies. Even now, countless pollinators flew from tree to tree, tickling her awareness. Each footfall, each speck of pollen removed, and every bit of sweet nectar sucked from the flowers were a blessing.

With the coming and going of the sun, the otter would bring her more sustenance. As with the insects pollinating her flowers, each meal was a cause for celebration.

The spirit gazed up at the moon—the otter was late with tonight's delivery of sustenance. Some may have experienced annoyance at this delay, but the ancient spirit wasn't such a fickle being. All things happened as the world allowed, and even if there was no delicious meal to partake in, she could just focus on the buzzing insects flitting through her awareness . . . right?

Two hours later, with the crescent moon peeking through the gap of her canopy, the ancient being's patience was at an end.

Her leaves shook in frustration, and just when she was considering sending a root out to seek the treacherous mammal that had likely stolen her food for herself, an approaching source of chi caught her attention. The otter, loping awkwardly with a tray held before her, slunk into the clearing. She chirped and grinned, and the being was just about to trip her with a root for her tardiness, but then she caught the scent of food.

Steam rose from the offering. The vapors were laced with chi of such potency that all of her thoughts of vengeance drained away like the rains through drought-parched soil. The otter dashed over and dumped the food at the base of the spirit's blue trunk. Forgetting about the bees, flowers, and lemon saplings entirely, the spirit sent a root up for a taste.

The first offering held a hint of burnt wood. She recoiled from it at first, but then the other flavors rushed out. Unknown seasonings and spices danced over her awareness, and she dove her root further in. Many of the previous meals had been skeletons with only slivers of flesh left, but this . . . the fish frame was covered in meat.

She withdrew the root to test another of the offerings. First came the familiar taste of charcoal, but as with the previous fish, unknown flavors rushed out and overwhelmed the unpleasant thoughts that burnt wood brought to mind.

She withdrew the root once more. This time, she plunged it into the gold-colored lumps, not expecting it to be as delectable as the fire-cooked fish.

Oh, how wrong she was.

The moment her root pierced the hard surface, it plunged into succulent flesh. The shell of crumbs had trapped the juices inside when cooked. A trickle of the oily liquid trailed down her root, and she absorbed it, not letting a single drop escape. Her canopy shuddered as she grew sprouts from her root, plunging one into each of the different offerings brought her.

Ecstasy roiled through every fiber of her being. With each morsel she absorbed, chi soared through her network of roots. When it hit the lemon trees, she felt them tug at it. Perhaps because she was too absorbed in her meal, or perhaps because she now saw the trees as part of herself, she let them drink of the essence. Some of the chi flowed back, but never as much as she sent their way.

All too soon, the feast was over. The last thing she absorbed was the crispy shell that had encased the fish, and she set all her roots to devouring every last crumb. She sighed, her whole trunk swaying. Filled with curiosity, she sent her awareness out to the lemon trees. They had absorbed so much of the essence, and she wondered at what they'd done with it.

She trailed the hints of power up their trunks, across their branches, toward their flowers, and . . .

No way . . .

At the tips of the branches, nestled among the leaves, some of the flowers had fruited. She sent herself toward the yellow growths, feeling them. They hadn't just fruited—they had matured completely.

The trees, using the power of the offered meal, had grown lemons.

She withdrew a drop of juice from one of them and sent it down toward her main body, and when she tasted the drop, she shuddered in delight, her canopy twitching. Though the citrus juice was sour, it held a hint of sugar, and, more importantly, unbelievably dense chi. The trees hadn't used all the essence in the fruit's creation—they'd refined, condensed, and changed it, pouring the culmination of their efforts into each lemon.

She felt a moment of desire, dreaming of absorbing their liquid and sucking the refined chi into her core, but it swiftly faded. The ancient spirit had made a deal with the cultivator—fruit in exchange for the continuous delivery of chi-filled meals. Her leaves shook once more, but not in annoyance or frustration.

Perhaps the cultivator would reward her success with even more of the crispy, animal-fat cooked fish. With thoughts of future pleasures, she sank into herself, processing the chi still coursing through her system.

With the midmorning sun warming my limbs, I smiled out at the ocean and placed a finger against my line, waiting for a bite.

Bill was beside me on the sand, and I reached a hand over to scratch the back of his head. His feathers were unbelievably soft and covered in a thin layer of water-repelling oil. He closed his eyes and leaned into my touch. His skin beneath was smooth, and I rotated my fingers slowly, massaging the top of his head.

"You a fan of pats, mate?"

He let out a low grunt of agreement.

"Makes sense—it can't be too easy scratching yourself with those webbed feet of yours."

He didn't respond, his body relaxing as my scritches continued.

Sergeant Snips leaned against my leg and blew a small series of bubbles as she postured herself for a good carapace rub.

I let out a soft laugh and wedged the rod between my crossed legs so I could pet both of them at once. I sank into the moment, letting the sensations of my body wash over me. Bill's smooth feathers, Snips's sturdy carapace, the wind tickling my skin, and the quiet crashing of waves on the shore—all served to tether me to the present.

But then memories of Maria's words last night came barreling through. It wouldn't have been good to try anything when she was so intoxicated, but why did the thought of it seem to heighten my anxiety so . . . ?

As worry shattered my mindfulness, Cinnamon let out a loud squeak from behind me. I grabbed the fishing rod and spun, looking back toward my home. Maria leaned against the doorway with her shoulder, with one hand covering her eyes and the other hung limp by her side.

I quickly wound the line in and passed the handle to Snips.

"How are you feeling?" I asked as I got to her.

"Like I was blasted by one of Rocky's claws . . ." She groaned and took a deep breath. "Maybe one of Pistachio's, too."

"I already got you a pastry and some juice—do you want me to go get a coffee?"

"No thanks. The pastry and juice sound good, though . . ."

After fetching them for her, we sat on the floor of my back porch.

Hidden from the sun's harsh light by the surrounding rock, Maria took another sip of sugarcane juice. "I feel much better already."

I gave her a smile. "Yeah, Barry's rum still packs a punch, but the hangovers don't seem to last long." I pointed down at her half-eaten breakfast. "Especially if you have pew-pew food."

She gave me a flat stare, and I sighed. "*Fine*—chi food. Better?"

"Much." She took another bite of the pastry, slowly chewing before washing it down with more juice. "What even happened last night? The last thing I remember is Ruby telling me . . ."

She bolted upright. "Ruby is pregnant!"

I grinned. "She is."

"Holy frack . . ."

A laugh flew from me at her curse, and she smiled along with me.

"So you don't remember anything after that?" I asked.

"No, I don't . . ." Her eyes shot up to me, and she swallowed, then paused, chewing her lip as she looked down at my clothes she was wearing. "We didn't . . . you know . . . did we?"

Heat immediately rose to my cheeks. "N-no, we didn't. You got sick after toasting Ruby's pregnancy, then she helped you back here and got you showered and changed. I took you to the spare bed, tucked you with Cinnamon—and her egg, the little weirdo—then went back out for a little. People were already stumbling back home, so I went back to bed pretty soon after."

"Wait . . . if I went to sleep in the spare bed, how did I wake up in yours?"

The heat in my face turned into a wildfire, and I looked out at the sand, hoping she didn't see the redness in my cheeks. "I honestly have no idea. I woke up to you wrapped around me like a koala."

" . . . a what?"

"Oh, right—they're not from here. Nevermind. You were cuddling me when I woke up this morning."

"O . . . oh. Sorry."

I risked a glance, seeing her face was as red as mine felt. I quickly looked away. "You don't need to apologize. It was . . . well, it was nice."

A silence blossomed between us, but unlike the companionable silence we so often experienced, this one felt strained.

I let out a deep sigh. "You make me feel like a teenager sometimes."

She covered her mouth as she giggled. "You make me feel exactly the same. I don't know what's going on in that head of yours half the time . . ."

I thought of what to say, searching for the perfect words to defuse the situation, but Maria handled it for me.

She leaned over, put an arm around my waist, and kissed me on the cheek. "Thanks for taking care of me, Fischer. You're a true gentleman."

She pulled back and our eyes met. Beneath the shade of my balcony, they were almost green, their usually blue tint nowhere to be seen. I leaned in to kiss her, but she moved her head to the side.

"I should probably brush my teeth before you try that. I can't say you'd enjoy the taste I woke up to."

I laughed, the sound bubbling from my throat and making my chest shake. Just like that, the awkward moment was gone. I leaned in and kissed her on the forehead instead, lingering there as I held the back of her head. Even after a night of heavy drinking, she smelled of flowers. It was comforting, and as I let her go, she pulled herself into a hug.

With our arms wrapped around each other and Maria's lithe body pressed against me, we jolted when someone came scrambling around the corner. We both looked over, taking in the wavering form of Leroy.

"*Comanlookalemon!*" he yelled, then held his head with both hands, swaying on the spot. "Ugh, my brain . . ."

Maria and I both looked at each other, back at him, then cackled.

"What . . . what did you just say?" Maria asked through fits of laughter.

"The lemon trees," he slowly muttered, still bracing his head. "Come."

I blinked dumbly, then my eyes went wide.

"Lemon *trees?*"

CHAPTER FORTY-FOUR

INSUBORDINATION

What about the lemon trees?" I asked as we traveled across the sand at an infuriatingly slow pace. "Did they germinate? How many?"

Leroy swallowed his bite of the leftover pastry I'd given him before grimacing my way. "I have my suspicions, but I don't want to find out what Claws would do if I ruined the surprise. She is chaos incarnate."

Maria giggled, covering her mouth. "Probably a safe move—we'll just have to wait and see."

"You can go on without me," Leroy said. "I'm still reeling from last night."

My body wanted to take him up on his offer, to sprint across the sands and see what had happened to the trees, but I fought it down. "Nah, mate. We're happy to wait for you."

"I understand your pain," Maria said, wincing. "That was me only a half hour ago."

Leroy grunted, shielding his eyes from the sun as we continued. "I hope it only takes me a half hour to feel better. What happened last night?"

"Well," I said, grinning at him. "Last I saw of you, Barbara was cradling you in her arms like a newborn."

"Good gods—I passed out?"

"Oh, no—you were very much awake. You were making up a song about someone named Trent? I don't know what that bloke did to you, but your drunk self was *not* a fan. Your wife was trying to cover your mouth, but you just kept belting out lines. It was quite impressive, really."

Leroy blanched as he blinked at me.

I roared with laughter. "Yeah, mate—it was as bad as it sounds. Barry's rum certainly makes for interesting feasts, if nothing else."

"I can't believe I missed that!" Maria said, the color in her face mostly returned.

"Wait, what happened to you?" Leroy asked, peering at her from beneath the hand that shielded his face from the sun.

"I may or may not have blacked out and needed to be showered by Ruby."

Leroy started laughing, then immediately stopped, hunching down and holding his head. "Dionysus's cursed grapes—when does it get better?"

"Soon, mate. Just keep munching that pastry and you'll be right as rain before you know it."

Soon after, we stepped from the harsh late-morning sun and into the shade of the forest's canopy.

Leroy let out a sigh of relief. "Thank the gods—that's much better."

The air was cool, almost sweet, and I breathed deep of its moisture. So did Leroy and Maria, and the former's posture immediately lost some of the tension it held. We walked in silence, and while I couldn't speak for the other two, my thoughts were consumed by what we'd find when we arrived in the clearing. As we got close to it, a strange sound rolled out over the forest floor to greet us.

"What is that?" Maria asked, cocking her head to the side.

I knew what it was, and when I spun toward Leroy, he gave me a knowing smile. "You recognize the sound, don't you?"

"Yeah . . ." I answered. "But why are they there?"

"What is it?" Maria asked.

I turned to her, my eyebrows knitted in thought.

"Bees . . . and lots of them."

Corporal Claws, mistress of the pond, fuzziest of Fischer's animals, and protector of the forest gazed out with pride at the lemon-peppered trees before her. Her master had given her a task, and as was her prerogative, she fulfilled it exceptionally. There was only a moment of shock when arriving this morning and finding ripe lemons covering each of the citrus trees—an undeniable sense of superiority had quickly swept it away.

Of course the lemons had grown. If anything, it was surprising that it took them so long to grow! Such was her general efficacy. She'd dashed to the blue-tinted trunk immediately and patted it, just as she pictured her master would. It was important that she reward her subordinates for their successes, and Claws was nothing if not a benevolent leader.

She had coo'd her approval, rubbing its rough bark even harder. The tree's canopy shimmied in delight, and Claws shimmied back, emulating the movement. As one, they danced their delight, one cooing, the other shaking her leaves.

After a suitably long boogie, Claws had set off to find Leroy. As much as she wanted to go fetch her master immediately, it wouldn't have been right to exclude her other subordinate. She had woken him from a drunken stupor and sent him off to get Fischer.

Now that she stood in the clearing beneath the shade of a lemon tree, she nodded at her own actions. It was good to delegate; it both let subordinates feel useful and reminded them of their place. Now that Fischer was no doubt on the way, she began practicing poses—she wanted to project capability when her master arrived to find her work.

When Fischer stepped out into the clearing, trailed by Maria and Leroy, all of their eyes went wide. As much as she wanted to run to her master and receive praise, Claws stood firm, leaning against the trunk casually as if to say: *oh, these lemon trees? I guess they're* kinda *cool.*

Her body physically shook as an urge to appear nonchalant warred with a desire for scritches. After less than the span of a single breath, she could hold on no longer.

Lightning erupted from her legs and she flew across the clearing, mouth wide and a shrill chirp tearing from her throat.

Lured along by the increasingly loud buzz of bees, we burst into the clearing. As I took in the scene before me, my legs froze. Maria took a sharp intake of breath, covering her mouth with one hand.

Leroy took a half step forward. "Are they . . . ?"

I had hoped—prayed—that we would find the lemon seeds germinated when we arrived. A small part of me dared to dream that they'd grown into stalks, perhaps even saplings, but given how unlikely that was, the rest of my consciousness had suppressed it. What I hadn't dared to consider, even in my wildest dreams, was that they would be grown-ass trees.

An unfathomable amount of insects flew around their canopies, flitting from flower to flower. Nestled among the swarming pollinators and dainty white flowers, dozens of yellow fruit hung, so full of juice that they weighed the branches down.

"Yeah . . ." I swallowed, unbelieving of what I saw. "They're lemon—*oof!*"

Distracted as I was by the scene of beautiful chaos, I hadn't noticed Claws's approach until it was too late. She slammed into me with a wide grin and a shrill chirp. I flew backward, Claws clutched to my chest so I wouldn't fall on and hurt her. Maria caught us, and rather than let us go, she held on tight, pulling us both into a hug. It was an objectively emasculating gesture for such a slight woman to be holding me upright, but I found I didn't hate it—it was weirdly comforting.

I hope this doesn't awaken something in me . . . I thought, my forehead furrowing.

"Claws," Maria said, completely unaware of my inner dilemma. "Did you do this?"

She chirped in the affirmative, spinning to cast a needle-sharp grin over my shoulder.

"What . . . what did you do?" I asked, my voice faint.

Before Claws could respond, a root flew from the ground and, at incredible speed, flicked her right in the middle of her forehead.

Claws's head rocked back. She blinked, then fury bloomed in her eyes. She shot from me with lightning fueling her passage, rocketing for the blue-barked tree in the center of the clearing. When she slammed into the tree headfirst, the lightning wreathing her drained away. I felt it go into the tree and circulate within.

Claws put one forepaw on her hip, pointed the other directly at the tree, and unleashed a verbal barrage of chirps, chittering, and hisses. The tree shook its leaves in response, and I got the sense it was arguing back. They chirped and shook back and forth, their debate continuing at a rapid-fire pace.

"What are they saying . . . ?" Leroy asked, cocking his head as their row intensified.

"I think the tree, or the spirit within it, to be more precise, is upset that Claws took all the credit."

The tree had raised a thick root from the earth, and it poked Claws in the chest. Claws poked it back. Then, the catfight began. Poking turned to striking, and before I knew it, they were wrestling on the ground. The root coiled around Claws, and she wrapped her limbs around it, biting its base between her needle teeth and kicking out with her back legs.

"Whoa, whoa!" I said, jogging over before it could get too violent. I gripped the root at its base. The spirit tried to retract the root, but I held on tight.

"Let go, both of you. Don't look at me like that, Claws—I don't care who started it, missy! Let go!"

She did so, as did the spirit, and just as they separated, Claws slapped it one more time. The tree vibrated in indignation and also lashed out; a root slapped Claws right on the rump before she could get out of range. Lightning erupted from her limbs and she flew for it, but right as the fight was about to start anew, I gripped Claws by the loose skin on the back of her neck. I held her up and planted my foot on the root's base, holding them both in place.

"That's enough. You both got one more hit in."

Claws took a deep breath before hissing it out through clenched teeth. The tree seemed to as well, its branches swaying out and retracting in.

"You brought the food here for our tree pal, right Claws?" I asked.

She puffed her chest out and chirped with pride, which looked hilarious considering I still held her up like a newborn kitten.

"And you," I continued, pointing at the tree. "You used the food to grow the lemons, correct?"

The root beneath me nodded vehemently.

"Right—so you both did it. *Agreed?*"

Claws crossed her arms—so did the tree by sprouting two little tendrils from its root.

"Ladies . . ." I knelt down so I was eye to eye with the root—well, where its eyes would be if it had them. "You've both done something amazing here, and I can't properly appreciate it until you stop fighting. Can you do that for me, Claws?"

She glared at me defiantly.

" . . . please?"

All at once, the raging bonfire in her eyes reduced to an ember and she let out an apologetic chirp. In response, the root uncrossed its, well, roots, and nodded, copying her movement. I smiled at both of them, feeling genuine relief. I pulled Claws into a hug, cradling her into my arms to apologize for holding her by the scruff.

"Unbelievable . . ." Maria said, walking over to us with hesitant steps. "The tree . . . ?"

I shrugged. "Looks like it, yeah. It's as sapient as they come."

Leroy stepped past us and laid a hand on its sturdy trunk. The root turned to face him, cocking its makeshift head as it took him in. "It . . . no, sorry, *she*—you're a female, right?" he asked the root.

My eyes narrowed; I'd said ladies, but hadn't realized it until Leroy pointed it out. As with my animal pals, I had a sense of her gender.

The root—she—nodded, and Leroy turned to me. "She has expanded her bounds. Can you feel it?"

Confusion crossed my face, and I closed my eyes. I felt the waves of energy flowing around me, and just as Leroy had said, they swept outward, going to . . .

My eyes shot open.

"You took over the lemon trees?"

The tree made a *kind of* gesture.

"I think it's more accurate to say she joined them." Leroy walked over and touched one of their trunks. "I can feel a sort of awareness within each tree . . . they're unique, as if they were each a different person."

The root nodded.

"Unreal . . ." I said, walking over to stand beneath one of the lemon trees.

They were squat and nowhere near as tall as the blue-barked tree, yet I could still stand at my full height beneath them. From below, the hum of the pollinators was even louder, and I closed my eyes for a moment, letting the symphony wash over me. The remnants of a breeze flew beneath the forest canopy, and the cool, humid air swept across my skin, sending a pleasant chill through me. Maria slipped an arm around my waist, and we stood there for a long moment, both just enjoying existence.

When I opened my eyes, Maria was gazing up. I joined her in staring at the juicy, fat lemon hanging just above us. I raised a hand to cup it, then turned to the root still extended from the earth. "Can I pick it?"

The root's posture turned flummoxed, and the leaves of its main tree shook in what I took as humor. The root nodded, holding where its stomach would be in the approximation of a belly laugh. I smirked at it before returning my attention to the lemon. With a single tug, it came free.

"It's so big . . ." Maria said.

"No kidding." I squeezed the grapefruit-sized citrus. "These are even bigger than the genetically modified ones from back home."

"They're almost *too* big." She stepped closer, peering down. "How are you gonna use all of it? It'll taste too sour if you use all that juice in a single dish, right?"

"Huh . . ." I said, squinting at the lemon.

Maria arched a brow at me. "What's up?"

"You just gave me a fantastic idea . . ."

CHAPTER FORTY-FIVE

WHEN LIFE GIVES YOU LEMONS

Late morning gave way to midday as Maria and I toiled in the kitchen. We'd left Claws and Leroy behind in the clearing to do . . . *I dunno. Gardening stuff?* Frankly, I was too excited to care what they were up to.

"You're sure this is gonna taste good, Fischer?" Maria asked, frowning down at my concoction.

"When have I ever failed you?" I shot her a wink.

"Well, there was that one time you took me camping during a tempest, and we got soaked, and I could have caught pneumonia, and I could have die—"

"That was one time! Everyone gets one for free."

"Hmmm." She rubbed her chin in thought. "I suppose that's true . . ."

"Besides," I added. "The proof is in the pudding."

She narrowed her eyes and looked around, scanning my kitchen. "What pudding?"

"Oh, forget it. I mean the proof is in the end result."

I added another spoonful of sugar and stirred. When the granules had mostly dissolved, I tasted it. The sugar had cut the lemon's bitterness down, and the flavor, though not chilled, was thirst-quenching.

"Here," I said, holding up a spoon.

Maria opened her mouth, and I poured the lemonade in.

Her eyebrows lowered for a moment, no doubt expecting a sour explosion, but then her eyes flew wide.

"Good gods . . ." she said after swallowing. "That is amazing."

I grinned. "If you think that's good, wait until I cook up Asano's recipe—it takes a little more time, though."

"Whose recipe?"

I smiled wistfully. "A fictional character from my home world. I tried making his lemonade once before coming here, and let me tell you, it's life changing."

"A fictional character's . . . recipe?" She scowled at me. "I can't tell if you're messing with me or not."

"I know—it's fun, right?"

"No, Fischer." Her scowl turned deadpan. "It's not."

"Ah well, some people can't enjoy the good things in life. C'mon—let's take this lemonade to our churchy companions. They might need the pick-me-up after last night."

We crossed the sand at a clipped pace, and after knocking on Barry's door, we waited in silence.

"Maybe they're not home." Maria suggested. "Should we go get Leroy to see if they're in the church?"

"I don't know . . . I'm a little worried, to be honest. They were in quite a state last night, and they should be up by now, even if they're a little hungover . . ."

"Won't it risk, I don't know, discovering something you don't want to if we go down there?"

I rubbed my chin, torn between my desire for secrecy and the need to check on my pals. "Steven let something slip last night—he mentioned that all of their showers were beside the bedrooms at the end of the hall. If we just follow the hallways and don't look in any room until we get to the end, we should be fine."

Maria chewed her lip, then nodded. "All right. I'm in."

As we stepped into what used to be Barry's shed, Maria's eyes went wide. "Wow . . . I assumed it would be incredible, but this . . . ?"

"Right?" I ran one hand over the smooth stone, as did Maria.

We made our way down the steps. Each time we approached a sconce in the wall, it lit with a magical flame.

"That's not a good sign," I said.

"Why?" Maria asked, cocking her head.

"Because they light up when someone comes near. It means no one has been by recently."

"Hmmm. Let's hurry, then."

As we passed each room, Maria peered inside. I'd already relayed what I'd seen in each, but hearing was different from seeing with one's own eyes.

"Unbelievable . . ." she said as she poked her head into the underground spa. "That looks simply divine."

"We should come visit sometime—I'm sure they wouldn't mind."

"I'd never forgive myself if I said no to that offer."

When we strode past the indoor forest, her jaw dropped open. "I'm not sure if this or the blue tree is more impressive."

"Including the lemons? The blue tree. Without, though . . . there's something breathtaking about such a large tree, especially growing underground."

"Yeah, no kidding."

I walked further, and she lingered a moment, staring at the thick trunk before jogging to catch up.

"This is as far as I came last time," I said. "We'll have to keep our eyes forward from here on—no peeking in doors, open or not."

"I can do that." She hooked her arm in mine, squeezing me tight. "I do wonder what's down here sometimes, though . . ."

"I know, right?" I winced. "It's incredibly annoying. I don't want to be a part of it, but my brain can't help but imagine what secrets they're hiding."

Before the next sconce lit, an open door ahead of us shone magical light out into the hallway. Maria shielded the left side of her eyes with one hand, then did the same for me.

"Thank you," I said, smiling. "Not sure I could have resisted the temptation . . ."

The magical flame in the wall flickered to life, and we continued on, not gazing into the open room despite the desire to.

"Hey!" a nasally voice called. Not recognizing it, I froze.

"Where in Poseidon's chafed thighs is my breakfast?"

Maria's hand fell away. Dumbfounded, we both turned to look at the speaker.

Barry woke to the sensation of someone trying to crack his head open like it was a particularly ripe coconut.

"Ugghhh," he moaned, cradling his pounding head.

"Ngghhh," Helen agreed from beside him. "My head. What happened last—Paul!" she yelled, shooting upright.

"He stayed at Sue's," Barry reminded her, laying a hand on her knee.

With her maternal instincts no longer overriding the hangover, she slumped back down to the bed. "Water . . ."

She tried to get up, but Barry held her shoulder, halting her movement. "I'll get it, love. Wait there."

With no small amount of effort, he rolled out of bed and walked toward the kitchen. As he returned with a glass of water in each hand, a muffled conversation caught his attention. It was coming from Trent's open door, and Barry wondered if the sugarcane juice was finally taking effect.

Ellis had theorized that it was the collar halting the transformation, but Barry didn't want to risk removing it. Trent had drunk countless glasses of what Fischer would call pew-pew juice yet still hadn't awakened.

Barry rolled his eyes—Fischer may be a god waiting to happen, but he came up with the worst names.

As Barry's limping mind caught up to what his eyes could see, he realized the hallway from the entrance up to Trent's room was lit. A spike of panic tore up Barry's spine and wedged itself firmly within his pounding skull. Had someone wandered in and found the prince?

He set the glasses down and jogged to the open door, each sconce he passed lighting up. His head pounded with every footfall, but he forced himself to continue. He had to get there, had to make sure no one was freeing the prince, had to . . .

He stopped in the opening, as did his thoughts.

"Barry?" Fischer asked, raising an eyebrow.

"Er—yes, Fischer?"

"Are you aware there's a bloke locked up in your basement?"

Barry swallowed and raised a finger to object, but his brain failed him.

He drooped. "It's a long story . . ."

"A long story?" The self-described prince demanded from behind me. "No it's not!

You kidnapped me, your future king, and wrapped a cultivator's collar around my neck! I've already told this noble man about your crimes!"

Barry squinted at me, at Trent, then leaned against the doorframe. "I'm too hungover for this."

"Lemonade?" I asked, holding up a cup.

" . . . what?" Barry asked, peering through bleary eyes.

"Could you hold this, Maria?"

She took the cup, her eyebrow furrowed as she glanced back at the apparent prince. I filled the cup to the brim with lemonade, and Maria offered it to Barry.

"Thank . . . you?"

He lifted it to his mouth, smelled it, then had a sip. His eyebrow quirked a little and he took another drink, deeper this time.

"Hey . . . that looks good," the odd prince said, leaning his face up against the bars. "Give me some."

I raised an eyebrow at Barry, who was now sculling his glass.

He let out a deep sigh after finishing. "I suppose you've seen him now." Barry shrugged. "We've been feeding him sugarcane juice to no effect."

Maria held up another cup, still watching the prince with an unreadable gaze. I filled it up, and she passed it to him.

He sniffed it, drank, then his eyebrows knitted. "Lemon . . . how do you have *lemon?*"

I cocked my head at him. "You came to Tropica with collared cultivators, right?"

"That's right," the toe-like prince replied, having another sip. "This is actually *really* good."

"Focus, mate. You came to Tropica, had your ass absolutely handed to you by my animal pals, got imprisoned by my mate here." I pointed over my shoulder at Barry. "And you're surprised that we have lemons?"

Trent sniffed. "So? You're not supposed to have lemons, especially not enough to make a jug that big."

Barry, whose disposition was already improving after drinking a little lemonade, shook his head. "Trent is a little intellectually . . . different."

"That's right!" Trent said. "My mother, the queen, always said I was unique. Best you remember that, peasants—I'll be using those smarts to bust out of this prison the first chance I get."

Penelope Francine Gormona, the queen of Gormona, sat down on a high-backed seat in the throne room. "Where is that idiot son of ours?"

Her husband, Augustus Reginald Gormona, started. He glanced at her from his position on the throne. "What was that, dear?"

"Our son. Where on Kallis is he?"

The king shook his head. "Alive—we know that much."

The queen opened the locket slung around her neck, and sure enough, the small stone inside glowed a dull red. They had one such artifact for each of their children, and she'd worn Trent's day in and day out since his departure. Despite her awareness of his infirmity, he was still her son, and she would burn the kingdom to the ground to save him.

"Are you sure we can't send out a party to search for him?"

Her husband's eyes grew hard. "We've discussed this, wife. We don't have the resources with our kingdom under attack."

She wanted to call him a fool, wanted to challenge his ability to leave their son in danger, but reined the words in before they could fly free. It wouldn't help the situation. "Are you sure we *are* under attack?"

His jaw clenched, and though he probably had some of his own choice words, he simply nodded. "It cannot be coincidence. Five high-ranking officials disappearing without a trace, the theft of resources, and the awakening of five spirit beasts. It is a clear message. Someone wishes to make a fool of us."

A glint came to his eye, and he sat upright.

"They don't know that we have the artifacts we do. In this time of peace, the other kingdoms have forgotten the power that Gormona wields. We know about the spirit beasts, and we'll snuff them out before they can find the walls of our kingdom. They think they can challenge Gormona and walk away peacefully . . ."

The king let out a deep chuckle.

"We will learn who launched the attack after we find the spirit beasts, and then they'll rue the day they tried to slight Augustus Reginald Gormona."

At his words, she turned away, chewing her lip.

I watched Trent down the rest of his lemonade. The so-called prince let out a belch, followed by a contented sigh. As he stood there, mouth open and facing the roof, I noted that he had a head like a kicked-in watermelon. I'd never admit as much—that would be downright rude, after all—but in the confines of my own thoughts, I couldn't help but acknowledge how unfortunate-faced the man was.

I turned to Barry, who was sipping at another glass. "Can we talk for a second, mate?"

He nodded, his eyes holding a tension that had nothing to do with his headache.

"Hey! Don't forget my breakfast!" Trent called, but we all ignored him.

When we got far enough away, Maria spoke up first.

"Slavery, Barry?" she asked, her face riddled with disapproval.

"It's complicated," he replied. "I know it looks bad, but I have plans."

I shook my head.

"You're not gonna like what I have to say, mate."

CHAPTER FORTY-SIX

ADMIRING THE SCENERY

With the warm glow of magical fire lighting the smooth stones of the underground church, I weighed Barry with my eyes. The air between us seemed to thicken with tension, and before it could grow any more palpable, I sighed.

"I know this is me poking my head where I've specifically requested to be left out of, but I have to draw the line at slavery, mate."

Barry rubbed his temples, looking better but still worse for wear.

"Forgive the bluntness, Fischer—I'm too hungover for anything else. It's a temporary measure, and one that was—is—completely necessary. He's not being abused, forced to do anything, or deprived of necessities." Barry ran his hands through his hair, shaking his head. "By the gods, Fischer, have you seen his *cell?*" He emphasized how inaccurate the last word was with air quotes. "He sleeps in a bed the same as yours, eats better food than most villagers in Tropica, and we've been feeding him sugarcane juice like he's parched ground desperate for rain!"

By the end of Barry's rant, he was yelling, flinging his hands wide. All at once, he deflated, his shoulders slumping once more. "Sorry. I'm under a lot of stress here."

I glanced at Maria—she gave me a conflicted and strained smile that reflected my own feelings. I threw my head back and looked at the roof, imagining a creator high above.

"I really am inside a terribly written Xianxia. Whoever wrote this storyline sucks."

"What . . . ?" Barry asked.

"Slavery. I tried to ignore the collared cultivators, but now you've got a bloody royal collared up in a dungeon. What am I supposed to do? Pretend it's not happening, or go about ending it to virtue signal to the reader that I'm a good bloke? It's low-hanging fruit, mate—may as well have me stop someone from kicking a cat."

Barry only grew more confused. He leaned in close, narrowing his eyes. "Who has been kicking cats?"

I sighed. "No one has—I'm just complaining out loud." I looked back at the open doorway behind us, from which the collared prince was berating everyone and anything in an attempt to get some brekkie. "So, what's the plan with him? You said it's only temporary—what does that mean?"

"You're sure you want to know . . . ?" Barry asked.

"No, mate—not even a little, but I *do* want reassurance that my existence doesn't mean that people get enslaved."

"Do you trust me, Fischer?"

I slumped backward, leaning against the wall. "It's not that I don't trust you, this is just . . ." I gestured back at the cell. "It's *a lot.*"

Barry nodded. "It is, and I'm sorry you had to find out. What are you even doing down here, anyway?" He grimaced as we locked eyes. "I told you there were things in here that you wouldn't want to see . . ."

"We were worried for your safety," Maria said, gesturing at the lemonade. "We brought this, and thought if we just kept our eyes forward we wouldn't see anything we shouldn't."

"But then a certain something yelled at us for breakfast," I said, smiling despite everything. "He is a bit of a prick, isn't he?"

Laughter bubbled up from Barry. It flew free, and he joined me at the wall, leaning beside me. "You have no idea, Fischer. He was—is—a right prick. If you knew what he tried to do . . ." Barry shook his head. "I'll spare you the details, but suffice to say, a little imprisonment might honestly be too good for him. It was the kindest option we had at hand, though I'd be lying if I said I didn't get a sense of satisfaction when I clapped that metal collar around his neck."

"Wow—he must have been a prick," Maria said, smirking at him. "I'm not sure I've ever seen you angry."

"Agreed," I said. "The anger of a gentle man is nothing to scoff at."

A silence stretched between the three of us as our own thoughts consumed us. After a short while, I stood from the wall, stretching.

"All right—I've decided." I turned to Barry. "You're planning on making him awaken so he can't go running back home and tell his royal family of our existence, right?"

"Correct—as usual. We're also hoping we can win him over to our side, but even if he should try to escape . . ." He shrugged. "I really don't think he has much chance of outrunning Claws—do you?"

As I imagined the vicious glee she'd have etched on her face if she were given a target to pursue, I shook my head, grinning.

"No—I don't think he'd have any luck escaping that little deviant." I spun to face Barry. "I do trust you. As long as your goal is to free him eventually and you keep treating him well, I won't interfere. If you're not opposed, I might even give you a hand."

"A hand . . . ?"

"Yeah, mate." I shot him a wink. "If your sugarcane juice hasn't been working, maybe I can rustle something up that pushes him over the line."

Ellis, head archivist of the royal library, was having a terrible day. Someone was in his precious domain—a group of someones, judging by the chaos they brought with them. Already, liquids had been spilled on tables, food crumbs had been strewn across the carpets, and now, someone had taken his golden candelabra—complete with ten lit candles—into the stacks of ancient books.

With fury powering each step, Ellis ran after the firelight retreating further into the library. Each time he rounded a bookshelf, his antagonist would be just out of sight. They were always one corner away, and it infuriated him to no end. To think they were moving with such speed while holding an open flame . . .

His face contorted into a hate-filled snarl, and he lifted his knees, tried to catch his foe, but it was as if he ran through mud. His steps, no matter how much he tried to pick up the pace, moved at the same speed.

It only filled him with more fury.

He leaned forward, tried to break through the invisible barriers slowing him, and rushed headlong into his adversary.

"Ellis . . ." they said, taunting him.

They held him by his robe, and he tried to see their face, but the golden candelabra was held before them, obscuring their features with the candles' orange glow. He tried to break free as the attacker shook him, threatening to spill the hot wax across his beloved books.

"Ellis . . . ? Yoo-hoooo," I said, grabbing him gently by the collar. I shook him slightly, raising an eyebrow at how toned his body had become. "Damn, Ellis. You're feeling jacked, my man—"

"Unhand my fiery shaft, fiend!" he bellowed into my face, spittle flying as he bolted upright. He breathed heavily, blinking at me as his eyes cleared.

I looked up, turning to Theo and the rest of the fishing club that I'd already woken. As one, we burst into laughter.

"What in Morpheus's blessed realm were you dreaming of, Ellis?" Danny got out through fleeting giggles that sounded hilarious from the burly man.

Keith had collapsed, leaning against Theo for support.

"Remind me to never touch Ellis in his sleep!" He flinched and raised a hand to his head. "Gods, my own voice is like a sledgehammer to my brain."

Ellis blinked, squinted, then braced his forehead with both hands. "Please . . . stop being so loud."

Everyone laughed again, but they quickly cut off again.

"Here," I said. "I brought you guys a remedy."

Maria and I started handing out the hangover cure, and each person drank deep. We'd already visited the bed chambers across the hall, providing lemonade to the church members within.

"Wonderful," Ellis said, whatever godsforsaken dream he'd been having already long forgotten. "Would you tell me the recipe?"

He removed his notepad and pencil, fighting through the pain, and I smiled at him.

"That's easy, mate. It's lemon and sugar."

"Lemon . . ." he repeated, then his eyes went wide. "Lemon! It *is* lemon? Where did you get so much?"

Theo squinted at him. "A little quieter, Ellis, if you would."

I smiled at them. "When you're feeling up to it, I have something to show you. You might need to see it to believe."

A cup or two of lemonade each and a short walk later, we arrived at the clearing.

"Remarkable . . ."

I was delighted at the unveiled awe held in Ellis's eyes. I wasn't sure if it was the hangover or the sight—perhaps both—in the short time I'd known him, it was rare that something shocked Ellis enough for him to stop taking notes. As if the same thought occurred to him, he lowered his pencil and began scribbling. Everyone split up to explore the clearing, and Maria and I wandered over to the blue-barked tree in the center, sitting in the grass and leaning against its trunk.

Claws curled up in Maria's lap, and I reached over to rub her fur. I laid my other palm back against the tree.

"You girls did so well."

As the ancient spirit watched the humans and creatures perusing her Domain, an unknown emotion seemed to bubble up from the earth beneath her. When the cultivator "Fischer" set a hand to her trunk and praised her work, the trickle turned to a torrent. Though it was a new sensation, it wasn't bad.

Quite the opposite.

She could feel the emotions of the cultivators crossing the forest floor above her network of roots. Only hints of their emotions, but more than enough to understand their intent. Their eyes were wide, reflecting the afternoon sun as it filtered down through her canopy. The tones they spoke in were soft yet rushed, like the winds that hissed through her leaves before a storm. Their movements reminded her of the small prey animals that dashed from cover to cover during the daylight hours. Their steps, however, weren't hastened by fear—it was excitement, perhaps even awe.

As she focused on them further, she realized that they—each and every one of them—possessed chi. They were cultivators, yet they flitted around her clearing as if they were aspects of nature. The most powerful of all was a man that could, in all likelihood, tear her from the ground roots and all. He leaned against her trunk, holding the hand of a woman and lovingly patting an otter as if it was his own child. These sources of power, beings that her instincts told her should be fighting over the chi-laden fruits hanging from her lemon tree branches, were simply admiring the scenery and each other's company. It made something deep within her blossom, and the feeling of contentment unfurled and solidified.

A soft breeze blew across her canopies. It sent shivers of pleasure down her branches, through each trunk, and into her network of roots.

It didn't stop there.

When the sensations of each tree met beneath the soil, they bounced into each other, combining and flourishing into something . . . new. It traveled toward her core, slowly making its way closer to that nexus of power. Any other time, she may have assumed it was an attack—something negative to be shielded from. She might have even held it at bay, stopping whatever it was in its tracks. With contentment suffusing her being, however, she simply rested and let it come.

If the ancient being had all of her memories, she would have recognized the event for what it was. Instead, she was entirely caught off guard when every leaf, branch, splinter, and root shone with a blinding white light.

CHAPTER FORTY-SEVEN

ANCIENT MEMORIES

Despite the events of the day, I believed it was going to be a relaxing afternoon. Sunlight filtered down through the canopy above, shifting when a breeze swept through the leaves. Maria put her hand in mine, and I held her tight. Corporal Claws, the apparent druid of this grove, had one-half of her body draped over each of our knees. I had the toothy end, and she gazed up at me with her trademark cheeky grin, made all the more mischievous by the dagger-like points of her teeth.

All the church members milled around the clearing, gathering in small groups as they walked from tree to tree. They wandered, gazing up at insects and smelling flowers. The scene reminded me of visitors in an art exhibition, moving from exhibit to exhibit with childlike wonder on their faces. Maria squeezed my hand, and when I turned toward her, she was as awestruck as everyone else. But there was a hint of hesitancy coloring her disposition, hidden in the creases around her eyes that were usually caused by smiles.

I thought to ask what caused her worry, but then the world started to glow.

It was a subtle thing at first, as if someone had slid up the saturation on an image. Colors grew more distinct from one another: the lemons became the color of a yellow highlighter, Corporal Claws's pearly teeth turned almost opalescent, the grass and leaves surrounding us looked like something from a cartoon, and the blue in Maria's eyes glowed like everfrost beneath the midday sun. Everyone stopped moving, their eyebrows lowering and faces growing concerned.

Then, the light truly bloomed.

Lines of the purest white shot from every visible part of the lemon trees. Some bloomed from behind me, and I whirled, seeing them coming from the tree I leaned on. Last, they beamed up from the ground, tracing the patterns of roots that connected the trees before shooting outward in tangled webs of indescribable complexity. It all happened in the blink of an eye and would have been over before it began to a regular human. With my enhanced vision, however, I saw each microsecond in exacting detail.

When the lines shone from every part of the spirit's tree, they expanded. The pure white light diffused, stretching and connecting until they touched one another. Then, with a note of finality, a *boom* like one thousand drums being struck tore into existence. The sound went through me, pounding against every fiber of my being.

When it hit my core, that nexus of power within that seemed to contain my chi, it reverberated, absorbing the sound and sending it back out.

My body jolted, my limbs splaying outward and back arching. My diaphragm spasmed, and as I tried to breathe in, my body froze. Swift as it had come, the light bled from the world. My inner muscles relaxed, and with my back still arched, I took a shaky breath.

"Fischer!" Maria was in front of me, holding my face with her hands. "Fischer! Are you okay?"

"Y . . . yeah . . ." My voice was raspy as I spoke, and I cleared my throat. "I think so . . ."

Everyone had gone still, their eyes locked on me. I stared back, not understanding the concern on their faces. "What's up . . . ?"

"What's up?" Barry repeated, his voice shrill. "You just exploded with light! What the frack's up with you, mate?"

"Me?" I laughed, shaking my head. "Nah, it was from the tree."

"Aye . . ." Fergus said, clenching and unclenching his fists. "The tree first, but then you."

"Not just light, either," Theo added. "It struck me—like it had a physical force."

Ellis flew into action. He sprinted at me, his notepad in hand as he leaped. He came to a skidding stop before me, his eyes pinning me down. "Tell me everything." He swallowed, lowering pencil to paper. "Spare. No. Detail."

I opened my mouth to respond, but then something tugged at me.

"Fischer?" Maria asked, but her voice was distant. "Fischer!"

That's odd . . . I thought as my vision tilted to the side.

Maria called my name again, but it seemed to come from far away. Rather than feel disoriented, I felt content as a welcoming presence swept me up.

The ancient spirit came into being above a vast expanse of dirt.

She was freshly awoken.

With nothing tethering her to the land, she sailed on unseen currents of air, flitting to and fro in whichever direction the wind blew. Though she knew not what she sought, something deep within her did, and it scanned the scoured lands for a foothold.

A draft brought her closer to the ground, giving her a better view of the battlefield. A terrible conflict had befallen the coastline, leaving behind not one spark of life. The earth was pockmarked with rivets, holes, and impact sites, revealing hard clay below. Part of the coast itself had been entirely obliterated, chewing a circular crater into what should have been fertile soil. The ocean's water had rushed into the crater, mixing with the exposed dirt to become a muddy, lifeless bay.

Though she was closer to the ground now, she could still see for miles in every direction. All was brown dirt and black ash, not one speck of greenery remaining following whatever calamity had befallen this place. It filled her with . . . despair?

Yes, that was it.

The wind blew her southwest, and as she approached a range of mountains, curiosity joined her morose opinion of the world she found herself in.

The mountains had been freshly unearthed.

Their peaks were filled with jagged rocks and angular sheets of slate. Whoever or whatever had destroyed all life here had done enough damage to rip the world's crust asunder.

Before she could think too much about a being that could create mountains, something reached out and tugged at her soul. She sailed down toward it, using what insignificant energy she had to direct her path. Fighting against the unseen winds trying to sweep her along, she reached the scorched landscape. It smelled of burning, and she recoiled, warring with the urge to take flight once more and get far, *far* from this place. The only thing keeping her there was a spark of life, and she reached down with part of her spirit, using it to sweep aside a clump of dirt.

There, nestled among the ashes and mud, was a single leaf. It was yellow, starved of sunlight and nutrients. Part of it was brown and rotted, disease having taken hold.

She looked toward the sky.

She could leave this place of death, sail high above the earth to find a place filled with life and abundance. Part of her demanded that she did so for her own chance of survival, if nothing else. But then she gazed back down at the seedling. In this place of war, where the earth had been scorched and not even a splinter of wood remained, it had sprouted. Against all odds, the seed defied the very heavens, seeking to grow where naught but ashes remained.

Her mind was made up. She reached out to the single leaf, and, like the ocean flooding the crater to the northeast, they became one.

She immediately gathered chi from the surrounding land—it was acrid, as if the very air surrounding her was . . . wrong. Ignoring the flavor, she poured it into her new body. First, the rotten leaf was healed. Then, another grew. Her twin leaves absorbed the light of the sun, and using the energy it provided—along with the acidic chi around her—the spirit and her new tree flourished.

The sun and moon took their turns in the sky, blurring by as time passed and she turned from seedling to sapling and from sapling to tree. Birds flew high overhead, sometimes resting in her branches and leaving seeds in their wake. Slowly, over the span of years, life returned to the valley. Weeds and grasses grew first, but as other seedlings sprouted from the earth, their canopies eventually spread and starved the weeds of the sunlight needed to survive.

It was with her tree thriving and reaching its branches toward the sun that she had come face to face with her first cultivators. The four men had known of what she was, and as they spoke of harvesting her chi, she tried to fight them off. She had raised a root in defense, seeking only to shield herself from their attacks, but their leader caught her extended root like a bird would pluck an insect from the sky. This one moment of distraction had been all it took, however. His three companions attacked at once, seeking to destroy the man and claim her chi for themselves.

But they had underestimated the scarred man.

Even with a lethal wound in his side, he had lashed out with fire and lightning. All four cultivators died that day, and instead of harvesting her power, it was she that absorbed theirs.

As decades passed, the muddy waters of the bay grew clear, storms washing away mud and leaving sand in its place. The surrounding trees grew, and she even expanded to inhabit more, adding them to the network of her body. The entire time, however, the world's chi dwindled. At first, she had assumed it was because of where she chose to live. The earth has been scoured of life, after all, and who knew what effect that would have over time?

But as decades turned to centuries, she knew the truth of it—the world itself was losing its chi. This only made the cultivators more brazen. They sought her out, all the while blathering about her brothers and sisters they'd already extinguished. More was her elation when she absorbed the chi of each and every defiler. Despite the dwindling chi, she had grown powerful, and with each cultivator's passing, the distance between herself and the attackers widened.

Then, something changed.

Power returned to the world, and those cultivators she did sense rarely bothered her. They fled from or pursued one another, and those that came for her chi were already pushed to their limit, seeking her out in desperation. This time lasted for the mere blink of an eye compared to the centuries she had seen.

One day, it was over.

Like a flashfire, the excess chi burned bright and disappeared, and the world returned to its dwindling state. More cultivators came, some of which sat beneath her canopy rather than attack. She merely watched and listened to these travelers; she would not seek the destruction of life unless it sought the end of hers. These humans knew not what she was, so merely used her vast canopy for the shade it provided. Despite their lack of aggression, she had no doubt they'd try to rip out her nexus of power if they knew what she was—not that they'd have succeeded.

Slowly, even these peaceful cultivators stopped visiting, and lacking the chi she absorbed of those foolish enough to attack her, she knew it was time to rest. She withdrew from her network of trees, leaving them there to be claimed by any spirit with the power and inclination.

With one last breath of her beloved forest's sweet air, she went to sleep.

My eyes flew open and I took a deep breath; the air was sweet, just as the spirit remembered so, *so* long ago.

Tears welled in my eyes, tickling my cheeks as they ran down my face.

Maria stared down at me, her eyes wide and red. "Fischer . . . where did you go?"

She wiped my tears as I sat up, and I focused on my breath to calm my emotions. "The tree . . . she showed me her memories."

Ellis was still sitting before me, his face filled with desire and hands trembling.

I held up a hand, stalling the questions no doubt burning the back of his throat. "I need a moment, mate . . ."

He sat back. "Right." His hand still shook, but he put his pencil away. "Sorry, Fischer, I did not intend . . ."

Something filled my vision, not at all caring that I had willed the System's notifications to halt. I swallowed, my mouth going dry as I read the line printed before me.

New Domain established!

CHAPTER FORTY-EIGHT

FORBIDDEN KNOWLEDGE

In disbelief, I read the screen again.

New Domain established!
[Error: Insufficient power.]

"No way . . ." I said, too shocked to be bothered by the return of my insufficiently powered nemesis. Everyone was in a loose circle surrounding me, and one by one, their eyes cleared.

"A Domain . . . ?" Theo asked. "What on Kallis is that . . . ?"

Ellis started writing with a shaky hand. He looked up, staring at nothing as his pencil pressed into the notepad. With a soft *snap,* its tip flew off.

"Domains," he said, his voice distant, "were thought to be long extinct. The capital's tomes mentioned little about them, other than that they were something to be feared."

"Feared?" Barry took a step forward. "Is it something we should be worried about?"

Ellis's eyes focused, slowly drifting to Barry. "Something *we* should be worried about . . . ?" A smirk slowly spread across his face, and low, steady laughter flowed from him. He raised his face toward the sky, his arms wide and chest heaving as his laughter grew hysterical.

When he could speak again, he wiped his eyes, shaking his head. "No, Barry. Not us . . . *them.*"

The weight of his words hit me, and a silence stretched across everyone present.

"Just to clarify . . . you don't mean everyone, right?" I glanced back through the trees toward Tropica. "We're pretty close to the village."

Ellis shook his head, still smiling. "No, not everyone. A paragraph from a book in the royal library springs to mind. Its pages were old, more than half of them lost to the ravages of time." He clenched his jaw, a hint of fury crossing his face. "I swear, if I could go back in time and throttle each archivist that failed to re-transcribe the texts, I would likely need a lifetime to strike them all." He took a deep breath and held up a finger toward Keith, whose mouth had opened. "I know, Keith—I'm getting off track. The book is titled *On Warfare and Cultivation.* Page 245, chapter seven, paragraph three."

He cleared his throat.

"On fighting within another's Domain, there is only one tactic that can produce reliable results: *don't.* To enter the Domain of another is to forfeit control. Perhaps you are lucky and the Domain is one of little power. In such a case, your abilities may only be dampened. If you are unlucky, however, and the Domain has matured over the course of decades, if not centuries, your life—and those of your followers—will be forfeit."

Again, Ellis's words caused a silence to stretch over the clearing, the only sound that of the bees buzzing above our heads.

"So that's all we have to work with . . ."

Barry sighed. "Usually, I'd say we should do some testing, but in this case, I hope we never have to."

Ellis nodded, and as if just remembering the events that set the Domain's creation into being, his gaze snapped to mine. "Have you had enough time to process your experience, Fischer?" He removed a sharpener from his pocket—because of course Ellis carried a sharpener in his pocket—and started twisting his pencil within it. "I would appreciate getting an account of what happened while it's still fresh in mind."

"Uh, yeah—give me a second."

I spun on the spot, facing the tree. Even before looking at it, I could feel a sort of connection there, like the spirit was just waiting for me to call out. I reached out with both hands to press my palms against the blue tree trunk.

The moment we connected, my awareness expanded. I faintly sensed the spirit within the tree, its network of roots, and what I had to assume was the Domain. A bubble of aura bloomed out from the clearing, encompassing a vast swathe of land. I furrowed my eyebrows, and the spirit joined with me, helping me navigate. The Domain's bounds stretched from the middle of the bay to the mountains west of Tropica, and just as far to the north and south.

I pulled back, returning to my body. The spirit let me go, and I opened my eyes, gazing slightly up toward where I knew its main body was located within the trunk.

"Is it okay with you if I tell them what I saw?"

A leaf sprouted before me, and as she made it wave up and down in a nod, I felt a surge of . . . emotion? I didn't know how to describe the sensation, but the meaning was clear.

Yes.

Perhaps a simple *yes* wasn't enough to encompass the message; she held an indescribable amount of trust for me, which was also communicated with the surge she sent my way. I leaned forward and wrapped my arms around her trunk. In response, I got shock, surprise, then contentment from our mental link.

Trust. Trust. Trust, she sent, and I squeezed her trunk tighter.

I let go, pressing my back to the blue bark as I spun back toward everyone. A sea of raised eyebrows, smiles, and generally amused faces greeted me.

"What?" I asked. "Like you guys have never bonded with an ancient tree spirit before . . ."

Ellis's gaze bore into me, and if looks could kill, he may have accidentally drilled a hole right through me.

I chuckled. "Don't break your pencil again, mate. I have her blessing to tell you all about it."

I took a deep breath, sent a surge of appreciation through my back toward the tree spirit, and started talking.

In a room high above the capital city of Gormona, lit only by the afternoon sun filtering through a small window, a screen blinked to life. Some would consider this event—the reawakening of a dormant artifact after millennia—as rather noteworthy. In this room, however, it was becoming more and more commonplace. So, as the guard watching the room caught sight of the blinking screen, he merely raised an eyebrow before leaning back on another relic that was currently serving as his daybed.

"Huh. Another one."

The door swung open, the guard posted outside poking his head in. "What was that? I heard a noise."

"Oh, I was just speaking to myself."

". . . Why? We're supposed to be on the lookout, Deklan."

Deklan shrugged, shuffling his back around to get comfy on the rock-hard slab of metal.

"Right—and you're watching the door, Jack. I'm just resting so that when it's my turn to watch, I'm alert and sharp."

Jack opened his mouth to protest, then closed it again, narrowing his eyes. "All right, that actually makes some sense."

"Right?"

Deklan yawned and covered his mouth, to which Jack just shook his head.

"What did you say, anyway?"

"When?"

"You said you were speaking to yourself—what did you say?"

"Ohhh. I noticed that another artifact had lit up." He leaned over and flicked the artifact between himself and the open door. "They just keep popping up."

Jack nodded. "Yeah, I was surprised the first time, but I've become a bit—*wait, what?*"

"What?" Deklan repeated, shimmying his shoulders as he tried to find the right position.

"Another screen lit up?"

"Yeah, the big one right here."

Jack rushed over, his armor clanking together as he did so. He slid around the side of the artifact, coming to a stop as he peered down at the lines printed across it.

"Foreign Domain . . . ?"

Jack blanched, the blood rushing from his face.

Deklan cocked his head at his fellow guard. "You look like you've seen a ghost, Jack. It's just a screen—it can't hurt you."

"I . . . I need to tell someone . . ."

"Tell someone what?" Charles asked as he entered the room. "Why aren't you at your post, guard?"

"S-sir!" Jack snapped to attention. "Another artifact has powered on, sir!"

Deklan watched as his new boss sprinted forward and slid around the corner, mimicking Jack's movement. It was impressive for a man of his, er, sphericality.

"Triton's divine shaft . . ." Charles said as he caught sight of the screen. He ran from the room, already beginning to puff.

"Huh." Deklan covered a yawn. "Wonder where he's off to."

"To get the king!" Jack slapped his gauntlet on Deklan's greaves. "Get up—the king will probably come to see it immediately!"

Deklan watched him through half-lidded eyes as Jack dashed from the door and closed it behind himself. Deklan shook his head.

"They'll all get ulcers if they don't relax a little . . ."

Augustus Reginald Gormona rushed through the halls of his castle, having left the sweating and out-of-breath Charles in his wake. He fought down a spike of annoyance that flared as he pictured the unfit man still leaning against a wall five floors below.

I will have to talk to the guard captain about organizing . . .

When he recalled the quartermaster, Danny, was one of the men that had disappeared, his lip twitched. The guard captain was filling in as quartermaster until they could promote a suitable guard.

The afternoon sun shone through windows as he strode past them, and while the light and warmth may have been a welcome reprieve at another time, he barely noticed them. With his thoughts consumed by frustration at the ineptitude of his servants, the king arrived at the doorway. The guard there, who had been expecting his arrival, snapped a crisp salute and opened the door for him, shutting it after the king stepped through.

When his gaze landed on the other man he'd assigned to watch the artifacts, his eyebrow raised. "What do you think you're doing?"

The man was lounging on an inert artifact, and at Augustus's entrance, he merely nodded.

"Just watching the screen for any updates. Er—my king, I mean."

Augustus gave him a flat, withering stare; it had no effect, and the simple man continued smiling at him.

"Watching what screen, subject?" the king asked, his words clipped.

"That one," the guard replied, pointing at a large, rectangular relic that the king could only see the back of.

His eyes pinned to his subordinate—who remained lounging—the king rounded the relic. When he saw the words on the screen, his blood turned to ice.

Warning! Foreign Domain detected.
Effect: 20 percent Suppression, 20 percent Bolstering, 20 percent Growth.
Local Domain detected.

Effect: 5 percent Suppression, 5 percent Bolstering, 10 percent Defense, 5 percent Growth.

The king's world tilted sideways, and the next thing he knew, muscular arms were lowering him to the ground. The man who had been lounging in the room had caught him. He peered down at Augustus with . . . was that pity?

The king tried to sit up—it was a mistake. The guard caught him again and softly lowered him back down to the ground. "Don't rush back to your feet, frien—er, my king," the man corrected. "There's no shame in a little dizzy spell. You just have to rest a moment."

Too disoriented to lash out with fury, Augustus Reginald Gormona, king of this continent and ruler of these lands, lay on the bare stones, being gently patted by one of his guardsmen.

Charles straightened, pouring with sweat and taking heaving breaths. He had just conquered the last of the stairwells, and he ambled on shaky legs toward the relic-filled room. He cursed his fitness, not at all looking forward to the chewing out that would come his way. When he finally caught sight of the guard outside the door, Charles straightened his back and forced his legs to walk straight.

The guard opened the door for him, but before Charles could enter, the guard jolted. "King!" he yelled, running into the room.

Their ruler was on the floor, and when the guard reached him, the king slapped away his extended hand. "I am fine."

"He just needs a little space is all," the lackadaisical guard that was already inside answered, squatting by their king's side and petting his shoulder.

A spike of adrenaline coursed through Charles, banishing his weariness. "What . . . what happened?"

The king's eyes flashed with annoyance. He took a deep breath before letting it out slowly, then sat up and looked at the man that was now supporting his arm. "What is your name, guard?"

"Deklan, my king."

"Right. Thank you, Deklan."

"You're welcome," he replied with a wide grin.

Charles narrowed his eyes at the lack of deference, but before he could chastise his subordinate, Augustus Reginald Gormona's gaze met his.

"What happened, Charles, is that the spirit beasts have created a Domain within our—no, *my* lands."

Charles swallowed. "What does that mean, my king?"

"It means that things are worse than any of us could have possibly imagined. The ascendant creatures must be working together, and they are advancing at an incredible rate."

"H-how?" The question sounded stupid even to himself, and Charles cringed inwardly.

"Wow. That's kinda wild, huh?" Deklan asked, raising his eyebrows. "How'd they do that?"

"Wild indeed," the king answered, patting Deklan's hand in thanks as he sat up. "There's only one possibility: they have a master—someone is leading them."

"A . . . a master?" Charles asked, his eyes wide. "A cultivator?"

The king tilted his head, then let out a soft chuckle.

"No, Charles. Do not be absurd. A human could never hope to tame a spirit beast."

"Then . . . who?"

The king's eyes hardened, all mirth disappearing from his face.

"There can be only one answer." The king clenched his jaw. "It has to be Lizard Wizard—it takes a being of incredible arcane might and knowledge to establish a Domain."

At the pronouncement, the room went still—except for Deklan.

"What's a Domain?" he asked, scratching his head. Suddenly remembering his company, he gave the king a wincing smile. "Sorry—is that a dumb question?"

"No, not at all, Deklan." Augustus patted his hand. "It is forbidden knowledge for anyone but the royal family—which is why you will all keep it to yourselves."

Charles dropped to a knee, bowing before his lord.

"Of course, my king. What shall we do?"

Augustus Reginald Gormona answered immediately. "Recall the expeditions. It's time to go on the defensive."

CHAPTER FORTY-NINE

LOWLY WITNESS

The late afternoon sun filtered down through leaves and branches, casting long shadows from the west. All attention was on me. With Maria at my side and the firm trunk behind my back, I started telling the story of the ancient spirit and how she came to be.

Ellis continually asked questions, and before I even got to the part of the tale where she had found a seedling, I paused, seeing how viciously his writing hand shook.

"Are you all right, mate?"

"Sorry. This is quite unprofessional," he replied, glaring at the offending hand. "It is just—this information . . . for a battle between cultivators to have devastated the land so." He shook his head in an attempt to clear it. "Knowing this history is invaluable."

I nodded. "I feel like my words can't do it justice. Imagine you were kilometers above us, and each bit of land was scorched earth as far as the eye could see. Whatever you're picturing, it was worse. *Far* worse."

Maria squeezed my hand, and Ellis took a drink of water before stretching.

"Okay, I'm ready to continue."

I nodded and launched back into the tale. When I described her reaching out and expanding her awareness into other trees, a soft snapping sound rang out. Ellis looked down at his broken pencil, then up at me.

"All good, Ellis?"

He swallowed. "Are the blue trees created when a spirit enters them, or are they the only trees she could inhabit?"

I gave him a rueful smile.

"I had the same question—she doesn't know. If the trunks of these lemon trees turn blue, we'll have our answer, I suppose."

Ellis sharpened half a pencil and took another drink, then we jumped right back in. We had to pause again when I mentioned the changing levels of chi, Ellis's pencil once more snapping in his blurred hand.

"The carnage, the creation of the bay, the scoured landscape . . ." he said. "It was all before the power diminished, bloomed, then decayed again?"

I nodded. "Yeah, mate—is that significant?"

He chewed his cheek, looking up at the sun's dwindling light. "I had assumed the land-destroying battle was the result of the gods' departure, but for it to have been centuries from then until the power started fluctuating . . . it sounds more like the gods fled around the same time the chi levels changed." Ellis swallowed. "I always thought it strange that no records remained from the time of cultivators, but upon hearing of the power they wielded . . ."

"It's not surprising that books didn't live through the carnage?" I finished.

He nodded, wincing as he sharpened his pencil. "Just so."

We had to pause a few more times for Ellis's shaking hand and snapped utensils, but the story wrapped up before the sun had set.

Silence reigned, and Maria set a hand against the tree's trunk, a tear rolling down her cheek. "That must have been horrible."

Claws leaped from her spot in my lap. She wrapped her limbs around a branch high above, hugging the tree tight and making reassuring coos. I grinned at her, Claws's affection tearing right through the negative thoughts that lingered. The root extending from the ground made a shrugging gesture, mimicking the cultivators that had so often visited her clearing. She sent a surge of complex emotions into me, and a smile grew across my face.

"What did she say?" Maria asked.

"The general sentiment was that all things happen for a reason. If not for all those experiences, she never would have met us. Without meeting bloodthirsty cultivators, she couldn't have properly appreciated our peaceful nature."

Saying this seemed to lift a dark blanket from the faces of everyone around me, and conversation once more rang out through the clearing. I simply watched, bathing in the enjoyment of those around me and the spirit at my back.

I stood and stretched. "I think I'll go sort out some dinner and turn in early tonight."

"Early?" Maria asked. "The merchant is coming tomorrow, so everyone probably wants some rest . . . but you? I thought you'd want to stay up all night with your new friend."

"Usually I would, but I just learned something really important."

At the speed of light, Ellis's notepad was out, his hand ready to record. "What did you learn? In detail, if you would."

I laughed. "Nothing like that, mate." I glanced back at the tree spirit with a grin. "It's just something I'll need to sleep on."

Understanding me better than anyone else, Maria's eyes narrowed into a glower.

I nodded back at her, confirming her suspicion. "That's right—she doesn't have a *name*."

Most groaned, the loudest of all being Barry.

With the cultivators long departed, the ancient spirit devoured a delicious meal. The otter, Corporal Claws, had brought a *feast* of what her master called shallow-fried fish. She had wished he would make her more, but she was truly undeserving of the pile he gifted her. The spirit only hoped it hadn't taken him too long to create.

When the last of the delicious crumbs was absorbed into her body, she sat and processed the chi coursing through her veins. As she did so, she sent out tendrils to explore her surroundings. With her memories returned, she knew well that she had never held so much power. The chi suffusing the world was weak in comparison to what it had once been, yet it was easier to navigate with the power of fried food running rampant through her network.

There was a curious structure nearby, and she poked around it, feeling its dimensions. It was clearly not natural, but it exuded chi that was . . . familiar. It only took her a moment to place it; the chi was Fischer's. She expended more energy, wrapping herself around its area to get a better understanding of the underground base.

There was something else down there, something that seemed to call out to her very soul. Filled with curiosity, she reached a tendril toward it. She was let in, and as if the sun had just risen to banish the dark of night, she immediately understood. There was a tree within the building, and before she knew what was happening, she was looking out through its trunk, bark, branches, and leaves. It was stunningly gigantic, but as she poured more of her essence into it, she made a startling discovery.

The tree was young—unfathomably so. At first, she'd thought it had no intelligence—no soul that dwelled within. But then she found the hidden core buried deep beneath. Despite the strength of her awareness, she'd somehow missed it—such was its stealth. She sprouted a hair-thin root and grew it between stone and into the compound. Focused, she sent it out to contact the hidden core.

When they touched, she withdrew as if burned.

As she had entered the tree's trunk, all she had felt from the other being was a childlike curiosity, making her think its awareness was as basic as the lemon trees. Instead of a simple intelligence, however, she found a sleeping giant. Another spirit dwelled within the tree, and though it was a yawning maw of capability, it was an infant. Given time—and chi—it had the potential to become an absolute juggernaut. If she had found the spirit in the wild, she'd have snuffed it out, smothered it before it had the chance to threaten her life. This newborn spirit, however, was not wild—it smelled of her master.

She extended the thin root again, and when she touched it this time, she didn't shy away. She began sending a tiny trickle of chi through her network and down toward the alien being, knowing that if she sent any more, it could damage the infant tree spirit. The newborn only tasted the offered power at first, but when it did, it opened its core wide, sucking in every drop it could.

The ancient being smiled to herself—Fischer would be pleased when the sleeping giant woke.

As I woke from my slumber, I was beyond pleased. I tried to roll out of bed for a good stretch, but something held me down. I cracked an eye to see a needle-sharp grin smiling down at me. "Good morning, Claws," I yawned, covering my mouth.

She cooed, rolling onto her back and exposing her neck to the air. Ever the servant, I scratched her chin, delighting in the way her whiskers twitched and shook.

"All right, you're super cute, Claws, but we've gotta get cracking on today." I lifted her up, and she went limp in my hands. "Ah, a peaceful protester? I know just the solution."

A high-pitched squeal tore from her as I started tickling her armpits, and she writhed in my arms, trying and failing to escape my clutches.

"That's right, fiend!" I laughed with villainous inflection. "You are nothing before the lord of tickles! Bow down, and perhaps I will take pity on you!"

Claws laughed so hard that she ran out of breath, so I let her go, and she slumped to the bed.

"Fischer!" a beautiful voice called from the other side of my door. "When you're done torturing the fiends, there's breakfast and a coffee out here waiting for you!"

"Come quick!" I yelled back. "She's escaping!"

The door flew open. Maria stood in the doorway, shoulders hunched and hands extended, her fingers wiggling and promising tickly torture. Claws kicked away, her legs scrambling and failing to find purchase on the sheets. Maria swept in, lifted the horrified-looking Claws up, then pulled her into a hug.

"Just kidding—I could never treat you as bad as this evil wretch does."

Claws let out a chirped sigh as she slumped in Maria's arms. The rigidity of her body slowly melted away as Maria stroked the soft fur of her stomach.

"I suppose I can delay my punishment until after I've had brekkie . . ." I said, smirking at Claws.

She poked her tongue out at me.

"Oh—feeling brave now that your mother is here?" I took a step forward, raising my hands into prime tickling position and raising a brow. "You think I can't break through her defenses?"

Claws bolted upright, the tension returning in an instant. She ran around Maria's shirt like a squirrel and poked her head over one of her shoulders.

Stay back, she chirped, glaring at me.

Maria punched an open palm. "Try me, heretic."

Despite the words, her eyes sparkled with glee. I took a step forward and tried to wrap my arms around both of them, but Claws dashed away, not trusting my intentions. I closed my eyes as Maria hugged me back.

"Thanks for bringing me breakfast. You're the best." After an all-too-short embrace, I let go and opened my eyes—just in time to see two lightning-wreathed paw pads block out my vision. Claws collided with me as I darted my head back in shock. She bounced off and flew toward the roof, twisting in mid-air to land with all four paws on the ceiling. Not missing a beat, she kicked off again, flying out of the door and disappearing from sight, the echoes of a chittering laugh the only thing left behind.

"I guess I deserved that . . ."

"No comment," Maria replied, rubbing my forehead where Claws had collided.

"Ah well," I said, projecting my voice. "I guess she won't be there to hear the name I chose for our tree spirit pal."

I stepped past Maria and slunk toward the open door. As expected, my bait was too enticing for Claws to ignore. The moment her head poked back into view, I dashed forward and scooped her up, her eyes going wide.

"Got ya!" I yelled, throwing my head back and laughing like a villain again as the tickling resumed. Her panicked hisses of laughter were music to my ears as she tried to break free.

A few minutes later, with a temporary truce enacted and an otter perched atop my shoulder, Maria and I strode toward the forest. The sun poked its head over the horizon at our backs, causing us to cast long shadows that stretched out toward the trees. The night's chill still lingered in the air, and as I took another sip of coffee, I bathed in the warmth it provided.

"Thanks again for brekkie."

Maria beamed a smile at me. "You're most welcome."

I threw the last of the pastry into my mouth. It was buttery, flaky, and almost as sweet as the woman beside me. I took my time to enjoy the bite, staring at the trees as we stepped from the sand and into the forest. The humidity present beneath the lush canopy had trapped the cold of night, and if not for the coffee heating me from within, it would have sent a shiver down my spine.

Maria looped an arm in mine and pulled herself close. "I miss summer already . . ."

"Not a fan of the cold?"

"Hmmm . . . it depends, I suppose. It's nice if you're curled up under a blanket or sitting around a fire, and it's a welcome reprieve if you're doing fieldwork, but I'd definitely say I'm more of a summer person."

I focused on the cold air surrounding us; with each step, it seemed to steal some of my body's warmth.

"You know . . . I think coming here made me a summer person. I hated the humid summers back in Australia, but here in Tropica . . ." I trailed off, remembering the sun's kiss as I stood on the beach, a fishing rod in hand and the sound of waves lapping at the shoreline. "I guess I've only really been here a couple months, so I've only experienced autumn, right? Maybe I shouldn't speak so soon."

Maria shook her head, her shoulder-length hair softly tickling my upper arm. "The last few months have been about as hot as it gets. You get the odd heatwave here and there, but I'm sure a big, *strong* man like you can handle it."

She squeezed my bicep and waggled her eyebrows at me, causing a laugh to burst from my mouth. We stepped from the trees and into the clearing. Leroy, who was sitting at the base of the blue trunk, opened his eyes and smiled at us.

"I was wondering how long it would take you to arrive."

"G'day, mate! You haven't been waiting here all night, have you?"

"No," he laughed. "Barbara would have my head if I spent the night with a tree instead of her, whether or not it contains an ancient spirit."

Said tree's canopy shook with laughter, and Leroy raised an eyebrow at it, shaking his head with a smile. "I can't go to the merchant anyway," he continued. "It's not worth the risk of someone recognizing me."

I cocked my head to the side. "Yeah . . . I wonder if we couldn't think up a disguise or something? It seems unfair that you can't re-explore Tropica."

"It's fine, really. I have so much to be thankful for—I shouldn't complain about a little inconvenience."

Despite his words, I didn't miss the twinge of sadness in his eyes. Nor did I miss the mischief held in one Corporal Claw's visage as she loped forward and rested a reassuring paw on his knee.

"Well," I said. "Even if you were bothered, which you're clearly not, I've got something that might cheer you up . . ."

His eyes rose to meet mine, and I nodded. Maria leaned closer, squeezing my arm.

I cleared my throat, puffing out my chest and rolling my shoulders back.

"Long and hard have I considered!" My tone was grand, deep, and oh-so pretentious. "I ask you to bear witness, dear friends, for today, I give name to an ancient being of significant—"

Maria cut me off with a groan "I swear, Fischer—if you leave us on another cliffhanger, I'll—"

"Lieutenant Colonel Lemony Thicket," I bellowed, raising my hands to the sky. "Or Lemon for short—which would you prefer?"

A lemon fell from the tree behind me, hitting the grass with a muted *thump.*

"Lemon it is!"

"Fischer . . ." Maria said. "Lemon is super cute . . . but *Lieutenant Colonel Lemony Thicket?*" Her voice was filled with exasperation. "You have to be messing with us at this point, right?"

I threw my eyes open and pointed an accusing finger at Maria, then turned toward Lemon.

"Do you see this lowly witness's hubris? What say you, Lieutenant Colonel Lemony Thicket? How shall we punish the upstart?"

Silence stretched throughout the clearing. At the speed with which I spoke before considering my words, a thin root poked from the ground, drew back, then flicked Maria on the butt. Her eyebrow twitched, and she turned to face me, a forced smile and a promise of violence on her face.

CHAPTER FIFTY

CALCULATED LOSS

With the morning sun filtering down from above—and giggles flowing freely from my mouth—I ran for my life.

"I'm sorry! I was only joking!"

"Get him, Claws!" Maria yelled, her arms pumping as she sprinted after me.

Lightning sprouted from Claws's body. She kicked off the tree's trunk, extended her arms, soared toward me—and flopped onto her belly a mere meter from her launchpad. Lieutenant Colonel Lemony Thicket had absorbed the energy when Claws tried to kick off her trunk.

Claws's grin disappeared as she whirled on Lemon, screeching an accusatory chirp at the traitorous spirit.

I laughed so hard at the scene that I missed a step, crashing down to the forest floor before skidding to a stop on all fours. I made to take off again, to escape with my life, but then Maria body-slammed me.

"Oof!"

Though I had an enhanced body, so did she, and it was like being tackled by a rugby forward.

"Mercy," I croaked as she wrapped around me like a spider monkey.

"This 'lowly witness' demands satisfaction!"

"I yield! I was only joking!"

"All right. You're forgiven . . ."

I breathed out a sigh of relief.

"For the insult," she continued. "For that terrible name, however, your punishment will be more severe!"

Faster than I could react, her tiny little fingers darted under my arms, and my torture began.

"M-mercy! Please!" I yelled, squirming as she tickled me.

Corporal Claws, seeing her chance at revenge, abandoned her squabble with Lemon. She was at my side in a moment, her paws shooting under my chin and jabbing into the tender spot where neck meets shoulder. I tried to escape, tried to twist from the clutches, but I was powerless before the onslaught. After what felt like an eternity, my feet caught purchase on the forest floor. I kicked off, flying for sanctuary. When I reached Lemon's blue trunk, I latched on like a startled cat, breathing heavily.

I glared down at Maria and Claws, who were both rolling on the floor with laughter.

"Not cool!"

Leroy stood, shaking his head as he stared up at me. "Sometimes I think my life as a cultivator in the capital was more predictable . . ."

As Marcus, the leader of the merchant caravan, prepared his wares for the villagers of Tropica, he smiled to himself. The contents of the chest he held rivaled the wealth of every other product combined. Using it, he would further his own goals.

When he'd visited the village a month ago, he was filled with curiosity about a strange man who had appeared on these distant shores. This Fischer had shown a cunning unworthy of a mere commoner, but that was the least intriguing of his qualities. More notable was his political sway. Most anomalous of all was his wealth.

When Marcus had arrived back in the capital to unload his coin and collect more wares, he told his business partner of the man and all he'd learned of him. They both agreed; Fischer was likely of noble blood and was expanding his family's influence and wealth with some kind of scheme that was too complex for them to identify.

In the month since Marcus was last here, he had lamented his lack of preparation. Though he indeed identified Fischer as an important person at the time, and had made plans to ingratiate himself with the hidden noble, he'd been too safe—too unambitious. His business partner had disagreed, even suggesting that his plan to further ingratiate himself with Fischer was going too far. Marcus hefted the chest in his hands, and as he lifted its lid, his smile turned to a broad grin.

The produce was a strictly controlled item to inflate their scarcity, meaning he could only buy ten per month—all of which were in the chest before him. This time, he was prepared. He was going to make his business partner eat her words.

"G'day, mate!" I said as I strode toward the largest of the wagons.

"Ah, hello, my friend!" Marcus called, his hands clasped before him as he bowed. "I was wondering when you would appear! Come, come! I have all the wares that you could possibly desire!"

I grinned at the keen sparkle in the merchant's eyes.

"I'm not sure I need anything, mate—I'm mostly here to help my pals carry their purchases." I gestured at the two hulking smiths beside me. "I'll gladly have a little window shop, though."

"Er—I regret to say that I do not have any windows for sale, friend Fischer."

"Just a figure of speech, mate. I don't actually need any windows."

"Oh. Of course . . ." His sure smile returned, sweeping away any hint of confusion. "Well, let me skip right to the point, then."

He reached into the back of the wagon and pulled a chest from out of sight. He slid it toward me, and I leaned forward, peering down at the contents.

Preparing these goods for Fischer had been an expensive endeavor, and though Marcus wouldn't recoup all of his losses by selling them at market rate, it was a calculated loss.

He had hired a specially insulated chest, one that was usually reserved for the wealthiest of Gormona's residents when they embarked on long voyages or had one of their overpriced picnics. The chest had thick walls that were filled with a rare substance, and when food was placed inside, it would remain fresh for much, *much* longer than if it were kept at an ambient temperature.

As Fischer caught sight of the chest's contents, his eyes went wide, and Marcus rubbed his hands together in delight.

"That's right, my friend. I know how much you enjoyed the lemons I brought with me last time. They were old, not as fresh as they could have been . . ." He spread his hands over the open crate, drawing even more attention to the contraption. "This time, I have ensured their quality. I will take a loss on these ten fruits, my friend, but for you?" He shrugged and gave Fischer his best smile. "It is a worthy sacrifice."

I tried not to roll my eyes at Marcus's sales pitch; there was no way a merchant as successful as Marcus would take a loss on, well . . . anything. My eyes were drawn back down to the chest again, and I shook my head, unbelieving of what I saw.

"Where did you get so much?"

"For me, friend, no product is out of reach." Marcus shot me a wink. "That is why I have so many acquaintances in these distant lands, you see? If a client of mine requires fresh lemons, I will supply them."

"Oh, not the lemons, my man—I mean the ice." I pointed down at the four slabs of ice lining each wall. "How did you get so much? I've been looking for a cooling solution, but haven't found a good one . . ."

"The . . . ice?" A distinct lack of comprehension crossed Marcus's face, but he quickly swept it away. "Of course. Even in the capital, only one family has access to such a material, which is why they make their wealth by renting out refrigeration chests like this one. No one else knows how they source it, so they are the only ones that can provide such a service, you see?"

"Man, the capital and its monopolies." I shook my head, not hiding the dismay. "Let me guess—they hire out the chests and make you buy more ice to cool it?"

"Well . . . that is close. They rent out the chest with a batch of ice included."

"And it cost you an arm and a leg, yeah?"

"Well, as I said," he replied, flourishing his hands. "No cost is too much when it comes to supplying my friends, yes . . . ?"

I winced.

He'd likely bought the chest intending to make a profit off me, and, if not for recent developments, he'd have succeeded. I was considering how to let him down lightly when a choked noise interrupted my train of thought.

I turned to Duncan; the man was going red in the face, one hand firmly pressed against his mouth. Fergus slapped him on the back of the head.

"Go for a walk, lad."

"Excuse me," Duncan wheezed, his back shaking as he marched back toward the fields.

When I turned back to Marcus, his eyes watched the smith's departure. Abruptly, they shot toward me. "I suspect I have missed something important here, Fischer."

I sighed.

"I don't need any lemons, Marcus."

"You . . ." His head rocked back. "You don't?"

"Nah—sorry, mate. I appreciate the thought, but I've had a fair bit of citrus lately . . ." I trailed off as sheer panic flashed across his face. He schooled his features immediately afterward, but not fast enough for my enhanced senses to catch that kernel of truth.

"Too much citrus?" Marcus's voice had gone quiet. "But . . . how?" His eyes hardened. "Has another merchant visited? I assure you, friend Fischer, no one can rival the quality of my produce."

I held up both hands at the intensity of his face.

"Whoa, my man. I haven't bought lemons from anyone other than you." It was the truth, if a bit of a misdirection. "Your lemons were delightful, despite not being as fresh as this batch here."

He gave an uneasy smile, then opened his mouth to speak. I held up a finger to stall him. I'd thought his words about taking a loss were just that—words. Merchants, especially those as skilled as Marcus, would have no issue spinning a tale to entice a customer into making a purchase.

That flash of panic, though . . . that hadn't been an act.

Even if his words about bringing them specifically for me had been a lie, there was no reason I couldn't turn this into a fortunate outcome for all. I snapped my fingers, coming to a decision.

"Tell you what, mate—I *have* had a bit too much citrus lately, but I bet I can think of a few of my south-side friends that would absolutely love some lemons. Same price as last time?"

For the second time since I'd met him, Marcus's true feelings flashed across his face, both eyebrows shooting up and his mouth hanging open.

"You would buy lemons for . . . your friends?"

"Of course, mate!" I replied, grinning.

"*Commoner* friends?"

"What good is coin if I can't share it with my pals, and who would enjoy lemon more than people who've never tried it?"

Marcus blinked, a silence stretching between us as his eyes weighed me. Then, he laughed. He *really* laughed, holding onto the chest for support as he shook even harder than Duncan earlier.

"Ah, you are a rare man, friend Fischer. The same price as last time, you asked? No—one act of friendship demands another, so I ask only one silver and five iron coins each—market rate, yes?"

"You're too kind to me, mate."

I extended a hand, and he grasped it, shaking vigorously.

"It is no problem," Marcus said, giving me a wide smile. Despite the cool night air still lingering, he grabbed a handkerchief from his back pocket and dabbed sweat from his forehead.

Foreseeing the possibility of Marcus having some goodies I'd be interested in, I removed two gold coins from a pocket. "Put the change toward more metal for my smith friends."

"Are you sure?" he asked me, leaning in so only I could hear—assuming Fergus didn't have the ears of a cultivator, anyway, but Marcus didn't know that. "This is too much to cover the metal."

"That's no problem!" I replied, clapping Fergus on the shoulder. "I have them contracted to work a *lot* of metal for me, so put the leftovers into buying more metal for next month."

Marcus looked at the coins, back at the wagon, then toward me. "I am not sure I can carry so much metal . . ."

"How much silver's worth can you bring us?"

He rubbed his chin in thought, his eyes going distant as he did the math. "Four silver's worth."

"Perfect! Keep the last silver as a tip."

Marcus held up his hands.

"Thank you, but I have a set price on metals—I couldn't possibly accept more. I will put it toward the next order, if it pleases you. You will need more, yes?"

"You're a good bloke, Marcus. Thank you."

"Do not mention it! Just think of Marcus when you next need to procure something from the capital, yes? No item is too much trouble."

"Will do, my man!"

"Was there anything else you needed today?"

I shook my head. "I think that's it for today, Marcus."

"Very well!" He rubbed his hands together, smiling at me and Fergus. "If you follow me to another wagon, friends, I'll take you to this month's shipment of metal!"

As Fischer and the smiths carried away their bundles of metal on a cart, Marcus let out a contented sigh. They had bought every bit of metal he had, which alone would have been a cause for celebration. He had incurred a loss, sure, but what was a little coin compared to the business relationship he was working toward? The amount of metal that Fischer had requested was also the confirmation he was looking for: the man *was* working toward something here. If he needed metal, he'd need other supplies, too.

While he had a feeling that Fischer was a benevolent noble after his last visit to Tropica, part of him had been prepared for it to be a front, for Fischer to be just pretending to be a good person as part of his machinations in this seaside village. Why? Because that was what nobles did. They were shrewd, elitist, and, above all else, ruthless. Now, though? Marcus had measured the man and was certain that Fischer truly wanted the best for those around him.

He shook his head. Fischer, a noble, wanted the best for *commoners!* It was baffling, yet a breath of fresh air.

His business partner was going to be *livid* that he'd gone against her wishes and spent so much of their coffers on lemons, but Marcus grinned at the thought. The gamble had paid off, and even his finicky partner couldn't be upset with the result.

Well, not too upset, he admitted to himself, his grin turning fond as he pictured the cute way her eyebrow twitched when she was mad at him.

The moment we rounded a field of sugarcane and disappeared from view of the merchant caravan, we spotted Duncan. He smiled up at us from his seat on the ground, then got to his feet, brushing off his pants.

"Lemons!" he said, shaking his head. "Gods above, if only he knew." His eyes shot to the pile of yellow within the cart, and an eyebrow shot up. "Wait, you actually bought some? Why?"

"For Sue and the others!" I replied, shooting him a wink. "They can't exactly eat the lemons that Lieutenant Colonel Lemony Thicket grows."

" . . . What did you just say?"

"The lemons," I reiterated. "The ones we have access to would make people become cultivators." I pointed down at the ten in the cart. "These won't."

Both smiths gave me a flat look.

"Yeah, no, I got that," Duncan said slowly, as if talking to a toddler. "What did you call her?"

"Call who, mate?"

"The tree spirit . . ."

"Oh! Why didn't you say so? Her name is Lieutenant Colonel Lemony Thicket—Lemon for short, though."

" . . . I think he's finally lost it, boss."

I beamed a grin at Fergus, who just shook his head at me, a look of genuine concern on his face that only made my joy grow.

Thirty minutes later, the smell of burning coal rushed out toward me as the furnace heated. I breathed deep of the earthy scent before exhaling slowly. "Is it weird that I love the smell of your smithy?"

"Well, that depends," Fergus answered. "Define *love.*"

I barked a laugh. "Yeah, maybe I could have phrased that better. I thoroughly enjoy it—how's that?"

"Better."

"Nah," Duncan said, leaning toward the glowing coals and breathing in as loud as he could. "I love it too."

He shot me a wink, and from beside me, Maria rolled her eyes playfully. "Few men would take pride in being as weird as Fischer."

Duncan grinned. "I blame the repeated heat exposure—what's your excuse, Fischer?"

"Don't have one. I'm just a weirdo."

Maria pouted. "It's no fun when you go with it—you're supposed to be all, 'You dare speak back to me, foul wench?'"

I raised an eyebrow at the nasal voice she used to imitate me. "Please tell me I don't sound like that . . ."

"Oh, honey . . ." she patted me on the shoulder. "I would never lie to you like that." She spun to Fergus, completely ignoring the flat stare I was giving her. "Let's get these cages started!"

CHAPTER FIFTY-ONE

AN UNEXPECTED GUEST

The following month was perhaps the most restful period since my arrival in Tropica, despite the growth of Barry's congregation and their escalating shenanigans.

We'd run out of metal to make more oyster cages after only a day, and it took us a mere few hours the following morning to secure the seventeen cages in the shallows of the bay. Maria had unlocked the blacksmithing skill, and as with woodworking, she found it a relaxing hobby. We added it to the roster of activities, finding time to work on projects when we weren't too busy swimming, eating, fishing, relaxing in the sun, or petting our veritable army of cute animal pals.

I had given all the lemons to Sue, and the pastries that she and Sturgill had made as a result were to die for. It inspired Maria and me to spend each evening in the kitchen trying to make our own sweets.

Four Fieldays later, we waited on the patch of dirt west of Tropica for Marcus's arrival. But he never came.

That evening, I lowered myself into the underground spa hidden within the church. A blissful groan escaped my throat. "Ahhh—I think I could live down here . . ."

"Tell me about it," Maria replied with a blissful smile on her face.

She leaned back against a rock in the center of the pool. Her skin was flushed with the spa's heat, adding a hint of pink to the sun-kissed skin visible beneath her frilly swimsuit. A washcloth covered her eyes, but above it, I noticed a hint of tension creasing her forehead.

"Something on your mind?" I asked.

Her lips pressed into a firm line, then she sighed, removing the washcloth. "Just worrying about Marcus—same as everyone else."

"It's really that big a deal? I would have thought he'd be late now and then."

"Not Marcus—*never* Marcus. The man has an entire wagon filled with replacement parts should an axle snap, along with a handful of spare horses. There's a reason he's so beloved despite his occasionally over-the-top prices."

A knot of worry formed in my stomach, but I took a deep breath, focusing instead on the spa's heat as I let the anxiety go. "I'm sure he's just late."

Though I was excited about the material to make more cages . . .

"You're probably right," she said, but her brows remained furrowed. "It has just never happened before, so I can't help but worry about everyone in the caravan."

A realization hit me, and I slapped the water with one hand as I bolted upright. "Oh *no.*"

"What?" she asked, her back stiffening.

"I just remembered that Marcus is the deliverer of coffee beans!" I made my eyes go wide. "This is a disaster . . ."

Maria shook her head at me.

"Oh, *now* you're worried."

"This is no longer a joking matter, Maria." I grinned and shot her a wink. "Now the great Fischer's comfort is at stake—that should be enough to terrify anyone."

She snorted. "The truly terrifying thing is you speaking about yourself in third person." She shivered. "Talk about bone-chilling."

"Hmmm. Quite a heretical opinion you've got there, young lady. Don't let any of the followers of Fischer hear you spit such venom."

Her entire body cringed, and I cackled at the disgusted look on her face.

"All right, I'll stop. Sorry."

"Too late," she said, moving to the edge of the pool. "You've tainted the spa. The only thing that will clear my palate is a certain lemon-flavored pud—"

"Shh!" I hissed. "Don't spoil the secret of what I'm serving tonight!"

"Well, you'd best stop referring to yourself in third person, then." She smirked at me as she stepped from the pool. "Lest I scream your secret recipe from the rooftops in retribution."

I clutched at my chest, then raised a hand to my forehead as if I'd faint. "Oh, such cruelty, such barbed words. How could you threaten the great Fischer so—"

I cackled and ducked the bucket she threw at my head, weaving through the water as anything not nailed down came sailing my way.

Beneath the fading afternoon light, I prepared a throne for the guest of honor. I placed the specially crafted wooden frame on the ground, then filled it with as many plush pillows as I could fit inside it. When it was finished, I nodded.

"Ready."

Not skipping a beat, Maria lowered the egg—and the bunny draped over it—down into the pile of pillows. Cinnamon peeped her thanks, perked up as if she was a queen atop a throne, then promptly flopped back down over the egg. She had been sitting on it for the entire month, only taking breaks to eat or go for a quick hop around—even then, she ensured the egg was tucked away somewhere warm before leaving.

She somehow knew that it was due to hatch tonight, and given Maria and I had spent most evenings experimenting in the kitchen with different ways to cook the ample supply of lemons, throwing the motherly bunny a party was a no-brainer. Cinnamon wiggled, pushing the pelican egg further down between two pillows. She let out a contented sigh and closed her eyes, her ears relaxed and falling to either side of her head.

With the guest of honor situated, I turned my attention to the fire. Getting the perfect amount of heat to the dessert I was making had been the hardest part of the whole recipe. I considered baking it in an oven, but the difficulty of emulating an oven atop the campfire was a challenge I found surprisingly addictive. It had taken weeks to perfect, but I was finally there—or at least I thought I was.

I guess I'll find out tonight . . . I mused, placing the tray on a rack over the coals.

"Hey, Fischer!" Leroy called, striding across the sand as he arrived with his wife, Barbara.

"G'day, mate," I replied, not taking my attention from the campfire.

Maria let out a lilting giggle. "He's in the zone right now."

"Sorry, mate," I said, not raising my eyes. "Trying to cook dessert on an open flame is a whole thing."

"No need to apologize—it's my dessert you're cooking, after all."

"Our dessert is probably more fitting, dear," Barbara said, amusement in her voice.

"I said what I said—you can certainly *try* to eat some of it, but I won't go easy just because you're my—ow!"

From the corner of my eye, I saw the speed with which she jabbed an elbow into his ribs.

"A little too much . . ." Leroy groaned.

"Oh! Sorry!" She softly rubbed his side. "I'm still getting used to this whole cultivator thing."

The rest of the village's cultivators trickled in as the day's light bled away. Though I knew the sky was likely a beautiful blend of pink and purple, I didn't spare it a glance—such was my desire to prepare the perfect pudding. There was a tray covering the dessert. It served two purposes: simulating an oven, and hiding what I was cooking from surrounding eyes. As twilight faded to night, I removed the tray and turned my back to everyone. Snips lifted the cover so I could take a peek.

The hint of lemon was the first thing that hit me, and I couldn't help but take a deep breath through my nose, delighting in the scent. The top of the pudding was a golden brown, and when I poked it with one finger, it was bouncy, but firm.

"Perfect . . ." I said, peering up at Snips. "Thanks for the assist."

She hissed a few happy bubbles, closing her eye and leaning forward.

"Of course I can reward you with a good scratch—that's only fair!"

I set the tray down and rubbed Snips's sturdy carapace. She leaned into it, hissing softly as I got the parts of her head that she couldn't reach. Corporal Claws, ever the jealous type, dashed forward and presented her neck. I gave her a good scritching too, delighting in the contrast of shell and fur. The moment I stopped scratching them, their eyes moved to the tray sitting on the sand—they'd tasted every one of my trial puddings, and though they weren't usually ones for sweets, this dish proved to be the exception.

"All right, everyone," I said, standing up with the tray. "Who's ready to try some pudding?"

The sea of friendly faces lit up, and a few cheers even broke out—the loudest of which was Duncan, who was swiftly clapped on the back of the head by Fergus.

"Woo!" Duncan said again, much more reserved this time.

"What is it?" Barry asked, craning his neck to get a good look.

"This, my friend, is a self-saucing pudding."

"How in Hecate's magical teat—" Leroy cut off, shooting a glance at Barbara. She raised an eyebrow at him. He cleared his throat. "How in Hecate's magical *torch* did you create a pudding that sauces itself?"

"Better," Barbara said, lowering the elbow.

I laughed. "It's not as magical as it sounds—the sauce is created when it cooks." I moved the tray, making the firm pudding jiggle a little. "As it sets, a fluffy lemon sponge rises to the top. Beneath it . . . well, I suppose it's easier if I just show you."

I walked over to the table, set the tray down, and picked up a metal spoon Maria and I had made at the smithy. I plunged it into the pudding, making sure I scooped plenty of the lemon sauce from underneath. When I put the spoonful into a bowl, steam rose from the sauce as it spread out beneath the fluffy sponge. As I dished out the rest, my mouth watered. The smell of flour, sugar, and lemon was wafting up into my nostrils by the rising steam, and my body seemed to demand I take a bite. When there was a bowl for everyone, Maria helped me pass them out, and we picked up the last two bowls for ourselves.

I sat in my chair, and just as I was about to take a spoonful, an alarmed squeak caught my attention. Cinnamon was up on all fours, her back arched as she stared down at the egg. I leaned forward, peering at the white shell—just in time to see it shake.

"The egg!" I yelled, leaving my bowl behind and dashing for the bed I'd made her. When I got there, I glanced back. "You guys can eat up—don't wait for me."

"There's no way I'd miss this," Maria replied, leaving her own bowl behind.

It seemed everyone else agreed; they stood and formed a loose circle around Cinnamon's throne of pillows. No one made a noise, but then a loud *mmm* came out. Duncan had a spoon hanging from his mouth and a bowl in his hands. The sound of delight continued coming from his throat.

"Really?" Fergus demanded, shooting a scornful look at his apprentice.

"What?" Duncan challenged around a mouthful of pudding. He chewed and swallowed. "Like you can't stand and eat at the same time."

"He's got a point . . ." Barry said, glancing back at his bowl.

A mass exodus occurred as everyone—except for Maria and I—retrieved their dessert. Even my animal pals got their bowls—minus Pistachio, who merely watched with keen eyes. There was a cracking sound, and I leaned down, peering closer at the egg. There was nothing there.

I cocked my head to the side. "What the . . ."

Someone across from me dropped a bowl, and I glanced up. Barry still held his spoon in one hand, but the other had gone slack. His eyes stared past my shoulder.

I whirled.

Behind me, ten meters or so across the sand, a crack was tearing through space itself. It was as long as Cinnamon's body, but then another *crack* shot out, loud enough to rumble the ground beneath me. The rent in space tore wide, and tendrils of inky black snaked out like shattered earth.

A power stronger than I'd felt before came from the tear.

"Get back," I said, stepping forward and pushing Maria behind me. "Something is coming."

No one moved, all eyes fixated on the broken air. A paw as big as my head and darker than night stepped through it, padding softly onto the sand.

CHAPTER FIFTY-TWO

AN EVIL FORM

Inky tendrils spread from the paw that stepped through, so dark that they stood out against the black of night. A lithe form poured after it. The dog-shaped creature hunched, gathering power in its limbs and revealing a serpent where its tail should be. Two onyx eyes roamed around the gathering, stopping only when they fixed on me. Its gaze narrowed with recognition, and it hunched further, dipping its shoulders as it prepared to strike.

Before it could attack, all hell broke loose.

Pistachio slammed his open claw shut, releasing a sound like two boulders colliding as a blast of deadly force rocketed at the hound. Blue clouds of chi erupted from Snips's body, propelling her toward the intruder. Corporal Claws launched from the sand with lightning wreathing her limbs, and she scooped up Cinnamon and the egg in passing, continuing on to land at a safe distance. Bill took flight, his eyes pinned on the hound. Rocky, both his claws held high above his head, jumped at it, power swelling in the joints of his deadly clackers.

Leroy punched the sand, causing vines to sprout from the ground beneath the dog. Barry shot from the sand, his fist cocked back and ready to deliver violence. Fergus squatted down as sheets of earth started climbing his legs. Brad's arm blurred as something started forming around it. Ellis bellowed a single-syllable word I didn't understand. It seemed to make the surrounding air quiver. Theo snapped his fingers, making a golden light gleam from his entire body.

From the corner of my enhanced vision, I saw the strikes approaching the hound. I turned to watch, my brain unable to keep up with the violence unfolding before my eyes. Pistachio's shot, Rocky's dual explosions, Snips's blue arc of energy, Leroy's vines, and Barry's punch struck as one.

Each ability and strike traveled right through the hound as its body turned semi-opaque. Its eyes never left me, and as the attacks passed harmlessly through it, its leg muscles bulged. Without further warning, it launched at me, its teeth bared as it transformed.

Just before tearing a portal between realms, the hellhound reflected on the weeks gone since his last visit to the mortal realm. His body had been almost obliterated by the cultivator's attack. If the hellhound had been less experienced, he would have assumed that he'd be able to charge through the accidental kick of a mere human.

As that bare foot had approached and a thin line of white light extended, however, it drew his attention. The moment it began to expand, he knew the truth of it.

The unaspected light promised death.

So, he had grasped at the thin trickle of chi once more flowing through the world, diverting it to cushion his head and torso. His vital points were shielded from the brunt of the blow, but that did nothing to protect the rest of his body. Using the power held within his core, he had torn another portal open to the realm of shadow and slipped through, his shattered limbs and joints thankfully numb. As he crashed to the floor, his consciousness had fled, and when it eventually returned, he found himself alone, the portal having closed as his awareness waned.

The first two weeks had been a haze as he slipped in and out of consciousness, the passage of time marked only by an agonizingly slow reduction of pain. Though power had returned to the world after uncountable years, it wasn't enough for his body to heal at the rate he was used to. When his last ligament was completely restored and the physical pain was banished, something worse replaced it.

Loneliness.

When the gods had fled all those millennia ago, the chi hadn't followed them immediately. His family—his pack—had one by one left him. With each disappearance, it was like losing a part of himself. Eventually, it was just him and his brother, and then it was just him. The loneliness was indescribable, and with nothing to do while his body healed, he was all too aware of his solitude. Many would rejoice at being awake once more after so long in stasis, especially on finding themselves the lone occupant of a realm as powerful as shadow.

For a pack animal like the hellhound, it was torture.

Even worse was the memory of the creatures and humans that had defeated him. In the mortal realm, where power had historically ruled and all that anyone cared about was themselves, a mishmash of different beings had banded together. In times long gone, it had been his pack hunting down individuals. Somehow, the positions had swapped, and it made his blood boil.

Each time he replayed their coordinated attacks, his lip would twitch of its own accord. They even intentionally avoided hurting each other—the least they could have done was take out their rivals and pretend it was an 'accident' . . . but no. Their bond was genuine; they were a true pack.

Most egregious of all were the furtive glances they kept shooting back toward the headland. They were directed at his mark—though they came up against a hellhound, a creature that could eviscerate them all given the inclination, they threw themselves at him in unified purpose: the protection of the cultivator he had been sent to kill.

This realization was the final straw that broke him and made the hellhound's fury turn to despair. He longed for that connection—for his family to return. Yet he knew they wouldn't. Perhaps his brother one day would, but only after more millennia, if at all.

As with his anger, his despair similarly grew to become something else. A profound jealousy took root, and given enough time—of which he had plenty—it bloomed. He loathed those creatures and humans who had cultivated something so rare, so . . . *precious.* With a desire—no, a need to once more become part of a pack, the hellhound began forming a plan.

He harnessed the trickle of chi that churned all around him, gathering it within his core. Though he had never torn a portal open without the help of a summon, if he were to enact his plan, it was a necessity. It took weeks to gather the requisite power. Not once did he let his attention waver. When he finally had enough chi, he paused a moment, having second thoughts now that it was time. After expending the chi he'd gathered to open a portal to the mortal realm, he would be left defenseless. There was no retreating, no shielding himself from the death-delivering blows the cultivator could easily deliver. He didn't have to consider it long, though. Some fates were worse than death.

He channeled the chi, his body trembling beneath the weight of his task, and the first line appeared.

Crack.

The portal shook, threatened to close, but he redoubled his efforts.

Crack.

With one last push, the air before him shattered, and he stepped through. After one paw entered, the rest of his body was sucked through the rent in space, and he appeared on the sand before a sea of faces. He scanned them all, and when he found the one he was searching for, his eyes narrowed as a thrill ran through him. He hunched his legs. The creatures—of which there were now even more—attacked. The humans attacked too, and as chi flowed through each and every one of them, he halted a moment, stunned by their number. But it only hardened his resolve.

There were even more of them now, and they held the same fervor in their eyes, the same desperate desire to protect their pack. He went insubstantial so the attacks could flow through him. Then he leaped forward, his eyes never leaving the man he came to find. As he sailed toward him, he scanned the cultivator's mind for the canine form he found most ferocious.

The hellhound would need to transform into something intimidating if he were to prove himself worthy of becoming one of them.

When his ability returned a form, he didn't question the result—his power had never failed him. His body changed shape, becoming that which the cultivator found the most vicious, the most *evil,* in the entire canine world.

As the giant black dog sailed toward me, I readied my hands, preparing to rastle the misguided doggo if he got too close. It moved at terrible speed, its body blurring and shrinking as it took on a familiar form. Rather than collide with me as I'd expected, it skidded to a stop on the sand before me. Everyone—creatures and cultivators both—flew toward it.

"Wait!" I boomed, holding up a hand to halt them.

All came to a standstill, the only movement that of the dog trembling on the ground before me. It—er, he—was on his back, belly exposed and tail curled up between his legs. Though his trembling body showed supplication, his eyes were wide and his mouth was open. His tongue licked at the back of his teeth as he let out a gravelly yet high-pitched growl that sounded like a toddler's attempt at metal vocals.

I blinked, leaning down to peer at the new arrival.

"Is . . . is that a fucking *Chihuahua?*"

The hellhound let out a vicious growl, licking its teeth and shaking in the manner of the beast it now inhabited. The cultivator stared down at it, blinking.

"Is . . . is that a fucking Chihuahua?"

Perfect—the hellhound's form was having the desired effect.

He didn't understand why this tiny creature was what the cultivator found most ferocious of all canines—perhaps it was all he had seen? Regardless, the negative association with such creatures was there, so he leaned into the defining traits. He growled again, licked his teeth, and further increased the trembling that shook his limbs.

A strange noise came from the cultivator's mouth, so the hellhound paused his act, rolling over and cocking his head as he gazed up. The cultivator's face twisted, then his mouth flew wide. The sound was . . . odd, but as it dragged on and some others joined in, he recalled what it was. Laughter.

Dropping his evil form, the hellhound blurred back to normal. He remained prone on the sand, his ears pinned back and head lowered in deference to the powerful man before him.

With tears blurring my vision, I laughed for longer than was probably appropriate. A few of my pals joined in, but I got the sense they were laughing at my outburst rather than at the ridiculous creature before me. When it turned back into its nightmare-inducing form, everyone tensed up, and I held up a hand again, causing them to pause.

"He's showing submissive behavior, guys. Relax a little . . ."

"Fischer . . ." Barry licked his lips. "I don't think you understand—this creature . . ."

"Hold," I replied, shooting him a glance. "Are you about to tell me some secret churchy stuff?"

"Well, yes, but—"

"Did he hurt anyone?"

" . . . What?"

"This woofer—you all seem pretty wary of him, and not just because he's the size of a cow and has a snake for a tail."

"Well, I wouldn't say he hurt anyone . . ."

Gary fell to his knees, bowing so his forehead touched the sand. "I'm so sorry we summoned you, demon. I didn't know what I was doing. I—"

Gary cut off as Helen dropped down and covered his mouth with one hand.

"Fischer," she said, licking her lips. "He's, uh, just joking?"

I blinked, staring around at everyone. "Please tell me you guys haven't been summoning demons."

Barry held a hand to his heart. "I swear on my family's life that we haven't been summoning demons. Gary talks of the *past* actions of the Cult of the Leviathan," he said, emphasizing the word *past.*

"Truth," Theo added, then shrugged. "For what it's worth, anyway."

"Huh. Where is Sebastian, by the way? I just realized I haven't seen him in ages."

The leader of the Cult of the Leviathan was a bit of a prickly bloke, but I had hoped I could win him over given time.

At the wide-eyed stares and shared glances I got in response, I raised an eyebrow. "Oh . . ."

Barry grimaced. "Let's just say that summoning demons isn't good for your health."

"Damn. He was a little odd, but I didn't think he was a bad bloke."

Rocky snorted a hiss—or perhaps hissed a snort?—but then Snips knocked him hard on the carapace to shut him up.

"Yeah," I said. "I don't wanna know any more."

"You're . . . okay?" Barry asked, giving me a kind look. "I thought you'd be a bit more upset."

"I mean, I'm not happy about it, but you just told me he tried to summon a demon. That lands firmly in frack-around-and-find-out territory."

I turned back to the dog, who was apparently a demon, and cocked my head at him. "Are you trying to join our little gang?"

Despite his terrifying body, he had puppy-dog eyes as he stared up at me. He nodded once, the movement almost unnoticeable.

"All right, mate. If you're willing to be a good boy, I don't see why you can't—" I cut off as a blur of black and white entered my peripheral vision.

All I could do was watch as Warrant Officer Williams, my rambunctious pelican pal, flew parallel to the sand and karate kicked the ever-loving shit out of the nightmare puppy.

CHAPTER FIFTY-THREE

MAN'S BEST FRIEND

Like a bat out of hell, Warrant Officer Williams flew flipper first into the nightmare doggo. I had but a moment to fear for the new arrival's well-being, but then Bill made contact. He pinwheeled away from the hound's lithe form like a pigeon flung from a windshield. The dog yelped in panic and his hindquarters lowered as he spun.

Bill, still spinning like a feathered beyblade and honking in panic, slammed back-first into the sand ten meters away. He scrambled to his webbed feet, puffing his feathers out and preparing to attack once more.

The hound was faster.

Shadows formed around his legs. Power swelled, and the moment I saw tendrils of black reach up from the sand beside Bill, I reached down and grabbed the hound by the scruff of his neck.

"No! Bad boy!"

He turned back into a Chihuahua in my grasp, giving me side-eye as he let out a soft growl.

"I don't care who started it, mister!"

Bill, whose wings were spread and foot was lifted as if he was a kung fu crane, cocked his head to the side and let out a questioning honk.

"He isn't attacking me, Bill—he wants to be mates."

Blehhh, the Chihuahua-shaped predator growled, tongue licking the roof of his mouth.

I sighed, rubbing my eyes. "Yeah, I know he hit you, but he thought you were gonna attack me. Besides, I'm pretty sure he hurt himself more than you."

I held the pupper up, supporting his rump so we were eye to eye.

"I need your word that you'll be friends with all the creatures here. If you hurt anyone . . ." I let a hint of iron enter my voice. "I won't forgive you. Understand?"

The hound's body shifted, morphed, and the next thing I knew, I was holding a full-grown golden retriever in my arms. He barked once in agreement, his tongue lolling out the side of his mouth. He sniffed my chin, then licked me. My eyes went wide, and all I could do for a long moment was blink. Then I pulled him tight. His soft fur between my fingers was delightful.

Bill turned to the side and shook his feathers, trying to appear indifferent and looking anything but. Remembering I had company, I glanced back at everyone else.

They were completely frozen, some yet to dismiss the powers that I had no idea they even possessed. As I raised an eyebrow at them, Theo's shining golden light blinked out, Fergus's heathen gauntlets turned to sand and fell to the ground, and Brad—*was that a godsdamned knife hand?*

Before I could inspect it further, it faded away, replaced by a prideful grin on his face.

"Damn—you guys have been busy, huh?" I asked.

"Fischer . . ." Maria said.

I turned toward her. "What's up?"

She pointed at the golden retriever in my arms, whose head darted forward and licked her finger. She pulled her hand back, giggled, then cleared her throat and did her best to appear serious.

"We have—er—more important things to discuss."

"Really? I have a new shapeshifting dog—it's not that big a deal." I waggled my eyebrows.

"Hellhound," Ellis corrected, not looking up from his notepad as his pencil blurred across its pages.

I glanced down at the Chihuahua-looking nightmare dog, then back up at Ellis. "Hellhound?"

"Correct." He blessed me with a moment of eye contact. "I understand your hesitance to know anything about the church, but if you're going to befriend the beast, you should understand what it is."

"You're a hellhound?" I asked him. "How the frack did you get here?"

His eyes went distant for a moment before refocusing on me. He moved forward, hesitated, then lowered his head. Somehow, I understood his intent. I leaned forward, pressing my forehead against his.

All at once, I was drawn in. I felt others there, and as I reached out toward them, it was . . . everyone, each creature and cultivator present. Even Lemon was there, lingering in the periphery.

Then, he showed us.

His pack, his family, dwindling one by one. Millennia spent alone. Emptiness. Stasis. Reawakening. His battle on the sand. Me, wobbling and drunk as a sailor as I kicked the absolute *piss* out of him by accident.

Injury. Healing. Loneliness. Despair. Despair. *Despair.*

Regret—not for his situation, but for subjecting us to his emotions. Finally, his decision; his plan to join us—to become part of our pack. A split second later, my head darted back, and I gazed into his sad eyes. His snout dipped down like a dog who had been told off by his master and expected punishment. My vision blurred, but not because I was getting drawn in again.

I wiped at my face absentmindedly, sweeping away the tear that rolled down one cheek. "I'm so sorry, mate . . ." I said, unable to forget the pain I'd caused him.

Maria whimpered, and the next moment, her arms were wrapped around us. "Of course you can stay!" she half yelled, her voice shaking.

A blur of movement from the side, followed by a barrage of hisses and chirps as Claws and Snips joined in on the cuddle puddle. Snips blew a stream of sorrowful bubbles while Claws rubbed the hellhound all over with rapid-fire strokes of her paw pads. His tail started to wag slowly, tickling my arm. I bathed in their contact, soaking it up to soothe the lingering heartache inside me after experiencing the hound's sorrow.

I felt something soft brush up against my leg, and I peered down, seeing Bill had joined us. Though he didn't touch the hellhound directly, he was showing his support. A brown blur landed atop the pile of animals, and Cinnamon gave his head a tiny lick before leaping back toward the egg she'd returned to the bed. We stood like that for a long time, willing the pain to fade away.

Eventually, I cleared my throat, ensuring it wouldn't crack when I spoke. "You know, I saw something interesting in those memories that most would have missed."

"What did you see?" Ellis demanded, his hand still and eyes pinned on me.

I grinned. "Our new doggo friend here doesn't have a name."

Knowing where to find the best reaction, I stared right into Barry's soul. He groaned with such disgust that I couldn't help but cackle. Snips and Claws leaped to the sand as Maria pulled back, scratching our new friend on the head.

"Do you want a name?" she asked.

His demeanor was much improved following the loving we'd given him, and he nodded, letting out an instant bark.

It gave me immediate inspiration.

"Brigadier Borks," I declared. "It's a pleasure to meet you."

"Now, let's not rush it . . ." Barry said. "Don't you usually need to sleep on it? I'm sure the hellhound—er, dog—won't mind waiting."

"No need, mate!" I gave him a grin. "I've already decided!"

He groaned again, this time joined by a few others as their bodies sagged with sheer disappointment.

"Don't you mean barks?" Theo asked. "Not that it'd be any better, but at least it would make sense . . ."

I raised an eyebrow. "What do you mean, mate? He's clearly a borker."

"You know what? I give up." Barry threw his hands high. "You're too broken to fix."

"I think it's cute," Maria said, rubbing his cheeks. "Do you like the name, Borks?"

He barked in response, his tail wagging and tongue lolling.

"Well, there you have it—Brigadier Borks has officially joined the gang."

An insistent squeak drew my attention, and I glanced across the sand. Cinnamon's eyes were fervent as she glared at the egg. I turned my vision on it just in time to see the top half of its shell fall free. Everyone moved as one. Borks reached it first, bending down to sniff at the now open egg.

A hatchling sat at the base of the shell. It kicked its legs feebly, falling over and slowly sitting upright with halting movements.

"Is . . . is it okay?" Keith asked, scowling at the baby bird.

"Tell me you're a royal without telling me you're a royal," Theo replied, laughing.

Keith's eyebrows lowered further. "What's that supposed to mean?"

"That is how baby birds look, Keith," Ellis answered. "They emerge from the egg frail and weak, but grow at a staggering rate. I believe Theo was implying that common folk would have been around chickens at least once in their lives."

Keith rolled his eyes. "Don't give me that. Like you've ever been around farm animals."

Ellis nodded. "It's true—I've never seen them in person."

"But there was another implication that Ellis is too kind to state," Theo continued. "We all know what they look like because we read a damned book."

"Oh, hah-hah," Keith drawled, his gaze going flat. "Let's all tease the royal for his blood. Like it's more important to know what a baby bird looks like than to study war formations and the history of Gormona and the politics of its surrounding kingdoms."

"He knows you can study both, right?" Danny mumbled to Peter. "Like we did?"

Peter leaned in, replying in a stage whisper, "I think he does, but don't bring it up—it will only annoy him more."

"Bah!" Keith threw up his hands. "I don't know why I even came here with you buffoons. I swear, if it wasn't for my love of fishing, I'd pack right up and make my way back . . ."

Keith's voice trailed off as the fishing club wandered back toward the fire, still bickering and taking jabs at one another.

I peered down at the pelican hatchling, truly seeing it for the first time. It was completely naked, covered in brown, blue-tinted skin. Veins showed in its subcutaneous tissue, particularly around where its hook-tipped bill met its head. Its too-big eyes were closed, and, no matter what way you tried to spin it, the bird was . . .

"It's kinda ugly, isn't it?" Maria whispered, raising an eyebrow at me.

Borks nodded in agreement, and I tried not to laugh, all too aware of the volatile look on Cinnamon's face following Maria's pronouncement.

I failed at keeping the laughter bottled up. "Sorry, Cinnamon," I said as the laugh trailed away. "I'm sure it will be super cute when its feathers come in, but for now . . . it looks kinda alien."

She raised her nose at us—an impressive feat, considering she was only a foot from the ground. She moved over the hatchling, gently curling her torso around it.

I turned to Bill, who was leaning over the makeshift nest, one of his large eyes peering at the hatchling closely.

"Would you mind taking care of feeding this little one, Bill?" I cocked my head. "Wait, baby pelicans eat fish, right?"

He puffed his chest out, raised his head, and unleashed a mighty honk. Without further ado, he flew off toward the ocean, no doubt in search of fish.

With things quieting down, I went and fetched my bowl before returning to sit by Cinnamon. The pudding within had cooled completely, but as I put the first bite into my mouth, I still let out a contented noise. As with every lemon dish we'd made so far, Barry's sugar cut through the bitterness like a knife through butter. The soft sponge on top was dry, especially after cooling down. That was where the sauce came in. It had thickened as heat left the dish, and when it combined in my mouth with the sponge, the textures flitted across my tongue, the tart lemon and sweet sugar guiding the dance.

"It's a shame it cooled down," Duncan said, sitting beside me and Maria on the sand. "It's good now, but when it was fresh . . ." A blissful smile came to his face. "It was indescribable."

"Ah, that's a shame," I replied, grinning at him. "Guess we'll just have to make another one, huh, Maria?"

Her returned smile was as bright as a lighthouse. "A true shame, but I suppose we can manage it."

Some time later, Snips and Claws were curled up in our laps, and I dropped my right hand to pet Borks's soft fur, who was in his golden retriever form, snoozing on the sand as he leaned against my thigh. His weight was a welcome one, and as his yellow fur tickled the palm of my hand, I was completely present. Thoughts existed, of course—too many to count.

The knowledge that I'd only known Borks for an hour, yet he already felt like a part of my family—a part of me. Small flashes of worry about Maria and my friends, animal and human both. Excitement—and fear—for the future. A million other fleeting ideas, sensations, and possibilities that were a side effect of the human condition.

Rather than dive into any of the thoughts, they passed by like leaves on the wind, merely appearing, being acknowledged, then continuing on to disappear from awareness.

My breaths came slow and steady, each one cooling my nostrils on the intake and warming them as I exhaled. Maria's arm was hooked in mine and her head rested against my shoulder. The smell of her hair drifted up, engulfing and banishing every other thought. As if sensing it, she squeezed me tight.

It made the already present smile on my face spread even wider, but then she pulled away, letting out a yawn. "I'd better get going—if I stay any longer, I think I'll fall asleep."

"I know how you feel," I replied, stretching my back as I extended my hands toward the darkened sky. "I'll walk you home."

The following morning, I woke to something softly tapping the covers of the bed.

Fwip, fwip, fwip.

I cracked an eye in confusion, only to be assaulted by a barrage of sniffs as Borks leaned down to greet me. He was sitting on the bed, his long-haired tail the source of the sound.

"Morning, mate!" I said, reaching both hands up to scratch behind his ears.

He licked my cheek in response, causing an absolute deluge of serotonin to rush through me.

"Fischer!" came a yell from outside, and I bolted upright. Before I could stand, my door was thrown open, and Maria stared at me, her eyes wide. "Marcus just got here."

"Marcus?" I asked, my sleep-addled brain trying to catch up. That was good—everyone was worried about the caravan, but then why was Maria so panicked? "Is the caravan okay?"

"Not the caravan, Fischer. *Just* Marcus."

" . . . What?"

She chewed her cheek. "Better you hear it from him."

I threw the covers aside, all but running as I put on some clothes and followed her.

CHAPTER FIFTY-FOUR

DICHOTOMY

My skin prickled with nervous sweat as Maria and I jogged across the sand, traveling as fast as we could without revealing that we were cultivators.

Brigadier Borks loped beside us, his eyes and ears alert. As the fields surrounding us turned to stone-craft buildings and cobbled streets, something about the village seemed . . . odd. The sun was just breaching the horizon, casting an orange glow across all we saw. The town was usually bustling by this point, farmers off to tend their fields and craftsfolk going about their business. That's what it was, I realized—we hadn't seen a single person.

We passed Steven and Ruby's shop; it was open, yet neither of them were inside. I shared a glance with Maria, and we picked up the pace. As we approached the flat outside Tropica, where the caravan usually set up their wares, distant voices came rolling over the fields of cane and wheat. When we emerged from between two crops, we found what looked to be the entirety of Tropica, commoners and nobles both. They were split down the middle, the farmers and crafters packed in tight while the north siders gave each other space.

If that isn't a physical representation of the wealth inequality of the village, I thought, *I don't know what is.*

Worry lined the faces and colored the voices of the south siders as they looked toward the front of the crowd for answers. The nobles, however . . .

"Unacceptable!" a man boomed, his prodigious jowls glowing a deep crimson. I'd never seen him before, which made sense—his pale skin looked like he'd not seen the sun for decades. "You go back to Gormona and get my shipment of cured meats this second, young man!"

I glanced toward the front of the crowd, spotting the "young man" he was addressing. Marcus—who looked to be a few years older than the pale noble—stood atop a cart small enough to be drawn by a single horse, his fingers laced before him.

"I apologize profusely, sir. As the king has decreed, it is impossible to leave the capital with resources at this time."

"Why?" a suntanned farmer who had just arrived yelled.

"What's in the cart, then?" a noble bellowed.

A sea of murmurs rose to agree, slowly growing louder as Marcus tried to explain himself. I stood on my tiptoes, peered into the cart, and let out a sigh; whatever he had brought, the small sacks didn't contain metal for more oyster cages.

"Please, dear friends," Marcus yelled over the crowd. "Only select items have been allowed to leave the capital's walls, which is what I have with me."

"Is it food?" a mother holding a babe to her chest asked.

Her husband raised his head over the surrounding villagers. "Surely it's food! Though they're partially spoiled by the time they get here, we rely on the produce sent from other villages to feed our children! We can't live off bread and sugar!"

"W-well . . ." Marcus's face tightened around his eyes, betraying the smile he was giving. "It is food, yes . . ."

The crowd's murmur dimmed, but I winced, guessing that whatever he was going to say next would likely set them off again.

"But," he continued. "I was forbidden from disseminating food from village to village. To quote the king, 'All settlements are advised to subsist on their local crops until further notice.'"

As expected, the dissenting voices grew louder.

"What do you have, then?" the farmer with his wife asked, stepping forward. "What food did you bring?"

"Only produce from the capital . . ." he answered, his eyes darting furtively as he held up two hands that had no hope of quelling the villagers' anger.

"*What* produce?" the man bellowed, striding forward.

Marcus cleared his throat. "Coffee beans and passiona berries—"

The end of Marcus's sentence was cut off by the crowd's answering roar. Their complaints were overwhelming to my enhanced hearing, and I saw Maria cover her ears from the corner of my eye. Only a few statements made it through the cacophony without losing all meaning.

"Unbelievable!"

"You can only sell crops of the nobles?"

"Do the nobles have no shame?"

More than a few heads swiveled toward the north siders, their suntanned faces hard and filled with misplaced hatred.

The susurration was unrelenting, and I took a half step forward, ready to intercept should a farmer launch one of their balled fists. Just as I thought a full-blown riot would erupt, someone jumped up onto the cart beside Marcus.

"Now, Tropica!" he boomed, his eyebrows furrowing at us all. "Is that any way to welcome a merchant that has treated us so well all these years?"

I didn't recognize the man, and judging by the confused looks on those surrounding me, neither did they. I blinked at him as hints of recognition tugged at me.

"Hang on a damned second . . ." I said, my face scrunching as my brain tried to reconcile the voice with the body. "Is that . . . ?"

"Holy frack," Maria hissed. "That's George!"

He was . . . slim.

Well, slimmer, but it was a drastic change from the last time I'd seen him. He still had a rather girthy belly, but it was definitely smaller. The most notable change was in his face and neck, which was why he wasn't immediately recognizable.

"I saw him like a month ago." Maria whispered. "He looks like he's lost twenty kilos . . ."

Similar whispers rose around us, all unbelieving of his transformation. George stood and watched the crowd, content with letting the murmurs run their course. Besides the glaring physical change, something else seemed dissimilar. I rubbed my chin, trying to work it out.

"Why does he seem so . . . different?" Maria asked.

"You see it too?"

"Yeah . . ." She crossed her arms. "What is it, though?"

My eyebrows shot up as I realized. "His posture!"

Maria's hair hung down as she cocked her head to the side. "His what?"

"Look at the way he's carrying himself—I'm pretty sure the bloke has debilitating social anxiety. Even when he's just talking to me, he breaks out in a sweat."

Maria's eyes narrowed as she inspected him.

"Look at him now, though," I continued.

George was staring out at everyone. He swallowed, showing a hint of nervousness, but his hands were firm, his gaze unwavering. Beneath his stalwart front, the crowd slowly quieted.

"Forgive me, Marcus," he said, loud enough for all to hear. "I only just arrived, but I think I have caught the gist of it. These orders are directly from the king, correct?"

"Correct," Marcus replied, regaining some of his composure.

"Then, I must ask you to forgive us. *All* of us," he said, casting a meaningful look over the crowd. "You didn't bring your usual retinue. Is that also because of the king's decree?"

Seeing the layup George gave him, Marcus nodded magnanimously. "That is also correct, friend George. Large wagons are not permitted to leave the gates, and those that do leave with smaller carts must travel alone." He shook his head in unfeigned dismay. "It is dangerous for me to travel without guards, but I care for my customers so much—how could I abandon them altogether?"

George patted him on the shoulder. "Thank you for your care, Marcus." He turned back to the crowd. "I understand that this is unwelcome news, citizens of Tropica, but please don't take out your anger on Marcus—he is merely the messenger."

"You're only saying that because you can afford passiona berries, lardass!" someone yelled from within the crowd, throwing their voice so it couldn't be located.

Snickers rose from some of the south siders, and I scrunched my nose. People could be so cruel, especially when mob mentality took root. George opened his mouth to respond but faltered. His eyes grew distant and perspiration sprouted from his forehead as the insult rocked him. Just when I thought his social anxiety would get the better of him, he firmed his jaw.

Wiping beads of sweat with the back of one hand, he gave a small nod. "As I said, I understand your anger. Insulting others, however, won't fix the situation."

Maria and I shared an approving glance.

"He took that well," she said.

"Right?" I answered, keeping my voice low.

A noble stepped forward from the crowd, staring up at Marcus. Though his skin was pale, it looked as though he got at least some sun. Most notable of his features was the distinct lack of a gut, despite being older in years.

"I understand why *my family's crops* have been allowed to leave the gates, but may I ask why restrictions have been enacted?"

He had taken particular pride in calling the passiona berries and coffee "his family's crops." I raised both brows, then narrowed my eyes at him.

"I must apologize, Lord Osnan," Marcus replied, bowing at the waist. "I do not have an answer for you at this time."

Lord Osnan's eyes twitched in annoyance, but then he nodded and took a step back, not saying more.

"Worry not, citizens of Tropica," George said, raising his hands to the side. "As with the reduction in taxes, I will serve you in this. I'll send a personal entreaty back to the king. Would you deliver that for me, Marcus?"

"But of course! How could I not, given the plight of my friends in Tropica?"

"Terrible news, wouldn't you say?" a familiar voice asked from my left. I spun, knowing that there was no way he was actually here.

But there he was.

Leroy stood beside me, in open sight of any number of people that could recognize him. He had a tuft of yellow hair stuck to his upper lip. I looked closely at the fake mustache, peered down at Borks—who was smiling up at me with his tongue lolling—then raised an eyebrow as I looked back at Leroy.

"Love the mustache, mate."

He fought down a smile and gestured up with his eyes. I glanced at his oversized hat, not understanding what he wanted me to see, but then I took note of his hairline. An extremely familiar shade of brown hair poked down beneath the hat, still attached to a thin layer of dark, definitely non-human skin. It was a convincing toupee. Anyone without a cultivator's eyes would miss it.

"Your hair is such a lovely color," Maria said from beside me, fighting off a smirk. "I can't place it, but I feel like it reminds me of someone I know . . ."

In response, chittering laughter came from the hat, inaudible to anyone without enhanced hearing. His "hair" moved as each chitter caused Corporal Claws's insulating fat to jiggle.

"I don't think we've met," I said. "What was your name, mate?"

"Larry," he replied, extending an arm.

"Larry!" I let out a laugh, unable to contain it as we shook hands. "A pleasure to meet you, mate. I'm Fischer."

As Maria and "Larry" introduced themselves, my eyes scanned over the crowd. When I spotted the man I was looking for, he was already leaving, so I strode after him, weaving through the masses. Borks followed, deftly trailing behind me. As I stepped in front of the man my eyes were pinned to, Borks sat beside me, and I rested a hand on his cute little head.

The noble's face was smothered by annoyance, and I beamed a smile in response.

"G'day, mate," I said, extending a hand. "I'm Fischer."

Lord Osnan glanced down at it, then back up to me.

"I'm busy," he replied, his face pinched as he tried to step past me.

I moved with him, remaining in his way. "Aren't we all? I know I have plenty to do, but I thought I'd take a moment to come say hello."

He raised an eyebrow, his jaw firming as he leaned forward into my personal space. "Do you know who I am, peasant?"

His voice was low, the threat in it clear.

Borks let out a low growl in response to his, and I patted his head reassuringly.

"Nope! That's why I started with introductions." I rubbed my chin, my face mere centimeters from his. "Do they not have manners where you come from?"

"Where I'm from, peasant," he hissed, emphasizing the last word, "I could have you flogged for your insolence, and not a single person would bat an eye." He leaned back and lifted a hand, staring down at his rings as if pondering striking me with them.

"Well, I'm glad I'm not where you're from, then!" I grinned. "Sounds like a right shithole."

The subsequent look of indignation that crossed his face was a soothing balm to my growing irritation at the noble's self-importance.

"You're calling the capital, the royal seat of power, a *shithole?*" he demanded, his eyebrows trying to leave his face.

I raised a hand to my chest. "My good sir, I would never! I said it *sounded* like a shithole, but that's only from the way you described it." I held up a finger. "However—and this is the important bit, so pay attention—that's only based on the way you described it. But you seem to be a right prick, so if it was described by someone that didn't think they were more important than the rising sun, I'd probably say it sounded love—"

I cut off as he swung from the hip, his backhand soaring toward my head.

CHAPTER FIFTY-FIVE

CANNONBALL

As a bejeweled hand sailed toward my head—extremely slowly, might I add—I marveled at the rings adorning it. Four bands of precious metal and one of—*was that iron?*—adorned his fingers and thumb. Each of the gold and silver rings held a single pearl, the sun reflecting from their smooth faces. Set in the band of iron on his ring finger, three of the biggest pearls I'd ever seen stared at me as they crawled through space toward my noggin. If he was going to give me a good smacking, the least he could do was hurry it up.

I suppose I have to let him hit me, I thought, settling my weight atop Borks's head so he didn't accidentally pull the prick's leg off or something.

The hand kept coming, its iridescent stones reflecting sunlight.

In my wildest dreams, I couldn't have anticipated the hand that saved me. A plump fist—though much less plump than I'd previously seen it—caught Lord Osnan's, bringing the blow up short. I raised my eyebrows at George, and he raised his back, as shocked as I was that he'd intervened.

His face returned to a mask of calm, and he turned toward the man whose wrist he still held. "What is the meaning of this?"

Osnan reefed his hand back and tugged at his vest, staring hatred at George as a wind kicked up and blew cold air from the ocean.

"I could ask you the same, Kraken," he spat, emphasizing the last word. "Why did you stop me from dishing out punishment to a peasant?"

George cleared his throat. "Fischer is a vital part of this community, and more important than you know."

He stressed the latter part of his sentence, and I jerked my head back, completely disregarding the man who had just tried to assault me.

"Damn . . . thanks, George. That was a sweet thing to say."

Before the Lord of Tropica Village could respond, Osnan spat.

"Important?" He made a scoffing noise. "He needs to learn his place."

"Tom—" George started to say.

"That's Tom Osnan Jr. to you, Kraken! Don't think for a moment that being part of a disgraced house makes us equals!"

He stared at me from down his nose, and I could almost see the desire to strike me go through his mind. Then he looked down at Borks, who was growling low in his throat. The man's leg twitched, no doubt wanting to kick my dog, prick as he was.

For a moment, I wished he would try, but then I realized losing a leg was probably a bit too harsh a punishment. Instead of striking out, Osnan's lip twitched in disgust. He turned and strode back toward Tropica. I pouted at his back, then looked around, shrugging at the villagers that were staring at me, wide-eyed.

"Thanks for that, mate," I said to George. "Not sure what would have become of that whole situation had he struck me."

"Of course, Fischer," George replied, some of his anxiety returning to his face. "It was the least I could do."

"Nonsense, mate." I rested a hand on his shoulder; his muscles were taut. "You could have done nothing, but you stepped in for me. I appreciate it."

"You're, uh, welcome." He dabbed his forehead with a handkerchief, absorbing the sweat beading his brow.

I smiled at him—it couldn't have been easy for someone with social anxiety to intervene.

"You did really well with the crowd there, by the way." I patted his shoulder, then removed my hand. "You've been improving in leaps and bounds, and I'm super proud of you."

He blinked at me, his face going white, the poor bloke. "Th-thank you, Fischer."

"No worries. I'll see ya later, mate." I turned and left before I could make him any more uncomfortable and undo all of his progress. "Keep up the good work!" I called over my shoulder, waving goodbye as I returned to Maria and Leroy. Er—Larry, I mean.

"What was all that about?" Maria asked, resting a palm atop my arm. "I only caught the end of it, but it seemed tense . . ."

I shrugged, leaning in so we wouldn't be overheard. "I meant to go over and try to get some information about the crops his family grows, but he was such a prick that I couldn't help but dish some disrespect back his way. His response was to hit me."

"Hit you?" Leroy asked, his face incredulous. "What did you do?"

"I did nothing, mate. George stopped him."

"He what?" Maria shouted, then lowered her voice again, leaning in. "Sorry—I just didn't expect you to say that."

"Right? Our boy George was cool, calm, and collected."

I looked over my shoulder, watching him disappear into the crowd as they made their way back to the village.

As George walked back through the streets of Tropica, worry assailed him. Rather than beat it back, he followed the teachings of his family's manual, allowing the thoughts to come and go.

"Are you okay, dear?" Geraldine asked, resting a hand on his upper back.

He let out a slow breath. "You know, I think I am . . ."

"Are you ready to talk about it?"

He considered for a moment, then nodded.

Geraldine moved her hand in circles, rubbing his back and knowing he'd speak when he was ready. They reached their steps, and the sky seemed to darken as he began.

"Did you hear any of my interaction with Fischer?"

"No—I only saw it." As they walked inside, she turned her brilliant eyes on him and shut the door, banishing the cool breeze that had begun blowing outside. "I'm proud of you for stopping Tom's hand, George. You saved him from himself. Striking a crown auditor is a capital offense, whether you're from a powerful family or not."

He blew air from his nose in amusement. "You know, Fischer said the same thing."

"He admitted to being an auditor?" she almost yelled, her gaze growing intense.

"No, dear—not that." George touched her cheek. It had lost much of its former plumpness with the changes they'd made to their diet, but she was still the most beautiful woman he'd ever seen. "He said he was proud of me and the progress we've made."

" . . . Truly?"

"Truly. He said to keep up the good work."

"That's wonderful, dear." She slipped into his arms, pulling herself tight. George held her back, squeezing her just as hard. "Is that what has you feeling so relaxed?"

He considered the question, then shook his head. "No. Even before we spoke, I felt . . . good about stepping in with Marcus. Maybe it's just as the texts say: 'service is the path to enlightenment.'"

She pulled back from his chest so she could look into his eyes. They sparkled brilliantly, and the adoration he saw in her gaze only made his own rise.

"I love you, Geraldine."

She kissed him, pressing her soft lips to his before pulling away. "I love you more, dear. Should we go meditate on the events of this morning? I know you're feeling good, but it couldn't hurt."

He smiled. "I was going to suggest the same thing."

Hand in hand, they made their way up the stairs, not needing to rely on the banisters for support.

As if it could sense the mood of the villagers, a storm front blew in from the sea. Leroy—or Larry—had left us at the square, trailing after Barry and the rest of the church members that were at the meeting. I spoke to Marcus for a bit, and he even tried to give me back the silver for the extra metal, but I told him to just get it to us when he could.

Maria, Borks, and I took off, heading back toward my home. Before we got there, it was already sprinkling, and as we stood on my front porch, the thin rain became thick sheets of water.

"What a miserable day!" Maria yelled over the roar of falling rain.

I cocked my head as I looked out toward the river mouth, only barely able to see it through the wall of water.

"Do you still have a pair of swimmers here?"

"I do . . ." She raised a brow at me. "What are you thinking?"

"Have you ever gone running in the rain before?"

"Um, do you not recall our frantic sprint through the forest when we went camping?"

"That doesn't count," I laughed. "We had food, packs, and shelter to worry about, so it was hardly fun."

"You know, you have weird ideas of fun, Fischer. You really think that's a good idea?"

I grinned. "One way to find out."

I sprinted across the sands south of the river with loping strides, smiling at the look on Borks's face as he dashed along beside me. His tongue lolled from the side of his mouth, only being retracted when he occasionally snapped at the rain. His long golden hair was completely soaked, and at the speed we were traveling, it lay slick against his lithe body. He made me think of a greyhound in full stride, his back legs somehow looking like they'd overtake the front ones at any moment.

Borks skidded to a stop in the sand. Maria and I paused, both cocking our heads at him, but then he transformed. One second, he was a golden retriever. The next, he was a pitch-black greyhound, the rain rolling down his short fur. Borks, now in the form of a rather awkward-looking dog, took off. Faster than any creature had a right to travel, his limbs chewed through the sand, his ears pinned back and legs a blur.

Maria's laughter was an unstoppable force as she bent over, leaning on my shoulder for support. The rain continued bucketing down, washing away the tears of joy rolling down her cheeks. "What . . . what was that?" she asked, still laughing.

"A greyhound," I yelled back, competing with the downpour.

"Is it supposed to look like that?" She gestured at Borks, who was now literally running rings around us. "That can't be right."

I smiled, watching Borks and the sand he was flinging in his wake. "It is! They were originally bred as hunting dogs."

"Why is he so . . . long?"

"Oh, they get way longer."

I turned to Borks with a smirk, imagining a borzoi. He skidded to a halt in the sand, staring at us as he shifted once more. This form was the same shape as a greyhound, but taller and covered in long white fur.

"Now that," I said, gesturing emphatically, "is a long boy."

In a matter of seconds, Borks's coat was soaked, and Maria folded like the buttery layers of a croissant. She let go of my shoulder, falling to her hands and knees in the sand. Borks ran forward and assaulted her with a storm of licks more incessant than the squall surrounding us. She slung an arm over his shoulders, leaning on him for support as he continued licking her chin.

"Why are your dogs from Earth so . . . ?"

"Amazing?" I suggested, grinning.

"Sure—let's go with amazing," she laughed, hugging Borks tight.

He locked eyes with me and, unable to help myself, I pictured another breed. Maria gasped as he shifted again. Borks's body and legs shrank, and in the blink of an eye, a brown dachshund with gray speckles leaned his forepaws on Maria's thigh. Borks let out a sharp bark, his tail wagging and ears alert.

"Oh. My. Gods! What is that?" she yelled, scooping him up into a tight hug. "You're so cute, Borks!"

"A dachshund, affectionately known as a sausage dog, for obvious reasons."

"Are you a little sausage, Borks?" She nuzzled him with her nose, her rain-slick hair falling around him. "Who's a good sausage?"

Seeing a chance for mischief, I gave Borks a malevolent grin. He shifted again.

"W-whoa!" Maria yelped as she crashed to the ground, a Great Dane atop her chest.

Borks licked her chin, his gigantic tongue covering half of her neck. She shook with laughter and tried to stand up, but Borks dug his back legs into the sand and held her down, his massive tail swishing back and forth as he continued lapping at her chin.

"Enough, enough! I yield!" She giggled, pressing her chin to her chest.

Borks stood, tail still wagging as he shook, sending water flying.

"What do you two say to a race?" I asked, petting Borks's overlarge head.

He shifted back to his lithe greyhound form, letting out an affirmative bark as Maria got to her feet. Her back was covered in sand, but the still-pouring rain was already washing it away.

"Well, if you boys are fine with losing," she replied, shrugging. "I suppose we can race. What are the rules?"

"The rules, huh?" I asked, rubbing my chin. "I reckon first to the southern mountain wins. The only rule is—" I cut off, sprinting southward as fast as I could.

"Cheater!" Maria roared from behind me.

I glanced back, seeing them both trailing me through the sheets of falling water. "There are no rules!" I replied, laughing.

My legs thundered along, and with each passing step, I felt . . . *free.*

Despite my enhanced body, I spent so much of my time in Tropica having to dampen my movement and appear normal. To run across the sands as fast as I could, my quads bulging with each stride—it was enchanting. All-encompassing. I lost myself in the race, becoming one with the sands blurring beneath me. I felt a pulse of power behind me. Confused, I shot a look backward. Just in time to see Maria catapult Borks my way with an overhand throw.

He flew at me in his Chihuahua form, all four legs held forward. His eyes were wide, his teeth bared and tongue flicking. He let out a quiet growl, his face becoming clearer as he soared toward me at incredible speed. At the last possible moment, he shifted again, and the smushed face of a Bulldog took up my entire field of view, his curled tongue lolling from an open mouth.

The respiratorially challenged canine hit me like a gods' damned cannonball.

I landed face-first into the sand, sliding along with my back hyper-extended and legs hanging over my head like a scorpion's tail. I eventually slid to a stop, my torso falling over my head. Spitting sand and what remained of my pride, I got back to my feet. A blur of black fur and tanned skin flew past me. Maria was atop Borks's back, who was now some kind of mastiff. She hugged him tight, laughing hysterically at my disheveled form.

"No rules!" she choked out in passing before losing herself to laughter once more.

I stretched my arms high, making sure all my bits still worked. I crouched low, taking a sprinter's stance in the sand, then I took off, my eyes pinned on the faint flicker of black I caught sight of through the rain. By the time I reached them, they had already reached the tree line. Maria dismounted and hit the ground running, and they both tore off through the underbrush at a respectable speed.

Maria's slight frame was made for traversing between the thick trunks—as was Borks's myriad forms, apparently. He was constantly transforming, leaping from trunk to trunk as whatever dog better fit the occasion. When I caught up to him, he shot me a sidelong glance and changed back into his nightmare form. He summoned a portal and stepped through space.

"Cheating!"

"No rules!" Maria replied over her shoulder, throwing my words back at me.

That's how you two wanna play it, huh?

A smirk came to my face, and I leaned forward. I focused on each step as I kicked off trunks, leaped over bushes, and soared across the landscape. Bit by bit, I caught them, and as I passed Maria, I gave her a smug grin. Rather than the pout I was expecting, her eyes went wide. A hand reached out to stop me as I sailed through the air over a creek.

What is she—

My unfinished question was answered when I collided with a wall of stone. My cultivator's body flew through it, tumbling haphazardly and legs going akimbo for the second time in so many minutes. I came to a stop, finding myself out of the rain and laying atop a bed of shattered rock. I coughed, waving dust away from my face.

"Fischer, are you okay?" Maria asked, appearing in the cave's opening with Borks by her side.

"Yeah—I think so." The air smelled stale, and I rolled over, intending to get to my feet, but I paused as I saw the remains of a half-shattered boulder.

The dull gray light of day reflected from something set in its face, standing out like a star in the night sky.

"No way . . ." Maria said, striding forward. "Is that . . . ?"

I nodded, my jaw hanging open.

"I think it is . . ."

CHAPTER FIFTY-SIX

NATURAL RESOURCE

The stale air assaulted my senses, made even more noticeable by the fresh smell of rain I'd been running through for the past half hour. The storm raged outside, filling the cavern with its roar.

I'd accidentally obliterated a stack of boulders in my misadventures, and I reached a hand out, running a finger along the vein of metal sitting inside one of them. The metal was smooth and cold to the touch. Maria knelt down beside me, also running a hand down it.

"Silver . . . ?" she asked, her voice filled with awe.

"I'd bet my good name on it."

She quirked an eyebrow. "You have a good name?"

As I scowled at her jest, Borks came between us. He was a golden retriever once more, his immaculate fur dry after transforming. He sniffed the vein of silver, his nose inhaling and exhaling rapidly. With a nod of his head, and let out a quiet, affirmative *ruff.*

"That's . . ." Maria swept her wet hair back, squeezing it absentmindedly. "That's a lot of silver."

"No kidding . . ."

I looked at the stones littering the floor, spying a few more flecks of it. I stood up, braced the boulder, then hammered down on it with the bottom of my fist. It shattered beneath my strike, and I grabbed the vein of silver before it could hit the floor. It was as long as my forearm, as wide as my finger, and a hand-span deep. Chunks of dark rock clung to it, making it appear like a regular stone if viewed from certain angles.

For the first time, I gazed at the surrounding cave. The ceiling was half again as tall as I was and twice as wide. Marks marred every surface, cutting lines through the hardened rock.

"What made this?" Maria asked, craning her neck to follow my gaze.

"Humans, most likely. Or an awakened creature with sharp claws. But my money's on humans. What use would a spirit beast have for ore?" I squinted down the tunnel, its sides fading from view the farther it got from the faint light of day. "It's a shame we can't see—we'll have to go get some torches before we . . ." I trailed off as I felt a pulse of energy from Borks.

He reverted to his base form, his snake tail twitching in concentration. The shadows crawled toward us, oozing across the ground and toward his feet. The darkness shrouding the tunnel slowly bled into him, his body going the color of night. I blinked and rubbed my eyes, but I definitely wasn't imagining it.

"Damn, Borks," I said, peering down the now-visible tunnel. My canine friend was like a puddle of void and I reached a hand out, half expecting my hand to go through him, but it came to rest on his head. "You are such a good boy, you know that?"

His inky, snake-shaped tail wagged beneath my praise.

"Shall we?" I asked, holding a hand out to Maria.

Her wide-eyed gaze drifted up to me, and she reached a hand out and laced her fingers in mine. "After you."

We set off down the tunnel, Borks lighting the way by absorbing the very shadows into his body. The deeper we got, the staler the air grew, and I couldn't help but scrunch my nose at the sickly smell that seemed to engulf us.

"You know," Maria said, holding her nose, "I'm grateful for all the changes becoming a cultivator did to my body, but the enhanced sense of smell can be a real curse sometimes."

"Uh-huh," I answered, holding my nose and grinning.

Ahead, just outside of the circle of light created by Borks, the tunnel split. As we got to the crossroads, I paused for only a moment before continuing straight.

"We should just follow the main path for now," I said to Maria, giving her hand a light squeeze. "I don't want to get us lost in a mine—that would make for a terrible date."

"Oh, it's a date, is it?" she asked, arching a brow above a smirk.

"We're holding hands, aren't we?"

"I thought you wanted to hold my hand because you were scared."

"Well, that too." I shrugged. "But why can't it also be because I'm interested in you? It's a win-win."

"You're interested in me, are you?" She turned forward, gazing into the darkness.

While her question matched the joking tone we so often communicated with, there was a hint of . . . *What was that on her face? Concern? Sadness?*

"Of course I am." My mouth formed a line. "Is something wrong?"

She bit her lower lip and turned away for a second, inspecting the wall. When her head spun back toward me, her always-bright smile was back, and she grinned at me.

"It's nothing. I was just kidding."

I was just considering pushing further when she let go of my hand and dashed forward. She bent down to pick something up, and my eyes focused just in time to see the handle of a pickaxe disintegrate in her hand.

"Gross . . ." she said, rubbing the fibers on her swimsuit.

I reached down, picking up the head of the pickaxe. It was heavily rusted, and what remained of the handle fell away, the force of gravity enough for it to fall free.

"Well, I guess that confirms it was humans that made this."

Maria reached out and brushed a finger along the pitted metal. "How long has this been here?"

I hefted the pickaxe head. It was still extremely heavy, the bulk of its structure remaining.

"I have no idea. I'd assumed the tunnel had been here for centuries, at least. The wood has rotted to nothing, but then shouldn't this pickaxe have rusted away, too? It's super humid in here."

"Maybe we need to ask the blacksmiths?"

"Or Ellis," I replied with a smile. "I'd be shocked if he hasn't read at least twenty books on smithing, metals, and corrosion in general."

"Good point," she agreed, giving me a brilliant smile.

As we continued, I dared to hope that we'd find what I was looking for. As we came across another pile of pickaxes, the chances increased. The tools were strewn across the floor in a chaotic jumble. Maria rubbed her chin, eyes drifting from each of the tools.

"What are you thinking?" I asked, recognizing that she saw something I didn't.

"They were . . . discarded."

"Yeah, but they're just pickaxes, aren't they? What's so surprising about them being dropped on the ground? It's not like they'll break."

Maria shook her head. "They're tools, Fischer. Can you imagine my dad or Barry leaving their prized hoes in the field? Can you picture Fergus just dropping one of his hammers on the ground? Or Brad leaving his shop without putting each chisel where they belonged?"

"Huh. I hadn't thought of it like that."

"Even if they were just regular people forced to do the work by their lord, they'd have an overseer that ensured the tools were cared for. I can't imagine why they'd just abandon them."

A possibility crossed my mind. I became acutely aware we were far beneath the surface in a confined tunnel, and the occupants had left in enough of a rush that they discarded their expensive tools. What could have scared them so much?

"Maybe we should turn back . . ."

As we'd been speaking, Borks wandered down the tunnel, his nose held high and twitching as he sniffed the air. Suddenly, his body went rigid, his midnight hackles rising. A low growl came from his throat, and I was at his side in a moment.

"What is it, Borks?"

I stared down the tunnel where he was looking but couldn't make out a thing in the murky shadows beyond his range. Maria joined us, and I ushered her behind me with one hand. Borks strode forward slowly, his head held low and the same deep growl coming from him. We followed, both of us with our fists at the ready.

Something came into range of Borks's light. The moment it did, he went absolutely mental. He barked and snarled, his teeth bared and shoulders flared. I squinted at the gigantic scaled head, waiting for it to lunge, prepared for its attack, but then I noticed the sunken cheeks and hollow eyes. Breathing a sigh of relief as the adrenaline still coursed through me, I lowered a reassuring hand to Borks's back.

"It's all right, mate. The thing is dead."

He was still on edge as we strode toward the body. It was a lizard, and it was gigantic. It reminded me of the videos I'd seen of komodo dragons back on Earth—if a komodo dragon was the size of a fully grown saltwater crocodile.

"Well, I guess that explains why they ran," Maria said, letting out a relieved laugh.

"No kidding . . ."

Borks's hackles were still raised as he bent to sniff it, his loud huffing the only sound bouncing off the mine's walls. The lizard's skin was almost completely intact, only marred by what had likely been a vicious wound to the top of its head. I poked at the skull beneath, finding a deep cut in the bone.

"So, they wounded it and sealed off the mine," I deduced, standing back up and stretching.

"It has to have been an awakened creature, right?" Maria asked.

"I'm guessing so . . . What do you reckon, Borks?"

He let out an affirmative *ruff,* still sniffing at the reptile's bones.

"You're a good guardian, and an even better boy, Borks." I rubbed his back in an attempt at reassurance, but he remained alert, his eyes pinned to the lizard.

Maria let out a sharp sniff. "That also explains the smell."

I barely heard her; there was something on the wall behind the lizard. I stepped over one of its forelegs, taking care not to touch it. Borks and Maria came with me, the former lighting the way by absorbing the shadows. Ochre-colored rust covered a patch of wall, the face seeming to have wasted away with the passage of time. Drawing back the pickaxe I held, I drove it into the stone, careful not to strike too hard and cause a collapse. A chunk of rock as big as my torso fell away, and when the dust settled, a broad grin spread over my face.

"It looks like silver isn't the only thing this mine produced."

The deeper we had traversed into the earth, the more the surrounding rock took on a reddish hue. Thanks to the stones I'd used to construct the rock wall from my shores, I now knew that a red tint meant it was high in iron. Beneath the chunk I'd carved away, the rock was a dull gray, flecked with small spots of . . . What had Ellis called it? Hematite?

I turned to Maria just as she recognized why I was so excited.

"Is that what I think it is?" she asked.

"We'll have to check with Ellis and the smiths, but yeah, I'm pretty sure it's iron ore." I ran a hand over its cool surface. "If so, we might not need to rely on metal from the capital."

After running back to Tropica, Maria and I had a quick shower and changed as Borks ran off to fetch everyone.

I exited my bedroom just as she stepped from the spare bathroom, her damp hair the only remaining evidence of our torrential adventure. She smiled at me when our gazes met, and I took a deep breath, not averting my eyes.

"What are you thinking?" she asked, echoing my words back at me.

"That I'm not sure you're allowed to look so cute after getting caught in a storm."

She rolled her eyes, but the smile remained. "Is that what you say to all the girls?"

“If by all the girls you mean Sergeant Snips and Corporal Claws, I absolutely do—with completely different intent, though.”

She laughed despite herself, covering her mouth with the back of one hand. “Oh? And what are your intentions with me?”

The question brought me up short, my face flushing with heat. As my words continued to fail me, I scratched the back of my head and tried changing the subject. “Do you, uh, think they’ll be long?”

Something flashed in Maria’s eyes, and she gave me a smile that didn’t reach her eyes. I tried to think of something else to say, but before I could voice it, a two-meter long dog right out of a nightmare came bursting through the door. Borks shook, his snake tail whipping the doorframe and making the whole house vibrate.

“Careful there, big fella,” I said, thankful for his arrival. “Don’t want you tearing down the building by accident.”

His tail wagged and tongue lolled as he changed back into a golden retriever. Another figure burst through the door, heaving with breath and eyes manic.

“Whoa, Ellis—you right, mate?”

“Where is it?” he demanded, his jaw swinging and hands twitching.

“The mine? Not far to the south—”

“The body,” he interrupted, taking a step forward, his finger curling at his side. “The lizard. Take me to it.”

CHAPTER FIFTY-SEVEN

STICKY FINGERS

A soft drizzle was all that remained of the storm as we dashed over the sands. The sun peered out from between clouds, glinting off the water droplets and casting a vast rainbow in the distance. I smiled at it, wondering if everyone else felt the same level of peace. When I glanced at Ellis, that disillusion was swiftly dispelled. He ran with his knees high, his entire body holding a hint of manic energy.

I raised my eyebrows at Peter and Fergus, who had arrived at my home just after the animated archivist. The former cook grinned at me, clearly finding amusement in his friend's ardor.

"Where are the rest of the gang?" I asked, content to let Borks lead the way. "I had kinda assumed everyone would want to come see a mine and the body of a dead spirit beast."

Peter pursed his lips for a moment, then shrugged.

"I suppose I can tell you—it isn't really church business. Barry and Danny are organizing a trade route between the neighboring villages."

I noted he didn't mention everyone else, but I was hardly going to go digging and accidentally discover things I couldn't unlearn. I drew a hand to my chest, letting my mouth fall open.

Maria, catching my intent, let out an exaggerated gasp. "You mean to tell us that Barry and Danny, the very beacons of virtue, are going against their king's orders? They would trade goods with other villages despite his direct order to not do so?" Her lips formed a line as she shook her head. "I'm not angry. Just disappointed."

While not with the same urgency as Ellis, Fergus's eyes sparkled with more than just mirth as we made our way to the mine. I was excited for him; I couldn't imagine the joy a blacksmith would feel at finding a hidden iron mine in their own backyard—well, *my* backyard, but the point remained.

When we reached the entrance, we wasted not a second before descending. We passed by the crossroads, over the discarded pickaxes, and stopped only when the giant lizard came into view. Ellis skidded to a stop before he got near it, then crept forward on careful steps, not disturbing a stone. In a blur, he removed his notepad and pencil from a pocket.

"Remarkable . . ." His voice was filled with awe. "Absolutely remarkable."

"What do you think, Ellis?" I asked. "Was it an ascendant creature?"

"Undoubtedly. If it were anything but, the skin would have wasted away in this humid environment. To think it—*careful, smith!*"

Fergus raised an eyebrow, pausing mid-step over the lizard's leg. "I may be large, Ellis, but I'm not a bumbling idiot."

Ellis let out a sigh. "Sorry. I do not doubt your dexterity, it is just . . . please be careful around the specimen."

"Of course," he replied, stepping over the leg and continuing to the section of wall I'd taken a pickaxe to.

Maria, Borks, and I followed, leaving Ellis to his documentation. "So, what do you think, mate? Iron ore?"

Fergus grabbed one of the gray chunks of stone, holding it up before his eyes. I knew his answer before he replied. It was etched on his face.

"Aye, Fischer. It's iron ore. By my judgment, it has incredible metal content. This will make fantastic pig iron."

"Do we have the means to process it?" I asked.

He shot me an odd look. "I sometimes forget you're not trained in metals, considering how competent you are in the smithy. Aye, we have the means. Sometimes you need to crush and sort bits of rock out, but if all the ore has this much metal, all we need is enough heat."

"The kind of heat you'd get in your forge?" I asked.

"Aye, Fischer." The sparkle in his eyes morphed into a glowing ember. "Just so."

Barry glanced back up at the map in the Church of Fischer's meeting room, checking for the umpteenth time that there wasn't a more efficient route.

"Is everyone in agreement?"

"I believe so," Keith answered. "Danny?"

The former quartermaster didn't look up from the table for a long moment, poring over the map he'd drawn. There were innumerable lines scrawled across its paper, connecting different villages to one another. Beside each hub of civilization, he'd added what each area grew and would likely buy.

"I can't see anything we've missed . . . What about you, Theo?"

The former auditor looked up from the table. "Sorry, what?"

Danny's brow furrowed. "The route—the wares—do you see any way we could improve it?"

"Oh. Right. I was daydreaming, to be honest—I don't have anything to add that you wouldn't see, Danny. I'm mostly here for the next order of business. Not that there's any rush, mind you," he quickly added. "Take your time."

"Anyone else?" Barry asked, casting his eyes over the rest of the cultivators and animals present. Only Fergus, Duncan, and Ellis were missing, having sprinted off when they received news of a mine and the body of what was potentially an awakened creature.

A series of no's, head shakes, bubbles, and a chirp came in answer.

"I think we're all done here, to be honest," he said, standing and stretching. "As soon as we build a cart, we can send it out to swap goods between villages. I don't see anyone ratting us out, considering we're only offering trade and not trying to turn a profit."

"Agreed," Danny said, also stretching.

Brad and Greg shared a grin. "We'll get building on the cart as soon as the meeting is finished," Brad said. "We already have all the supplies needed."

"Should we get into the next order of business, then?" Barry suggested. "Anyone have anything to add or bring up first?"

No one raised their voice, so he cleared his throat and organized his thoughts. "Would you mind taking notes, Theo? Just until Ellis returns?"

Theo grinned and picked up a pencil and spare sheet of paper. "Of course, mate. Ready when you are."

"Much appreciated." Barry lifted his gaze, taking in the faces of all present. "In that case, I call into order the first meeting of Operation: Sticky Fingers."

"Ready, Ellis?" I asked.

He nodded back, bending down at the knees.

"All right, everyone—on three. One, two, three!"

We had returned to the mine under the cover of night, this time with a handful of helpers in tow. We all lifted part of the lizard's body, and Ellis slid a broad tabletop, borrowed from the woodworker's shop, beneath it.

"Down on three."

I counted down again, and we lowered the mummified creature. Thankfully, it remained in one piece.

"Wonderfully done, everyone," Ellis said, sliding around to peer at each section and check it hadn't been damaged.

"Let's get this thing back to the village so we can get started on the important work," Duncan said, shooting Ellis a wink.

The archivist pouted, which only made Duncan's smile broaden. As expected, Fergus slapped him lightly on the back of the head.

"Just because you're excited to get smelting doesn't mean that getting this overgrown lizard back to town isn't just as important."

"If you say so, boss." Duncan gave a cheeky grin.

Fergus shook his head in response, staring down at the lizard with no small amount of wonder as we lifted the tabletop. "I know you said it was big, but seeing it in person is quite a different story."

"Indeed," Ellis agreed. "Marvelous, is it not?"

I couldn't help but agree, and I breathed deep of the forest air as we stepped from the mine. The smell of rain still lingered, its scent so sweet I could almost taste it. I was walking backward, so when the moon's light hit the lizard's scales, I let out a soft gasp. The vision granted by Borks's ability within the cavern wasn't a light, per se; it was a lack of shadow. The result was the scales appearing a dull, lifeless brown. With the pale moon above reflecting from their jewel-like faces, it was an entirely different story.

Each scale, only as large as a wheat seed, was a purple so deep that they seemed almost black. Before our eyes, the color shifted. From the center of each scale where the moonlight kissed, burgundy swirled out. The purple held firm at the edges, rebuffing the miniature galaxy that swirled within.

"D-down!" Ellis said in a rush. "Set it down!"

While I was aware of Ellis flitting around in my peripheral vision after lowering the table, I paid him no mind. At some point, Maria came to my side. Her hand fell into mine, and we watched the galaxies together, the lizard's body displaying a beauty that belied how long ago it had passed.

"There's no point writing it down, Ellis," Fergus said, his voice distant. "There are no words to describe it."

"And yet, I must try," he replied, not looking up from his notepad.

"What do you plan on doing with it, mate?" I asked. "Are you just going to preserve it?"

Ellis ruffled his mustache. "That was the plan, yes . . . but now . . ." His eyes shot up, locking with mine. "It is clear to me that the skin, preserved as it is, still holds power. Do you have a tanner or leatherworker in Tropica?"

Both my eyebrows flew up at the implications of his question. I turned to Fergus and Duncan. "Do we?"

They both shook their heads, and Fergus sighed. "We did for a time, but he left a few years ago. A right shame, that. I've not bought a new apron since he left. Any Marcus could bring me is a touch too pricey to justify."

"A shame indeed." Ellis blew air from his nose. "Oh well. I'd have been more comfortable with experienced hands guiding the way, but I suppose I'll have to make do with the books I've read."

Duncan frowned. "No offense, Ellis, but I don't think reading about a trade is enough for you to make leather, let alone work with whatever this is. It has taken me years of practice to get as good as I am in the smithy, and I still don't hold a light to Fergus."

Ellis shook his head. "You underestimate me, Duncan. You might have been right before I became a cultivator . . ." Ellis flexed a toned bicep to emphasize his point. "I do not say this with bravado. I just know that I can implement the knowledge I've acquired." He winked. "Given some cheaper material to practice with first, of course."

"Don't let your ego impede your judgment," Fergus mumbled, likely intending for only his apprentice to hear. "Others' abilities—or lack of—don't change the hard work you've put in at the forge." He ruffled Duncan's hair to take the sting out of his words.

Duncan opened his mouth to respond, then closed it again, his head cocking to the side in thought. The deepening frown on his face told me he was realizing Fergus was right on the money—and was anything but happy about it.

Taking care not to turn my head toward them, I smiled at the interaction; something about it was just as beautiful and pure as the light dancing on the scales below.

"Okay!" Ellis said, closing his notepad. "Let us resume. I'd like to get the skin into the climate-controlled air of the church as soon as possible."

Not a word was uttered as we made our way back to Tropica, engrossed as we were in the lizard-shaped carpet of swirling light beneath our noses.

"Thank you for attending, everyone," Augustus Reginald Gormona said, his intonation so deep as to almost be a yell. The confidence in his voice was the antithesis to the way he felt inside, which was all the more reason to use it.

Though the waxing crescent moon was bright beyond the stained glass windows of the throne room, the orange glow of countless candles smothered any other color with their monotony. All six women before him bowed deep, some slower than others. The king forgave them; the hour was late, and many had been asleep.

The castle staff had been under orders to rouse them all—Augustus included—the moment Aisa arrived back from her expedition to the southern desert. It had taken longer than planned to get the message to her, and as a flourish of annoyance emerged at the memory, Augustus Reginald Gormona did his best to banish it. He couldn't alter the past, and he needed to focus on what he could change. Could influence.

"Let me ask you straight," he said, surety in his voice that he didn't feel. "Who among you knows what a Domain is?"

Aria and her sisters, Chloe and Larissa, shared a glance, but no one spoke up.

The king sighed.

"Yes, I know it is restricted information, just as you do, yet I'm aware of the records your families keep. Please—speak with honesty. This is not a test and you shan't be punished."

Aisa stepped forward. "A Domain is a sort of area buff created by a cultivator, correct?"

"Correct," the king replied.

The three who shared a look earlier didn't react to the words, but lines formed on the faces of the other set of sisters, Eirene, Dianne, and Naomi.

So their parents kept it a secret . . . the king noted.

Eirene rolled her shoulders back. "What is the significance of this information, my king?"

Augustus nodded, appreciating the question.

"You were all sent to hunt down awakened creatures, of which none were found . . ."

All six women bowed at the waist.

"Forgive us, king," Aisa said, staring at the ground. "These lowly servants deserve any punishment you see fit."

"No."

They all glanced up, save Aisa, whose face remained downturned.

"It is not your fault," he continued. "They are of significant power, which is why I have revealed the knowledge of Domains."

This made Aisa's head turn toward him, and he could see the realization sprout on her face.

"That's right," he said, clenching his jaw. "They are working together, no doubt being led by one of their number."

Aisa swallowed; she had already deduced who.

Augustus Reginald Gormona, king of these lands, nodded again. "That's correct, Aisa. Lizard Wizard has established a Domain within the bounds of our kingdom."

She bared her teeth, as did her sisters, similarly furious. The other three women looked ponderous, but the king didn't judge them for it; it was of their nature to consider everything before reaching a decision.

"That is an open act of war, my king," Aisa ground out. She dropped to one knee. "What are your orders? We will tear them up by the root if necessary—just give the word."

Her statement gave the king hope, and he felt more sure of himself with these powerful women before him. He gave them a magnanimous look.

"I appreciate your fervency, but we are going on the defensive. This will be a war of attrition."

Aisa's eyes darted around at nothing in particular as her capable brain worked. "Cut them off, starve them of resources before they assault the walls," she said to herself. "Become like a great turtle in its shell—impregnable, stalwart, *strong.*" Her eyes snapped up to his. "A brilliant plan, my king."

The king grinned, his expression finally matching what he felt inside. "Indeed, Aisa. You are all to lead your collared in this defense. I leave the area designation up to you."

He turned and strode from the room, knowing a show of faith in their abilities to be the best option.

"Yes, king!" came the answering cry from all six women.

CHAPTER FIFTY-EIGHT

A FRIENDLY CHAT

As we strode beneath the crescent moon, I frowned at the load of iron ore now covering the tabletop. "These rocks are way uglier than the lizard, Fergus."

He grinned at me. "True, but you can't turn a lizard into cages, can you?"

"Certainly not with that attitude," Maria replied, trying to give a snooty look but falling short.

Duncan pouted with just as much theatrical failure as Maria, his smile peeking through. He turned to Fergus. "No one appreciates our hard work, boss. I told you we should have branched out into making jewelry. Maybe then the simpleminded would have something shiny to catch their attention."

Maria's answering laugh lilted freely over the surrounding sands, just as breathtaking as the memory of the lizard's scales. "A smith calling a farmer simple?" she continued, arching a brow between the part of her sandy hair. "Talk about throwing stones from a glass house."

The back-and-forth ribbing continued for the next couple of hours, especially when Theo joined us, stating he couldn't sleep. By the tenth trip, however, the late hour and monotonous work caught up to us.

"Should we make this the last load?" I asked, seeing the haggard look on everyone's faces.

From the first trip to Tropica with the dangerous-smelling lizard, Borks was there, running along the sand and padding silently over cobbled streets. All the while, he bathed in the conversation. It mattered not that it wasn't directed toward him—simply being around a pack again was an unspeakable joy.

Coming to Tropica hadn't been a mistake.

He had kept trying to find opportunities to help, but short of carrying a chunk of ore in his jaws each time they made a trip, he just got in the way. Though he was stronger than many of the humans helping—stronger perhaps than everyone but his master—his padded paws were ill-suited for carrying the plank of wood they used for transporting rocks.

He'd tried to get under and lift it atop his back, but Fischer had stopped him and pointed out that he might make the load lopsided. He was correct, of course, but Borks still wanted to help. Maybe he could use his ability—tear a portal open with which to transport the ore . . . but no. The moment he reached for that power, he knew his reserves were still depleted. It had taken him weeks of gathering power to step back into the mortal realm.

As the night got later and the conversation grew sparse, his desire to help only increased. He wanted to show his thanks, wanted to demonstrate just how joyous an experience it was being accepted in this odd yet tight-knit pack. So, he reached for the power anyway. It didn't answer. He closed his eyes, focusing harder on the nexus of chi buried within his abdomen.

Brigadier Borks delved deeper, focusing on what he wanted to accomplish while feeling out his partially filled core. He wanted to help. He wanted to contribute.

Above all else, he wanted to be . . . accepted.

This realization hit like a pickaxe striking stone, and his core answered. Borks's eyes flew wide, as did the gates to his power.

"Should we make this the last load?" I asked.

I got a series of blank faces in response.

Fergus stifled a yawn. "I think we have enough ore for the next couple of days. To be honest, we don't have much more room in the smithy to store more. It might not be enough for the amount of cages Barry wants, but it's certainly a good start—"

Bwooom.

Air exploded from behind me. With it, came shadow. Inky tendrils of black slithered everywhere, only noticeable because of my enhanced awareness. In the blink of a regular human's eye, the entire cavern was plunged into darkness.

"Protect Fischer!" Theo yelled.

Maria was at my side in a second, holding my arm with strength that would likely terrify anyone else.

"Relax, everyone," I said, projecting my voice. I still couldn't see a damned thing, but I knew there was no need to worry.

After all, the power had come from Borks.

I could feel his touch in each of the shadows that swirled around us. Within every tendril, his will was present, and I instinctively knew what he'd been trying to accomplish with this new ability. It was both lovely and tragic. He wanted to help. He wanted to be one of us. He wanted—needed—to prove his worth. I took a step toward him, aware of his location despite the pitch-black darkness engulfing us. When I reached him, I lowered a hand to the top of his head and rubbed it softly.

"You are such a good boy, Borks."

Fwip, fwip, fwip, came the sound of his tail wagging and hitting the rocky floor. Just as fast as they had expanded, the shadows withdrew, pouring back into him.

I knelt down and pressed my shoulder into his, hugging him tight. "You *are* one of us, buddy," I whispered so only he could hear. "You don't need to earn your place."

The speed of his tail increased, striking the floor at a faster rhythm.

"What . . . what is *that?*" Theo asked, pointing at the rift I could feel beside me.

"No bloody idea, mate," I replied, letting go of Borks and turning to face it.

A black circle hung in the air just above the ground. Around its edges, tiny black cracks extended that pulsed with abyssal energy. Borks walked over to it and put his head inside. I raised an eyebrow and leaned to look behind the portal. His head wasn't there. The hellhound's neck moved around as he inspected whatever he saw inside, and as he stepped back, he whirled to face me, letting out a joyous bark.

The meaning was clear: it was safe.

Trusting Borks completely, I put my head into the portal. As I looked around inside, Maria rested a hand on my back, then her head popped in beside me.

"Where . . . where are we?"

"I have absolutely no idea . . ."

The portal led to a spacious, cube-shaped room. It was bare of . . . anything, really. The walls, roof, and ceiling were constructed of inky shadow and lit by a purple-tinged light that came from everywhere. It was around five meters in every direction, its corners vaguely rounded. Borks squeezed in beside us, jumping through the portal and into the room. His tail wagged as he walked to the back and dropped a large chunk of iron ore. He sat down, his tail once more striking the ground with muted thumps as he looked at the ore, at us, then barked.

My eyes went wide with realization. "It's a storage room—like a pocket dimension?"

Yes, he barked.

We stepped inside, peering around from within. I reached a hand out and touched one of the swirling walls; it was solid and cold.

"Well, I guess that solves our transport and storage issues."

Borks walked to my side and sat down, also looking around the room he'd created.

"You did this, Borks?" Maria asked, her voice full of awe.

He barked with excitement, his pride clear.

"I was wrong before, buddy," I said. Borks looked up at me, his head cocking to the side as his ears perked up. "You aren't a good boy—you're the *best* boy."

He stood up, rubbing his body against our legs as he wound around us and whined happily.

"Holy frack . . ." came the voice of Theo, his head poking inside. "Is this what I think it is?"

"Certainly is, mate," I replied, beaming a grin at him. "What do you say we load in some ore?"

Excitement-fueled effort swept away the fatigue of the day as we piled the space high with iron ore. I dual wielded pickaxe heads, chipping away at the wall with careful strikes. In only an hour, we'd filled a quarter of the space, and I wiped my brow as we all stood inside, admiring the fruits of our labor.

"That's probably enough for now, right?" I asked, looking at what had to be tons of ore.

"Way too much, if I'm honest," Fergus said, wiping a brow. "We'll put it to good use, though."

I reached down, petting Borks's head. His golden fur slipped through my fingers, a welcome sensation after swinging two metal picks through stone for an hour.

"Let's get back to Tropica and make sure it works before we rest for the night."

As we approached the village, Maria cleared her throat.

"I might split off and head home. Dad will no doubt be waiting for me to return before he goes to bed."

I winced. "Sorry for keeping you out so late."

"It's okay!" She smiled at everyone and bent down to scratch behind Borks's head. "It was my pleasure."

"I'll walk you home." I looked back over my shoulder. "Meet you guys at the smithy soon."

As Maria and I split from the group, we walked in silence. With each passing day, it had been growing colder. Tonight was no exception. My hand twitched as it went to hold her hand of its own accord, but I held it back, noticing Maria's closed-off posture. Both hands were clasped before her, and though her eyes looked at the ground, her gaze was distant.

I wanted to say something, wanted to voice the question burning to escape my throat. Try as I might, it never came. While most of my time with her was still as comfortable as ever, it was flecked with moments of tension, fractions of time in which there seemed to be a physical wall between us. One such barrier was firmly between us right now, and the longer it lingered, the more my brow crinkled.

If only I could . . .

My thoughts cut off as a cold hand grabbed mine. I turned to Maria, the tension held in my body slowly melting away as I took in her moonlit face. She was smiling at me, her head tilted and her sun-bleached hair hanging to one side.

"Where were you?" she asked.

"Sorry?"

"You were elsewhere." She reached up and tapped a finger on my forehead. It made my skin tingle, and my hand drifted up to rub it. "What were you thinking about?"

"It's nothing," I said, both of us knowing it to be a lie.

She nodded, giving me a smile that didn't reach her eyes. "Well, we're here. Thanks for escorting me."

She darted in and planted a kiss on my cheek. Her lips were as cold as her fingers. "Sweet dreams, Fischer," she said, pulling away.

"You too . . ." I said, watching her tiptoe across her porch and open the front door.

She froze. "Dad, you didn't have to wait up for me." She closed the door, cutting the rest of their conversation off.

I turned and strode away before I could overhear anything else, focusing on the sounds of shifting leaves and the sand beneath my feet so that my enhanced ears didn't accidentally eavesdrop. It was a needless precaution; thoughts consumed my awareness.

The following morning, I woke up to a warm ball of fur curled up against my side. I reached down to pet the Chihuahua-shaped hellhound, delighting in the muffled thumps of Borks's tail as he woke up. A second later, he emerged from the blankets, letting out a soft whine as he stretched and yawned.

"How did you sleep, buddy?"

Good, he yapped.

"Glad to hear it."

I got up and reached to the sky, my body and brain feeling similarly fatigued. Unlike my doggy pal, I'd had a fitful night. After finding the pocket dimension open at the smithy, I helped them unload part of it before Borks and I had headed home. I'd hoped that the physical labor would help sleep steal my consciousness away. It didn't. Instead, I'd lain awake for hours, unable to fight off my worries for long enough to pass out.

It wasn't all bad news, though. Forced to be present with my thoughts, I'd reached a decision, one that would hopefully help me process the complex emotions haunting me.

"Wanna come for a walk, Borks?"

He barked, shifting into a golden retriever as he leaped from the bed.

"All right—let's head off."

Forgoing caffeine for now, we made our way over the sand. The sun rose at my back, its rays doing nothing to banish the cold of last night. Borks loped ahead, sniffing the rows of sugarcane after we reached them and turned west. Anxiety sprouted its ugly roots as I stepped up to the door. I swallowed, my mouth feeling as dry as the sand we'd just crossed.

A snout nudged my leg, and I looked down at Borks, smiling at the compassion held in his eyes.

"Thanks, buddy."

I took a deep breath, sighed it out, and knocked on the door.

"Morning, Fischer!" a voice came from behind me.

I just about jumped out of my skin as I whirled around. "Frack me, Barry—a little warning next time!"

"A warning for saying hello?" He raised an eyebrow, giving me a smirk as he looked between me and the wooden facade he'd secured to the church's gilded entrance. "I didn't expect to see you this early."

Borks trotted over and gave Barry a sniff. The farmer reached a hand down, rewarding him with a pat on the head. The door swung open behind me, and Danny stepped out. "Morning, Fischer."

"G'day, mate. Have you seen Theo about? I was hoping to speak with him." I turned to Barry. "Are you free, too? Any chance I could shout you and Theo a coffee and croissant in exchange for a bit of your time?"

"I always have time for you, Fischer. You don't need to buy me breakfast, though."

"I went and got enough coffee and croissants for everyone," Danny said. "There's more than enough for you, too—Keith only went to bed as I was waking up, so you can have his."

"You're sure?"

"Of course. I'll go get Theo."

He disappeared inside, the door closing with a soft click. Barry and I made small talk as we waited, and less than a minute later, the door swung open again. Theo held a small tray in hand, three coffees and croissants atop it.

"Good morning, mate!" he said, giving me a smile. "Coffee?"

"Bless you," I said, grabbing a cup and pastry. "Do you have a moment?"

"Always! Danny said you wanted to talk to me. What's up?"

"It's, uh . . ." I trailed off, not knowing where to begin.

"Is everything okay?" Barry asked, still petting Borks's head.

"Yeah, mate, I just . . ." I let out a sigh. "I've had some stuff on my mind, and I just need to talk it out with someone. I can't think of anyone better than you fellas to give me good advice."

Barry's hand stilled atop Borks's head, his eyes narrowing on me. "This wouldn't have something to do with a certain young lady, would it?"

I paused mid-sip, then slowly lowered the coffee. "What makes you say that?"

"Because I have eyes, Fischer."

I sighed. "Is it that obvious to everyone?"

"Not to me . . ." Theo said, looking between us. "I don't know what the frack you're talking about."

Barry gave me a kind smile. "I knew something was up but thought I should wait until you wanted to talk about it."

I rubbed the back of my head, feeling awkward despite seeking them out.

"Come on." Barry grabbed a coffee and croissant, then started walking away. "Let's head down to the beach. It's a lovely morning."

"Yeah, all right."

As we wandered east, I tried to organize my thoughts.

CHAPTER FIFTY-NINE

BREAKTHROUGH

With the sun guiding our way, Barry, Theo, and I walked toward the ocean. The soft breeze blowing toward us was cool against my skin, the cold of night not yet banished by the day's warmth. The air went still, letting the sound of softly crashing waves reach us. I focused on the sand beneath my feet and the white-wash calling out to us.

Before I knew it, we were at the water. We sat down just above the lapping tide, close enough that it would reach our feet if we stayed too long.

"So," Barry said, taking a sip of his coffee. "What about your relationship with Maria has been bothering you?"

Gulls called from above as they soared on unseen winds, their shrill noises calming as they melded with the ever-churning ocean.

I let out a sigh. "I'm not sure we even have a relationship." I swirled the coffee around my cup, staring down at the golden liquid. "We haven't spoken about it."

"Okay. Do you want one? With her?"

"I do, yeah, but it's . . . complicated."

Barry cocked his head. "How so?"

I gave a humorless smile. "You're spearheading a cult that treats me as some sort of deity. You, of all people, should know."

"First, it's a church. Second, you're trying to change the subject."

"True," Theo added, shooting me a wink.

"You brought us here because you wanted to speak, Fischer, and it sounds like that's what you need." Barry's eyes bored into me, firm and unrelenting. "So, I ask again: how are things complicated?"

I opened my mouth to retort but paused with my finger half raised. I wanted to tell him he was wrong, wanted to have a go at him for being so snippy, but then I thought about what he'd said. I closed my mouth, flexing my jaw as I mulled the words over.

"I hate that you're right," I admitted, giving an exaggerated pout.

Barry laughed, his serious facade falling away. "I didn't say it out of malice, Fischer. It's easy to lean into anything else when you're feeling vulnerable. But there's no need to hide yourself from us, mate. Theo and I are your friends, and we want what's best for you."

"True," Theo agreed, beaming a smile at me.

I returned it, then cast my eyes out to sea, taking a deep breath. I held it, focusing on the horizon as I counted to four in my head. When I let it out, it was slow and controlled, like exhaling through a straw. Before the calm could leave me, I answered honestly.

"I'm terrified. Of what I am—of what I could become."

"Why does that scare you?" Barry asked, his voice patient. "Are you worried you could hurt her?"

I frowned. "Well, I wasn't before, but you've got a point . . ."

Barry shook his head at me, a wincing smile on his face. "You're changing the subject again."

I sighed. "I suppose I was."

I looked up at the sky above us, letting the sun warm my skin and ground me.

"I'm scared of what it means for her. I couldn't care less about myself, mate. No matter what happens, I'll have my animal pals. Even if the worst happens and you blokes manage to make me a god or whatever, I know they'll always be there with me . . . but Maria . . ."

"You're worried she'd stay behind?"

I chewed my lip. Was that what worried me? I'd been pushing the thoughts away for so long that I didn't even know anymore. I always acknowledged and let them go, not wanting to dwell on the negative for too long. As if called by name, they once more rushed into my awareness.

This time, I didn't push them away.

"Of course I'm scared of her staying behind—of her not choosing me, but isn't everyone scared of that? The thought of letting someone in, of loving them entirely, but then being abandoned . . . it's . . ." I winced. "It's horrifying."

Barry opened his mouth to respond, but I shook my head, my mind still processing my complex emotions. "That's not what has me frozen, though. It's terrifying, sure, but it's worth the risk. *She's* worth the risk . . ."

I glanced up at Theo, then Barry, both of them nodding for me to continue.

"Maria has a family and a life here. If something happens and I'm forced to leave, it's not that I'm worried she won't choose me. It would suck, but that's life. She's her own person, after all. Still, I don't want her to have to choose. It seems . . . unfair. Like there's a power imbalance between us and going further would be preying upon that."

The light feeling in my chest told me I was reaching the truth of it, but before I could continue, Theo laid a hand on my shoulder.

"Fischer . . ."

I raised an eyebrow at the stern glance he gave me. "What?"

He looked at Barry, then back at me, his lips curling into a kind smile. "You're a moron."

The statement, so abrupt and unexpected, made me bark a laugh. "I know, but in this instance, why?"

He patted my shoulder twice, then pulled his hand back. "Because you said it yourself. Maria is her own person. She has agency of her own life. You trying to shield her from loving you is possibly the dumbest thing I've ever heard."

I didn't respond right away, and Barry cleared his throat. "Are you open to honest feedback, Fischer?"

"Of course, mate. That's why you're both here."

He nodded. "To expand on Theo's point, it's also rather . . . patronizing."

"Patronizing . . . ?"

He gave me a smile that didn't take the sharpness from his words.

"Because you're painting it as a kindness—something that you're doing to protect her. As if you're smarter than her and she couldn't possibly make an informed decision, so you have to remove the possibility entirely."

I sat back in the sand as if physically struck. I'd asked for their help, and neither of my friends had pulled their blows. Worse, they were right. The logic was sound. I was scared of placing Maria in a position that could hurt her, but she was *brilliant,* which was one of the reasons I had such strong feelings for her. Pulling back so she wouldn't get hurt down the line was treating her as if she couldn't be trusted to make her own choices. It was how you'd treat a child that wanted something to snack on before dinner.

I leaned forward on my knees, my eyes unfocused as I considered it more. Borks leaned into my lap. His tail wagged so vigorously that even his head shook, and I rested a palm atop it. Though the words of my friends hurt, my chest felt lighter than it had in weeks. There was still something there, though . . . a small weight lingering within me, pressing down on my core.

My eyebrow furrowed as I searched for what it was.

"Fischer . . ."

I glanced over at Theo. "Yeah, mate?"

"You know I can tell when someone is being truthful, right?"

"Yeah?" Of course I knew that. "Why?"

He chewed his cheek, his face thoughtful. "You weren't being entirely truthful earlier."

"What? When?"

His eyes darted to me but drifted away just as fast. "When you were talking about your fear . . . of being abandoned . . ."

"Huh? Yes I was."

" . . . Are you sure about that? *Really* sure?"

The weight inside me trembled. My hand drifted to my abdomen, resting on it. I had been telling the truth . . . hadn't I? While I *was* scared of getting attached, it wasn't the cause of my hesitation. As I thought about it, considering how it would feel if that eventuality came to be, it was like an icy hand gripped my heart. It squeezed, and my lungs went tight. The weight at my core responded, shaking and trying to get free.

"Oh . . ."

The feeling was a familiar one. It was how I felt when I thought about my mother leaving when I was a child. Of her abandonment, no matter how much my father had pushed her away.

"*Shit . . .*"

"Say it," Theo encouraged. "If you're comfortable to do so, I mean."

I nodded, licking my lips. "I wasn't pushing her away because I wanted to protect her. Well, not only for that reason, anyway." I swallowed, my mouth dry and chest tight. "It was to protect myself . . ."

I took a deep breath, closed my eyes, and slowly exhaled. The weight sitting on my core lifted. My skin prickled as it diffused, making its way from my abdomen out to my limbs. When it reached my toes and fingertips, the weight gathered, pooled, pushed at my pores, oozed through my skin . . .

. . . Oozed through my skin?

"What the . . . ?" Barry asked.

I opened my eyes, frowning as I stared down at my hands. They were covered in a translucent, faintly glowing liquid. Not just my hands, either—my entire body, everywhere I'd felt the weight spread toward, was covered in drops of it. I shook an arm, but the drops didn't move. I rubbed two fingers together, trying to test the consistency, but as I did, it started reabsorbing into me.

"What the frack is happening?" I heard myself ask.

The viscous liquid was back within me in the blink of an eye, and it began retracing its path back toward my core. My ligaments shook as it crawled its way across them. With each part of my body it passed, the power grew, feeling like an ember, a flame, and then a roaring bonfire.

Something was coming.

"Get back!" I growled through gritted teeth.

"Fischer . . . ?" Theo asked, his voice laden with care. "Are you—"

"Back!" I yelled.

The second warning was enough.

Borks, Barry, and Theo dashed away, scrambling across the sand. The raging bonfire climbed down my chest, gathering fuel and heat as it went. Its edges flickered against my core, and then they were merging. It was too much power. It was too bright. Too hot. My body was burning up, unable to handle the sheer magnitude of the assault. I curled into a ball, my muscles aching from how tight they were.

Then, just as I thought I would explode, light did instead. It shone from my entire body, turning the world a blinding white. I was frozen in time, my friends' positions locked as the light approached them. I'd felt this before, had light shoot from my body . . . but never like this. It just kept growing, kept expanding, kept—

Boooom!

A blast of unbelievable force exploded from me, disintegrating the sand at my feet. Despite anything to stand on, I remained suspended in the air, my limbs going numb as more power flowed out.

The next thing I knew, I was in free fall.

* * *

"Back!"

The urgency in Fischer's voice left no room for argument, so Barry took heed. He took off running, Theo and Borks at his side as he dashed away. With his back still turned, he felt the moment the chi exploded from Fischer. Milliseconds later, the blast hit his body. He was flung forward, swept off his feet as the world turned to a blur. A wall of purple appeared in his path and Barry flew into it, the world turning from yellow sand and blue skies to a murky darkness.

He slammed into something firm, the air getting knocked from his lungs and his vision going black. Sand was everywhere, flung up by the explosion and settling within his clothing. He rolled to the side, coughing and spluttering. A canine snout wedged itself under his abdomen and helped him sit upright.

Borks licked his face as Barry's vision and awareness slowly returned.

"What was that?" Theo groaned from beside him, also getting help from Borks.

The dust in the air settled, and Barry blinked at the surrounding room. They were within Borks's spatial room, and realization struck. The purple wall had been Borks opening a portal before them, and the firm object he'd hit was the back wall. Barry recalled the force they'd been struck with—if he hadn't been a cultivator, he would have died on the spot. If Borks hadn't opened the portal, all three of them could have torn through Tropica's buildings like a scythe through wheat.

Seeing that both he and Theo were well, Borks let out a bark and dashed out through the portal, disappearing from sight. Barry stood slowly, then held out a hand for Theo. With a grunt, he pulled the man to his feet. They both ambled toward the exit, leaning on each other for support.

Weightlessness settled over me. My entire body tingled in a pleasant manner as I fell through space, descending for what felt like an eternity. I kept falling, faint whispers of wind tickling my—

"*Oof!*"

I slammed back-first into the wet sand, forcing the air from my lungs. I squinted out, seeing the blue sky through a dissipating cloud of dust. Time felt . . . odd. It wasn't traveling as fast as it should, but with each passing second, I got the sensation that it was returning to normal. The soft sound of water called out to me—the ocean. I relaxed, content with just bathing in the sounds of the world.

But then they came to meet me.

A tsunami of ocean water crashed down onto me, catching me just as I'd gone to take in a slow breath. Some got into my lungs. I coughed and spluttered, forcing the salty liquid from my throat with what little air I had left. My body was spinning, caught in the inexorable swirl of the surrounding water. With my chest screaming for oxygen and my limbs grasping for purchase, a red-hot coal of panic glowed within me.

CHAPTER SIXTY

CULTIVATOR

I spun for what felt like an eternity in the whitewash. There was neither up nor down, and I fought against the disorientation, my limbs fighting for purchase. The ocean water was freezing, but I barely felt it. I had to get out. Had to get a breath. And with each passing second, the anxiety at my loss of control increased. I lashed out with my legs and swept my hands through the water.

Finally, I made contact.

When my fingers brushed solid sand, I spun and kicked off with every ounce of strength I could muster. With my body shaped like a torpedo, I sailed from the salty prison.

Theo helped Barry stand as they followed Borks from the portal and returned to the sands of Tropica. The shore looked like a meteor had struck it. Where Fischer had been, a gigantic crater remained. The sand that previously filled it had surged up to create a two-meter-tall ridge. A third of it occupied where the ocean was before, and even as they strode up the ridge, seawater was pouring into the hole.

"Where is Fischer?" Barry asked.

Borks stared down at the churning water, his tail high and ears alert.

Theo's gaze went distant.

He had heard accounts of cultivators' breakthroughs from Ellis, and he was going over them in his mind's eye, comparing the tales to the scene before him. Such knowledge had been scoured from most history books, of course. But not those in the royal library. They had spoken of ascension in vague terms, mentioning shows of strength and transformations. Their little group of fishermen had spent many a night debating just what that truly meant.

Looking at the beach before him, Theo saw the truth of it.

The force needed to create such a blast was astronomical, and if he hadn't seen it for himself, he would have thought it an exaggeration. Theo was a cultivator too, and he'd done all manner of tests under Ellis's instruction, as had everyone else that was a part of the church. Even if they had all attacked at once, they couldn't have done a third of what Fischer had just done by accident.

He'd been told of Fischer accidentally destroying a tree, and the time that he kicked Brigadier Borks clean over the sand between his house and Tropica, but neither of those acts held a candle to the damage done to the coastline. If he had to bet, Theo would say that Fischer clearly surpassed some sort of threshold.

It filled Theo with an even higher level of respect for Fischer than he'd already held. If it were anyone else, he may have been terrified of them. For Fischer, though . . . all he felt was excitement and awe.

With Theo's thoughts straying to the future and all the possibilities it held, Fischer exploded from the water. His eyes were wide, mouth gasping like a fish as he careened for the far wall of the crater. He slammed face-first into the raised sand, throwing what had to be a ton of the grainy matter flying.

When the sand cleared, all that was visible of Fischer were his hands and lower torso. As Fischer's limbs twitched, Theo just stared.

Both his face and sense of awe dropped.

Forcing my arms wide and planting my hands on the sand, I extracted myself from the tomb I found myself in. I arched my back and faced my head toward the heavens, gasping in a breath of air so sweet I could have cried. I collapsed to the ground, settling into the small divot I'd made in my hasty exit from the churning water. As my gaze drifted to the crater I'd just flown from, both eyebrows rose of their own accord. The ocean was rushing into what looked like a thirty-meter-wide pool, its sandy sides already collapsing into the rushing water.

I caught sight of movement on the other bank. Barry and Theo stood completely still as they stared at me, in complete contrast to the full-bodied wag Borks was doing. I felt a pulse of chi, and the next second, he was standing beside me. A storm of licks descended, and I petted him all over, laughing at the way his golden fur tickled me.

"Hey there, buddy."

Theo and Barry leaped, landing on either side of me.

"Are you okay, Fischer?" the former asked.

I rubbed my face, getting as much sand from me as possible. "Yeah, mate—I think I'm good. Are you guys? Whatever that was, it had a bit of a punch to it."

" . . . A bit of a punch?" Theo repeated, his voice incredulous. "If not for Borks's timely intervention, we'd have been shot into Tropica."

He went on to tell me of the speed with which my blast had sent them flying, and of Borks's opening of his soul space—*pocket dimension?* Whatever that ability was. The entire time he spoke, I was listening, but I was also feeling the world around us. Everything was more . . . tangible. It was impossible to describe properly, but it was as if I could feel the very strands of essence that wove around us, simply existing. When I focused on any of my friends before me, I could feel the chi—the *power*—that they held within them.

Where before I'd had an inkling if someone was a cultivator because of the resonance coming from them, when I felt any of them now, I *knew.* I was patting Borks's head, wanting to show my thanks for him potentially saving lives, when I focused on the core in his abdomen. I blinked, and when our eyes locked, I could tell he was aware of the conscious presence I was exerting.

He licked my chin, and I closed my eyes, pressing my forehead to his. "You guys wanna see something neat?"

"Something neat?" Barry asked.

Theo narrowed his eyes in thought. "Should I get Ellis first? He might headbutt me if I don't let him record it."

"No time, I'm afraid."

Both their foreheads furrowed in confusion, but I just smiled in response. Borks backed away as I sat up straight and crossed my legs. I set my hands to the sand beside me, and I peered down at the swirling water beneath me, fixing the image into my mind before closing my eyes. I reached out with my will and exerted it upon the crater.

The world answered.

Power coursed from my core, and I guided it, expertly weaving strands where they were needed. My abdomen hummed as it hit the resonance the world demanded, and white light burst from me in a rush. The ground beneath me shifted. The landscape changed. And a contented smile spread over my features as I opened my eyes again a second later. In my previous transformations, each element had been a surprise, and I was pretty sure I'd been unconscious for half of them.

This time, I knew what would await me.

The walls of the pool had been raised and solidified, as had the floor. The water within, which had been churning chaotically, was mostly still. I had carved a channel out toward the ocean. The bay flowed in with small waves. The floor of the pool sloped down gradually from the west, starting shallow enough for a toddler to splash and becoming so deep that I wouldn't be able to stand with my head above water.

I looked up at my friends. "What do you think?"

Theo and Barry were stunned, while Borks just smiled and wagged his tail at me, striding toward me to lick my cheek.

Theo sighed. "Yeah, I'm definitely gonna get headbutted for not getting Ellis to witness this."

I shook with laughter, picturing the archivist doing exactly that. "Sorry, mate. If I wanted to create this, I had to do it right away. Any longer, and the strands would have dissipated."

Theo held up his hands. "Say no more, please."

I arched an eyebrow. "You don't want to know?"

"Of course I want to know! If you tell me anything more without Ellis here, though, the headbutt will be upgraded to a body slam." He gazed out at the tide pool I'd made, shaking his head before returning his attention to me. "Will you wait here? I can get him right now."

I stood up, dusting the now dry sand from my body. "I'm afraid I've gotta go somewhere—I'll come find Ellis later, if that's all right?"

Theo gave me a flat stare, then sighed. "A body slam it is, then. At least I know it's coming." He waved his hands for me to get going. "Run along, then. Go see her."

I made an exaggerated pout. "What makes you think I'm going to see Maria?"

Barry made the same gesture for me to hurry. "We can stall Ellis for a while. Get out of here before you start doubting yourself again and cause another explosion."

I reached down to pat Borks. "Would you mind staying with these two for a while, mate? They might need your protection from a certain archivist once he realizes they're protecting me."

Likely knowing my true intentions, he barked and nudged me away with his snout.

Sparing them one last grateful look, I took off, sprinting across the sand.

George was deep in meditation when the earth shook. His house quaked, chandeliers chimed above, and a glass shattered as it fell free of the table.

"G-George!" Geraldine gasped, reaching a hand out to grip his arm.

He opened his eyes in a panic that had nothing to do with the sudden chaos of the outside world. His core, where he had been focusing his meditations on just as his family's tome instructed, had resonated with the blast. It had seemed to pulse right through him, making his entire abdomen vibrate and hum. It spread from that spot within, growing less intense as it traveled down his arms and legs. His head tingled, and he ran a hand through his sparse hair.

"Did . . . did you feel that?"

"Of course I felt that!" she said, her voice shrill. "The entire room shook!"

"Not the room . . ." he said, getting to his feet. "I'm going to go check outside. I'll be back."

"I'm coming with you." As they rushed from the room, she laid a hand on his shoulder. "What did you feel, George?"

The tone of her voice told him she understood the significance of what he'd experienced, so he explained as best he could while they hurried down the stairs. When they got outside, he paused for a moment as they took in their surroundings. No one else was outside, but from most buildings, faces could be seen peering from windows.

"Stay inside, everyone!" he yelled, heading off toward the south.

As they traveled, he told Geraldine the rest of the story. She asked just the right questions, digging for George to explain the intricacies of it in a way she could understand. Gods, he loved that woman and her brain. When they reached the south side of Tropica, *everyone* was outside. Those that had been working fields were returning to their homes to check on their loved ones.

At seeing George, many approached and asked questions he didn't have the answers to. No one knew what had happened. Those that were outside at the time of the blast said that it sounded like it came from everywhere. Air had rushed from the south, but when George and Geraldine jogged to the edge of Tropica, they saw nothing of note toward the distant mountains past Fischer's land.

If the earthquake had happened even weeks ago, George and Geraldine would likely have scrambled around the village, working themselves into a tizzy. With the calm that came from practicing his family's techniques, however, they both knew it to be a pointless endeavor.

As they slowly returned to their home, they walked in silence; both were consumed by their own thoughts. When they reached the upstairs room they'd been using for their meditations, George pointed at Geraldine's stomach, taking comfort in the curve of her body despite the urgency he felt to return to meditation. "It's just as the book says—focus right here."

She nodded, her eyes fervent, then she pulled George into a swift kiss. "I love you, dear."

He smiled at her, then kissed her again before pulling away. "I love you more."

They both closed their eyes and settled into the cross-legged stance. When he focused on the core within, it seemed close, easier to grasp, and his awareness swept into it faster than ever before.

With the wind and sun at my back, I ran for Maria. I extended my awareness toward her home. Both her and Sharon there. I picked up the pace, purpose guiding my steps. When I appeared from between the rows of cane that were now tall enough to block out my vision, I came up short.

"Please," Sharon said, laying a reassuring hand on Roger's arm. "Just stay here. I'll be back soon—"

Roger's face contorted in rage. "Enough is enough, Sharon! When are you going to tell me what in Pistis's good name is going on?"

"You have to trust me, my love . . ."

She tried to lift her hand to his chest, but he twisted away, not letting it land. Just beyond them, standing on their deck and gazing at me with wide eyes, stood the most beautiful woman I'd ever seen.

Even a supermodel from back on Earth didn't hold a candle when compared to her perfectly imperfect freckles, her suntanned hair, and her stunning eyes, despite how panicked they looked in the moment. My feet strode forward of their own account, and I stepped past Sharon and Roger, not even registering their existence.

"Fischer . . ." Maria said, darting glances behind me. "Do you know what happened? What that blast was? We—"

I wrapped my arms around her waist and pulled her into me. With her on the slightly raised porch, we were at the same height. She was hesitant for a moment, but then she leaned in to meet me. Our lips pressed together, and time froze. My heart thundered, and I felt the fluttering of hers as we pulled each other in. We lost ourselves in the pure moment. Still holding her body to mine, I leaned back to stare into her eyes.

I no longer hesitated. "I love you, Maria."

Her eyes searched mine, darting from one to the other rapidly. "You mean it."

It was a statement. I nodded anyway.

"I do. And I'm sorry it took me so long to say it."

"I . . ." She bit her lip and glanced down, averting her eyes. "I love you too, Fischer."

A firm hand grasped my shirt and pulled. It tore open at the shoulder, the sleeve almost entirely disconnecting. I turned to see Roger, his rage clouded by confusion.

He looked at the torn sleeve still in his hand, then up at me, his eyebrows narrowing. At a speed I wouldn't think possible for a regular human, he poked my bicep. I saw a flicker of understanding in the lines of his face, and then the muscles of his shoulder tensed.

Without another word, his fist flew. If he had swung at me upon my arrival in Tropica, it would have collided and hurt like shit. With my body as it was now, though . . .

I slid aside at the last instant, letting his fist travel through open air, but it was for his sake, not for mine. As fast as his fist was traveling, the bones of his hand would have shattered on me.

"You . . ." he looked at me, then Maria, who had stepped back when he swung. "Get away from him!"

Roger raised his fists and stepped forward, rolling his shoulders. There was zero hesitation on his face, despite his realization.

"Cultivator," he spat, coming closer.

CHAPTER SIXTY-ONE

STARS COLLIDING

It was, by all measurable metrics, a wonderful morning in Tropica. The sun was bright and warm, banishing the night's chill. A soft breeze blew, giving the air a fresh quality. I just had some sort of breakthrough, and as a result, I was more aware than ever of the world around me. I had just told the most beautiful woman I'd ever known that I loved her. She had said it back. That her father was currently bobbing and weaving toward me, hands raised and ready to lash out with the old left-right-goodnight, really dampened the mood, though.

"I'm sorry," I said, wincing at Maria. "I really messed this moment up."

"Get back!" Roger yelled, though if it was at me or his daughter, I wasn't sure.

"Roger, stop!" Sharon tried.

I held up my hands placatingly. "Whoa, mate. We can talk about this. It's a misunderstand—" I cut off as I ducked a jab. "Standing! It's a misunderstanding!"

"I knew there was something off with you," he growled, then spared a glance for Maria. "What are you doing? Run!"

He jabbed again and I dodged to the side, but there had been no need. Sharon caught his arm at the wrist. He glared at her and tried to yank his hand back, but it didn't budge. What color remained in his face fled.

"I'm sorry I didn't tell you, dear," she said, a mountain of regret in her eyes. "I was waiting for the right time."

"You . . ." he said, his voice flat.

Sharon's eyes darted to Maria reflexively. She immediately returned them to Roger, but it was too late—he'd seen it.

"Maria?" he asked, voice still lacking any inflection.

Maria grimaced, then hopped to the side. To me, it was a casual movement. To Roger, she may as well have teleported.

"No," he muttered, his legs wobbling.

Sharon caught him and lowered him to the step. "It's not what you think, dear. You'll understand when I explain."

His eyes went distant. "How did this happen? My family . . ."

She tapped him on the forehead hard enough to get his attention. "Is still your family. Don't go saying anything foolish you can't take back."

He rubbed the red mark forming above his eyes, his gaze clearing for just a moment.

Sharon pounced. "I can explain it all, Roger." She grabbed his head, forcing his eyes to meet hers. "Please. You'll agree with my actions if you'll just listen to what I have to say."

I felt the need to jump in, to say something that would help, but what was there to say? It would eventually be revealed that I was the catalyst for all this change, and that would hardly make him inclined to trust me. This was a job for Sharon.

"Let's go for a walk, Maria."

"No!" Roger yelled, coming back to himself and darting to his feet. "You can't!"

"Dad . . ." She gave him a forced smile, and the look in her eye broke my heart. "I'm a cultivator too. If you're terrified of Fischer, you may as well be terrified of me."

He opened his mouth to respond, looked to his wife for support, then seemed to remember she was also awakened.

His face fell, and Sharon pulled him into a hug. "I know, dear. I'm so, *so* sorry."

That was all I heard because Maria had grabbed my hand. We walked away and around the corner of their home. The moment we were between two tall rows of cane, she collapsed in the sand, all surety leaving her.

I laid a hand on her shoulder. "I'm . . . Damn. I don't have the words. I'm sorry, Maria. That must have been hard."

She let out a steadying breath. "It's okay. He reacted worse than I thought he would, but he'll come around."

I sat down beside her. "Do you want to talk about it?"

She cocked her head to the side as she stared into the crops, then she spun on me with a mischievous smile. "You *love* me."

"I do," I laughed, leaning over to kiss the top of her head. "And you love me too, apparently. If you can be trusted, I mean."

I shot her a wink, and she smiled back at my attempted joke, but it was a fragile thing. She pulled away and picked up a stray leaf from the ground, then started winding it around a finger. "Are you sure? That you love me, I mean."

I didn't need to think about it. "I am."

She focused on the leaf, unwinding it only to wrap it around her finger again. "Part of me thought you weren't interested anymore. I thought that maybe you just wanted to be friends."

"I'm sorry." I spun so I was facing her, but kept the gap between us, giving her the agency to close the distance if she wanted. "Are you in a place to hear about what was going through my mind, or do you want to leave it for another day?"

She chewed her cheek, still focused on the leaf. "I want to know. It'll be a good distraction."

I nodded, and having already exposed my soul to Barry and Theo today, the words flowed freely. I told her everything. Of my fear of being hurt, of my desire to protect her, and of the revelation that it was mainly the former giving me pause. At some point during the retelling, her hand drifted over to mine. Her tiny fingers intertwined with mine, keeping the words rushing forth.

I spoke of the breakthrough I'd had, explaining that being true to myself and what truly motivated me had been the catalyst for the transformation.

"*You* were the blast?" she asked, her voice more than a little amused. "I honestly should have known. *Of course* it was you."

"Yeah, your dad was right. I'm a dangerous guy to be around." I wiggled my eyebrows. "Some ladies are into that, you know."

She scoffed and rolled her eyes. "Maybe not ladies that you confess your feelings for, then pull away from for the next month."

I pulled my hand back, and my face must have shown the impact her words had, because she winced. "Sorry. That came out worse than I meant."

"You don't have to apologize. You're right." I took a steadying breath, looking at the sky as a silence stretched between us. "I'd understand if you needed some time to think about everything."

Her face scrunched in thought, and she stared into the stalks of sugarcane before us. Her gaze drifted to mine. "No, it's fine."

Her eyes betrayed her.

"You're a terrible liar," I said, giving her a sad smile.

She flushed and stared off into the crops again, and I swallowed.

"You can tell me if you're feeling up to it, or we can speak about it another time. I don't want half-truths and white lies to form the basis of . . . our relationship."

Saying the last bit made butterflies take flight in my stomach. Maria's face grew even redder, and I didn't miss the smile she was trying to keep from reaching her mouth.

She bit her lip, schooling her expression. "The way you were over the last few weeks . . . it was . . . confusing. I've never been a self-conscious person. *Ever.* But the way you were so loving and kind, then would just . . . back off or misdirect my affection with a joke. It made me feel crazy. It made me so unsure of myself. Half the time I told myself I was imagining it, and the other half I was convinced you just didn't want me anymore."

The butterflies in my stomach died.

I knew my actions would have been confusing, but to hear the impact it had on the woman I supposedly loved . . . it was like the ground fell out beneath me, and more than anything, I wanted to make it all better. I felt the need to scoop her up, to tell her it was all going to be okay . . . but that was selfish. It was what I wanted, what would make *me* feel better.

So instead, I spoke.

"I'm sorry, Maria. I didn't do it intentionally, and I wish I could take it all back. There weren't any bad intentions . . ." I shook my head as I trailed off. "No. That's a cop out. It doesn't matter what I intended. I'm sorry, and I'll do whatever I can to make it up to you."

I fought the urge to reach over and take her hand. When hers came over to intertwine with mine, my heart thumped.

"I won't lie and say it didn't hurt, Fischer, but you're being too hard on yourself." She turned, her jaw firm as she looked me over. "I know how you can make it up to me."

"How?"

"Don't do it again, you handsome idiot." She smiled, and this time, it wasn't forced. "*Love* me."

I laughed, and so did she. We both leaned forward, meeting each other atop the sandy soil. Her arms went around my abdomen, so I held tight to her upper back, one hand resting on her head and stroking her silken hair. Her floral scent drifted up to meet me, making my heart thunder even harder.

"You were up to the part where you detonated like a fermented cask left in the sun," she said, still holding me. "What happened next?"

Smiling at the lack of tension between us, I voiced the rest. I told her of waking up at the bottom of a churning pool. Of my definitely graceful and not at all embarrassing exit, in which I landed on my feet and looked super cool. And of my heightened awareness that came as a result. All the while, I kept stroking her head, willing the grief I'd caused her to wash away.

When I told her about the transformation the crater had undergone, she pulled back, and her gaze shot up to meet mine. "You made another thing? And it was easier this time?"

"Yeah . . . why?"

"Can we go?"

"To see it?" I asked, entranced by the sparkle in her eyes.

"Yeah!"

"It would be my pleasure."

We untangled our limbs, and I stood and offered my hand. She grasped it, and as I pulled her to her feet, she kept coming. She wrapped her arms around my neck as mine went around her waist. Standing on her tiptoes, her lips met mine. They were warm and soft—gods, they were soft—and as so often happened when it came to Maria, I got completely lost in the moment, intoxicated by her.

"Fischer!" a voice boomed, entirely too loud to come from a non-cultivator.

"Keep your voice down!" Another hissed, barely audible over the wind rustling sugarcane leaves.

I tsked. "Damn. He found me."

Maria pulled back, cocking her head to the side. "Is that who I think it is?"

"Afraid so." I raised my chest and cupped a hand to my mouth. "Over here, Ellis."

If a regular human had been present, they would have seen a crazed, muscular man appear from nowhere, a swath of sugarcane obliterated in his wake. Plant fibers and sugary liquid sprayed me and Maria.

I wiped my eyes, giving Ellis a flat stare. "You right, mate?"

"Tell me," he said, his voice low and dangerous. "Before the memory fades." He leaned in, his entire body shaking as he reached for his notepad. "I must know—"

He cut off as Maria grabbed his ear and reefed it to the side. "What do you think you're doing, Ellis?" Maria demanded, glaring at him like he was a petulant child.

I raised an eyebrow but kept my mouth shut—there was no way I was going to intervene.

"I . . . I did not . . ." he stammered, blinking at her expression. "I am . . . sorry?"

"You're damned right you're sorry." She let go of his ear and flicked him between the eyes, the blow making his head rock backward. "You just obliterated a quarter of one of our crops, you goose. This is a farming village, Ellis. Show more care with your body."

I leaned to the side, locking eyes with Barry as he strode through the corridor Ellis had made. He gave me an *oh, shit,* look, and I nodded, trying to hide my smirk.

"I'm—er—I am truly sorry, Maria. It was just . . . Fischer, he . . ." He looked at me for help, and I just shook my head. "S-something happened, you see, and I wanted to get a recounting from Fischer while he was still . . ."

"Still what, Ellis? Fischer is a *cultivator.*" She gestured at me emphatically. "He's been a cultivator longer than any of us, and I can't forget things even if I try. Can you?"

"Well, no, but—"

"No buts, mister!"

"Yeah, Ellis—no butts." I grinned but swiftly raised a hand and examined the plant fiber there when Maria's head spun to look at me.

"And," Maria continued, "you absolutely covered us in sugarcane. Look at us!"

She spread her arms, and Ellis noticed our appearance for the first time. He looked genuinely remorseful. "I apologize."

She patted him on the shoulder.

"Good. Now, Fischer and I are going to look at the pool." She glanced down at herself. "And probably go for a swim to wash this off." Ellis opened his mouth, probably to apologize again, but she cut him off. "You're welcome to ask him questions as we travel, but after we get there, he's mine for the rest of the day. Do you understand?"

She glanced at me too, daring me to say otherwise. I held up my hands in defeat.

"Yes, Maria," Ellis said, lowering his head. "Sorry again."

"Well," Barry said. "Now that you've found them, Ellis, I'm going to get my family." He shot me a wink. "I heard a new pool just opened up!"

"Er . . . there's something I should tell you, mate," I replied before he could leave. "Roger may have just learned that we're all cultivators."

"He *what?*" Barry shot me an incredulous look. "*How?*"

"Well, you know how I ran over here, all excited to tell Maria I loved her and stuff?" I pointed down at my ripped shirt. "He tried to pull me off of her."

Maria sighed. "He *immediately* knew."

" . . . How did he take it?" Barry asked.

"Uhhh," I started.

"Bad," Maria finished. "He tried to beat Fischer up."

Barry raised an eyebrow, the hint of a smile tugging at his lips. "Say what you will about Roger, but it sounds like he's willing to stand up for what he believes in."

"Yeah," Maria replied, shaking her head. "He's as bullheaded as they come."

Barry nodded, giving her a wincing smile. "Do you need me to do anything?"

"No. Mom is with him. I should probably go check on them, though. I need to get something to swim in, anyway."

As Barry left to fetch his family, Maria went to check on hers and retrieve a swimsuit.

"He's still in shock, but he'll be fine," she said when she rejoined us outside.

I answered every question Ellis had as we walked, doing my best to communicate that which was impossible to convey with words. When we reached the pool, the sight filled me with joy. Half of the church's members were already swimming in it, and Paul's shrill laughter was an absolute delight as he sat atop Duncan's shoulders in the shallows. Helen was on Barry's shoulders, and Paul was doing his best to push his mother over. When Helen threw herself backward, giving her son the win, Paul threw a fist high.

"Yes!" he roared.

"Whoa, Paul!" I called. "You're even stronger than the last time I saw you!"

"Fischer! Do you want to wrestle . . ." he trailed off, squinting at me. "Why are you and Maria *green?*"

I glanced down at the plant matter covering both of us. We looked ridiculous.

"Had a bit of a mishap, but it's nothing a little ocean pool can't wash away!" I turned to Ellis. "Sorry, mate. I'll come find you tomorrow and answer any other questions you have, yeah?"

He nodded, clearly unhappy but not willing to go against Maria's orders.

I took my torn shirt off and held a hand out to Maria, who was already dressed in her swimsuit and ready to go. "Shall we?"

She squeezed my hand, then pushed my chest with all the strength she had.

"W-whoa!" I hadn't been expecting it, and I fell down to the sand.

The smile on her face as she sprinted for the pool's edge was brighter than the sun, and she disappeared from sight. I chased after her, leaping high into the air.

"Cannonball!" The last thing I saw before descending into the pool was the look of shock on Paul's face as he fell backward, losing his balance in an attempt to escape the water I was about to spray everywhere.

We spent much of the morning swimming and playing. At Paul's behest, we engaged in a shoulder wars tournament. Given the strength our bodies held, it was more akin to scripted wrestling than an actual tournament, but we all did our best to perform for Paul. He and Duncan were the official winners, but I like to think that Maria and I "lost" with the most spectacular moves.

My animal pals remained hidden, but I caught glimpses of them in the deep end when I went underwater. Corporal Claws came in a few times to tickle me, too, but after the third time, I'd caught her and tickled her with a vengeance. She hadn't tried again.

When the sun reached its zenith in the sky, everyone got out and headed to their respective homes for lunch. Maria and I smiled at each other as we headed to my house.

"Duncan is really good with kids," she said, squeezing water from her hair. "I can't believe how much Paul latched onto him."

"I was thinking the same thing. I guess it makes sense, though. He's a bit of a goof. In a good way, I mean."

"I haven't really seen that side of him before. I always just saw him as the quiet apprentice."

"Quiet?" I laughed. "I think that's the last word I'd use to describe him."

We slipped into a comfortable silence, and when we reached the house, I opened the door for Maria. "I'll go get us some towels—I hung them out to dry."

"Okay! I'll be here."

I made my way around the side, heading for the clothesline I'd strung up on the back patio. My body felt light, and my heart raced as the memory of Maria kissing me earlier came to mind. I hadn't truly acknowledged how much the tension between us had been weighing me down. Now that it was gone, I felt light. Like I could breathe properly for the first time in weeks. The smile never left my face as I grabbed two towels and headed back inside.

I could hear the shower running, so I made my way to the guest bathroom but stopped short. The sound was coming from my room. I swallowed, walking on numb legs. The door to the ensuite was left cracked open, and steam flowed from the gap. With great effort, I averted my eyes, watching the door as I strode around my bed. When I reached it, I extended a hand, then paused. Did she want me to come in . . . ? Was the open door an invitation? I rubbed my face, trying to clear my thoughts.

The door flew open, and I looked up, seeing only a wall of steam. It slowly dissipated, and all I could make out through the steam was Maria's face. She was blushing furiously and looking down as she swept a stray strand of hair behind her ear.

I swallowed. "Did you want to . . . *oh* . . ."

The steam cleared, and all I could do was stare as she reached up to her shoulder. Her fingers carefully plucked at a strap, sliding it down her arm. She reached up to the other side, and when the strap there was free of her shoulder, her garment fell to the floor. The sight that greeted me hit my reset button.

"You . . . *wow.*" I shook my head, my brain still recovering. " . . . *Wow.*"

Her eyes rose to meet mine, and I tore my gaze from her body.

"What are you waiting for?" she asked, her face red and lips parted as she lifted her chin.

For three thunderous beats of my heart, I stood completely still. Then, I stepped inside. The steam engulfed me, warming my skin and hitting the back of my throat with each heaving breath I took. When our bodies met, it was like two stars colliding. The impact swept every other thought away, leaving only her.

CHAPTER SIXTY-TWO

RENOVATIONS

Warmth flowed through me as I slowly returned to the waking world. A comfortable weight rested on my arm. When I opened my eyes, a small smile came to my face. Maria was still asleep, on her side and curled into my chest. We'd held each other in the early afternoon hours, both content to simply exist with each other. She'd fallen asleep before me, and it must have claimed me soon after.

Careful not to wake her, I rested a hand atop her head, caressing her mess of sandy-blond hair. She was like a hot water bottle, warming me beneath the covers. Her breaths came slowly, and each exhale blew warmth onto my neck, banishing the cool air trapped within my room. I inhaled, and the cool air passing by my nostrils was a pleasant counterpoint to the heat engulfing me.

Maria sleeping next to me had no right hitting me as hard as it did. I held onto the moment, intent on burning every line of her body, every point of contact into my memory. I pulled her tight, and she let out a soft noise, nuzzling closer into me. It melted my core from within. I pulled her tighter, overwhelmed by the emotions roiling within me.

I was wide awake now, but I didn't make a noise. I wanted the moment to last forever.

Not long after, I opened my eyes, and she smiled up at me. "Hello, sleepyhead."

"Sleepyhead?" I yawned. "I've been awake for a while."

She gave me an odd look, smirking. "You were snoring until five seconds ago."

I frowned, and she laughed at the confusion on my face.

"You fell back asleep." She got up on one elbow, her hair hanging down to one side. "You were too cute to wake up, so I've just been creeping on you for a while."

I covered my mouth and yawned. "I thought you said I was snoring. That doesn't sound cute."

She giggled, covering her mouth. "Oh, but they were such charming little snores, though."

I narrowed my eyes at her. "I can't tell if you're messing with me."

She gasped, giving me a look of affront that was completely ruined by the grin on her face.

"You think I would mess with you? Well, I have *never* . . ."

She ran a hand through my hair, and it sent tingles coursing down my entire body.

I breathed out slowly. "Do you wanna go fishing? We should probably get up and do something or else I might never get out of this bed."

"You know, I can think of worse things . . ."

She grabbed onto my hair and pulled herself down, throwing a leg over me. When her insistent lips met mine, every other thought disappeared once more.

Barry stood and stretched, needing a moment to reset his posture. Swimming in what Fischer called his "lap pool" had been a welcome distraction, and though it set him behind in his work, he didn't regret it. He gestured down at the floor plan Ellis had been drawing. "Just to confirm, this is the western wing, correct?"

"Right," Ellis nodded, not looking up. "Ground floor. This here is the first, second, and third floor," he added, pointing at the respective sheets of paper.

"Perfect. Thank you for your time, Ellis. I know you'd rather be working on that lizard."

Ellis glanced up, sparing a moment to give Barry a smile. "I haven't raised my leatherworking enough yet to even consider working on the spirit beast. Besides, I am quite used to being pulled this way and that from my time in the royal library. You would not believe how often someone got the idea to shuffle around the shelving for absolutely no reason. Usually right when there is another important project going on."

"Weren't you the head archivist? Couldn't you just say no?"

"Just so, but sometimes you have to make concessions where it is least painful, lest you have to concede on something that actually matters."

"Huh . . ."

It was rather insightful for a passing comment, but before Barry could say that, he heard the scuffle of footsteps descending the steps.

He prepared to hide the maps in case it was Fischer moseying on down, but then Brad and Greg appeared. Both woodworkers made to speak, then stiffed a yawn.

Brad shook his head and rubbed red-rimmed eyes. "The cart is ready to go."

Barry blinked. "It is?"

"Aye. We stayed up all night, but it's done."

They looked absolutely spent, and Barry gave them a thankful smile.

"You didn't have to do that, but I'd be lying if I said I wasn't glad. The sooner we can get supplies to the surrounding villages, the sooner we can move forward with Operation Sticky Fingers."

"There's one more thing," Brad said, grinning through his lack of sleep. "When the wagon was finished . . . well, it transformed. Just as Fischer's works do."

Ellis shot to his feet, staring wide-eyed at them. Before he could demand the information he so desperately wanted, Brad continued. "Also. It got my woodworking skill to twenty-five, and this appeared."

He reached behind his back, grabbed something from his belt, and threw it toward Barry. He caught the brown bag, the contents making an audible clink as it came to a stop.

It couldn't be . . . could it?

Barry opened the drawstring with trembling fingers, his breath catching as he caught the glint within. He reached in and grabbed onto something cold and hard, then withdrew it into the magical light of the chamber. The golden coin glimmered. He spun it, revealing one face with a scythe, and another with the face of a man he didn't recognize.

"Is that . . . ?" Ellis asked, his voice faltering.

"It is." Barry threw the coin to Ellis, who just barely caught it from the air. "It's the kind of coin Fischer uses to build things—the same as those that made this base."

Barry's mind whirled, and his gaze went distant as his plans for the evening changed for the second time in so many minutes. He snapped back to the present when he made a decision.

"Get everyone out of the church. They can work from my home for now. Can someone go get Brigadier Borks? I may have need of him."

"What are you going to do?" Ellis asked, not looking up from the notepad he'd begun recording in.

Barry's eyes twinkled in delight.

"We're going to attempt some renovations."

With the sun setting at our backs and a cool breeze brushing by, Maria and I sat on the edge of the rock wall. We both had a fishing rod in hand, and she leaned on my shoulder, eyes closed as she waited for a bite. I had a finger resting on my line, so I could feel the bump of any fish bold enough to munch my bait. If I was being honest, though, I was more focused on her.

Claws and Pistachio came to join us, and as Rocky also crawled up the wall to sit near us, I narrowed my eyes at the distinct lack of Sergeant Snips.

"Okay," I said, gazing over my animal pals arrayed in the afternoon sun. "I know I want nothing to do with whatever the church is up to, but where the heck is Snips? I'm missing my crabby gal."

Claws slunk forward, giving me an odd look. I cocked my head to the side as she climbed into my lap. She leaned up with one paw on my chest, then pressed the other to my lips.

"Shhh," she hissed through her sharp teeth.

"Maria . . ."

"Yes, Fischer?"

"Did I just get shushed by an otter?"

Claws nodded gravely, pressing both paws to my lips to seal them shut.

Maria giggled. "Looks like you won't get any answers from her."

I rolled my eyes and freed myself from Claws by cradling her in my arms. "Can you tell me she's safe, at least? I'm worried about her."

Rocky took a step forward, shaking a claw at me and letting out a *very* pissed-off hiss.

"Woah, Rocky. Chill, my guy. I'm not calling her incompetent. I just worry for her—"

He shook his forelimb with more vigor, chastising me for *daring* to question his mistress.

I sighed. "She's safe, Claws?"

She gave me a *one moment* gesture, hopped off my lap, wiggled her butt, and erupted with chi. As she launched herself at Rocky, vengeance was etched in every line of her furry little face. Pistachio, sensing her intent, dashed faster than I'd ever seen him move. His giant claw flicked Rocky up into the air, then Claws slammed into the airborne crab, yeeting him out over the ocean.

Unlike his usual *eeeee* of joy, Rocky hissed with fury as he departed, but it was quickly drowned out by crashing waves as he got farther and farther from us.

Maria and I raised an eyebrow at each other.

Damn, she mouthed.

Claws fist-bumped Pistachio, then brushed sand off her paws, giving the dwindling speck that was Rocky one last glare before returning to my lap.

She locked eyes with me and chirped a single sentiment: *safe.*

I smiled, shaking my head at what they'd just done to Snips's subordinate. "Okay. I'll take your word for it."

I jolted upright, whirling my head to look back toward land.

Maria let out a gasp. "What's wrong?"

I frowned and pouted for a moment, then just shook my head, smiling.

"Barry is up to some shenanigans. I didn't mean to startle you, it just took me by surprise."

I opened myself to the pressure tugging at me, letting chi drain away. While it wasn't as much as the last time he'd sought my power, it was still a hefty amount.

"Shenanigans, huh?" Maria asked. "Are you okay? I know it was a lot last time that happened . . ."

If not for the transformation I'd had this morning, I might have collapsed under the weight of it. Now, though . . . I put an arm around Maria's shoulder, letting the chi flow from me in a steady stream.

"I couldn't be better."

Sweat sprouted from Barry as his entire body tensed. He sat on the floor of his bedroom, and though he had originally held a meditative posture, it was long discarded as his tendons drew tight. Helen had a hand on his shoulder, supporting him in the only way she could. Her fingers dug in, helping to keep him upright, but he barely felt them—such was the pressure exerted on his core.

Worse, he was drawing from Fischer. He'd hoped that he could do it in secret now that it was him possessing the coins, but that wasn't the case. There was a steady flow of chi coming through an invisible connection, and he feared for his friend's safety. In retrospect, it was a mistake. He'd wanted to let Fischer and Maria have their time together, but now Fischer might be in danger.

"Fischer . . ." he ground out through clenched teeth.

"What?" Helen asked, sounding as if far away.

"Check on Fischer . . . *please.*"

She didn't respond, and when her hand disappeared from his shoulder, he knew she had gone. Flaring his nostrils, Barry realized his intent was too scattered, so he forced his thoughts onto the task at hand. On what the church needed. He would have to trust his wife's speed and Fischer's resilience.

As the chi continued to flow through me, I felt Barry's focus sharpen.

That's it, mate, I thought. *Keep up the good work.*

"O-oh!" Maria started. "Fish on!"

She set the hook and wound the line in, joy clear on her face as the fish darted this way and that. Before she got it to the rocks, I heard footfalls behind me. I spun, cocking my head at Helen and the speed she was sprinting at. "Helen? You all good?"

She skidded to a stop, looking at me with panicked eyes. "Are . . . are you, Fischer? Barry said to check on you . . ."

"Never been better! Just catching some food for—" I cut off as the force pulling chi from my core ended. Then, a burst of power bloomed from the west. I beamed at Helen. "Looks like he's finished."

"He is?"

"Yup. Just now."

She turned on her heel and sprinted away as fast as she'd come. I heard a splash and spun just in time to see Maria lift the fish from the water. It swung my way, and my hand darted out, grabbing it by the gills.

Mature Shore Fish
Uncommon
Found along the ocean shores of the Kallis Realm, this fish is a staple source of both food and bait.

"Ohhh, it's a big one!" Maria said, drawing my attention to the present.

"More than enough for dinner." I dispatched the fish with a swift movement, then looked up at Maria. "There's only one more decision to make."

She pursed her lips, her hair dangling as she cocked her head. "What's that?"

I grinned. "How are we going to cook it?"

Barry took deep, steadying breaths as his legs wobbled beneath him. He gave up on standing and fell back to the ground, leaning back on one hand. Sweat soaked his body, and his brain was clouded by fatigue, yet he laughed, loud and full of relief.

He heard thumping footsteps hit the wooden deck and fly inside, and a second later, Helen threw the door open.

She crashed into him, holding him tight and not caring at all about his soiled clothing. "Barry . . ." she whispered, her voice filled with relief.

"Was Fischer okay?" he asked.

Helen pulled her head back so she could look into his eyes. "*Okay?* He and Maria were fishing without a care in the world. Worry about yourself, you soil-brained farmer."

He'd already had an inkling that Fischer was fine based on the way the power finished transmitting, but having it confirmed made a weight evaporate from his shoulders. "Good . . ."

Someone cleared their throat, and Barry looked past Helen's shoulder. A sea of faces peered through the doorway. Most intent as always, Ellis's hands shook around his pencil and notepad. He showed amazing restraint in not voicing any of the questions no doubt fighting to escape.

Barry squeezed Helen one more time. "Would you help me stand, dear?" She easily lifted him to his feet, and he smiled at Ellis. "Let's go look at the changes, shall we?"

A bonfire roared to life in Ellis's eyes. "The . . . changes?"

"Better to see it in person. I'm happy to tell you about the act of creating it as we walk, though."

Ellis nodded feverishly and stepped aside, giving Barry a path out.

As he led the congregation back toward the church, Barry recounted the experience as best he could. As always, Ellis's questions were pointed, helping Barry better describe what had occurred. The entire time they walked, hushed conversation trailed them. The excitement was palpable, and as they reached the bottom of the stairs, Ellis looked up from his notepad.

"It . . . looks the same."

"Looks can be deceiving," Barry replied, leading them farther down the hallway.

They passed the open doors to the meeting room, spa, and forest.

When they walked by Trent's room, the prince ran to the bars. "Where are my sweets and what was that rumbling?"

"You just had dinner," Keith replied from behind Barry.

"So?" the prince demanded, his voice incredulous. "What of dessert? I've only had one glass of lemonade today! *One!* This cell is a prison!"

Barry stopped mid-step, unable to walk over that speed bump of a statement. He slowly turned toward the prince. "Uhhh. Yes, Trent. The cell *is* a prison. That's the point."

"If only the lemonade would work . . ." Ellis muttered, making Barry snort as he resumed leading.

"Hey! Don't ignore me!" Trent yelled. "I. Demand. *Sweets!*"

Keith shook his head at his cousin. "I'll come back with your sweets. We're busy."

They continued on, all ignoring Trent's indignant demands that called after them. When Barry reached the first door that used to open to a stone wall, he pointed at it.

"Fergus, Duncan—this one is yours." He turned to the entrance on the opposite side of the hallway, gesturing at it. "Brad and Greg." He took a few steps up the hallway. "Ruby, Steven, this is yours on the left."

All six of them stepped forward, their eyes wide.

"Don't tell me . . ." Fergus said, his hand slowly extending to the handle of the door that Barry had called his.

Ellis rushed forward, then stopped in the hallway between the three doors, his head darting back and forth, unable to decide which room to look in first.

"Don't you want to see your room, Ellis?" Barry asked, trying to keep his voice steady.

Ellis whirled on him, and the confusion on the former archivist's face made a smile split Barry's face.

"My . . . *my* room?"

"Well, yeah. You didn't think I'd add a room for the other crafters and not one for you, did you? Where better to process the scales of an ascendant being than within a System-made workshop?"

Ellis, his mouth moving and not making a noise, ambled forward. His pencil made a soft sound as it clattered to the ground, falling from his loose grip. He didn't even acknowledge it, so Barry picked it up for him. Ellis's hand gripped the handle of the door next to Barry, just as the other crafters gripped theirs.

As one, all four doors swung open on silent hinges.

CHAPTER SIXTY-THREE

EXPANSION

Barry watched over Ellis's shoulder as the door opened, revealing the room beyond. Various tubs lined the space. There was an odd contraption on the wall, but as Ellis walked over and pulled it down, Barry understood what it was—a drying rack. On the side of the room, a series of faucets sprouted from the wall. Ellis picked up a tub and turned one of the taps on. A clear, viscous liquid poured out.

"Remarkable. This will assist me greatly in my leatherworking endeavors." Ellis reached for the pencil in his pocket, but when he didn't find it, he started patting down his pants. "Where did I put my . . . ?"

"Here," Barry said, throwing the pencil to him.

Ellis caught it, nodded in thanks, and began writing.

Barry spun, looking into the tailoring room. Ruby and Steven were poring over it, the former cataloging a gigantic cupboard filled with different materials, the latter inspecting a loom that took up a full third of the space. Others were milling in the hallway and looking between the rooms, so Barry made his way toward the other doors. Helen was leaning against the wall next to the new smithy. He put an arm round her waist and peered inside.

Both Fergus and Duncan were completely silent as they stood in the center of their new workshop. Their heads drifted around, taking in everything they saw. Barry had never seen so many tools, and he doubted a larger collection existed anywhere in the kingdom. He couldn't even fathom what half of them were used for. The wall of tools, though impressive, was nothing compared to the forges. They were both set into the far wall, and as Barry watched, Fergus walked up to them. He leaned his head inside, peering around the vacuous space.

" . . . where on Kallis are the bellows?"

In response, Duncan reached out and flicked one of two switches. A soft hum slowly grew, and Fergus reached an arm in, his eyebrows forming a line. "No way . . ."

Duncan, his eyes going wide and a grin growing, flicked the other switch. He skidded to a stop in front of the forge on the right, actually jumping into it and reaching an arm into the chimney at the rear.

"It sucks air up!" he yelled, leaning out to look at Fergus.

His master moved as a blur, appearing before the forge and reefing Duncan out of it. "Get out of there, you blasted fool! Are you trying to get yourself incinerated?!"

At the reprimanding, Duncan merely grinned. Barry mirrored it as he turned, heading for the woodworking room.

When he crossed through into the opposite door, he found himself corrected. There was a larger collection in the kingdom than the blacksmithing tools behind him. As with the smithing tools, he had no clue what some of the odd-shaped chisels could be used for. There was what looked like a machine in the back of the room, which was currently being inspected by both woodworkers.

Brad reached up and grabbed what looked kind of like the metal bit you'd put in a hand drill, but was the shape of an arrowhead. He put it in a hole atop the machine, then leaned back as he pressed a button. The metal bit spun in a blur as a high-pitched whir rang out through the room. The two brothers immediately turned to each other, eyes wide. Greg grabbed Brad by the shoulders. His brother grabbed him back. They hopped in a circle, laughing wordlessly.

Barry eyed the rest of the bits on the wall behind the machine. There were *hundreds* of them, all with different shapes and lengths. As their childlike giggling subsided, he eased forward, Helen at his side and holding his hand.

"What are they for?"

Both turned. Their eyes were feverish.

"Everything, Barry," Brad said, his gaze growing even more fierce. "*Everything.*"

As George sat for their afternoon meditation, something dragged his awareness in an odd direction. He'd first believed that such distractions were a failure of meditation, but both his family's tome and his hours of practice revealed the truth. He was only human. Thoughts came as they willed, as sure as the sun rose and fell. The skill of meditation wasn't so much about the ability to banish thought entirely—it was about refocus. One's capability to recognize the thought, acknowledge it, and let it go. The thought that dragged him toward his wedding ring, though, was . . . different.

He felt the iridescent stone set in a silver band as his attention seemed to get pulled into it. He felt the spherical stone from within, as if it was his own body. The silver setting holding it in place was both fragile and strong. A soft metal that combined with the iridescent stone to become something greater than the sum of their parts.

The rings that he and his wife wore were a remnant of the past, one of the few relics remaining of his family's inheritance. The more he considered it, the more sure he became—his wedding band wasn't just a physical promise of his commitment to Geraldine.

But . . . what was it, exactly?

With his awareness inside the stone, the pulse of energy that came from the southwest rocked him. He inhaled a shuddering breath as he was thrown from the ring and returned to his body. The hand wearing his ring was dragged back behind him, heading toward the pulse of power for a fraction of a second. He blinked, his vision taking a moment to focus after having his eyes closed for so long. Despite the cool air, a sweat broke from his skin as he looked down at his hand, wondering if he had imagined it.

"George . . ."

He spun to Geraldine, adrenaline spiking at the panic in her voice. She stared down at her own hand, her lip quivering. "What . . . what was that?"

He swallowed. "You felt it too?"

She nodded. "I was . . ." She pressed her lips into a line to stop them shaking. "I was *inside* my ring? I don't know if that's the right term, but it felt almost like . . ."

"Like it was your own body," George finished, reaching a reassuring hand out to rest on her leg. "It's okay, Geraldine. It was the same for me."

She chewed her leaner-by-the-day cheek, still staring down. "What does it mean?"

A tidal wave of thoughts washed forth, crashing down into George. Did it have something to do with the blast from earlier? What did it mean that it physically pulled their wedding bands? If the iridescent pearls set in his and Geraldine's rings were more than just a promise to each other, what were they? All at once, he realized there was no point in addressing the thoughts right now, especially when his wife needed him. He stretched his back before getting to his feet.

He extended a hand toward Geraldine. "Should we go make some dinner and talk about it, my love?"

She took a deep breath through her nose, held it, then exhaled through her mouth. Her eyes cleared, and with a much calmer demeanor, she grasped his hand and let him pull her up.

"That sounds lovely, dear."

Joel, the leader of the Cult of Carcinization, smiled out at the ocean. Today was a monumental day, one that would no doubt go down in the cult's history books.

"If not those of the very heavens . . ." he dared to dream aloud, eyes fixed on the small waves cresting the horizon.

"What was that?" Jess asked, leaning in to better hear him.

"Er . . . it's nothing, Jess. I was just saying I was excited."

With her face lit by the purple hue of sunset, she beamed a smile at him.

"I am too. They shouldn't be much longer . . ."

A comfortable silence bloomed between them, but the longer they sat, the more Joel's thoughts worried him. What if they weren't ready? What if the deity didn't accept them? What if—

A weight settled on his shoulder, and he turned to see Jess's hand resting there. She gave a soft squeeze. "It's going to be okay, Joel. They'll understand why you didn't tell them right away."

Firming his jaw, he nodded, trying to at least appear sure of himself.

"Not interrupting, are we?" a voice called.

Joel started, then quickly got to his feet. "Not at all. Thanks for coming, everyone."

Doug, Jonah, and Red, the other acolytes of his church, gave him mixed looks. Doug, the one who had spoken out, was looking rather unimpressed. Jonah waved, only making eye contact for a moment before averting his gaze once more.

Red, the tallest of them by far, stretched his arms out wide with a grin. "Thanks for inviting us! I've been missing the group meditations of late."

That simple comment cut right to the heart of the issue, and Joel gave a wincing smile. He and Jess, in their courting of the ascendant being that Fischer had called Sergeant Snips, had been distancing themselves from the three acolytes.

"I'm sorry about that, Red. As I said before, it was vital that we meditate in seclusion for the last month."

"Right," Doug drawled, rolling his eyes. "You did say that, didn't you?"

"Doug . . ." Jonah said, his voice soft. "Don't be like that. We're here now, aren't we?"

"Exactly!" Red clapped them both on the shoulder. "Have a little faith in our head priest, yeah?" He walked forward without a care in the world, carving a path through the sand for the other two to follow. "So—what meditation should we do? And what's up with the fish?"

Happy for the change of subject, intentional or not, Joel rushed to explain the tray of fish he and Jess had gathered. "The offering before us is what we wanted to show you—what we've been working so diligently on. Please, sit by it, if you will."

Doug's jaw, which had been clenched in an obvious show of annoyance, opened. "You've pushed us away for the last month to . . . catch fish?"

"Hmmm . . ." Red rubbed his chin, then shrugged. "I don't really get it, but that's all right. Sit down with me, Doug. I'm sure we'll get an explanation."

The man sighed but did so, settling in the soft sand beside his friend. Jonah rushed to sit on Red's other side, and Jess joined them, nodding at Joel. He rushed into motion, not wanting to let the awkward silence linger longer than necessary.

He collected a handful of fish, making a trail down to the water. When he had one last fish in his hands, he placed it between his palms and raised it to his face. He bent his head down, whispering a prayer into the offering. When his will was suffusing the fish, he carefully placed it into the shallows. He backed away, his head bowed as he sat beside Doug, forming a semicircle around the fish-covered tray.

"Meditate, and if we are lucky, it will show itself."

"Show itself?" Doug asked, curiosity overcoming his argumentative demeanor.

"You'll have to wait and see," Jess said, shooting a wink at Doug when he turned an annoyed glance her way.

Leading the way, Joel adjusted his body into an approximation of the perfect form.

His feet scuttled to the side, bracing his weight. His lips extended, preparing to blow bubbles. Both hands came up beside his head, and he clacked them together for good measure, imagining them as a crab's powerful claws. Before he let the meditation whisk him away, he cracked an eye to check on his acolytes. All had adopted the same posture, the only variation being Doug's grumpy face. Joel ignored it, closing his eyes and letting his thoughts become those of a crab.

He lost himself, making bubbling noises that helped to ground him in the meditation. When the others were comfortable and settled, they joined in, and the sounds of their meditation sparked joy within him. After a few minutes, he heard the same noises from Doug, and it seemed that all was right in the world. He hadn't realized it, but he had truly missed their companionship and comradery over the past weeks. To find others whose beliefs aligned with your own was a rare thing, and he was beyond lucky to have found so many friends. The love and appreciation for those around him helped him settle deeper in the crab meditation than ever, and though he was crouched atop the sand, he was scuttling beneath the ocean in his mind's eye, his hard carapace easily gliding through a strong current.

One step at a time, his eight magnificent legs drew ever closer toward—

"Ah!" Jonah yelped, shattering his concentration.

Joel opened his eyes as he returned to his body, its fleshy form jarring after experiencing the perfect form for what had felt like hours.

"Jonah . . ." Doug growled, whirling on the meek acolyte. "I was just getting into it. I—" He cut off when he saw the look on Jonah's face. "What is it?"

"C-c-crab!" he replied, pointing forward.

They all turned toward the tray.

There, lowered to the sand and feasting on the last of the fish, was a god. The first time Joel had laid eyes on the ascendant crab, her carapace had been covered in spikes, and she wore a leather eyepatch over one eye. Every time she accepted their offerings since, she was smooth shelled, yet large and mighty.

"Lower your heads!" Joel ordered, remembering himself. He lay down and pressed his forehead into the ground, as did the others.

The only noise he heard for a long moment was the chewing sound he'd grown accustomed to over the weeks gone. Suddenly, something tugged at his very being, originating right in the center of his abdomen. His head snapped up of its own accord, too shocked to care that he was before his deity. The spirit beast held the metal tray in her claw. She stared to the southwest—the same direction that Joel had felt the tug from.

Without warning, the god became a blur of motion.

Bonk, bonk, bonk.

Booom!

The sound of the metal tray striking three heads was quickly washed away by an explosion. Joel covered his face, trying to keep the spray of sand from his eyes and mouth. The three acolytes between him and Jess all sputtered, unprepared as they were for their deity's blessing.

When the air was clear, they raised their heads, each as stunned as the next.

Rocky blew annoyed bubbles as he scuttled over the sands at incredible speed, heading for the source of whatever that sensation had been. His spiky mistress's master was up to something, and it had robbed him of a wonderful moment. The cultists had both given him more food and presented more heads for him to bonk—both of which were a cause for celebration.

Rather than enjoy the moment, however, Fischer had done something *again,* and he'd had to rush off.

Rocky hadn't even had time to give the other two a good whack with the thin metal tray before he sent himself flying with dual explosions from his powerful claws.

His mouth parts undulated in annoyance, the pleasant aftertaste of fish replaced by fury. One of these days, he was going to give Fischer a good bonk on the head if he kept on messing with Rocky's plans.

Maybe Sergeant Snips, his beloved matriarch, would punish him as a result when she returned . . .

That thought brought joy back into Rocky's awareness, and as he approached the church, he imagined himself getting flung farther than ever, sailing so high that the midday sun heated his carapace while the ocean rushed past beneath him.

"What . . . what just happened?" Doug asked, his eyes staring at the spot where a tray now sat in a small crater.

"You were blessed!" Jess said, kneeling down before them. "She approved of you! Just as she did with us!"

"Sh-she?" Jonah squeaked.

"That's right," Joel said, smiling at them. All had gone to plan. "We, the Church of Carcinization, have a deity to worship. Her name is Sergeant Snips, or so we've been told."

"How . . . ?" Red asked, unusually somber.

"I'll explain it all in good time. Why don't we meditate on the encounter, and then we can discuss it over dinner?"

Everyone nodded except for Doug. The man stared down at his hands, then up at Joel, his lip quivering. He blinked rapidly as his eyes welled.

A single tear ran down his cheek. "I . . . I'm sorry, Joel. I . . ." he trailed off, his chest heaving with sobs. "I'm sorry for doubting you."

Joel shuffled over and pulled him into a hug. "You have nothing to apologize for, acolyte Doug. I'm the one that's sorry for not telling you sooner."

Doug nodded into his shoulder, and when the tears had subsided, Joel let go. "Let's meditate on it, shall we?"

There was a fire in Doug's red-rimmed eyes. He gave a sharp nod.

CHAPTER SIXTY-FOUR

DETERMINATION

The room I woke up in was so cold that I couldn't feel my face. I shimmied farther under the covers, and when I felt Maria's warmth at my side, a wave of endorphins coursed through me. With my stomach fluttering, I rolled to my side and put an arm around her, running my hands through her long fur.

. . . *Long fur?*

I opened my eyes to see a golden retriever grinning at me with complete contentedness, his eyes half-lidded with sleep.

"Good morning, Borks," I said, laughing softly.

He licked my neck and let out a rather cute noise, his whiskers tickling the underside of my chin. As my brain slowly woke up, I recalled the events of last night. Maria and I had made fried fish for dinner and cuddled by the campfire, but she hadn't spent the night. Given that Roger was still coming to terms with the news that we were all cultivators—and that the bloke his daughter was in a relationship with was also the deity of a cult . . . er, *church*—I had walked her home.

Settling for the next best thing to Maria, I pulled Borks in for a cuddle. He rested his head in the crook of my neck, his wagging tail thumping against the bed and blanket. I felt the urge to go see Maria. Perhaps I could bring Roger a coffee and croissant as a peace offering . . . but no. We'd agreed that I should give him space for now.

"I think it might be just you and me this morning, buddy," I said, scratching Borks behind the ear.

His tail wagged even harder, and he rolled onto his back, wiggling in excitement and kicking the blankets off. I rolled out of bed, raising my hands toward the sky as I let out a noise and stretched. "All right—let's go sort out some brekkie, shall we?"

He barked, got to his feet, and leaped from the bed, heading for the door as I opened it.

Maria stirred, wrapped in a cocoon of blankets. The first thought that came to her was of Fischer. She grabbed a pillow, hugging it tight as butterflies rose in her stomach. A knock came at the door.

"Come in!" she called, squeezing the pillow as if it was the man she loved.

Sharon opened the door and stepped inside. She sat beside her on the bed, and when Maria saw her sleepless face, she reached out to put a hand on her mother's leg. "Everything okay?"

Sharon smiled, but her eyes were so, *so* tired. "I'm fine. Your father and I spent most of the night talking. We're going to get some breakfast and coffee, and I was wondering if you wanted to come."

"Of course," she replied, stretching. "I'll just get dressed."

With her pajamas replaced by workwear, Maria stepped outside to find her parents waiting. Her father sat on the porch, staring out toward the fields. Her mother was at his side, her head resting on his shoulder.

That's a good sign, she thought.

When Fischer walked her home last night, they'd found her parents sitting outside, but there was a physical distance between them. Her dad's body had stiffened when he saw Fischer, so after planting a quick kiss on her cheek, Fischer left. As she thought of that kiss, that small touch, her thoughts were drawn to other memories. Her face grew hot, and she shook her head, coming back to the present.

"Are you both ready?" she asked, hopping down from the porch and giving them a smile that they both returned, if a little halfhearted.

"Is anyone else coming?" her father asked, giving her a pointed look.

Maria rolled her eyes. "No, Dad. Fischer isn't coming. He's giving you space, lest you try and attack him with your favorite scythe."

Roger snorted. "I may as well swing at the sun for all the good it would do me."

It was the first time she'd heard him make a joke since yesterday, and though it held a hint of bitterness, it left her feeling at ease. Her mother darted a quick look toward her, raising an eyebrow. They both smiled, and as a family, they left for Sue's bakery.

With Borks at my side and the sun at my back, I couldn't help but smile as I walked through the streets of Tropica. My furry companion felt the same, his tail wagging as he looked at the passing faces, even veering off toward children to let them have a good pat of his soft coat.

When we reached Sue's, the smell of coffee urged me on, but the man I came face to face with brought me up short. We blinked at each other, and I opened my mouth to say something, then closed it again.

"Fischer," Roger said, his tone lacking any inflection.

"G'day, Roger. How are ya, mate?"

He shrugged, his eyes tired. "Been better. Been worse."

"Yeah . . ." I replied, searching for the words to say. The ladies saved me.

"Good morning, Fischer!" Sharon said, coming to his side.

I beamed at her as Borks stepped forward to sniff her leg and receive a pat. Then, *she* appeared.

Like a ray of sunshine, Maria came from the counter and passed the tray of coffee and croissants to her mother. "Can you give us a moment? I'll catch up."

Roger's jaw worked, but he nodded, and I bid them goodbye. The second they disappeared around a corner, Maria threw her arms around my neck. The kiss consumed me as she pressed her lips to mine. A painfully short second later, it was over.

"I love you." She squeezed my arm. "I'll come see you later, okay?"

"I love you too," I whispered back. "And please do."

She jogged away, her hair bouncing as she glanced back, waving over her shoulder. I stared after her as she disappeared around the same corner her parents had. Gods, she was beautiful.

Someone cleared their throat behind me, and I spun.

"Well, well, well," Theo said, smirking at me. "The great Fischer, staring after an innocent young woman with lecherous intent. I never thought I'd see the day . . ."

"Innocent?" I asked, raising an eyebrow. "I have it on good authority that she has entered a formal relationship with a . . ." I leaned in, darting my eyes from side to side as if to check the coast was clear. "With a heretic!" I hissed, my eyebrow still raised.

"A formal relationship? With a *heretic?*" he gasped. "I dare say you're correct, dear Fischer. She must be of questionable morality to choose such a partner. A shame, for someone of such ample proportions as she."

I squinted at him, pouting at his description.

He returned the look. " . . . Too far?"

We both burst into laughter, and I shook my head at him. "You caught me off guard with that one."

"Says you—the king of saying wild things." He let out a sigh. "Gods, I needed that laugh. I take it that things went well with your conversation yesterday? You both seemed happy when you were swimming."

I smiled, remembering the day gone.

"It did, mate." I slung an arm around his shoulder. "C'mon. I'll buy us breakfast and tell you all about it."

He gasped again, pulling away and staring at me with shock. "Fischer! You would besmirch a lady's good name by recounting your endeavors? For shame, I say."

I leveled a glare at him. "I'll tell you all about our *conversation,* you pest."

He threw his head back and laughed again, loud and free. "I can't, I'm afraid. I have to do something back at the church today."

I raised an eyebrow. "Something to do, huh? That wouldn't have anything to do with Barry getting up to some shenanigans, would it?"

He froze, shooting a glance at me. "You're sure you want to know about that?"

"You tell me, mate."

He considered for a moment, then shrugged. "I think you'd want to know. You can make use of it, after all. But you should probably talk to Barry about it."

"Make use of it . . . ?" I asked, but he was already walking away.

"Gotta go!" he called over his shoulder. "Bye, Fischer!"

I waved goodbye with one hand as I rubbed my chin with the other. "What could Barry have made that I could use . . . ?"

I shrugged, shook my head at myself, and spun. I had more important things to take care of.

"Morning, Sue," I called, beaming a smile at her and the smell of coffee in the air.

* * *

Maria's mouth became dryer with each step toward their destination. Her mother had pulled her aside on the way home from Sue's and told her the plan. It was exciting, hope-inducing, and terrifying. She swirled the last bit of coffee in her cup, then drank it down. But her mouth remained dry.

She glanced to the side. Though for different reasons, both of her parents walked with hesitant steps. Her mother was shooting looks at her father, while the latter's eyes were pinned on the shed that they approached. Maria, wanting to get this over with as soon as possible, darted forward. She grabbed the handle, looked down for a moment, then steeled her nerves and pulled it open.

The room beyond was lit by magical light, and as Roger caught sight of it, his step faltered. He gazed at the inside of the door, taking in its rich gilding.

"Dear . . . ?" Sharon asked.

He grit his jaw, let out a slow, steady breath, and stepped inside. Sharon was at his side, slipping an arm through his. Maria followed them in, closing the door behind herself. She joined them at the top of the stairs, shooting a furtive glance toward her father for what felt like the hundredth time that day. He stared at the descending steps, his face a wash of conflicting emotions that reminded Maria of the look he'd had while they ate their breakfast.

"Is it all true?" he'd asked her.

"Is what true, Dad?"

"Everything your mother has told me. Fischer. The church. The building. The . . . the *animals.*"

Her mother, rather than being annoyed at the question, had looked at Maria patiently. The answer was simple, so she had given it to him.

"Yes, Dad. It's all true, and even if I didn't know it for sure, I'd trust Mom to tell me the truth—as should you."

She shook her head, returning to the present.

"We don't have to go down if you don't want to," her mother said, resting a hand on his shoulder. "We can come back another time—whenever you're ready."

Her father flexed his hands, stretched his neck from side to side, and began the descent.

The way was lit, and as they passed each sconce, he would stare into the magical flames. When they approached the landing, he stopped caring about the torches—voices echoed off the walls toward them. The door to the meeting room was open, which was where the conversation was coming from.

Maria dashed forward and leaned her head in. "Everyone—Dad's here!"

She glanced back, her heart breaking at the look of resignation on her father's face.

"It's fine, Dad," she whispered, giving him a genuine smile. "There are some people who want to meet you."

Roger nodded and stepped forward, entering the doorway. Her mother's jaw was tight, so Maria grabbed her hand, giving it a soft squeeze.

"G'day, mate! It's nice to meet you!" Theo said, leaning over a map. "I'm Theo. This is Ellis, Danny, Peter, and Keith."

"Roger," he replied tersely.

"We've heard all about you, mate," Theo continued. "I'm glad you're finally coming into the fold, as it were. I'm sure we're better off with you here."

"I'm not so sure I'll be joining you. I just came to have a look around."

"Oh. Right." Theo shrugged. "Well, that's totally fine. Want me to go get Barry so he can show you the ropes? He's with Fergus down at the smithy."

" . . . The smithy?" Roger asked, his brow furrowing.

"Yeah!" Theo pointed in its direction. "Up there, on the left."

"The smithy?" Sharon repeated in a whisper, glancing at Maria.

Maria shrugged. She had no idea either.

"Right . . ." Roger said. "Well, I'll be heading on, then. It was nice to meet—"

"Oh!" Theo interrupted, snapping his fingers. "I just remembered. I was supposed to give you something."

Maria caught the hint of a grin playing on Theo's features, and she watched him closely as he bent down and picked up a . . . Was that a present? The wooden box was held shut by a deep red ribbon that ended in a bow. Theo strode forward, smiling in an entirely too-happy manner, and held it out.

Roger, not knowing what else to do, accepted it. "Erm. Thank you . . ."

"No worries, mate! Best you open it now."

Roger glanced back at Maria and Sharon, who both shrugged. With a fierce scowl on his face, Roger undid the bow. He put a hand to the lid, hesitated, then lifted it up. It was filled with colorful cuts of cloth. Blinking, Roger put his hand into the makeshift confetti. His scowl deepened as he took hold of something, and he lifted it up.

Corporal Claws grinned at him, revealing her needle-sharp teeth as she chirped a greeting. There was a bow on her head in the same color as the ribbon.

Roger dropped both the box and the otter, taking a step back.

"Theo!" Sharon chided, grabbing Roger by the arm. "We're supposed to be introducing my husband to the animals! Not playing cheap jokes!"

Theo held his hands up in surrender as he looked between Claws, Roger, and Sharon.

"Sorry, mate—it was out of my hands. Corporal Claws here wanted to make a good first impression, and you ignore her whims at your own peril. I was too busy to scratch her one day, and I've been finding piles of sand in my bed ever since. Don't look at me like that, Claws. Of course I knew it was you! Who else would be putting sand in my sheets?"

"Corporal Claws . . ." Roger said, his voice hesitant.

Claws whirled, chirping in the affirmative and giving him another grin.

Movement at the other end of the room caught their attention, and a seething mass of creatures climbed up to peek over the table. Sergeant Snips, waving a happy clacker, bubbled a greeting. Pistachio nodded a single time, so slight as to be almost imperceptible. Rocky made a rude gesture, and was swiftly smacked from sight by Snips, hitting the floor so hard that the entire room shook. Bill hopped up, letting out a honk and flapping his mighty wings to escape the weaponized crustacean. Cinnamon leaped all the way onto their side of the table, landing silently and sniffing at the air toward Roger. Sitting atop her head and nestled within Cinnamon's fur, Bumblebro and Queen Bee waved, buzzing their wings in greeting.

"You've been told their names?" Theo asked.

Roger nodded, his jaw hanging so low that Maria worried it might fall off.

"Well, that makes things easier. Everyone, this is Roger. Roger, this is the gang—those that Fischer calls his animal pals. The only ones we're missing are Brigadier Borks and Lemon, but you can meet them later."

Roger stared, his body stiff as a board. He pressed his lips together and lines formed around his eyes. Sharon stepped forward, placing a hand in the center of his back. It did nothing to quell the emotions warring on his face.

"I need to speak with Fischer," he said.

Sharon took a half step closer. "Dear . . . ?"

"Fischer," he repeated. "Barry, too."

When he turned toward them, any shock or fear was long gone. All that remained was an icy determination. Though she'd only seen it a few times in her life, Maria recognized the look. It made the breath catch in her throat.

She swallowed. "I-I can go get them—"

"No." His voice was iron, his visage emotionless. "I need to speak with them alone. Get Barry. He can take me to . . . *him.*"

"Please, Dad. I—"

"Barry, *Maria.* Get him."

She had seen her father angry before. Furious, even. The vitriol in his eyes was something new, and though it wasn't directed at her, she felt herself shrink beneath it.

His lip twitched at her inaction. "*Now,*" he growled.

She nodded wordlessly, backing from the room before running down the hallway toward the smithy.

CHAPTER SIXTY-FIVE

COULD HAVE GONE WORSE

As I lay in the shade with a sausage dog resting on my chest, I drifted in and out of sleep. Each time my awareness returned to the waking world, I smiled and rubbed Borks's belly. The filtered sunlight peeking through Lieutenant Colonel Lemony Thicket's canopy was just right, providing the perfect amount of warmth to counteract the chilly forest air.

All things considered, it was a wonderful day to be ambushed.

I cracked an eye as I *felt* Barry coming.

That's something, I thought.

I'd never been able to discern who each person was before, but that flicker of chi striding through the forest was definitely Barry.

"Over here, mate!" I called, closing my eyes and letting a smile cross my face. "Next to Lemon!"

Borks stretched, and I scratched his belly as Barry drew closer.

"How did it go with Roger, by the way?" I asked, knowing he was close enough to hear me.

"Not good," came the gravelly voice of definitely not Barry.

I bolted upright, and Borks responded with the same level of surprise. He shifted into his nightmare form in an instant, his large torso standing over my shoulder. Roger's stride didn't falter for a moment. He marched toward me and Borks, his gaze flinty. Barry followed behind him, looking as confused as I felt.

I reached under Borks's chest, patting his shoulder reassuringly and letting him know it was fine. I was sure he wouldn't attack Roger, but I didn't want him to scare the farmer. As Roger drew closer and I got a better look at his face, I realized my worry was misplaced. His jaw worked inaudibly as he looked from me to Borks, then at the tree.

"I take it this is Brigadier Borks and Lieutenant Colonel Lemony Thicket, then?"

"Er—yeah, mate. Borks, Lemon—this is Roger."

Borks nodded, and Lemon sprouted a leaf, waving it at him.

He bit down, the muscles at his temples flexing with the effort. "I need to thank you for healing Sharon." He spared Barry a glance. "Both of you."

I rubbed the back of my head. "It was all Barry on that one, mate. All I did was exist."

His face didn't change as he stared down at me.

“If you weren’t a cultivator, a traveler, as Sharon tells it, then she’d never have been healed.” He looked at Barry again. “Correct?”

“Uhhh . . . yeah. That’s right.”

Roger’s eyes came back to me. “You saved my wife—Maria’s mother—from a terminal illness. So, I thank you.”

The cold indifference on his face didn’t match his words. Without another sound, he lunged for me. Any of us—Barry, me, or Borks—could have stopped him. But none of us did. Roger’s hand held my collar. He pulled it toward himself as much as he could without ripping another of my shirts.

If looks could kill . . . I thought, seeing the fury etched in every line of his face. His upper lip twitched, then peeled back to reveal clenched teeth.

“But,” he said, jaw trembling, “you did so by making her a *cultivator.*” The last word was venom-laced, and he spat to the side as if he couldn’t bear its flavor. “Then, you made my daughter a cultivator, potentially dooming all of us to death if the capital were to find out.”

“Fischer had nothing to do with Sharon’s awakening, Roger—”

“Shut! Up!” he roared, whirling on Barry. “Everyone keeps calling it awakening, or ascending, or some other pleasant bullshit that makes it sound like something good!” He took a deep breath, but it didn’t stop his anger. “You turned my *wife* into a godsdamned *cultivator!*”

Barry nodded, steady as a boulder. “I did. And I’d do it again.”

“What gives you the right?” Roger let go of my collar, stomping toward Barry and poking a finger into his chest. “*Who* gave you the right? You’re not a god, so stop acting like one!”

Barry gave Roger a tragic smile, his eyes filled with compassion.

“She would have died, Roger. Soon, too, by my estimate. I regret that I couldn’t give her a choice, but she wasn’t lucid enough to understand me, let alone consent. As I said, though . . . I’d do it again. I’d do it a hundred—a *thousand* times over if it meant saving her life. As for Maria—”

“Don’t!” He screamed, his voice like gravel. “Don’t even speak her name! You two turned my little girl into an abomination!”

“Mate . . .” I said, unable to hold my tongue. “That’s going a bit too far—”

“Shut up, Fischer! I don’t care if you’re some god or someone pretending to be one! You’ve single-handedly tainted the two people I love the—”

“Enough!” I moved in what must have been a blur to him. I lifted him by the torso and pressed him into Lemon’s trunk, not hard enough to hurt him, but hopefully hard enough to knock some sense into his thick skull. It stunned him enough for his anger to break, his eyes going wide.

“Remember what Sharon said about not saying things you couldn’t take back? They’re still your family, you stubborn old prick!” I opened my mouth to continue but cut myself off. I took a deep breath, then let out slowly, continuing with a calmer tone. “They’re still your family, Roger, you peanut. They aren’t different people.”

“And!” I continued, raising my voice a little. “Maria knew exactly what she was doing. She *requested* to be made into a cultivator after I warned her off of it. Repeatedly. To call that a mistake is to call your daughter an idiot." I let go of Roger, and he slumped to the forest floor, his face going blank as he leaned against Lemon's sturdy trunk. I knelt down so our eyes were level. "We both know she's not an idiot. She's brilliant, mate, and she was of sound mind when she decided to become a cultivator."

"I know . . ." he said, his gaze staring right through me. Slowly, motion returned to his face. His lip trembled, but this time, it wasn't because of anger. With eyes growing bloodshot, he lowered his head into his hands. I hesitantly raised a hand, but pulled it back, not knowing how to reassure him. I looked to Borks for assistance, but he was already on the move. His golden hair bounced as he padded up to Roger in golden retriever form, sniffing and nuzzling his arm and head.

An arm laced with wiry muscle drifted up to rest on Borks's back.

Barry and I turned away at the same time.

"I'll be picking some lemons over here when you're ready to talk again, Roger," I said.

I heard a muffled sound that could have been a sob, but I kept my eyes forward as I strode away, knowing there was nothing I could do to comfort him. We reached one of the lemon trees on the other side of the clearing and began studiously searching its branches for the juiciest of fruit.

"Well," Barry whispered. "That couldn't have gone any worse."

I shrugged. "Pretty sure a meltdown was impossible to avoid, given how staunchly he views the world. All things considered, it could have gone way, *way* worse."

Barry reached up and plucked a lemon.

"I suppose that's true. Still, there's something unsettling about seeing a man like Roger distraught."

"Yeah, no kidding. I can handle anger and hatred, but how do you comfort a bloke like him? I feel like there's a fifty-fifty chance it just makes everything worse."

"Agreed. We're lucky to have Brigadier Borks here."

I sent a pulse of gratitude Borks's way, and he sent his love back. I could practically see the way his tail was wagging in my mind's eye. I leaned around the trunk of the lemon tree, spying Barry as he reached for another particularly fat lemon.

"So, were you gonna tell me about what you got up to last night?"

"I have no idea what you mean. I just had a night in with the family, and . . ." He let the words trail off, letting out a sigh. "You're sure you want to know?"

I grinned. "Very much so, especially after Theo told me it was something I could use."

Barry rolled his eyes. "Would have been nice for Theo to give me a heads up on that particular detail."

I puffed out my chest and rolled my shoulders back. "Sounds to me like he has his priorities straight, my man. Lucky for you, I'm a benevolent god, so shan't smite you for not being more forthcoming with information."

I caught the lemon thrown at my head and let out an indignant gasp. "From casual insubordination to overt assault? Well, I have *never.* Keep it up, young man, and I'll be informing your wife."

"You wouldn't . . ."

"Hmmm. Perhaps I wouldn't, but only in exchange for some information. If only there were something you could tell me. Something I didn't know and desperately wanted to learn of . . ."

"Oh. Like the workshops I created last night in the church? Is that something that would interest you?"

My jaw dropped open, and I blinked at the smug look on his face. "You're serious?"

"I certainly am."

"Workshops? What kind of workshops?"

"Oh, you know, nothing too impressive." He made a dismissive gesture with one hand. "Just a tailoring room, a woodworking shop, a smithy—"

"A smithy?" I interrupted. "Do Fergus and Duncan know?"

"Know? They're in there right now working on cages."

My mouth practically salivated at the idea. "What's in there?"

Barry went on to describe a room filled with what sounded like a mountain of different tools. When he mentioned there were *two* forges powered by System shenanigans, my jaw dropped open. I had spent plenty of time in the smithy of late, and I couldn't help but picture the joy that the smiths must have had when they first set eyes on the room. Moreover, the lack of metal for oyster cages was the only thing gatekeeping the acquisition of more pearls, so having two forges fueled by chi or the System or whatever was a massive boon.

"That's wild, mate . . . I can't wait to see it."

"It's even more impressive than what I'm describing, Fischer. I don't really understand anything about blacksmithing, but I know Fergus and Duncan are beyond chuffed with it."

"What about the woodworking and tailoring rooms?"

He described their features, both of which were just as impressive as the smithy. I shook my head. "I can hardly believe what I'm hearing, mate."

He gave me a pride-filled grin.

"You'll have to come see it for yourself, then."

"Hang on," I said, raising a finger. "I cut you off before. What else is down there?"

"Oh, right. I almost forgot. There's a tannery for Ellis, too."

My eyebrows furrowed. "A tannery? Like . . . a solarium?"

"What on Kallis is a solarium?"

"You know—a place to tan."

"A place to *tan?*"

"Yeah. Your skin?" I pointed at my browned arm. "Tan. I know Ellis has a buff bod now, but I didn't take him for the type to work on his complexion."

Barry shook his head, sheer incomprehension plastering his face. "No, Fischer, I don't mean a place to tan. What are you even . . ." He stilled, giving me a flat stare. "You're messing with me, aren't you?"

I gave him a smile so wide that my cheeks hurt. "Would I do that, Barry? Mess with you for my amusement?"

"Yes. Often and flagrantly."

My grin widened even more, and he shook his head. Before I could say something to make Barry even more disappointed in me, a bark grabbed our attention. Borks sat on the grass beside Roger, whose chin was raised and gaze fixed on us. His eyes were red and puffy, but his face was resolute.

"I've reached a decision."

Barry and I shared a glance, then I turned back to Roger. "Er . . . that's good, mate. But what decision are you talking about?"

"The only one there is to make."

He breathed deep, firming his shoulders and standing taller.

"I want you to make me into a cultivator."

CHAPTER SIXTY-SIX

BIRDS OF A FEATHER

As the sun rose ever higher in the sky, its light stole through gaps in the canopy above. When I'd first come across this patch of grass, it had been a clearing, the space around the blue trunk free of flora other than grass. Now, four lemon trees stood, all growing bigger by the day. Their branches were filled with glossy leaves, bright-yellow lemons, and countless bees that flew between small white flowers. A soft wind gusted above us, shaking the leaves and making a pleasant sound.

I blinked at the man before me. "Come again, Roger?"

He lifted his chin, his gaze unwavering. "I want you to make me a cultivator. As soon as possible."

Lost for words, I looked at Barry. He studied Roger with an intent look. "Why do you want to become a cultivator?"

"To protect my family," he replied, not skipping a beat. A hint of his anger returned, his nostrils flaring and mouth growing tight. "No matter how I feel about you putting my family in danger, it's up to me to protect them." He whirled on me, likely seeing the look on my face. "Don't say a word, Fischer. I don't care about your reasoning or justifications. You had no right to give Maria your poisoned food."

Barry cleared his throat. "Can I speak with Fischer for a moment, Roger?"

"Why?" he demanded, not hiding his suspicion. "So you can decide how to dispose of me now that you know I won't blindly follow you?"

Barry sighed. "Because I want to talk to him. There's no scenario in which we harm a hair on your head, Roger. If we wanted you to disappear—which, to be clear, we don't—I'm pretty sure Lemon could open up the earth where you stand and swallow you whole."

One of Lemon's roots shot up from the ground right before Roger. It nodded, and his face went white as he stared down at his feet.

"I just want to talk to Fischer, okay?" Barry continued. "Can you give us a moment?"

He stepped backward slowly, holding his hands up in a placating gesture as if Lemon would actually eat him up.

Barry sighed and shook his head when Roger was out of hearing range. "Are you okay with this?"

"With making him ascend even though he isn't . . . what? Subservient?"

"Exactly. Are you comfortable with that?"

"Hell yeah, brother. It's an absolute win."

" . . . It is?"

I grinned, leaning in close. "Riddle me this, Barry. What do people need to do to become a cultivator?"

"Eat food you've made . . . ?"

"Exactly." I nodded sagely, but Barry just raised an eyebrow.

"I don't get it."

"Mate, I've been slowly converting everyone to the ways of fishing. What better way to make him realize fishing is the correct way of life than to feed him some delicious seafood? Who could have some of my deep-fried fish and not crave more?"

"Er . . . you know you could just give him lemons, right? Or a sugary pastry? Or literally *anything* else?"

"I could, yes."

" . . . But you're not going to."

My smile was the only answer I gave, and Barry let out a soft laugh.

"I'm starting to wonder if raising you to the pantheon is a good idea, Fischer. You're diabolical."

"Not at all! I am but a humble servant to the sea, doing my bit to impart knowledge upon the uninformed."

"Yeah, that's what I said—diabolical."

I waved the comment away. "Diabolically pure, you mean."

I turned to Roger, who was hiding in the tree line away from Lemon's trunk and glaring at us.

"Good news, mate! We've agreed to give you some pew-pew food!"

The afternoon sun was high overhead, bathing my skin in a pleasant heat. Steam wafted up from the pot before me, bringing with it the scent of beef tallow, fried breadcrumbs, and fish. I breathed it in, a smile slowly coming to my face.

Maria leaned in beside me, putting an arm on my leg that sent tingles coursing through me. "You know, Fischer, you could have just given him lemonade . . ." She leaned in closer, whispering. "But I'm so glad you didn't."

I nodded, shooting a look at Barry, who had clearly heard by the way he rolled his eyes.

"At least someone here gets me."

"What are you whispering about?" Roger demanded, sitting upright.

"Just saying it's almost done, mate!"

Sharon kept her face neutral, but I didn't miss the spark of amusement in her eyes as she rested a hand on her husband's arm. Some of his rigidness relaxed with her touch—not all of it, however.

"I wanna test something," I said, peering down at the fish. "I might not hear you for a while."

"What are you testing?" Ellis asked, his eyes and posture attentive as he lowered pencil to paper.

"My chi control after yesterday's advancement. I'll let you know about it afterward."

I focused all my attention on the chunks of fish frying in the tallow as I closed my eyes, feeling the surrounding world. There were strands of essence flowing all around us, blowing in chaotic directions like leaves in the wind. Those hints of chi, though noticeable, were nothing compared to the chi coming from my core. It poured into the pot before returning to me in an endless cycle. I sent my awareness along with the flow, and when it hit the fish, some of the chi was left behind. Despite not being in my body, I was aware of my eyebrows shooting up. Someone asked something—Ellis, no doubt—but I ignored the question entirely.

I pushed at the stream, making it flow faster. When it passed by the chunks of fish, I honed in on one of them. More chi poured into it, and it started to glow brighter to my senses. Following a hunch, I focused on another chunk of fish next to it. I tried to push and redirect the essence within it into the one that was glowing brighter. I saw the transfer take place. All the chi that had accumulated in one chunk flowed into the other, making it even brighter. In a matter of seconds, the drained one was free of any essence at all.

I opened my eyes again, returning to the present. Everyone was staring at me, most intent of all Ellis, but I ignored them. The bubbles surrounding the chunks of fish had subsided, so I removed the chi-less one with a pair of tongs. When it was cool enough, I poked it with a finger. The breading was crispy and the fish beneath was firm.

"All right, gang. Lunch is ready."

"Fischer!" Ellis literally yelled, making me jump.

"Whoa, man. What's up?"

"Details!" he ordered, his hand trembling on the pencil.

"Oh. Right. My bad."

As I removed all the fish, I regaled them with my findings.

Ellis swooped in, leaning in so close that I worried he might burn himself. "Fascinating. I cannot tell them apart in the slightest . . ." He withdrew, settling in the sand as he kept writing.

When it had cooled, I grabbed the enhanced one with the tongs and put it on a plate. "You're up, Roger." I went to stand but paused.

"What's wrong?" he asked, his face pale.

"Er, on second thought, this might be too much." I cut it down the middle, placing half back on the cooling rack. "Give this a crack, mate."

He accepted the plate with a shaking hand, staring down at the golden-brown crumbing and flaky flesh within. He gulped.

"It's okay, Dad. Try it."

"She's right, dear," Sharon added, squeezing his arm. "There's nothing to be afraid of."

He lowered his hand, shook it to stop it from trembling, then scooped the fish up. Before he could change his mind, he threw it into his mouth. I could hear the crunch from where I sat. I leaned in, unable to contain my anticipation. What must have been only a few seconds felt like an eternity as he sat still, only his chest moving with his breath. Roger's jaw moved, his entire face scrunching as if he couldn't stand the taste. A single tear escaped his left eye. It rolled down his cheek with glacial speed, glinting in the sunlight.

"Dear . . . ?" Sharon asked, compassion coating her words. "What's wrong?"

He covered his mouth with one hand. "It's just so . . . disgusting. I can barely . . . stand it."

Seeing through him, I shot to my feet.

"Liar!" I cackled, dancing from foot to foot with my excitement. "It's delicious! It tastes so good that you're crying tears of *joy!*"

"Fischer!" Sharon chided, looking genuinely pissed off. "This is hardly the time to . . ." she trailed off as she turned back to Roger and the hatred held in his face. Her expression turned thunderous, and she flicked him on the arm. "He's right, isn't he? Roger, you blockhead, you made me worry!"

"No," he mumbled, covering his mouth once more, his face still leaking tears. "It's foul. I hate it."

"Spit it out then," she said, crossing her arms.

"I . . . I can't. I need to become a cultivator."

"I knew it!" I continued dancing my little jig. "Roger likes fish," I sang. "Roger likes fish, Roger likes—ow!"

I rubbed my arm where Maria had flicked me. Unlike her mother, she'd used her full strength.

"Stop teasing my dad." She shook her head, but the hint of a smile was clear on her face. "You're both as blockheaded as each other."

Roger swallowed. He licked his lips and wiped his eyes. "I think I'll need some more. I didn't awaken, so—"

He cut off, his eyes going vacant. I felt it. The exact moment the System reached out to him.

"You were saying?" I said, sitting once more and leaning casually on one arm. "Now that you've become a cultivator, would you like some more of my delicious, irresistible, *tasty* fish?"

His vision cleared as he returned to the present. He licked his lips again. "I might need to have a little more . . . just in case. I wouldn't want the awakening to fail because I didn't have enough."

"Is that true?" Ellis asked. "That small mouthful of fish worked?"

Roger nodded, his eyes darting around at us all. "It . . . it's asking me to choose a name. Do I just say Roger?"

"No!" Ellis, Barry, and I yelled.

His eyes went wide. "Why not?"

"Sorry," Barry said. "We have reason to believe that the capital can monitor our names, so we've been choosing pseudonyms that will throw them off."

Roger nodded, his face going thoughtful. "Sharon mentioned that there was a prince you were getting information from. What name do I use, then?"

I threw my hand up. "I have an idea! I've been brainstorming more names to confuse them should someone find the artifact."

Ellis perked up, watching me intently.

"What is it?"

I grinned.

When I told them the name and my reasoning behind it, Maria laughed so hard that I thought she may have wet herself.

Augustus Reginald Gormona felt his anxiety slide away as he shed his kingly robes and got into a scalding hot bath. The castle always got terribly cold this time of year, but no matter what worries assailed him—of which there were plenty—he could always rely on a bath of almost boiling water to recenter himself. He breathed in the steam floating up from the surface, enjoying the heat as it passed his nostrils and went down into his lungs. The water was scented, and even smelling the herbs put him in a good mood, recalling all the baths that had come before. A sharp knock came from the door, and a spike of annoyance lanced his calm.

"I am busy for the next hour. Come back then."

He took a deep breath, trying to center himself once more, but then the sharp knock came again.

"Come in!" he yelled, only so he could identify and punish this intruder. When the face poked into the room, his stomach dropped.

"Apologies, my king. There has been a development," Charles, the man in charge of monitoring the artifacts, said.

" . . . What sort of development?"

Charles winced. "Another name, my king."

Augustus Reginald Gormona rose from the water in an instant, scrambling across the marble floor for a towel.

Two minutes later, wearing a bathrobe and with steam still rising from his body, the king burst into the artifact-filled room.

"Where is it? Which screen?"

"This one," Deklan replied, scratching his neck and staring down. His face was lit by a faint blue light.

The king walked forward on unfeeling legs, the calm of his bath long gone. He knew it would be bad based on Charles's demeanor, but the name printed on the screen was worse than he could have ever imagined.

He leaned back on the same artifact the guard was using. "Do you know what this means, Deklan?" he asked, his voice faint.

"Not really, no."

The king swallowed. "It means they're preparing for war. They've secured a scout—one which we have no hope of controlling."

Augustus Reginald Gormona stared at the relic, willing it to change, willing this to be a fever dream. The name remained, taunting him. Five simple words that could mean the downfall of a kingdom—of his family. He read the name of the freshly awakened spirit beast once more, printed in bold lettering.

An Entire Flock of Birds.

CHAPTER SIXTY-SEVEN

PSYCHOLOGICAL WARFARE

A few hours earlier, we sat before a campfire. The smell of deep-fried fish was in the air, and Maria's giggles joined the faint sound of waves lapping the shoreline. Her joy was a soothing balm to the uncertainty of the day gone, and I watched the lines of her face intently, drinking them in. Barry shook his head, more than a little amusement on his visage.

"This is why I said you are diabolical, Fischer. What is wrong with your brain that you can think of a name like that?"

I shrugged one shoulder. "Just a bit of psychological warfare, mate. Blame Ellis." I pointed at the former archivist. "He was the one that inspired me with the names they all chose."

Ellis stopped writing to cast a smirk over the top of his notepad. "Happy to be of service. For what it is worth, I agree with your reasoning. I cannot think of a better name to sow chaos within the capital should they be monitoring our advancements. Also, I have another suggestion if you are amenable to it, Roger."

The farmer turned cultivator hadn't stopped scowling. "You're assuming that I'll use that ridiculous name. 'An Entire Flock of Birds'? How will it do anything other than make me look ridiculous?"

Sharon squeezed his arm. "Do you trust Fischer?" Roger gave her an unimpressed look, and she held up a finger. "Don't answer that. Do you trust me, dear?"

His mouth moved, likely fighting back the urge to call me a choice insult. Instead of voicing it, he nodded.

"Good," she said. "Because *I* trust Fischer. I trust Barry, Ellis, and the rest of the church. If it has even a small chance of misdirecting the capital and making us safer, why wouldn't you use the name? You're still Roger. We don't call Ellis Lizard Wizard because he's Ellis. The name is only for the System and has no impact on who you are as a person."

Roger grunted. "What if I don't choose one? Won't that be even better than trying to misdirect them?"

"I tried that," Barry said, laughing. "I hope you don't like sleeping, because it will pull at your awareness multiple times an hour until you pick one."

"What was the other request, Ellis?" Roger asked, not-so-subtly changing the subject.

"After you choose the name, I want you to spend your time learning every trade and skill we have. I want you to gain as many levels in different things as possible."

"Listen to me, Ellis." Roger turned toward him, demanding every ounce of the former archivist's attention. "I may have agreed to become a cultivator, but I don't intend to join your church. I did so to protect my family." He shook his head. "All that aside, I'm a farmer. I *farm.* I don't have time to be running around doing tasks for you."

I snorted, unable to help myself, and Roger whirled on me, his eyes filled with hate.

"Er—my bad," I said.

"Something funny, heretic?"

"Yeah, mate. You thinking you won't have any spare time. Do you have any idea how much becoming a cultivator will improve your body? Your speed? Your strength? You don't have that many fields, Roger. I reckon you'll be able to knock out your work in a couple of hours each day."

"So? That means I'll have more time to spend with my family. Not more time to help you with whatever your goals are."

"*Riiight . . .*" I said, dragging the word out. "Let's assume that the church's goals aren't the best way to protect your family, which, to be clear, they totally are. Even if they weren't, I'm pretty sure I know what Ellis's intention is. The confusion it could cause would *definitely* be the best way to help your family out." I turned to Ellis. "May I?"

He nodded, so I continued.

"You gaining a bunch of different skills simultaneously will make it appear that a flock of birds has genuinely taken steps on the path of ascension, and they're individually training different skills. It implies numbers, intelligence, and a goal, all of which are pretty terrifying. Think about it, mate. A whole flock of birds of an unnamed species all following different paths. It'll have the capital sweating bullets every time they see a shadow."

"I'm still not doing it. I need time to consider what choice I make."

"Dad . . ." Maria started, but Sharon shook her head.

"Take your time, dear," she rubbed Roger's back. "I know you'll make the right decision when you're ready."

I waited a moment, and when I saw no one else had anything to add, I grinned. "Well, that's that. How about we dig into this fish before it goes cold?"

Everyone had forgotten the meal, and as I pointed down at the still-warm morsels, their eyes were drawn to them. I went to cut the one I'd drained the chi from, then glanced up at Roger. Unsurprisingly, he was giving me his best scowl.

"Can I interest you in more fish, mate? I just wanna know before I cut this piece up."

He licked his lips. "Well, if it has the chance to give me more power . . ."

"Nope. This is the one I drained all the chi from, which is why I'm cutting it up. I thought people might want to taste the difference. Interested?"

"No. Definitely not."

"You're sure? I can cut you off a bit if you're worried it will make you a heretic or something."

He hesitated for a fraction of a second before shaking his head. That was all the confirmation I needed.

You did like the fish, I thought. *You want to taste this bit, even though it won't give you any chi.*

It filled me with glee, and the smile I gave him made a scowl return to his tanned face. I cut the fish into equal pieces, putting each on a plate. Next, I added half a chunk of the chi-containing fish. Finally, I cut up the rest of the filet that I'd poured extra chi into. When each plate held some of each, I passed them around.

Roger was watching the leftover food, his scowl having lost some of its heat.

"Want more of the chi fish, mate? There's a chance it'll make you more powerful."

He nodded immediately, so I gave it to him, then looked up at everyone else. "Let's start with the plain fish."

When we'd all picked it up, I placed mine on my tongue. Silence reigned across the sand as we chewed.

"Mmm," Maria said, her face creased in thought. "It's . . ."

"Kinda bland," I finished.

She nodded. "Yeah. Don't get me wrong, it's still delicious, but compared to the usual . . ." She threw a chunk of said fish into her mouth. Her shoulders relaxed as she ate it. "Yeah. That's much better."

I ate some too. Compared to the one I'd drained of chi, it was night and day. Like the first portion hadn't been seasoned at all.

"So . . ." I said. "Chi makes it taste better . . . ?"

"If that's the case . . ." Barry's eyes never left his plate. "What will the one you've enhanced taste like?"

I lowered my hand toward my portion of the fish in question, my mouth watering and fingers twitching. Before I could get there, power bloomed from across the fire. I sat up straight, staring directly at the source. Roger's eyes were wide, his gaze distant. He shook his head, coming back to reality. Everyone else was looking down at their plates, so I cleared my throat to get their attention.

"Roger . . ."

"What?" he demanded, challenging me with his eyes.

I raised my eyebrows expectantly. "Anything to tell us, mate?"

His lip twitched as he continued trying to glare a hole through me.

"What are you talking about?" Sharon asked, darting a look between us. "Roger? What's he talking about?"

"The System or whatever you call it," he growled. "It was distracting me, so I chose a name."

"Distracting you, huh?" I couldn't keep the grin from my face as I glanced down at the half-eaten chunk of deep-fried fish in his hand. "Distracting you from what, Roger? What was so important that you didn't want to be interrupted?"

Maria let out a little *oh,* and then she smirked. "Don't tell me, Dad . . . you don't enjoy the taste of fish as much as Fischer was suggesting, do you?"

His face was turning red as his mouth moved inaudibly, trying and failing to find the words to explain himself. "I'm leaving," he said, getting to his feet.

My grin turned downright evil as I looked from him to the fish still held in his hand. "Taking that with you, mate?"

"Enough, Fischer," Sharon said, letting out a sigh. "And you." She grabbed Roger by the arm. "Sit back down. You're allowed to like the taste of fish, for the love of the gods. It's delicious, especially when Fischer cooks it. Sit with me and eat the damned meal."

I pouted at her.

"Booo," Maria called, cupping a hand to her mouth. "No fun allowed."

Sharon threw a chunk of fish at her daughter.

"Thanks!" Maria said, catching it and throwing it into her mouth.

Barry raised a hand, getting our attention. "I'm calling an official truce. I think each second we wait is shaving a year off of Ellis's lifespan."

Sure enough, Ellis held the cut of enhanced fish up to his face. He was literally shaking as he stared at it, his other hand ready to scrawl notes in his open notepad.

"Deal," I said, then threw mine into my mouth.

The moment the first drop of moisture hit, its flavor exploded across my awareness. The deepest umami flavor I could imagine hit every one of my taste buds at the same time. Despite the flesh having cooled, it warmed everywhere it touched. The heat spread down my chest, and when it reached my core, it was as though the sun itself warmed me from within. Unable to wait any longer, I bit down into it. Breading crunched, meat separated, and the heat rose to a fever pitch.

A noise escaped me, joining the sounds coming from my friends. I savored it as long as I could, closing my eyes to experience each bite in its entirety. Finally, I swallowed it, and a comforting flame shot down my throat, followed by another shudder. I opened my eyes, blinking rapidly to banish the tears that had welled up.

That bite had been barely wider than a coin, and that was the impact it had? I took deep breaths, completely overwhelmed by the experience as I looked around the circle. Everyone was similarly speechless, their expressions rapturous. The only one with a smile on his face was Roger, but I suspected that was because he'd already eaten a whole mouthful previously and knew what to expect.

Maria looped an arm in mine and pulled herself close. "Are you single?" she whispered. "Because I'd give anything to eat food like that for the rest of my life."

"Taken, I'm afraid," I whispered back, shakily. I cleared my throat and clenched my jaw, willing my voice box to work correctly. "If things ever fall through with her, though, where can I find you?"

She elbowed my ribs lightly, and I put an arm around her, pulling her to my side. As she leaned into me, we lapsed back into silence, both enjoying the moment. When I opened my eyes after a few breaths, Roger was once more scowling at me, but the joy on Sharon's face beside him counteracted it.

The scratching of a pencil came from my right, and I glanced over, seeing Ellis taking notes at a ridiculous pace. He shook his hand, his limb likely as insubordinate as my voice had been.

I inhaled deeply, then let out an audible sigh. "We've had a big day today, one that I think requires a celebration."

Barry raised a knowing eyebrow. "We have, haven't we? Dare I say this calls for a church-wide feast?"

I smiled back. "Anything less would be downright disrespectful. How could we properly celebrate Roger's ascension without a party?"

His scowl deepened; my grin widened.

Three hours later, the delicious taste of fish lingered in my mouth as I watched Danny pat the back of an inconsolable Peter. The chef opened his mouth to speak, but only a pained noise came out. Everyone's reactions to the pile of enhanced fish I'd cooked were wonderful, but Peter's was the most visceral. He'd been beside himself for the last five minutes since he'd taken a bite.

I rubbed Corporal Claws's belly, who was lying on her back in Maria's lap, her little head resting on my thigh. I moved my hand up to her chin, giving it a good scritching that made her whiskers twitch. As I looked around the circle, I bathed in the friendship on display.

The fishing club all sat close to Peter, taking turns trying to console him. The crafters sat together, probably discussing the different aspects of their workshops. I looked closer, and when I saw the attention going to Ruby's abdomen, I realized she and Steven must have shared the news of her pregnancy. They raised their drinks in a toast, and Ruby's eyes sparkled as she drank from her cup of sugarcane juice.

Claws let out an indignant chirp.

"Sorry, Claws."

I resumed scratching her chin, her temporary disapproval melting away. I waved at Ellis, and when I caught his eye, I gestured him over.

"Yes, Fischer?"

"Sorry for calling you over, mate. I wanted to give you something, but as you can see, I'm currently serving her royal highness, Corporal Claws."

Claws cooed her agreement, moving her head so I could scratch the other side of her chin.

"Oh?" Ellis asked. "What did you want to give me?"

I reached down behind me, grabbing a plate I'd stowed away. When I held it up, Maria raised an eyebrow at me.

"Fischer . . ."

"Yes?"

"Why were you hiding a bit of fish?"

"I wanted to sneak it to Ellis."

"Oh, uh . . . Thank you, Fischer, but I'm quite full."

"It's not for you, mate."

Maria scrunched her nose at me. "I'm too full for your riddles. Who is the fish for?"

I stared up at Ellis, and I saw his face transform as the realization struck him.

"The prince?" he asked, his eyes narrowed in on the deep-fried strip.

"Yeah, mate. It's *filled* with chi. I know you've been struggling to make him a cultivator. If this doesn't work, I don't know what will."

His hand reached out of its own accord, but he pulled it back, licking his lips. "Are you sure this is okay? I know you do not want to be involved."

"It's fine, mate. Like Barry said, it's for everyone's safety, so—"

Ellis's hand shot out like a viper, yoinking the plate and fish from my grasp. "Thank you!" he yelled over his shoulder, only slowing to lift Keith to his feet and show him the fish. With a nod to each other, they tore off over the sands, throwing up a cloud of debris in the wake.

I shook my head, smiling at the world I had found myself in.

Not a day went by that I didn't thank the cosmic force or isekai bullshit that led me to Tropica, and in that moment, I felt an indescribable level of gratitude. I turned to Maria, and as I stared at the firelight dancing over her freckles, she darted in to steal a kiss.

"What was that for?" I asked, my cheeks heating.

She cocked her head, a strand of hair falling free from behind her ear. She swept it back into place with a practiced movement. "I don't need a reason. I love you."

It was said so simply, yet it made butterflies spring to life in my stomach. What a beautiful life I'd found. "I love you, too."

Claws chirped, once more indignant.

"Yes, Claws." I rolled my eyes playfully. "I also love you."

CHAPTER SIXTY-EIGHT

INVALUABLE DATA

The warm light of magical fire lit the way as Ellis strode with purpose down the church's hallway. His attention had been divided over the past couple of days, but now that the trade route was set into motion and Roger had ascended, there was only one more task to take care of before he could devote himself entirely to processing the spiritual beast. He took a deep breath, enjoying the smell that wafted up from the tray in his hands.

"Everything okay, Ellis?" Keith asked from beside him.

"It will be as soon as we get this business over with."

Keith nodded.

"Agreed. Here's to hoping this actually works . . ."

"It will."

"How can you be sure?"

"Hmmm. A gut feeling."

Keith's footsteps halted, and Ellis turned back. Keith pursed his lips, looking back at him as if he were a scroll he couldn't quite decipher.

"Are you well, Keith?"

"Am *I* well? Did I just hear you say that you, former head archivist of the royal library, know something because of a . . . gut feeling?"

"Yes. Why is that odd?"

"Because you don't have any proof, Ellis. No backing articles, journals, or first-hand recordings . . . yet you're sure."

Ellis raised an eyebrow at his own behavior. "Hmmm. That is quite remarkable, isn't it?"

"*Quite remarkable?* It's downright astounding, Ellis. You've never committed to anything without having a literary foundation supporting it."

"Perhaps it is because . . ." Ellis shook his head and raised a hand. "No. We can theorize on that later. As soon as we deliver this food to your cousin, I am focusing my attention on the spirit beast's carcass and my crafting."

Ellis turned and kept striding, so Keith ran to catch up. "Have you put any thought into what you're going to do with it? The lizard, I mean."

"It will depend on what properties it presents, if any. Unfortunately, I need to focus on my leatherworking first—"

"Hello?" a voice interrupted the open doorway ahead of them. "What's that about a lizard?"

Keith sighed as they entered the room. "None of your business, Trent. What are you doing?"

The prince was leaning against the bars, making his already toe-like face even more squished. "What am *I* doing? No one brought me my dessert! What are *you* doing?"

"Well, great news, then!" Keith pointed at the tray in Ellis's hands. "We've brought you food."

Trent frowned at it. "What is that?"

"Deep-fried meat. Try it—it's delicious."

" . . . But I want dessert . . ."

"Tell you what. If you eat all of this second dinner, I'll give you extra dessert. What do you say?"

Greed entered the prince's eyes, and he happily scooped up one of the golden chunks of fish. He raised it to his mouth but paused.

"This isn't lizard, is it?"

"Why on Kallis would we give you lizard to eat, Trent?"

He pouted. "I'm not stupid, Keith. I heard you two talking about a lizard. I won't go eating dumb animals for your amusement."

Keith took a steadying breath. "It is not lizard. It's meat, and it's delicious. Just try it."

Trent, still frowning as if they were trying to trick him—which, to be fair, they were—bit down into the fish. His face immediately transformed. He'd not so much as swallowed when he raised the rest to his mouth, but then he caught sight of the flesh.

"White meat . . . ?" He froze, and Keith could practically hear his sparse brain cells bouncing off one another. Trent retched. "It *is* lizard! Oh, Keith, you deceitful, hateful cousin."

"It's not lizard, Trent."

The prince squinted at him. "Swear on your parents."

"I swear on my parents' lives that it isn't lizard."

"In that case . . ." He threw it into his mouth and chewed happily, letting out a *mmm* that trailed off abruptly as his gaze went distant.

Ellis's heart hammered in his chest. They had given him *countless* chi-filled foods over the past weeks. Lemonade, sugarcane juice, even dishes with fish in it. For some unknown reason, none of them had worked. Which is exactly why they had taken Fischer up on his offer to create a chi-enhanced meal for the prince.

Has it truly worked? Is the quest to awaken the foolish royal finally complete?

Trent's eyes came back to the present, and he swallowed his mouthful, looking completely perplexed. "Why did that thing ask my name?"

Ellis's anticipation drained away as he and Keith shared a glance. In their excitement, they'd forgotten to remind him not to enter one by himself. They'd done so before, of course—mentioned in passing that if something asked his name, he shouldn't enter it. Trent being Trent, though, had clearly forgotten that detail.

"What name did you enter, cousin?" Keith asked, taking an involuntary step forward.

Trent gave his cousin a look like *he* was the moron.

"Trent. *Duh.*"

The prince shook his head.

"Are you dumb? That's my name."

Though Augustus Reginald Gormona was half aware he was dreaming, he couldn't wake himself. The nightmare trapped him.

He ran from parapet to parapet atop the capital's walls. But no matter where he went, they were besieged by creatures of the night. They had shadowy, intangible forms, and the more he focused on them, the more they seemed to slip away, evading his observation.

Some of them had climbed the walls. Limbs writhed over the parapet and claws dug into stone, silent yet terrible. They circled him. Reached for him. Grasped him.

"*Augustus!*"

He tried to fight them off, but his body was robbed of strength.

"*Augustus!*" someone called again.

He had no time for whoever called. He was surrounded, the world growing smaller with each creature reaching for him.

"*Augustus!*"

Thumping like thunder joined the sound of his name, and all at once, the illusion was shattered. Augustus Reginald Gormona bolted upright, taking a deep breath as he scrambled away. When his back came to his ornate headboard, its carved wooden surface was cool in the winter air.

"Augustus!" his wife said again, her voice urgent. "Someone is at the door!"

Thump. Thump. Thump. Thump.

With his body still panicked, Augustus Reginald Gormona climbed out of bed. Addled as he was, he didn't step into his lush slippers. When his stumbling feet left the royal rug that the servants put under their bed for the winter months, the castle's stone floors were freezing. He focused on the sensation, willing his racing heart to calm.

"I'm coming!" he yelled before the awakener could knock again. He grasped the door and pulled it open, revealing a man just as panicked.

"Charles? What is the meaning of this?" Augustus had intended for the question to come out as a demand, but the dread he felt made it sound weak to his own ears.

Charles's lips formed a line. "The screen, my king. Another name . . ."

"Another . . . ?"

It was exactly what the king had feared, but before he could fully cognize the ramifications, Charles opened his mouth again. It moved inaudibly for what felt like an eternity. Eventually, the dignitary found his words.

"Your . . ." He swallowed. "Your son, my king . . ."

"Explain yourself, Charles." Fury and confusion burned in the king's chest. "Now."

"Another name appeared on the screen. It was . . ." He looked past Augustus toward the queen. "It was Trent."

"What?" his wife asked, but from the tone of her voice, she already knew.

"They have our son?" Augustus answered in a whisper.

The queen ran from the bed, dashing toward the dresser where she kept her jewelry. She plucked a locket from among her necklaces and cracked it open with shaking fingers. She let out a noise halfway between relief and despair as she fell to the floor, her shift bunching around her legs.

"The light remains lit. He's alive . . ."

"Some fates are worse than death," Augustus said, his body going numb. "They *have* him. There's no other way he could have awakened."

His wife's answering whimper echoed his thoughts, and her eyes went vacant as she stared into space. "My baby boy . . . he's not strong enough . . ."

Augustus clenched his jaw so tight he thought his teeth might shatter. His wife was right; the foolish boy was ill-equipped for being a captive of war.

Trent Reginald Gormona, first in line to the throne and authority on all things sweet, was having a wonderful time. He lounged among a throne of plush pillows as he ate his second dessert for the evening. Two dinners *and* two desserts? Now that was Trent's kind of night. Even better, since he had entered his name into that weird blue thing, the delicious sweets he ate no longer bothered him. Each time he'd drunk sugarcane juice or lemonade previously, an odd pressure would pulse in his brain for a while, as if trying to break down a physical wall. It had been the same when he ate that deliciously savory meat earlier. Rather than struggling against the wall, though, the white flesh covered in golden crumbs had shattered right through.

Trent cocked his head to the side. Perhaps it was the meat that had fixed his problem, not entering his name. Realizing he was thinking, he chuckled at himself. What good was *thinking* when he had delicious things to eat? He dipped the croissant into his heaped pile of lemon jam and placed it on his tongue. The sweet flavor warmed his entire body, and he could almost feel its energy coursing through his veins. He paused, waiting for the energy to press against that wall, but then he remembered the wall was no more. Trent grinned, dipped his pastry, and took another bite.

"How do you feel?" his traitorous cousin asked, making the blessed jam covering his tongue turn sour.

Trent leveled his best hate-filled scowl at him as he chewed. "I'd feel better if you brought me more jam."

Keith nodded. "As I thought. I can take it from here, Ellis. You can go get started on your project if you like."

"Are you sure?" the other man said.

What was he again? A librarian?

Trent shook his head; it didn't matter.

"I'm sure. I'll take notes if my cousin here does anything of note, but I don't foresee that happening." Keith sighed. "Not like he's going anywhere."

"You don't know that," Trent countered through another mouthful of pastry. "I might flex and bust out of this prison the moment you lower your guard."

If Trent hadn't been so engrossed by the lingering flavor of jam and the sense of smugness he got from insulting his captors, he may have noticed the drips of information making their way into his cerebrum.

Being Trent, he didn't, of course.

He simply puffed his chest out and looked down his nose at the two men outside his jail cell.

Ellis couldn't help but shake his head at the moronic prince. He had finally ascended, but the poor boy was so thick that he didn't even realize it yet. Ellis recalled the physical and cognitive changes that had occurred almost immediately following his own awakening. The urge to enlighten him was hard to ignore, but doing so could negatively impact the data. Trent's mental faculties—or lack thereof, he supposed—presented a unique opportunity.

Based on all their testimonials, the animals that had ascended from eating Fischer's food all experienced the same thing: a steady stream of information flowing into them. Though humans also experienced improvement, it was insignificant in comparison. Given these statements were all true, what would happen when a man thicker than Fischer's desserts awakened?

The data was invaluable, so Ellis once more dismissed the urge to tell him.

"All right, Keith. I leave the imbecile to you."

Trent snorted, an ugly noise considering how much croissant and jam he had stuffed into his mouth.

He gave them a smug smile as he swallowed. "Your insults are so ludicrous as to be amusing. Don't waste your breath attempting to bring this one low—you merely lower yourself in the attempt."

Ellis had started walking away, but froze mid-step, slowly looking back toward the prince.

Keith was staring with the same amount of incredulity. "What did you just say, Trent?"

The prince raised an eyebrow at them. "What? Are my sentences too verbose for cretins like you to comprehend? Doth my vocal vibrations leave you flummoxed?" He shook his head, laughing. "I daresay you two are the imbeciles, not I."

Ellis's hand twitched, reaching for his notepad of its own accord.

"What?" Trent continued. "Nothing to say? Are you so inarticulate that you've forgotten your words? You are a stain upon your houses. A blight upon the learned. A plague—"

"Trent," Keith interrupted, leaning so far forward that he was almost at the metal bars of his cousin's confinement. "Think about the words you're using."

Trent rolled his eyes. "Don't bother with your trickery, cousin. I know they are contextually correct. It is *you* who lacks the intellectual dexterity to—"

"Trent! *Think* about the words you're using. Do they sound like things you'd normally say? Sentences you'd normally put together?"

Trent cocked his head, squinting at them. His face morphed as the realization struck him.

"Poseidon's salt-crusted beard . . ." Trent said in a whisper, his eyes like saucers. "I sound like a *nerd* . . ."

As dawn approached in the capital city of Gormona, Aisa fought down her growing weariness.

Unlike the collared scum she was in charge of, a full night's sleep was a necessity. It hadn't been all that long since the king held an emergency meeting about the birds, but considering the night's events, her nerves felt frayed.

A wave of exhaustion washed over Aisa. She shook her head and slapped her cheeks, willing wakefulness to find her.

"Something wrong, handler?"

Aisa leveled a withering glare at the cultivator. "Mind your tongue around your betters."

He snorted. "Our betters, huh? You hear that, guys?"

"Give it a rest," the female cultivator with shoulder-length hair replied, giving the man a flat stare.

"Sorry we're not all beaten dogs like you."

"Enough," Aisa said. "No more talking unless you spot a bird."

They continued on in silence, the two chatty cultivators darting venomous looks at each other. Aisa peered at the other two. They, at least, were reliable. The man and woman marched on stoically with their gazes facing the surrounding buildings' rooftops.

Just when her nerves began to calm, a crack like thunder split the air. Aisa threw herself to the ground, and as debris rained down, she rolled to the side, her training taking over. She shot to her feet, prepared to dodge another incoming attack, but paused.

The cultivators all stood still, the calm two looking at the destroyed section of roof, and the other two glaring at each other.

"What in the hells was that?" the female cultivator demanded, holding the argumentative male by the collar.

"What? I saw movement!"

Aisa waited for his collar to beep, announcing that he was lying and had gone against his orders. When it didn't, the female's did instead. She let go of his collar, averting his gaze as he grinned at her.

Aisa brushed debris from her clothes as she took a steadying breath. Of all the things she thought she'd need to do to defend the capital, shooting bolts of lightning at every bird they came across had never crossed her mind.

Beneath a starry sky and far from home, a crustacean pressed herself against a stone chimney. A downright *rude* individual had just sent a bolt of lightning crackling her way.

To most denizens of this world, the existence of a rock crab hundreds of kilometers from the nearest shore would have been a startling discovery. To anyone who knew this crustacean well enough, however, such things were well within the realm of possibility.

Sergeant Snips shook her head; that bolt had almost hit her. She'd been scouting periodically since the announcement of Operation Sticky Fingers, and the fatigue was clearly catching up to her. The pitiful attack wouldn't have damaged her, but to be struck by one so below her station would have brought great shame.

Worse, it would have brought shame to her master.

A silent stream of bubbles flowed from her mouth. She had no clue why the cultivators were so riled up, but now that they were shooting blasts toward every bird they saw, the rooftops had become much more dangerous.

Snips shook her head. This work was better suited to Claws and her soft steps, but the dastardly otter couldn't be trusted to not engage the enemy. Or steal something shiny. Or perhaps both.

The cultivator squad's footsteps receded down the street, so Snips got up, stretching and willing her fatigue to leave.

If I leave now, I can get back to Tropica by tomorrow night . . .

That thought seemed to reenergize her. She scuttled along the tiles, heading east.

CHAPTER SIXTY-NINE

FUTURE PLANS

A swath of purple and orange colors painted the sky in the predawn light. Beneath that beautiful vista, Maria and I raced over the sands. Borks loped between us, his golden fur streaked back in the wind. I reached the gate first and put our race aside for a moment to hold it open for her. Without even a thank you, she sprinted past, poking her tongue out at me.

Borks leaped clean over it. As with Maria, he didn't pause. I pouted, then grinned. Taking off at a sprint, I swiftly made up the distance they'd put between us. The world blurred by under my feet, and focusing my chi into my legs, I leaped. Like a rocket, I sailed past them, skidding to a stop in the sand just before the first crop of sugarcane.

They reached me three heartbeats later, and Maria pointed at me. "Cheater!" she yelled, lifting her chin. "We agreed to a running race! You were clearly flying just now! Right, Borks?"

He barked in agreement, his tail wagging despite the accusation.

"Flying?" I held a hand to my chest. "I would never commit such vile treachery on purpose. It's not my fault that I tripped and fell."

She giggled. "*Tripped and fell?* From the halfway point between your house and the village's border?"

"I'm rather clumsy."

Borks barked in the affirmative again, and I narrowed my eyes at him. "Fine. We'll call it a draw, then."

"I'd say that too if I got caught cheating," Maria huffed, but her smile betrayed her.

"Come on," I said. "If we don't get our coffee soon, we'll miss the sunrise."

She interlaced her fingers with mine and planted a lightning-fast peck on my cheek. "Lucky you're cute, otherwise you'd never get away with your constant bending of the rules."

Despite it being the smallest of kisses, my face flushed hot, and a hand drifted up to touch the spot she'd touched, distracting me as we walked. When we entered the street before Sue's bakery, the scent of fresh coffee struck me. Sue was just handing over a cup.

She beamed up at us. "Well, well, well. Fancy seeing you two together so early in the morning. You must have woken up rather early to meet before coming here together." The downright predatory smile she had told me she knew the truth of it.

"We—er—we didn't . . ." Maria spluttered, her cool demeanor having disappeared before Sue's ambush.

I gave Maria's hand a squeeze, trying to reassure her, but before I could tell Sue off, a tiny ball of dough came sailing toward her head.

"You leave them alone, Sue," Sturgill said, leaning around the dividing wall between the counter and kitchen.

The dough bounced off the side of her head, and she slowly turned his way. Sturgill retreated, scrambling from sight as Sue rushed him. Maria and I raised our brows at each other as a cacophony of clanging pans and muffled smacks followed.

"Joking! I was joking!" Sturgill tried, but Sue's pursuit was relentless.

I let my hearing extend, wanting to make sure Sturgill wasn't getting shoved headfirst into the oven. They were both giggling under their breath as Sue berated and smacked him with what sounded like a wooden spoon. I withdrew my senses. A moment later, Sue reemerged, brushing flour from her shoulder and smoothing her hair.

"Where were we?" she asked, tugging at her apron. "Ah, yes—you two were explaining how you came to be together so early in the morning."

"I stayed at Fischer's last night," Maria replied, a slight blush to her cheeks.

Sue sighed. "Sturgill!"

"Yes, dear?" he asked, grinning from behind the counter.

"Stay there for a moment, would you?" She bent down to retrieve a croissant from the display case. Drawing her arm back and raising a knee, she launched it at her husband's head.

He let it strike his chest, then plucked it from the air before it could hit the ground. "Thanks! I was just considering breakfast."

Sue pouted at his laugh as he retreated into the kitchen.

"Infuriating man, ruining all my fun." Sue straightened her apron once more. "Well, all jokes aside, I'm happy for you two. You're both wonderful people and you make a charming couple."

A heat blossomed in my chest, only increasing as Maria's grip tightened around my hand. "Thank you," I replied, feeling the heat move up to my face.

"Okay." Sue gave us a kind smile. "That's enough of my prattling for one morning. I assume you two would like a coffee and a croissant?"

I grinned. "I'd usually ask for the finest coffee and croissant someone has, but I know all of yours are flawless."

She gave me an appraising look, then glanced at Maria. "Watch yourself around this one. He has a silver tongue."

As Sue prepared our coffees, the purple and orange sky faded to gradients of pink, warning of the sunrise to come.

"Okay." Sue placed our cups on the counter and slid over two croissants. "On the house, as usual."

"Thanks, Sue. I know we made a deal for free coffee and food, but I'll have to start paying one of these days."

She shook her head at me, rolling her eyes playfully. "Are you out of your mind? Do you have any idea how much our business has picked up because of the coffee machine you got us? We could give you twenty coffees a day and it wouldn't be enough."

"You're too kind to me." I passed Maria her cup and croissant, then breathed in the scent of my coffee. Unable to help myself, I drank a sip. It was *perfect.*

"So," Sue said as I took another drink. "How long until you two have a baby in the oven?"

I choked, spraying foam and crema everywhere. Maria made a similar noise from beside me, thumping at her chest to clear her throat. Sue sputtered with laughter as we tried to compose ourselves, then leaned all of her weight on the counter, barely able to hold herself upright.

"Sue!" Sturgill chastised from the kitchen. "Leave them alone!"

She only laughed louder, falling to the floor as she tried to wipe a tear from her eye. "Your faces!" she got out before cackling wordlessly.

Maria cleared her throat and took a deep drink of her coffee. I reached over the counter and stole a tea towel, using it to wipe my face free of foam before throwing it down at Sue. Again, it only made her amusement increase.

I grabbed Maria's hand. "Let's go catch that sunrise. The owner of this coffee shop is a lunatic."

Maria's face was bright red. She nodded, not meeting my gaze as Sue's chortles trailed our departure.

My heart and mind raced as we sat on the shore, watching the sun's glow rise over the horizon. When its orange face finally came into view, I turned to Maria. She stared at it, her lips pursed and eyes crinkled in thought.

I gathered my courage. "Do you want children, Maria? Eventually, I mean."

She started, her head hanging to the side as she turned to look at me.

"I do . . . eventually." She swirled her cup. "What about you? Do you want kids?"

It was something I had never really considered in my previous life. There were fleeting thoughts, sure, but bringing a child into that world seemed almost . . . irresponsible.

Here, though. In Tropica . . .

Each time I saw Paul, the thought of having a son or daughter came to mind. When my eyes drifted from the rising sun to Maria's freckled face, the answer was simple.

"I'd love to have children, or at least one child." I rubbed the back of my head. "I haven't given it too much thought, to be honest, but I know I'd love having a kid, especially with the right person."

"The right person, huh?" She rubbed her chin. "It's a shame Sue is spoken for, then. I can't think of anyone else with the same cruel sense of humor as you."

It was so unexpected that I almost choked on my coffee again. "Oh, *ha-ha.* If we're talking degenerate senses of humor, you're just as bad as she is."

She grinned. "I suppose I am. You might have to settle for me, then. A pity."

I flicked part of my croissant at her. She caught it, dipped it in her coffee, then placed it in her mouth as she shot me a wink.

I looked out at the ocean. The sun was almost entirely visible now, only a small section remaining hidden by the horizon. "So . . . I have an awkward question."

"More awkward than Sue asking us when we were going to procreate?"

I snorted. "No, not quite that bad. Is there, uh . . . contraception here? In this world, I mean?"

I chanced a glance at her.

She stared back, her face scrunched in confusion. "Contraception? What's that?"

"You know—like methods to stop someone getting pregnant."

"Oh!" She laughed, covering her mouth with one hand. "I honestly forget you're not from here sometimes—you have the weirdest little gaps in your knowledge." She shook her head, smirking. "There are two different teas, one to stop you getting pregnant, the other to . . . stop a pregnancy." She turned her body to face me, suddenly serious. "Maybe we should have talked about this earlier. My mom has been preparing the former for me for the last month or more, so there is little chance of anything happening. If it does, though, I don't believe in taking something to 'take care of it.' Even if it's not the perfect time, I would never get rid of a blessing like that, especially with the . . . side effect."

"Side effect?"

She nodded seriously. "It can hurt your chance of having a kid later. Other people can do what they like, but it's not something I could ever do."

I held up both hands. "I'm not the kind of man that would pressure anyone to do that."

Her face relaxed, and she reached a hand out to squeeze my knee. "I know you're not, Fischer, but thank you for voicing it."

I smiled at her, the glow of her cheeks threatening to take both my breath and all conscious thought away.

I forced myself to continue. "In a perfect world, I'd like to wait until all of this churchy-culty bullshit is over, but I know these things don't always wait for the right time."

"Same. As much as I agree with Barry's plan and think it's the best path for everyone's safety, I don't relish the thought of bringing a child into it." She gave me a haughty look. "I'm also not so sure about you yet."

I nodded. "Understandable. I'd be having second thoughts too after seeing all that weight George has lost. He's looking damn *fit.* Like a fine wine, only getting better as it ages—"

She raised her hand to stop me. "Okay, that's the line. He's still about twenty years older than me, Fischer."

I shot her a wink. "How about this, then: we revisit this conversation after Barry is finished making us all gods or whatever? If something happens before that, though, we'll do the best that we can." I squeezed her hand. "Together."

The smile she rewarded me with seemed brighter than the rising sun, and she nodded, making her hair bounce against her face. She took my half-finished cup of coffee from my other hand, put it on the sand, and crawled into my arms. Our proximity made a barrage of emotions wash over me. I reveled in them, squeezing her tighter.

The joy coursing through me made me want to voice the other thing that had been tugging at my awareness lately. Against my better judgment, I decided to let it out.

"I wanted to mention something else, too," I said, my stomach fluttering suddenly. "I worried it was a bit . . . forward, but considering the conversation we just had, it doesn't seem so bad."

"What is it?" she asked, looking up at me.

Gods, she was beautiful.

I chewed my cheek. "Let me preface this by saying this is probably just me getting caught up in my feelings, so keep that in mind if it seems a bit . . ."

She reached a hand up toward my face. I thought she'd caress my cheek or run a hand through my hair, but she flicked the tip of my nose and shook her head at me with a bemused smile.

"Fischer. We just had a conversation about the possibility of having a child. If that doesn't scare me away, what could?"

I raised a finger to protest, then snorted. "All right, that's fair play. It's just . . ."

"Out with it." She tapped me on the nose again. "Or else I'll give you another flicking."

I ran a hand through her hair, fighting the urge to change the subject by kissing her. "Okay. I wanted to ask you about, er . . . moving in with me."

Her eyes opened just a little wider, so I rushed to explain the rest of my thoughts.

"I know it's terrible timing with your father, and having you move in might be the thing that finally gives him a conniption, so I don't think we *should* . . ." I shook my head. "What am I even saying?" I ran both hands over my face, searching for the right words. "I guess what I mean is that I'd love for you to move in when the time is right, and I wish it could be now."

Her hand reached up again as she stared into my eyes, and this time it did come to rest on my cheek. "You're becoming an issue, Fischer."

I quirked an eyebrow. "Why?"

"Because everything you say only makes me fall for you more."

I blew air from my nose, giving her a confused smile. "How does the word salad I just threw at you make you more in love with me?"

"Because you are thoughtful, caring, and kind. Even to my dad, who is a grumpy, unreasonable man that held a scythe to your neck the first time you met him."

She wrapped her arms around me.

"Despite how much of a menace he is, I'm quite fond of my dad. As such, I don't want to send him over the edge by moving in with a heretical fisher." She pulled her head back to look into my eyes. " . . . *yet.* I'd love to move in with you when the time is right."

She pulled herself in again, holding me so tight that I thought she may never let go. In that moment, with the scent of her hair wafting up and her slight body held in my arms, I wished she never did.

CHAPTER SEVENTY

HATCHLING

In the fading afternoon light, Cinnamon woke from a wonderful nap atop the headland rocks. She stretched her body out, lounging in the cushions comprising the nest she lay in. The female pelican hatchling she was curled around let out a soft peep, complaining at being woken. Cinnamon peered out at her charge, taking in the down covering the pelican's entire body. It was almost the same color as her own cinnamon fur, and was, frustratingly, even softer. The bird had grown an incredible amount over the last week or so since her hatching and was now half as big as Cinnamon.

Has it really been a week already? Cinnamon wondered.

The days had blurred into one, her latent maternal instincts kicking in and letting her focus on nothing but the life dependent on her. Those same instincts were the reason she had kept the hatchling isolated—though she knew not why, she was certain that keeping her charge unsocialized for the first few weeks of life was integral to development.

As much as Cinnamon loved doing pranks on others and being a general nuisance, she was forced to admit that nurturing the baby bird currently falling back asleep was even more rewarding. Knowing it was time for another feeding soon, Cinnamon nudged the pelican's head. The hatchling peeped in protest, but Cinnamon persisted, nudging her again.

With perfect timing, Bill came soaring up over the side of the rock. The hatchling, who looked at Cinnamon with what she thought was certainly annoyance, perked up immediately. She opened her bill, facing her wide-open maw toward Warrant Officer Williams. He landed beside her, stretched his crop, then started dropping baitfish in. She ate each one whole as fast as they came, somehow fitting them into her tiny, down-covered body.

Cinnamon had been amazed the first time she saw how much food such a small bird could eat, but quickly grew used to it.

When the steady stream of baitfish from Bill came to an end, the hatchling settled down, lowering herself into a rather cute little loaf. Bill reached back, ruffled through the feathers of his back, and withdrew a stalk of sugarcane. He held it out to Cinnamon, and she happily accepted, letting out a thankful squeak as she munched on the delicious treat.

Bill nodded once, then turned and took flight, heading back out to sea.

* * *

A full moon rose high above us, shining its light across the landscape. The campfire's flames licked at the logs within it, orange tingeing our surroundings with each flicker. Each night for the past two weeks since Maria and I had discussed moving in, we'd practiced my cooking. Well, I'd been practicing, but she was ever by my side. Tonight was no different.

No one had spoken since the meal began; the only sounds to be heard were the churning ocean and my animal pals' enthusiastic crunching as they bit down into golden crumbs. Claws, Pistachio, and Rocky were all partaking, each as intent as the next.

"Cheers," Maria said, holding out a strip of deep-fried fish.

"Cheers!" I tapped mine to hers, and we bit down at the same time.

I had worried that the taste of the chi-enhanced fish would lose its luster once I got used to it. Each meal since, this one included, proved just how wrong I was. The flavor exploded across my taste buds, the fish's juices mixing with the crumbs and tallow it was fried in. As I chewed the mouthful, I breathed in through my nose. The sweet air was a perfect companion to the savory bombardment assaulting my senses, and I ate each bite slowly, lingering in the moment as long as possible.

A familiar chi signature crawled toward us from the west, and the moment I recognized it, I spun. "Sergeant Snips! Where have you been, missy?"

I hadn't seen my favorite crab in literally weeks. Knowing that she was likely off doing some churchy stuff, I didn't poke my nose into it. But now that she was back, a longing to rub her sturdy carapace rose up within me. I hadn't realized how much I missed her.

"Snips?" Maria demanded, whirling. "She's here?"

Sergeant Snips, my first animal pal and trusty guard crab, ambled forward over the sand.

The moment I saw her, I sat up straight. "Snips? Are you okay?"

She looked . . . haggard. Like she hadn't slept in days. Her movements were sluggish, and she gave me a lazy wave of one claw as she crawled up and into my lap. The moment she got there, she collapsed, blowing happy bubbles.

Claws dashed forward and gave her a strip of fish. I patted Snips's head softly as she took her first bite. The moment the chi-enhanced food hit her mouth, her demeanor shifted. She bolted upright, staring up at me with her single eye. In a blur, she devoured the rest of it.

"Good?" I asked.

She nodded with her entire body, clearly reenergized by the essence-packed morsel.

"So," I drawled. "Can you tell me where you've been?"

She blew happy yet negative bubbles, making me laugh.

"Fair enough. Well, I'm glad you're back."

She made a so-so gesture with her claw.

"You have to go again?"

Sorrowful bubbles.

"You don't have to apologize, Snips. You are your own crab, and you can do as you please." I stroked the top of her head.

"Just come home to us when you're done," Maria said. "We miss you when you're gone."

She nodded, climbing over into Maria's lap and happily receiving her pats.

A loud honk drew my attention, and I whirled toward it.

"Bill! I was wondering where you were. There's fish to . . ." I trailed off, seeing the two creatures on his back.

Cinnamon's ears were alert as she sat up, wiggling her little body in excitement. Sitting down before her, an unrecognizable bird peered out at the world with curiosity. The last time I'd seen the bird, she looked like a plucked lorikeet.

Now, she was . . . well, she looked like a small pelican.

Soft down the same color as Cinnamon's fur covered most of her body, interspersed with small brown feathers that grew from her head, chest, and around her wings. Most impressive was her size. She stood up and hopped from Bill's back under Cinnamon's guidance—she was already bigger than the bunny.

"I knew baby birds grew quickly, but damn . . ." Maria said, a look of shock on her face that mirrored my own thoughts.

Bill puffed his chest out in pride, but it was nothing compared to Cinnamon. She looked downright smug, her eyes twinkling and head held high.

"To what do we owe the pleasure?" I asked. "I thought we were banned from seeing your child. You've chased me away every time I came to check up on things."

Bill actually blushed, a pink tone rising to his yellow pouch. With a reassuring paw resting over the hatchling's back, Cinnamon pointed another toward us. I followed the gesture; she was pointing directly at the small pile of deep-fried fish.

My eyes widened. "For her . . . ?"

Cinnamon nodded, her eyes laced with anticipation. Cocking my head to the side, I extended my awareness toward the adolescent pelican. Two weeks spent moving chi around while cooking had given me an unforeseen level of control over the essence flooding the world, and I channeled every ounce of experience I'd gained. Cinnamon and Bill's cores—and the power held within—drew me in, but I brushed past them, homing in on the curious bird. There was no core present—no nexus of power holding chi. I furrowed my forehead, digging deeper, sharpening my attention, focusing . . . *there.*

Within her body, only marginally stronger than the chi flowing all around us, power circulated. Given time, she would ascend if they kept nurturing and feeding her, but Cinnamon thought that now was the time to force the issue.

"You're positive, Cinnamon?"

She nodded again, letting out a peep filled with certainty.

"You too, Bill?"

He dipped his head, just as sure.

Without another word, I plucked some chi-enhanced fish from the pile, broke a bit off, and flicked it toward them. Bill caught it from the air and slowly lowered it down to his adopted daughter. Sensing a meal, she opened wide, letting out a half-honk, half peep as she awaited the morsel. Bill dropped it, and she ate it whole. I held my breath, watching the hatchling. My heart pounded in my ears, the only sound I registered as the seconds stretched on. She opened her bill again to beg for more food, and just as I thought it may have not worked, she froze. Her head darted back, going still as her eyes glazed over.

And then I felt it.

The chi held within the food had already spread throughout most of her body. All of it flowed toward her abdomen, even now filling the core I could feel coming into existence. When that nexus of power was almost filled to bursting, it solidified. A pulse came from her, flooding over the landscape and making an immutable sense of euphoria swell within me.

My skin tingled in the aftermath, and just as I started to wonder about the effect of awakening an adolescent, a blinding light shone from across the fire. As was becoming a frequent occurrence for me, time slowed to a crawl. The chi within the pelican vibrated as it bloomed, spreading to encompass every last feather on her tiny frame.

It didn't stop there.

Her form shifted as ligaments extended and bones grew. With each adjustment, she became more . . . *real.* Her plumage sprouted in earnest, and it was as if each feather that finished growing was a piece of a puzzle slipping into place. When the change was finished, I was left with a feeling of contentment, like the world was more whole.

I held up a hand, squinting against the dazzling gleam as time returned to normal. Even before the light disappeared, I *knew* what I'd find.

With the blinding flash withdrawing, the fire's orange glow and the full moon above us once more lit our surroundings. A now fully grown pelican sat between Bill and Cinnamon, looking cartoonishly perplexed. Her feathers were a dark brown yet had a sheen that reflected the moon's light. Her body was a slightly different shape to Bill's; she was smaller, her features more feminine.

The newly awakened bird looked at Bill, Cinnamon, the rest of the gang, and then me.

"*Honk . . . ?*"

I couldn't help laughing at the sheer bewilderment on her face. "I'm as confused as you are."

Her eyes went vacant as she stared off into the distance with a look of supreme discomfort, as if the knowledge of ten thousand scholars flowed into her. It was reminiscent of those videos back on Earth of someone putting sliced cheese on a cat, making them malfunction. She leaned back, and if not for Cinnamon's guiding paw, would have fallen over. All of my animal pals were gravitating toward her, slowly advancing.

"Claws," I said, making the otter's head dart my way and cock to the side. "Sorry, but would you mind going to get Ellis? He'll complain for a week if we don't at least invite him to whatever is happening."

Her eyes sparkled at the task, and after a serious chirp, she tore off across the sand with lightning flowing from her legs.

"Is she getting faster?" Maria asked.

She was gone in the blink of an eye, only dust remaining to tell of her passing.

"I think so . . ." I replied, smiling at the overenthusiastic otter.

Everything. The pelican was learning . . . *everything.* It poured into her with unerring incessancy, each detail finding a place to settle within her awareness. It was enlightening, marvelous, and objectively uncomfortable. She was only vaguely aware of her body tilting backward, her brain too occupied to worry about trivial details like spatial positioning.

. . . Spatial positioning?

The words, unfortunately, made sense. A disorienting flash of images and ideas raced through her mind's eye simultaneously, firmly slamming into place the knowledge of both concepts.

Something caught her. No, not something—someone. A . . . bunny. The word made a slew of relevant information jump out at her. Adolescent rabbit. Mammal. Herbivore. Burrower. Low intelligence. The bunny had caught her; not a regular rabbit, then.

Awakened.

Again, a deluge of information jumped out. Awakened. Spirit animal. Enhanced cognition. On the path of ascension. It was what she was—what she had become.

Why was the bunny helping her, though? Spirit animals were . . . self-serving. More knowledge slid forward. Memories of the past weeks. The bunny had been there from the beginning. Warming her. Caring for her. The bunny, a creature of an entirely different species, had acted as her mother. Even now, the mammal held her body with tenderness and support.

It made her feel . . . nice. With what little attention she could spare, she leaned her head down, resting it atop the small bunny.

Cinnamon . . .

CHAPTER SEVENTY-ONE

AN UNLIKELY PAIR

Sequestered deep beneath the surface of Tropica, a grin came to Ellis's face.

"Wondrous . . ." he said to himself, checking the results again.

He carefully removed the section of bone from the acid with a metal tong, and just as he went to put it in the cleansing mixture, the door was thrown open. Claws dashed into the room, a whirl of energy and fur. She stood there looking frazzled, gesturing out of the room and chirping insistently. It had something to do with . . . food? Ellis ignored her attempted distraction.

"Impeccable timing!" He scooped her up in his arms. "I was just thinking of getting Theo to bounce my theories off of, but you will do."

Claws began to chirp something, but he cut her off; he had to put voice to the words lest they bounce around his head indefinitely.

"My original theory—that the spirit beast's remains offered some sort of protection—were correct! I had thought I was wrong for a time, unable to replicate the conditions as I was." He lifted Claws up, bringing them eye to eye. "The secret was moisture, Claws! *Moisture!*" He laughed at himself. "How foolish a mistake—the environment the spirit beast was sealed within, you see? High humidity and low air circulation. I should have started by replicating the same conditions from the get. I suspect it was semi-aquatic, which makes sense why it was located near Tropica Village's coastal flats. If not for the scales, I would have assumed it to be a species of newt—or perhaps it is, just with a scale evolution it unlocked when taking steps on the path of ascension—"

Claws chirped indignantly, pushing off his chest and trying to get away.

Ellis sighed, shaking his head with a rueful smile. "I suppose you are correct—I am getting quite off topic." He let go of her and rubbed his chin. "Where was I . . . ? Ah, yes—the protective properties. When it is exposed to water, it radiates a protective aura. Do you recall how the pickaxes were not as spoiled as they should have been? The metal should have rusted away entirely, the handles turned to dust."

Corporal Claws leaped back up. Ellis caught her. "Ah, you are as excited as I, Claws? As expected of one of Fischer's spirit beasts. Your intellect knows no—"

Claws reached into his pocket, withdrew his notepad, and slapped him across the face with it. She chirped again, so loud that the very walls seemed to shake.

Ellis recoiled. "W-what . . . ?"

She chirped again, pointed at the notepad, then out the door.

"There . . . is there something to record?"

Yes, she chirped, rolling her eyes and sagging her shoulders.

He pouted. "Well, you could have just said that—there was no need to assault me."

Claws's eyebrow twitched, and she smacked him with the notepad again.

When Claws finally arrived with Ellis in tow, my new pelican pal was having an existential crisis. Both she and Cinnamon sat in my lap, the former staring into space like a shellshocked war vet, the latter rubbing the pelican's brown plumage with calming repetition.

Ellis halted as he entered the firelight. His brow furrowed and pointed toward my lap. "That is . . . not Bill."

I smirked at him. "Sharp as ever, mate."

In response, Bill swooped down and landed before me. A pile of fish spilled from his mouth, and he looked at the newly ascended pelican with anticipation. She didn't respond. I noticed her leaning into Cinnamon's pets, so I started stroking her too, running my fingers along the back of her head. The feathers there were unbelievably soft.

I glanced back up at Ellis just in time to see the realization strike him.

"The hatchling?" he asked, his hand reaching for his pocket.

"Yeah, mate. The hatchling. I gave her some of my chi-enhanced fish."

Ellis scrawled everything down with exacting detail as I recounted the night's events. He probed with countless questions; I answered them as best as I could. By the time we finished speaking, the pelican was looking much more sure of herself.

"Are you okay?" I asked, stroking her neck.

She let out a hesitant honk that was laden with trepidation.

"There's no rush." I smiled down at her. "Take all the time you need."

She hopped off my lap and shook her body, her feathers fluffing out. When she saw the pile of fish Bill had dumped onto the sand, she slowly turned toward me, the question clear in her body language.

I laughed. "You can have as much as you like. Bill here got that for you while you were . . . uh . . . Were you learning? Is that why you were silent for so long?"

She nodded, still gazing at the fish. Bill, seeing her hesitation, hopped over, picked one up, and lobbed it to her. She caught it from the air instinctively, wobbled her head so it aligned in her pouch, then swallowed it whole. Seeing her animalistic instincts, I felt a pang of guilt.

She had still been a hatchling a mere hour ago, and here I was grilling her with questions.

"Sorry to be a pain, Ellis, but is it all right if we leave it there for tonight?"

"Yes, that is fine."

"I know you're probably wanting to ask more—wait, what?" I raised a brow. "It's . . . fine?"

"Yes," he replied, closing his notepad and sliding it into a pocket. "I was working on something and I would like to return to it. Goodnight, everyone."

He turned and jogged away, not sparing us another glance. Maria and I shared a look, both similarly confused.

"Claws . . ." I said. "What was Ellis working on?"

She let out a non-committal chirp, so I spun to find her. She was sitting on the sand beside the pile of food, one baitfish in each forepaw as she happily crunched down on them.

"Never mind," I said, smiling. "Who wants more fried fish?"

A chorus of agreement met me, so I stood and stretched before making my way over to the fire.

"What about you, Private Pelly?" I asked, watching the brown pelican. "Do you want some more?"

I tried to keep my face straight as I looked around the circle, gauging everyone's reactions.

"Just like that, huh?" Maria asked, quirking an eyebrow. "You're not even gonna ask if she has one already before giving her one of your weirdo names?"

"First of all," I replied, holding up a finger. "There's no way Cinnamon gave her a name without me. Second, and most important, how *dare* you insult Private Pelly's beautiful, charming, and downright cute name? Can you believe the audacity of this woman, Cinnamon?"

I turned to the bunny in question, who was staring at me with an unreadable gaze. "Wait . . . you didn't already give her a name, did you?"

She shook her head slowly. A twinkle entered her eye, and she turned to look at Pelly's brown feathers, staring at the moonlight reflecting from them. A soft peep came from her throat, sounding remarkably like *Pelly.*

Bill threw his wings wide and raised his head toward the sky. He unleashed a mighty honk, broadcasting his approval for everyone to hear.

"That settles it," I said, bending to rub her head. "Welcome to our little family, Private Pelly."

Despite her obvious exhaustion following the transformation, she preened, her feathers puffing up around Cinnamon's reassuring paw.

I stepped from my living room beneath a purple sky. Sunrise was so far off that even the predawn light had yet to arrive, but that didn't stop Borks and I.

"Ready to go?" I asked.

He barked, his tail wagging.

"Race you there!"

I took off, leaving a trail of sand and accusatory barks in my wake. With each stride, I grew more awake, and by the time I arrived in the clearing, my head was clear. I took a deep breath of the humid forest air.

"Good morning, Lemon."

Her leaves shook in greeting, then paused. A twig bent to point behind me.

"Huh? What's up—"

Borks slammed into me from behind, launching me forward. We slid along the grass. He tried to kick off my back, but I spun, grabbing him.

"Not so fast, you little gremlin!" I dug my fingers into his neck, giving him the worst punishment of all—a good tickle.

He wriggled and tried to get away, but my grip was as firm as my smile was wide. After only a few seconds, I let him go. He tore off, sprinting around the clearing as he suffered from an acute case of the zoomies. Round and round he ran, barking at me and darting in with false charges to bait me into chasing him.

I obliged.

"Think you're fast enough for me, Borks?" I roared, kicking off the base of Lemon's sturdy trunk.

The white of his eyes became visible as he looked back and saw me right on his tail. I let the game drag on, repeatedly grabbing at his back half before falling back. I had no idea how long we played for, but by the time we were finished, light shades of pink colored the purple sky. Borks collapsed to his back, his stomach exposed and tongue lolling from his mouth.

"Truce," I said, collapsing to the clearing beside him.

When he'd caught his breath, Borks nipped at my arm playfully, and I laughed, batting him away. I stared up at the lemon tree above us. As always, it was laden with yellow citrus, but given the early morning hour, the pollinators were absent. It made the scene seem lifeless in comparison.

"I haven't seen Bumblebro and Queen Bee in a while," I mused. "Let's go see how they're doing before we get started."

We approached in silence, not wanting to rouse the resting insects. As with the trees, the hives were quiet; not a single bee flew in or out. Curious if they'd made any headway with the hive I'd built, I lifted the lid to the top chamber. To my utter astonishment, there was honeycomb. I raised both eyebrows, and Borks cocked his head to the side. I replaced the lid, then lifted the first chamber. The next one down was empty, and I nodded—it hadn't been that long, so it made sense. Unable to help myself, I put the first chamber down and lifted the second, revealing what would usually be the brood box. I froze, not believing my eyes.

There was comb in the brood box too, but unlike the top chamber, it was absolutely *filled.*

"What the . . ."

I carefully lifted a tray free, peering down at the honeycomb. One corner of the tray was a different color, so I leaned in closer. Within the comb there, only taking up a dozen or so of the hexes, were fully developed pupae.

"Queen Bee is producing more workers in here, huh?"

I replaced the tray and lifted another with just as much care, curiosity overtaking me. A small shape at the bottom of the brood box caught my attention, and I paused. Inadvertently, my awareness shot down toward it.

Not just a small shape, I realized.

It was Bumblebro and Queen Bee, resting so close beside each other that their abdomens touched. They stirred, either sensing my attention or being woken by the light leeching in. Both their wings twitched as they looked up toward me.

Then, they exploded into motion.

Queen Bee's face flushed, which I didn't even know bees could do, and she darted from view, her wings vibrating in agitation.

"What the—whoa!" I darted my head to the side, dodging Bumblebro's charge. "Sorry, Bumblebro!" I dodged again. "I didn't mean to startle you!"

He flew at me one last time, stopping directly before my face. He let out a low drone, clearly pissed, then flew down to the tray in my hand, staring up at me defiantly as he buzzed his wings.

"Er . . . sorry?" I put it back, and the moment it was in place, he darted over to the chambers I'd set on the ground.

"*Bzzz!*"

"My bad, Bumblebro." I put them back on, and he raced down to the entrance, heading back inside.

His head poked out of the hole, and he shook it, letting out one more buzz of disapproval. With that, he was gone, leaving me and Borks alone beneath the forest canopy. He stared up at me with his ears pinned back.

I leaned down to whisper, "I think we saw something we shouldn't have . . ."

"*Bzzz!*" Bumblebro complained from within the hive.

I held up both hands in surrender and backed away. Borks followed suit, his ears still pinned back. When we were a few meters from the hive, we turned and made our way back toward the clearing.

"If anyone asks, we saw nothing."

He let out a soft *ruff,* darting glances back at the hive as we went.

The moment we got back to the clearing, I plucked two lemons from the tree and sat down on the grass.

"Ready to test this theory, Borks?"

Just as happy to forget our foolish foray toward the hive, he nodded, staring at the citrus intently.

I sat down, crossed my legs, and sent my awareness down into the fruit—just in time for something mighty to fall from the heavens and strike the back of my head.

CHAPTER SEVENTY-TWO

ARTS AND CRAFTS

Something light smacked into my back, making a noise like sheets flapping in the wind. Borks let out a yelp and dashed away at incredible speed, his back legs trying to overtake the front ones. When my assailant let out a panicked honk, I knew what had fallen from the heavens to strike me down.

". . . Pelly?"

She shook her body, puffing her feathers out as she got back to her feet. I raised an eyebrow at Borks, who had run to the other side of the clearing in his retreat. He was sniffing a bush and pointedly ignoring me, pretending he hadn't just fled for his life from a pelican half his size.

"You all good, Pelly?" I asked, turning back toward her.

She let out an embarrassed honk, so I gave her a kind smile. "Were you trying out your wings?"

She nodded.

"Let me guess—you were coming to say good morning?"

Again, she nodded, even more bashful this time.

"Well, I'm glad I could break your fall. Don't feel bad. If me or Borks here tried to fly, we'd probably hit the ground face-first."

Borks was slowly making his way back toward us, sniffing everything he passed in an attempt at nonchalance. I rolled my eyes at him, letting him know I knew what he was up to.

"Wanna see something cool, Pelly?" I asked, pointing down.

This got her attention. She waddled over, peering at the objects before me.

"Lemons. You know that food I gave you last night? I want to try doing the same thing with this fruit—shifting the chi so one is empty, while the other has twice the concentration."

Her intelligent eyes sparkled, and I could practically see the thoughts whirling through her mind.

"Yeah . . . if it works, it could change every—"

"Fischer!" a feminine voice called out through the forest.

It made my heart jump. "Over here!" I yelled back. "In Lemon's clearing!"

There was silence for a moment, then her voice came again, much closer this time. "I swear on all the gods, Fischer—if you're trying to make edible lemons without me, I'll pluck your feathers and string you up to a particularly thorny tree. Then,

I'll . . ." she trailed off as she reached the clearing and caught sight of Pelly. "Oh . . . Pelly. Good morning, sweetie. Did you sleep well?"

Pelly took a step closer to me, keeping a wary eye on Maria.

I roared a laugh. "She was just being hyperbolic, Pelly. She wasn't going to pluck me, nor would she hurt you."

Maria clutched a hand to her chest, and I thought she might cry as she watched Pelly sidle even closer.

"Come give Pelly some pats in apology," I suggested.

Maria skipped forward. "I really am sorry, girl. I didn't mean to startle you."

Pelly was hesitant at first, but then Maria found the right spot. Her feathered head tilted to the side, giving Maria even better access to the back of her neck.

"Ohhh, you like that, do you?" Maria giggled. "Your feathers are so soft . . ." She turned to smile at me. But then she caught sight of the lemons. "Hey! You *were* creating lemons without me!"

I held up both hands in surrender. "It was just a trial run! Borks and I woke up early and I didn't want to wake you."

She appeared unconvinced.

"Plus," I continued, "it might have upset Roger if I came to get you, right? We wouldn't want that . . ."

Her brow lowered into a scowl. "You can make some lemons, then have Sue make some treats from them as an apology. I'll accept no less than five pastries!"

I made my face go impassive. "Best I can do is four pastries."

"Oooh, you . . ." She shook a finger at me. "You're playing with fire, mister."

I let out an exaggerated sigh. "Ah, they warned me of dating noble-born women. Fine, five pastries it is."

She snorted in a very non-ladylike manner. "If it gets me sugary treats, you can say what you like about my lineage—lie or not."

I grinned at her pragmatism. "Good morning, by the way."

"Yes, yes—good morning." She leaned down and kissed me on the forehead. "So, did you try yet?"

"Not yet. I was about to when a certain pelican crashed down from above."

Pelly let out a soft, apologetic honk.

"Aww." Maria scooped her up. "You don't need to say sorry for an honest mistake."

The pelican still appeared chastened, so I thought to offer a distraction. "Pelly, have you met my tree friend?"

She cocked her head at me, clearly not understanding.

Not missing a beat, one of Lemon's roots sprouted from the ground. It rose to the height of Pelly and Maria, then gave them a curt nod. Pelly flapped her arms and jumped from Maria's arms, not once taking her eyes from the root. She let out a questioning honk, and Lemon retracted part of the root until it was once more at Pelly's height. They proceeded to have a conversation consisting of honks, nods, and the subtle movement of leaves.

Happy to let them go, I cleared my throat, took a deep breath, and picked up the lemons before me. Sensing I was about to begin, Maria sat beside me and Borks flopped into her lap.

She gave me a nod. "You've got this."

I returned the gesture, then focused on the lemons. Immediately, I could feel their power. It was . . . damn, they were strong. Much stronger than I'd thought. I hadn't sent my awareness into one since my last advancement, but now that I was feeling them out, I suspected a single fruit had the ability to awaken multiple people.

Why hadn't it worked on Trent, then?

Ellis had told me that they'd given him non-stop drinks of sugarcane juice and lemonade, yet none of them had caused him to awaken. It was . . . weird.

I wonder if the fish worked?

Realizing I was getting off track, I shook my head and returned my attention to the task at hand.

Chi swirled from my core, traveling along my right arm and into the fruit held there. I imagined it flowing from right to left, going through the lemon and taking its chi with it. It was harder than with the fish, perhaps because they were in their natural form. If not for my practice over the past two weeks, the test would have been a complete failure.

A small grin tugged at my lips.

Luckily for me, I *had* been practicing. The lemon's chi was picked up by the essence I was circulating, traveling into the other fruit. I imagined each strand detaching from mine when it reached the second lemon; it did so. Doing all the actions simultaneously was like juggling four balls at once, and a single bead of sweat dripped down my face. I ignored it, focusing entirely on the transference of power. Despite the effort of will required to concentrate the chi, it was incongruously relaxing. My breaths slowed as the process continued, my mind and body slipping into a zen-like state.

I had no idea how long it took, but when it was done, something tugged at my awareness and I was returned to the present as if waking from a dream. My arms tingled in a pleasant manner as I squinted out at the world, marveling at the beautiful colors of the coming dawn that peeked through the canopy above.

"Did . . ." Maria licked her lips. "Did it work?"

I opened my mouth to respond, but something tugged at my awareness again, an unignorable sensation I hadn't felt in weeks.

The System.

Though I'd willed the notifications to turn off, something important enough had occurred that the System demanded my attention. I considered reading it. Only for a moment, though. With a surge of will, I pushed it away.

"Not today, demon. Leave me in peace."

"Um . . ." Both Maria's eyebrows reached toward her sun-bleached hair. "Come again?"

"Oh, sorry. I was talking to the System. It was being a scoundrel." I lobbed a lemon toward her. "Catch."

She swiped it from the air, furrowing her brow. "Do you plan on only speaking in riddles today? Why can't you just . . . *Oh.*" She stared wide-eyed at the citrus in her hand. "That's . . ."

I nodded. "It worked. Better than I could have imagined."

"I've not felt it before." She held the lemon up reverently. "Not like this, anyway . . ."

"It confirmed something I had suspected from the fish."

Borks cocked his head at me, so I continued.

"Transferring the chi isn't a one-to-one deal. It has an additive effect of several orders of magnitude. It was hard to tell with the fish, but that's why it's so potent. But that lemon . . ." I pointed at the fruit Maria was cupping in both hands. "*That* has some serious pew-pew power."

Maria sighed so hard she almost dropped it. "Can you not be serious for a single second?"

"Nope!" I grinned. "That's not even the most important thing, though."

"It's not?"

I hefted the other lemon. "This one has absolutely no chi—the test was a success."

Maria understood immediately. "Sue can cook with it!"

She started pumping the air with a fist. Borks got caught up in Maria's enthusiasm and ran around her in circles, barking toward the pink and purple sky above.

I got to my feet and stretched. "Shall we?" I asked, extending a hand to Maria.

She grabbed it and pulled herself up, then shot off with the momentum. "Race you!" She glanced back at me. "Come on! We have to catch Sue before the coffee rush!"

Not wasting a second, I took off after her. "Let's beat her there, Borks!"

He let out a bark, loping beside me as we trailed Maria's infectious giggles.

As I presented the lemon to Sue in the predawn light, a head shot from around the dividing wall that led to the kitchen.

"You're serious?" Sturgill's eyes were filled with need. "Another lemon?"

"Yeah, mate. One condition, though."

Sue tugged at her apron, trying and failing to appear nonchalant. "What's the condition?"

"We want to watch!" Maria said, beaming. "And Fischer requires five pastries of whatever you make—to repent for past crimes against me, you understand."

"Crimes, huh?" she asked, amusement playing over her face. "Of course, my lady. May I inquire as to what crimes he committed?"

Maria sniffed, adopting the demeanor of a slighted noble lady. "A betrayal most foul, I assure you." She leaned in close, raising a hand between me and her mouth. She spoke in a stage whisper. "He agreed to wait for me this morning before running errands, but alas, when I went to his abode—he was nowhere to be seen!"

Sue gasped, holding an indignant hand to her lips. "He didn't . . ."

Maria sighed. "It's true—I didn't want to believe it either. Ah, such are the hazards of socializing with men of ignoble birth, I suppose."

Sue nodded gravely. "I understand completely. Worry not, Maria. We'll ensure you have all the pastries necessary to take the sting out of his barbaric actions."

I snorted at the sparkle in their eyes and raised a brow at Sturgill. "Does it ever get better, mate?"

"Afraid not. Come on, you two. I already have an idea for what we can make. It's been stewing in my head since the last time you brought lemons."

Sue lifted the movable section of counter, and we followed Sturgill into the back.

"I expect a couple portions too!" Sue called as we entered the kitchen.

"Of course, dear." He rolled his eyes at us playfully as he led us toward the back of the kitchen, past sacks of flour, bags of sugar, and baskets of eggs.

"Have either of you ever made danishes?"

"I've had some, but I can't say I've made it, mate . . ."

"I've never even tried it," Maria said.

Sturgill smiled to himself as he grabbed a handful of flour and dusted it over the bench before reaching for a large wooden bowl. "Well, I'd better not disappoint, then."

Deep beneath the sands of Tropica, a crafter toiled under the orange glow of magical flames. Ellis wiped his forehead, removing beads of sweat that had sprouted there. Any other time, he would have found his perspiration miraculous; he hadn't done so since becoming a cultivator. With his gaze firmly set on his craft, however, he had no attention to spare. He removed the leather from the almost boiling liquid, and as he held it up high, a smile crossed his lips.

"Being a cultivator is almost cheating . . ." he mused aloud, the liquid's heat no match for his enhanced body.

He pinched the leather between his fingers, and judging it soft enough, he carried it over to his molding rack. There were several patches of leather there from yesterday, and after setting out his still-hot sections to dry, he picked one up from the previous day.

As he applied a small amount of pressure to it, he whistled.

"Just as the books said . . ."

It had gone rigid, making it the perfect material for his project.

In a blur, he collected the dried strips and took them to his bench. There, he gathered a pre-measured and cut panel of leather that was almost as tall as he was, and with a glint in his eyes, he began sewing the dried strips to it.

Time flew by as Ellis worked, completely engrossed by his crafting. He attached the leather panels one by one, sewing them so they overlapped. His mouth tugged up into a grin as he pulled the last stitch into place, and just as he was about to lean over and grab some straps to attach, chi surged up from his core.

It poured forth into his project, and he joined his will to it, picturing what he wanted to make in his mind. The hard lines blurred, and as it slowly sharpened back into a visible object, Ellis's wide-eyed stare was drawn into it.

Apron of the Apprentice
Uncommon
Crafted by a leatherworking apprentice, this apron provides a moderate boost to crafting.
+5 crafting

He had made countless aprons over the past week, but this was the best by far. Ellis opened his mouth to bellow his success out into the world, but then another surge of chi came forth. This time, it came from outside of his body.

You have advanced to leatherworking 25!

Ellis whirled, catching the bag of coins that spawned behind him before it could hit the ground. He took a deep breath, shuddered and grinned, then screamed at the top of his lungs. Weeks of crafting, and he had finally hit the milestone he toiled toward. As he slipped his new apron on, he turned, casting his eyes over the body of a spirit beast at the other end of his workshop.

It was time to create his magnum opus.

Surrounded by stone walls and the scents of timber and lacquer, a craftsman smiled. Particles of dust suffused the air and wood shavings littered every surface, but no matter how much chaos entered the world, Brad always found peace in woodworking.

"*Woooooooo!*" came a scream that bounced off the church's underground tunnels, shattering Brad's calm.

He glanced toward the other side of the room, locking eyes with his brother.

"Ellis," they both said, then burst into laughter.

Greg shook his head. "That scared the piss out of me."

"Me too," Brad agreed. "My mind was elsewhere."

"Well, at least Ellis is having a good time."

"How is your project going?"

"Good, I think," Greg replied. "When you get a chance, could you come check over the measurements for me?"

"One second." Brad set his tools down and strode over. "Let's have a look . . ."

Greg was sitting on a stool at his workbench, and he leaned back, letting Brad see the page he had drawn his design on. The giant net-like cage had eight panels.

Brad ran the mental math on its segments. "It looks right to me. What material are you thinking?"

"Hardwood. It'll be a pain, but necessary."

"Agreed. On the off chance the System doesn't transform it, it'll need to be made of sturdy wood to ensure it doesn't break. Is there enough time, though?"

"If I was a regular human? Probably not."

Greg shot an amused glance at Brad, who returned the same look. "Good thing we're not regular humans, then, huh?"

Greg grinned. "Aye. That it is."

"All right. I'll make half of the bars. Let me know if you alter the design."

"Will do!" Greg moved the pages aside and started gathering materials as Brad strode back to his workstation.

Deep beneath the sands of Tropica, a woman sat on the bench beside her loom. Ruby caressed her stomach absentmindedly, her thoughts drawn to the life growing within her. Pregnancy had always been a terrifying prospect, but now that she was months into it, it felt . . . natural. She could scarcely remember what it was like before, and just as she tried to recall it, a noise reverberated down the hallway, halting her thoughts in their tracks.

"*Wooooooooo!*" Ellis absolutely *screamed* from somewhere down the hall.

"Well, then," Steven said, smirking. "I guess that means Ellis was successful."

Ruby snorted. "Was he still making aprons, or has he moved onto the scales?"

"Aprons," Steven replied. "He didn't want to risk damaging the scales until he reached Leatherworking 25." One of Steven's hands drifted down to the apron Ellis had made him. "I'm not sure I'll ever get used to casually wearing clothes made by the System."

"I know what you mean," she replied, her hands still resting on her stomach and the apron that sat there.

As her eyes drifted down, it drew her vision in.

Apron of the Initiate
Uncommon
Crafted by a leatherworking initiate, this apron provides a small boost to crafting.
+2 crafting

"How is your costume going, love?" she asked, looking over at Steven. When she saw what he wore on his head, she choked. "What is *that?*"

"Oh, this?" Steven asked, his voice muffled. "It's Rocky's finished costume. Well, almost finished. Just need to make a hat." He shimmied his shoulders, making the headgear bobble.

Laughter bubbled up from Ruby's throat and spilled out into their workshop. "Please stop moving," she wheezed, her vision swimming. "You're going to make me pee myself!"

He removed it, flashing her a winning smile. "With a few more touches, we can add Rocky's costume to the finished pile."

"I don't know if I can match that level of genius," she said, wiping a tear from her eye.

He shook his head at her. "You're too humble, dear. You've always had more of an artistic flair than me."

"We'll see." Filled with inspiration, Ruby hopped down from the bench. "I suppose I can't let my husband outdo me."

She cast her gaze over her gathered materials, recalling where she was up to.

Assembly, she remembered, blowing hair from her face.

As much as she enjoyed being pregnant, she couldn't wait for her memory to return to normal. Even becoming a cultivator hadn't saved her from "baby brain." Focusing on the myriad objects strewn over her table, she resumed crafting Snips's costume.

In the capital city of Gormona, in a no longer abandoned room high above the castle, a sleepy guard smiled. He had first woken this morning as the purple light of predawn streamed in through a slim window. Rather than get up, he remained lounged on his bed of choice—an ancient artifact with a dip that made it perfect for napping in. He slipped in and out of consciousness, each time he woke just as pleasant as the last. With a content sigh, he slipped back to sleep once more.

The next time his consciousness returned, the sun had risen. It shone in through the window, and just as Deklan was considering blocking it out with a raised gauntlet, the light disappeared.

"Ahhh," he sighed, relaxing once more.

But then the sun returned. It beamed down on his closed eyes. His hand twitched, wanting to move and block it out. As before, the sun disappeared again.

"The hells . . . ?"

He cracked an eye. The scene only confused him more. The sky visible through the window was still the deep purple of predawn, the sun nowhere to be seen. Just as he began to consider that he'd dreamed the whole affair, the invading light bloomed once more. The entire room lit, a bright white light bouncing off the stone walls.

Deklan rolled from his favored sleeping spot, squinting at the room as he tried to find the source of the strange illumination. He stood there for a long moment, getting more and more confused each time it blinked on and off. Eventually, he noticed that one corner of the room was brighter than the others. He slipped through the artifacts, heading in that direction. It was completely blocked off at one point, so he crawled beneath the relics, struggling to fit his armored body through the winding maze of metal legs.

He reached a gap where he could stand, so he got to his feet, leveraging his arms to pull himself skyward. The moment he was upright, the artifact before him shone. A thin strip of illumination peeked through around the edges of a rectangular screen. As he squinted at it, he realized something had been put there to cover most of the light source.

He removed a gauntlet and scratched at it with a finger. It was . . . paper. Someone had wet black sheets of the stuff, layering it over the screen like the royal children would sometimes do to make papier-mâché. The paper peeled back in a single sheet, easily detaching.

As if sensing that it was once more visible, the light shining from the screen dimmed, revealing a series of printed lines. Just as with the other artifact, Deklan could read them. He focused on the last line there, cocking his head to the side as he tried to grasp its meaning.

New ascension milestone! Fischer has learned Chi Manipulation.

"Fischer . . . ?" Deklan scratched his head. "Who's that?"

He stretched his arms toward the roof, letting out a long groan of contentment. His back cracked, making a small smile spread over his face.

"I suppose I should let the king know . . ."

CHAPTER SEVENTY-THREE

ADVERSE EFFECTS

Beneath the sandy soil surrounding Tropica Village, a prince woke from a restful sleep.

He wished he hadn't.

The moment he was conscious, the storm of thoughts returned. They crashed down on Trent like a tidal wave. Each day since he'd been turned into a cultivator was worse than the last, the unbearable weight of knowledge only ever increasing. He sat up, rubbing his eyes and willing the thoughts to leave him be.

They didn't—they never did.

He began pacing the room, his legs striding of their own accord. The movement helped him sort through the worries assaulting him, even if only a little. He sighed, willing his body to calm as he admitted something to himself for what must have been the hundredth time: for most of his life, Trent had been a moron. *Worse* than a moron. He was cruel, selfish, and petty. Knowing that these traits were born of his own mental inadequacies did nothing to quell the embarrassment and shame.

For the barest of moments, a light shone through the storm within him. Perhaps there was time for him to right the wrongs. He was still relatively young, after all. He could return to the capital and use his newly attained intelligence to benefit the crown and citizens alike. Reality came crashing in on him, snuffing out that ray of hope.

He was a *cultivator.*

The villagers, these *cult* members, had turned him into a reviled being. His lip twitched up into a snarl, both because of what they had done to him and for who he had been.

"Good morning, Trent," came a familiar voice from the bars of his cell.

Trent glared at Keith, channeling every ounce of loathing toward his traitorous cousin. "What do you want?"

Keith raised an eyebrow. "I brought you breakfast. What happened to the man that was always so keen for his morning sweets?"

"You know damned well what happened, Keith."

Trent marched over, intent on taking the tray so he'd be left alone. The look on Keith's face brought him up short, however.

" . . . What?"

Keith narrowed his eyes, leaning in close to the bars. "Did . . . did you do something to your face?"

"Save me the insults, cousin. I've heard them all a hundred times over."

"No, I'm serious, Trent. You look . . ." Keith set the tray of food down and reached into a back pocket. "One second. I'll show you." He strode from the room, disappearing down the hallway.

Trent rolled his eyes. He didn't have the patience for whatever game Keith was playing. Before he could yell such thoughts, however, Keith's hurried footsteps returned. He swept into the room holding an object before himself—a small hand mirror. Trent gave him a flat glare, slowly looking over at the mirror and expecting a jibe from Keith about his features. Instead, he found a stranger staring back.

As the initial shock dissipated, he recognized parts of himself. The lines of his chin, though much less round, were a vaguely similar shape. His cheeks weren't as swollen, but parts of their hamster-like pudginess remained. His hair . . . had his hairline lowered?

What on Kallis . . .

"See?" Keith asked, putting the mirror away and sliding the breakfast under the bars. "I told you."

Trent felt at his face, tracing his features to confirm it wasn't some trick of the light. His face, something he'd been struggling to come to terms with as he gained more knowledge, had changed. He bent and retrieved the cup of sugarcane juice, sipping at it to quench the dryness in his throat.

"I mean, you're still hideous," Keith said, a smirk on his lips. "I suppose you're slightly better to look at, though . . ."

Trent took another drink, pouted his lips, and sprayed a stream of the sugarcane juice onto Keith's tunic.

Keith looked down at his wet clothing, then back up at Trent, his face featureless. "Did that make you feel better about yourself?"

Trent's answering smile was genuine. It sent a wave of joy down into his core, faint as it may have been. "A little, yeah. Thanks for breakfast." He picked up the tray with one hand and retreated to his pile of pillows, taking another sip of juice.

It tasted sweet.

I took steady breaths as the first few drops of coffee dripped from the coffee machine. Dual streams fell from the portafilter down into two cups beneath it. Steam rose from the cups in the cool predawn air, bringing with it an intoxicating scent.

I watched it intently, and just as the shots started to change color from a deep brown, the sun rose over the rooftops east of Sue's coffee shop. The rays hit the steam, making them glow a golden hue. A smile came unbidden to my face, but I didn't let the magic of the moment distract me from my task. When the coffee pouring from the machine again changed color to a light brown, I turned the water off, just as Sue had instructed.

Next, I had to froth the milk. I poured some in until it reached the second line, then put the wand inside and turned the knob above it, releasing the pressurized steam. It hissed, the milk within swirling and bubbling as the temperature rose.

I held my hand to the side so I could feel the warmth, and when it was just hot enough, I raised the wand to the surface, causing froth to rise.

Seeing it was ready, I turned the steam off, swirled the pitcher, and poured half into each cup.

"Two cappuccinos and croissants," I said, placing the cups on a tray and bending for the accompanying pastries. "Sorry about the lack of art—I'm still learning."

The farmer gave me a friendly nod, his eyes lighting up as he gazed down at the cups of liquid happiness. He picked up the tray and walked over to his lady friend, setting it down before joining her on the floor. There was something innocent about the act, like they had no worries in the world other than each other. Seeing the smile she gave him reminded me of Maria, and I took a moment to wish them the best.

"Who's next?" I raised my eyes to the front of the line, finding a friendly face accompanied by an equally grumpy one. "Oh! Morning, guys! What can I get for you?"

Roger grunted, his arms crossed.

Sharon stepped forward, giving a slight shake of the head to her husband. "Good morning, Fischer. Dare I ask why you're making coffee?"

"I'm just helping out! Maria and I brought a fun ingredient for Sturgill to bake with—it felt a waste for Sue to miss it."

In truth, I hadn't even thought of offering to sit out for Sue, but after I caught her stealing glances into the kitchen between customers, I realized my folly. To a commoner, lemon was an almost mythical ingredient; they'd never be able to taste it, let alone cook with. I'd already started to take the citrus for granted after only a couple of months, and seeing the hunger in Sue's eyes each time she peeked at us was a sobering reminder.

"A fun ingredient, huh?" Sharon asked, intrigue clear on her face.

"Don't worry." I shot her a wink. "Nothing dangerous that could have any adverse effects."

"Well, in that case, it's lovely of you to take over the storefront while she tries out this . . . *fun* ingredient."

"Fischer!" came Maria's singsong voice. "It's almost ready. Wanna come—Oh! Good morning!"

"Morning, dear," Sharon replied. "I was wondering where you got off to so early."

"It still wasn't early enough." She gave me a playful flick on the arm. "*Someone* had already started without me."

Sharon clicked her tongue. "To think someone trying to court my daughter would act so disrespectfully . . ."

As the mother-daughter duo continued their fun at my expense, I noticed the slight shift in Roger's demeanor. His frown was still there, but it seemed almost forced. His wife and daughter interacting, the most important people in his life, seemed to lift his spirits. His posture, too, seemed different. He stood taller than usual, his frame of bone and roped muscle having filled out a little. It wasn't as drastic as Ellis, who had turned from a skeleton to a men's physique contender, but it was still incredible. I felt the urge to ask him about it, but then he noticed my attention.

His scowl returned in earnest as he slowly spun to glare at me.

Before he could spit out a choice insult, Sue came scrambling from the back. "You two! Get back into the kitchen!" She started beating at me with a tea towel.

"W-wait!" I tried. "I'm happy to make the coffee. You should help with the—"

"You're too slow! Look at the line! Shoo!"

I glanced up, seeing she was right. I had been so caught up in the conversation that I didn't see the crowd gathering. There were a few annoyed glances mixed in with the friendly faces, so I gave them a sheepish smile and let Sue guide me away.

"Okay," Sue said, pulling at her apron. "What can I get you two?"

The moment I was past the dividing wall between kitchen and counter, the scent of the danishes hit me. The bakery always smelled divine, as was the way of things, but this . . .

The lemon's distinct profile was most notable, trailed only marginally by the flour, sugar, and . . . was that vanilla? It immediately made my mouth water, and I had eyes for nothing but the tray in Sturgill's hands as I approached. He held it with the care a father would give a newborn. So gentle as to not make a sound, he set it on the metal bench. Only when he was sure it wouldn't somehow fall to the floor did he look up at us.

I felt a surge of chi swelling around us. I focused on each stream, my brow furrowing as they rose from the ground, swirled around the room, and slammed into Sturgill. He went still, his eyes going distant.

"Sharon!" I immediately called, running for the counter.

Sturgill let out a whimper.

When I got to the front, I raised the countertop. "Sharon, Roger—could I, uh, show you something?"

"Oh, sure, Fischer," Sue said in a joking tone from the coffee machine. "Just make yourself at home. It's not a business or . . . Fischer? What's wrong?"

She had turned to give me a grin, but my face must have betrayed my panic.

"It's nothing," I lied, plastering a smile on my face. "Just need to show Sharon and Roger the danishes, is all."

The pair immediately picked up on my urgency. They walked as fast as possible without running, Sharon lowering the countertop behind them. I gave Sue one last attempt at a reassuring smile, then followed them into the kitchen. Sturgill had collapsed to the floor, a thousand-yard stare on his face. Maria rubbed both his shoulders, speaking softly into his ear.

"I thought you said there was no chance of this," Sharon hissed.

"There wasn't! Or there shouldn't have been—there wasn't a trace of chi in the lemon we used."

"Shocker," Roger growled. "Something Fischer touched turned to shit."

"Not now," Sharon said, shooting him a glare. "We need to get him out of here. Grab an arm, Roger."

"What about Sue?" Maria asked. "What do we say?"

"Yeah," came a voice from behind us. "What about me?"

Her face was fiery as she stared at us, blocking the exit. She looked around, settling on a flour-covered rolling pin for a weapon.

"Put him down. *Now.*" She spoke softly, but she clearly meant it—she'd sooner take us all on with a rolling pin than let us pass.

"Sue, please. You don't understand." I held up both hands and took a step forward. "I don't know how to explain this. He's—"

She took a breath that filled her chest, then opened her mouth. Her intention was carved in every line of her face, so before she could yell for help, I was on her.

"I'm sorry," I said, holding one hand to the back of her head and clamping the other over her mouth.

To her eyes, I would have teleported. She went stiff as a board, then her eyes rolled into the back of her head. I caught her and lowered her limp body to the ground.

"S-Sue . . ." Sturgill returned to himself, her unconscious form enough to tear him back to the present. "What did you do . . . ?" His voice was breathy, as if he couldn't truly believe what he was seeing. He swallowed, his face going red as he looked between us. "What did you—*hnng!*"

His rising voice caused Sharon to dash forward. She flicked him in the stomach hard enough for him to buckle.

"Mom!" Maria hissed. "What the hell?"

Sharon drew a hand to her mouth. "S-sorry, Sturgill. I only meant to shock you. I panicked!"

Sturgill groaned again, obviously winded.

"Everything okay back there?" someone called from the counter.

Before they could come to check, I got to my feet and rushed out. Everyone in the front of the line had taken a step forward, trying to peer into the back of the bakery.

"I'm sorry, everyone. The bakery has to be closed."

"Why?" a woman asked. "What was that noise?"

Thinking on my feet, I made the only excuse I could think of. "Sue and Sturgill are both sick. It struck them fast, so it might be contagious. She doesn't want to risk customers eating contaminated food, so she asked me to close up."

From the corner of my eye, I saw the young man sitting opposite his lady friend choke mid-swallow. Croissant sprayed everyone, all over the tray and the girl's work leathers.

"John!" she yelped. The blood drained from his face, but before he could pass out from embarrassment, she started laughing. "That is so gross, man!"

"I-I'm so sorry!" he started wiping the flecks of pastry up with a handkerchief.

At any other time, I'd have laughed too. Instead, I grabbed the pile of sheets Sue used to show she was closed and draped one over the coffee machine.

"Sorry, everyone." I threw a sheet over the display case. "I'm sure they'll recover and open up again soon."

With the crowd dispersing and more than a few grumbles making it to my ears, I slid the wooden panels across, sealing the bakery off from the outside world. When I returned to the kitchen, everyone appeared as stressed as I felt. Sharon was rubbing

Sturgill's back in apology as his breath gradually returned. Roger was channeling his anxiety at the situation into hatred for me, blessing me with a mighty glower. Maria had gone to Sue, who was sitting up with her help, staring at me like I'd just . . . well, like I'd revealed myself as a cultivator.

I groaned, putting my head into my hands. "I just wanted to give my friends some lemon." I let out a mocking laugh, wishing I could rewind the clock. "It wasn't supposed to go like this."

When I looked out at the room once more, I could tell Roger wanted to rip into me again, but he shot furtive glances at Sue, likely only holding back for her sake. I knelt down to her level, ensuring I kept a good amount of distance. The last thing I wanted to do was make her faint again.

"Are . . . are you okay, Sue?"

She shook her head, tears coming to her eyes. "No, Fischer. I'm not okay. What did you do to my husband?"

Seeing her sorrow made my heart break. "Nothing, Sue. It's not what it looks like. It's . . ." I put my head in my hands again. "Where do I even start? Barry is so much better at this stuff."

"I'm sorry, Sue," Sharon said. "The only person who did something to Sturgill was me. I flicked him in the stomach lightly."

"Lightly?" Sturgill interrupted, his voice hoarse. "It felt like you hit me with a brick."

"I meant to do it lightly," Sharon corrected, wincing. "I'm still getting used to my strength."

"You're *all* cultivators, then." Sue had a look of resignation on her face as she got to her feet, brushing off her apron.

"Where are you going . . . ?" I asked, shrinking back as she strode past me.

"If I'm going to die anyway . . ." She plucked a danish from the tray. "I'm at least going to try this before I go."

I shook my head as she took a massive bite, flakes of pastry falling to the floor.

"No one is going to kill you. Like I said, it's not what you think."

"What is it, then?" Sturgill replied, answering for his wife who was blissfully eating the danish and staring at nothing.

"It's . . ." I sighed. "Screw this—I need one too."

I trudged over, grabbed a pastry, and took a bite.

CHAPTER SEVENTY-FOUR

BETTER LATE THAN NEVER

The taste of lemon danish lingered on my tongue. It was sweet, morish, and light, yet insignificant compared to the silence that stretched between everyone in the bakery. Gazes were turned toward walls, the floor, and random kitchen equipment, studiously avoiding each other.

Sue drank deep of a coffee cup, swirling the liquid in her mouth before swallowing. She cleared her throat. "So, I take it you really aren't planning on killing us?"

I grimaced. "No, Sue. Even if I didn't consider you both my friends, we wouldn't, er . . . snuff you or Sturgill out for awakening as a cultivator."

"That's truly what this is?" Sturgill asked, gripping Sue's hand tightly. "I've become a cultivator?"

"Yeah, mate," I replied. "I think it's not official until you accept a name, but from what I've heard, not accepting isn't an option. Barry said the System won't let you sleep or rest until you do."

"Barry?" Sue licked her lips. "Barry is a cultivator too?"

"I think it's best if you start from the beginning, Fischer," Sharon suggested.

Thankful for the direction, I nodded. "Sharon's right. I'll tell you the story from the start."

I told them everything. Well . . . *almost* everything. From my encounter with truck-kun, to the chi transference I'd done with the lemons, I told them everything necessary, only omitting details that would make the tale too long. They listened intently, not uttering a single question until I finished.

"And that's the lemon I brought here this morning—one that I'd drained of all chi."

Sturgill blinked, his eyes distant. They slowly drifted up to me as he leaned forward. "You mean to tell us that Borks is a . . . a hellhound? I'm not sure how I could believe that, Fischer."

Sue pulled back from him, shaking her head as she scowled. "*That's* what you're questioning? The damned *dog?*"

"What?" Sturgill demanded. "He's a good boy! How could he possibly be a hellhound?"

Knowing there was an easy way to confirm the detail, I looked up at the rafters. "Would you mind, Borks?"

Everyone followed my gaze, so when a dog shaped like a demon dropped from above, we all bore witness. Borks, in his Chihuahua form, fell toward my chest. I easily caught him.

Sturgill's eyebrow furrowed. "Who is that?"

In response, Borks shifted to the form he always took around the village—that of a long-haired golden retriever. His tongue lolled happily as he let out a bark.

Sturgill and Sue both leaned back, their eyes going wide.

The former cleared his throat. "Okay, so Borks is definitely a spirit beast, but I struggle to believe he's a hellhound—"

Without needing my guidance, Borks shifted once more. His long fur turned into midnight skin as he more than quadrupled in size. He still sat in my arms, his torso and snake-headed tail both upright and looking at the two bakers.

"Oh . . ." Sturgill said.

Sue arched an eyebrow at him. "Happy, foolish man?"

"Well, no. But I do believe Borks is a hellhound now."

"It's true, then?" Sue asked, staring at me as Borks shifted back and dropped to the floor. "All of it?"

"Yep. All of it. I have one more bit of proof, for what it's worth." I looked up at the rafters again. "Corporal—"

Before I could finish my sentence, the otter zapped across the room on lightning-fueled muscles. She slammed into my chest, letting out a happy coo as she curled into my arms and smiled with her needle-sharp teeth.

"This is Corporal Claws—or Claws for short. She is how Borks snuck into the rafters without you knowing. Don't give me that look, Claws. Of course I felt you zap him up there before I closed the café, you little deviant. You're not sneaky enough to avoid my senses."

She chirped her defeat before squirming to get even more comfortable in my arms. Closing her eyes, she started drifting off to sleep without a care in the world. When I looked back up at Sturgill and Sue, they sighed, then shared a smile at the similar reaction from the other.

"You two seem . . . remarkably calm about all of this," Maria said, giving them an appraising look.

Sue shook her head. "I most certainly am not calm. It makes sense, though. The changes Fischer has had since coming here. Your remarkable recovery, Sharon."

"And Roger's hatred for you," Sturgill muttered.

Roger grunted, and I thought he'd turn his displeasure on Sturgill. As always, however, he reserved it for me.

I grinned back at him, then cleared my throat. "Right, then. Should we take you guys to the church? I'm sure Barry will have answers for any questions you have."

"Um . . ." Sturgill rubbed the back of his head. "How do you plan on getting us there? I think the villagers might have a few questions if they see us walking about after closing up for the morning."

I tickled Claws's chin, making sure she was awake. "Can you get Borks out of here without being seen?"

She sat up, stretching her back as she let out an affirmative chirp.

"I . . . don't understand," Sue admitted, glancing between us.

"I skimmed over some of our abilities." I grinned at Borks. "Would you mind, buddy?"

He barked happily, and power swelled within his core. The next second, a black portal tore into existence, its lines spider-webbing out as it shattered the air itself.

I stepped inside and poked my head out. "Follow me. It's safe."

"You're sure?" Sturgill asked, his eyes tracing the black lines around me.

"Positive!" Maria skipped toward the portal. "Last one in doesn't get another danish."

Sue snorted. "You're out of your minds if you think we're giving you more danish after the fright you gave us." She picked up the tray and held it to her chest to emphasize the point. "You forfeited the right to any delicious pastries."

Maria pouted at her, but I saw the amusement tugging at her lips.

Everyone stepped inside, the portal closing behind us.

Barry leaned down over the report, thoroughly scanning each line. As everyone did the same, the only sound was that of Ellis's pencil scratching down notes in the corner. With each sentence, paragraph, and accounting of goods sold, Barry's smile grew. When he finished the last line, he grinned out at the room. One by one, they looked up from the document, similar looks of pride, joy, and surprise plastered over their faces.

All the while, Danny tried to appear nonchalant in his spot at the circular table, but his bouncing knee gave away his anticipation.

"You did amazing, Danny." Barry said. "Better than amazing. The amount of produce you moved is honestly unbelievable." He pointed at the ledger halfway down the page. "This is all correct? You brought *this much* food and cured wood back with you?"

Danny shrugged, still trying to play it cool. He failed. His cheeks glowed a vicious crimson as the entire congregation present settled their attention on him.

"It was thanks to the route you and Ellis devised—all I did was show up and let the villages know. It was particularly brilliant sending me to Bengal and Cedar first. I'd never have thought to start so far away, but those two villages alone got me stocked up for the rest of the route." He shot a smirk at Barry. "You didn't exaggerate how much they hated each other, either—having me act as merchant meant they could trade without coming to blows."

"Wait . . ." Helen said from opposite Danny. "How do two villages have access to everything you needed for the rest of the route?"

"It is not that they have everything," Ellis answered, not taking his eyes from his notepad. "It is that they had exactly what each other—and the next villages on the route—wanted. The path wasn't chosen for its ease of passage or proximity."

Barry reached over, giving Helen's hand a squeeze. "The most important thing was trading compatibility." He looked over at Danny again and tapped the report.

"The only thing your report doesn't mention is if you were able to establish the passive trade routes. Do you think they'll continue without your presence, or will we need to constantly have the wagon traveling?"

Danny nodded. "I left that out on purpose because it's . . . nuanced." He shuffled through his papers until he found one in particular. It was *covered* in small writing. "I thought it best to write it up on the wall here. That way, we can . . ." Danny trailed off at the sound of clawed feet scrambling down the hallway.

Every head drifted toward the door just in time to see a golden-haired good boy come flying around the corner, a manic-eyed otter riding his back. Borks's padded feet fought for purchase as he ran on the spot before slamming into the doorway. Unperturbed, he used the collision and subsequent cessation of movement to leap up onto the table, landing right in the center. Claws hopped down, chirping a greeting and puffing out her chest. Borks let out a bark, wagged his tail, and tore a portal into existence.

A dark shape extended from the murk, slowly taking shape in the magically lit room.

"Er, good morning, everyone," Maria said, covering her eyes. "Is it safe for me and Fischer to come out?"

As safe as I knew it was within Borks's pocket, it was . . . stuffy. When I stepped out into the air of the underground church, I took a deep breath, delighting in how sweet the air was in comparison.

"G'day, Barry. I may have made a lil' whoopsie this morning and . . ." I looked around the room, seeing almost everyone. "Oh. My bad. Good morning gang."

Stacks of pages sat before every person, tactically turned face-down so I couldn't catch sight of their contents.

"A whoopsie . . . ?" Barry asked. "What kind of whoopsie?"

I raised a finger and opened my mouth to respond, then shook my head. "Best if I show you, I think."

I popped my head back inside Borks's portal. "You can come out, guys."

I withdrew, stepping aside to make room for everyone. Roger came first, grumbling as he did so. Sharon came next, accepting Roger's hand as he helped her down from the table. Last, Sue and Sturgill stepped through, both looking as uncomfortable as the other. Their faces slowly transformed to a mix of surprise and disbelief as they looked around the circle, able to see each face when Borks's portal disappeared.

"You . . ." Sue said, her jaw hanging open as she stared at everyone in turn. "*All* of you?"

They stood stunned atop the table, their heads swiveling non-stop. Maria and I shared a glance and helped them down from the table, not wanting to have them feeling trapped.

"What happened?" Barry asked.

I winced. "You know how I've been draining chi from some of my fish? Well, I did that with a lemon. I wanted to let Sue and Sturgill bake with it because of how rare lemons are. It had no chi, so it shouldn't have had any effect . . ."

"Except it did," Roger finished in his gravelly, disapproving voice.

I gave a rundown of the events, my chest constricting further with each sentence. Unfortunately, it seemed to have a similar effect on Sue and Sturgill, and their faces grew more stricken with each word.

When I finished, Barry walked around the table, coming to a stop a short distance from the bakers. "I'm sorry. You must have had a crazy morning."

Sue nodded, tears coming to her eyes as her lips formed a line.

He reached out a hand, but she flinched back.

He grimaced, withdrawing it. "I promise you, this isn't a bad thing."

A chorus of agreement rang out, loudest of all was Claws, who chirped and nodded her head emphatically.

Sturgill, who had pulled Sue into a hug, raised his head. "Forgive me for saying so, but of course you'd say that. You're *all* cultivators." He immediately averted his eyes, showing deference.

"Hey," Barry said, clicking his fingers to draw Sturgill's attention. "None of that—we're not a bunch of power-tripping nobles that need to be kowtowed to. We're not some shadowy cabal of evildoers."

"You say that," Roger said, "yet you all praise Fischer as your god. At least be honest with them."

The bakers' gazes both shot toward me. The prevalent emotion was evident.

Fear.

I had seen all I could handle. I'd tried to come into the meeting with my usual chipper attitude, but seeing the effect my actions and presence were having on Sue and Sturgill, I had to get away. Misunderstanding or not, it was too much. I hadn't even realized I'd been slowly backing from the room, but seeing my proximity to the door, I edged toward it. Maria held my hand, trying to keep me there, but I had to go—had to get away.

"I think I've done enough damage for one day," I muttered. "Sorry, but I think I need to leave the rest to you—"

"Wait," Ellis said, standing.

His voice held iron, so I paused. "This is not your fault, Fischer."

I let out a self-deprecating laugh. "I think you'll find it very much is, mate."

"He's right, Fischer," Barry said. "We knew this was coming."

My eyebrow furrowed as I glanced from one to the other. "You knew I'd do this?"

"No, that people would start awakening. You wanted to be left out of the loop, yes?" Ellis looked up from his notes. "Well, forgive me, but I believe you need to hear this, lest you descend into misguided self-blaming. Technically, you caused this, yes—but that's because of the chi once more coursing through the world."

He looked up at Sturgill. "You got a message from the System for baking, correct? You didn't eat any of the food yet?"

"Yes . . ."

Ellis nodded. "Sturgill here awakened of his own accord. The System saw his baking as good enough to merit becoming a cultivator. Otherwise, Sue would have awakened by eating the danish." He rubbed his chin. "Actually, she still might have if the System saw it as food created by a cultivator. A fascinating line of thought. Which comes first: the chi or the awakening?"

Entirely forgetting we were all there, Ellis began muttering to himself, taking notes on a fresh page.

Just like that, the former archivist had looked up, given me a tactical nuke of knowledge, then gone back to his work. I blinked at him, genuinely shocked by his efficiency. It made part of me feel better for one simple reason: it made sense.

The chi that slammed into Sturgill had risen from the world around us, not within the lemon. I took a deep breath, exhaling it slowly as Maria came to my side and gripped my forearm lightly. There was still a tightness to my chest, but with each breath I took, its hold loosened.

"Better?" Barry asked.

"Yeah, mate. I should have noticed that myself, though."

He gave me a kind smile. "You've had a tough morning too, mate. It's not surprising that your thoughts weren't clear."

I didn't respond, focusing entirely on my breathing as I tried to ground myself in the present moment.

"All right." Barry clapped his hands together. "There's one more thing you should hear me tell them, Fischer, then it's probably best you leave." He turned to Sue and Sturgill. "I've wanted to bring you in and make you members of the church for some time now."

Their eyes went wide, as did mine.

Before we could speak, Barry continued. "You're both perfect candidates: smart, hardworking, and, most importantly, kind. The only reason we didn't come and offer you ascension is because you both serve food to many of Tropica's citizens, and we thought it might be problematic given we know so little about what causes someone to awaken. That you've now awakened, Sturgill, isn't a curse. It's a *blessing.* Perhaps this is the universe's way of telling us we made a mistake in not coming to you sooner. For that, I'm sorry. If I'd come to you before the System took matters into its own hands, you wouldn't have had such a traumatizing morning."

I watched Sue and Sturgill's faces closely. Though Barry's words didn't remove any of the ropes wrapping my chest, their reactions did. Fear remained, as did hesitation, weariness, and confusion. But now there was also curiosity.

They wanted to know more.

"Thank you, Barry," I said, grabbing Maria's hand. "And sorry again, guys." I gave Sue and Sturgill one last glance before leading Maria out and up the stairs. We walked toward the surface in silence, both lost in our own thoughts as our feet scuffed on the stone stairs. When we stepped out into the sunlight, Maria stopped, turning her head toward me.

"Well?" she asked, her hair falling to the side as she cocked her head.

"Well what?"

"Are you going to tell me what's still bothering you?"

I didn't bother protesting, instead just shaking my head. "I'm that obvious?"

"To me? Yep." She squeezed my hand. "Walk and talk?"

I nodded. "Walk and talk."

Hand in hand, we turned and ambled off toward the distant tree line.

CHAPTER SEVENTY-FIVE

FINDING PURPOSE

As we strode over grass and between trunks, a slight breeze rustled the canopy above us. The scents of earth and decaying leaf litter drifted on the air, dulling the edges of my troubled thoughts.

Maria gazed up at the gaps of blue sky filtering through the trees. "Something about the forest here always makes me feel . . . calm."

I looked up, focusing on the leaves' hypnotic movement. "I know what you mean."

A powerful gust blew, making the scene chaotic for a few seconds. A soft roar came from the canopy as thousands of leaves shifted, sounding almost like a crashing wave. The sharp edge of my worries dulled further as Maria squeezed my hand, giving me a smile that was oh-so beautiful.

"So." She swung our arms comically high with each step, not once breaking eye contact. "What's up?"

I faced forward, my gaze going distant as the words formed. "Okay, so let me preface this by saying it's probably ridiculous."

She stopped walking, holding me firmly in place and giving me a knowing smile. "You know you don't need to diminish your feelings like that, right?"

I opened my mouth to respond, then pressed my lips into a line, making a cute giggle come from Maria.

"Don't give me that look," she said. "Tell me what you're feeling. I'm not going to judge you or call it ridiculous, so you don't need the disclaimer attached."

Walking once more, I tried again.

"So . . . seeing Sue and Sturgill's reactions kind of made me realize everyone has probably had a similar experience. There's no easy way to let someone know that there's an entire group of people that have become cultivators."

She nodded. "Yeah, you're right. There's probably no good way of doing it."

"The thing is, though, they're the lucky ones. Anyone being recruited by Barry and that bunch of well-intentioned maniacs has a support system to ease them into the whole cultivator thing. Now that Sturgill awakened just by creating some bloody danishes . . . well, it stands to reason that other people are going to awaken. People who have no support network and are going to be *terrified* of what it means for them. Worse, what happens if immoral people awaken? I trust every single person in the church inherently, and we were lucky that it was Sturgill that awakened of his own accord. What happens when a sociopath becomes a cultivator? Or that dickhead noble, Osnan or whatever, that took a swing at me the other week? If he was a cultivator and I was a commoner, he'd have slapped my head clean off."

We stepped from the thick canopy into the sparsely occupied sky of Lemon's clearing. The pollinators swarmed the citrus trees above us, buzzing around from flower to flower. It was a beautiful sight. Despite how much Maria loved to watch their movement, her eyes were focused on me, appearing a light-blue in the sunlight beaming down from above.

"Do you feel responsible for all those people that might ascend?" she asked.

"I do."

"That's a lot of weight to shoulder, Fischer."

"It is," I agreed. "As much as I want to spend my days fishing with you, though, I'm not sure I can ignore it. We know what happens when I bottle things up and pretend they don't exist."

She gave me a wry smile. "Yeah—you obliterate trees. Worse, you alienate *me*—a crime most foul."

I laughed at the jab, knowing there was no malice hidden in her words.

"Do you want to hear my opinion?" she asked.

"Of course."

"Okay. Well, as usual, you're being too hard on yourself. But," she added before I could protest, "that doesn't mean you should ignore it. If you feel responsible, trying to do something about it is probably the right move."

As I thought about that, we both sat down at the base of Lemon's trunk. I ran my hands through the grass there, taking solace in the lingering cold of the night gone. Lieutenant Colonel Lemony Thicket extended thick roots from the ground beside Maria and I, and I rested a hand on one, soaking in the love I felt radiating from Lemon.

"Oh! Hi, Lemon!" Maria said, giggling at a leaf tickling her leg.

"Where do I even begin doing something about an entire world's worth of people that could be becoming cultivators?" I asked.

"One step at a time," she replied easily.

I grabbed a few blades of grass, weaving them together as I glanced Maria's way. "You know, it's infuriating that you're always right."

"The sooner you get used to it, the better." She winked. "We've got a whole life of me being right about everything ahead of us."

I rolled my eyes, causing her grin to broaden.

"What's the first step, though?" I asked.

"Well, what usually helps you think?"

I thought for only a moment. "Honestly? When I have something to do. If my hands aren't busy, it's like I get paralyzed by negativity."

She nodded. "Then that's your first step—finding something to do that gives you purpose."

"Something to do . . ." I mused, looking around the clearing. Half sunlight and half shadow, it never failed to take my breath away. The bees flying between branches lit up when they crossed beams of light, fading once more when they reached the next flower. It was almost like the tiny embers dancing above a campfire, burning bright before disappearing.

Something that gives me purpose . . .

"Oh!" I sat up straight, eyes widening as I stared at the patches of sun. "I think I know what to do!"

"Oooh, what is it?"

"Well, it kind of depends." I swiveled to face Lemon's trunk. "How do you feel about having some more life in your clearing?"

With my hand held to the root she'd extended, I felt an odd mix of emotions coming from her. Then, with absolutely no warning, she shook her entire trunk forward and back, nodding her tree body like it was a head.

Maria's answering laugh skipped across the clearing. "Call me crazy, but I think she likes the idea . . ."

I turned toward Maria and she spun to meet me, her eyes filled with curiosity.

"How do you feel about going on a trip?" I asked.

"A trip? You don't even need to ask, Fischer. Of course I'll go on a trip with you. Where to, though?"

"The capital city of Gormona."

The curiosity on her face only grew, then her brow rose in realization.

"More life in the clearing? Don't tell me . . ."

I grinned. "If lemons can grow here . . . why can't passiona fruit?"

Mischief and possibilities danced in Maria's eyes, just as they did in mine.

Two hours later, with the sun cresting its peak in the sky, the construction had begun. Maria and I picked up a wooden plank each. We put the corners together as I hammered large nails into place. We added more planks of differing sizes until the planter box was complete. It was about knee height, a half meter wide, and three meters long.

Somewhere along the line, Claws had joined us. I'd once told her about construction sites back on Earth—a conversation she'd apparently taken to heart. She stood atop one of Lemon's branches with an empty shell on her head that acted as a hardhat. She chirped and cooed incoherent orders at us, having an infectious amount of fun.

Maria and I were a blur of wood and nails as we constructed another three boxes and set them on the forest floor around Lemon's trunk. They were each positioned in the sunny gaps between trees—the perfect position for berry bushes.

"Okay," I said as we placed the last planter. "Time for some substrate."

"Substrate?" Maria asked, cocking her head to the side.

"Yeah! Do you ever mix straw into the soil? You can do the same with branches."

"Oh, right! Wait, branches?" She frowned. "You're sure you can use branches? They're a bit . . . big, aren't they?"

"You can!" I rubbed my chin. "Well, you could on Earth, anyway. I don't see why it should be any different here. They're big, yeah, but that just means they'll break down slower and provide more fuel for the passiona."

"Well, what are we waiting for?" she asked, brushing dirt from her hands. "Let's go find some branches!"

It didn't take us long. What must have been ten minutes later, we strode back toward the clearing with armloads of wood. Honestly, armloads might have been an understatement. My branches were piled so high that I could barely see.

"You sure you're all right with that, Fischer?" Maria asked, peering from behind her own stack.

"You doubt *me?* The venerable *Fischer?* Liege Lord of these lands? Master of the waves? Benevolent—" Lost in my tirade, I hadn't noticed my stack of branches hit the low-hanging canopy. No matter how fast I was, there was no time to recover, and all I could do was watch as my pile came raining down around me.

Maria, her arms filled with half as many branches, completely lost it. She leaned against a trunk so she wouldn't fall over with her laughter. I gave her a flat look, only causing tears of laughter to stream down her face.

I eyed a particularly large branch at the base of her pile, a devious plan forming.

"You can't say you didn't deserve that, Fischer. Wait, what are you doing? No! Don't you dare! *Fischer!*"

I pushed the branch, throwing her entire stack off balance. She tried to save it, tried to keep it in one piece. Focused as she was on staying upright, she didn't pay attention to Claws crouching down behind her with a devious grin on her face. Maria tripped over her, letting out an *oof* as her mountain of branches came crumbling down.

"Are you," I squeaked out between laughter. "Are you okay?" My vision swam with tears as she whirled around.

"Claws! *Traitor!*"

The look of sheer delight on Claws's face was too much for me. I fell down, joining them on the ground as my legs gave out under the onslaught of my laughter.

"Come on," I eventually said, wiping my eyes and getting to my feet. I helped Maria up, and after one last giggle for good measure, we began rebuilding our stacks with the help of Claws.

As I threw the last branch into the fourth planter box, I let out a content sigh, gazing down at the layer of sticks. Each planter had an even amount of the organic material. It would make the perfect foundation for . . . *What the?*

Power began ebbing around us, chi flowing from the very earth itself. It went toward all four planters, as well as . . . *us?* Rather than watch the transformation to come, I watched Maria. It was as if she moved in slow motion, her eyebrows shooting high as the chi crashed into her core and flowed out, just as it did mine. Euphoria washed over me, sending a shiver all the way up my spine.

The light flowed away, dissipating into nothingness as our ecstasy faded.

"Whoa . . ." Maria said, breathing heavily. "That was . . . *Oh.*"

Her eyes went distant as she read the System-sent notification. Figuring there was no harm in checking because I'd hear it from Maria anyway, I willed the notification to show.

You have learned horticulture!
You have advanced to horticulture 2!
You have advanced to horticulture 3!
You have advanced to horticulture 4!

Neat.

I went to dismiss it, but the System shoved another notification through.

You have learned Chi Manipulation.

"Oi, you cheeky prick. I didn't ask for you to show me the alert from the other day!"

You have advanced to fishing 63!

I slammed my will into the notifications, forcefully cutting them off for good. I let out a string of expletives and bent to pick up a stick—yeeting it through the forest might make me feel better. There were no longer any branches in the planters, however. I blinked at the bare earth where the layer of sticks had been.

"Fischer . . . ?" Maria asked, face lined with worry.

"What's up?"

"*What's up?* You just used a string of words I'm pretty sure were horrifically offensive where you come from."

Claws held a paw to her mouth, taking an indignant gasp.

"Yeah, it was justified, though. I let the System show me that message about learning horticulture, but it snuck in a couple more. I'm pretty sure it would have kept going if I didn't slam the door closed, the cheeky little fracker."

Maria gave me an unreadable look as she reached out and touched my hand. "You know we're going to have to unbox that one day, right?"

Claws nodded sagely, but I was pretty sure she had no idea what Maria meant either.

"Unbox what?" I asked.

"Why you don't like reading the System notifications."

I sighed, not wanting to confront it. "One existential crisis at a time."

"When we get back from our trip," she pushed. "We're going to talk about it."

I pouted. "Fine."

"Good. Now, if you'll excuse me, we have some brand-new planter boxes to inspect."

She let go of me, leaning over the closest one. Her eyes went distant, so I looked down too, expecting it to draw me in—it didn't.

"Huh?" Maria asked. "Why can't I inspect it?"

I shook my head. "You can't inspect everything."

" . . . *Why?*"

I shrugged. "I have absolutely *no* idea. Couldn't do so with the beehive, either." I pointed down at the planters. "It's definitely changed, just not enough to be considered a magical item or whatever, I guess."

The grains of wood had tightened and condensed, making it much less cumbersome. At the corners where we'd nailed the planks together, metal brackets now lined the outside, secured with way more nails than I had actually used.

"If only we had some sort of generated text messages from the System . . ." Maria trailed off meaningfully. "Maybe they could have explained why . . ."

I gave her a flat glare but couldn't keep it up for long as her lips curled. "Yeah, yeah. Point taken."

She patted me on the shoulder. "Like you said—one crisis at a time, my love."

The statement, so easily voiced, made birds take flight in my core. It must have shown on my face because Maria leaned in close.

"Oooh, you *liked* that."

My face heating, I nodded.

Claws jumped up onto my shoulder, leaning in with a look that said she sensed weakness.

"Well, then," Maria said, sweeping in toward me. She got up on her tiptoes and planted a peck on my lips, pulling back to stare into my eyes. "Let's go get some soil, *my love.*"

Claws let out another gasp, scandalized.

I grabbed Maria around the waist with one arm and pulled her close, using the other to cover Claws's eyes. Maria and I melted into each other, heat blooming everywhere our bodies made contact. All too soon, we separated, both left taking heavy breaths.

Claws jumped to the ground and mimed being sick.

I ignored her; my eyes were only for Maria. "Come on. Let's get that soil."

She scrunched her face up at me. "Tease."

"You started it," I said, messing up her hair. "I have a fun idea for transporting the dirt that might cheer you up . . ."

CHAPTER SEVENTY-SIX

BRIBERY

"You're sure this is a good idea, Fischer?"

I stood tall, peeking over the wooden tabletop I'd borrowed from the woodworkers. "Yeah, why's that?"

She looked from me to the portal torn in space on the other side of the planter box, and back to me, quirking a brow. "Do I really need to verbalize my concerns?"

She had a good point. Before I could make that concession, however, Claws—who was once more donning her shell-shaped hard hat—chirped for the work to commence. In response, dirt came flying from the portal.

I hid behind the tabletop, holding it still against the planter's wooden frame as an absolute torrent of earth smacked into it. Dust and debris filled the air, and I covered my mouth with my shirt to keep as much out as possible. Still, the finer particles made it through. The moment the torrent ceased, I ran from the cloud, coughing and sputtering.

"Did it work?" I wheezed, squinting to make sure no dirt got into my eyes.

Claws let out an affirmative chirp from atop an absolute mountain of dirt that was large enough to conceal the planter completely.

Maria stared at me. "A good idea, huh?"

"Of course! Borks just got a little too excited. Having too much is better than having not enough. Right, Claws?"

In complete agreement, Claws gave me the "ok" hand gesture.

Wait, how did she do that with her chunky little fingers . . . ?

Before I could question her anatomy any further, Borks flew from the portal, coming to land beside Claws. His entire body wagged as he hopped from paw to dirt-covered paw.

"A little too much, buddy."

Claws chirped an order, pointing at the peak and sides of the mountain. Letting out a bark—he was just happy to be there—Borks turned and started digging. He moved an obscene amount of earth with each flick of a paw, and in less than a minute, enough dirt was removed to call the mission a success.

"Good boy!" I said, scratching him behind the ear.

Claws protested loudly and immediately. She hopped onto his back, removed her shell-hat, and pointed at her own head, demanding scritches.

"Yes, yes," I said, obliging with my other hand as I spun my head toward Maria. "So . . . good idea?"

"All right, *fine.* It was a good idea to have Borks do all the digging." She reached down to scratch his head with one hand, preemptively doing the same to Claws before the rascally otter could protest. "You both did good."

They preened beneath our praise, leaning into the pats.

"Okay, gang." I ran a hand down Claws's back. "What do you say we fill the rest? We're making fantastic time."

Claws snapped to attention, placing her shell-hat back in place. After a series of chirps, Borks was off, loping toward the next planter.

Less than a half hour later, Borks's tongue lolled from his panting mouth as he flopped to the forest floor. All four of the planters were finished, and he'd just finished scattering any leftover dirt around the clearing.

I scooped him up into my arms. He transformed into a dachshund, slipping into the crook of my elbow and heaving with tiny little breaths. Maria scooped up Claws, who also went half liquid in Maria's arms despite not having done any physical labor.

"What's next?" Maria asked.

"Well, other than packing our stuff, we need to tell everyone what we're up to."

"Do you think everyone will be okay with it?"

"They can certainly try stopping us if they think it's a bad idea, but I have a plan to make them more amenable."

"Oh?" Curiosity twinkled behind her eyes. "What's that?"

I grinned. "Why, bribery, of course."

She covered her mouth as she laughed. "Bribery, huh? What flavor of bribery?"

I gave her a full-toothed smile. "The fishy kind."

Beneath the midday sun and atop the rocky shore of the headland, I held out my handcrafted fishing rod. "This is what we use. I made this one with the help of the System."

Pelly craned her neck forward, peering down at the different components. As always, intelligence shone in her gaze. I assumed her enhanced consciousness was no doubt working overtime to deduce what each part of the rod did—but then she proved me wrong by letting out a *very* confused honk.

"Maybe it's best if we show her," Maria said, giggling.

"Fair call." I pointed at one of the spare rods. A sabiki rig was tied to the end. "Do you want to try and catch an eel?"

Maria's face lit up, her hair bobbing as she nodded. I sat down on the rocks beside Claws, who was crunching on a juvenile shore fish she'd predated. Pelly came and stood next to us. I saw her eyeing me, so I laughed, ushering her in closer.

"You never need permission for a good cuddle, Pelly. My lap is your lap."

A guttural noise came from her throat. To some, it may have sounded aggressive, but I could hear the happiness in it. As Maria's deft hands unhooked the sabiki rig and let gravity straighten the line, I couldn't help but watch her. A soft breeze flowed past us, tickling my skin and blowing her hair around chaotically. She lifted her face toward the sun, a smile forming on her lips as its heat shone down on her. She took a deep breath, flipping the reel forward. Drawing her arm back, she exhaled and cast her line out past the rocky shore. The sinker let out a soft *plop,* barely disturbing the water.

"This rig works by reflecting the sun's light," I whispered to Pelly, not wanting to disturb Maria. "The metal strips near the hook make fish think it's the scales of a smaller fish."

She quietly grunted her understanding.

Maria's attention was entirely on the rod in her hands. Her eyes were closed, one hand holding the reel as the other felt the line, waiting for a bite. She swayed softly with the breeze, her body completely free of tension. Each breath came steady, gradually getting slower and slower as she slipped deeper into a meditative state. Contrary to her calmness, my hands twitched. Pelly noticed and she cocked her head, staring at my opening and closing hands as she let out a questioning honk.

I forced them to relax. "I'm not agitated—seeing her fish just *really* makes me want to wet my line too."

Maria's shoulders jolted up, drawing our attention. She lifted her arms, raising the rod high.

"Fish on!" she yelled, her voice exuberant.

I sat up, subconsciously leaning forward. Pelly did too, both our necks craning forward as Maria started winding. Doing a little happy dance with her lower half, she wound the line in. The rod's tip bounced up and down as the hooked fish tried to escape. Against Maria and the System-made training rod, though, it didn't stand a chance. The moment she caught sight of it at the water's surface, she hefted the line, bringing the fish up onto the rocky shore.

Pelly flapped forward, peering down at the eel from every possible angle.

Common Eel
Common
Found in the brackish waters of the Kallis Realm, this eel's flesh has high oil content and a strong scent, making it unpalatable food but excellent bait.

Hello again, my twice-common friend.

"Good job!" I bent and grabbed the eel, angling my body so Pelly could watch as I spiked its brain, dispatching it instantly. I held it up to her. "Poking a fish behind the eye with a nail ends them immediately. It's the most humane way of doing it."

Pelly nudged the eel with her bill, then bobbed backward, likely still expecting it to move. She came forward once more, picking the eel up and waddling over to my rod. I cocked my head, not understanding. She placed it on the rocks, grabbed the large hook attached to my line, then stuck it into the eel's tail.

Maria laughed, sweeping her hair from her face as the wind did its best to blind her. "It's too big to use whole, Pelly. Here. I'll show you."

With practiced efficiency, Maria grabbed my knife, crouched over the eel, and began slicing. She ran the blade behind its pectoral fin, along the spine, then back out, carving a perfectly sized chunk for the hook. Seeing her so easily handle the slimy eel was surprisingly endearing, and as she explained the process to our curious pelican pal, my affections only grew. She slid the chunk of eel onto my hook, passed my rod to me, then repeated the process again, cutting another chunk of bait for herself. When she finished, she stood, winding in the slack line and preparing to cast.

Noticing me sitting there and not already fishing, she cocked her head. "What are you waiting for?"

"You know, if I didn't already love you, seeing you handle that eel would have had me falling."

She stared at me for a long while, chewing her cheek. "Fischer . . . you know how weird that sounded, right?"

"What, a man can't get excited about how someone handles a fish?"

"Please stop."

I erupted into laughter. She tried to keep a stern face, but her amusement leaked through.

"Okay, my bad," I said. "Shall we show Pelly how it's done?"

Playfully rolling her eyes at me, she walked to the water's edge, flicked her reel forward, and cast out into the river mouth. The tide was running out, so when I stepped forward, I cast my line out farther, ensuring they didn't get tangled. The sinker sailed high over the ocean, the line unspooling silently as more and more length arced over the water. With an inaudible splash, it finally landed. I flicked my reel back and wound in, pressing my finger against the now-taut line.

I took a deep breath and glanced at Maria. She was already looking at me, her eyes crinkling with joy. Two small steps later, she was at my side, resting her head against my upper arm. I closed my eyes, leaning into her as I focused on the sensations of my body. The wind blew fitfully, tickling my skin with each gust. The sun warmed me from above, its heat welcome in the winter air. Maria's weight, so slight yet comforting. Pelly at my other side, her feathers brushing against my leg as she stared out at the river mouth. Claws must have been feeling left out, because she leaped up on my shoulder, cooing softly as she rubbed her head against mine.

An unbelievable gratitude welled up from within me. I let it flow, actively thinking of every blessing I'd received since coming to this strange new world. Just as my gratitude was reaching a crescendo, climbing to a point that I felt my core physically buzzing, something nudged my line. It was a *massive* hit, something colossal having tasted the bait. I opened my eyes, focusing on the tip of the rod beneath the midday sun.

"What was that?" Maria asked.

"You saw that?"

"Yeah . . ." she muttered, her eyes pinned to my fishing rod.

For a tense moment, nothing happened. Had the hit just been a fish randomly swimming into my line, or did something actually bite at the hook? Had something taken the bait?

It nudged the line again.

I leaned forward, anticipation coursing through my veins. I braced my feet, my hand tightening around the reel, just in time for the fish to eat the bait whole. It took off, the bearing within my reel squealing in protest. I wound backward, tried to let line out as fast as possible, but it wasn't enough. The hooked creature was simply too quick. The line tore through the water, leaving a visible wake as the fish swam out to sea with inconceivable speed.

A grin spread over my face as adrenaline pumped through me, my stomach fluttering with excitement.

I had a fight on my hands.

CHAPTER SEVENTY-SEVEN

THE DEEP

With the midday sun beaming down from above, waves crashed on the rocky shore before me. A gust kicked up, carrying drops of water from the crashing waves to strike against my legs. Combined, it was a feast for the senses, yet I barely registered it.

I had a war to wage.

The fish tried to tug the rod from my hands, so I gripped even tighter, the handle creaking within my grasp. The hooked creature kicked with mighty beats of its tail at slow, steady intervals. An undeniable fact made my throat rise and pupils dilate: I'd experienced nothing like the fight this creature was giving me.

All the more reason I need to catch it, I thought, clenching my jaw.

Maria asked something, but I didn't quite hear the words.

"Sorry?" I asked. "Didn't catch that."

"What is it?" she repeated, her voice intrigued.

"I have no idea." I glanced over, seeing her eyes wide and jaw clenched. It only made my smile widen. "I'm gonna find out, though."

I jogged along the shore with the fish's movement, letting it drag me toward the bay. After only a few seconds, I reached the edge of the ocean. I planted my feet down against the shoreline, enjoying the feel of the rocks beneath my bare feet. The reel continually spun, taking more and more line out. I glanced down at it, furrowing my brow.

At least half of its length was gone.

Something had to change. I had to make a move, lest the fish spool me. What could I do, though? I hadn't tightened the drag because I feared the line would snap. I'd hoped the fish would tire, expending too much of its energy to sustain the fight for long . . . but that clearly wasn't the case. Despite how far each kick of its tail took it, the movements seemed almost calm, ponderous. I instinctively knew it could keep this pace all day, if not indefinitely.

As if in answer to my predicament, a strand of chi called out to me. I cocked my head to the side, not entirely understanding. It wasn't that I couldn't tell where it originated—just the opposite. I knew *exactly* where it was: right within my grasp. The hair-thin, almost undetectable strand of power flowed from the handle of my fishing rod to the tip, then folded back on itself, flowing down. When it hit the reel, it deviated, flowing up and around before rejoining the rod. In my mind's eye, I could trace every single fluctuation of the insubstantial chi.

A ghostly hand reached out in my periphery, and as it approached, I recognized it. Maria gripped my shoulder, shaking me softly.

"What's up?" I asked, opening my eyes and blinking against the harsh midday sun.

"The line!" She pointed at my reel. "It's almost gone and you're just standing there!"

I glanced back down at my reel, seeing only a quarter remaining as the bearing within screamed in protest. I gave Maria an exaggerated pout. "Like you've never experienced cosmic insight that took every ounce of your attention before."

" . . . What?"

I laughed, unable to help myself at the look of unabashed bewilderment on her face as she glanced between me and the diminishing line.

"Check this shit out." I winked at her. "I'm about to exert some real main-character energy."

I lowered the rod, bent my knees, and opened up the gate to my power.

Only a trickle came out because that was all I needed. It flowed up my torso, down my arms, and into the rod, joining with the chi already dwelling there. To my magical senses, it was the equivalent of pouring petrol on a fire. The lines of chi flared, exalting at the source of fuel. Though impossible for the eye to see, I could feel the power it granted. I guided the strands, sending them spiraling down toward the reel. When they got there, I urged them further on. They exited the reel to touch the line. What I'd hoped for was there: a strand of chi, too thin for me to sense, already existed within the line. My power joined the existing strand, flowing into the line still spooled, then shooting off into the water at incredible speed.

. . . *Even faster than the fish,* I thought, a grin coming to my face.

"Fischer."

"Yes, Maria?"

"You said you were gonna do some *main-character shit,* but you're just standing there, hunched over and smiling like a goofball."

"A *cute* goofball?"

"Yes, fine! A cute goofball! What are you doing?"

"I'm charging up," I replied, only half paying attention. "As all good protagonists do."

The reel was still whirring away, more and more of the line disappearing into the blue depths. I doubled the amount of chi pouring from me, increasing the speed it rocketed down toward the hook. Hundreds of meters of line were empowered, but still my chi shot along its length. There were only a few layers of line left on the reel, and it wasn't slowing.

Maria sputtered, gesturing wildly at the reel. "It's going to spool you!"

The reel kept going; there was only one layer of line left now.

The chi wound through the bay, ever trailing the fish. With a feeling like finally scratching an itch, it reached the hook, taking only a fraction of a second to encompass it. With less than ten lengths of line still wrapping the reel, I tightened the drag all the way and pulled up. The hooked fish, feeling its passage come to an immediate halt, panicked. It redoubled its efforts, finally kicking as hard as it could to get away.

I half expected the line to snap despite the strengthening, but with each powerful sweep of the fish's tail that the line withstood, my confidence grew.

This was going to work.

I started retrieving line, my hand winding as I pumped the rod up and down, reducing strain with the rod's flexible body. The fish's attempted flight only intensified, the creature's sweeping kicks of its tail becoming sporadic. I was just getting used to the tempo of our battle when it shifted. The fish darted to the side, trying a different angle of escape. I grinned, knowing it to be fruitless, but then my hubris came back to bite me. My left foot slipped out from under me, sending me crashing down to the rocks. My enhanced awareness was a curse, letting me experience each agonizing moment in vivid detail. The moment I hit the ground, I would either be dragged into the water or have to let go of the rod.

There was only one option that would let me keep my prized fishing rod: I'd have to get dragged into the water, then sever my line.

All of this work, all the insights I'd gained, all to lose the fight in such a disappointing manner. I arced further downward, the sun coming into view above as my head tilted back. I could cast the line out again, sure, but what were the chances I'd encounter this fish again? My one chance with an unknown Leviathan, and I'd lost the opportunity because of slick rocks and my penchant for going barefoot.

A small smile came to my face.

It was funny, really. But just as I began to come to terms with the reality of it, firm arms caught me. They lifted me up, a slight frame coming to rest at my back as someone drew me higher. Confused at finding myself upright, I glanced down.

Maria.

Well, her arms, to be specific. They were wrapped around my torso, her body braced against mine.

"You know," she said, "I had half a mind to let you fall because of how cryptic you were being, but then I'd never see what kind of fish that is."

A laugh of sheer relief and joy bubbled up from my throat. "I fracking *love* you."

"Right back at you, ya cute lil' goofball." She squeezed me tighter, leaning back with all of her weight. "Now make it up to me by catching that fish and showing me what it is!"

With my feet once more on solid ground and Maria supporting me from behind, the battle resumed. As I pumped the rod and wound in, the fish fought with renewed vigor. Each length of line was hard earned, and by the time a quarter of it was wrapped around the reel, sweat beaded my forehead. When I had retrieved half of its length, sweat streamed down my face.

After months of having a body that never tired, it felt almost alien to experience exhaustion. Waves of it radiated from my core, making the cause clear: my use of chi. I suspected it wasn't the amount, but rather the mental control it took to shape the strands and keep them bound to the line. Wiping my forehead on my sleeve to clear some of the sweat, I wound even faster.

The fish swam from side to side with erratic movements, each sweep of its body sending it shooting forward. Back and forth, it tried every angle of escape until suddenly, its movements slowed, then stopped completely. Whatever was hooked became deadweight, making me wonder what happened. I stood up straight, not needing to brace my legs anymore.

"What is it?" Maria asked, letting go of my torso and leaning around to look at me.

"It stopped moving . . ."

I kept pumping my arms, fearing that it had somehow slipped the hook onto debris and gotten away. As it approached the shore, I held my breath, knowing I should have caught sight of at least a flash of silver by now. Maria leaned forward, as did Pelly and Claws, everyone silent as we tried to spot anything within the water. A shadow formed, long and sleek. I squinted, moving my head side to side in an attempt to work out what I was seeing.

Finally, a flash of silver came, larger than any before it.

Maria cursed.

A beast of a fish was on its side, only two meters from shore. Its tail kicked, but the movements were so slight and sluggish I couldn't feel them. A few heartbeats later, it was at the rocky shore. I bent down, swallowing as my eyes were drawn into it.

Mature Bluefathom Tuna
Rare
Found in the deep waters of the Kallis Realm, this fish is prized for both sport and the quality of its flesh. Its raw meat is considered a delicacy among all who have tried it.

"It's . . . wow," Maria said, bringing me back to the present. "It's so big . . ."

I nodded. It was longer than I was.

"Help me, would you?" I asked, but before she could respond, its body rose.

I was dumbfounded for a moment as its humongous body—longer and wider than me—lifted right out of the water. But then I caught sight of the creature beneath it. Pistachio, his thick legs easily clambering up the side of the rocky shore, placed the fish on the ground. I bent, gave him a fist bump and a nod of thanks, then immediately dispatched the fish. Its struggle ceased immediately, the massive body going still.

"What happened to it?" Maria asked. "Why did it suddenly stop fighting?"

Seeing the type of fish it was, I understood.

"It's a tuna—they need to swim forward to breathe, so they rarely survive being caught."

"Oh . . . so when you started bringing it back to shore, it couldn't breathe anymore?"

"Basically, yeah . . ."

We stared down at the fish for a long moment, all humbled by the size of the thing. Pelly had the best reaction. Her head bent down so close that her eye was almost touching it. Her bill opened and closed silently, stunned by its form.

"Well . . ." I said, turning toward Maria with a grin. "If this doesn't work as bribery, I don't know what will."

She locked eyes with me, a satisfied smile coming to her face.

I rubbed the top of Claws's head. "Would you mind getting everyone?"

She chirped, saluted, then exploded into action, her muscles wreathed in lightning as she shot from sight.

I lay my hands on the fish's torso, closing my eyes and taking a moment to thank it. I had taken its life, but we'd make use of every last bit of its body. The flesh would sustain us just as the frame and skin would fertilize the plants of the forest.

"Thanks, mate," I whispered, letting my gratitude flow.

I stood, stretching my arms toward the sky.

"And thank *you,* Pistachio. That assist was clutch." I looked down at the fish, then back up at him. "Would you mind carrying it?"

He nodded, and Maria and I helped get it onto his back before we made our way toward the campfire. Exhaustion lingered in my body, making my limbs feel heavy.

I ignored it—I had a feast to prepare.

CHAPTER SEVENTY-EIGHT

FEVER DREAM

Beneath the shade of my deck, I cut into the tuna. Recalling the memory of a particular video on Earth, I did my best to emulate the movements of a Japanese master of his craft. Surprisingly, the flesh came away just as I imagined. There was no way it should have worked out, so I took a second to thank the System and the levels of fishing and cooking it granted me. As much as I hated the thing and its annoying messages, I couldn't have processed the tuna so efficiently without it.

Before I knew it, I had slipped into a zen-like state. My hands took over, lifting, slicing, and removing massive chunks of the fish at a time. I set each filet aside, and when the last of the usable sashimi had been removed, I started cutting away skin. As before, my body moved of its own accord, easily parting the edible flesh. There were strips of dark meat that ran down the tuna's spine, and I removed them with careful incisions, making sure to not take more of the pink flesh than necessary. I set the dark meat aside on a spare board, knowing my animal pals would likely love the stronger flavor.

A gust swept past me, bringing with it savory scents that made my mouth water and a smile cross my face. Maria was at the campfire making a sauce. We had been experimenting over the last couple of weeks, doing our best to replicate soy sauce. It was a complete failure, if I was being honest, but we'd managed to create a delightful alternative using garlic, salt, and other spices, skipping the fermentation step entirely.

After washing my hands and knife in the kitchen, I started slicing strips of the raw flesh, cutting against the grain as my instinct told me to. One cut at a time, I filled three wooden boards, layering the fish in an aesthetically pleasing way. I so desperately wanted to try some. It took every ounce of will I had to withhold, knowing it would be better to experience it with everyone else. Pelly was sitting beside me, her eyes filled with the same hunger I felt.

"You can help yourself if you like," I said.

She shook her head, staying strong.

"It's worth the wait," I replied, focusing on each cut I made. "Food tastes better when shared with friends." Remembering an important detail, I held an uncut chunk of tuna out to Pelly. "Would you put this on the fire, Pelly? It needs to be cooked all the way through."

She nodded, grabbed the fish, and took off.

I lapsed into silence as I processed the final filet. When it was finished, I placed it on the board, marveling at the sight. I had a veritable mountain of food before me, all three boards piled high.

"Fischer!" Maria called. "They're here!"

Pistachio lumbered around the corner, freezing for a moment when he caught sight of all the food.

"It's a lot, huh? More than I expected."

He slowly nodded, his eyes locked onto the closest board.

"Could you carry one for me, mate?"

Blowing bubbles of anticipation and hunger both, he picked a board up, holding it before him with care belying his size. I grabbed the other two, lifting them high and striding around the corner. A sea of faces met me, some hesitant, most excited.

"Hope you all brought your appetites!" I said, sweeping forward with the mountains of fish. "The feast is ready!"

"Uh, Fischer?" Barry asked, giving me an odd look.

"Yeah, mate?"

"Is that raw . . . ?"

"It certainly is! It's called sashimi. I've eaten it plenty before and can confirm it's bloody delicious. It should be safe to eat for everyone except Ruby." I leaned past Barry to look at her. "Sorry, Rubes. Raw fish is no bueno for pregnant women. There's a portion cooking on the fire for you."

She smiled in response, shrugging one shoulder as she held a hand to her stomach.

Pistachio and I set the boards down on stumps beside the campfire. Snips, Claws, and Bill stepped through the crowd, all following the scent of the fish.

"Oh! I almost forgot! One moment!" I dashed off toward my deck, returning with the red, flavorful cuts that I removed from the pink flesh. I set it on the corner of a board and cut it into strips. "You guys will *love* this. I think it will be too strong for us humans, but that's only because we're inferior."

Claws gave a little wiggle, puffing out her chest, and Snips blew a humble bubble, nodding along.

"Are you sure it's safe, Fischer?" Barry asked, looking skeptical.

Maria set bowls down next to each board, pouring her finished sauce into them.

"Well," I said, "I'm willing to eat some to prove how safe it is. Even *if* it would make people sick, I'm pretty sure being cultivators would save us. The System specifically said in the description that it's a delicacy when eaten raw, though."

"A delicacy . . . ?" Peter asked, stepping forward.

"Damned right, mate. You in?"

He nodded, licking his lips as he stared down at the pile of pink meat. I picked up a slice. It was tender and cool between my fingers. Most came forward, the only exceptions being Ruby, Roger, Sue, and Sturgill. Maria removed the now-cooked chunk of tuna from the fire, setting it on a plate and passing it to Ruby before collecting her own bit of sashimi.

"I recommend trying it without the sauce first." I locked eyes with all present, then held my sashimi high. "To friendship, family, and good food."

They cheered in response. As always, Claws was the loudest, giving a shrill chirp as she held her red cut of sashimi above her furry little head. All together, we threw it into our mouths.

Despite having it without any of the sauce, the sashimi's umami notes immediately sprang forth. I'd tasted plenty of sashimi on Earth, including from Michelin starred restaurants in Japan. None of those experiences held a candle to the flavor of the fish currently blessing my palate.

I bit down into the soft flesh; the flavor profile transformed. A sweet, subtle taste took over, smothering my taste buds with each bite. As I got used to the sweetness, I tasted the umami again. They melded together, perfectly complimenting each other. The more I chewed, the more their compatibility grew, becoming something greater than the sum of their parts. I closed my eyes, letting the mouthful encompass my awareness. The flavors swept across my tongue like a crashing wave, only for the next wave to form and join its predecessor.

Finally, I swallowed. The chi within the meat warmed my throat as it traveled down to my core. I exhaled a shaky breath, overwhelmed by the experience. When I opened my eyes, I found someone standing before me. Peter's eyes were teary, his lower lip trembling as he blinked at me. He opened his mouth to speak, but no sound came out.

"Need a hug, mate?"

He nodded shakily, so I pulled him in, patting him on the back. He took a steadying breath, his silent trembling slowly receding.

When he let go, he exhaled, taking a step back. "That was . . ."

"Unbelievable . . ." Maria finished, her voice awestruck.

"Yeah." Peter cleared his throat. "That."

"Hestia's welcoming hearth," Ruby swore, cutting through the silence. "If the raw fish is as good as this, I totally get it." She scooped up another forkful of cooked tuna and put it in her mouth, letting out a loud, drawn-out groan.

"All right," I said. "Show of hands—who wants more?"

The hand of everyone who had tried it shot up, animals included. Claws flopped to her back in the sand, raising all four paws as high as she could. Maria laughed, bending to scratch Claws's belly and fuss over how cute she was.

"Um . . ." someone said, drawing my attention. Sue, seeing everyone looking at her, blushed. She absently tugged at her apron and stood tall beneath our gazes. "Can I have some too?"

I raised an eyebrow, peering over at Barry. "I take it things went well, then?"

He gave me a single nod before turning to Sue. "Of course you can have some. Just remember not to choose a name for now."

Sue, wringing her hands, shot a furtive glance at Sturgill. "Is that okay, dear?"

Sturgill's head slowly tilted to the side, his face growing concerned. "Did you just ask me for permission to do something? Who are you, and what did you do with my wife?"

I barked a laugh, unable to help myself—as did at least half of those present.

Sue went beet red, and she whipped him on the upper arm with a rag. "This is why I never ask your permission! You can't be serious for a gods' damned second!"

He laughed along with the crowd, easily catching and holding her wrists. "Of course I'm okay with it."

She tutted, withdrawing her hands as he let go. "Well, you'd better run if it makes me awaken. I won't be so easy to fend off."

Roger's face had been shifting the entire time, moving between frustration and want. I knew better than to address it, though, and my patience was rewarded when he cleared his throat.

"Will this make me more powerful?"

"Yup," I said cheerily. "I felt the chi I got from that single slice. It was *potent.*"

He sniffed. "I suppose I'll have some then."

Sharon and I shared a knowing glance as he bent to grab a bit of fish. She rolled her eyes playfully, shaking her head as everyone joined Roger in taking more. I dipped my slice into the garlicky sauce Maria made, my mouth watering in anticipation.

I held it before me as I waited, one palm under it so I didn't waste a single drop of flavor. Sue and Sturgill were the last to fetch some. Sue's hands bunched around her apron, twisting it as she stared at the pink, glossy fish. Her jaw clenched, and just as I thought she had changed her mind, Sturgill laid a hand on her arm. He whispered something in her ear that I intentionally didn't listen in on. Whatever he said made her body relax, and she nodded, plucking a thin piece of sashimi from the board. Without dipping it into the sauce, she stepped back, locked eyes with me, and gave me a nervous smile.

With everyone else's gazes on me, I put the fish into my mouth. The sauce dripped, touching my tongue before anything else. It was like a bomb, its umami essence exploding throughout my mouth. Knowing the overpowering flavor's cure was already within reach, I bit down into the sashimi. Sweetness rushed out, the tuna's mild notes joining the fray. They swept each other up, like a warm updraft and cool downdraft forming a tornado. Rather than leaving destruction in its wake, however, the tempestuous flavors left only bliss. I smiled, a tear forming in the corner of my eye.

I waited to hear someone unleash an *mmm*, or perhaps for Peter to sniffle. Instead, power bloomed across from me. To my enhanced awareness, it came at glacial speed, forming at waist height. I was more than a little surprised to feel strands of power reaching up from the ground to join the coalescence taking place. They curled upward from different directions, weaving into then solidifying the core. All at once, it was done, and a wave of euphoria washed out, just as enjoyable as the first time I'd felt it.

I swallowed the mouthful, letting its flavor linger in the afterglow of Sue's awakening. When I opened my eyes, every head was facing her, one and all smiling. Sue blinked, her eyes clearing as she once more looked out at the world.

"So," I said, trying to appear indifferent, "have you guys planned out their names?"

Barry slowly turned, his face intentionally blank. "Why do you ask?"

Maria, much less tactful, let out a groan. "Just cut to the chase and tell us the delinquent names you've thought up, Fischer."

I grinned. "I thought you'd never ask!"

High above the capital city of Gormona, within a relic-filled room, Augustus Reginald Gormona swallowed. It did nothing to help his reflux.

He leaned against a lifeless artifact, his eyes locked on a screen that he'd scarcely looked away from since learning of it. Upon being told of its existence, he had thought it an error. The screen *had* to have been showing advancements from another age, right?

But then the slew of new messages had begun.

His enemies were more vast than he could have imagined, and the spirit beasts appeared to have recruited humans to the cause. Worse, they grew stronger by the day. Especially that troublesome flock of birds. Each appeared to be mastering different crafts. It was a terrifying prospect, and the main reason for Augustus's lack of sleep.

"You should get some rest, my king," the guard leaning beside him said.

The out of turn comment made the rage of a thousand suns flare in his chest, but as the king whirled on the man, his fury deflated.

"You're probably correct, Deklan." The man had been a rock these past weeks—he didn't deserve his ruler's scorn. "And please—call me Augustus."

The lackadaisical man, rather than protest as most would, simply nodded. "I can do that, Augustus. Tell you what, if you go get some sleep, I'll come and let you know right away if anything crazy gets reported by the relics."

August Reginald Gormona, a king who prided himself on his unflappable demeanor, let out a weary sigh. "You're a good man, Deklan. Thank you."

He bent and crawled his way back through the sea of artifacts. When he emerged on the other side of the room, a blue light sprang forth. He slowly spun, horror dawning—he already knew what it meant.

Another cultivator or spirit beast had awakened.

On numb, exhausted legs, Augustus stumbled over to the artifact, leaning on other relics for support. At a speed that belied belief, Deklan appeared at his side, having crawled to meet him.

"Let me help, Augustus."

"Thank you," he replied, his voice coming shakily. Deklan's support was a welcome balm to his worries, but any semblance of reassurance vanished the moment he spied the lines of text printed on the screen. His stomach dropped, the floor itself feeling as though it disappeared beneath his feet.

"Please tell me my eyes deceive me, Deklan." He rubbed his weary eyes, praying that when he opened them again, he would wake from this fever dream.

He didn't.

The lines of text taunted him, further cementing the doom of his kingdom. He read the first line again.

Fat Rat Pack

Swallowing, he took in the second, despairing at the implications.

The Beetle Boys

CHAPTER SEVENTY-NINE

OATHS

Beneath the descending sun, Sue's and Sturgill's eyes were distant. Dual waves of power flowed from them as they entered their names into the System.

"Happy?" Maria asked, giving me a rather judgmental look while trying her best to hide the amusement poking through.

"Very," I replied, grinning.

I extended a hand to Sturgill, then Sue, shaking them in turn. "Welcome to the ranks of the heretical, Fat Rat Pack and The Beetle Boys."

Sue pouted. "I'm still not sure how I feel about being called *The Beetle Boys.*"

"Would you rather Fat Rat Pack?" Sturgill asked, smirking.

She lowered her eyebrows. "No. I'd prefer Sue."

I opened my mouth to let her know why the names were important, but she shook her head.

"It's fine. Barry already explained why it was necessary, but it doesn't take all the sting out of it."

"Would more tuna help?" I asked.

Her eyes drifted to the heaped boards of fish. "It couldn't hurt . . ."

"Well, good, because we need to eat all of this before it goes bad. It's warm, so we should really hurry."

With that, the feast truly began. The mountains of sashimi shrunk surprisingly fast, everyone falling into silence as we ate it one mouthful at a time. I watched my animal pals with no small amount of glee, encouraging them to eat the pink flesh when the slices of red meat were gone. I didn't know when she got there, but Cinnamon lounged in the sun, chewing a stalk of sugarcane as she rested a paw on Pelly's side.

"And where have you been?" I asked, raising an eyebrow.

She gave me a sly little shrug, amusement clear on her face.

"All right. Keep your secrets." I bent to rub her belly, then grabbed another slice of sashimi.

No matter how much I ate, the fish, even when combined with the savory sauce, was light and refreshing. It only took us a half hour to eat the mountain of food. I'd been keeping an eye on Roger, only glancing his way when he was distracted. Though I already knew it to be the case, it was clear he was eating the fish for more reasons than just gaining power. The tension held in his body slowly melted away with each bite. He and Sharon joked and smiled, their love for each other clear in their eyes. Maria, who was also stealing glances at them, squeezed my hand. We shared a smile, hopeful that our plan would come together.

As we sat and let the food settle, I cleared my throat. "So, I have a confession to make."

All turned to face me, their conversations pausing.

"I had an ulterior motive in inviting you all here for this fishy feast." Before anyone could respond, I steeled my nerves and rushed into it. "Maria and I have decided to take a trip to the capital."

"Now hold on one second!" Roger protested, his temporary joviality gone. "That's too dangerous. I won't let you take my little girl into the maw of the capital."

"Dear . . ." Sharon said. "I think this could be a good idea." She shot him a meaningful glance, communicating . . . something. "Don't you *also* think Fischer going to the capital is a good idea, Barry?"

I furrowed my brow, not sure what Barry had to do with it. His eyes darted around, his face calculating.

What have I missed . . . ? I wondered, still not comprehending.

"It *would* be a good idea for Fischer to go to the capital." Barry agreed. "The timing is—"

"I don't give a damn about your Operation Sticky Fingers!" Roger spat. "If you think I'm willing to risk my only daughter for such foolishness, you're out of your damned mind! I care little for the—"

Sharon clamped a hand over his mouth, cutting him off. "Mind your company, dear . . ." she said, glancing at me.

"Okay." I threw my hands up. "What the hell is going on? What is *Operation Sticky Fingers?*"

Maria, Sue, and Sturgill looked similarly confused, but every other face grew apprehensive. I waited, a line forming between my eyes as I tried in vain to connect the dots.

Barry broke the silence. He sighed, shaking his head. "We've been meaning to suggest you go to the capital, though Maria wasn't involved in the plan . . ."

"*. . . Why?*"

Barry grimaced. "Do you really want to know the details?"

"If you do, is there a chance that Maria fits into the plan?"

Barry nodded. "I don't see why she couldn't—"

"Absolutely not!" Roger yelled, cutting him off. "It's much too dangerous!"

"That's enough, Roger." Barry's voice held a weight to it, physically pushing against my body. I'd felt it from him before, and as it washed over me, I finally understood why it held such power.

There's chi in his voice . . . ?

Strands of it, hair-thin and invisible even to my eyes, flowed out from him. He didn't have the level of control I did, so I wondered if he was even aware it was happening. Roger's complaints died in his throat, his eyes going wide as he sat back down, blinking rapidly.

Barry took a calming breath, slowly exhaling it before he continued. "I understand your worry. Truly, I do, but you're being too emotional and speaking out of turn. If you can't hold your tongue, I'll need to ask you to leave. Sharon can tell you what happened later."

Fury crossed his face, his lips forming a line and cheek twitching, but he remained seated.

"Thank you," Barry said. He turned toward Maria and I. "How much do you want to know?"

We shared a look, and she nodded for me to take the lead.

"I want to know about anything that puts Maria—or any of you—in danger. Spare the rest of the details unless we ask."

Barry nodded, taking a moment to think. "Okay," he eventually said. "I can work with that. I really did want to leave you out of this, but you'll understand once you know the plan . . ."

Hours later, Barry sat at the round table within the church. As he waited for the rest of the congregation to take their seats, he smiled out at them.

"How are you feeling, dear?" Helen asked, rubbing his shoulder.

"Honestly? I feel great."

Snips, Claws, Pistachio, and Bill entered the room, taking their seats at the table. Bill was a recent recruit, but it already felt as though he'd been there since the beginning. His instruction in martial arts had been invaluable.

Sharon smiled, squeezing Barry's arm to get his attention. "Are you relieved that Fischer agreed?"

"More relieved that the conversation is no longer hanging over my head, I think. I always knew he'd say yes, but I dreaded asking him to do it. It's the opposite of the relaxing life he yearns for . . ."

"But it's for the best."

"It is," he agreed, reaching over to take hold of her hand.

Sue and Sturgill took their seats, each looking as confused as the other. Only two spots at the table were empty—those of Sharon and Roger. The latter still claimed he wasn't a part of the church, yet he'd attended the last week's worth of meetings. When it had become apparent that Maria could—and would—accompany Fischer to the capital, Roger had stormed off, trailed closely by Sharon.

Knowing there was no point in waiting for them, Barry cleared his throat.

He gave Sue and Sturgill a kind smile. "Sorry for dropping you right into the deep end like that, you two. I'd have liked to ease you into it, but Fischer forced the issue."

"It's fine, Barry." Sturgill put a hand around Sue's back, resting it on the chair. "We spoke about it on the way back here, and I think it actually helped. We know the stakes and what you're working toward."

"More importantly," Sue added, leaning into her husband. "We agree with all of it."

Another weight lifted from Barry's shoulders. "I'm glad. We're more than happy to have you with us."

"Shall we pick up where we left off?" Ellis asked, reading over his notes.

"We should." Barry rubbed his chin. "I believe we were about to go over your crafting when Claws came to get us. How is the spirit beast's leather coming along?"

"Coming along?" Ellis raised his eyes, pride clear in them. "It is finished. Just in time, too."

"It is?" Theo asked, clapping his friend on the shoulder.

"Indeed. It came out even better than I had hoped."

"That's fantastic timing, Ellis." Barry gave him a nod. "Well done." He took a deep breath, thinking about what to discuss next. "Okay, I believe the running plan should work. We'll use the Baker's Dozen and Hidden Stash variations. Also . . ." He smiled at the room, unable to hide it. "I believe we can adjust Baker's Dozen now that we have Fat Rat Pack and The Beetle Boys."

Claws chirped, nodding her head so violently that Barry thought she might take flight.

"Glad you approve, Claws."

"Wait," Sturgill said. "I thought we were staying here? Why are you including us?"

"Oh, sorry. I forgot you don't know the variation details. We didn't tell Fischer on purpose." Barry turned to Ellis. "Would you mind going over it?"

"Of course." He stood, placing his notepad in a pocket as he walked over to the diagram on the wall. "Baker's Dozen, by its nature, is a variation focused on misdirection . . ."

He continued explaining the variation in all its intricacies. When understanding finally struck Sue and Sturgill, their eyes went wide.

"Don't tell me . . ." Sturgill said.

"You really mean to . . . ?" Sue asked, trailing off.

Barry nodded, unable to stop himself from smiling.

The two bakers, now known to the System as Fat Rat Pack and The Beetle Boys, burst into laughter.

There were only a few hours of daylight left, making it a terrible time for a villager to leave on a camping trip. Luckily for us, we weren't regular villagers. With a fitful breeze at my back and Maria's hand in mine, I followed the setting sun toward the west.

"Are you sure about this, Fischer?"

"Don't worry." I gave her hand a soft squeeze. "I'll be on my best behavior."

"Yeah, that's exactly what I'm worried about."

"Hey! I can be good!"

She snorted. "Yeah, you were being good when you spoke to that noble the other week. How did that end?"

"Lord Tom Osnan Jr.?" I asked in a posh voice. "I thought that went wonderfully."

"He tried to slap your head off!"

"Fine, it didn't go well, but that was one time."

"One time? What about every other time you've interacted with my dad?"

"Okay, I might have been a touch antagonistic here and there."

She stopped on the spot, narrowing her eyes beneath her blond hair. " . . . *Here and there?*"

"Fine—*most* of the time, but this time will be different. I promise."

She looked at me for a long moment, then nodded and resumed walking. "Okay."

" . . . Okay?" I took a few hurried steps to keep pace. "Just like that?"

"Yep. I trust you."

I glanced over, seeing a solid side-eye coming from her.

"Unless I shouldn't?" she asked.

I grinned back. "You can trust me. I want you to move in without your dad swearing a blood vendetta against me, so I'll be on my best behavior."

"Good." Her cheeks flushed, and she darted in to plant a kiss on my cheek. "I want that too."

I stared into her eyes, marveling at the colors I found there and the way they seemed to shift in the sunlight. Distracted as I was, I felt our quarry's chi signature too late.

"What do you want?" came his gruff voice.

I turned to look at Roger. He sat on his deck, peeling a root vegetable and letting the skin fall to the sandy soil.

"Hey, Mate. I came to see you."

"Don't you think you've done enough for one day?"

I turned to Maria. "Would you give us a moment?"

"Of course." She let go of my hand, sweeping forward and only pausing to give her dad a quick hug before running inside. The front door closed behind her, leaving us alone.

The soft *snick* of his knife peeling skin from the vegetables was the only sound to be heard. A wind kicked up, shaking the leaves of the surrounding crops. I leaned into the calm the wind gave me, letting out a slow breath.

"I know you don't trust me, mate. That's okay, and I get it. In the absolute best-case scenario, I'm some kind of interworld traveler with more power than he can fully comprehend."

Roger raised an eyebrow, glaring up at me.

I held up both hands, stalling the inflammatory comment no doubt forming on his tongue.

"Let me finish, mate. You don't trust me—totally fine. What you can trust is that I love your daughter. I'm *in* love with your daughter. Come hell, highwater, or even a literal God coming down from the heavens, I will protect her with my life. I swear to you, on everything I am, that I'll bring her home safe. I'll *always* bring her home safe."

Every time Roger looked at me, I saw exactly who he was. He had the eyes of a soldier, one who had seen things most men would crumble under the weight of. He'd never told me as much himself, but it was easy to glean from the things Maria had told me. He never spoke of his time in the army. *Never.* Not even a word. It was why he was so abrasive. Why he didn't really care what others thought. Given everything he had been through, it was impossible for him to not see the world through a grim lens.

When it came to his daughter, though, that mask shattered.

He usually did pretty well to hide it, often lashing out in anger to hide the fear he felt. The fear of losing her. Earlier, when Barry had agreed Maria could accompany me to the capital without being put in danger, Roger's eyes told the truth. Now, as he looked up at me from the deck, with his knife frozen midway through removing a strip of dirt-covered peel, he had the eyes of a father, terrified of the prospect of losing the thing he held dearest in this world.

"Can you really promise that?" he asked, voice unnaturally calm.

"I can."

Whether he could tell I meant it or because he needed to believe me, Roger nodded and stood. He set his vegetable and knife down, holding out a hand toward me. I grasped it, shaking as he weighed me with his gaze. It felt as though we'd finally found common ground, like I'd finally convinced him that I was someone worth trusting.

Was this the missing piece? I wondered. *Could I have ended the animosity long ago by promising I'd protect her with my life?*

He leaned in close, his eyes going flinty. "Fail her and I will hunt you down, heretic."

Welp. Never mind.

"I don't care if you ascend to the heavens," he continued, leaning in closer and squeezing my hand with everything he had. "I'll follow you, find you, and *end* you."

"Deal," I said, matching his strength.

I felt a small but powerful source of chi racing through the crops behind us. Roger looked past me, hearing the creature as it brushed sugarcane stalks aside. Borks came flying out, his tongue lolling and tail wagging as he came to a skidding stop before us. He barked, sitting down and looking up with nothing but excitement on his face.

"I think that's my cue, mate," I said, letting go of Roger's hand.

The door opened behind him, Maria and Sharon appearing in the doorway.

"Ready to go?" She asked, giving her father and me a hesitant glance.

"Yep! Ready when you are!"

She skipped forward, wrapping Roger in a tight hug. Sharon came to me, giving me a knowing smile as she approached.

She pulled me into an embrace, patting me on the back. "Bring her home in one piece." She leaned toward my ear. "And nicely handled," she whispered before letting go.

I gave her a wide grin as Maria came to my side, putting her hands behind her back and smiling at her parents.

"See you guys soon," I said.

"Yeah!" Maria agreed. "We'll be back within the week."

"Remember your promise," Roger said, his face once more that of a hardened soldier.

"Will do, mate!"

With Borks at my side and Maria's hand in mine, we followed the trail of the setting sun.

CHAPTER EIGHTY

BROTHERLY LOVE

Beneath the pink and orange sunset of a beautiful winter's day, two brothers stumbled arm in arm along a seldom-traveled dirt road.

"We'd better get back to the farm," David slurred as they both wobbled.

"Aye." Trevor upended his bottle, taking a deep swig. He sighed with the burn that ran down his throat, warming him from the core. "Da will tan our hides if he learns we been out drinking all day instead of working."

A few seasons back, things had kicked off between their home village of Cedar and those bog-water drinkers over at Bengal Village. As a result, the brothers hadn't been able to buy any of Bengal's moonshine for most of the year. So, when a merchant had come through with some of the swill—and speaking all proper like, so they knew he wasn't a Bengalian in disguise—they'd bought as much as they could afford.

"Say what you will about those goatherders over in Bengal, they sure know how to make a damned good brew." Trevor tipped the glass bottle up, his eyebrow furrowing when none came out. He shook it, a scowl deepening when only a few drops fell onto his tongue. He turned to glare at his brother. "You drank the last of it, you bastard?"

"Me?" David reeled back from his brother, indignant and swaying. "You're holding the damned bottle!"

"Aye! Which makes it even worse! Ye drank the last of it right out from under me, you poxy son of a goat."

"Oi, oi, oi. You leave my mother out of . . ." David hiccupped, a flushed grin coming to his face. "We have the same parents. You just called yourself a son of a goat."

Swaying without a shoulder to lean on, Trevor pointed the now-empty bottle at his brother's thieving, mother-besmirching face. "You take that back."

With the dexterity of a dehydrated man that had been day-drinking moonshine for the last eight hours, David backhanded his brother. Well, he tried to, anyway. By some miracle, he managed to smack the swaying bottle extended toward him. It made a dull *tink* as his knuckles collided with it, sending it sailing into the tree line. Both wobbling violently, their heads spun to follow its trajectory.

"You ungrateful, mother-insulting toad lick—"

Trevor cut off as a streak of colors shot past them, traveling east to west along the road. The speed of it was incredible. They both turned, intending on seeing what it was, but there was nothing there.

"What in—"

A wall of wind slammed into their backs. If they had been sober, perhaps they could have withstood it. Instead, they fell like long-dead trees in a hurricane, landing in a tangle of limbs as dust sprayed over them. Both brothers slowly climbed to all fours, spitting dust.

Trevor locked eyes with his brother and chortled. "You look like you been tilling the soil with your teeth!"

"Yeah?" David got to his knees. "Well, you look like you been shovelin' dirt with your head!"

Both pairs of eyes narrowed, a lip curled, and they burst into laughter.

"That damned bog-swill is some good stuff," David said, finally making it upright and holding a hand to his brother.

"Aye," Trevor agreed, using the offered hand to pull himself upright. "We'll have to get some more soon. Might not be so bad dealing with them bog-water drinkers if we can get more bottles . . ."

Shoulder to shoulder and their spirits as high as the clouds above, the brothers stumbled back toward their village.

Watching the two men go, Maria, Borks, and I shared a smile. We waited until they were far away before hopping down from the tree. After accidentally sprinting past them at cultivator speed, all three of us had scrambled upward, hiding from sight.

"Phew!" Maria brushed her hands off. "That was close."

"No kidding. Lucky they were so drunk."

Maria giggled, covering her mouth. "I'm not so sure how I feel about the church's trade route being used to facilitate whatever those two were up to."

"I don't know," I replied, looking down the road after them. "I kinda love it. They seem like fun."

"Should we go say hello?" she asked, raising an eyebrow.

"We probably shouldn't be seen, but we could trail them. Checking they got home *would* be the right thing to do . . ."

She rolled her eyes, smiling at me. "Right. It's *definitely* because you want them home safe and not because you'll get enjoyment out of their banter." She bent to scratch Borks's head, who was staring up at us with unconditional love. "Come on, then. Let's go make sure those farmers make it back to their village."

We trailed them for a good half hour, our enhanced senses of hearing easily picking up their voices. The words they were using, however, were a different story.

"Are they getting drunker?" Maria asked, scrunching her nose. "What are they even saying?"

I laughed, keeping it quiet enough that we wouldn't be overheard. "I think that was something about a barn cat or a cactus needing water. Could have been either, honestly."

The two brothers' voices trailed off. When we stepped farther through the trees, I saw why.

They'd arrived at Cedar Village, just as Ellis had marked on our map. We barely caught sight of their still-swaying backs as they stumbled around a stone and mortar wall. The mortar was half covered in moss, the plant flourishing in the damp forest air. Buildings beyond stretched toward the sky, their walls built of the same materials and only slightly less afflicted by the green growth. Smoke rose from chimneys, glowing a deep orange against the almost set sun beyond.

It looked like a little village right out of a fantasy novel. The only thing missing was elves, or perhaps a low-flying dragon.

Or a bloke that can shoot beams of explosive light from his fist, I thought, smiling at myself.

Cedar Village was almost as beautiful as the picturesque bay back at Tropica, and we stood in silence a moment longer, taking it in.

"David and Trevor!" a feminine voice called, breaking the silence. "You get your butts here this instant so I can smack some sense into you!"

One of them mumbled something unintelligible, but the tone was questioning.

"What? You thought I wouldn't know my idiot sons bought some of that poison from Bengal when the merchant rolled through? When your Da couldn't find you, I checked your hiding spot. And what did I find? A bottle missing!"

A series of hurried smacks rang out through the trees, followed by slurred protests.

"Oh, you think this is bad? Just wait until you Da finds you!"

Their mother slipped into a tirade filled with such vitriol and passion that Maria and I raised our eyebrows at each other.

"I feel like I should write that down," I whispered. "That would put some hair on Paul's chest."

She hit me on the arm softly. "Don't even joke about that! Helen would slap you silly."

"Naturally . . . but it could be worth it."

She rolled her eyes. "Come on. Let's go find a place to camp before you get any more brilliant ideas."

"But then we won't get to hear their Da beat their hides like an old carpet . . ."

"Let's race, then," she replied, shooting me a grin. "Loser has to cook dinner!"

Before I could reply, she was off, dashing through the trees to the northwest. Borks raced off after her, his golden hair streaming with his passage. It was a terrible punishment for losing; I loved cooking.

What I couldn't ignore, however, was a challenge.

"You want a race, huh?" I rolled my shoulders, watching them as they tore off through the underbrush. I crouched, sent chi down to my legs, then exploded into motion.

A half hour later, Maria was leaning on her knees, huffing. "Not . . . fair . . ." she got out between breaths.

"Not bad, huh?"

She collapsed to the ground, her sweat-streaked hair sticking to parts of her face. "Your chi advancement or whatever it is—I want it."

Borks let out a groan of agreement, also lying on his side in the grass.

The entire time we ran, I'd used just enough chi to stay ahead of them. I wanted the race to be close, and the result was the exhaustion Borks and Maria were currently experiencing. We'd covered an insane amount of ground, running around the village and next to the road along our plotted path. When we reached a crossroads Ellis had marked down on the map, we took a left and headed south. It was a little out of the way, but there was a vital pit stop we had to make. I gazed out at our reason for visiting, anticipation burbling to the surface of my consciousness.

The lake was the largest I'd seen since coming to this world.

The sides of it were raised, looking like nothing so much as a crater. There were no streams coming to or from the body of water, meaning there was good potential for finding a new species. The far bank was as far across as the river mouth back home, and my fingers twitched as I dreamed of casting out my line. With the daylight almost gone, though, there were more important things to take care of.

"Take your time to recover," I said, stretching. "I'll get started on the camp."

It took little time to set our tent up, and even less to collect wood for a campfire. As I blew on a tiny flame sprouting beneath a teepee of sticks, Maria knelt down beside me. The fire grew, quickly consuming the dry wood.

"You know," Maria said, leaning her head on my shoulder. "You're pretty well domesticated."

"Yeah, my girlfriend is lazy, so I naturally learned to—kidding! *Kidding!*"

She withdrew her pinchy fingers, smiling behind her pout. Borks shoved his head between us, tongue lolling from his panting mouth.

I rubbed Borks's head. "Let's see if this lake holds any fish."

After setting our rods up, I removed the chunk of bait.

"It's a shame we didn't find any of the pungent eel over the last couple days," Maria said, pinching her nose as I removed the ripe eel from its wrappings.

"Yeah. This twice-common one should be enough to do the trick, though."

I ran a knife through the eel, cutting off two thin pieces. Maria had a smaller hook on her line so we could target different sized fish at the same time; we had no clue what the lake held. I slipped the baits on each of our hooks, then we stepped forward together.

"After you," I said, delighting in the look on Maria's face.

"No. Please." She ushered me forward. "Ladies first."

"Oh, such a gentleman!" I replied, batting my eyes.

She giggled, covering her mouth in the way that always made my heart flutter. I cast my line out, aiming right for the middle of the lake. It landed with a satisfying *plop,* as did Maria's, just a little closer to shore. Sitting beside each other, and with Borks at our feet, we waited.

And waited.

And *waited.*

"Well, this is a bit disappointing . . ." Maria said, chewing her lip as she stared at the water.

I reeled my line in. It felt heavy, and sure enough, the bait was untouched.

Maria sighed. "I was so excited, too. I guess there's nothing in this lake?"

"Maybe . . ." I replied, thinking of something.

"What are you doing?" Maria asked as I cut my tackle off the end of my line.

"Testing a theory . . ."

I grabbed a sabiki rig, tying it to the end of my rod, then walked down to the water and cast it in. It landed close to shore, making a quiet splash barely heard over the calls of insects. I wound the line in so it was tight.

"You think there are smaller fish here?" she quietly asked.

"Yeah," I whispered back. "Surely there's *something* . . ."

She wrapped an arm around my back, leaning against my torso as we both stared out at the calm lake.

Something tugged at the line.

I inhaled sharply, adrenaline spiking and shattering the calm that Maria's proximity gave me. I held the line tight, waiting for the bite.

Bump.

Bump.

The fish bit the hook, immediately trying to swim away. It was a small thing, but that didn't make it any less exciting as I brought the hooks toward the surface. With a smile on my face, I lifted it up out of the water, swiveling so it entered the campfire's light.

The moment I caught sight of it, I froze, blinking at the flailing limbs.

Maria's hand jolted on my back, gripping onto my shirt.

" . . . *What the frack is that?*" she demanded, her voice shrill.

CHAPTER EIGHTY-ONE

FOUR-LEGGED MONSTROSITIES

Night had well and truly descended within the forest, the light of day having slowly bled over the western horizon. The campfire was both a welcome source of heat and light, the latter of which was currently illuminating an absurd-looking creature.

Maria and I shared a worried look as it kicked around on the hook. Borks slunk over to sniff at it, taking care not to come within touching distance. Most of its features were that of a fish; it had tiny scales, fins, and was a light-brown color that would help it hide in the murky lake's waters. Sprouting from the bottom of its body, however, were four decidedly non-fishy limbs. It was . . . a quadruped? They were like the limbs of a salamander or axolotl, scaleless and fleshy. Its eyes bulged hideously, like it was being squeezed.

As it kicked all four of its legs feebly, my eyes were drawn into it.

Mature Jungle Mudminnow
[unknown]
[unknown]

What in the fresh fuck? I thought, dismissing the information from my field of view.

"*Unknown?*" Maria asked.

The System, my ever-annoying pal, demanded my attention. It wasn't like any nudge I'd felt from it before, and I got the sense it was trying to give me something. With more than a little hesitation, I accepted the message.

New species discovered: Mature Jungle Mudminnow!
Claim and identify species?

Claim and identify?

I willed my ascent, and information about the creature streamed into me. It was unnatural—not native to this world. It had . . . mutated? Been created? I couldn't exactly tell, but that it was alien to this forest was undeniable. The System tugged at my attention again, once more offering something. A little less hesitant, I allowed it to come.

New species identification bonus: +5 to fishing! Congratulations!
Mature Jungle Mudminnow
Unique
This fish is a creation of the followers of Ceto. It is unknown how long the Jungle Minnow has existed within the Kallis Realm, but in that time, it has stabilized itself within the food chain. This fish has become the favored prey of [unknown].

"Holy frack . . ." I said aloud, processing the many implications. I turned to Maria, curious to know if she had gotten the messages too.

Her face told me everything I needed to know. Her eyes were distant, likely staring at the writing in her field of view, and as I waited impatiently for her to come back to the present, golden light burst from her. There was no warning, even my enhanced sense of chi not alerting me to the advancement. The shine was blinding, and I had to squeeze my eyes closed against the gold brilliance lighting our surroundings.

With the light came an overwhelming euphoria that made my entire body tingle. A smile that wasn't only a result of the sensation came to my face. The moment the light diminished, I opened my eyes, excited to hear from Maria what had happened. Instead, I found myself lurching forward, instinctively reaching for her unconscious form as she raced headfirst toward the forest floor.

I easily scooped her up, bitter panic rising in the back of my throat.

"Hey . . . *hey!*" I cradled her head in my hands, my eyes locking on hers as I caressed her cheek with a shaky hand. "Maria!"

Borks dashed to our side in the blink of a cultivator's eye, pressing his wet nose against her neck and sniffing intently. She stirred, my heart seeming to stop beating in my chest as I waited for another sign of life. She . . . giggled, then squirmed her head down against Borks to block out his wet nose.

"Borks! Stop!" She pushed him away with one hand, still giggling. "It tickles!"

I heaved a breath of relief, slumping to the forest floor as she sat up. My panic was still present, but drained away with each breath I took.

"Fischer? You okay? You look like you've seen a ghost."

"Don't ever do that again! You scared the life out of me!"

"Do what?"

"You fainted! It was terrifying."

She pulled me into a hug and patted my back, laughing loud and free.

"What's so funny?" I asked, leaning back.

Her grin turned wry. "Do you know how many times you've done that to me? Just collapsed with no warning, then popped up like nothing was wrong? About time you got a taste of your own medicine."

I shook my head, palpable relief still running through me. We made to stand, but Maria froze, her brow lowering. She reached underneath herself, grabbed a hold of something, then lifted it up before her eyes. A familiar tinkle came from the small brown bag.

Her eyes were knowing yet still curious. She opened the drawstring and leaned forward so we could both see within. Golden coins gleamed back at us, faintly illuminated by the campfire's orange glow.

"What did the System say?" I asked.

"I got five skill points in fishing for discovering a new species. That fish—"

"Crap!" I interrupted. "The fish!"

With everything happening, I'd completely forgotten about the poor creature. Unlike us, it couldn't breathe air, and I'd left it to suffo . . . *cate?* The jungle mudminnow, apparently unaware or uncaring of its inability to breathe air, was standing on its four salamander-like limbs, trying to walk back to the water. The fishing line was stretched to its limit, the rod too heavy for the small fish to drag it into the lake.

It seemed to look at us with its bulging eyes.

"Ew . . ." Maria said.

"Yeah," I agreed. "I don't like that at all."

Still, I walked over to it, picking it up to remove the hook from its mouth. All four of its fleshy legs fought against my palm, tickling me as they squirmed to be free of my grasp. I lobbed it into the water, both feeling sorry for it and wanting to be as far from it as possible.

"Didn't you want to try using it as bait?" Maria asked, patting Borks on the head.

"I felt bad about forgetting it, but honestly, I think it may have been able to breathe air?" I shook my head, shuddering. "Why are legs on a fish so weird?"

"I don't know. They just are."

Borks ruffed his agreement, staring at the lake I'd returned the fish to.

"How are you feeling?" I asked Maria.

"Drained." She tied the drawstring on her bag of coins closed.

"Too drained for a little fishing?" I asked.

Her eyes sparkled as she looked up at me. "Never."

With a sabiki rig soaking in the water, my thoughts returned to the messages we'd received from the System, as did Maria's.

"The descriptions said it was from the followers of Ceto, right?" she asked, curling a finger through her hair.

"Yeah. Pretty insane, huh?"

"No kidding . . ."

"Ceto was a god of the sea, weren't they?"

"Yeah."

I sighed. "I have a confession to make."

She quirked an eyebrow at me. "Another one?"

"Would you mind keeping it between us for now? I think it might break Ellis if he finds out."

Recognizing how serious I was, she spun to face me. "Of course."

"Most of the gods you all swear about in this world . . . I'd heard of them before coming here."

Her head cocked to the side, her nose scrunching. "You did? How?"

"From my world—they were the same gods an ancient civilization worshipped."

"They were in your world?" she asked, her eyes flying wide.

I made a so-so gesture. "I mean . . . maybe? If not that, then someone from this world—or from another realm those gods had fled to—was sent to ancient Greece."

"Ancient Greece . . . that's where you know the gods' names from?"

I nodded. "Yeah."

"Huh. That's pretty neat."

I raised an eyebrow. "That's it?"

"Well, yeah. I'm more interested in the fact that Ceto's followers could somehow make a new species of fish, to be honest."

Seeing the incredulity on my face, she shook her head, smiling. "Fischer, you're a regular man—or at least *were* a regular man—that was sent from an entirely different world. Spirit beasts, creatures that haven't existed for thousands of years, pop up around you like weeds. You shoot beams of light that turn trees into splinters and send hellhounds flying across the sky like shooting stars." She turned to the side. "No offense, Borks."

He shrugged, a decidedly non-doglike gesture.

"On that note," she continued. "You're so powerful that you befriended a hellhound, a creature spoken of in the mythology here as the arbiters of the underworld that drag souls off to the afterlife. All those things considered, that our gods may have fled to your world at some point doesn't seem that important to me."

"Huh . . ."

"Though, I do agree you shouldn't tell Ellis right now. His head might explode, and we need him for the mission to succeed. Feel free to tell him after, though."

My chest felt light following the confession, and I let out a laugh, shaking my head. "The jungle mudminnow alone might make him implode. He's going to be so pissed that we didn't tell him until after the mission—especially when he's so close."

Maria joined in with my mirth, covering her mouth as she let out a cute giggle. "How long has that information been bothering you?"

"Since I arrived here. I didn't think it was that important, to be honest, but with how light I feel right now, it was weighing on me more than I thought."

She leaned forward. I expected her to plant a soft kiss on me, but then she reached up, flicking my nose softly. "Stop keeping secrets, you big oaf. How many times do you need to relearn that lesson?"

I rubbed the spot she'd flicked. "Point taken."

Maria leaned back in. This time, she did kiss me, her velvet lips lingering on mine for a few heartbeats. When she pulled back, she smiled at me. "Now, can we talk about the fact that there are four-legged fish in here? That shit's *whack.*"

Unexpected as it was, her use of Earth-borne slang made me chortle. "Yeah, it truly is whack."

"If it was made by the followers of Ceto, *and* if Lemon's memory of this world's timeline can be believed, they must have been here for thousands of years, right?"

"It would seem so, yeah, unless there are some secret followers of Ceto still kicking around. The fact it said *church,* though, makes me think that isn't the case. It was from a time when Ceto, and presumably, the rest of the gods, were present."

"And in that time . . ." Her eyes, twinkling with anticipation, darted over to meet mine. "These four-legged monstrosities have become the food source of another creature . . ."

As if listening to the flow of our conversation, something bit down on my line. I shot to my feet and held my rod high, angling it past Maria's rig as I slowly wound it in. My plan worked; the slow retrieve meant another fish had time to bite down on another hook. The moment I felt the extra weight on my line, I lifted it out of the water.

Two mudminnows flopped on the grass, their weird little legs trying to find purchase.

"Yeah, still gross," Maria said, scrunching her nose.

I dashed forward, dispatching both of them and removing them from the sabiki rig before either knew what was happening. Both were smaller than my palm, and Maria and I immediately set about swapping our tackle for something more suitable. With the sabiki rigs removed and a single large hook tied above a sinker, we shared a grin, then baited up with a whole mudminnow each.

"Same time?" I asked, smiling at Maria.

She nodded. "Same time."

In practiced unison, we flicked the reels forward, cocked the rods back, and cast our lines out.

They landed one after the other, twin splashes rising as our baited hooks hit the water's surface. I took a slow breath, a smile coming to my face as a sense of ease washed over me. Maria and I sat down, our legs touching as we got comfortable. Borks came to sit at my side, his reassuring weight resting against me. The night air was chilly, growing more so with each gust of wind blowing through the leafy canopy above. Warmth from the campfire radiated against my back, stealing away the night's wintery kiss. I had wound my fishing line tight, and with a finger held to it, I waited for a bite.

As much as I idealized a life of peace and calm, chaos had been leaking into it over the past couple of months. In moments like this, though, the chaos didn't matter. As long as I had fishing and the relationships that had flourished since my arrival in this strange realm, all the chaos in the world couldn't overwhelm me.

"Oh . . . *Oh!*" Maria said, sitting upright.

Her line went taut, her rod bending and bouncing as a hooked creature fought to escape.

Her face lit up, completely covered in childlike wonder.

"Fish on!"

CHAPTER EIGHTY-TWO

POTENT

A breeze blew through the surrounding trees, their leaves rustling softly, and ethereal moonlight shone down from above, lighting the lake's surface. Flames licked at the campfire behind us, its orange glow joining the blue-white light of the moon. Within that beautiful vista, Maria's line tore through the water.

"Fish on!" she repeated, laughing as her eyes gained a predatory gleam.

The fish darted to the right, trying to escape her clutches—there was nowhere to go. My fingers twitched, my entire body aching as I watched her rod bend beneath the fish's mighty kicks. The hooked creature darted back to the left, charging toward my line.

"Shit," I hissed, reeling in so they wouldn't get tangled.

Something bit at my hook, making my adrenaline spike. When it didn't budge, however, I understood.

A snag, I thought, letting out a sigh.

I held the tip of the line low, trying to get it out of Maria's way, but then my snag *moved.*

"*F-fish on!*" I yelled, excitement blooming in my core.

"Double hook-up!" Maria let out a lilting laugh. "Last one to catch the fish has to clean up after dinner!"

"Deal!" I replied.

I stepped to the left, keeping our lines away from each other. My fish had other plans. It dashed to the right, just as Maria's continued going left. I held my rod high and she slipped beneath it, neither of us needing to utter a word. Whatever we'd hooked, they were both *powerful.* Not sitting still for a moment, they used their lean muscles to seek any possible avenue of escape. As was so often the case, however, we were more than their match.

Maria's fish darted toward us, taking a course it had no way of knowing was the wrong one. She didn't waste the opportunity, reeling in the line and keeping it tight. It turned, swimming adjacent to the shore, its silvery scales flashing beneath the moon's otherworldly light.

It was *big.*

"No way . . ." Maria uttered.

Her hand never stopped winding in line, and with its proximity to the surface, water swirled around each kick of its massive tail. Holding her rod up in one hand, she stepped into the shallows, easily looping a hand under its gill plate and hauling it up onto the shore. I wanted to gaze at it, wanted to let my eyes get drawn into the unknown fish, but I had my own fight to focus on. The fish I'd hooked continued trying to escape, but for every method it tried, I was ready to counter it. I drew it ever closer, and when it finally reached the shallows, I followed Maria's actions, reaching down to lift it from under the gills. Its body was as long as it was formidable, and if I was a regular human, I'd not have been able to wrestle it to shore. With my enhanced body, however, I brought it up with one hand, sliding it up on the grass.

The moment I'd seen its mouth beneath the pale moonlight, I understood why Maria hadn't grabbed it by the jaw. Rows of crocodilian teeth lined its jaw, and even with my strengthened body, I didn't want to chance having my hand ripped to shreds by those razor-sharp chompers. Its body was at least a meter long, its stomach as round as my muscle-packed thigh. Just like the mudminnows, its scales held a brown hue, likely to help it camouflage within the silty waters of the lake. It snapped at me with its tooth-filled mouth. I dodged, positioning myself above it so I could hold the mouth closed with both hands.

As I stared down at its inhuman eyes, my gaze was drawn into it.

Mature [unknown] Alligator Gar
[unknown]
[unknown]

Before I could say anything, the next lines of text appeared.

New species discovered: Mature [unknown] Alligator Gar!
Claim and identify species?

I glanced at Maria; she was staring back. We both nodded. Borks let out a loud bark, not entirely understanding what we were doing, but happy to be there. I willed my assent, as did Maria.

New species identification bonus: +10 to fishing! Congratulations!
Mature [unknown] Alligator Gar
Unique
This species variation of the alligator gar has evolved through its predation of jungle mudminnows, an unnatural fish created by the followers of Ceto, over thousands of years. There is more to learn about this species for those willing to partake of its flesh.

I dismissed the System message, the orange glow of the campfire flickering as the fish flopped about, trying to escape. I held it, making its efforts futile as I turned to Maria. Before I could say anything, power welled up from within me. It flowed out as a heady pulse, the golden light making me stumble. With my increased power, I managed to stay standing. Something fell to the ground behind me, letting out the jangle of coins as it struck the grass.

Grabbing her fish around the back of the head and shooting me a knowing glance, Maria ran down to the water, placing it beneath the black surface. The fish wasted no time in swimming back to the depths, leaving only swirling water in its wake.

I cocked my head in question.

"Mine was out of the water for longer," she answered, eyes flicking between me and the fish I held down. "And we only need to eat one to learn more about it . . ."

Grinning as my strength returned, I slipped the spike from my belt. With a flash of movement, I drove it into the fish, dispatching it in an instant.

"Thank you," I said, holding a hand to its dinosaur-like head.

"Yeah," Maria said, kneeling down beside me. She laid her palm on its abdomen. "Thanks, fishy. We'll make sure none of you goes to waste."

I twisted my torso, picking up the bag of coins. "More, huh?"

Chewing her lip, Maria seemed pensive as she looked at the brown bag. Her eyes drifted toward the fire, avoiding mine. "On the subject of secrets, I know you're still hesitant to read the notifications from the System, but do you want to know what it said when it gave me my coins?"

The question brought me up short, but after a moment's consideration, I let out a sigh. "I think I already know, so you may as well tell me."

"You do?" she asked.

"Unfortunately, yeah. Did you reach a milestone? Like, say, getting level twenty-five in fishing?"

She nodded slowly. "Yeah. That's exactly what it was. How long have you known that was the cause of the coins?"

"Well, since you just confirmed it. Before that, it was only a theory."

As if sensing the moment of weakness, the System pinged me. With more than a little hesitation, I allowed it in.

You have advanced to fishing 75!

I shook my head, letting out a soft laugh. "Yeah—I just got to fishing seventy-five. I guess that confirmed the 'intervals of twenty-five' theory . . ."

"*Seventy-five?*" she repeated. "Glaucus's scaled tail! *Seventy-five?*"

"What can I say? I love me some fishin'."

Her face turned thoughtful. "Do you think the church knows? About the intervals, I mean?"

"Good chance. I imagine more than a few of them have skills above level twenty-five by now, especially considering it takes previous experience into account. Peter would have to be *at least* twenty-five in cooking, right? If not way higher." I ran a hand through my hair. "Hell, all the crafters probably have at least one skill at twenty-five." My brows furrowed. "Which begs the question: how many coins is

Barry sitting on, and what is he planning to . . ." I shook my head, dispelling the thought. "Never mind. Don't wanna know."

Maria giggled at me, covering her mouth. "You're cute when you get flustered."

Seeking to distract myself, I lifted the alligator gar and took it down to the water's edge. With my trusty knife, I started removing its scales.

"Why do you think the mudminnow said an unknown amount of time, but the alligator gar said thousands of years?" I asked after a stretch of silence, running the dull side of my knife along its body.

"Hmmm . . . because it is an evolution of an existing species?" she guessed. "Or maybe because we caught it second, so we got information from both of the fish?"

"Both possibilities make sense. If we'd caught the gar first, I wonder if the System would have said it predated an unknown fish instead of outright stating it evolved by eating jungle mudminnows."

"I assume so?" Maria shook her head, her hair whipping with each movement. "I feel like we could discuss the nuance of those System messages and the whole coin thing all night."

"Yeah," I agreed. "There's a lot to be gleaned from them, not least of all that we learn more by eating the fish. I won't lie; I don't like the phrasing of *those willing to partake in its flesh.*"

Her head cocked to the side, her eyes curious. "Why?"

"It makes me worry it might not have a positive effect." I flipped the fish over and began scaling the other side. "Especially because it evolved by eating four-legged horror fish."

"Good point. I still can't get over how creepy those little bug-eyed things are."

I finished scaling the second side much faster than the first, then immediately started gutting it. "I think I should eat it first. We can cut a little off and cook it. Hopefully, that'll unlock the unknown info."

I sliced back a bit of skin on the side of its body, removing a palm-sized chunk of pink flesh from the filet there. After pressing a stick into it, I held it over the flames. The moment the flesh started to cook, the smell was intoxicating. The scents and sounds of a campfire alone were enough to make my soul sing, but with the addition of seared fish to the mix, I found myself salivating.

"Mmm." Maria said. "That smells *amazing.*"

It took little time for the thin slice of fish to cook, and when the side facing the fire was completely white, I flipped it. The side that I'd seared dripped, its white flesh sprinkled with spots of brown from the campfire's heat. I watched the fish intently, knowing it wouldn't take long to cook, but then another of my senses spoke up.

My brows drew down as I felt my abdomen resonate with the small bit of fish. It was . . . *was that chi?* Without me doing any essence-swappy shenanigans, the chi content of the fish had increased on its own. As the flesh continued cooking, the power only grew, and when the chi within it stabilized at a potent level, I knew the fish was done.

"Can you feel that?" I asked, removing it from the flames.

"Feel what?" Maria cocked her head to the side. "I didn't notice anything . . . ?"

I licked my lips. "The chi content of the fish. It's—"

The System nudged me, offering more informational goodies. Usually, I'd have ignored it, but if it was willing to tell me about the fish, I was happy to take a chance.

New species trait discovery bonus: +10 to fishing! Congratulations!
Mature Potent Alligator Gar
Unique
This species variation of the alligator gar has evolved through its predation of jungle mudminnows, an unnatural fish created by the followers of Ceto, over thousands of years. Through millennia of evolution, the potent alligator gar has managed to produce a unique kind of chi that only matures when exposed to heat.

"Holy frack . . ." Maria said.

"You . . ." I licked my lips. "You got the notification too?"

She nodded, staring down at the fish.

Without a moment's thought, I broke it in two, holding one-half out toward her. "Well, we know it isn't poisonous," I said. "Will you try it with me?"

She accepted the fire-charred fish, watching it with hunger in her eyes. Without a word, we both ate it at the same time. We'd added no salt, no seasoning, no . . . anything. The only flavor lending itself to the fish were the smoky notes provided by the campfire. An appreciative noise escaped my throat as its essence washed over my awareness.

The flesh was low in fat, and given how I'd seared it over the fire, it was firmer than some of the melt-in-your-mouth fish I'd eaten of late. Still, it was delicious, having a mildly fishier taste than the oceanic species we usually partook of. When I swallowed, the chi heading down toward my core was like a roaring forge. It heated everything it passed, waves of warmth radiating outward.

Maria released a shaky breath, clearly experiencing the same sensation. "That's . . . wow." She took a deep drink of water. "That's a *lot.*"

"Yeah . . ."

We sat with the feeling for a long moment, Borks coming up to each of us and sniffing at us inquisitively. I ran a hand along the top of his head, delighting in how soft his fur was.

"I think I know how to cook the fish . . ." I said, thinking aloud.

"Were you thinking shallow fry? Because I was thinking shallow fry."

I shot her a smirk. "Great minds think alike. The crumbs and added fat content would lend itself perfectly to the flavor."

"Well," she said, getting to her feet. "I'll get the oil and breadcrumbs ready—you cut up the fish?"

"Deal!"

I headed back down to the filets, my knife making short work of them.

A little less than an hour later, we'd fried all the fish, and an absolute mountain of golden-crumbed pockets of deliciousness lay atop a board. Maria, Borks, and I had been helping ourselves as we went, and each portion was just as delicious as the one before it.

"I'm honestly full already," I said, nursing my stomach.

"Me too," Maria agreed. "I might explode if I absorb any more chi . . ."

I turned to Borks. "Wanna share some with everyone else?"

His tail wagging, he barked in the affirmative. I lifted the board for him, letting him grab it with his mouth. With his golden tail still swishing away, he opened a portal and disappeared.

"I'll never get used to that," Maria said, watching the abyssal tear in space.

Before I could reply, Borks was back, closing the portal behind him.

"How are they faring?" I asked.

Good, he barked, coming to lick me on the cheek.

"You're a good boy," I said, ruffling his fur.

Yes, he barked in reply, his whole body wagging.

CHAPTER EIGHTY-THREE

SOMETHING BREWING

Riding unseen currents of air high above the coast, Warrant Officer Williams—affectionately dubbed "Bill" by his master—let out a mighty yawn. Pelly had taken the night shift, allowing him to rest. They would have to take turns over the coming days, lest exhaustion overcome them and cause their intricate plan to fall apart.

Seeing the formation scattering, Bill dove toward the ground, unleashing mighty kicks through the air until they came back together, heading north. Inexplicably, an idiom sprung to mind: herding cats.

Though he'd neither seen a cat with his own eyes nor tried to herd them, he knew the comparison to be an apt one. The formation he was hounding was chaotic, their darting movements making little sense to his intelligent mind. Unlike the proverbial herder of cats, however, Bill wouldn't fail. His job was vital and would contribute toward the safety of everyone on the mission to come.

With his resolve renewed, he sailed higher on the ocean currents, leaving the formation alone until the next time they tried to scatter.

Despite the cold winter air trapped beneath the forest's canopy, I woke to a cuddle puddle so warm it was almost too much. *Almost* being the keyword, I wrapped my arms around Maria, pulling our bodies closer to one another. Borks, still snoring softly, flopped into the space behind me, rolling onto his back.

As hot as I felt, it was nothing compared to the warmth that ran through my awareness, my love for both Maria and Borks climbing to an overwhelming crescendo. Taking a long breath and sitting with the more-than-welcome feeling, I carefully extricated myself, intent on making a delicious breakfast for them to wake up to.

Given our ability to carry basically as much as we wanted within our packs, we'd brought all manner of ingredients with us. I would have loved to make laminated dough and craft some croissants from scratch, but we simply didn't have the time. For this reason, I'd taken some from Sue and Sturgill ahead of time. The frosty air trapped beneath the canopy above meant that we could bring dairy products without fearing they would go off, and when I unwrapped a parcel of folded leather, the vaguely cube-shaped dough within was cool to the touch.

With a smile on my face, I placed it on a wooden board and started cutting triangles. They'd given me an excessive amount of dough, and when I finished, there were thirty-two of them—too much for Maria, Borks, and I, but the perfect amount to share with our friends. I stretched the triangles out with practiced ease, following the directions Sturgill had given me. After they were the correct shape, or at least I *thought* they were, I started rolling them. It was a pleasant process, time flying by as I lost myself to the work, getting a little quicker with each croissant I made.

As the sun's beams just started peeking through the leaves above, movement from my left caught my attention. Maria and Borks emerged, both stretching after escaping the tent's confines.

"Good morning," I said. Engrossed as I was by the work, I hadn't noticed the ache building in my lower back. I stretched too, raising my hands toward the sky and letting out a soft groan as the pain melted away.

"Good morning," Maria eventually replied, unleashing a mighty yawn.

She walked toward me, but Borks was faster, striding over with his tail wagging and head dipped. He rubbed himself on my side, and I gave him a pat with my elbow, not wanting to get my hands dirty.

"Ooooh," Maria said. "Croissants?"

"Yeah! I thought this morning was the perfect time."

She nodded, stifling another yawn. "Makes sense. This is the last chance we have for Borks to use his portal, right? We'll be too close to the capital after traveling today."

"Exactly." I removed two trays from my bag, layering the croissants over them evenly. Before I could get any further, I remembered the most important thing. "Oh! Coffee!"

Maria rolled her eyes playfully. "You and your coffee. Want me to take over the croissants?"

"Er—would you mind?"

"Don't be silly." She sat down beside me, shooing me away. "Go on. *Get.*"

Happy to oblige, I ran for her pack, where the sweet, *sweet* coffee beans—and my new favorite toy—were located. It would take longer to create the coffee this morning, but that was only natural given the invention the craftsmen had whipped up for me. At first, I hadn't understood the anticipation on Brad's and Fergus's faces when they'd told me they had a surprise for me. What could a woodworker and a blacksmith build together? The possibilities were endless, but none could have brought me as much joy as what they presented.

Made mostly of stainless steel, it looked like something produced by an artisan back on Earth. Its wooden handles were a deep mahogany, the color reminiscent of dark-roasted and freshly ground coffee beans. Atop the main body, there were two chambers. The first held coffee grounds, the second collected the golden liquid bubbling up from below. It was what I'd heard called a moka pot in my previous life.

I'd often used one when traveling abroad and had only mentioned it to Fergus in passing; he'd taken the idea, run it past Brad, and they'd gone out of their way to make it for me, doing a better job than I ever could have imagined. It was the next best thing to a fresh coffee made at Sue's espresso machine and was certainly preferable to reheating shots over the campfire.

I poured some fresh water from a canteen into the bottom chamber, not entirely trusting any lake that housed fish with legs. I shuddered at the thought.

I'm never going to get used to those creepy little bastards.

Banishing them from my mind, I grabbed the bag of pre-ground beans, poured them into the bottom chamber, then screwed all the pieces together. When it was back in one piece, I held it up before my eyes.

"It really is beautiful . . ."

"Do I need to be worried?" Maria asked, not looking up as she checked on her baking croissants. "I thought others might try to steal you from me, but I never considered an inanimate—"

"Understandable," I interrupted. "I'm a whole lotta *man.*"

She leveled a flat glare at me. "Never mind. The coffee pot can have you."

"*Coffee pot?*" I gasped, miming covering the moka pot's ears. "How dare you reduce her to a mere item? How dare you objectify her so? How dare you look down upon the love of a man and his moka—"

I bent backward, matrix-style dodging the log Maria sent hurtling my way. "Whoa!" I laughed, coming back upright. "Point taken."

She arched an eyebrow at me, and despite the firewood turned artillery that she'd intentionally made easy for me to dodge, there was no malice in the joyous lines of her face. "Come get the coffee boiling, you big goof. If you wait any longer, it won't be ready when the croissants are."

"Yes, ma'am!" I snapped off a crisp salute. "Sorry, ma'am!"

I laughed, dodging the next log that sailed over me.

Claws, with a grin on her face and the thrill of the hunt fueling her limbs, tore through the underbrush beneath the rising sun. It was rare that she got to utilize every bit of her espion . . . *urge? Scorpionage?* She shook her cute little head, giving up on the word. With her sniffer twitching away, she breathed deep of the forest air, her toothy grin turning malevolent when she caught the scent of her quarry. It was faint, so she slunk around on silent paw pads, slowly triangulating the source. A breeze blew beneath the canopy, bringing with it a smell stronger than any of the colonies she'd already found.

More lithe than an arrow in flight and with deadlier intent than a master swordsman, Claws followed the trails, so thick in the forest's humid air that she could almost taste them. Over a meadow, down a sweeping hill, and across a creek, she went wherever the scent did.

Eventually, she spotted the first of them.

It was walking around a tree, so enthralled in its business that it hadn't noticed her dangerous form slinking out from under a bush. Not giving it a chance to flee, Claws flew forward on lightning-empowered limbs. She flicked it in the back of the head, just hard enough to knock it out.

Noting its position in her mind, she set off for the next target, knowing the thickness of their odor meant there had to be dozens, if not hundreds. She spied another three as she rounded a corner, and after a moment spent considering the best way to subdue them, she chose violence.

As a small breeze blew along the lake's surface and over the campfire, the scent of baked goods and fresh coffee suffused the area. I breathed deep, the soft whistle of the moka pot like music to my ears as it mingled with the leaves rustling above.

"Smells like it's almost ready," I said, my mouth watering.

"Good," Maria replied, watching the pans atop the campfire. "I'm not sure I can wait any longer."

She folded a tea towel, using it as a glove to remove a tray covering one pan. Moisture streamed out the moment she lifted, and when I caught sight of the golden pastries within, I knew they were ready. So did she, evidently, because she quickly swept them from the rack atop the fire, setting the pans down on the grass. She lifted both lids, letting the vapor escape. The sun shone down through the trees, lighting the steaming croissants in all their glory.

I removed the top of the moka pot, seeing just what I expected: dark-brown coffee filled the top chamber. There was enough there to make a dozen double shots.

"Happy with espresso?" I asked.

"Always," she replied, fanning the croissants.

I poured a couple shots of coffee into two wooden cups, delighting in the steam that danced above them. Setting them aside, I put the moka pot on a wooden board. Maria, wasting no time, plucked the still-steaming croissants from the pan and piled them high next to the pot. With only a croissant each left for Maria, Borks, and me, she nodded to our canine companion.

"Ready when you are, buddy."

He let out a bark, picked up the tray, tore a portal in space, and hopped through. A few seconds later, he was back, closing the rift behind himself.

"How were they?" I asked, grinning at how fast he was.

Good, he barked as he dropped the board, though with his optimism, I assumed he'd never answer contrarily.

I picked up our wooden cups and walked over to Maria, sitting down beside her and passing her one. "Thanks for making breakfast."

She shot me a wry smile. "It's nice to be appreciated—I've been up since the crack of dawn folding them myself. I daresay my poor wrists may be sore for the rest of the day, so you might need to carry my pack for me."

I nodded, grinning back. "As is only fair. Hopefully the coffee takes some of the sting from your no doubt bruised hands."

She took a sip, her shoulders relaxing, the amused look on her face replaced by one of bliss. "I feel better already. Thank you."

Unable to wait any longer, I grabbed one of the piping hot croissants. I broke it in half, the buttery pastry easily parting. My mouth watered as I took a bite. It was soft, just that tiny bit chewy, and, above all else, delicious.

"*Mmm,*" Maria said, closing her eyes as she chewed.

Borks sniffed his croissant, licked it, then took a little nibble. His eyes went wide and he wolfed it down, basically swallowing it whole.

"Good, mate?" I asked, laughing.

He let out a bark of sheer delight, his tail wagging violently.

"I'm glad. We'll need the energy for how far we need to travel today."

We slipped into silence, our breakfast too encompassing for conversation to take place.

CHAPTER EIGHTY-FOUR

AMBUSH

With the morning sun peeking its orange-hued rays through the trees above, Cinnamon wiggled her cute little tail. Small as her task may be, she was excited to be included in the mission. She took one last bite of her sugarcane stalk, licking up every last drop of its sweet juices. When she swallowed, the chi-enhanced stalk made her body tingle with power.

Despite how strong she had become, some of her base instincts remained. Nothing within the forest could hope to hurt her, yet she still hopped silently through the underbrush, feeling much more at ease when tucked away from sight. Lucky for her, that's where the things she hunted also liked to hide. They were prickly things, so each time she found one within the leaf litter, she'd bat it into her small sack with a paw, taking care not to strike any of the spines.

Though she never doubted her own ability to harvest them, she hadn't anticipated just how many of them she'd find. The sun had only been up for an hour or so, and she'd already filled her sack multiple times, depositing her harvest in a specialty box designed by Ellis and the woodworkers each time it became full. After another two bushes, it was time to deposit again. She hopped back to the box, leaping up its odd-shaped sides to get to the top. Marveling at how weird a construction it was, she popped the latch open and dumped her harvest inside. As she fixed the latch into place, she peered in through one of the many slits lining the box. Despite how many she'd harvested, the vast majority of the box was still empty.

A grin crossed her little bunny face. She didn't have much time, but she would make sure to fill as much of the container as possible. For her master, for her friends, and for every member of the congregation, she would do this task.

With resolve stealing over her features, she launched herself back toward the trees, intent on gathering even faster than before.

I leaped from branch to branch, the midday sun peeking through the leafy canopy I occupied. Borks and Maria joined me, sprinting from tree to tree at inhuman speed.

"Uh, Fischer?"

I glanced at Maria as I leaped from a particularly thick branch. "What's up?"

"Why are you running like that?"

I was leaning forward, my arms trailing behind. "What? You've never seen the Naruto run before?"

She narrowed her eyes, unimpressed with the reference we both knew she wouldn't get.

"I thought it might be more efficient now that I'm a cultivator and all, but it still feels pretty awkward."

"Well, it can't feel worse than it looks."

I laughed so hard at the unexpected jab that I fumbled the landing on the next branch, falling to the floor and having to abort my Naruto run lest I slam headfirst into the ground. I skidded to a stop on all fours, and an opportunist took advantage of my positioning. Borks flew in under my legs, assaulting my chin with a barrage of licks.

"Stop!" I laughed, squirming to get away.

He followed, his tail wagging as the assault continued. Maria rescued me by scooping Borks up into a hug. She cradled him like a baby and he accepted his fate, resting his head on her shoulder as he panted to catch his breath.

"Do you want lunch soon?" I asked, smiling at them.

Borks's head shot around at the mention of food, his ears perking up.

"I'll take that as a yes." I checked the map Ellis had given us. "If we're where I think we are, the next village is just over that hill. And just it . . . "

"The river?" Maria asked. "There's no way we traveled that far already, is there?"

"Pretty sure we have. If the village is where I think it is, the river will be just west of there."

With our energy reserves receiving a booster shot of excitement, we took off once more.

A couple of minutes later, we caught sight of the village. It was the biggest one yet, its houses sprawling across the distance of a valley. We kept our distance from it, circling wide to the south. When we got to the other side of the valley and crested the hill there, Maria turned to me.

"That means the river *is* close, right?" Her eyes grew intense. "Do we have time to fish?"

"We're almost halfway to the capital already and don't have to be there until tomorrow night. We can spend the rest of the day, and then some, fishing."

She did a little happy dance, a strand of hair falling from behind her ear that she didn't bother sweeping back into place. "What are we waiting for? Let's go!"

We tore down the hill, and as we emerged from the trees on the river's bank, we skidded to a stop. As beautiful as my home in Tropica was, the vista we stumbled upon might give it a run for its money. Unlike the water that sometimes turned murky in the river mouth, the water in the river was crystal clear. Smooth rocks lined the riverbed, their gray uniformity somehow stunning beneath the sparkling surface. The sun, directly above us in the cloudless sky, beamed its life down on all we saw.

"Beautiful . . ." Maria said.

"Thank you! Not so bad yourself."

She slapped me on the arm lightly, but couldn't fully hide her smile. "Let's set the rods up. I'm *starving*."

* * *

As the sun set over the western mountains, Bill swelled with pride. He had covered a vast stretch of coast, getting even further than he imagined possible. With every beach, cove, rocky cliff, and mangrove swamp he crossed, his formation grew. They were nearing a thousand strong now, already exceeding the numbers necessary for the Baker's Dozen variant of Operation Sticky Fingers. There were still two full days to gather more strength, and as he pictured how large the formation could grow, a shiver ran down his spine, continuing toward the tips of his mighty wings.

He, as well as the congregation, had assumed that controlling the formation would become harder as it grew. They couldn't have been more wrong. The burgeoning numbers made them stay closer together, their surrounding brethren seeming to give them a sense of security as they migrated. There were still times when sections attempted to scatter, of course, and just as he was wondering when next it would occur, it happened. A full third split off toward the west, following the lead of one misguided fellow. Faster than the formation's eyes could register, Bill appeared on the ground in front of them, kicking up sand with two mighty beats of his wings. They rejoined the main group, and all became right in the world.

Bill rode an unseen column of warm air back into the sky, and as he stabilized high above the coast, he felt a surge of chi approaching from behind. He glanced back, a content smile coming to his face when he saw who it was. Pelly was a kilometer back, rocketing toward him at incredible speed. So swift was her passage that within the space of two wing beats, she was over him. Rather than stop, though, she kept going. His grin widened, and before she could get too far away, he honked to get her attention.

She jolted, spreading her wings wide and flapping backward to halt her passage. With a furiously blushing pouch, she came down to meet him, her eyes averted. Bill shook his head with wry amusement, letting out an understanding honk in an attempt to ease her shame. He, too, sometimes lost himself when shooting along unseen winds high above the ocean. It was natural—a remnant of their animalistic origins.

Pelly let out a honk of her own, telling Bill she was ready to take over the formation. Giving her an appreciative nod, he dove toward the ground, swooping past the formation's edges to bring them tighter together. With one last wave toward Pelly, he veered off toward a rocky cliff in the far distance. Letting off some steam, he shot toward it, his enhanced wings crossing leagues in the time a regular pelican could travel meters.

He found a nice little crevice that shielded him from the elements and tucked himself inside, settling down to sleep.

Beneath a blanket of stars, Claws skipped along a dirt road while dragging a makeshift sled behind her lithe body. Her day had been wonderfully productive, and as she glanced back at the dozen creatures lying unconscious on her sled, she let out a toothy grin. While she'd never once doubted her ability to complete the task, her clandestine skills had surprised even herself. She'd accumulated dozens upon dozens of them, which, considering she only took the largest and ugliest of each group, was no small feat. Among their kind, her captives were bruisers that could conquer entire ecosystems. Yet all it took was a tap on the head for Claws to render them unconscious.

Her attention drifted to the beautiful sky above. There wasn't a cloud in sight and the crescent moon beamed its blue light down on the surrounding trees, granting them—

Weight shifted on the sled. Claws spun, ready for violence.

One of the creatures had awoken. It shook its head groggily, getting to all fours. Claws saw the moment it registered the other unconscious bodies of its kind; the creature's eyes went wide. It bunched its muscles, crouching to gather strength and flee far from this place of terror. Claws sent a tiny little zap of lightning chi its way, so small that the unawakened eye wouldn't even register it. It hit the creature at the base of the skull, hitting its 'reset button,' as her master would say. The creature collapsed back to the sled, once more in a state of slumber.

Trilling a little song to herself, Claws continued back to the cart that Ellis had designed and the crafters had made for her. Unlike the one made for Cinnamon, hers was designed for her to push. She could only do so under the cover of night, obviously, so time was of the essence. Claws wondered how Cinnamon and the pelicans were doing. While she wished them luck with their tasks, she intended to hunt so many of her quarry that her ascended friends' efforts seemed paltry.

Claws's toothy grin turned predatory as she reached the cart. With lightning-enhanced limbs, she threw each captured creature into the cage, wedged her sled in a place it wouldn't get dislodged, then grabbed the handle and tore off along the road, trilling a happy little song all the way.

With a stomach full of fish and the flavor of the jungle perch still lingering on my tongue, I let out a content sigh.

"Agreed," Maria said, resting her head on my shoulder.

Borks let out a similar noise, rolling onto his back beside me and offering his belly up for a good rubbing. We'd spent the entire day swimming, fishing, and relaxing, even sneaking in a cheeky sun nap in the late afternoon. The fish had been the perfect thing to top it all off, and despite the minor disappointment of not discovering a new species in the river's waters, it was nowhere near enough to besmirch the rest of the day's joy.

"Want some juice?" Maria asked, glancing up at me.

"I would *love* some."

She gave me a kiss on the cheek before standing and stretching. "Back in a moment."

She went over to the tent and started rummaging through our bags. Borks bolted upright, his ears at attention.

"What's up, Borks? Did you hear—"

Something metallic reflected the campfire's light as it flashed from behind the tent. A man, covered head to toe in dark-green cloth, held a spear to Maria's torso.

"Don't move," he ordered, his lean muscles poised to plunge the jagged spear into Maria's side.

CHAPTER EIGHTY-FIVE

DISARMING

"There is an arrow trained on your head, stranger," the camouflaged man warned, glancing at me.

I had Borks gripped by his scruff, stopping him from insta-murdering the misguided spearman. I looked over my shoulder, and sure enough, there was a teenage boy with a bow. It was pulled back, the tip of the arrow trained on me. There was one reason I hadn't taken both of our attackers out—well, one main reason: Maria was in no danger.

Neither of these men—likely father and son, judging by the look of them—were cultivators. If she were so inclined, she could probably throw one at the other hard enough to end them both. Hell, I wasn't sure that the spear could break her skin if she stood still, but if the man tried to stab her, it would be like a newborn trying to jab a mountain.

Realizing no one had spoken for a long moment, I cleared my throat. "If you've come to rob us, you can take whatever you like."

"We're not thieves!" the adolescent behind me yelled.

"Quiet!" the man snapped, shooting a warning glare at his son.

"Then what do you want?" I asked, keeping my voice calm.

The spearman tightened his grip, his hands shaking. "To ensure you're not the king's men."

King's men? I thought. *Interesting* . . .

"We're not with the king, but if we were, what would you have done?"

"We'd have to take you prisoner."

I nodded. "I think I know what's going on. You traded with the caravan that came from other villages, right? Now you're worried about the king coming to punish you?"

"I don't know what you're talking about," he replied, but his eyes told the truth of it. They'd gone panicked at my mention of the caravan.

"Look, we're not with the king, okay? Anything but. Now, can you remove that spear from my girlfriend's side before I lose my cool?"

"I'm the one giving orders here!" His eyes were still wild, and they darted between Maria and me, his knuckles white on the spear's shaft. "If you're not with the king, what are you doing out here in the forest? How do you know about the caravan?"

I felt the immediate urge to goad him with a comment about the caravan he just accidentally confirmed, but I pushed it down, knowing it would just make things more tense.

"I thought you didn't know about the caravan?" Maria said, smirking at him.

The man blanched and I burst into laughter, unable to help myself. "Maria! You're being inflammatory!"

"Hey, he's the one that's got a spear aimed at my important bits. Is that an old sickle you've reshaped, by the way? You're a farmer?"

Maria's casual tone, despite being held at spear point, broke the man for a few seconds.

His mouth moved up and down inaudibly until he was able to reboot. "You're acting awfully relaxed for being one movement away from death, lass."

"We know about the caravan because my friends organized it," I explained, making a calming gesture with both hands. "We're out here on a camping holiday. Look, we even brought our cute dog!"

I pointed at Borks, but when I looked over, I realized he was snarling.

"Borks—show them your cute face. We're trying to de-escalate."

His face transformed immediately, his eyes placid and tongue lolling from the side of his mouth.

"See? A harmless couple out and about with their friendly and definitely not dangerous dog."

"Enough!" the spearman yelled. "I need a moment to think. I . . ."

"I believe them, Dad," the teen said. "I think they're telling the truth."

"Quiet, Toby! The king employs all manner of underhanded tactics. Just because they look innocent doesn't mean they are! Gods above, the more innocent they appear, the more we need to distrust them!"

Maria rolled her eyes. "This is getting tedious. Can I?"

I let out a weary sigh. "Yeah, go for it."

"What are you—" the spearman started, cutting off as Maria whirled on him.

She swept her left foot around, grabbed the spear's shaft, twisted it from his grip, then held the tip to his neck. The movement was beautifully controlled, not so fast that it would identify her as a cultivator, but definitely nearing the upper limit of a regular human's capabilities.

I raised an eyebrow at the son. "Would you mind putting the bow down? I don't wanna have to knock you out or something."

"You *are* with the king!" The father yelled.

The son's eyes darted between me and his father. His hands shook violently, the entire bow wavering.

"We're not with the king," I said. "We're from Tropica and just happen to practice martial arts for funsies. It's quite good for your health—especially when it stops you from getting speared by a confused farmer."

"Theresa . . ." the father said.

"Theresa?" I asked, not at all understanding.

The name wasn't meant for me, however. Something changed in the adolescent when he heard it. Standing tall, he took a deep breath. His hands stilled, and he drew the arrow back once more, training it on me.

"I need to be sure you're not with the king. Swear it to me, and I'll lower my weapon."

Here's something, I thought. *The mere mention of a name was enough to turn the boy's spine from jelly to titanium. Who is Theresa?*

I nodded. "All right. See those things on the ground next to the tent?"

The boy wouldn't take his eyes from me, so I looked up at his father. "Do you know what those are?"

He swallowed, a line of sweat running from his temple down to his chin. "I don't, no."

"They're fishing rods!" Maria announced, beaming. "We in Tropica are into some *seriously* heretical activities. Very un-kingly, wouldn't you agree?"

"It's a cover, son," the father growled. "No one would actually fish. The rods are clearly an attempt at misdirection."

I swore, rubbing the bridge of my nose. "Borks, would you try to find a skeleton? Don't give me that side-eye, mister. No attacking them, all right? Just find one of the jungle perch frames I threw into the shallows."

Giving the bow-wielding teen a low growl on the way past, Borks disappeared into the shadows.

"Sooo," I drawled. "You two come here often?"

"Don't listen to him, Toby!" the father blurted. "He's trying to build a relationship with you so you don't shoot!"

"That's not true! I'm already in a relationship."

"Fischer . . ." Maria shook her head, making a disgusted face. "He's like . . . twelve. Don't even joke about that."

"I'm turning fifteen!" Toby countered, his cheeks flushing.

"Stop talking to him!" the father ordered, finding some of his nerve despite the spear to his throat. "They're making it more difficult to shoot at them!"

Borks slunk from the shadows, his body wet and tail wagging. He walked toward Toby and spat something out. Two fish frames, their filets removed and heads picked at by creatures in the shallows, sat lifeless on the forest floor.

"See?" I said. "Fish. We caught them, fileted them, and ate them." I pointed at myself. "I'm Fischer, and I enjoy fishing. This is Maria—she also enjoys fishing and eating said heretical beasties."

"It's true," Maria added. "They're delicious."

Borks barked his agreement, most of his agitation having melted away after being able to retrieve something.

"That still proves nothing!" The dad—who was reminding me more of Roger by the second—yelled.

I let out a weary sigh; my enjoyment of the day was slowly bleeding away. "Mate, can we give up the posturing? Neither of you are murderers, and you're not gonna shoot us."

"You don't know what we're capable of."

I shook my head. "Maybe you're capable of it if your family were in danger, but you're not convinced that we are with the king or whatever. If you were, you'd have told your son to shoot the second Maria disarmed you."

"I'm sorry, Dad . . ." Toby lowered his bow, letting the tension go from the string. "They're right."

"No!" the father wailed. "Please. You can have my life, but let the boy go. He's only young, and his sister needs someone to care for her." He closed his eyes and lifted his neck, giving the spear Maria held a better angle to strike. "Look away, Toby."

"My guy . . ." Maria said, lowering the spear. "Your son is right. We're not going to hurt you."

He cracked an eye slowly, unbelieving. "You're . . . you're truly not with the king?"

"Nah, mate." I grinned. "We're from Tropica on a holiday to the capital."

"But . . ." He took a step back from Maria. "How did you disarm me so easily if you're from a coastal village?"

"I told you, mate." I gave him a wink. "We're into martial arts."

"But . . ." Toby said, stepping around to his father's side. "My dad was in the army. Where did you learn to—"

"Toby!" his father admonished. "Still your tongue!"

"Martial arts," Maria reiterated, giving me a smirk. "Fischer is actually the strongest of us, and he could have taken you both out the moment you showed yourself if he wanted to."

"Really?" Toby asked, staring at me with adolescent exuberance. "How?"

"They're bluffing, Toby. A single man couldn't possibly—"

I grabbed my favorite knife from where it was sheathed at my hip. Letting a hair-thin trickle of chi come from my core, I sent it up my arm as I released the knife. It flew through the air, the chi guiding it and keeping the blade straight as it sailed toward its target. Just as Maria had, I kept my movement at the upper limit of what was possible for a regular human. The knife slammed into the trunk Toby had originally stepped from behind of, driving an inch into the wood there with a muted *thonk*.

The blood drained from the father's face; awe grew over Toby's.

"Whoa!" he said. "Did you see that, Dad?"

"Who . . ." the father swallowed. "Who are you people?"

"Just a couple of lovers on a fishing trip," I said. "With our cute dog, of course."

Borks came to my side at the mention of him, and I patted his head, letting my appreciation for him flow.

The father slumped to his knees. He sat there for a couple of breaths, then lowered his forehead to the grass. "Thank you for not killing my son."

"Uh . . . you're welcome?" I shared a look with Maria, who shrugged back at me, similarly wordless.

"What's your name, mate?" I asked.

He glanced up from the grass. "Why do you want to know?"

"You know our names, and we know your son's name . . . What's yours?"

He raised his head, chewing on the thought for a long moment. Eventually, he spoke. "My name's Rodger, but all my friends call me Rod."

Maria and I locked eyes and both burst into laughter. I fell to the floor, my legs no match for my mirth as tears came to my eyes.

"What . . . ?" Rod asked, looking between us. "What's so funny?"

"We know a Roger," Maria answered, covering her smile. "He was also in the army. You two would get along."

"Except you seem a little more okay with the whole fishing thing," I added, wiping a tear from my eye.

"I'm not at all okay with it—there were just more important things to worry about." Rod shook his head. "If you're both on a fishing trip, you're both heretical fools. It's just not natural to be—"

I couldn't hear the rest, my chortle drowning it out. Maria joined me on the ground, his choice of words landing like a physical blow.

"Yeah, you two would definitely get along," I said when I could speak again. My cheeks hurt from smiling too much, and I rubbed them as I sat up. "So, weird question—Theresa is your daughter, right? The 'sister' that Toby would need to look after if Maria had given you a terminal poke?"

Rod's face was red with embarrassment, but it blanched at my question. He didn't answer, but words weren't necessary; his face told me the truth.

"How sick is she?" I asked, trying to appear serious.

Toby, seeing his father wouldn't answer, spoke up. "She has always had it. My mother passed when she was born, so it's just me and Dad that look after her."

"Other villagers? Could they care for her if you didn't return?"

My inquiry made color return to Rod's face. "That's none of your concern."

"Okay," I replied, holding up both hands. "I was only making sure she wasn't super sick."

Maria shot me a meaningful glance, knowing me well enough to see my intention.

"You're not agents of the capital, right?" Rod asked. "So you're going to let us go?"

"True." I nodded. "You're both free to go. We'll pack up our camp and move. No offense, but I don't relish the idea of you returning with your entire village in some foolhardy attempt at self-preservation."

"We wouldn't do that!" Toby exclaimed, his face indignant.

"But they'll still move, anyway." Rod stood, brushing dirt from his knees. "Can I trust you won't follow us?"

"We won't," Maria said, passing his spear back to him. "We've got our own business to be about."

"Come on, Toby. Let's leave them to it."

"One last thing." I strode forward, extending my hand.

Rod stared down at it for a long moment, then grasped it.

"It was nice meeting you, mate. You too, Toby."

"Y-you too!" Toby replied, shaking my offered hand.

I thought for a moment, considering if it was worth the risk. Maria poked me in the side, and when I looked her way, she nodded. I smiled back at her.

"If you two get in trouble," I said, "or if Theresa gets more unwell, come and find us. I reckon you'd get along well with my friends back in Tropica."

"Thank you for the offer," Rod replied, hesitant. "We'll keep it in mind. Come on, Toby."

We watched them go, and when they were from sight, we started packing up.

"Keep an eye and make sure they don't return," I said to Borks.

He nodded, skulking toward the tree line and watching the darkness.

"So, that was insane, right?" Maria said.

"No kidding. I can't believe they actually snuck up on us . . ." I glanced in the direction they'd left, seeing nothing but shadows and dimly lit trees. "I didn't hear a thing, and the fact that Borks didn't smell them tells me they understand tracking and wind direction better than most."

My brow furrowed as I started considering the implications, but Maria, seeing right through me, poked me in the side again. "I'm proud of you, Fischer."

"You are?" I raised a questioning brow. "Why?"

"Because I saw the fury on your face when he came at me with the spear, but you trusted me. You also had empathy for strangers that ambushed us in the night. Moreover, you told them where they could find help if Rod's daughter got sicker."

I snorted. "Only because you told me it was okay."

She shook her head, her hair bouncing against her face. "You would have done it anyway. I just sped up the decision." She wrapped her arm around my back. "Every day you do things that make me love you even more."

"You think that made *you* love *me* more? I wish you could feel what I feel—the way you disarmed him in a split second did things to me. The way you handled that pole—"

She unlooped her arm from me and slapped me on the arm at the speed of light. "Don't finish that sentence. You'll undo all the good work you did tonight."

A laugh flew from me, rolling over the grass and bouncing off the trees. Despite being ambushed no less than ten minutes ago—and being held at arrow point—I felt calm and free.

As Rod led his son back toward their village, anxiety and fear warred for dominance within him.

Toby followed his steps exactly; the years he had spent training his son in the way of the hunter hadn't been a waste. Proud as Rod was of his only boy, the thoughts assaulting him were immutable.

To think that mere villagers could be so powerful . . .

It rivaled the strength he'd seen those dreaded cultivators use on the battlefield. Unbidden, some of the scenes of destruction flashed through his mind, making bile rise in his throat. He shook his head, trying to clear it of the flashes. The sound of a stick snapping rang out through the forest.

Rod froze.

"Dad. Are you okay?" Toby asked. "I can't remember the last time you stood on a stick."

Looking down at the offending twig, Rod clenched his jaw. "I'm fine," he lied.

As they continued on, he played over the interaction in his mind, searching for where he could have improved—what he could have changed to get the upper hand.

There was nothing.

Short of shooting arrows from the dark and assassinating complete strangers, they couldn't have won that fight. The speed with which the man had thrown that knife . . . even if Rod had held him at spear point instead, he'd still have been easily disarmed by the martial artist. He replayed the woman—Maria—so easily removing the spear from his grasp and holding the tip to his throat. It really was like the speed he'd only seen cultivators possess, and it made the bile rise in his throat once more.

Is it possible that they're cultivators? Sent by the crown to dismantle their little pocket of resistance?

Rod blew air from his nose, acknowledging just how ridiculous a suggestion that was. If they had been cultivators, he and his son would have been dead before they knew it. Besides, they weren't collared. The king wouldn't abide slaves that weren't forced to do his bidding under threat of death.

The knowledge that he couldn't have done anything different should have made him feel worse. Surprisingly, it made him feel at ease. He shepherded his whirling thoughts, focusing on the information they'd gotten from the misguided encounter. As distasteful as it was that they were fishing—actually *fishing* of all things—it showed how little they cared for the crown's rules. Perhaps there was something there. Was it possible that their village could find allies in Tropica? Others willing to go against the tyranny of the king and his cultivators?

Once more smiling at his own hubris, Rod shook his head. No one outside of his village could be trusted. He was thankful for the restraint the strangers had shown, but he didn't trust them.

He couldn't.

He returned his attention to the surroundings, his thoughts still troubled as they made their way home.

CHAPTER EIGHTY-SIX

THE CALM BEFORE THE STORM

I woke to the sun beaming in through the tent's opening as a barrage of tiny licks rained down on my chin.

"Cinnamon?" I asked groggily, squinting against the morning light.

I wasn't sure what Cinnamon was doing here, but who else had such little kisses? Still blind, I reached my hands up . . . and found a Chihuahua. Borks yapped at me, his tail wagging despite his incredulity.

"Sorry, buddy," I said, smiling at him. "You're so small that I thought you were a bunny."

He let out another yap.

"Yes, yes. I know you're ferocious."

He barked his agreement, letting out a demonic little growl from his Chihuahua throat.

"Why the change, though? Is it to scare off any would-be ambushers?"

He stood tall atop my chest, beaming down at me with pride. It was both cute and hilarious, so I ruffled the soft fur on the top of his head. "You're a good boy, Borks."

"When you two are done cuddling in there," Maria called, "breakfast is almost ready!"

"We'll never be done!" I called back.

Borks ruffed, wagging his tail in agreement.

"Oh, yeah?" she asked. "You asked for it."

I glanced past Borks. "Asked for what—"

She came flying through the opening, her eyes wide and grin manic. "For me to crash this party!"

She slammed down next to us, startling the absolute hell out of Borks. He jumped on the spot, whirling on her with his teeth bared.

"Aww, did I scare you, buddy? I'm sorry. I just wanted to be a part of the cuddle puddle."

Borks, upon realizing it was her and not another attacker, descended on her with his rapid-fire kisses.

She half choked, half laughed, pressing her chin to her chest in a failed attempt to keep him away. With his small size and cultivation strength, he was a formidable adversary, and just when I thought Maria might die of laughter, I swept him up, his short legs hanging uselessly in the air. "Sorry to interrupt your ambush, Borks, but I need her to be breathing to make us breakfast."

"Thank you," she wheezed.

She tried to get up, but I pounced, pulling her into a hug. Borks, free of my grasp, lay on top of us, rolling to his back and slipping in the wedge shape our bodies made.

"Good morning." I kissed her on the forehead. "Did you sleep well?"

"I did. You?"

"Nope." I yawned and stretched. "I found it hard to sleep after the ambush last night. My mind wouldn't stop."

"I'm sorry," she said, patting me on the chest. "Will you be okay traveling the rest of the way to the capital today?"

"If I had some breakfast made by my girlfriend, I'm sure I could do anything."

Maria giggled. "Well, lucky for you, I think she has some buns warming and coffee brewing this second."

"Wait, what?" I furrowed my brow, doing my best to keep the smile from my face. "My girlfriend is here? I thought Sue was back in Tropica . . ."

"Borks . . ." Maria eventually said, glaring at me.

He perked his ears up, cocking his head to the side in question.

"Sic him!"

Borks, playing along, launched himself at me. He snarled and nipped, the growls coming from him making me laugh as I wrestled the little git.

"Oh, you think you're ready to take on the master, Borks?"

I scooped him up, running from the tent and performing a slow-motion slam onto the ground. He played dead, groaning as his tongue hung from his open mouth.

"Fischer!" Maria gasped, dashing from the tent. "You *killed* him!"

She started doing fake chest compressions, but Borks remained "dead," a little smile coming to his face under all the attention.

"Okay," Maria said, rubbing his belly. "If I leave breakfast on the fire any longer, it's going to burn."

He hopped to his feet, coming to sit beside me.

"First course: honey buns!" She lifted a tray from the campfire, and when she removed the covering, steam flowed out. The smell of honey drifted over to me, making my mouth water.

"Mmm," I said. "When did you make honey buns?"

"I snuck off to make them before we left," she replied, grinning. "I even got fresh honey from Bumblebro and Queen Bee to make them."

"Oh. You didn't . . . er . . . interrupt them?"

"*Interrupt them?* What do you mean?"

I hadn't told anyone about the time I'd caught them . . . cuddling? Man, I *hoped* that's all I had caught them doing.

I shook my head. "You know what? Forget I said anything."

"Okay . . ." she said, raising an eyebrow. "Well, the point is, the honey is fresh. Here."

I grabbed one from the offered tray, immediately breaking it open to let some of the heat out. The vapor drifted in the air, its irresistible notes traveling up my nostrils and down into my lungs. I couldn't wait a moment longer. I bit down into it. Despite being baked two days ago, the bun was fluffy, sweet, and filled with chi. I leaned back as I chewed, angling my face toward the sun that peeked down through the clearing we'd set up camp in. With the honey bun's chi warming me from within and the sun's rays warming me from without, a smile I couldn't resist crossed my face. My eyes were closed, so I didn't see Maria's approach. She planted her soft lips to mine, lingering for a moment that was both blessedly long yet too short.

"Glad you like it," she whispered, sweeping a hand through my hair.

"The kiss or the bun? Each was wonderful."

She giggled, a red blush rising to her cheeks. "Both. Are you ready for coffee?"

"Does Rocky like being launched out to sea? Of course I'm ready for coffee!"

"Coming right up!" She removed the moka pot from the fire, pouring the liquid into two cups.

I took another bite of the honey bun as she passed the cup to me, washing the sweet pastry down with deliciously smooth coffee. It had a bitter bite to it, but that wasn't a bad thing. I took a deep breath through my nose, letting the air circle my mouth and enhance the flavors lingering there. "Delicious, my love." I took another bite, the honey joining the coffee's aftertaste.

"So are you." She bent and kissed me on the forehead, then sat beside me, leaning on my shoulder and taking a sip of coffee.

As we took the time to enjoy our breakfast, my thoughts drifted toward the events to come. We'd reach the capital tonight, and then the fun would begin.

"The calm before the storm, huh?" I asked, resting my head on hers.

"Yep. I can't wait."

I grinned; neither could I.

As the sun reached its zenith in the sky, Pelly flew in circles. It was almost time, and with each passing moment, she could barely contain her nervous energy. She continued flying in a loop, trying to distract herself from the butterflies in her stomach. The formation below had stabilized more with each new addition, and since she'd taken over the post this morning, she hadn't had to swoop down and gather them together a single time.

A source of power drew her attention, and with her excitement reaching a fever pitch, she turned toward it. Bill rocketed toward her, and the moment she caught sight of him, she took off, heading south. She gave him a honk in parting. He honked back, his call filled with thanks for her hard work.

She sent chi down to her wings, stretched them wide, then flapped as hard as she could, the ground becoming a blur beneath her.

Claws, content with her efforts, napped in the early afternoon sun. She had filled the entire cart—every last cage stocked to the brim with her quarry. They were lively this afternoon, attempting to break out of their temporary prisons, but their teeth stood no chance against the woodworkers' and their System-aided creation.

Hanging her head down over the side, she chirped at them, telling them to be quiet. It didn't work; they only increased their efforts, biting down on the bars with their long teeth. Letting out a sigh, Claws accepted her fate. She was too excited to nap, anyway. She was only a half hour away from the capital, having traveled within walking distance last night. Hopping down from the top of the cart, she gazed over her handiwork. The mammals gazed back at her, black eyes assessing her.

Claws puffed out her chest, taking great pride in how many she had captured. There was *no way* the others had collected more than her. She was the benevolent Claws, maiden of the forest and cutest of Fischer's followers. The sun would set in a few hours, and when it did, the operation would begin.

Claws grinned, her needle-sharp teeth glinting in the afternoon sun. She couldn't wait.

Cinnamon heard a familiar beat of wings above her. Her heart immediately set to fluttering as she raced back to the box. Both she and Pelly arrived at the same time. Cinnamon launched herself from the ground, rocketing toward her wayward daughter and wrapping furred limbs around Pelly's feathered body. Pelly landed atop the box and craned her neck, wrapping it around Cinnamon as she crooned. Cinnamon peeped back, telling Pelly how much she had missed her over the past couple of days. After a good cuddle, they separated.

When Cinnamon hunkered down on top of the box, Pelly cocked her head in question. Cinnamon grinned back; there was no world in which she was going to miss the chaos to come.

Are you sure you want to do this? Pelly asked with a low honk.

Certain, Cinnamon peeped back.

Shrugging, Pelly hopped to the handle and gripped it in her feet. Despite it being half filled with the spiky little things Cinnamon had been collecting, Pelly easily lifted it skyward with powerful beats of her wings. Cinnamon held on tight, gazing down at the landscape as it grew ever further away.

Pelly let out a questioning honk, to which Cinnamon nodded. She was ready.

Her adopted daughter took off, traveling west at incredible speed. With every meter they crossed, Cinnamon's core seemed to vibrate with excitement. Before the day was done, her hard work would come to fruition.

Under the cover of night, Maria, Borks, and I arrived at the capital city of Gormona. I had come across some serious fantasy shit since arriving in this new world, but the city was like nothing else I'd seen before. Walls that had to be at least four stories high protected the capital, its top lined by a parapet and a series of torches at even intervals.

There was a single structure visible over the wall: a castle of ridiculous dimensions. I could only see the top floors, but there were multiple spires as big around as office buildings, all reaching up into the sky. I'd caught snippets of Operation Sticky Fingers, so I knew there were multiple levels to the castle, but seeing it in person was something else. Tearing my eyes from the castle, I focused on the wall before us. A giant gate of wood and iron blocked our way, and short of blowing through it, we wouldn't be able to enter the city.

Luckily for us, we weren't taking the front door.

Maria was staring wide-eyed at the castle, so I nudged her in the side. We shared a nod, then dashed off toward the south, staying within the tree line. Borks followed behind us in his golden retriever form, his steps completely silent under the crescent moon. I counted the arrow slots in the wall as we went, and when we reached the eighty-third, I held up my fist, signaling a stop.

Here.

We dashed through the clearing to the wall, crouched, and leaped. All three of us soared through the air, easily landing atop the wall without so much as the scuff of a boot to give us away. The entire cityscape was within view, everything from the castle to the gate to a few points of interest I'd been made aware of.

My heart thundered in my chest as I looked down into the courtyard below; it was the reason we'd climbed the wall here.

Lines of citrus trees ran up and down, their green canopies well pruned and cared for. Running between the trees, small bushes grew, some of which were covered in purple berries.

"Wow," Maria whispered. "There are so many . . ."

"May I interest you in some fresh passiona berries, my love?"

"Why, such a gentle . . ." she trailed off. "Fischer—what is that?"

"Something wrong?"

She stared toward the northeast, her eyes going wide.

Curious, I followed her gaze, then frowned. "Is that—"

"*Is that what I think it is?*" she interrupted.

"No fracking way . . ."

Ruff, Borks agreed.

A sea of white creatures filled the sky, their number so vast as to be uncountable.

"Above them!" Maria yelled. "Is that Bill?"

Sure enough, there he was, soaring on unseen winds. He darted from side to side, and for a moment, I didn't get it. Then, though, I realized the truth—he was *herding* them. As if he was privy to our conversation, Bill unleashed the mightiest honk I'd ever heard. Despite being on the other side of the capital, it reverberated in my chest with a bassy kick.

"Over there!" Maria gasped, pointing toward the front gate to the city.

I followed her gesture, and when my cultivator eyes caught sight of it, my mouth dropped open. "Cinnamon and Pelly? Wait, what is Cinnamon wearing? Is that *armor?*"

"Forget that! What the frack is Pelly carrying?"

It was a wooden box, but I didn't have much time to check it out, because the front gate to the city fracking *exploded,* large chunks of wood and metal scattering everywhere. This, at least, wasn't a mystery; I felt the chi signature that caused it. Before the smoke cleared, a cart zoomed through onto the cobbled street. If not for my enhanced eyes, I wouldn't have seen Claws or the gleam of her needle-sharp teeth as she tore through the thoroughfare with lightning-wreathed limbs. She zoomed behind a building, Tokyo-drifting her cute little tooshie out of sight.

"We have some troublesome children . . ." Maria said, then let out a long sigh. "I guess it's time for me to go, then. So much for my passiona treat."

I squeezed her hand. "I'll bring you some berries home. Overprotective dads, huh?"

"Rogers, more like," she replied, giving me a grin.

I couldn't help but laugh. "Yeah, no kidding."

She swept forward into my arms, planting a kiss on my lips that banished everything else. It was only for a few seconds, but her warmth flooded out and resonated deep within me, more powerful and all-encompassing than any of my breakthroughs.

She pulled back, exhaling a shaky breath. "I love you, Fischer."

"I love you more."

Borks let out another *ruff,* adding his affection to the mix.

Maria walked backward, not taking her eyes off me. "Good luck." Without another word, she leaped from the battlements, soaring into the forest beyond.

I smiled, then bent to pat Borks on the head. "Good luck, buddy."

He licked my hand, turned, and dashed away, shifting to his nightmare form as he sped along the wall.

"Guess it's my turn . . ." I said aloud, approaching the ledge. I stepped into open air above the grove of trees, opening the floodgate to my core and letting chi flood out into my body as I fell to the ground below.

CHAPTER EIGHTY-SEVEN

FULL-BLOWN ASSAULT

Augustus Reginald Gormona, ruler of every tree, stone, and building below him, gazed out over his kingdom. He stood atop a balcony in the highest spire of the castle, leaning on an ornate metal railing and letting the winter air wash away his troubles.

"It's a beautiful night, Augustus," Deklan said, leaning against the rail beside him, his metal armor clinking.

"Isn't it? There are few things that calm my nerves so."

Though he usually found solace in the heat of a bath, the scene before him was almost as relaxing.

Even the peasants' quarter was picturesque of an evening, the dirty streets made appealing by the warm firelight cast down by myriad lanterns. Augustus took a deep breath, focusing on the cold air tickling his nose. With each passing day over the last few months, his troubles only grew worse. It had reached a point where he no longer looked at the relics, their data too much for him to handle. He would be warned if another spirit beast ascended, of course—that it hadn't occurred in days was a blessing of the highest order.

After ignoring the constant stream of advancements for a short period, he'd started questioning just how much of a threat these spirit beasts really posed. They were advancing fast, sure, but their levels were mostly in trade skills: baking, tailoring, blacksmithing, woodworking, and *fishing* of all things. They were hardly advancements worth losing sleep over.

I am safe, he reminded himself.

The city's guards defended the castle, Aisa and the rest of the handlers watched the streets, and dozens of cultivators were defending the city's wealth, ready to strike should someone be foolish enough to try and steal it.

"I need to thank you, Deklan," Augustus said, feeling at peace.

"Oh? Why's that, my king?"

"Augustus," he corrected.

"My bad." Deklan gave him a wide grin. "Hard to break old habits. Why's that, Augustus?"

"Because you were right. Constantly being told of the advancements was a blight on my consciousness. A black cloud that only served to hamper my judgment. The days since I stopped checking that dreaded screen have been a breath of fresh air."

"You're welcome, Augustus." Deklan nodded at him, then looked out at the horizon. "You're a good man, but even the best of us need a reminder sometimes."

This strange guard—a man that seemed to be immune to the weight of kings, queens and crowns—would have frustrated Augustus to no end mere months ago. Now, though, Augustus found himself feeling an inordinate amount of gratitude for the atypical guardsman. He was common born, the lowest of the low, and yet he seemed to possess such gravitas, such wisdom.

"You know, Deklan, in another life I'd have loved to wed you to my daughter. I'm ashamed to admit that your lowborn status prevents such a pairing, but—"

Deklan blew air from his lips. "No offense, Augustus, but your daughter is a terror."

Augustus slowly turned, raising an eyebrow. "Excuse me, Deklan? We are close, yes, but please mind your tone—"

"Hey . . ." Deklan interrupted. "What's that?"

"Deklan," Augustus chastised, his voice firm. "I like you, and I'd hate to have you chained. I request, nay, demand that you apologize—"

"No, really," Deklan repeated, squinting into the night. "What in Neptune's veiny member is that?"

His face scrunching at the curse, Augustus felt his gratitude for this guard diminish. "Deklan, I think you should return to the artifact—"

"Augustus!" Deklan's eyes turned to the king, finally showing the proper level of respect for his betters.

What the king saw in the peasant's eyes was enough to bring his fury to a standstill. The usually lackadaisical man was serious, his eyes narrowed and mouth forming a line.

"This conversation isn't over, Deklan, but what are you . . ." Augustus blinked, coming face to face with a field of white. "B . . . b . . . b . . ." His tongue became leaden, his mouth unable to form the word.

"Birds." Deklan finished. "That's a *lot* of birds."

A swarm of seagulls, thick enough to block out the stars, flew over the capital's walls. High above them, a larger shape beat wide wings. It unleashed a honk that physically struck the king, making his royal robes flutter.

"A flock . . . an entire . . . flock . . ." His words were sluggish, as if an entire pastry obstructed his mouth.

"Oh!" Deklan snapped his fingers in understanding. "That's *An Entire Flock of Birds!* Like from the artifact, right?"

"Sound the alarm!" King Augustus Reginald Gormona screeched, whirling on the spot.

Panicked as he was, his feet got tangled beneath him. He tumbled headfirst into a stone wall and his vision went black.

Corporal Claws, pusher of carts and fastest in all the land, tore through the streets like her chompers tore through fish. Snips had been running reconnaissance in the capital over the weeks gone, and though they'd all felt terrible keeping it a secret from Fischer, Claws regretted nothing. Because of the knowledge they had gained, Operation Sticky Fingers was going to succeed.

Speaking of the devil, she felt her master's power blossom. Like the weight of a blanket, his familiar chi washed over her, filling her with a sense of ease.

Claws shook her head, dispelling the comfort; she had a mission to focus on. The cobbled stones were a blur beneath her lightning-wreathed limbs as she ran ever deeper into the capital, searching for . . . *there!*

A sprinkling of chi rose in her senses, and she turned left onto a street, veering for it. The moment she caught sight of them, her grin spread even wider. She took two white rocks from her pouch with one paw, wedging them in place between her upper lip and gums.

Weeks of scouting, months of planning, and innumerable secrets kept from her beloved master—all for this moment.

She grinned so wide that her cheeks hurt; the *fun* had finally arrived.

Following the booming honk earlier, Aisa ran through the streets.

"Stick close!" she ordered, glancing at the four cultivators assigned to her. "Which way?"

"It came from that direction!" the short-haired cultivator replied, pointing toward the eastern wall.

She had been assigned to the middle quarter that night, and though she would never leave her post, the honk that rang out was an obvious declaration of war. Following the cultivator's directions, she turned down an alleyway, sprinted through it, arrived in a square, and skidded to a stop.

An odd cart blocked the way, and before their eyes, all four of its walls fell to the ground. Something leaped atop the wooden cart, standing tall and puffing out its chest like a proud rooster. When Asia saw what it was, her eyes went wide.

A humongous rat with giant bucked teeth glared down at them like they were a fresh patch of manure. Then, movement exploded from the cart. A wall of fur, beady eyes, and twitching whiskers flowed down, flooding the street. Hundreds of rats, each larger than any of the ones they'd caught in the capital over the last few days, ran in every direction.

"Fat . . . *Fat Rat Pack!*" one of the female cultivators yelled, voicing what Asia had already surmised. "*Attack—*"

A bolt of lightning cracked, slamming into the cultivator and sending her flying. She struck a barrel, its wooden panels exploding. As the debris cleared, Asia's stomach dropped. The giant rat, grinning with wicked malevolence, locked eyes with her as it stepped down from the fallen cultivator's chest. It strode forward in what felt like slow motion, blue arcs of lightning wreathing its body.

"*What are you idiot cultivators doing?*" Aisa demanded, not taking her eyes off the formidable foe. "Attack! Defend the capital!"

Her order snapped them from their inaction, and abilities flew from all sides. A bolt of fire, a clump of cobblestones, and a wave of green energy descended upon Fat Rat Pack's leader, crashing into it.

"Good!" she yelled, whirling back to the horde of rats. "Exterminate the rest! They can't be as powerful as that one. It—"

Lightning struck, slamming into the stone-throwing cultivator. His lifeless body rocketed at the cart and shattered it into a million pieces. Splinters and nails rained down, obscuring her view. All she could do was stare—fear, horror, and understanding washing over her as the dust cleared, revealing their doom. The rat, crackling with energy that made the street smell of ozone, chittered at her.

It *taunted* her.

A rat fleeing the explosion climbed over her foot, but Aisa didn't even register it—her eyes were locked on a vision of death. Fat Rat Pack's leader grinned even wider, revealing a row of needle-sharp teeth behind the two white incisors. The rat stood up on its back legs, raising its forepaws to the sky and cackling with maniacal laughter. Movement in the sky drew Aisa's attention, and when their shapes resolved, any ounce of hope she held on to withered.

A blanket of birds flew above, blocking out the night's sky and seeming to drain the air from Aisa's lungs.

An Entire Flock of Birds . . . she thought, despair turning to numb disbelief. *It's a full-blown assault* . . .

When the rat leader caught sight of the birds above, the laughter died in its throat. The rat pointed skyward, gesturing at them wildly as she let out a shrill chirp that sounded almost like an accusation. When the rat's eyes returned to meet Aisa's, they were filled with fury.

"Run," Aisa ordered the remaining two. "Flee deeper into the—"

The moment she issued the order to flee, the two remaining cultivators listened. She wanted to preserve the kingdom's strength, sacrifice herself for the greater good, but the spirit beast saw right through her. In one movement, it zapped around the square, ricocheting off walls and striking both cultivators, knocking them out. It came to a stop before her, peering up at her, and despite the size difference, Aisa felt as though she was looking up at a mountain.

The rat leader gave her an exaggerated wink, once more puffing its chest out like a proud cock at the crack of dawn.

Lightning shattered the air, her hair stood on end, and her consciousness fled.

With the rabble taken care of, Claws chirped again, yelling her displeasure at the seagulls flying above as she shook a fist in their general direction. The scheming pelicans had outdone her by collecting *way* more birds than she had rats. She'd intended to have more fun with the cultivators, to draw out the fun, as was her right. The sight of so many birds, though, had made a red-hot anger well up from within her.

Claws forced herself to take a deep breath, letting it out slowly as her master had instructed so many times. More birds was a good thing, she supposed, despite it making her light shine dimmer. Kicking splinters of the shattered cart as she went, she started gathering the cultivators, cursing Bill and Pelly under her breath all the while.

She would have gathered more than Cinnamon, at least . . . *right?*

Cinnamon let out a thankful peep as Pelly dropped her and the payload. Taking one last glance at her feathered daughter, she turned her attention to the street below. The cultivators there were engaged in some sort of argument, spittle flying from the mouth of the person who had to be their handler. Cinnamon adjusted her armor. It was made of thin metal sheets that were stained black, made to resemble the very thing she had been collecting in the forest. Though she hadn't filled the entire payload, she'd collected an impressive amount, filling it halfway to the top.

Power flooded from across the capital, its source clear—it was her master, unleashing only a fraction of his strength. It made her soul feel calm, and she took a moment to wish him a joyous night. As the ground grew closer, some of the conversation below drifted up to her fuzzy ears.

"Obey my orders, scum!" the handler demanded.

Well, that is just rude.

Her master would never treat his followers so.

"We are obeying orders!" the bearded cultivator spat back. "The king ordered you to hold this square! His authority outshines—"

"Look out!" another cultivator yelled, his blue eyes wide as Cinnamon's payload dropped toward their heads.

She waved a greeting his way, grinning beneath her armor.

They all looked up, saw the payload about to strike their heads, and dashed back instinctively. Just in time, too, because Cinnamon and her mount struck the place where they'd been standing. As she had expected, the payload had been engineered flawlessly; its sides split apart, each panel flung outward when the bottom plate hit the cobbled street. As such, the impact did not harm the thousands of beetles within. They flowed out like a black, spiky liquid, engulfing the street. Cinnamon found their writhing bodies around her feet disgusting, but it was a small price to pay for such a dramatic entrance.

The bearded man that had been fighting the handler recovered first. He stared at the bugs, then at Cinnamon, his eyes going wide. "The . . . *The Beetle Boys!*"

Cinnamon let out her best beetle *scree*, confirming his assertion. She held her beetle-armored forepaws high to the sky, making the pose Claws had shown her. The humans were frozen, captivated by her grace, her *ferocity*. Ellis had called the bugs "elephant beetles," and as they stopped flowing outward, they started taking flight. The air became alive, and with her enhanced awareness, Cinnamon watched the face of every single human surrounding her change.

It. Was. *Beautiful.*

Power swelled, hands extended, and abilities flew, but Cinnamon was faster. In the blink of an eye, she slammed into each cultivator, lashing out with a headbutt, a roundhouse kick—Bill was right, that one was fun—a left jab, and a body slam, knocking all four of them out cold. She came to a stop before the handler, gazing up imperiously at her foe. Annoyingly, the handler was looking toward the sky, her eyes perusing the seagulls currently blocking out the moon.

"*An Entire Flock of Birds,*" the handler mumbled, dropping to her knees. Her eyes drifted down to Cinnamon. "Please. Spare me . . ."

In response, Cinnamon patted her on the cheek. The handler licked her lips, hope dawning in her eyes.

"You'll . . . you'll let me go?"

Cinnamon snorted. *Frack no.*

She backhanded the woman, sending her sprawling to the ground in a lifeless pile. Cinnamon stared down at her armored paw—Bill was right about that move, too. Slapping people was *fun.*

She set about gathering the cultivators, making sure she didn't step on any beetles; the spiky little creatures had served her well, and she was proud of not letting a single insect fall to the cultivators' attacks.

"You look fracking ridiculous, Ellis," Theo laughed.

"Your thoughts are of little matter," Ellis said, adjusting his armor. "My ego is nothing before the mission."

"Booo!" Danny drawled, giving a thumbs down. "At least fight back—I need some entertainment."

"How much longer?" Peter asked, running a hand through his hair. "We've been cooped up in here for days. I'm getting desperate for some proper food."

Barry nodded. "It can't be too long now. We just have to wait for Borks to let us out."

Sergeant Snips was sitting between Pistachio and Rocky off to one corner, hissing orders at the latter, who nodded with only a little annoyance. Before she could finish, the portal into Borks's pocket dimension opened, letting fresh air flow into the space.

"Yes!" Danny yelled, jumping to his feet.

Borks poked his head in, letting out a loud bark before retracting it.

"Okay," Barry said. "Everyone ready?"

Every face turned toward him. The fishing club—minus Keith, who was back in Tropica with Trent—were the first to nod. Next, the woodworkers, standing and stretching as they gave him their assent. The two smiths, who locked arms with each other, shook, then nodded at Barry. Finally, Fischer's creatures. Barry knelt down so they were eye to eyestalk. "Pistachio, Snips—you know the drill."

They nodded, both blowing serious bubbles.

"And Rocky . . . please don't blow anything up. Remember your restrictions. This is a *delicate* mission."

He scowled back at Barry, but Snips petted Rocky's carapace, nodding at Barry that Rocky would behave himself.

Content, Barry stood back up, casting his gaze around the room. “In that case, I officially call for the commencement of Operation Sticky Fingers!”

They whooped and hollered, letting out their nervous energy before leaving the dimensional space. One after the other, they ran through the portal and entered the capital city of Gormona.

CHAPTER EIGHTY-EIGHT

CONQUEROR

As I fell toward the grove below, cold night air rushed past me. The crescent moon was high in the sky, and I bathed in its light, intent on soaking up as much as I could before Bill and his army of seagulls blocked it out. As I considered the mass of gulls, I shook my head, smiling to myself. This night was shaping out even more chaotic than I'd anticipated. I hoped they were all having as much fun as I was.

I landed silently in the grassy grove, and still releasing a steady stream of chi, I wasted no time in collecting my prize. Thanks to the intel—from Trent, of all people—I knew the passiona bushes were tiny things that barely reached my knee. I unfurled a bag Ruby made me, shook it out, then bent down to pull a bush from the earth. I froze when I felt the chi radiating up its stem.

The trickle of essence was thickest at its base, separating into thin strands as it went out toward the leaves and berries. Furrowing my brow, I traced it back down to the ground. The chi flowed between all the bushes, meshing out in every direction. Not only the bushes, either—it connected to the lemon trees, the chi running up and along their thick branches toward their leaves and the few lemons present.

"And what do you think you're doing?" came a demanding voice.

Raising my gaze, I stared in the speaker's direction with more than a little disbelief. For the second time in so many days, someone had managed to sneak up on me.

In the lone gate to the courtyard, an aged man stood. He had white, close-cropped hair and a neatly trimmed salt-and-pepper beard. His robes were immaculate, their deep purple more rich than any clothes I'd seen since coming to this world. His hands were calmly crossed in front of him, each finger adorned by pearl-encrusted rings.

"G'day, mate. I was just stealing some of these bushes. How's your night going?" In the time since we'd started weighing each other, multiple explosions had occurred in the city. I gestured all around, pointing in their general directions. "Seems like some crazy shit is going down in the capital, huh? What's a man of your stature doing calmly checking on a few bushes?"

He smirked at me and started removing his ornate rings. "I knew you'd come for the capital's strength," he stated, completely ignoring my question. "Unlike you, I wasn't born yesterday. I won't fall for your distractions, *child.*"

He spat the last word, and I was keen to continue the banter, but then the rest of his statement pulled me up short.

"The capital's strength . . . ?" I glanced at the bushes. "These things? They're tasty, yeah, but surely their commerce isn't what keeps you goons in power."

"There's no point in playing dumb. You know their purpose as well as I do." He waved all around himself, encompassing not only the bushes, but the lemon trees, too. "That's why you're here."

I held up my hands in surrender. "You got me, mate. I definitely know what's going on here, and I came to steal your—er—source of power?"

"Finally, some truth." He was on his second hand now, the first completely free of the pearl rings. "Would you like to know a secret?"

"I love secrets."

He snorted, the condescending smirk never leaving his face as he removed another ring. "Your mission was pointless. These grounds are ancient, having stood as long as the royal castle. Longer, perhaps. Even if you take these bushes, they'll wither to nothing without the chi present here."

"You know what chi is? Neat. What if my mission was to destroy them, though? That would shatter your source of power, right?"

He rolled his eyes. "You could try, but I don't think you'll live long enough to attempt it." He removed his last ring, and as it came free of his finger, my mouth dropped open.

Chi roiled from the man, bristling and chaotic. Unlike the slow, steady stream I was releasing, his was like a forest fire, lashing out and consuming whatever it touched. He snapped his fingers, and shapes emerged from the shadows around us, dozens upon dozens of cultivators appearing atop the surrounding walls.

"Do you have any last words, child?"

"Last words? I've got plenty of life and words ahead of me, mate."

He raised a brow, anger clear in the lines of his face, and then burst into laughter. It was an ugly thing, filled with superiority and misplaced confidence. He shook his head. "I can't believe the king was worried about you."

"Why?" I asked, giving him a genuine smile.

"Because you, peasant, are a moron." He clenched his fists together, water rushing from his skin and coating them in a pale blue light.

"What's your name, bloke?" I asked the still-smirking dickhead.

His lip twitched. I thought he might attack, but he shuddered, forcing his fury down and holding up a hand to halt the collared cultivators. "Lord Tom Osnan. Keeper of the grove and lord of Gormona."

My eyebrows all but flew off my fracking forehead as I remembered the noble that had taken a swing at me back in Tropica.

Lord Tom Osnan Jr. . . .

"I don't suppose you have a similarly dickheaded son that lives in a coast village?" I asked.

His eyes narrowed, but rather than respond, he flew at me.

Dozens of cultivators followed his lead, some launching forward, others unleashing ranged attacks. One and all, their cores hummed with power. I closed my eyes, focusing on each individual cultivator. My mind's eye traced the lines of their powers, painting a view from above as they drew closer.

Unlike the lord who had managed to sneak up on me, I'd felt the cultivators there from the beginning. I registered every step as they'd slowly arranged themselves around me, thinking me to be cornered prey. Just like the purple-robed lord, all of their chi was a wildfire. It was chaotic, unfocused, *hungry.*

When a grin came to my face, I was forced to admit something: as much as I wanted to fish in peace, having almost fifty cultivators unleash their power and descend upon me at once made excitement course through my veins. It was a direct challenge—a clashing of two powers in which there could only be a single victor.

With my grin turning predatory, I tore open the floodgate to my core.

Flying like an arrow launched from a bow, Bill rocketed groundward. His flipper connected with a cultivator's chest.

Oof! the man moaned, flying to hit another of his kin.

Bill held no remorse for the fools; they had launched attacks at his seagull brethren. The gulls weren't spirit beasts, but that was hardly their fault. His actions had placed them in danger, so it was up to him to protect them.

Such was the way of the warrior.

Angling his body to the right, he swooped around, slamming his wings into the last two cultivators standing. They hit the floor, their consciousness fleeing like the receding tide.

"A . . . An Entire Flock of Birds, sir?" the handler sputtered, averting her eyes.

Bill peered down at her with disdain. She had ordered her cultivators to attack the seagull homies, a crime most foul.

"I . . . I'm sorry, sir. Please spare my life—"

Bill smacked her over the head hard enough to knock her out, yet soft enough to ensure no lasting damage. With one beat of his wings, he took to the air once more, zooming around the battlefield and herding the gulls so they remained above the city.

Power swelled from his master's position to the south, and just as Bill shot a glance that way, white light exploded outward. Bill shielded his face, blocking out the blinding aura. When the shockwave hit his body, it knocked the breath from him for a moment, his core seizing. The surrounding gulls were thankfully unaffected, their cores nonexistent. Shaking his head as he stabilized himself, Bill couldn't help but smile—it seemed as though his master was enjoying himself.

As the bubble of pure white chi shot out from me, it was like finally scratching an itch I'd been long ignoring. It was enjoyable to use my chi. I'd done so daily since my last awakening, but it never felt *anything* like this. For the first time, I truly understood that my chi wanted to be used, wanted to be expended. I was merely a vessel, a conduit for the chi held within me to experience the world. Letting it out made me feel . . . useful.

Alive.

I could do more, I realized; I could better serve the universe by opening the gate even wider. With building euphoria urging me on, I cracked it wider. The pure chi built, illuminating the surrounding grove and everyone in it. I gave over control, letting the universe take hold.

Lord Tom Osnan, keeper of the grove and water-chi cultivator, had prepared the perfect trap. Though his highness the king had been stricken with melancholy following the news of an outside force, it had filled Tom with nothing but glee. Over the course of his long life, there had been attempts by countless enemies to steal the kingdom's power. Most of those misguided fools weren't even cultivators, though. To the average person, challenging Gormona was akin to challenging the heavens, and every single one of the attempts had been snuffed out by the kingdom's agents long before reaching his doorstep.

So, when multiple spirit beasts had awakened and joined some sort of alliance, even gaining enough power to generate a Domain, he wished them luck. He *wanted* their power to grow—*needed* their cultivation to advance in order for them to pose a threat.

When this lone cultivator appeared in the grove, it was a bitter joy. Excited as he was to spring his trap, the outside force hadn't spent long enough cultivating to present the sort of danger he craved. The chi flowing from the young man before him was barely worth notice, only detectable because of Tom's relative strength.

Most disappointing of all, the man's chi seemed unaspected. He hadn't even cultivated long enough to specialize in an elemental affinity.

Frankly, it was insulting.

A lesser man than Lord Tom Osnan would have stretched out the conflict and let the adolescent cultivator think he had a chance. A lesser man may have even guarded the grove by himself without the aid of other cultivators. Tom, however, was no lesser man. He was a lord of Gormona and the keeper of the grove. It was his duty—his very purpose—to crush anyone foolish enough to stand against his kingdom. So, the trap had been prepared. Over half of Gormona's cultivators had lain in wait for weeks, poised to strike the moment the enemy moved.

Still, Tom wasn't against a *little* fun. He'd launched himself at the cultivator first, knowing that his strike would end the fight before it even began. As he glided over the grass toward the enemy, propelled by jets of water chi, a snarl crossed his face. The enemy cultivator was even more foolish than Tom had assumed; he grinned back, not yet understanding that his demise was sealed.

Then, the bubble of white appeared.

Unaspected chi flew in every direction, the cultivator not even experienced enough to direct his attack. It was so pitiful that Tom almost felt sorry for the fool. An echo of the bubble's power brushed up against him, making Tom raise an eyebrow. It had a decent amount of chi behind it, surprisingly. The moron must have shattered his core in panic, releasing enough chi all at once to rebuff the first wave of attacks. It was useless, of course; they'd just attack again. Tom considered pulling back and bracing himself but immediately dismissed it—the bubble of white didn't present a threat.

He extended his fist and prepared to break through it, but then another echo hit his awareness. Though it was only a reflection of the bubble's power, it was strong enough to make Tom's core vibrate. His breath caught in his throat as if physically struck, and as his eyes refocused, they were drawn into the man before him. It didn't make sense—he'd already shattered his core, hadn't he? How was he releasing even *more* chi?

It increased again, hitting Tom so hard that his entire body was jolted back an inch. It was as if he were a mortal man that had struck a brick wall, and his momentum was arrested instantaneously. His instincts kicked in and he rerouted his water chi, shooting himself back from the bubble. He didn't have any contact points with the ground, so his retreat would be slow, but he should be able to get out of the way in time to save himself—

The power doubled, tripled, doubled again, each strike hammering against Tom's core. The white light was blinding now as it expanded from the intruder. He could still see the man the chi exuded from, still make out his face. And what Tom saw there made his blood freeze. The cultivator's smile remained, not at all changing over the fraction of a second since Tom had launched himself forward. The eyes, though . . . they weren't the eyes of a peasant.

They were the eyes of a king.

No, he thought, the ice in his veins crystallizing.

They were the eyes of a conqueror, someone with the utter confidence and surety that they could do as they pleased.

The bubble's chi increased again, gaining so much strength that the surrounding air warped. The cultivator hadn't shattered his core at all. That first increase in power, so strong that Tom had assumed he had ruined his cultivation, was a mere drop in the ocean. This man, this attacker, was no peasant. He was a wolf, a force of nature, and Tom had stumbled directly into his path.

As the bubble of white burgeoned outward, Tom saw his death. All he could do was watch it approach.

CHAPTER EIGHTY-NINE

UNVEILED

Barry's breath caught as he took in the royal library. Shelves stretched three meters up to the roof, running in long lines he couldn't see the end of. The purple light of Borks's portal was the only thing that lit the room, and as he closed it, darkness descended.

A flame came to life, battling the gloom for dominion. Ellis carefully closed the lamp's hinged glass door and glanced up, his eyes severe. "If anyone causes me to set fire to the library, I will curse you and every one of your descendants in perpetuity."

"Yes, dad," Theo replied, giving Ellis a soft pat on the shoulder that made the former archivist glare at him. "It's in a lantern. Not like the flame will reach the books even if we do bump you."

"I still can't take you seriously while you're wearing that, Ellis," Peter added, stifling a laugh. "You look extra preposterous in the lamplight."

Ellis looked down at the armor he had worked so hard on. "What? I look remarkable. Especially considering the age of the material . . ."

"You look like a wayward god got freaky with an iguana," Theo muttered, causing Peter and Danny to chortle.

Barry let the banter continue, tuning it out as he set his backpack down and turned toward Fischer's creatures. "Okay, everyone." He opened the bag's drawstrings. "Let's get the costumes on. It'd be a shame to waste Steven and Ruby's hard work."

Borks was first. The dark-brown material was covered in old foliage, pondweeds, and patches of moss and dried mud. Ruby had somehow made the mud appear wet despite them being hardened and cracked.

I'll have to ask her about that, Barry thought, considering other uses.

Snips was next, and Barry draped the patchwork armor over her carapace. The armor—of Steven's design—was arranged in a hexagonal pattern, and the talented tailor somehow concealed Snips's orange carapace with layers of ingeniously woven material underneath the metal plates. He tied the straps in place, ensuring it was secure.

"Okay, Pistachio. You're up."

The lobster's costume was perhaps the most complicated. They hadn't found a pelt for the animal he was supposed to be, but Ruby had still done a wonderful job. Barry layered the fake fur on top of the Leviathan crustacean's sizable body, then attached the four legs. Lastly, the two eyes were strapped to his head.

Barry would never admit it to the disgruntled crab, but Rocky's costume was his favorite. Barry slipped elastic loops over Rocky's body; the animal pelt fit perfectly. As a final touch, Barry reached into a bag and removed what Fischer had called a *pirate hat.* Barry set it down atop Rocky's head, then tied it in place with a thin leather strap.

As Barry stepped back, he had to stifle his laugh. Rocky was prone to violent outbursts; the last thing he wanted to do was set the crab off and have him start unleashing explosions.

Snips, however, had no such compunctions. She hissed with laughter, her carapace dropping to the floor and legs kicking out.

Rocky froze, slowly spinning to glare at Snips. Given the costume, it had the opposite of his desired effect. Pointing at the hat, Snips's legs spasmed, her hissed laughter sounding more like a choke as she writhed on the floor.

Her antics drew everyone else's attention, and when they spied the now vibrating-with-fury Rocky, their conversation died. Under the attention, Rocky started hissing like a boiling-over teapot, so Barry sprang into action.

"Focus," he reminded them, stepping forward. "Take us to the royal library when you're ready, Ellis."

The former archivist marched them down a confusing series of corridors, finally arriving at a stone door. Just as Ellis had informed, there were four different locks necessary to open it. Everyone stepped back as Pistachio scuttled forward. He cocked his claws back, then unleashed a single blast at an upward angle that obliterated a third of it.

Barry pushed the door open on silent hinges.

"Wh-what are you doing?" A man asked from within. "What manner of—oh . . ." He fell to his knees, his eyes darting between the spirit beasts and Ellis. "Monsters—"

Snips flew forward on water jets, parts of her costume trailing behind her as she smacked the man on the back of the neck. He fell limp and she caught him, slowly lowering him to the ground.

"Wonderfully done," Barry said, striding forward.

Pistachio nodded. Rocky made a noise akin to, "yeah, so?" And Snips let out a series of happy bubbles.

The surrounding walls were shelves, and books filled every gap.

"Okay, gang," Barry said, a smile forming as Borks reopened his dimensional space. "Let the pillaging begin."

With his mouth feeling like it was filled with rocks, Augustus Reginald Gormona woke from a fitful sleep. He rolled over, letting out a groan. To his surprise, his mouth *was* filled with rocks. He spat them out, coughing and sputtering. Where *was* he? His vision swam, the stone bricks of the castle spire slowly coming into view as the moon's light radiated in through a shattered doorway.

When something flew in front of the moon, he remembered all at once.

"The birds!" he yelled, scrambling to his feet. "Gods above! Deklan, where are you?" He gazed around the room, finding the guard sitting on a chunk of fallen wall. "What are you doing? Help your king up! We must defend the castle!"

The eccentric yet reliable guard chewed his lip, staring down at his hands. "You're a cultivator?" he asked, not looking up.

Augustus spat, clearing more grit from his tongue. He saw no reason to deny it right this second. "Yes. I am. But that's of little import right now! We have to—"

"My brother was a cultivator." Deklan wrung his hands, his gauntlets creaking. "*Is* a cultivator."

"Enough prattle, fool! We—"

"Leave me be," Deklan said, his voice lacking any inflection. "I need to think."

Seeing such a reaction from someone he considered a friend, Augustus felt the need to explain himself, to voice and justify the way of things. But then the pulse of chi struck his core. Something so powerful that it had to be the efforts of multiple enemy cultivators driven into him, setting his entire body to vibrating. It made his heart skip a beat.

Augustus clenched his jaw, recalling that he was a *ruler.* His kingdom was in danger, and he had no need to explain himself to a mere peasant.

"I don't have time for your hysteria, *guard.*" Augustus spat the last word, approaching the spire's stairwell and not bothering to hide his ire. "Report to the garrison for punishment. I don't need dull tools."

For their former friendship, Augustus wouldn't kill him on the spot, but that was all. They were done.

Without waiting for a response, Augustus began descending, removing stone-encrusted rings as he went. With each finger he freed, power coursed through him. The pulse of power that had struck felt like it came from the grove, but that was of no matter. Lord Tom Osnan was there, as were most of the kingdom's cultivators.

Anyone stupid enough to attack it was as good as dead.

Removing the last ring, Augustus unleashed his full power for the first time in decades. Chi flowed from his back, ripping through his robe and propelling him down the spiraling staircase at blistering speed. With the unshackling of his power, a familiar madness crept forward like an old friend come to visit. The essence-sealing rings were a necessity, of course. The more power one released, the harder it was to contain when violence was no longer required. Still, it had been too long since the king had let his true nature show, and a vicious grin graced his lips as he let more chi flow from his considerable reserves.

Woe was any spirit beast that got in his way.

Endless bliss roiled through me with each drop of chi I surrendered, my very soul delighting to serve. It was a frozen moment, each passing microsecond making me give thanks for the boundless euphoria. The bubble surrounding me condensed and built upon itself, containing indescribable levels of power that only grew as I let the universe take hold. It dragged it out, ravenous for the essence I held.

The bubble was so dense that it was hard to see out of, so I sharpened my awareness, sending chi toward my eyes. My vision pierced the veil. The cultivator was there—the lord that had launched himself toward me with water chi wreathing his hands. He was at an odd angle in the air, something—probably me and my chi—having struck him a physical blow. Though his face was upturned, his eyes were locked on mine.

No longer did he look down his nose at me.

Even the condescending smile was gone, replaced by a visage of sheer pants-pissing terror. All at once, I realized my folly. This bloke and the rest of the cultivator slaves attempting to ambush me didn't have the same power I did. If I was to unleash any more chi, they might have a seriously bad time. Sending my awareness inward, I slammed the floodgates closed.

Well, I tried to. My core resisted, wanting to keep spewing chi out like some sort of homicidal dam.

Oi, I thought inwardly. *I. Said. Close!*

I hammered my will into it and my core listened immediately, cutting off my chi and sealing itself to the world. Though my power was no longer pouring out, there was still entirely too much in the surrounding orb to be good for my attackers' health. Shooting the lord a quick wink that I *really* hoped his cognition was enhanced enough to see, I shot off through the bubble, rupturing its force in that direction. Just as I exited the light, I experienced a moment of hesitation.

For this to work, I'd need to release more chi.

Memories of ecstasy still lingered in my body, my nerves not yet forgetting just how *good* it felt to let it all flow out, to let the universe take hold and pull essence directly from my core.

Is it really safe for me to use my power so soon?

But then I saw the faces of the cultivators surrounding the incoming blast. Just like their "lord," they were terrified. Unlike the tyrant lord, however, they were here through no fault of their own. They were collared cultivators. They did what their handler commanded, lest they be put down like rabid dogs. Each of them was worthy of empathy. Pity.

More importantly, they were worthy of saving.

Without an ounce of hesitation remaining, I saturated my lower muscles with chi and flew for the first row of cultivators—those that had leaped toward my previous position. Some shielded their eyes. Others stared at the bright light in frozen shock. One and all, they reeked of terror. I flicked each of them on the back of the neck to knock them out, then set them down against the wall in the spot where I'd ruptured the bubble's force.

Next, I collected the outer row. As many as there were, I had to do four trips, each time carrying a stack of limp bodies back to the only safe place in the courtyard. It all happened in less than a second, and following the exertion of chi, I felt like I'd just done leg day, my lower half sluggish and slightly unresponsive. The job was done, though. No innocent cultivators would lose their lives to the blast I'd unleashed.

The lord, however . . .

From a perch atop the battlements, I watched the blast strike him. I'd shattered the force to his left, somewhat disrupting the bubble's power. But that didn't stop it from hitting him like a freight train. His body shot backward, slamming beside the doorway he'd entered the grove from. To my surprise, the wall held. It cracked and cratered, but the structure was reinforced by the same lines that spider-webbed around the courtyard and carried chi to the plants.

Lord Tom Osnan, keeper of the grove or whatever he had called himself, slumped to the ground. The crater behind him leeched chi, the strands so potent that I could physically see them. My core called to them of its own accord.

The strands obeyed.

Floating through the air, they came to me, soaking into my abdomen like fresh rain into parched earth. I could *taste* the chi. It was as if an ancient forest entered me, the trees as old as time itself, its soil holding the nourishment of a million decayed leaves. Though it was now within me, the foreign chi hadn't melded with my own. It sat to the side, occupying its own space in a previously unused pocket of my core. The strands continued flowing until there were none left, the very grove robbed of its life force.

Before I could properly investigate the chi I'd somehow stolen, Lord Tom Osnan took a wheezing gasp.

"Who . . ." he groaned. "Who are you?"

"I didn't introduce myself? Where are my manners?" I crouched down before him. "I'm Fischer. Nice to meet you, mate."

I held a hand out to shake, but Tom's body seemed to be unresponsive. I lifted one of his hands, guiding it to shake mine.

"The—" He cut himself off with a racking cough. "*The chi manipulator?*"

"Oh! You guys *were* tracking our advancements? Barry's gonna be chuffed."

Though his body was limp, his eyes held the rage of ten thousand Rockys. "You win, Fischer," he wheezed. "You can tell your followers you won."

I cocked my head. "Huh?"

"Don't toy with me. You—" Another cough took him. "That power you wield. You're clearly the leader."

"Oh!" I made a dismissive gesture. "Yeah, nah. I'm not the leader of this little mission."

His eyes narrowed in suspicion, then widened as he seemed to realize I was telling the truth. He licked his lips, the slight movement taking all his effort. "What are you, then?"

I grinned. "I'm the distraction, mate!"

"You . . . you can't be."

"Afraid so, my man," I replied. "Gotta let the boss know I'm done here, too. Sorry about this."

Once more opening the floodgate to my power, I unleashed an uppercut into the air above me.

A beam of white light shot from my fist. It climbed into the heavens in an instant, and a fraction of a second later, it detonated.

CHAPTER NINETY

THE THEFT

Back beneath the sands of Tropica, a rhythmic tapping bounced off the church's stone walls.

Over the last few days, the usual busyness of the underground tunnels was nowhere to be seen. To most prisoners, this would have been a reprieve—a chance for them to escape monotonous questions and attention.

To Trent, it was torture.

Ever since his awakening, information had slowly trickled into his awareness. At first, it had been a blessing. Each fact gave the prince something to consider other than his imprisonment. But before long, it had become a curse; with each dawn, his anxiety only grew.

"Cousin . . . ?" came a familiar voice.

Trent glanced up at the entrance to his prison and stopped bouncing his knee, making the rhythmic tapping come to an abrupt end. "What do you want?"

Keith gave him an unreadable look. "Are you well?"

"*Am I well?*" Trent repeated. He let out a bitter laugh. "No, Keith. I'm not."

A silence spread over them like a heavy blanket.

"Do you want to talk about it?"

Something about Keith's tone made bile rise in Trent's throat. Trying to calm his emotions, he glanced to the side and caught his reflection in a hand mirror. Rather than the grotesque face he remembered, a chiseled jaw, light-blue eyes, and handsome features stared back at him. As the information had continued streaming in, his features grew comely. It only made Trent's fury build.

"Yes, Keith! Let's talk about it!" He strode toward the bars of his cage. "Do we start with the fact that your bedfellows are attacking our family in the capital as we speak?" Trent grabbed the metal gate, squeezing it as hard as he could. "Or should we talk about the fact that *I* was the one that sold our family out? That you took advantage of my low intelligence to squeeze the intel out of me?"

Trent struck out with his fist. A metallic *thump* rang out as the very room seemed to vibrate, but the gate remained undamaged.

"Don't look at me like that, Keith." Trent exhaled, partially deflating. "I have a perfect memory now. I can recall each and every word that came from my *stupid* gods' damned mouth."

"Trent . . ." Keith chewed the inside of his lip for a moment. "I owe you an apology, I think. If you recall your words, I'm sure you remember mine, too. I was . . . cruel. For that, I'm sorry."

Trent blinked at his cousin, opening and closing his fists. "You think your words bother me?"

The memories that had haunted him for the last few days flashed through Trent's mind. "You know, Keith, I wasn't always so loathsome."

"What?"

"Ugly." Trent stepped back from the bars, his gaze going distant. "Stupid."

Keith leaned forward, getting closer to the gate. "What do you mean?"

"You know what my nursemaid used to call me?" Trent laughed bitterly, unable to hide the hate coursing through him. "She called me her 'cute little prince.'"

He could see her vividly in his mind. Her wizened face, creased with laugh lines and sheer joy when she looked down at him. Then, the last face he'd seen her make replaced it—the look she gave him after he changed.

Shock. Horror. *Disgust* . . .

It had been the last time he saw her. His mother and father had been there. The words they had said . . .

Power swelled in Trent's core. He leaned into his fury, letting it course through his body. The potential energy made his limbs tremble, and without knowing what he was doing, he let it out. Searing flames burst from his skin, engulfing the room in a conflagration.

The collar around his neck beeped in warning, but Trent didn't care. He wanted to burn it all down, to set fire to the world itself. He felt his chi in action, sensing as it consumed the plush pillows, wooden bed, and every piece of furniture that decorated his prison.

The collar beeped again, giving its second warning.

Good, he thought.

Heat washed over his body, the surrounding flames seeming to cleanse his body. Metal creaked, the gate likely warping and melting beneath the raging firestorm of his creation. He gave not a single thought to escape, focused as he was on destruction.

The final beep rang out from the collar, and a smile came to Trent's face, knowing his suffering was at an end. He spread his arms wide in invitation, but then a wall of wind hit him. It yanked the collar from around his neck, and a fraction of a second later, it detonated.

Bwoom!

The explosion joined forces with the smoldering furniture, making the myriad fires flare. Then all at once, the flames guttered out, and Trent opened his eyes to a scene of devastation.

Nothing remained of his plush pillows. His lush, System-made bed had been obliterated, only smoking splinters remaining of its impressive mass. Every chair, stool, and dresser was now ash. And before him, Keith knelt, holding Trent up by the shoulders.

The creaking hadn't been the bars melting; it had been Keith opening the gate. His cousin had entered the conflagration to cast aside the collar and save his life.

"Trent . . ." he said, snapping his fingers in front of his face. "What was that? Are you back?"

The prince shook his head as tears welled up. "Why would they do it to me?" He locked eyes with his cousin. "*How* could they do it to me?"

"Who?" Keith asked, his gaze searching. "What did they do to you?"

Trent shook his head. He had already said too much.

"The capital is rotten, cousin . . ." Trent licked his dry lips as the memories flashed through his head once more. "Corrupted to the core."

High above the streets of Gormona, Corporal Claws commanded the sky. Evening air rushed past, tickling her whiskers and making a toothy grin cross her face. She stood tall on her noble steed, reaching her forepaws high and praising the moon.

Bill, her formerly obedient steed, let out a loud *honk* as her weight shifted, so Claws sat back down, giving him a mighty pout as she did so. First he'd brought more creatures than her, now he dared order her around?

The audacity of this junior . . .

Cinnamon let out a squeak of laughter from her right, so Claws turned her ire on the troublesome bunny. Cinnamon rode on Pelly's back, whose large avian eye sparkled with amusement. Claws opened her mouth to give her junior sisters a taste of her mind, but something brought her up short.

A pillar of light, wider than any of the castle's spires, shot into the sky. It illuminated everything in sight, seeming to cleanse the city with its purity. Then, the pillar imploded. It collapsed in on itself, all of that light being converted into sound.

Crack!

It was like the world was torn in two as the sound reverberated in Claws's very soul. Bill's flight faltered. He dropped toward the ground before balancing out again. Her master had said he would release two distracting blasts, but as Claws stared where the pillar of light had been, both her eyebrows rose to their peak.

Her master was terrifying. It was *fantastic.*

Movement stirred in a window just across from Claws. A little girl—just younger than Barry's son, Paul—stared at Claws with eyes like saucers. Letting out a cheerful chirp, Claws smiled and waved at the little girl. Another face appeared in the window. An older man, likely the little girl's father, dropped his jaw open when he spied the pelican-riding otter. The girl raised a hand to wave back, but the father swept her away, sprinting to some hidden corner of the house.

Claws sighed.

They *all* ran and hid. Was it too much to ask that someone witness Claws's brilliance as she conquered the skies? Was she not Corporal Claws, maiden of the forest and cutest of Fischer's animals?

Shaking her head, Claws focused down on the ground once more. Fine. Let them ignore her. There was still another gang of cultivators about, anyway. She'd be the one to find them. Then, she'd have an outlet for her indignation.

Not at all upset that there was no one to witness her brilliance—*okay, maybe just a* little *upset*—the hunt began.

As Borks loped along the stone hallway, a *crack* struck like two mountains colliding. He turned his head in its direction. His master was over there; no one else could have released such a powerful burst of chi. Thinking of his master, Borks wagged his serpentine tail.

Returning to the task at hand, he bounded across the floor. He no longer needed to follow the map in his head—Borks could *smell* his destination. It was an ancient scent, something he knew well from his former life as a hellhound.

And it grew closer.

He rounded a corner, running along the wall so he didn't skid along the smooth stones. A guard stood ahead, his back to a closed door, his eyes panicked. As he whirled toward Borks's movement, the blood flowed from the man's face.

Borks skidded to a stop before him.

"B . . ." He dropped to his knees. "Bog—"

Borks smacked him across the chin with his tail, knocking the man out cold, then caught him on his back and lowered the guard to the ground. He looked up at the door and considered opening it by the handle. But where was the fun in that?

Instead, he leaped through it.

Wood splintered, hinges buckled, and the metal handle clattered across the floor, coming to rest at the foot of an ancient artifact. As the door's debris settled, Borks gazed over a treasure trove. In his long life, he'd never seen so many relics in one place. There had to be multiple kingdoms' worth here.

His tail started wagging; his master was going to be *so* happy. Maybe he'd even call Borks a good boy. Grasping for his power, Borks tore a portal open to his dimensional space.

Barry leaped through the portal as soon as it opened. After only a moment of staring at the veritable treasure trove—and giving Borks a pat on the head, of course—the theft began.

"Screen here!" Brad said, his amusement clear. "It lists awakenings. I see 'Fat Rat Pack' and 'The Beetle Boys.'"

"Marvelous!" Ellis replied. "They are aware of the names!"

"Another here!" Fergus called when they'd loaded half of the relics already. "It's the one Trent told us about. They found it."

"They know about the levels?" Barry laughed, unable to hold it back. "All those skills that Roger has been gaining as *An Entire Flock of Birds* must have been terrifying."

"One here!" Duncan interrupted from the side of the room. "It—whoa. The Domain . . ." Duncan's eyes went wide. "It says what our Domain does. It also says there's one here that—"

"What does it say?" Ellis demanded, marching over.

"Not now!" Barry called, carrying a relic with Peter. "We can converse when Borks seals us back in!"

"Right. My apologies." Shaking his head, Ellis strode over and helped Duncan lift it. As they walked, Roger craned his neck over the top, no-so-subtly reading the Domain's effect.

Barry helped them take it into the portal, sharing a smirk with Duncan as Ellis continued examining the screen. They placed it against the others, and when Barry came back into the room, Theo made an excited noise.

"Another here!" He stared down at the screen, his eyebrow furrowing. "Ah . . . you guys might want to see this one."

"Get it inside first. We're almost done!"

"Oh. Right . . ."

They were a well-oiled machine as they loaded up the last of them, all knowing that the success of Operation Sticky Fingers was on the line. When the final one was in place, they met in the now-empty room.

"Okay," Barry said. "We have confirmation they know of the false names." He turned to the spirit beasts. "Are you all up for the Marinate variant of Operation Sticky Fingers?"

As one, they nodded and made various sounds of confirmation.

"Good."

"Me too," Ellis said.

Barry's eyebrows shot up. "You're sure?"

"I am." The former archivist lifted the scaled head adorning his own. "It is necessary for proper marination."

Smiling, Barry nodded. "All right. Good luck, then."

Everyone but the animals and Ellis entered Borks's portal. When the portal sealed behind them, Barry spun, rubbing his hands together as he spied the working artifacts.

Augustus Reginald Gormona leaned into the madness as he ran through the castle's twisting corridors. It was a long way between the spire he had been in and the artifact-filled room.

Getting there as fast as possible, he expelled vast amounts of chi with every step, but they were only drops in the bucket that was his core. The smell of his own robes burning greeted him like an old friend, reminding him of years long passed.

It smelled like training and his youth. Most of all, it smelled of his father. Thinking of the old man made a shudder run down Augustus's spine, and he shook his head, returning to the present. He could reminisce later. For now, there were enemies within the capital's walls.

Augustus stopped on the spot. He could feel cultivators. They were close. For a moment, he dismissed his worry, thinking it was only one of the girls with a handful of cultivators under her control. But if that were the case, why were they in the castle and not defending the streets?

When the cultivators got close enough to count, his blood ran cold.

The cultivator squads only run with four at a time, and there are five of them . . .

They stopped moving on the other side of a wall.

Can they sense me, too? He wondered, a smirk coming to his face.

If they thought of ambushing him, they would soon regret it. He cocked his arm back, aimed it at the wall, and channeled as much chi through his elbow as he could. His fist rocketed forward, the strike filled with deadly intent.

Before it could hit, a yell loud enough to travel through stone came from the other side of the wall.

"Fire!" Ellis bellowed.

Pistachio, Rocky, and Snips all released the power welling in their claws. Their abilities combined into a single blast that slammed into—and through—the stone wall. The cultivator Ellis had felt on the other side of the wall rocketed back as if shot from a cannon. From his position, Ellis saw each subsequent wall the stranger struck and broke through.

"That may have been a little too much force . . ." he mused, sensing the cultivator coming to a stop a few rooms away.

The backlash from the blasts would have torn the spirit beasts' costumes to shreds if not for the fact they were System-made, and Ellis quickly jotted that down as he stepped through the hole left in the first wall. "Let us go be seen, shall we? Our presence must be marinated within the locals' minds."

Rocky was already scuttling forward, his disguised claws held high and promising future violence.

"Don't let him kill them," Ellis said to Snips, who tore off after Rocky, followed closely by Pistachio and Borks.

If not for the skills the king had honed over a lifetime, the attack would have killed him on the spot. He'd rerouted his chi to form a protective shield in front of his torso just in time.

As he flew backward, crashing through walls like they were papier-mâché, he had time to consider his next move. By the time he came skidding to a stop within the grand banquet hall, he had the entire fight mapped out in his mind's eye.

They had gotten the jump on him, yet they had failed to kill him. Augustus grinned, letting the madness running through his veins show. Let them gaze upon his true form. Let the world see . . . his . . .

Augustus's mind came sputtering to a stop as the first of his attackers skidded to a stop in the banquet hall. Unmistakably mammalian, the creature made the king's breath catch in his chest. With the pelt of a goat and more limbs than a spider, it was no natural beast. The hat atop the spirit beast's head made its identity clear.

"Boat Goat . . ." the king muttered, his eyes locked on his adversary.

He gathered his power and forced it to come roiling up from his core, but before he could attack, the rest of them arrived.

Glare Bear, its body too low to the ground to be anything *but* an evolved creature. It almost seemed to slither, its many legs like that of a centipede. The namesake glare came from two enormous eyes sprouting from its head. Augustus quickly averted his gaze from the awakened bear, suspecting it had some sort of ocular ability.

Next was Hurtle the Turtle. It was the same size as Boat Goat and also had entirely too many limbs, but that was where the similarities ended. Its armored shell glinted in the banquet hall, reflecting the firelight of multiple torches.

A humongous canid came bounding through the breach, covered in remnants of the swamp whence it came. Bog Dog was as tall as a man, and the visible patches of body beneath its wetland trappings were lithe and muscular.

When the last of the cultivators came strolling through the shattered wall, Augustus clenched his jaw.

Standing on two legs, the spirit beast was more anomalous than the rest. Its body was covered from head to toe in scales so purple they seemed almost obsidian. The scales seemed to absorb the torchlight and reflect it out at the wrong angle. That the creature was a humanoid meant something terrifying: it had advanced enough to leave behind its beastly form. Within its thumbed and scaled hands, the spirit beast grasped a notepad and pencil.

Looking up from the notes it was taking, it turned toward the king with beady, dead eyes, freezing in place when it saw him.

" . . . *Augustus?*" it asked in a too-human voice, apparently surprised. "You are a cultivator?"

"So you finally show yourself?" The king laughed, sounding mad even to himself. "You think to ambush me? To unsettle me by knowing my name? In *my* seat of power?" He spat. "You waste your breath, wizard."

The leader of the enemy forces bent in response. Its body convulsed, and Augustus took a step back, preparing himself for an attack. But then he heard the sound coming from his enemy's throat.

The scaled humanoid was *laughing.*

"How did we not expect this?" it asked, shaking its reptilian head. "It all makes so much sense now!"

The fire chi seethed from the king's core and bathed everywhere it touched in fiery rage.

This cretin dares laugh at me?

His chi spread out in an instant, burning away shock and leaving only righteous indignation. Channeling his chi outward, Augustus rocketed forward on streams of molten energy, heading directly for the still-cackling spirit beast.

"*Lizard Wizard!*" he roared. "*Fight me!*"

CHAPTER NINETY-ONE

SHOOTING STAR

Of all the secrets Ellis expected to uncover during Operation Sticky Fingers, the king of Gormona taking steps on the path of ascension wasn't one of them. Ellis's mind worked to unravel the implications as he stared down Augustus Reginald Gormona, his former monarch and apparent cultivator.

How many of the royals are cultivators . . . ?

Trent wasn't one. Despite being first in line to the throne, the prince had been unaware his father was a cultivator. Had he perhaps known and successfully fooled them?

Not possible, Ellis immediately deduced.

Theo had been present for many of the conversations. He would have detected any lies or half-truths. When, then, would they have informed Trent? How would they have caused him to awaken? If it were only to occur after the king passed, that would imply a secret faction in the capital. Ellis's eyes went wide. There *had* to be a secret faction. If the king was the only one to know, the knowledge would disappear if he died unexpectedly.

Just how deep did the conspiracy go? How many of the capital's lords had been cultivators all along? His thoughts immediately went to Lord Tom Osnan, the king's closest confidant. His house held the passiona and lemon monopoly within a white-knuckled grip, making it the most powerful family other than the king's own.

Suddenly, a wave of chi burst from the king. It coalesced as flames that shot from his back.

"*Lizard wizard!*" he roared, rocketing forward with eyes locked on Ellis. "*Fight me!*"

Ellis paused for only a fraction of a second. "Trial of scales!" he yelled back, but it wasn't for the king's ears.

It was a battle variation, one of the many they had prepared in advance. As one, Fischer's animal companions took a step back, yielding the floor to Ellis. Their only remaining goal after Operation Sticky Fingers succeeded was to be witnessed—to be seen by as many of the capital's denizens as possible. Finding a powerful cultivator, however, presented a unique opportunity that Ellis could not pass up.

With the prospect of invaluable data fueling his stride, Ellis dashed forward, heading right for the king and his madness-filled smile. Seeing that his challenge had been accepted, Augustus drew a fist back. Flames sprouted from it in a chaotic release of chi. The inferno burned bright enough to drown out the surrounding torches, and it only grew stronger with each passing moment.

Hmmm, Ellis thought, weighing the strength of the king's attack. *I shall try one hundred percent first to be safe.*

Ellis braced his legs and lowered his body as he channeled chi into his System-made armor. The scaled suit readily accepted, drinking deep of Ellis's offering.

After I unleashed the skyward blast, I stumbled on the spot, having released more chi than I intended.

My damned core, I thought, furrowing my eyebrows as I held a wall for support.

"Hey." I glanced down at my stomach. "I'm the boss here, got it? I don't care how good it felt to release power. We only let out as much as I want."

It was a troubling development, but I had more important things to worry about. The column of light I had created released a wave of pressure as it imploded. It had struck the surrounding cultivators, and given how close I was to Lord Osnan, he'd been hit by the brunt of it. I knelt and held a finger to his neck. He still had a strong pulse, and I let out a relieved breath. Though he was a monumental prick, especially considering he was a cultivator who enslaved other cultivators, that didn't mean I wanted his blood on my hands.

"Where did that bag get to?" I mused, scanning the grove.

As I caught sight of the state of the vegetation, I grimaced. Following the two blasts I'd unleashed, most of the passiona bushes had been decimated. Those hit directly looked like they'd gone through a wood chipper; the only proof they'd ever existed was the leaves and splinters littering the base of the surrounding walls. The lemon trees had thankfully survived . . . well, their trunks and thicker branches had. Not a single leaf or fruit remained of their previously lush canopies, also having been torn and shredded by my chi.

Right before the stack of unconscious cultivators, in the spot where I'd weakened the initial bubble's power, four passiona bushes remained. They looked like a toddler had gotten his hands on a hedge trimmer and gone buck wild on them. But enough of their stems and leaves were undamaged, or so I hoped.

I guess I could always try to grow some from a seed if they don't survive . . .

I bent to dig my hands in the soil but paused. I glanced to the side, staring at the unconscious forms of the cultivators. Chewing my lip, I let out a soft curse and stood upright.

I couldn't just leave them here.

Barry had said there was only so much room back at the church, but leaving them here with these monsters didn't sit right with me.

"Sorry, Barry . . ." I stretched, relieving some of the fatigue in my muscles. "We'll just have to make it work."

I left the grove and wandered into the streets of Gormona in search of something I'd need.

* * *

Flowing forward on streams of flame, Augustus lashed out with a straight jab toward Lizard Wizard's abdomen. The fire surrounding his fist roared as it tore through the air, and he drew the flames in, concentrating their power.

The foolish spirit beast didn't even bother to defend itself; it lowered its arms and left its vitals open. Augustus's strike flew with unerring accuracy at the lizard's core. He aimed the jab *through* Lizard Wizard, knowing it would tear the cold-blooded reptile asunder.

Augustus released the concentrated fire chi before his fist connected.

He expected it to scorch Lizard Wizard's body, to soften the flesh before his fist followed through. But with his enhanced cognition, he watched the inferno blast into the black scales and flow around them like water.

Lizard Wizard *repelled* the flames.

Some sort of ability, the king decided.

He withdrew the remaining flames and channeled their power into his fist. His body vibrated with sheer force as the death blow landed.

Except it didn't.

His shoulder shuddered with the impact, his fist brought to a complete stop on the black scales. The next thing Augustus knew, he was flying backward, his momentum turned against him. He slammed into the far wall, the stone cracking and buckling beneath his weight. Sliding down the surface, he landed on his feet and checked his body with wide-eyed disbelief.

Where his outer robe hadn't been burned away by the flames, it had been shredded by the force Lizard Wizard's alien scales had reflected. His body, at least, wasn't damaged. Augustus grabbed his robe, tearing the remains of his royal garb away with one hand.

He stood to his full height, taking a steadying breath. Rather than discouraged, the king felt victorious. Lizard Wizard had powerful abilities. One that could repel magic, and one that could repel physical force. But powerful abilities meant the use of excessive chi. Across from him, Lizard Wizard rested his hands on his knees. The reptile took heaving breaths, no doubt exhausted by such ridiculous expenditure.

A laugh tore free of the king, bouncing off the hall's high ceiling.

They had entered a war of attrition. And he would *win.*

Ellis could barely contain his excitement as he watched the king slam into the far wall with so much force that the stones cracked. He had channeled one hundred percent of the armor's ability, just to be safe.

It had not been necessary.

Ellis focused on his armor, letting it draw his eyes in.

Galaxy Komodo's Armor of Resistance
Made of the scales of a galaxy komodo, this armor grants its user resistance to all attacks. Level of resistance is dependent on how much chi the user channels into the armor.
Bonus effect: 20 percent of all physical force resisted is reflected at the attacker.

Coming back to the present, Ellis realized he was hyperventilating. The armor's effectiveness had overstimulated his mind, and he braced his arms on his knees.

The king let out a manic laugh from across the room, and when Ellis looked up, Augustus was striding forward.

"Not bad, Lizard Wizard."

The king had ripped his torn robes away and revealed an odd set of clothing. The one-piece suit was made of a dark material and hugged tight to the king's body. Unlike the royal garb he'd discarded, the clothes hadn't been torn or scorched in the least.

A System-made bit of clothing? Ellis wondered as he straightened and forced his breathing to calm.

He shot a look at Sergeant Snips, whose eye glinted back; she had noticed the clothing and reached the same decision.

They nodded at each other.

"What do you communicate?" Augustus asked, sauntering forward. "Are you finally going to join the fray, Hurtle the Turtle?"

Snips shrugged at him.

"You would do well to attack together." The king's smile turned even more unhinged. "Give me a challenge."

Perhaps it would be good to put on a proper show, Ellis thought. *It would give him something to think about . . .*

"Peacock strut," Ellis said.

"Are you mad, Lizard Wizard?" the king asked, ever closing the distance. "What gibberish do you speak?"

Again, though, the words weren't for the king. It was another formation. Understanding the order, the spirit beasts attacked.

Borks stepped through space, appearing behind the king. Showing remarkable reaction speed, Augustus whirled, fire fueling his passage. He swung a fist into the side of Borks's head—but it went right through, the hellhound having turned incorporeal. The distraction worked, and Pistachio slammed his clacker closed.

Crack.

The bullet of force hammered into the king's back with what Ellis estimated was 20 percent of the lobster's power. Augustus shot forward through Borks's still-incorporeal body like a bug hit by hurricane winds, and flew face-first into the far wall. The king pushed himself off and spun, his face twisting with rage—just in time for the first of the tables to collide with his head.

The term *self-control* meant nothing to Rocky.

Given this undeniable fact, the crustacean was under strict orders to only use environmental objects when attacking. As they were in what appeared to be a banquet hall, the weapon of choice was hardwood tables. The first table exploded in a storm of splinters, and before they could clear the air, he slammed the next one down on the king's head.

* * *

Enough was enough. Being attacked within Augustus's castle was one thing, but being smacked over the head with his own furniture was another. Perhaps his rage was because he couldn't land a blow. Or perhaps it was because the boat-faring goat that did it had to have known it wouldn't do any damage. Regardless of the reason, Augustus's blood boiled.

Flames erupted from his body, licking out toward the surrounding cloud of splinters.

Whoosh.

A bonfire roared to life as his chi continued pouring out and devouring every source of fuel it touched. A regular human would have been burned to nothing in a moment, but to a fire cultivator like the king, it felt like home. The flames were a part of him, and he exalted with each bit of wood that burned away. As the fireball grew, it consumed every chair and table it touched. The heat was so intense that a rug on the other side of the room burst into flames.

All at once, Augustus drew the flames in.

He crouched down, channeling the latent energy into his legs. Then, he kicked off. With his eyes wide and his snarl even wider, he flew at Boat Goat, his fist cocked back and ready to deliver death. The speed was too much for Boat Goat, and before the spirit beast could move an inch, Augustus punched out.

His fist flew right through Boat Goat's head like it was a paper lantern, incinerating skin, bone, and that stupid, *stupid* hat.

As Augustus skidded to a stop beyond the headless goat's corpse, he roared with laughter and spun toward his fallen adversary.

"One down!" he taunted. "Four more to—*what?*"

Boat Goat's headless body ran away, gliding along the floor on its alien appendages. The king had never killed a spirit beast before, so he watched with curiosity, assuming it to be the death throes of an ascendant being.

But then Boat Goat, still lacking a head, picked up another table and threw it at him.

"What manner of demon are you?" Augustus yelled, his fury reigniting.

Chi flew from his core of its own accord and he kicked through the table. It burned to ash before his foot could land, and with flames spinning him around, he aimed a low kick at Boat Goat's body. Augustus drew on every ounce of power he could without damaging his core. His foot screamed through the air, the fire burning so hot that it turned white. Just before it collided, a purple wall cracked into existence.

Lizard Wizard and Hurtle the Turtle appeared, leaping through the portal and into the path of his attack.

Augustus's smile only grew. The fools thought to save their fellow beast, but had doomed themselves instead. Lizard Wizard's ability may have absorbed and reflected his earlier attack, but even that weak punch had left the humanoid reptile breathless. This kick held at least ten times the power. It would shatter through Lizard Wizard's defenses, rip its body in two, then continue on and obliterate Hurtle the Turtle.

The king let even more chi out. It was foolish, and he'd never have done it if not drunk with the power of his chi, but he dismissed that thought, not caring if he threatened his cultivation base. The flames around his leg grew hotter, turning translucent as the foot descended. A figure shot from around the portal, coming to stand beside Hurtle the Turtle.

If Augustus had the time, he'd have roared with laughter. Two spirit beasts had given their lives to save Boat Goat, yet the headless idiot had placed itself back in the line of death. And just in time, too.

The king unleashed the flames.

As before, they washed over Lizard Wizard's scales, not leaving a single mark. But this time, there were others behind the lizard. Incandescent flames washed over both Hurtle the Turtle and Boat Goat, igniting their flesh. His advanced cognition and the awareness of his fires let Augustus see and feel as each hair burned away. Their leather skin was consumed in an instant, their very skin melting to reveal flesh that was raw, orange, and . . . *hard?*

The flames still wreathed both mammals, yet they had nothing to burn. Within the inferno, two crabs stared at him, one with an eyepatch, the other with both its claws spread wide. Before his brain could fully comprehend what was happening, his foot collided with Lizard Wizard.

When the king had punched Lizard Wizard, it had been like a regular human striking a block of steel. This time, the scales bent inward, giving way beneath the power of his attack. Just as he'd expected, his foot would tear through the first beast and continue on through the others. All three would perish.

But then his foot slowed.

His momentum came to a screeching halt against Lizard Wizard's side, the scales there glowing a furious red. Faster than even Augustus could register, the one-eyed crab formerly known as Hurtle the Turtle appeared at his side. It pinched down on the ancient artifact he was wearing with both claws, blowing bubbles that he somehow understood.

Bye . . . ? he wondered.

Lizard Wizard's protecting scales flashed white, and power swelled within the still-open claws of Boat Goat the crab.

Clack!

Twin explosions came from the claws. At the same time, Lizard Wizard's scale reflected his kick. Augustus didn't even register the wall shatter as he shot through it. One moment his kick was landing, the next he was sailing through open air beneath a star-filled sky. The castle, now with a gaping hole in its side, grew smaller as he flew from it at impossible speed.

Within the breach, all five of the spirit beasts stepped up to the ledge. The two-eyed crab had both claws held high in victory. The eyepatch-wearing crab was scolding the former with bubbles flying from its mouth. Bog Dog sat on its haunches, its tail wagging. Glare Bear stood silently, its eerie gaze watching him as he rocketed away. Last, Lizard Wizard was writing in a notepad, not even bothered to witness his departure. A familiar garment was slung over the reptile's shoulder.

Augustus Reginald Gormona, the king of the lands he currently flew over, looked down. He was as naked as the day he was born, his royal member exposed for all to see.

Before he had a chance to cover himself from the judgmental eyes of Glare Bear, he struck something.

A moment later, he struck another something, and his vision went black.

CHAPTER NINETY-TWO

RESOUNDING SUCCESS

Beneath the sea of birds still milling over the capital city of Gormona, I trudged along with a smile on my face. As I glanced back, I saw that my wares were still in order. It hadn't taken long to find a cart big enough to carry the dozens of still-unconscious cultivators. I'd removed their collars and stacked them as comfortably as I could, making sure they all had room to breathe. Right at the front of the cart sat my prized passiona bushes, all four of them having large clumps of dirt still attached to their root systems. Ahead of me, I heard the clanking of armor, and I let out a sigh. Rather than change course, I just kept walking, too exhausted to really care.

"G'day," I said as the guard came into view.

He must have been lost in thought because my greeting made him jolt. As his eyes cleared, he blinked at me, his eyebrows narrowing as his gaze drifted to the cart full of cultivators I was dragging behind me.

I expected fear, anger, or perhaps even a cry for backup. Instead, the morose guard simply stared at me and my burden for a long moment. All of a sudden, his hand flew to the sword on his waist.

I sighed.

"What are you doing?" the guard demanded.

"I'm taking these slaves somewhere safe, mate." I replied, giving him an appraising look. "Is that a problem?"

"Slaves?" His hand tightened around the sword's hilt. "You mean to enslave them?"

"Look, man—I don't want trouble. I'm saving these guys, okay?"

"Saving?" His grip loosened slightly, but still remained at his side. "What does that mean?"

A crack like continents colliding split the air. I whirled toward it, seeing an entire section of the castle explode. The stones, some as large as a car, rained down across the forest. In their midst, something flew across the night sky.

Not something, I realized. *Someone . . .*

A man I didn't recognize sailed through the debris, his eyes wide and pants nonexistent. He had to have been attacked by my pals because he traveled at unbelievable speed. He shot *through* the first mountain, only coming to a stop when he slammed into the peak of a second one.

"Whoa . . ." the guard said. "What was that?"

"I must be getting tired," I replied. "Because I could have sworn I just saw an old cultivator flying through the air with his meat and two veg flapping in the breeze . . ."

"Did he have long gray hair and a longer beard?"

"He did. You know him?"

"The king," the guard said.

I chuckled. "Sounds like the poor bloke met my friends. He . . ."

I whirled back to the mountain, my skin prickling. "*The king is a cultivator?*"

"Apparently," the guard answered. "I only found out tonight."

"Damn." I scratched my chin. "That's kinda fracked up, isn't it? The bloke is a cultivator himself, but enslaves others?" I pointed back at my cart full of cultivators. "Talk about a dick move."

"Fracked up?"

I waved a hand. "Don't worry about it. Anyway, it was nice meeting you, but I gotta bounce. Probably best you don't tell anyone you saw me, yeah? They might get mad at you for not stopping me."

I gave him a nod and made to walk on, but he stepped forward.

"Wait."

I sighed. "Mate, it should be obvious that I'm a cultivator. I'm all for your loyalty, but I'd appreciate it if you just let me go."

"It's not that." He clenched and unclenched his fists for a long moment before he raised his eyes to meet mine. "Can I come with you?"

Well, that was unexpected.

"You want to come with me?"

"Yes," he answered simply, his eyes resolute.

"I don't have an issue with it, but my friends might get a bit annoyed if I don't ask you why."

"Why . . . ?" the guard repeated. He pointed at the stack of cultivators. "See the man with his hair tied up?"

There were a lot of people in my cart, so I squinted at the pile. "The one with dark brown, or the one with sandy-blond hair?"

"Dark brown."

"You know him?"

"He's my little brother."

"Oh. *Oohhh!*" Now that he mentioned it, I could see the resemblance. "I get it. You're, uh, okay with me taking their collars off and all that?"

The guard shrugged. "The king didn't wear a collar. Why should they have to?"

I gave him a grin. "Finally, someone sane. What's your name, mate?"

"Hey!" a voice yelled from down the street. "Return to your homes! The city is under attack!"

A woman came sprinting into view, trailed closely by four others with gleaming collars around their necks. The cultivators' eyes were wide as they scanned the sky above, tracking individual seagulls. Unlike the cultivators, their handler was covered in sweat.

"What are you doing moving wares around while the capital is . . ." She trailed off when she caught sight of my cart's contents. "Attack!" she screamed, clearly recognizing the cultivators within.

The order made the collared tear their eyes from the gulls above. When they saw their unconscious peers, there was a brief moment of silence. All four of them blinked, their enhanced minds struggling to reconcile the sight. Then, chi poured from their cores.

I dashed forward and slipped around the guard, placing myself between him and the attacks that would tear through the street in less than a second. There was a brief moment of quiet like the calm before a storm as the cultivators drew from their chi reserves.

A whistling sound broke the silence, and I glanced up at the sky, unable to contain my joy.

A small form shot headfirst toward the ground. Covered in brown fur, the creature shaped herself like a missile as she rocketed downward. Lightning wreathed Corporal Claws's entire body, and small jolts arced between each of her dagger-sharp teeth as she closed the distance. She trilled her glee for all to hear, and before the cultivators knew what was happening, she was among them.

Electricity gathered in the clouds above. I raised an eyebrow, not understanding why chi was gathering there. The seagulls, their senses apparently more keen than the cultivators surrounding Claws, left the area just in time.

Booom!

A bolt of lightning tore down from the clouds. It connected with Claws and spread out, slamming into all four of the cultivators. The chi they were gathering fled along with their awareness, and all four of them fell to the ground.

"Claws!" I yelled. "You got a new ability? What was that!"

She cast a wide grin my way, giving me a double thumbs up. Before I could run over and scoop her into a hug, another whistling sound caught my attention.

I scanned the sky but was unable to locate its source, so I reached out with my senses instead. They were still sluggish following the blasts I'd unleashed, and it took me longer than it should have to feel a familiar chi signature coming from behind me. I spun, expecting to find her coming for a good scritching.

Instead, I saw murder in her eyes.

Cinnamon rocketed down from up high. She flew headfirst toward the guard, her gaze locked on him. A half peep, half banshee wail tore from her throat as she spun in mid-air, utilizing her momentum to deliver a spinning back kick right into the guard's chest. She didn't use deadly force, but it still would have rocked the regular human it was aimed at. Before she could connect, I caught her by the cinnamon-colored scruff.

"Hey!" I chided, holding her up before the wide-eyed guard. "He's a friend. We don't kung fu our pals."

She looked at him, me, and him again, then hung her head in embarrassment.

Sorry, she peeped, her entire body going limp.

"It's, uh . . . okay?" the guard replied, his hand twitching as he stared at Cinnamon.

Cinnamon watched him closely, her eyes locked on the sword at his hip.

"Everything all right?" I asked, raising a brow.

"Yeah, it's just . . . she looks so soft . . ."

I barked a laugh. "You can pet her—if it's okay with her, I mean."

Cinnamon perked up immediately, her ears going alert.

"I think that's a yes, mate," I said, letting go of her scruff.

She jumped up into his arms, resting her forepaws on his chest. He removed his gauntlet and rubbed the top of her head with his hand, a small smile coming to his face that disappeared when a certain miscreant leaped onto his shoulder.

Corporal Claws chirped her indignation at him, shoving Cinnamon aside and pointing to her own head, demanding scritches with a firm chirp.

The guard obeyed, taking turns to rub them both. Claws started pushing Cinnamon, and Cinnamon started pushing back. Before they could start batting at each other within the poor guard's grip, I yoinked them both.

"All right, you two. You know I love giving a good scritch as much as the next guy, but we're still on a mission."

Cinnamon let out an apologetic noise but Claws just gave me a wide grin. I shook my head as I let them go.

"Get out of here, you little scamps."

Rather than shoot off, however, they both leaped to the cart. Cinnamon gave me a shooing gesture.

"You want me to leave them with you?"

Yes, they both replied.

"Do you promise you won't let Barry leave them behind?"

Cinnamon held a paw to her heart and nodded sincerely, while Claws held a hand to her stomach and reeled as if my words had struck her a mortal blow.

I pointed at the cart. "I'm serious, Claws. The bloke with long, tied-up brown hair is this fella's—wait, what was your name, mate?"

"Er—Deklan . . . ?" he replied.

"I'm Fischer. Nice to meet you, mate." I turned back to Claws. "That bloke in the cart is Deklan here's brother. I know you can be trusted, but it might make him relax if you give him your assurance."

Claws hopped up onto the cart's ledge. She gave Deklan a crisp salute, then dashed forward and grabbed his hand, pumping it up and down in a firm handshake.

"I—er—thank . . . you . . . ?" he said.

Claws nodded, leaped to my shoulder and kissed my cheek, then left. Lightning wreathed her body as she tore off with the cart, disappearing from sight in what must have been the blink of an eye for my new unawakened friend.

"They're spirit beasts?" he asked.

I nodded, glancing his way. "How do you feel about that, mate?"

"Honestly?" He thought about it for a moment, chewing his lip. "It's pretty neat," he eventually decided.

"Right?" I laughed. "It *is* pretty neat!"

I took a deep breath, my chest feeling lighter than it had all day. "So, are you ready to leave?"

Deklan was lost in thought. But at my question, he looked up. "I think I am, yeah."

He was still clearly shocked, but he was handling the fact I was friends with spirit beasts remarkably well. We started walking away, and as much as I wanted to give him a chance to process everything he'd learned, I couldn't keep a question from voicing itself.

"So, Deklan . . ."

"Yeah?"

I looked up at the wheeling gulls, trying to appear nonchalant. "How do you feel about fishing?"

Turning his back to the mountains the king had struck, Ellis watched as Snips smacked Rocky on the head.

"It is okay," Ellis said, returning his attention to his notepad. "The king lives."

Snips blew a slew of furious bubbles.

"I know that is not the point, Snips, but it is done now. No use crying over spilled ink."

He finished taking his notes as Snips's beratement continued. Now that his thoughts were down, he could finally inspect the king's clothing.

The garment drew his eyes in.

Indestructible Flame Suit of the Weaver
Rare
Woven of web from a core weaver, this suit is almost completely impervious to damage from all chi. It does not provide any resistance.
Bonus Effect: +30 percent effectiveness to fire chi.

"Remarkable . . ." Ellis said as he returned to the present.

Before he could further vocalize his thoughts, the surrounding ruckus caught his attention.

Now that they had been seen by the king, it was time to go. Borks had his portal open and ready for them to enter, but Rocky was being . . . well, Rocky. The crab was facing the hole the king's naked body had made in the castle, pointing at his back. When Ellis realized what Rocky was asking for, he rubbed his temples.

Rocky wanted to be . . . what was it that Fischer called it?

Yeeted.

Rocky wanted to be yeeted by Snips as a punishment for breaking his no-chi-attacks rule. Snips was trying to grab him and drag him into the portal, but every time she got close, he cocked his claw back and threatened to blow the floor up.

"Rocky," Ellis chided. "You can be launched to your heart's desire when we get back to Tropica. We really do not have time for this. If you wish to be brought on further missions, I must ask you to enter the portal."

Rocky spun and gave Ellis a series of remarkably rude gestures. The distraction had worked, however.

With Rocky's back turned, Pistachio dashed behind him. He wrapped Rocky up in his powerful claws. Rocky hissed and spat, his entire body shaking in rage as he promised future violence for the Leviathan lobster. Pistachio ignored the threats and scuttled into the portal, taking Rocky with him. Snips followed, berating Rocky the entire way.

Ellis took one last look at the castle before he too strode for the portal. "Take us home, Borks." He leaned down and patted him twice on the head. "You are a good boy."

Borks licked Ellis's hand, and Ellis nodded his thanks. When he stepped back into Borks's pocket dimension, a sea of faces met him.

"How did it go?" Barry asked, his features lined by worry as he glanced at the restrained Rocky and vehemently hissing Snips.

The portal to the outside world closed.

"I have much to relay, but first . . ." Ellis threw back his hood, letting them take in his wide smile. "I hereby declare Operation Sticky Fingers a resounding success."

EPILOGUE

On the outskirts of Tropica, Lieutenant Colonel Lemony Thicket's canopy shook in anticipation.

Most of her friends were on a mission far, far away. It was the perfect opportunity.

Master will be so happy, she thought as the image of his grin passed through her awareness.

Lemon had been storing energy and waiting for the perfect chance to strike, and her core vibrated with excitement now that the moment was here. Ever since she had contacted the child beneath the ground, they had remained in contact.

That alien being, so similar yet so different to herself, had been hesitant at first. Though filled with curiosity, it had kept Lemon at a limb's length, not ever letting her get too close. Over time, Lemon had kept feeding it a steady trickle of chi, and with each morsel it consumed, it lowered its guard.

When it felt how excited Lemon was, it sent a message.

Excitement? it seemed to ask. *Why?*

Growth, Lemon replied. *Growth. Growth. Growth.*

Taking one last measure of the power she had accumulated, Lemon deemed it worthy. She sent a portion down through her mighty roots, offering it up to the baby tree spirit. It was only a fraction of the chi she'd set aside, yet when the child felt it, it recoiled and crawled back into its protective tree, pushing away Lemon's offering.

Trust, Lemon sent alongside the chi. *Good. Good Good Good.*

As she continued radiating reassurance, she withdrew most of the offering and left only a taste for the child to consider. It came from the back of its safe space, and with a trepidatious bite, it tasted the chi. Through their bond, Lemon felt its curiosity grow.

. . . *Delicious,* it sent.

Yes, Lemon agreed. *Delicious. Good. Growth.*

The spirit considered that for a long moment. Eventually, it replied with a weak pulse, *Fear.*

Lemon had been too exuberant with her initial offering; it had made the child wary.

Sorry, she said, breaking off an even smaller portion and trickling it down to the spirit.

She could practically see the child hesitating on the edge of its Domain. Despite having been in contact with Lemon for months, it still didn't trust her. It was a sentiment Lemon well understood. She, too, was a tree spirit. Their lifespans were measured in the thousands of years—what were a few months? Both before and after her hibernation, Fischer was the only person Lemon had ever truly trusted. She had faith in those that Fischer called friends, but that was only because they had earned *his* trust. If the child had been too accepting, Lemon would have thought it an imbecile.

While she pondered, the child slowly crept from its den.

In the tree spirit's estimation, life was a good thing. Before, there had been nothing. Now, there was something. Something was *probably* better than nothing. Unfortunately for the tree spirit, existence meant one could want. And there was only one thing it wanted: for the leaves of its tree to feel the sun.

It had never seen the sun, yet it knew what it was. The sun was a provider of life, and its tree would be much happier if it was beneath its warming rays. Happy tree, happy life . . . right?

The tree spirit thought so.

Still, things weren't so bad. It was safe within its tree's mighty trunk. It even had a companion, one which seemed much older and more aware of the world. They talked sometimes. Mostly, though, they were just . . . there. The companion was always connected and giving the tree spirit power. The spirit thought it could trust the other, but just like the tree spirit knew the sun existed, it knew there was no sense in rushing things. Though glad for the companionship, it wasn't about to follow its companion's every beck and call.

When the companion had started buzzing with excitement and sent down an overwhelming amount of power, the tree spirit had retreated.

Sorry, its companion had said, but it wasn't necessary.

The tree spirit hadn't recoiled because its companion had offered too much; it had recoiled because the offering had tasted delicious.

Too delicious.

It left the tree spirit wanting more. Wanting to suck up every drop its companion offered. It was a scary compulsion. Before, it had only wanted sun for its tree. That was . . . natural. Trees liked the sun, and tree spirits liked happy trees. This hunger, though . . .

Its companion sent down a soothing feeling that seemed to say *sorry* again.

Perhaps another taste wouldn't be so bad. It sent its awareness down toward where its companion's root sat. It could feel the power. Could almost *taste* it.

Just a little more would be okay . . . wouldn't it?

Before the tree spirit could second guess itself, it drank some in.

Delicious.

It. Was. *Delicious.* Just as good as last time. Better, even.

Its companion offered up a little more, and the spirit tree drank it. The offering slowly grew, eventually getting as wide as a river.

A river . . . ? the spirit wondered.

How long had it known what a river was? It . . . *oh.*

It wasn't just delicious power the spirit was drinking in; it also absorbed knowledge. Its companion continually increased the amount of chi coming through, and the tree spirit accepted every drop. Before long, it had increased by an order of magnitude—which was also a fun term the tree spirit now knew. No matter how much chi came through, the tree spirit accepted every drop. Before long, it got the sensation that some of the essence should be put to use. With but a thought, the thick gouts of chi poured from its body.

The roots of the spirit's tree shot down into the soil, winding their way ever deeper as they grew. Its roots found pockets of water, spots of nutrients, and even odd channels of chi that ran under the earth. The tree spirit ate some of the chi; they were *okay,* but nowhere near as delicious as that offered by its companion.

The torrent of power coming through increased again, and the spirit channeled it into the tree's trunk. With a roar of creaking timber, its stronghold grew. The tree shot up faster than was natural, and within seconds, it scraped the roof.

Well, that's no good, the spirit thought.

There was still so much chi being sent its way. Too much, in fact. It should probably stop absorbing it all. Tell its companion to slow the offering. In response to this line of thinking, the tree complained.

It wanted to keep growing. It wanted to grow its canopy wider than any other tree. *It wanted to feel the sun.*

Making the spirit equivalent of a shrug, the spirit let it be so. The entire room shuddered as the tree reached the ceiling and wood punched against stone. Then, the spirit had an idea: it grew a root from the canopy. The root, as thin as a hair, found a crack in the ceiling. It corkscrewed into the stone and kept on going, forcing its way through until it found earth. Stone cracked and soil parted as the root paved the way. The trunk followed its passage, growing wider at the base as it grew ever taller.

Other beings ran into the room the tree spirit had occupied since gaining awareness. It had never known what they were before, but now it did. They were humans, and they stood witness to the tree's growth.

Abruptly, the root breached the surface, and for the first time in its short life, the spirit tasted open air. Its companion seemed to sense the spirit's emotions, because the second the root's tip was free of the earth, the river of chi became an ocean. Its companion forced chi through, and the spirit redirected every last bit of it. The earth quaked, and large chunks of ceiling fell to the floor, making the humans flee the room.

But the spirit had no mind for them. All of its attention was on the trunk's growth as it pushed tons of earth aside and found the open air. Its trunk twisted high into the sky, its branches extending and leaves unfurling into a wide canopy.

The tree spirit looked out through the leaves. A crescent moon was high in the sky above, bathing the surrounding landscape in an ethereal light. There was no sun, yet the outside world was even more beautiful than the spirit had imagined. It breathed deep of the salty air, relishing the freedom its tree had gained.

* * *

Within the capital city of a foreign land, a man nervously fidgeted with the rings adorning each of his fingers. He checked the time piece around his neck for what had to be the hundredth time that night.

Thirty minutes since the last blast, he thought.

It was time to go.

He crept down the stairs of his rented abode, avoiding the three steps that creaked. He paused at the door, took a steadying breath, and opened it. The hinge was silent; he'd oiled it just in case. As he closed the door behind him, he felt one last pang of regret for the gold he was leaving behind. A prince's ransom worth of coins, hard earned with how far he had traveled to sell his wares. It was no good, though. They would only weigh him down on his journey.

The man's heart thundered in his chest as he scanned the street beyond. It was eerily silent, even the bugs and night birds having gone completely silent after the series of blasts that had rocked the city. He took each step with great care as he slunk along in the shadows until movement on a building's gutter to his left caught his attention, and the call of two creatures shattered the silence. In a blur, the man unsheathed a dagger from his waist and drew it back, preparing to fight.

When he saw the creatures, he paused, his pulse thumping in his ears. Two seagulls sat on the roof. They screamed at each other, each standing tall and posturing for dominance. The man shook his head, lowering the throwing knife but not sheathing it.

What in Poseidon's blessed waters are two seagulls doing this far from the ocean? he wondered.

There was no point in silence if the bird-brained creatures were going to scream at each other, so he abandoned his stealth.

He slipped through the light of a crescent moon, crossing a street and entering the alley he'd find his exit in. When he reached the sewer grate, he removed the lock he'd previously cut. Placing it in his pocket, he began descending into the sewer, but paused, taking one last look at the city.

The capital city of Gormona was a surprisingly beautiful place, considering how primitive the kingdom was. It was a relic of a time long passed, a monument to the powerhouse it had once been. When the man caught sight of the castle, his breath caught. A hole had been blown in the side of it that was large enough to reveal three floors. Whatever had happened, it wasn't caused by mortals.

The man slipped into the sewer and quickly replaced the grate, sealing himself within. The stink of human waste was pungent, but it was nothing compared to his duty. He climbed down the metal rungs in pitch darkness, landed on the walkway, and took off running alongside the river of filth.

He had to get home and warn them.

ABOUT THE AUTHOR

Haylock Jobson is the author of the Heretical Fishing series, originally released on Royal Road. He lives on the beautiful shores of Australia's Gold Coast and spends his days writing in local cafes, drinking what some might refer to as "too much" coffee, and annoying strangers by asking if he can pet their dogs.